# DICK FRANCIS

## THREE COMPLETE NOVELS

# DICK FRANCIS

## THREE COMPLETE NOVELS

### DECIDER

### WILD HORSES

### COME TO GRIEF

G.P. PUTNAM'S SONS
NEW YORK

G. P. Putnam's Sons

*Publishers Since 1838*

a member of

Penguin Putnam Inc.

200 Madison Avenue

New York, NY 10016

Library of Congress Cataloging-in-Publication Data

Francis, Dick.
[Novels. Selections]
Three complete novels / Dick Francis.
p.   cm.
Contents: Decider—Wild horses—Come to grief.
ISBN 0-399-14306-8
1. Detective and mystery stories, English.   2. Horse racing—Fiction.   I. Title.
PR6056.R27A6   1997                96-40080 CIP
823'.914—dc21

Printed in the United States of America
1   3   5   7   9   10   8   6   4   2

Book design by Julie Duquet

# Contents

# DICK FRANCIS

## THREE COMPLETE NOVELS

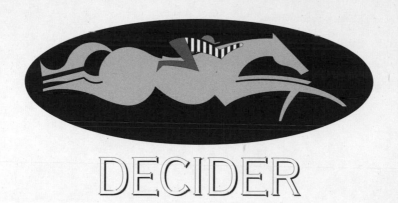

# DECIDER

# 1

O K, so here I am, Lee Morris, opening doors and windows to gusts
of life and early death.

They looked pretty harmless on my doorstep: two middle-aged civil Eng-
lishmen in country-gent tweeds and flat caps, their eyebrows in unison raised
inquiringly, their shared expression one of embarrassed anxiety.

"Lee Morris?" one of them said, his diction clipped, secure, expensive.
"Could we speak to him?"

"Selling insurance?" I asked dryly.

Their embarrassment deepened.

"No, actually . . ."

Late March evening, sun low and strong, gold light falling sideways onto
their benign faces, their eyes achingly narrowed against the glare. They stood
a pace or two from me, careful not to crowd. Good manners all around.

I realized that I knew one of them by sight, and I spent a few extended seconds wondering why on earth he'd sought me out on a Sunday a long way
from his normal habitat.

During this pause three small boys padded up the flagstoned passage from
the depths of the house behind me, concentratedly threaded a way around me
and out through the pair beyond and silently climbed like cats up into the
fuzzy bursting-leaf-bud embrace of an ancient spreading oak nearby on the
lawn. There the three figures rested, becoming immobile, lying on their stom-

achs along the old boughs, half seen, intent, secretive, deep in an espionage game.

The visitors watched in bemusement.

"You'd better come in," I said. "They're expecting pirates."

The man I'd recognized smiled suddenly with delight, then stepped forward as if in decision and held out his hand.

"Roger Gardner," he said, "and this is Oliver Wells. We're from Stratton Park racecourse."

"Yes," I said, and made a gesture for them to follow me into the shadowy passage, which they did, slowly, tentatively, halfblinded by the slanting sun outside.

I led them along the flagstones and into the cavernous room I'd spent six months converting from a rotting barn into a comfortable house. The revitalizing of such ruins was my chief livelihood, but recently the inevitable had finally happened and my family were currently rebelling against moving to yet another building site and were telling me that this house, *this one* was where they wanted to live.

The sunlight fell through tall west-facing windows onto the sheen of universal slate-gray flagstones which were softened here and there by rugs from Turkey. Round the north, south and east sides of the barn now ran a railed gallery bearing a row of bedrooms, with a staircase giving access at either end.

Under the gallery a series of rooms stood open-fronted to the great room, though one could close each off with folding doors for privacy. They offered a book-lined room for watching television, an office, a playroom, a sewing room and a long capacious dining room. A breakfast room in the south-east corner led into a big half-visible kitchen with utilities and a workshop wholly out of sight beyond. The partition walls between the open-fronted rooms, partitions which looked merely like space dividers, were in fact the extremely strong load-bearers of the gallery above.

Furniture in the central atrium consisted chiefly of squashy armchairs scattered in informal groups, with many small tables handy. A fireplace in the western wall glowed red with logs.

The effect I'd aimed for, a dwelling built like a small roofed market square, had come out even better than I'd imagined, and in my own mind (though I hadn't told the family), I had intended all along to keep it, if it was a success.

Roger Gardner and Oliver Wells, as was usual with visitors, came to a halt and looked around in frank surprise, though they seemed too inhibited to comment.

A naked baby appeared, crawling across the flagstones, pausing when he reached a rug, wobbling onto his bottom and looking around, considering things.

"Is that yours?" Roger asked faintly, watching him.

"Very probably," I said.

A young woman in jeans and sweater, fair hair flying, came jogging out of the far part of the kitchen in businesslike running shoes.

"Have you seen Jamie?" she demanded from a distance.

I pointed.

She swooped on the baby and gathered him up unceremoniously. "I take my eyes off him for *two seconds . . .*" She bore him away, delivering a fleeting glance to the visitors, but not stopping, vanishing again from our view.

"Sit down," I invited. "What can I do for you?"

They tentatively sat where I indicated and visibly wondered how to begin.

"Lord Stratton recently died," Roger said eventually. "A month ago."

"Yes, I noticed," I said.

"You sent flowers to the funeral."

"It seemed merely decent," I agreed, nodding.

The two men glanced at each other. Roger spoke.

"Someone told us he was your grandfather."

I said patiently, "No. They got it wrong. My mother was once married to his son. They divorced. My mother then married again, and had me. I'm not actually related to the Strattons."

It was unwelcome news, it seemed. Roger tried again.

"But you do own shares in the racecourse, don't you?"

Ah, I thought. The feud. Since the old man had died, his heirs, reportedly, had been arguing to a point not far from murder.

"I'm not getting involved," I said.

"Look," Roger said with growing desperation. "The heirs are going to *ruin* the racecourse. You can see it a mile off. The rows! Suspicion. Violent hatreds. They set on each other before the old man was even cold."

"It's civil war," Oliver Wells said miserably. "Anarchy. Roger is the manager and I'm the Clerk of the Course, and we are running things ourselves now, trying to keep the place going, but we can't do it much longer. We've no *authority,* do you see?"

I looked at the deep concern on their faces and thought about the difficulty of finding employment of that caliber at fifty-something in the unforgiving job climate.

Lord Stratton, my non-grandfather, had owned three-quarters of the shares in the racecourse and had for years run the place himself as a benevolent despot. Under his hand, at any rate, Stratton Park had earned a reputation as a popular well-run racecourse to which trainers sent their runners in dozens. No Classics, no Gold Cups took place there, but it was accessible and friendly and had a well-laid-out racing circuit. It needed new stands and various face-lifts but old die-hard Stratton had been against change. He appeared genially on television sometimes, an elder conservative statesman consulted by interviewers when the sport lurched into controversy. One knew him well by sight.

Occasionally out of curiosity I'd spent an afternoon on the racecourse, but racing itself had never compulsively beckoned me, nor had my non-grandfather's family.

Roger Gardner hadn't made the journey to give up easily.

"But your *sister* is part of the family," he said.

"Half-sister."

"Well, then."

"Mr. Gardner," I explained, "forty years ago my mother abandoned her infant daughter and walked out. The Stratton family closed ranks behind her. Her name was mud, spelt in capitals. That daughter, my half-sister, doesn't acknowledge my existence. I'm sorry, but nothing I could say or do would carry any weight with any of them."

"Your half-sister's father . . ."

"Particularly," I said, "not with him."

During the ensuing pause while the bad news got chewed and digested a tall fair-headed boy came out of one of the bedrooms on the gallery, skipped down the stairs, waved me a flapping hand and went into the kitchen, to reappear almost at once carrying the baby, now clothed. The boy took the baby upstairs, returned with him to his bedroom and shut the door. Silence fell.

Questions hovered on Roger's face but remained unasked, to my amusement. Roger—Lt. Colonel R. B. Gardner, according to the Stratton Park racecards—would have been a thorough flop as a journalist, but I found his inhibitions restful.

"You were our last hope," Oliver Wells complained, accusingly.

If he hoped to instill guilt, he failed. "What would you expect me to *do?*" I asked reasonably.

"We hoped . . ." Roger began. His voice faded away, then he rallied and manfully tried again. "We *hoped,* do you see, that you might knock some sense into them."

"How?"

"Well, for one thing, you're big."

*"Big?"* I stared at him. "Are you suggesting I *literally* knock some sense into them?"

It did seem that my appearance had given them instant ideas. It was true that I was tall and physically strong; very useful for building houses. I couldn't swear I'd never found those facts conclusive in swinging an argument. But there were times when to tread softly and shrink one's shoulder-span produced more harmonious results, and I leaned by nature more to the latter course. Lethargic, my wife called me. Too lazy to fight. Too placid. But the ruins got restored and left no trails of rancor in local officials minds, and I'd learned how to get around most planning officers with conciliation and reason.

"I'm not your man," I said.

Roger clutched at straws. "But you do own those shares. Can't you stop the war with those?"

"Is that," I asked, "what you mainly had in mind when you sought me out?"

Roger unhappily nodded. "We don't know where else to turn, do you see?"

"So you thought I might gallop into the arena waving my bits of paper and crying 'enough,' and they would all throw down their prejudices and make peace?"

"It might help," Roger said, straightfaced.

He made me smile. "For one thing," I said, "I own very few shares. They were given to my mother all those years ago as a divorce settlement, and I inherited them when she died. They pay a very small dividend now and then, that's all."

Roger's expression went from bewilderment to shock. "Do you mean," he demanded, "that you haven't heard what they are fighting *about?*"

"I told you, I have had no contact with them." All I knew was what I'd learned from a brief paragraph in *The Times*'s business pages ("Stratton heirs dispute over family racecourse") and some blunter remarks in a tabloid ("Long knives out at Stratton Park").

"I'm afraid you will soon hear from them," Roger said. "One faction of them want to sell off the racecourse to developers. As you know, the course lies just to the north-east of Swindon, in an area that's growing all the time. That town has exploded into a center of industry. All sorts of firms are moving there. It's heaving with new life. The racecourse land is increasing in value all the time. Your few shares might now be worth quite a lot, and they might be worth even more in the future. So some of the Strattons want to sell now, and some want to wait, and some don't want to sell at all, but to go on running the racecourse for racing, and the sell-now lot should have been onto you by now, I would have thought. Anyway, someday soon they'll remember your shares and they'll drag you into the fight whether you like it or not."

He stopped, feeling he'd made his point; and I supposed he had. My sincere desire *not* to be dragged into any fracas looked like being a casualty of "the real world," as one of my sons described all calamities.

"And naturally," I commented, "you are with the faction that wants racing to continue."

"Well, yes," Roger admitted. "Yes, we are. Frankly we hoped to persuade you to vote your shares *against* selling."

"I don't know that my shares even have a vote and there aren't enough of them to sway anything. And how did you know I had any?"

Roger briefly consulted his fingernails and decided on frankness.

"The racecourse is a private limited company, as I expect you know. It has directors and board meetings and the shareholders are informed each year when the annual general meeting is to take place."

I nodded resignedly. The notice came every year and every year I ignored it.

"So last year the secretary who sends out the notice was ill, and Lord Stratton told me just to do it, there's a good chap . . ."—his voice mimicked the old man's splendidly—"so I sent out the notice and it happened that I put the list of names and addresses in a file for the future . . ." He paused, hovering, ". . . in case I had to do it again, do you see?"

"And the future's upon us," I said. I pondered. "Who else owns shares? Did you by any chance bring the list with you?"

I saw from his face both that he had brought it and also that he was unsure of the ethics of passing it over. The threat to his job, though, conquered all, and after the briefest of hesitations he reached into an inner pocket in the tweed jacket and produced a clean once-folded sheet of paper. A fresh copy, by the looks of things.

I opened it and read the ultra-short list. Shorn of addresses it read:

William Darlington Stratton (3rd Baron).
Hon. Mrs. Marjorie Binsham.
Mrs. Perdita Faulds.
Lee Morris Esq.

"Is that all?" I inquired blankly.
Roger nodded.

Marjorie Binsham was, I knew, the old lord's sister. "Who is Mrs. Perdita Faulds?" I asked.

"I don't know," Roger said.

"So you haven't been to see her? You came here, though?"

Roger didn't answer, but he didn't need to. That sort of ex-soldier felt more at home with other men than with women.

"And," I said, "who inherits the old man's shares?"

"I don't *know*," Roger answered exasperatedly. "The family aren't saying. They've shut up like clams about the will, and of course it's not open to public inspection before probate, which may be *years* away, at the rate they're going. If I had to guess, I'd say Lord Stratton left them all equal shares. He was fair, in his way. Equal shares would mean that no single one of them has control, and that's the nub of the problem, I'd think."

"Do you know them personally?" I asked, and they both nodded gloomily. "Like that, is it?" I asked. "Well, I'm sorry, but they'll have to sort it out themselves."

The young fair-haired woman strolled out of the kitchen with a glass in one hand and a feeding bottle of milk in the other. She nodded vaguely in our direction and went up the staircase and into the room where the boy had taken the baby. My visitors watched in silence.

A brown-haired boy rode a bicycle up the passage from the front door and made a controlled circuit of the room, slowing slightly as he passed behind me and saying, "Yeah, yeah, you told me not to," before returning along the passage towards the outside world. The bicycle was scarlet, the clothes purple and pink and fluorescent green. The very air seemed to quiver with vibrant color, settling back to quiet slate when he'd gone.

Tactfully, no one said anything about obedience or keeping children in order.

I offered the visitors a drink but they had nothing to celebrate and murmured about the length of the drive home. I went with them into the softening sunlight and proffered polite apologies for their non-success. They nodded unhappily. I walked across with them to their car.

The three pirate-ambushers had dematerialized from the oak. The scarlet bicycle flashed in the distance. My visitors looked back at the long dark bulk of the barn, and Roger finally came out with a question.

"What an interesting house," he said civilly. "How did you find it?"

"I built it. The interior, that is. Not the barn itself, of course. That's old. A listed building. I had to negotiate to be allowed windows."

They looked at the neat dark oblongs of glass set unobtrusively into the timber cladding, the only outward indication of the dwelling within.

"You had a good architect," Roger commented.

"Thank you."

"That's another thing the Strattons are fighting over. Some of them want to tear down the stands and rebuild, and they've engaged an architect to draw up plans."

His voice was thick with disgust.

I said curiously, "Surely new stands would be a good thing? Crowd comfort, and all that?"

"Of course new stands would be good!" Irritation finally swamped him. "I implored the old man for years to rebuild. He always said, yes, one day, one day, but he never meant to, not in his lifetime, and now his son Conrad, the new Lord Stratton, he's invited this dreadful man to design new stands, and he's been striding about the place telling me we need this and we need that, and it's all rubbish. He's never designed stands of any sort before and he knows bugger-all about racing."

His genuine indignation interested me a lot more than a fight about shares.

"Building the wrong stands would bankrupt everybody," I said thoughtfully.

Roger nodded. "They'll have to borrow the money, and racing people are fickle. The punters stay away if you don't get the bars right, and if the owners and trainers aren't pampered and comfortable, the buggers will run their horses somewhere else. This lunatic of an architect looked totally blank when I asked him what he thought the crowds did between races. Look at the horses, he said. I ask you! And if it's raining? Shelter and booze, I told him, that's what brings in the customers. He told me I was old-fashioned. And Stratton Park will get a horrendously expensive white elephant that the public will shun. And, like you said, the place will go bust."

"Only if the sell-now or sell-later factions don't get their way."

"But we *need* new stands," Roger insisted. "We need *good* new stands." He paused. "Who designed your house? Perhaps we need someone like *him.*"

"He's never designed any stands. Only houses . . . and pubs."

*"Pubs."* Roger pounced on it. "At least he'd understand the importance of good bars."

I smiled. "I'm sure he would. But you need big-building specialists. Engineers. Your own input. A team."

"Tell that to Conrad." He shrugged dejectedly and slid behind his steering wheel, winding down the window and peering out for one more question. "Could I possibly ask you to let me know if or when the Stratton family contact you? I probably shouldn't trouble you, but I *care* about the racecourse, you see. I know the old man believed it would carry on as before, and he wanted it that way, and perhaps there's something I can do, but I don't know *what,* do you see."

He reached into his jacket again and produced a business card. I took it and nodded, making no promise one way or another, but he took the acknowledgment as assent.

"Thank you very much," he said.

Oliver Wells sat impassively beside him, showing his certainty that their mission had been, as he'd all along expected, unproductive. He still failed to raise guilt in me. Everything I knew of the Strattons urged me strongly to stay away from them in every way I could.

Roger Gardner gave me a sad farewell and drove off, and I went back into my house hoping I wouldn't see him again.

"WHO WERE THOSE people?" Amanda said. "What did they want?"

The fair-haired woman, my wife, lay at the far side of our seven-foot-square bed, emphasizing as usual the distance between us.

"They wanted a white knight act on Stratton Park racecourse."

She worked it out. "A rescue job? You? Those old shares of yours? I hope you said no."

"I said no."

"Is that why you're lying there wide awake in the moonlight, staring at the canopy?"

The pleated silk canopy roofed our great four-poster like a medieval sleeping tent, the only way to achieve privacy in those days before separate bedrooms. The theatrical glamour of the tester, the tassels and the bed's cozy promise beguiled friends: only Amanda and I understood the significance of its size. It had taken me two days of carpentry and stitching to construct, and it was understood by both of us to be a manifestation of a hard-won compromise. We would live in the same house, and also in the same bed, but apart.

"The boys start their Easter holiday this week," Amanda said.

"Do they?"

"You said you'd take them somewhere for Easter."

"Did I?"

"You know you did."

I'd said it to defuse an argument. Never make rash promises, I told myself. An incurable failing.

"I'll think of something," I said.

"And about this house . . ."

"If you like it, we'll stay here," I said.

"Lee!" It briefly silenced her. I knew she had a thousand persuasions ready:

the scattered hints and sighs had been unmistakable for weeks, ever since the gravel had been laid in the drive and the building inspector had called for the last time. The house was freehold, finished and ready for sale, and we needed the money. Half my working capital lay cemented into its walls.

"The boys need a more settled existence," Amanda said, not wanting to waste her reasons.

"Yes."

"It's not fair to keep dragging them from school to school."

"No."

"They worry about leaving here."

"Tell them not to."

"I can't believe it! Can we afford it? I thought you'd say you couldn't afford it. What about the mansion near Oxford, with the tree growing in the drawing room?"

"With luck I'll get planning permission this week."

"But we're not going there, are we?" Despite my assurance, her anxiety rose sharply.

"I'll go there," I said. "You and the boys will stay here for as long as you want. For years. I'll commute."

"You *promise.*"

"Yes."

"No more *mud?* No more *mess?* No more tarpaulins for roofs and brick dust in the cornflakes?"

"No."

"What made you decide?"

The mechanics of decision, I thought, were mysterious. I could have said it was indeed because it was time to settle down for the children's sake, that the eldest had reached the examination time zone and needed continuity in teaching. I could have said that this area, the smiling countryside on the Surrey-Sussex border, was as wholesome as anywhere nowadays. I could have made the decision sound eminently logical.

Instead, I knew in my private mind that the decider had been the old oak. It had appealed to me powerfully, to the inner boy who had been brought up in London traffic, surrounded by landscapes of stone.

I'd seen the oak first a year earlier, fuzzy then as now with the promise of leaf. Mature, perfect, its boughs invited climbers, and as I'd gone there alone I climbed it without embarrassment, sitting at home in its ancient embrace, looking at the rotting great eyesore of a barn that the hard-up landowner had been forbidden to demolish. A historic tithe barn! A local landmark! It would have to stay there until it actually fell down.

A lot of crap, I'd thought, descending from the tree and walking into the ruin through a creaking gap doing duty as a doorway. History-worship gone mad.

Parts of the roof far above were missing. Along the west side the timbers all leaned drunkenly at wild angles, their supports wholly weathered away. A rusted abandoned tractor and heaps of other assorted junk lay among saplings struggling up from the cracked concrete floor. A stiff breeze blew through the tangled desolation, unfriendly and cold.

I'd seen almost at once what could be built within there, almost as if the design had been hovering for a long time in my mind, awaiting life. It would be a house for children. Not necessarily for my own children, but for any. For the child I'd been. A house with many rooms, with surprises, with hiding places.

The boys had hated the place at first and Amanda, heavily pregnant, had burst into tears, but the local planners had been helpful and the landowner had sold me the barn with a surrounding acre of land as if he couldn't believe his luck. When each son found he would be having a separate bedroom as a domain all his own, the objections miraculously ceased.

I'd brought in a conservationist to check the oak. A superb old specimen, he'd said. Three hundred years in the growing. It would outlive us all, he said; and its timeless strength seemed to give me peace.

Amanda repeated, "What made you decide?"

I said, "The oak."

"What?"

"Common sense," I said, which satisfied her.

ON WEDNESDAY I received two direction-changing letters. The first, from an Oxford District Council, turned down my third application for planning permission for restoring the mansion with the beech tree growing in its drawing room. I telephoned to discover why, as I'd understood the third plan had met with their unofficial approval. They now were of the opinion, a repressive voice told me, that the mansion should be restored as one dwelling, not divided into four smaller houses, as I'd suggested. Perhaps I would care to submit revised plans. Sorry, I said. Forget it. I phoned the mansion's owner to say I was no longer a potential buyer, sending him into predictable orbital rage: but no planning permission, no sale, had been our firm agreement.

Sighing, I disconnected and dropped three months' work into the wastepaper basket. Back, literally, to the drawing board.

The second letter came from the lawyers acting for the Stratton family, inviting me to a Stratton Park shareholders' extraordinary meeting the following week.

I phoned the lawyers. "Do they expect me to go?" I asked.

"I don't know, Mr. Morris. But as you are a shareholder, they were required to alert you to the meeting."

"What do you think?"

"Entirely your decision, Mr. Morris."

The voice was cautious and noncommittal, no help at all.

I asked if I held voting shares.

"Yes, you do. Each share has one vote."

ON FRIDAY I did the end-of-term school run, collecting the boys for their Easter break: Christopher, Toby, Edward, Alan and Neil.

What, they wanted to know, had I planned for their holidays?

"Tomorrow," I said calmly, "we go to the races."

"Motor?" Christopher asked hopefully.

"Horses."

They made vomiting noises.

"And next week . . . a ruin hunt," I said.

Deafening disapproval lasted all the way home.

"If I don't find another nice ramshackle ruin, we'll have to sell this house after all," I said, pulling up outside. "Take your pick."

Sobered, they grumbled, "Why can't you get a *proper* job?" which I took as it was meant, resigned acceptance of the program ahead. I'd always told them where the money came from for food and clothes and bicycles and because they'd suffered no serious shortage they had inexhaustible faith in ruins, and were apt to point them out to me unprompted.

Since the thumbs-down letter on the mansion I'd checked through the files of replies I'd had to an advertisement I'd run in the *Spectator* three months earlier—"Wanted, an uninhabitable building. Anything from castle to cowshed considered"—and had inquired of several interesting propositions to see if any were still available. As, owing to a recent severe slump in property prices, it seemed they all were, I promised an inspection and made a list.

I hardly admitted to myself that the uninhabitable buildings niggling away on the fringes of my mind were the grandstands at Stratton Park.

Only I knew the debt I owed to the third baron.

# 2

It rained on Stratton Park's steeplechase meeting, but my five elder sons—Christopher, fourteen, to Neil, seven—grumbled not so much about the weather as about having to wear tidy, unobtrusive clothing on a Saturday. Toby, twelve, the rider of the red bicycle, had tried to avoid the trip altogether, but Amanda had packed him firmly into the mini-van with the others, providing a picnic of Coca-Cola and ham omelettes in burger buns, which we dealt with in the parking lot on arrival.

"OK, ground rules," I said, collecting the wrappings into a single bag. "First, no running about and banging into people. Second, Christopher looks after Alan, Toby takes Edward, Neil goes with me. Third, when we've chosen a rallying point, everyone turns up there immediately after each race."

They nodded. The family crowd control measures were long established and well-understood. The regular head counts reassured them rather than irked.

"Fourth," I went on, "you don't walk behind horses as they're apt to kick, and fifth, notwithstanding the classless society, you'll get on very well on a racecourse if you call every man 'sir.' "

"Sir, sir," Alan said, grinning, "I want to pee, sir."

I trooped them in through the gates and acquired Club enclosure tickets all round. The white cardboard badges fluttered on cords from the sliders of the zips on five blue-hooded anoraks. The five young faces looked serious and well-intentioned, even Toby's, and I went through a rare moment of being both fond and proud of my children.

The rallying point was established under shelter not far from the winner's unsaddling enclosure and within sight of the men's room. We then went all together through the entrance gate into the Club itself and round to the front of the stands and, once I was sure they all had the hang of the whereabouts, I let the paired elder ones go off on their own. Neil, brainy but timid when not in a crowd of brothers, slid his hand quietly into mine and left it there as if absentmindedly, transferring his hold to my trousers occasionally but running no risk of getting lost.

For Neil, as for imaginative Edward, getting lost was the ultimate nightmare. For Alan, it was a laughing matter; for Toby, an objective. Christopher, self-contained, never lost his bearings and habitually found his parents, rather than vice versa.

Neil, easy child, made no objection to walking around in the stands instead of going to see the horses currently plodding wetly round the parade ring before the first race. ("What are the stands, Dad?" "All those buildings.") Neil's agile little brain soaked up vocabulary and impressions like a sponge, and I'd grown accustomed to hearing observations from him that I would hardly have expected from adults.

We popped our heads into a bar that in spite of the rain was uncrowded, and Neil, wrinkling his nose, said he didn't like the smell in there.

"It's beer," I said.

"No, it smells like that pub we lived in before the barn, like it smelled when we first went there, before you changed it."

I looked down at him thoughtfully. I'd reconstructed an ancient unsuccessful and dying inn and turned its sporadic trade into a flood. There had been many factors—reorganized ground plan, colors, lighting, air management, parking. I'd deliberately *added* smells, chiefly of bread baking, but I didn't know what I'd taken away, beyond stale beer and old smoke.

"What smell?" I asked.

Neil bent his knees and put his face near the floor. "It's that horrid cleaning stuff in the water the pub man used to wash his lino tiles with, before you took them all up."

"Really?"

Neil straightened. "Can we go out of here?" he asked.

We left hand in hand. "Do you know what ammonia is?" I said.

"You put it down drains," he explained.

"Was it that smell?"

He thought it over. "Like ammonia but with scent in it."

"Disgusting," I said.

"Absolutely."

I smiled. Apart from the wondrous moment of Christopher's birth I'd never been a good man for babies, but once the growing and emerging minds had begun expressing thoughts and opinions all their own, I'd been continually entranced.

We watched the first race, with my lifting Neil up so that he could see the bright action over the hurdles.

One of the jockeys, I noticed in the racecard, was named Rebecca Stratton, and after the race, when the horses returned to be unsaddled (R Stratton unplaced), we happened to pass by while she was looping girths round her saddle and speaking over her shoulder to downcast owners before setting off back to the changing rooms.

"He moved like a torpid stumblebum. Might try him in blinkers next time."

She was tall with a flat body and a thin scrubbed face with high hard cheekbones, no compromise with femininity in sight. She walked not in a heel-down scurry like the male jockeys but in a sort of feline loping strut on her toes, as if she were not only aware of her own power but aroused by it.

"What's a torpid stumblebum?" Neil asked, after she'd gone.

"It means slow and clumsy."

"Oh."

We met the others at the rallying point and I issued popcorn money all round.

"Horse racing is boring," Toby said.

"If you can pick a winner I'll pay you Tote odds," I said.

"What about me?" Alan said.

"Everyone."

Brightening, they went off to look at the next race's runners in the parade ring, with Christopher explaining to them how to read the form lines in the racecard. Neil, staying close to me, said without hesitation that he would choose number seven.

"Why seven, then?" I asked, looking it up. "It's never won a race in its life."

"My peg in the cloakroom at school is number seven."

"I see. Well, number seven is called Clever Clogs."

Neil beamed.

The other four returned with their choices. Christopher had picked the form horse, the favorite. Alan had singled out Jugaloo because he liked its name. Edward chose a no-hoper because it looked sad and needed encouragement. Toby's vote went to Tough Nut because it had been "kicking and bucking in the ring and winding people up."

They all wanted to know my own choice, and I ran a fast eye over the list and said randomly, "Grandfather," and then wondered at the mind's subliminal tricks and thought it perhaps not so random after all.

Slightly to my relief, Toby's Tough Nut not only won the race but had enough energy left for a couple of vicious kicks in the unsaddling enclosure. Toby's boredom turned to active interest and, as often happened, the rest responded to his mood. The rain stopped. The afternoon definitely improved.

I took them all down the course later to watch the fourth race, a three-mile steeplechase, from beside one of those difficult jumps, an open ditch. This one, the second to last fence on the circuit, was attended by a racecourse employee looking damp in an orange fluorescent jacket, and by a St. John's Ambulance volunteer whose job it was to give first aid to any jockeys who fell at his feet. A small crowd of about thirty racegoers had made the trek down there besides ourselves, spreading out behind the inside rails of the track, both on the take-off and the landing sides of the fence.

The ditch itself—in steeplechasing's past history a real drainage ditch with water in it—was in modern times, as at Stratton Park, no real ditch at all but a space about four feet wide on the take-off side of the fence. There was a large pole across the course on the approach side to give an eye-line to the horses, to tell them when to jump, and the fence itself, of dark birch twigs, was four feet six inches high and at least a couple of feet thick: all in all a regular jump presenting few surprises to experienced 'chasers.

Although the boys had seen a good deal of racing on television I'd never taken them to an actual meeting before, still less down to where the rough action filled the senses. When the ten-strong field poured over the fence on the first of the race's two circuits, the earth quivered under the thudding hooves, the black birch crackled as the half-ton 'chasers crashed through the twigs, the air parted before the straining bunch risking life and limb off the ground at thirty miles an hour: the noise stunned the ears, the jockeys' voices cursed, the colored shirts flashed by kaleidoscopically . . . and suddenly they were gone, their backs receding, silence returning, the brief violent movement over, the vigor and striving a memory.

"Wow!" Toby said, awestruck. "You didn't say it was like *that.*"

"It's only like that when you're close to it," I said.

"But it must be always like that for the jockeys," Edward said thoughtfully. "I mean, they take the noise with them all the way." Edward, ten, had led the pirate ambush up the oak. Misleadingly quiet, it was always he who wondered what it would be like to be a mushroom, who talked to invisible friends, who worried most about famine-struck children. Edward invented make-believe games for his brothers and read books and lived an intense inner life, as reserved as Alan, nine, was outgoing and ebullient.

The racecourse employee walked along the fence on the landing side, putting back into place with a short-handled paddle all the dislodged chunks of birch, making the obstacle look tidy again before the second onslaught.

The five boys waited impatiently while the runners continued round the circuit and came back towards the open ditch for the second and last time before racing away to the last fence and the sprint to the winning post. Each boy had picked his choice of winner and had registered it with me, and when people around us began yelling for their fancy the boys yelled also, Neil jumping up and down in excitement and screaming, "Come on seven, come on seven, come on *peg.*"

I had put my own trust on Rebecca Stratton who was this time partnering a gray mare called Carnival Joy, and as they neared the fence she seemed to be lying second, to my mild surprise, my own expertise at picking winners being zero.

At the last minute the horse in front of her wavered out of a straight line, and I glimpsed the strain on the jockey's face as he hauled on a rein to get himself out of trouble, but he was meeting the fence all wrong. His mount took off a stride too soon and landed right in the space between take-off pole and fence, where, frightened, it dumped its jockey and veered across into the path not only of Carnival Joy, but of all the runners behind.

Things happen fast at thirty miles an hour. Carnival Joy, unable to see a clear path ahead, attempted to jump both the fence *and* the horse on the take-off side, a near-impossible task. The gray's hooves caught the loose horse so that its whole weight crashed chest-first into the fence. Its jockey willy-nilly flew catapulting out forwards over the birch and in a flurry of arms and legs thudded onto the turf. Carnival Joy fell over the fence onto its head, somersaulted, came down on its side and lay there winded, lethally kicking in an attempt to get up.

The rest of the field, some trying to stop, some unaware of the melee, some trying to go round it, compounded the debacle like cars crashing in a fog. One of the horses, going too fast, too late, with no chance of safety, took what must have seemed to him a possible way out and tried to jump right off the course through the nearside wing.

Wings, on the take-off side of each fence, were located there precisely to stop horses running out at the last moment and, to be effective, needed to be too high to jump. Trying to escape trouble by jumping the wings was therefore always a disaster, though not so bad as in the old days when all wings had been made of wood, which splintered and ripped into flesh. Wings at Stratton Park, conforming to the current norm, were made of plastic, which bent and gave way without injuring, but this particular horse, having crashed through unscathed, then collided with the bunch of onlookers, who had tried to scatter too late.

One minute, a smooth race. In five seconds, carnage. I was peripherally aware that three more horses had come to grief on the landing side of the fence with their jockeys either unconscious or sitting up cursing, but I had eyes only for the knocked-down clutch of spectators and chiefly, and I confess frantically, I was counting young figures in blue anoraks, and feeling almost sick with relief to find them all upright and unscathed. The horror on their faces I could deal with later.

Alan, born seemingly without an understanding of danger, suddenly darted out onto the course, ducking under the rails, intent on helping the fallen jockeys.

I yelled at him urgently to come back, but there was too much noise all around us and, powerfully aware of all the loose horses charging about in scared bewilderment, I bent under the rails myself and hurried to retrieve him. Neil, little Neil, scrambled after me.

Terrified for him also, I hoisted him up and ran to fetch Alan who, seemingly oblivious to Carnival Joy's thrashing legs, was doing his best to help a dazed Rebecca Stratton to her feet. In something near despair I found that Christopher too was out on the course, coming to her aid.

Rebecca Stratton returned to full consciousness, brushed crossly at the small hands stretched to help her and in a sharp voice said to no one in particular, "Get these brats out of my way. I've enough to contend with without that."

She stood up furiously, stalked over to the jockey whose mount had caused the whole pile-up and who was now standing forlornly beside the fence, and uttered loud and uncomplimentary opinions about his lack of horsemanship. Her hands clenched and unclenched as if, given half a chance, she would hit him.

My brats predictably detested her immediately. I hustled them with their wounded feelings off the course and out of further trouble, but as we passed near to the lady jockey Neil said, suddenly and distinctly, "Torpid stumble-bum."

"*What?*" Rebecca's head snapped round, but I'd whirled my small son hastily away from her and she seemed more disconcerted than actively directing fire at anyone except the other unfortunate rider.

Toby and Edward, impervious to her, were more concerned with the mown-down spectators, two of whom looked badly hurt. People were in tears, people were stunned, people were awakening to anger. Somewhere in the distance, people were cheering. One of the few horses that had side-stepped the calamity had gone on to win the race.

As on most racecourses, the runners had been followed all the way round by an ambulance driven along on a narrow private roadway on the inner side of the track, so that help was at hand. The racecourse official had unfurled and urgently waved two flags, one red and white, one orange, signaling to the doctor and the vet sitting in a car out in the middle of the course that they were both needed at once.

I collected the boys together and we stood in a group watching the ambulance men and the doctor, in an identifying arm band, kneeling beside the fallen, fetching stretchers, conferring, dealing as best they could with broken bones and blood and worse. It was too late to worry about what the boys were seeing: they resisted my suggestion that we should go back to the stands, so we remained with most of the spectators already there, and were joined by the steady stream of new spectators ghoulishly attracted down the course by chaos and disaster.

The ambulance drove off slowly with the two racegoers who'd been felled by the crash through the wing. "The horse jumped on one man's face," Toby told me matter-of-factly. "I think he's dead."

"Shut up," Edward protested.

"It's the real world," Toby said.

One of the horses couldn't be saved. Screens were erected round him, which they hadn't been for the kicked-in-the-face man.

Two cars and a second ambulance swept up fast from the direction of the stands and out leapt another doctor, another vet, and racecourse authority in the shape of the Clerk of the Course, Oliver Wells, one of my visitors from Sunday. Hurrying from clump to clump, Oliver checked with the doctors, checked with the vets behind the screens, checked with the first-aid men tending a flat-out jockey, listened to a horse-battered spectator sitting on the ground with his head between his knees and finally paid attention to Rebecca Stratton, whose brief spell of daze was still resulting in hyperactivity and a het-up stream of complaints.

"Pay *attention,* Oliver." Her voice rose imperiously. "This little shit caused the whole thing. I'm reporting him to the Stewards. Careless riding! A fine. Suspension, at least."

Oliver Wells merely nodded and went to have a word with one of the doctors, who looked across at Rebecca and, leaving his unconscious patient, attempted to feel the all-too-conscious lady's pulse.

She pulled her wrist away brusquely. "I'm perfectly all right," she insisted. "You stupid little man."

The doctor narrowed his eyes at her and took his skills elsewhere, and across Oliver Wells's bony features flitted an expression that could only be described as glee.

He caught me looking at him before he'd rearranged his expression, and changed the direction of his thoughts with a jolt.

"Lee Morris," he exclaimed, "isn't it?" He looked at the children. "What are they all doing here?"

"Day at the races," I said dryly.

"I mean . . ." He glanced at his watch and at the clearing up going on around us. "When you go back up the course, will you call in at my office before you go home. It's right beside the weighing room. Er . . .*please?*"

"OK," I agreed easily. "If you like."

"Great." He gave me a half-puzzled final glance and dived back into his duties and, with things improving on the turf and slowly losing their first intense drama, the five boys at length unglued their feet and their eyes and walked back with me towards the stands.

"That man came to our house last Sunday," Toby told me. "He's got a long nose and sticking-out ears."

"So he has."

"The sun was making shadows of them."

Children were observant in an uncomplicated way. I'd been too concerned with why the man was there to notice the shadows on his face.

"He's the man who mostly organizes the races here," I said. "He runs things on race days. He's called the Clerk of the Course."

"A sort of field marshal?"

"Quite like that."

"I'm hungry," Alan said, quickly bored.

Neil said "Torpid stumblebum" twice, as if the words themselves pleased his lips.

"What are you talking about?" Christopher demanded, and I explained.

"We were only trying to help her," he protested. "She's a cow."

"Cows are nice," Alan said.

By the time we reached the stands the fifth race, over hurdles, was already being run, but none of my five much cared about the result, not having had a chance to pick their fancy.

No one had won on the fourth race. Everyone's hopes had ended at the ditch. Edward's choice was the horse that died.

I gave them all tea in the tea-room: ruinously expensive but a necessary antidote to shock. Toby drowned his brush with the real world in four cups of hot sweet milky pick-you-up and every cake he could cajole from the waitress.

They ate through the sixth race. They all went to the men's room. The crowds were pouring homewards out of the gates when we made our way to the Clerk of the Course's office beside the weighing room.

The boys entered quietly behind me, unusually subdued and giving a misleading impression of habitual good behavior. Oliver Wells, sitting at a busy-looking desk, eyed the children vaguely and went on speaking into a walkie-talkie. Roger Gardner, racecourse manager, was also in attendance, sitting with one hip on the desk, one foot swinging. The Colonel's worry-level had if anything intensified during the week, lines having deepened across his forehead. Civilized habits of behavior would see him through, though, I thought, even if he rose to full height at our entrance looking as if he had expected Lee Morris but not five smaller clones.

"Come in," Oliver said, putting down his instrument. "Now, what shall we do with these boys?" The question seemed to be merely rhetorical as he had recourse again to his walkie-talkie, pressing buttons. "Jenkins? To my office, please." He switched off again. "Jenkins will see to them."

An official knocked briefly on an inner door and came in without waiting for a summons: a middle-aged messenger in a belted navy raincoat, with a slightly stodgy expression and slow-moving reassuring bulk.

"Jenkins," Oliver said, "take these boys into the jockeys' changing rooms and let them collect autographs."

"Won't they be a nuisance?" I asked, as parents do.

"Jockeys are quite good with children," Oliver said, making shooing motions to my sons. "Go with Jenkins, boys, I want to talk to your father."

"Take them, Christopher," I encouraged, and all five of them went cheerfully with the safe escort.

"Sit down," Oliver invited, and I pulled up a chair and sat round the desk with the two of them. "We're not going to get five minutes without interruptions," Oliver said, "so we'll come straight to the point." The walkie-talkie crackled. Oliver picked it up, pressed a switch and listened.

A voice said brusquely. "Oliver, get up here, pronto. The sponsors want a word."

Oliver said reasonably, "I'm writing my report of the fourth race."

"Now, Oliver." The domineering voice switched itself off, severing argument.

Oliver groaned. "Mr. Morris . . . Can you wait?" He rose and departed, whether I could wait or not.

"That," Roger explained neutrally, "was a summons from Conrad Darlington Stratton, the fourth baron."

I made no comment.

"Things have changed since we saw you on Sunday," Roger said. "For the worse, if possible. I wanted to go and see you again, but Oliver thought it was useless. And now . . . well, here you are! Why are you here?"

"Curiosity. But with what the boys saw at that fence today, I shouldn't have come."

"Terrible mix-up." He nodded. "A horse killed. It does racing no good."

"What about the spectators? My son Toby thought one of them, too, was dead."

Roger said disgustedly, "A hundred dead spectators wouldn't raise marches against cruel sports. The stands could collapse and kill a hundred, but racing would go on. Dead *people* are irrelevant, don't you know."

"So . . . the man *was* dead?"

"Did you see him?"

"Only with a dressing covering his face."

Roger said gloomily, "It'll be in the papers. The horse came through the wing into him and slashed him across the eyes with a foreleg—those racing plates on their hooves cut like swords—it was gruesome, Oliver said. But the man died of a snapped neck. Died instantly under half a ton of horse. Best that can be said."

"My son Toby saw the man's face," I said.

Roger looked at me. "Which is Toby?"

"The second one. He's twelve. The boy who rode his bike into the house."

"I remember. Poor little bugger. Nightmares ahead, I shouldn't wonder."

Toby was anyway the one I most worried about, and this wouldn't help. He'd been born rebellious, grown into a cantankerous toddler and had never since been easy to persuade. I had a sad feeling that in four years' time he would develop, despite my best efforts, into a sullen world-hating youth, alienated and miserable. I could sense that it would happen and I ached for it not to, but I'd seen too many other suffering families where a much-loved son or daughter had grown destructively angry in the mid-teens, despising attempts to help.

Rebecca Stratton, I surmised, might have been like that, ten years earlier.

She came into Oliver's office now like a whirlwind, smashing the door open until it hit the wall, bringing in with her a swirl of cold outside air and a towering attack of fury.

"Where's that bloody Oliver?" she loudly demanded, looking round.

"With your father . . ."

She didn't listen. She still wore breeches and boots, but with a tan sweater in place of her racing colors. Her eyes glittered, her body looked rigid, she seemed half-way demented. "Do you know what that stupid bloody doctor's done? He's stood me down from racing for *four* days. Four days! I ask you. He says I'm concussed. Concussed, my arse. Where's Oliver? He's got to tell that bloody man I'm going to ride on Monday. Where is he?"

Rebecca spun on her heel and strode out with the same energy expenditure as on the way in.

I said, closing the door after her, "She's concussed to high heaven, I'd have said."

"Yes, but she's always a bit like that. If I were the doctor I'd stand her down for life."

"She's not your favorite Stratton, I gather."

Caution returned to Roger with a rush. "I never said . . ."

"Of course not." I paused. "So what has changed since last Sunday?"

He consulted the light cream walls, the framed print of Arkle, the big calendar with days crossed off, a large clock (accurate) and his own shoes, and finally said, "Mrs. Binsham came out of the woodwork."

"Is that so momentous?"

"You know who she *is?*" He was curious, a little surprised.

"The old lord's sister."

"I thought you didn't know anything about the family."

"I said I had no contact with them, and I don't. But my mother talked about them. Like I told you, she was once married to the old man's son."

"Do you mean Conrad? Or Keith? Or . . . Ivan?"

"Keith," I said. "Conrad's twin."

"Fraternal twins," Roger said. "The younger one."

I agreed. "Twenty-five minutes younger, and apparently never got over it."

"It does make a difference, I suppose."

It made the difference between inheriting a barony, and not. Inheriting the family mansion, and not. Inheriting a fortune, and not. Keith's jealousy of his twenty-five-minute-elder brother had been one—but only one, according to my mother—of the habitual rancors poisoning her ex-husband's psyche.

I had my mother's photographs of her Stratton wedding day, the bridegroom tall, light-haired, smiling, strikingly good-looking, all the promise of a splendid life ahead in the pride and tenderness of his manner towards her. She had that day been exploding with bliss, she'd told me; with an indescribable floating feeling of happiness.

Within six months he'd broken her arm in a fight and punched out two of her front teeth.

"Mrs. Binsham," Roger Gardner said, "has insisted on a shareholders' meeting next week. She's a dragon, they say. She's Conrad's aunt, of course, and apparently she's the only living creature who makes him quake."

Forty years back she had implacably forced her brother, the third baron, to behave harshly in public to my mother. Even then Mrs. Binsham had been the dynamo of the family, the manipulator, the one who laid down the program of action and forced the rest to follow.

"She never gave up," my mother said. "She would simply wear down any opposition until you would do what she wanted just to get some peace. In her own eyes, you see, she was always *right,* so she was always certain that what she wanted was *best.*"

I asked Roger, "Do you know Mrs. Binsham yourself?"

"Yes, but not well. She's an impressive old lady, very upright. She comes to the races here quite often with Lord Stratton—er, not Conrad, but the old lord—but I've never had any really private conversations with her. Oliver knows her better. Or at least," he faintly grinned, "Oliver has obeyed her instructions from time to time."

"Perhaps she'll sort out the present squabbles and quiet things down," I said.

Roger shook his head. "What she says might go with Conrad and Keith and Ivan, but the younger generation may rebel, especially since they're all coming into some shares of their own."

"You're sure?"

"Certain."

"So now you have an informant in the nest?"

His face grew still; wary almost. "I never said that."

"No."

Oliver returned. "The sponsors are unhappy about the dead horse, bless their little hearts. Bad publicity. Not what they pay for. They'll have to reconsider before next year, they say." He sounded dispirited. "I'd framed that race well, you know," he told me. "Ten runners in a three-mile 'chase. That's good, you know. Often you'll only attract five or six, or even less. If the sponsor pulls out, it'll be a poorer affair altogether, next year."

I made sympathetic noises.

"If there *is* a next year," he said. "There's a shareholders' meeting next week . . . did they tell you?"

"Yes."

"They're holding it here on the racecourse, in the Strattons' private dining room," he said. "Conrad hasn't moved into the big house yet, and anyway this is less personal, he says. Will you be coming?" It was less a question, I thought, than an entreaty.

"I haven't decided," I said.

"I do hope you will. I mean, they need an *outside* view, do you see? They're all too *involved*."

"They wouldn't want me there."

"All the more reason for going."

I doubted that, but didn't bother to argue. I suggested collecting the boys, and found them "helping" the valets pack the jockeys' saddles and other gear into large laundry hampers while eating fruitcake.

They'd been no trouble, I was told, and hoped I could believe it. I thanked everyone. Thanked Roger. "Vote your shares," he said anxiously. Thanked Jenkins. "Well-behaved little sods," he said helpfully. "Bring them again."

"We called everyone 'sir,' " Neil confided to me as we left.

"We called Jenkins 'sir,' " Alan said. "He got us the cake."

We reached the mini-van and climbed in, and they showed me all the jockeys' autographs in their racecards. They'd had a good time in the changing room, it seemed.

"Was that man dead?" Toby asked, reverting to what was most on his mind.

"I'm afraid so."

"I thought he was. I've never seen anyone dead before."

"You've seen dogs," Alan said.

"That's not the same, plank-head."

Christopher asked, "What did the Colonel mean about voting your shares?"

"Huh?"

"He said 'Vote your shares.' He looked pretty upset, didn't he?"

"Well," I said, "do you know what shares are?"

"Pieces of cake," Neil guessed. "One each."

"Say you had a chessboard," I said, "there would be sixty-four squares, OK? Say you called each square a share. There would be sixty-four shares."

The young faces told me I wasn't getting the idea across.

"OK," I said, "say you have a floor made of tiles."

They nodded at once. As a builder's children they knew all about tiles.

27

"Say you lay ten tiles across and ten tiles down, and fill in the square."

"A hundred tiles," Christopher nodded.

"Yes. Now call each tile a share, a hundredth part of the whole square. A hundred squares. OK?"

They nodded.

"What about voting?" Christopher asked.

I hesitated. "Say you owned some of the tiles, you could vote to have yours blue . . . or red . . . whatever you'd like."

"How many could *you* vote on?"

"Eight," I said.

"You could have eight blue tiles? What about the others?"

"All the others, ninety-two, belong to other people. They could all choose whatever color they liked for the tiles they owned."

"It would be a mess," Edward pointed out. "You wouldn't get everyone to agree on a pattern."

"You're absolutely right," I said, smiling.

"But you're not really meaning *tiles,* are you?" Christopher said.

"No." I paused. For once, they were all listening. "See, say this racecourse is like a hundred tiles. A hundred squares. A hundred shares. I have eight shares of the racecourse. Other people have ninety-two."

Christopher shrugged. "It's not much, then. Eight's not even one row."

Neil said, "If the racecourse was divided up into a hundred squares . . . Dad's eight squares might have the stands on!"

"Plank-head," Toby said.

# 3

Why did I go?

I don't know. I doubt if there is such a thing as a wholly free choice, because one's choices are rooted in one's personality. I choose what I choose because I am what I am, that sort of thing.

I chose to go for reprehensible reasons like the lure of unearned gain and from the vanity that I might against all odds tame the dragon and sort out the Stratton feuds peacefully, as Roger and Oliver wanted. Greed and pride . . . powerful spurs masquerading as prudent financial management and altruistic good works.

So I disregarded the despairing plea from my mother's remembered wisdom and took my children into desperate danger and by my presence altered forever the internal stresses and balances of the Strattons.

Except, of course, that it didn't seem like that on the day of the shareholders' meeting.

It took place on Wednesday afternoon, on the third day of the ruin hunt. On Monday morning the five boys and I had set off from home in the big converted single-decker bus that had in the past served as mobile home for us all during periods when the currently-being-rebuilt ruin had been truly and totally uninhabitable.

The bus had its points: it would sleep eight, it had a working shower room, a galley, sofas and televisions. I'd taken lessons from a yacht builder in creating storage spaces where none might seem to exist, and we could in fact store a sizable household very neatly aboard. It did not, all the same, offer privacy or much personal space, and as the boys grew they had found it increasingly embarrassing as an address.

They packed into it quite happily on Monday, though, as I had promised them a real holiday in the afternoons if I could visit a ruin each morning, and in fact with map and timetables I'd planned a series of the things they most liked to do. Monday afternoon we spent canoeing on the Thames, Tuesday they beat the hell out of a bowling alley, and on Wednesday they'd promised to help Roger Gardner's wife clean out her garage, a chore they bizarrely enjoyed.

I left the bus outside the Gardner house and with Roger walked to the stands.

"I'm not invited to the meeting," he said as if it were a relief, "but I'll show you to the door."

He took me up a staircase, round a couple of corners, and through a door marked "Private" into a carpeted world quite different from the functional concrete of the public areas. Silently pointing to paneled and polished double doors ahead, he gave me an encouraging pat on the shoulder and left me, rather in the manner of a colonel avuncularly sending a rookie into his first battle.

Regretting my presence already, I opened one of the double doors and went in.

I'd gone to the meeting in business clothes (gray trousers, white shirt, tie, navy blazer) to present a conventional boardroom appearance. I had a tidy normal haircut, the smoothest of shaves, clean fingernails. The big dusty laborer of the building sites couldn't be guessed at.

The older men at the meeting all wore suits. Those more my own age and younger hadn't bothered with such formality. I had, I thought in satisfaction, hit it just right.

Although I had arrived at the time stated in the lawyer's letter, it seemed that the Strattons had jumped the clock. The whole tribe was sitting round a truly imposing Edwardian dining table of old French-polished mahogany, their chairs newer, nineteen-thirtyish, like the grandstands themselves.

The only one I knew by sight was Rebecca, the jockey, dressed now in trousers, tailored jacket and heavy gold chains. The man sitting at the head of the table, gray-haired, bulky and authoritative, I took to be Conrad, the fourth and latest baron.

He turned his head to me as I went in. They all, of course, turned their heads. Five men, three women.

"I'm afraid you are in the wrong place," Conrad said with scant politeness. "This is a private meeting."

"Stratton shareholders?" I asked inoffensively.

"As it happens. And you are . . . ?"

"Lee Morris."

The shock that rippled through them was almost funny, as if they hadn't realized that I would even be notified of the meeting, let alone had considered that I might attend; and they had every reason to be surprised, as I had never before responded to any of their official annual bits of paper.

I closed the door quietly behind me. "I was sent a notification," I said.

"Yes, but—" Conrad said without welcome. "I mean, it wasn't necessary . . . You weren't expected to bother . . ." He stopped uncomfortably, unable to hide what looked like dismay.

"As I'm here," I said amiably, "I may as well stay. Shall I sit here?" I indicated an empty chair at the foot of the table, walking towards it purposefully. "We've never met," I went on, "but you must be Conrad, Lord Stratton."

He said, "Yes," tight-lipped.

One of the older men said violently, "This is a disgrace! You've no right here. Don't sit down. You're *leaving.*"

I stood by the empty chair and brought the lawyer's letter out of a pocket. "As you'll see," I answered him pleasantly, "I *am* a shareholder. I was properly given advance notice of this meeting, and I'm sorry if you don't like it, but I do have a legal right to be here. I'll just sit quietly and listen."

I sat down. All of the faces registered stark disapproval except for one, a younger man's, bearing a hint of a grin.

"Conrad! This is ridiculous." The man who most violently opposed my presence was up on his feet, quivering with fury. "Get rid of him at once."

Conrad Stratton realistically took stock of my size and comparative youth and said defeatedly, "Sit down, Keith. Who exactly is going to throw him out?"

Keith, my mother's first husband, might have been strong enough in his youth to batter a miserable young wife, but there was no way he could begin to do the same to her thirty-five-year-old son. He hated the fact of my existence. I hated what I'd learned of him. The antagonism between us was mutual, powerful and lasting.

The fair hair in the wedding photographs had turned a blondish gray. The good bone structure still gave him a more patrician air than that of his elder twin. His looking glass must still constantly be telling him that the order of his birth had been nature's horrible mistake, that *his* should have been the head that engaged first.

He couldn't sit down. He strode about the big room, snapping his head round in my direction now and then and glaring at me.

Important chaps who might have been the first and second barons looked down impassively from gold-framed portraits on the walls. The lighting hung from the ceiling in convoluted brass chandeliers with etched glass shades around candle bulbs. Upon a long polished mahogany sideboard stood a short case clock flanked by heavy old throttled-neck vases that, like the whole room, had an air of having remained unchanged for most of the old lord's life.

There was no daylight: no windows.

Next to Conrad sat a ramrod-backed old lady easy to identify as his aunt, Marjorie Binsham, the convener of this affair. Forty years earlier, on my mother's wedding day, she had stared grimly at the camera as if a smile would have cracked her facial muscles, and nothing in that way, either, seemed to have been affected by passing years. Now well into her eighties, she flourished a still-sharp brain under disciplined wavy white hair and wore a red and black hound's-tooth dress with a white, ecclesiastical-looking collar.

Rather to my surprise she was regarding me more with curiosity than rigid dislike.

"Mrs. Binsham?" I said from the other end of the table. "Mrs. Marjorie Binsham?"

"Yes." This monosyllable came out clipped and dry, merely acknowledging information.

"I," said the man whose grin was now in control, "am Darlington Stratton, known as Dart. My father sits at the head of the table. My sister Rebecca is on your right."

"This is unnecessary!" Keith snapped at him from somewhere behind Conrad. "He does not need introductions. He's leaving."

Mrs. Binsham said repressively and with exquisite diction, "Keith, do stop prowling, and sit down. Mr. Morris is correct, he has a right to be here. Face facts. As you cannot eject him, ignore him."

Mrs. Binsham's direct gaze was bent on me, not on Keith. My own lips twitched. Ignoring me seemed the last thing any of them could do.

Dart said, with a straight face covering infinite mischief, "Have you met Hannah, your sister?"

The woman on the other side of Conrad from Mrs. Binsham vibrated with disgust. "He's not my brother, he's *not.*"

"Half-brother," Marjorie Binsham said, with the same cool fact-facing precision. "Unpalatable as you may find it, Hannah, you cannot change it. Just ignore him."

For Hannah, as for Keith, the advice was impossible to follow. My half-sister, to my relief, didn't look like our joint mother. I'd been afraid she might: afraid to find familiar eyes hating me from an echo of a loved face. She looked more like Keith, tall, blonde, fine-boned and, at the moment, white with outrage.

"How dare you!" She shook. "Have you no decency?"

"I have shares," I pointed out.

"And you shouldn't have," Keith said harshly. "Why Father ever gave them to Madeline, I'll never know."

I refrained from saying that he must know perfectly well why. Lord Stratton had given shares to Madeline, his daughter-in-law, because he knew why she was leaving. In my mother's papers, after she'd died, I came across old letters from her father-in-law telling her of his regret, of his regard for her, of his concern that she shouldn't suffer financially, as she had physically. Though loyal in public to his son, he had privately not only given her the shares "for the future" but had endowed her also with a lump sum to keep her comfortable on the interest. In return she had promised never ever to speak of Keith's behavior, still less to drag the family name through a messy divorce. The old man wrote that he understood her rejection of Hannah, the result of his son's "sexual attacks." He would care for the child, he wrote. He wished my mother "the best that can be achieved, my dear."

It was Keith who later divorced my mother—for adultery with an elderly illustrator of children's books, Leyton Morris, my father. The resulting devoted marriage lasted fifteen years, and it wasn't until she was on her own one-way road with cancer that my mother talked of the Strattons and told me in long night-time outpourings about her sufferings and her fondness for Lord Stratton; and it wasn't until then that I learned that it was Lord Stratton's money that had educated me and sent me through architectural school, the foundations of my life.

I had written to thank him after she died, and I still had his reply.

My dear boy,

I loved your mother. I hope you gave her the joy she deserved. I thank you for your letter, but do not write again.

Stratton.

I didn't write again. I sent flowers to his funeral. With him alive, I would never have intruded on his family.

With Conrad identified, and Keith, and Marjorie Binsham, and Conrad's offspring Dart and Rebecca, there remained two males at the meeting still to be named. One, in late middle age, sat between Mrs. Binsham and Keith's vacated chair, and I could make a guess at him.

"Excuse me," I said, leaning forward to catch his attention. "Are you . . . Ivan?"

The youngest of the old lord's three sons, more bullish like Conrad than greyhound like Keith, gave me a hard stare and no reply.

Dart said easily, "My uncle Ivan, as you say. And opposite him is his son Forsyth, my cousin."

"Dart!" Keith objected fiercely. "Be quiet."

Dart gave him an impassive look and seemed unintimidated. Forsyth, Ivan's son, was the one, I thought, that had reacted least to my attendance. That is to say he took it less personally than the others, and he slowly revealed, as time went on, that he had no interest in me as Hannah's regrettable half-brother, but only as an unknown factor in the matter of shares.

Young and slight, he had a narrow chin and dark intense eyes, and was treated by the others without the slightest deference. No one throughout the meeting asked his opinion about anything and, when he gave it regardless, his father, Ivan, regularly interrupted. Forsyth himself seemed to find this treatment normal, and perhaps for him it was.

Conrad, coming testily to terms with the inevitable, said heavily, "Let's get on with the meeting. I called it . . ."

"*I* called it," corrected his aunt sharply. "All this squabbling is ridiculous. Let's get to the point. There has been racing on this racecourse for almost ninety years, and it will go on as before, and that's an end to it. The arguing must stop."

"This racecourse is dying on its feet," Rebecca contradicted impatiently. "You have absolutely no idea what the modern world is all about. I'm sorry if it upsets you, Aunt Marjorie, but you and Grandfather have been left behind by the tide. This place needs new stands and a whole new outlook, and what it doesn't need is a fuddy-duddy old colonel for a manager and a stick-in-the-mud Clerk of the Course who can't say boo to a doctor."

"The doctor outranks him," Dart observed.

"You shut up," his sister ordered. "You've never had the bottle to ride in a race. I've raced on most courses in this country and I'm telling you, this place is terminally old-fashioned and it's got my name on it too, which makes me open to ridicule, and the whole thing *stinks.* If you won't or can't see that, then I'm in favor of cashing in now for what we can get."

"Rebecca!" Conrad's reproof seemed tired, as if he'd heard his daughter's views too often. "We need new stands. We can all agree on that. And I've commissioned plans . . ."

"You'd no right to do that," Marjorie informed him. "Waste of money. These old stands are solidly built and are thoroughly serviceable. We do *not* need new stands. I'm totally opposed to the idea."

Keith said with troublemaking relish, "Conrad has had this pet architect roaming round the place for weeks. *His* choice of architect. None of us has been consulted, and I'm against new stands on principle."

"Huh!" Rebecca exclaimed. "And where do you think the women jockeys have to change? In a partitioned-off space the size of a *cupboard* in the ladies' loo. It's pathetic."

"All for want of a horseshoe nail," Dart murmured.

"What do you mean?" Rebecca demanded.

"I mean," her brother explained lazily, "that we'll lose the racecourse to feminism."

She wasn't sure enough of his meaning to come up with a cutting answer so instead ignored him.

"We should sell at once," Keith exclaimed, still striding about. "The market is good. Swindon's growing. The industrial area is already on the racecourse boundary. Sell, I say. I've already sounded out a local developer. He's agreed to survey and consider."

"You've done *what?*" Conrad demanded. "And *you've* consulted no one, either. And that's never the way to sell *anything.* You know nothing about business dealings."

Keith said huffily, "I know if you want to sell something you have to advertise."

"No," Conrad said flatly, as if that settled it. "We're not selling."

Keith's anger rose. "It's all right for *you.* You inherit most of Father's residual estate. It's not fair. It was *never* fair, leaving nearly all to eldest sons. Father was hopelessly old-fashioned. *You* may not need money, but none of us is getting any younger and I say take out our capital *now.*"

"Later," Hannah said intensely. "Sell when there's less land available. Wait."

Conrad remarked heavily, "Your daughter, Keith, fears that if you take the capital now you'll squander it and there'll be none left for her to inherit."

Hannah's face revealed it to be a bull's-eye diagnosis, and also showed disgust at having had her understandable motives so tellingly disclosed.

"What about you, Ivan?" his aunt inquired. "Still of the same indecisive mind?"

Ivan scarcely responded to the jibe, even if he recognized it as one. He nodded with a show of measured sagacity. "Wait and see," he said. "That's the best."

"Wait until you've lost the opportunity," Rebecca said scathingly. "That's what you mean, isn't it?"

He said defensively, "Why are you always so *sharp*, Rebecca? There's nothing wrong with patience."

"Inaction," she corrected. "Making no decision's as bad as making the wrong decision."

"Rubbish," Ivan said.

Forsyth began, "Have we thought about tax on capital gains . . ." but Ivan was saying, "It's clear we ought to shelve a decision until . . ."

"Until the bloody cows come home," Rebecca said.

"Rebecca!" Her great-aunt's disapproval arrived automatically. "Now stop it, all of you, because at the moment I and I alone can make decisions and I have the impression that none of you realize that."

From their expressions it was clear that they neither knew nor cared to be told.

"Aunt," Conrad said repressively, "you have ten shares only. You cannot make unilateral decisions."

"Oh, but I can," she said triumphantly. "You're so ignorant, all of you. You fancy yourselves as men—oh, and *women,* Rebecca—of affairs but none of you seems to realize that in any company it is the directors, not shareholders, who make the decisions, and *I . . .*" she looked round, collecting undivided attention, "I am at present the sole remaining director. *I* make the decisions."

She brought the meeting to its first taste of silence.

After a pause, Dart laughed. Everyone else scowled, chiefly at him, disapproval of a grandson being more prudent than defying the dragon.

The splendid old lady took folded sheets of paper from an expensive leather handbag and shook them open with an almost theatrical flourish.

"This is a letter," she said, putting on reading glasses, "from the Stratton Park racecourse lawyers. I won't bother you with the introductory paragraphs. The heart of the matter is this." She paused, glanced around at her attentive and apprehensive audience and then read from the letter. "As two directors are sufficient, it was quite proper for yourself and Lord Stratton to comprise the whole Board and for him, as by far the major shareholder, to make all the decisions. Now that he has died you may wish to form a new Board with more directors, and while these *may* be members of the Stratton family, there is no bar to your electing outside, non-shareholding directors if you should wish.

"We would accordingly suggest you call an extraordinary meeting of shareholders for the purpose of electing new directors to serve on the Board of Stratton Park Racecourse Ltd., and we will be happy to assist you in every possible way."

Marjorie Binsham looked up. "The lawyers were willing to conduct this meeting. I said I could do it and they weren't to bother. As the sole remaining director of the company I make a motion that we elect new directors, and as director I also second the motion, and although this may not be exactly regulation procedure, it will have the desired effect."

Conrad said, feebly for him, "Aunt . . ."

"As you, Conrad, are now titular head of the family, I propose that you become a director forthwith." She looked down at the letter. "It says here that any director may be elected if he obtains at least fifty percent of the votes cast at a shareholders' meeting. Each share, in this company, bears one vote. According to this letter, if I and the inheriting family shareholders all attend this meeting, there will be eighty-five votes available. That is to say, my ten shares, and the seventy-five now inherited by the rest of you." She paused and looked down the table to where I sat. "We did not expect Mr. Morris to attend, but as he is here, he has eight votes to cast."

"No!" Keith said furiously. "He has no *right.*"

Marjorie Binsham replied implacably. "He has eight votes. He can cast them. You cannot prevent it."

Her verdict had surprised me as much as it had astounded the others. I'd gone there out of curiosity as much as anything else, ready to upset them slightly, but not to this fundamental extent.

"It's *disgraceful,*" Hannah yelled, rising compulsively from her seat like her still-pacing father. "I won't have it!"

"According to our lawyers," her great-aunt went on, totally ignoring the tantrum, "once we have elected a Board of Directors it is *they* who decide the future of this racecourse."

"Make *me* a director," Rebecca demanded.

"You need forty-seven votes," murmured Dart, having done some arithmetic. "Any director needs forty-seven, minimum."

"I propose we elect Conrad at once," Marjorie reiterated. "He has my ten votes." She looked round, challenging them to disagree.

"All right," Ivan said. "Conrad, you have my twenty-one."

"I suppose I can vote for myself," Conrad said. "I vote my own twenty-one. That's, er, fifty-two."

"Elected," Marjorie said, nodding. "You can now conduct the rest of the meeting."

Conrad's manner regained confidence and he seemed literally to swell to fill his new role. He said kindly, "Then I think we should vote to keep Marjorie on the Board. Only right."

No one demurred. The Honorable Mrs. Binsham looked as if she would chew any dissenter for breakfast.

"I, too, must be a director," Keith asserted. "I also have twenty-one shares. I vote them for me."

Conrad cleared his throat. "I propose Keith for director . . ."

Forsyth said too quickly, "That's asking for trouble."

Conrad, not hearing, or at least choosing not to, hurried on. "Keith's twenty-one, then, and mine. Forty-two. Aunt?"

Marjorie shook her head. Keith took three fast paces towards her with his hands outstretched as if he would attack her. She didn't flinch or shrink away. She stared him down.

She said with starch, "That's exactly why I won't vote for you, Keith. You never had any self-control, and you've grown no wiser with age. Look elsewhere. Ask Mr. Morris."

A wicked old lady, I saw. Keith went scarlet. Dart grinned.

Keith walked round behind Ivan. "Brother," he said peremptorily, "I need your twenty-one votes."

"But I say," Ivan dithered, "Aunt Marjorie's right. You'd fight Conrad all the time. No sensible decisions would ever get made."

"Are you *refusing* me?" Keith could hardly believe it. "You'll be sorry, you know. You'll be sorry." The violence in his character had risen too near the surface even for his daughter, Hannah, who had subsided into her seat and now said uneasily, "Dad, don't bother with him. You can have my three votes. Do calm down."

"That's forty-five," Conrad said. "You need two more, Keith."

"Rebecca has three," Keith said.

Rebecca shook her head.

"Forsyth, then," Keith said furiously, at least not begging.

Forsyth looked at his fingers.

*"Dart?"* Keith shook with anger.

Dart glanced at his sweating uncle and took pity on him.

"OK, then," he said, making nothing of it. "My three."

Without much emotion, a relief after the storm, Conrad said flatly, "Keith's elected."

"And to be fair," Dart said, "I propose Ivan also."

"We don't need four directors," Keith said.

"As I voted for *you,*" Dart told him, "you can do the decent thing and vote for Ivan. After all, he has twenty-one shares, just like you, and he's got just as much right to make decisions. So, Father," he said to Conrad, "I propose Ivan."

Conrad considered his son's proposal and shrugged: not because he disapproved, I guessed, but because he didn't think much of his brother Ivan's brains.

"Very well. Ivan. Anyone against?"

Everyone shook their heads, including Marjorie.

"Mr. Morris?" Conrad asked formally.

"He has my votes."

"Unanimous, then," Conrad said, surprised. "Any more nominations?"

Rebecca said, "Four is a bad number. There should be five. Someone from the younger generation."

She was suggesting herself again. No one, not even Dart, responded. Rebecca's thin face was in its way as mean as Keith's.

Not one of the four grandchildren was going to give power to any other. The three older brothers showed no wish to pass batons. The Board, with undercurrents of gripe and spite, was established as the old lord's three sons and their enduring aunt.

Without difficulty they agreed that Conrad should be chairman (*"Chair,"* Rebecca said. "Don't be ridiculous," said Keith), but Marjorie had another squib in reserve.

"The lawyer's letter also says," she announced, "that if the shareholders are dissatisfied with any director, they can call a meeting and vote to remove him. They need a fifty-one percent vote to achieve it." She stared beadily at Keith. "If it should become advisable to save us all from an irresponsible director, I will make certain that Mr. Morris and his eight votes are encouraged to attend the meeting."

Hannah was as affronted as Keith, but Keith, besides being infuriated, seemed almost bewildered, as if the possibility of his aunt's vitriolic disapproval had never occurred to him. Similarly it had never occurred to me that she wouldn't demand my execution rather than my presence. Marjorie, I then reckoned, would use any tool that came to hand to achieve a desired end: a wholly pragmatic lady.

Dart said with deceptive amiability, "Isn't there some rule in the setup of this company that says all board meetings are open? I mean, all shareholders may attend."

"Rubbish," Keith said.

Forsyth said, "Attend but not interrupt. Not speak unless asked . . ."

Ivan's voice drowned his son's. "We'll have to read the articles, or whatever."

"I did," Forsyth said. No one paid any attention.

"It never mattered before," Conrad observed. "The only shareholders besides Father and Aunt Marjorie were Mr. Morris, and of course before him, Madeline, and . . . er . . . Mrs. Perdita Faulds."

"Who exactly *is* Mrs. Perdita Faulds?" Rebecca demanded.

No one replied. If they knew, they weren't telling.

"Do you," Dart asked me directly, "know who Mrs. Perdita Faulds is?"

I shook my head. "No."

"We'll find her if necessary," Marjorie declared, making it sound ominous. "Let's hope we won't have to." Her malevolent gaze swept over Keith, warning him. "If we have to remove a director, we will find her."

On the brief list of shareholders that Roger had shown me, Mrs. Faulds's address had been care of a firm of lawyers. Messages to the lady would no doubt routinely be relayed, but actually finding her in person might take ingenuity. Take a professional bloodhound, perhaps. Marjorie wouldn't blink at that, I guessed, if it suited her.

It also occurred to me that if she were so certain the mysterious Mrs. Faulds would vote as Marjorie wanted, then Marjorie, at least, knew who she was. Not really my business, I thought.

Conrad said, with a show of taking a grip on the meeting, "Well, now that we have directors, perhaps we can make some firm decisions. We must, in fact. We have another race meeting here next Monday, as you know, and we cannot ask Marjorie indefinitely to be responsible for authorizing everything. There was a lot Father used to do that none of us know about. We simply have to learn fast."

"The first thing to do is sack the Colonel and stupid Oliver," Rebecca said.

Conrad merely glanced at his daughter and spoke to the others. "The Colonel and Oliver are the only people at present who can keep this place running. We need, in fact we rely entirely on, their expertise, and I intend to go on consulting them over every detail."

Rebecca sulked angrily. Marjorie's disapproval grew vigorous runners in her direction, like a rampant strawberry plant.

"I put forward a motion," Ivan said surprisingly, "that we continue to run the races as before, with Roger and Oliver in their normal roles."

"Seconded," Marjorie said crisply.

Keith scowled. Conrad, ignoring him, made a note on a pad in front of him. "The Board's first decision is to continue without change, for now." He pursed his lips. "I suppose we ought to have a secretary to write the minutes."

"You could use Roger's secretary," I suggested.

"No!" Rebecca jumped on it. "Everything we said would go straight to bloody Roger. And no one asked you to speak. You're an outsider."

Dart launched into verse, "Oh wad some power the giftie gie us to see oursels as others see us! It wad frae monie a blunder free us, an' foolish notion."

*"What?"* Rebecca demanded.

"Robert Burns," Dart said. " 'To a Louse.' "

I smothered the least appearance of a laugh. No one else seemed to think it funny.

I said to Rebecca mildly, "You could reposition the women jockeys' changing room."

"Oh really?" She was sarcastic. "Exactly where?"

"I'll show you. And," I went on speaking to Conrad, "you could double the take in the bars."

"Ye *gods,*" Dart said comically, "what have we here?"

I asked Conrad, "Are there already detailed plans for new stands?"

"We're not having new stands!" Marjorie was adamant.

"We must," Conrad said.

"We sell the land," Keith insisted.

Ivan dithered.

"New stands," Rebecca said. "New management. New everything. Or sell."

"Sell, but later," Hannah repeated obstinately.

"I agree," Forsyth nodded.

"Not in my lifetime," Marjorie said.

When the meeting broke up it became apparent why it had been held impersonally on the racecourse, as none of the people attending lived with any of the others.

They walked out as individuals, each in a seeming barbed-wire enclosure of self-righteousness, none of them anxious to acknowledge my continued presence.

Only Dart, half-way out of the door, looked back to where I stood watching the exodus.

"Coming?" he said. "The fun's done."

With a smile I joined him by the door as he thoughtfully looked me over.

"Care for a jar?" he said and, when I hesitated, added, "There's a pub right outside the main gates that's open all day. And, frankly, I'm curious."

"Curiosity's a two-way street."

He nodded. "Agreed, then." He led the way downstairs by a different route than the one I'd come up, and we emerged into an area, within the paddocks and near the unsaddling enclosures, that had been crowded with people on the race day but now contained only a number of parked cars. Into each car a single Stratton was climbing, none of the brothers, offspring or cousins grouping for friendly family chat.

Dart took it for granted and asked where my car was.

"Down there." I pointed vaguely.

"Oh? Hop in, then. I'll drive you."

Dart's car, an old dusty economical runabout, was standing next to Marjorie's chauffeur-driven blackly-gleaming Daimler, and she lowered her rear window as she glided slowly away, staring in disbelief at my acceptance by Dart. Dart waved to her cheerfully, reminding me vividly of my son Alan's similar disregard of the power of dragons, a lack of perception as much as a matter of courage.

Car doors slammed, engines purred, brake lights went on and off; the Strattons dispersed. Dart put his own car into gear and steered us straight to the main entrance, where a few forlorn-looking individuals were slowly walking up and down bearing placards saying "BAN STEEPLECHASING" and "CRUELTY TO ANIMALS."

"They've been here trying to stop people coming in, ever since that horse died here last Saturday," Dart observed. "The woolly head brigade, I call them."

It was an apt enough description, as they wore a preponderance of knitted hats. Their placards were handwritten and amateurish, but their dedication couldn't be doubted.

"They don't understand horses," Dart said. "Horses run and jump because they want to. Horses try their damnedest to get to the front of the herd. Racing wouldn't exist if it weren't for horses naturally busting their guts to get out in front and win." The grin came and went. "I don't have the instincts of a horse."

But his sister had, I thought.

Dart bypassed the demonstrators and drove across the road into the parking lot of the Mayflower Inn opposite, which looked as if it had never seen Plymouth, let alone sailed the Atlantic.

Inside, it was resolutely decorated with 1620 imitation memorabilia, but not too bad for all that. Murals of Pilgrim fathers in top hats (an anachronism) and white beards (wrong, the Pilgrims were young) were reminiscent of Abraham Lincoln two hundred years later, but who cared? The place was warm and welcoming and had at least tried.

Dart bought us two unadventurous half pints and put them carefully on a small dark oak table, settling us into wooden-armed reasonably comfortable old oak chairs.

"So why," he said, "did you come?"

"Eight shares in a racecourse."

He had steel-gray eyes: unusual. Unlike his sister, he hadn't honed his bone structure to angular leanness. Not for him the agonies and bad-temper-inducing deprivations of an unremitting battle with weight. Thirty or thereabouts, Dart already showed the roundness which could develop into the all-over weightiness of his father. Unlike his father he was also showing early signs of baldness, and this did, I slowly discovered, upset him radically.

"I'd heard about you," Dart said, "but you were always cast as a villain. You don't look villainous in the least."

"Who cast me as a villain?"

"Hannah, mostly, I suppose. She's never got over being rejected by her mother. I mean, mothers aren't supposed to dump infants, are they? Fathers do, regularly, male prerogative. Rebecca would kill me for saying that. Anyway, your mother dumped Hannah but not *you*. I'd look out for knives between the shoulder blades, if I were you."

His voice sounded light and frivolous and I had the impression I'd received a serious warning.

"What do you do?" I asked neutrally. "What do you all do?"

"Do? I farm. That is to say, I look after the family estates." Perhaps he read polite surprise on my face because he grimaced self-deprecatingly and said, "As it happens, we have a farm manager who runs the land and also an agent who sees to the tenants, but I make the decisions. That is to say, I listen to what the manager wants to do and to what the agent wants to do, and then I decide that that's what *I* want them to do, so they do it. Unless Father has different ideas. Unless Grandfather had different ideas, in the old days. And of course unless they've all been listening to my great-aunt Marjorie whose ideas are ultimate." He paused quite cheerfully. "The whole thing's bloody boring, and not what I'd like to do at all."

"Which is?" I asked, entertained.

"Fantasy land," he said. "Private property. Keep out." He meant no offense. The same words in Keith's mouth would have been a curse. "What do *you* do, yourself?" he asked.

"I'm a builder," I said.

"Really? What of?"

"Houses, mostly."

It didn't interest him greatly. He trotted briefly through the occupations of the other Strattons, or at least the ones I'd met.

"Rebecca's a jockey, I suppose you guessed? She's been besotted with horses all her life. She's two years younger than me. Our papa owns a racehorse or two and goes hunting. He used to do my own job until he decided I was too idle, so now he does even less. But to be fair, he does no harm, which in these days invests him with sainthood. My uncle Keith . . . heaven knows. He's supposed to be in finance, whatever that means. My uncle Ivan has a garden center, all ghastly gnomes and things. He potters about there some days and trusts his manager."

He paused to drink and gave me a glimmering inspection over the glass's rim.

"Go on," I said.

"Hannah," he nodded. "She's never done a hard day's work. My grandfather poured money over her to make up for her mother—*your* mother—rejecting her, but he never seemed to love her . . . I suppose I shouldn't say that. Anyway, Hannah's not married but she has a son called Jack who's a pain in the arse. Who else is there? Great-aunt Marjorie. Apart from Stratton money, she married a plutocrat who did the decent thing by dying fairly early. No children." He considered. "That's the lot."

"What about Forsyth?" I asked.

A shutter came down fast on his easy loquacity.

"Grandfather divided his seventy-five shares of Stratton Park among all of us," he stated. "Twenty-one shares each to his three sons, and three shares each to his four grandchildren. Forsyth gets his three like the rest of us." He stopped, his expression carefully noncommittal. "Whatever Forsyth does isn't my business." He left the clear implication that it wasn't mine, either.

"What will you all do," I asked, "about the racecourse?"

"Besides quarrel? In the short term, nothing, as that's what the great-aunt is set on. Then we'll get some hopeless new stands at enormous cost, then we'll have to sell the land to pay for the stands. You may as well tear up your shares right away."

"You don't seem unduly worried."

His quick grin shone and vanished. "To be honest, I don't give a toss. Even if I get myself disinherited by doing something diabolical, like voting to abolish hunting, I can't help but get richer as time goes by. Grandfather gave me millions nine years ago, for a start. And my father has his good points. He's already given me a chunk of his own fortune, and if he lives another three years it'll be clear of tax." He stared at me, frowning. "Why do I tell you that?"

"Do you want to impress me?"

"No, I don't. I don't care a bugger what you think." He blinked a bit. "I suppose that's not true." He paused. "I have irritating holes in my life."

"Like what?"

"Too much money. No motivation. And I'm going bald."

"Marry," I said.

"That wouldn't grow hair."

"It might stop you minding."

"*Nothing* stops you minding. And it's damned unfair. I go to doctors who say I can't do a bugger about it, it's in the genes, and how did it get *there,* I'd like to know? Father's OK and Grandfather had the full thatch, even though he was eighty-eight his last birthday, and look at Keith with enough to brush back with his hands all the time like a ruddy girl. I hate that mannerism. And even Ivan has no bare patches, he's going thin all over but that's not as *bad."* He looked balefully at my head. "You're about my age, and yours is *thick."*

"Try snake oil," I suggested.

"That's typical. People like you have *no idea* what it's like to find hair all over the place. Washbasin. Pillow. Hairs which ought to stay growing in my scalp, dammit. How did you know I wasn't married, anyway? And don't give me the stock answer that I don't look worried. I *am* worried, dammit, about my hair."

"You could try implants."

"Yes. Don't laugh, I'm going to."

"I'm not laughing."

"I bet you are, inside. Everybody thinks it's hilarious, someone else going bald. But when it's you, it's tragic."

There were irretrievable disasters, I saw, that could only get worse. Dart drank deep as if beer would irrigate the failing follicles and asked if I were married, myself.

"Do I look it?"

"You look stable."

Surprised, I said yes, I was married.

"Children?"

"Six sons."

*"Six!"* He seemed horrified. "You're not old enough."

"We married at nineteen, and my wife likes having babies."

"Good Lord." Other words failed him, and I thought back, as I did pretty often, to the heady student days when Amanda and I had taken to each other with excitement. Friends around us were pairing and living together: it was accepted behavior.

"Let's get married," I said impulsively. "No one gets *married,"* Amanda said. "Then let's be *different,"* I said.

So we married, giggling happily, and I paid no attention to my mother, who tried to tell me I was marrying Amanda with my eyes, marrying a half-grown woman I didn't really know. "I married Keith Stratton for his beauty," she told me, "and it was a dreadful mistake. It's always a mistake."

"But Amanda's lovely."

"She's lovely to look at and she's kind and she clearly loves *you,* but you're both so young, you'll change as you grow older and so will she."

"Mum, are you coming to the wedding?"

"Of course."

I married Amanda for her long legs and her blonde hair and her name, Amanda, which I loved. It took ten years for me to face a long-repressed recognition that my mother had been right about changes.

Neither Amanda nor I had known at nineteen that she would almost at once develop a hunger for babies. Neither of us could possibly have envisaged that she would ecstatically enjoy the actual birth process, or that she would plan the next pregnancy as soon as the last was accomplished.

Both Christopher and Toby had been born by the time I'd struggled through my qualifying exams, and feeding and housing the four of us had seemed an impossible task. It was then, in my first week out of college, that I'd gone to drown my sorrows in a depressing old pub and found the land-lord weeping bankrupt tears into warm beer amid the crash of his own per-sonal dream. The place had been condemned as unfit to live in, he owed money everywhere, his wife had left him and his license to sell liquor would run out the next day.

We negotiated a rock-bottom price. I went to the council to get a stay of demolition. I begged and borrowed and mortgaged my soul, and Amanda, the two boys and I moved into our first ruin.

I began to make it habitable while I looked around for a job, and I found a lowly position in a large firm of architects, an existence I disliked but stuck to grimly for the pay packets.

Unlike Dart, I knew well what it was like to sweat at night over which bill to pay next, over how to pay *any* bill next, over which did I need most, elec-tricity or a telephone (electricity), and do I pay the plumber (yes, but I learn his job) or do I pay first for roof tiles (yes) or new bricks (no).

I'd carted away free rubble and improvised and sanded old mortar off by the bucketful and given glamour to old stones and built a chimney that never smoked. The ruin came to life again, and I left the firm of architects and ir-revocably grew and changed.

I hadn't known at nineteen that I would be unsuited to work as part of a team, or that my true *métier* was hands-on construction, not simply the draw-ing board. Amanda hadn't imagined that life with an architect could mean dirt, upheaval and months without income; but to the extent that we'd settled for what we hadn't expected, she had coped with the ruins and I had agreed to the babies, and each of us had had what we needed for our own private ful-fillment, even if we'd grown apart until even our sexual interest in each other had become perfunctory and sporadic, an effort, not a joy.

After Neil's birth, during a patch when nothing had seemed to go right, we had nearly split finally asunder, but the economics of feeding the nestlings had prevailed. I took to sleeping alone under the tarpaulins while the rest slept in the bus. I worked eighteen hours a day as a form of escape. After four increasingly prosperous but unhappy years, when neither of us had met anyone to supplant the other, we'd made a great effort to "start again." Jamie had been the result. He still kept Amanda happy and, even though the new start had slowly fizzled, we had, because of it, achieved a sort of tolerant to-our-mutual-advantage stand-off which I reckoned enough for the foreseeable future, at least until the boys were grown.

So where was free choice in all of that? I chose to marry to be different and to stick to what it brought me because of an inability to admit failure. I'd chosen to work alone because I hadn't the qualities needed for a team. Every choice a result of given factors. No free choice at all.

"I choose to be what I am," I said.

Dart, startled, said, "What?"

"Nothing. Only a theory. Was it inevitable that Conrad, Keith, Ivan and the rest of you should make the choices you all have about the future of the racecourse?"

He looked at his beer for answers and glanced up at me briefly. "Too deep for me," he said.

"Would you ever have expected your father to want to sell? Or Keith to potter along as things are?"

"Or Rebecca to love men?" He grinned. "No, in all three cases, I wouldn't."

"What do you yourself want for the racecourse?" I asked.

"You tell me," he said amiably, "you're the expert."

I felt in him an encompassing lassitude. Not the sort of thing to say to a virtual stranger.

"Another half?" I suggested, indicating our almost empty glasses.

"No, don't bother. What about totally random choice? Pick a card, that sort of thing. What about rational choices? Like do I take an umbrella because it's raining?"

"Many people don't."

"Because it isn't in their natures? Because they think it wimpish?"

"More or less."

"How did we get into this?" He seemed to tire of the subject. "Go back to the meeting. When you asked Father if he already had detailed plans of the new stands he's set on, was it because you're a builder?"

"Yes," I nodded.

"Well . . . if you could see the proposals, would you have an opinion?"

"I might."

He thought it over. "I do know where you could see the plans, but no one will want you to, except me. If I get you a look at them, will you tell just *me* what you think of them? Then at least I'd have some idea of whether new stands are a good idea or not. I mean, I don't know *how* to vote about the future of the racecourse, because I don't really know the significance of the options. So yes, you're right, if I had to choose now it would be a gut reaction. I'd choose because of the way I am. Right?"

"Right."

"How about taking a look-see at Conrad's pet architect's plans, then?"

"Yes," I said.

He grinned. "This choice game's a knock-out. Come on then, we'll do a bit of breaking and entering." He stood up decisively and turned towards the door. "Can you pick locks?"

"It depends on the lock. But given due warning and high need, possibly."

"Good."

"How long," I asked, "will it take?"

He paused, eyebrows rising. "Half an hour, maybe."

"OK."

I followed him out of the Mayflower and into his runabout, and we set off with a jolt to a destination undisclosed.

"How about I choose not to go bald?" It amused him in a bitter sort of way.

"Not a choice."

We were heading east, Swindon behind us, Wantage, according to the signposts, ahead. Long before we reached there, however, Dart put his foot on the brake and swerved in through some open gates set in a stone wall. Up a short driveway he came to a halt in front of a large house built of smooth gray bricks with bands of smooth pink bricks and inset patterns of smooth yellowish bricks, all in all (to me) an eyesore.

"I was brought up here," Dart said encouragingly. "What do you think of it?"

"Edwardian," I said.

"Near enough. Last year of Victoria."

"Solid, anyway."

A turret. Big sash windows. A conservatory. Affluent middle-class display.

"My parents rattle around in it now," Dart said frankly. "They're out, by the way. Father was going to meet Mother from the racecourse. They won't be back for hours." He pulled a bunch of keys out of the ignition and stood up out of the car. "We can get in round the back," he said, sorting out one key. "Come on."

"No breaking and entering?"

"Later."

At close quarters the walls were still repulsive and also slippery to the touch. The path around to the rear was edged with gloomy evergreen shrubs. At the back of the house, a red brick extension had been added to provide bathrooms: brown-painted drains zig-zagged over the exterior, an invitation to ice. Dart unlocked a brown-painted door and let us into the bowels (well, literally) of the house.

"This way," he said, marching past a cloakroom and other plumbing, briefly glimpsed through half-open doors. "Through here." He pushed aside a swing door which led from utility to opulence; to the black-and-white tiled floor of a large entrance hall.

We made our way across this to a polished door and into a cluttered oak-paneled room whose chief eyecatchers were endless pictures of horses; some, in oil paintings, hanging thickly on the walls with individual lights on the frames, some in black-and-white photographs in silver frames standing on every surface, some on book jacket covers. Horse-head bookends supported leather-bound classics like the *Irish R.M.* and *Handley Cross.* A silver fox held down papers on a busy desk. Silver and gold coins were displayed in collections. A hunting crop lay casually coiled on a broken-springed chair. Copies of *Horse and Hound* and *Country Life* filled a magazine rack to overflowing.

"Father's sanctum," Dart said unnecessarily. He strolled unconcernedly across the room, skirted the desk and the large chair behind it, and stopped beside a section of paneling which he said was a cupboard door always kept carefully locked by his parent.

"The racecourse plans are inside," Dart said. "How about opening it?"

"Your father wouldn't approve."

"I dare say not. Don't tell me you're going all moral and starchy. You pretty well said you could do it."

"This is too personal."

I went round beside him, however, and bent to take a closer look at the lock. All that was to be seen from the outside was an inconspicuous keyhole: without Dart's knowledge of its existence the door itself would have remained more or less invisible, particularly as a painting of a meet with huntsman and foxhounds adhered on it, to make it indistinguishable from the walls around.

"Well?" Dart asked.

"What does its key look like?"

"How do you mean?"

"I mean, is it a small short key, or one with a longish narrow shaft with a clump of wards on the end?"

"A long shaft."

I straightened up and gave him the bad news.

"I'll not touch it," I said. "Won't the key be somewhere in this room?"

"I tried to find it for years in my teens. No good at all. How about a bit of force?"

"Absolutely not."

Dart fiddled around with things on the desk. "What about this paper-knife? Or this?" He held up a long buttonhook. "It isn't as if we're going to *steal* anything. Just to take a look."

"Why does your father have the plans locked up?"

Dart shrugged. "He's secretive by nature. It takes such a lot of *energy* to be secretive. I can never be bothered."

The lock was an old and undoubtedly simple warded-bit key job, probably surface-mounted on the inside of the door. The keyhole itself was about an inch from top to bottom, a healthy size that made picking it a cinch. Failing a filed-down key, two wires would have been enough. I was not, however, going to undo it, on the grounds that Conrad would be legitimately furious if he found out, and also because my interest in seeing the plans was not uncontrollable.

"Wasted journey, then?" Dart asked.

"Sorry."

"Oh, well." It seemed his appetite for the enterprise had easily subsided, as if common sense had somewhere raised its wiser head. He looked at me assessingly. "I've a distinct feeling you *could,* but you won't."

The trip had been an anticlimax. I looked at my watch and asked if he would mind taking me back to the racecourse. He agreed, seeming to feel the same deflation. I had not, it was clear, come up to his expectations.

We set off again in his car and I asked where he lived now, himself.

"Actually," he said, "in Stratton Hays."

"Is that a village?"

"Lord, no." He was amused. "A house. Though, come to think of it, it's as big as a village. Grandfather's house. The old fellow was lonely when Gran died, so he asked me to stay for a while. That was about ten years ago. Keith didn't like it, of course. He tried to get me out and himself in. He'd lived there a lot of his life, after all. He said it wasn't natural for a twenty-year-old boy to move in there, but Grandfather wouldn't have Keith back. I remember all the shouting. I used to get out of the way whenever Keith was around. That wasn't anything new, mind you. Anyway, I *liked* Grandfather, and we got on fine. We used to dine together every evening and I drove him most days round the estate and the racecourse. He ran the racecourse himself, really. That's to say, the colonel that Rebecca was complaining about, Colonel Gardner, he's the racecourse manager, he would do whatever Grandfather wanted. He's an excellent manager, whatever Rebecca says. Grandfather had a real knack of picking people to run things, like Colonel Gardner, and those two that I depend on, the farm manager and the land agent. Just as well, because to be frank we only ever had one genius in the family and that was the first baron, who was a merchant banker with a super-plus Midas touch." His voice was light and self-deprecating, but there was a depth of feeling in his next statement. "I miss the old man rotten, you know."

We droned along until the woolly-head marchers were again in sight.

"Stratton Hays," Dart said, "is straight on past the gates. Not far. On the edge of the racecourse land. Do you want to see it? It's where your mother lived with Keith. Where she dumped Hannah."

I looked at my watch, but curiosity prevailed over parental responsibility. I said I would be very interested, and on we went.

Stratton Hays was everything Conrad's house was not, an ancient homogenous pile in the manner of a smaller Hardwicke Hall. Early seventeenth-century stone and glass in lighthearted proportional harmony, built by the golden fortunes of the Elizabethan age, it looked exactly as it had done for almost four hundred years and certainly as it had forty years earlier when my mother had gone there as a bride.

She had spoken of "the Stratton house" as a heartless heap, projecting her own unhappiness into its walls, so that I was unprepared for its easygoing grandeur. It looked friendly to me, and welcoming.

"My great-great-grandfather bought it," Dart said offhandedly, "as being a suitable seat for a newly ennobled baron. The first baroness is on record as thinking it not aristocratic enough. She wanted Palladian pillars, pediments and porticos."

As before, we went into the house via an unobtrusive side door, and as before found ourselves in a black-and-white hall, this time floored with marble. There was more space than furniture and no curtains at the high windows and, as my mother had said, it echoed with vanished generations.

"Keith used to have the west corridor," Dart said, heading up a wide staircase. "After he divorced your mother he got married again, and Grandfather made him and his new wife take Hannah and find somewhere else to live. Before I was born, of course. It seems Keith didn't want to go but Grandfather insisted."

Dart headed across a large unfurnished area and turned a corner into a long wide corridor with a dark wood floor, a runner of crimson carpet and a tall window at the far end.

"West corridor," Dart said. "The doors are all unlocked. The rooms get dusted once a month. Browse around, if you like."

I browsed, feeling uncomfortable. This was where my mother had suffered beatings and what was now called marital rape. Time had stood still in their bedroom. I shivered there.

A dressing room, a boudoir, a study and a sitting room, all with tall uncurtained windows, also opened onto the corridor. A Victorian bathroom and a twentieth-century kitchen had been fitted into what had probably once been another bedroom. No sign of a nursery.

I went back along the corridor and thanked Dart.

"Did these rooms never have curtains?" I asked.

"They rotted away," Dart said. "Grandfather got rid of them and wouldn't let Gran replace them." He walked towards the stairs. "Grandfather and Gran lived in the east corridor. It's the same architecturally but it's a proper home. Carpets, curtains, pretty. Gran chose everything there. It feels so empty, now, without either of them. I used to spend most evenings with Grandfather in their sitting room, but I don't go along there much any more."

We went down the stairs.

"Where do you live, then?" I asked.

"This house is E-shaped," he said. "I have the ground floor of the south wing." He pointed to a wide passage leading away from the main hall. "Father has inherited this house but he and Mother don't want to live here. They say it's too big. I'm negotiating with Father to be allowed to stay here as a tenant. Keith wants me out and himself in, sod him."

"It must cost a fortune to run," I commented.

"There's no roof on the north wing," he said. "Ridiculous, but if part of the house is uninhabitable, they reduce the tax on it. The north wing needed a new roof, but it was more economical to take the roof right off and let the weather do its worst. The north wing's a ruin. The outside walls still look all right, but it's a shell."

I would come back one day soon, I thought, and ask to see the ruin, but at the moment was concerned only to relieve the Gardners of their extended baby-sitting.

Dart obligingly drove me the mile back to the main gate, where our way in through them was barred by a large bearded man in a woolly hat who stepped into the path of our car. Dart, swearing, jolted to a stop, his only option.

"They were doing this earlier," he said. "They stopped Aunt Marjorie on her way to the shareholders' meeting. And Father, and Keith. They were furious."

Owing to Roger Gardner having directed me to his house through a down-the-course entrance, I hadn't had to run the gauntlet myself. The boys, I knew, would have enjoyed it from the safe, high ground of the bus.

The large beard carried a red message on a placard—"HORSES RIGHTS COME FIRST." He stood without budging in front of the car while a sharp-faced woman rapped on Dart's window, signaling that he should lower it. Dart stolidly refused, which made her screech her own message, which was that all persons to do with racing were murderers. Her thin intensity reminded me vividly of Rebecca, and I wondered which came to them both first, a leaning towards obsession or an activity worthy of it.

She carried a black-edged placard saying ominously "DOOM TO RACE-GOERS," and she was joined at the window by a jollier woman whose notice-on-a-stick read "SET HORSES FREE."

Someone rapped peremptorily on the window my side, and I turned my head and looked straight into the glaring eyes of a fanatical young man showing the blazing fervor of an evangelist.

He yelled "Murderer" at me and shook for my attention a blown-up photograph of a horse lying dead beside white racecourse rails. "Murderer," he repeated.

"They're potty," Dart said, unconcerned.

"They're doing their thing."

"Poor buggers."

The proselytizing group had now all gathered round the car, but were staring balefully rather than making overtly threatening movements. Their dedication to the cause stopped short of physically harming us. Their kicks would be a nice warm glow that evening at having expressed their caring natures. They would be unlikely, by themselves, to close down an industry that employed the sixth-largest workforce in the country, but that probably made them feel all the safer in attacking it.

So far, I thought, looking at their angry committed faces, they hadn't been adopted by professional bully-boy saboteurs. A matter of time, perhaps.

Dart, having had enough, began edging his car forward. The bearded way-barrer leaned against the bonnet. Dart waved to the obstruction to remove itself. The obstruction shook its fist and continued leaning. Dart pushed his hand down irritably on the horn and the obstruction jumped to one side, galvanized. Dart rolled slowly ahead. The placard bearer stalked beside us for several paces but stopped abruptly as we crossed through the gates themselves. Someone, it seemed, must have instructed them about trespass.

"Such a bore," Dart said, accelerating. "How long do you think they'll keep it up?"

"For your race meeting here next Monday," I suggested, "I would get a police cordon."

# 5

Where's your car?" Dart asked. "I'm going out the back way. I'm tired of those hate merchants. Where's your car?"

"I came in the back way," I said. "Drop me somewhere down there."

His eyebrows rose, but all he said was, "Fine," and he headed on the inner way past the grandstands and down the narrow private inconspicuous road to the racecourse manager's house.

"What's that monstrous bus doing there?" he demanded rhetorically when he saw it.

I said, "It's mine," but the words were lost in a sharp horrified exclamation from my driver who had seen, past the bus, the black parked shape of his great-aunt's chauffeured Daimler.

"Aunt Marjorie! What the hell is *she* doing here?"

He braked his rusty runabout beside the gleaming ostentation and without much enthusiasm decided to investigate. The view that presented itself as we rounded a corner of the manager's neat modern house had me helplessly laughing, even if I laughed alone.

Double garage doors stood open. Within the garage, empty space, swept clean. Out on the drive, the former contents lay untidily in clumps of gardening tools, cardboard boxes, spare roof tiles and rolls of netting for covering strawberry beds. To one side a discard section included a gutted refrigerator, a rotted baby buggy, a battered metal trunk, a mouse-eaten sofa and a heap of rusty wire.

Standing more or less to attention in a ragged row stood five young helpers deep in trouble, with Mrs. Roger Gardner, sweet but threatened by authority, trying ineffectually to defend them.

Marjorie's penetrating voice was saying, "It's all very well you boys carrying all that stuff out, but you're not to leave it there. Put everything back at once."

Poor Mrs. Gardner, wringing her hands, was saying, "But Mrs. Binsham, all I wanted was for them to empty the garage . . ."

"This mess is insupportable. Do as I tell you, boys. Put it all back."

Christopher, looking desperately around, latched onto my arrival with Dart as if saved at the eleventh hour from the worst horror movie.

"Dad!" he said explosively. "We cleared out the garage."

"Yes, well done."

Marjorie swiveled on one heel and directed her disapproval towards Dart and me, at which point my identification as the father of the workforce left her temporarily speechless.

"Mr. Morris," Roger Gardner's wife said hurriedly, "your children have been great. Please believe me."

It was courageous of her, I thought, considering her husband's vulnerability to the Stratton family's whims. I thanked her warmly for keeping the children employed while I'd attended the shareholders' meeting.

Marjorie Binsham stared at me piercingly but spoke to Dart, her displeasure a vibration in the air.

"What are you doing here with Mr. Morris?"

Dart said with cowardice, "He wanted to see Stratton Hays."

"Did he, indeed? Stratton Hays is no business of his. This racecourse, however, is *yours,* or so I should have thought. Yours and your father's. Yet what have either of you done to look after it? It is I who have had to drive round to see that everything is in order. Colonel Gardner and I, not you and your father, have made a thorough inspection of the course."

I could see, as easily as she could, that it had never occurred to Dart that he had any responsibility for the state of the racecourse. It had never been his domain. He opened and closed his mouth a couple of times but came up with no protest or defense.

A frazzled-looking Colonel drove up in a jeep and, springing out, assured Marjorie Binsham that he had already put in hand her requirement that spectators should be kept further away from the fences, to save them from injury henceforth.

"It isn't my job," she complained to Dart. "A few posts, and some rope, some instructions to stand back, that's all it takes. *You* should have thought of it. The racecourse has had too much bad publicity. We cannot afford another debacle like last Saturday."

No one mentioned that it had been the horses, not the spectators, which had caused the grief.

"Also," Marjorie continued, "you and your father must get rid of those people at the main gates. If you don't, they will attract extremists from all over the place, and the race crowds will stay away because of the aggravation. The racecourse will be killed off as quickly as by any of the crackpot schemes of Keith and your father. And as for Rebecca! If you notice, there's a woman just like her in that group at the gate. It's only a group now. Make sure it doesn't grow into a mob."

"Yes, Aunt Marjorie," Dart said. The task was beyond him, perhaps beyond anybody.

"Demonstrators don't want to succeed," Marjorie pointed out. "They want to *demonstrate*. Go and tell them to demonstrate for better conditions for stable lads. The horses are pampered enough. The lads are not."

No one remarked that injured stable lads usually lived.

"You, Mr. Morris." She fixed me with a sharp gaze. "I want to talk to *you.*" She pointed to her car. "In there."

"All right."

"And you children, clear this mess up at once. Colonel, I don't know what you're thinking of. This place is a *dump.*"

She headed off vigorously towards her car and didn't look around to make sure I followed, which I did.

"Mark," she told her chauffeur, who was sitting behind the steering wheel, "please take a walk."

He touched his chauffeur's cap to her and obeyed her as if accustomed to the request, and his employer waited beside one of the rear doors until I opened it for her.

"Good," she said, climbing into the spacious rear seat. "Get in beside me and sit down."

I sat where she pointed and closed the door.

"Stratton Hays," she said, coming at once to the point, "was where your mother lived with Keith."

"Yes," I acknowledged, surprised.

"Did you ask to see it?"

"Dart offered, very kindly. I accepted."

She paused, inspecting me.

"I never saw Madeline again, after she left," she said at length. "I disapproved of her leaving. Did she tell you?"

"Yes, she told me, but after so many years she bore you no animosity. She said you had urged your brother to close family ranks against her, but she was fond of your brother."

"It was a long time," she said, "before I found out what sort of a man Keith is. His second wife killed herself, did you know? When I said to my brother that Keith was an unlucky picker he told me it wasn't bad luck, it was Keith's own nature. He told me your mother couldn't love or nurse the baby Hannah because of the way the child had been conceived. Your mother told my brother that touching the baby made her feel sick."

"She didn't tell me that."

"I am now," Marjorie said, "offering you a formal apology for the way I behaved to your mother."

I paused only briefly to check what my parent would have wanted. "It's accepted," I said.

"Thank you."

I thought that that must conclude the conversation, but it seemed not.

"Keith's third wife left him and divorced him for irretrievable breakdown of marriage. He now has a fourth wife, Imogen, who spends half of the time drunk."

"Why doesn't she leave him too?" I asked.

"She won't or can't admit she made a mistake."

It was close enough to my own feelings to strike me dumb.

"Keith," his aunt said, "is the only Stratton short of money. Imogen told me. She can't keep her mouth shut after six glasses of vodka. Keith is in debt. That's why he's pushing to sell the racecourse. He needs the money."

I looked at the appearance Marjorie presented to the world: the little old lady well into her eighties with wavy white hair, soft pink and white skin and hawk-like dark eyes. The pithy, forceful mind and the sinewy vocabulary were, I imagined, the nearest in quality in the Stratton family to the financial genius who had founded them.

"I was furious with my brother for giving Madeline those shares," she said. "He could be obstinate sometimes. Now, all these years later, I'm glad that he did. I am glad," she finished slowly, "that someone outside the family can bring some sense of proportion into the Stratton hothouse."

"I don't know that I can."

"The point," she said, "is whether you want to. Or rather, how much you want to. If you hadn't been in the least bit interested, you wouldn't have turned up here today."

"True."

"You could oblige me," she said, "by finding out how much money Keith owes, and to whom. And by finding out what relationship Conrad has with the architect he's committed to, who Colonel Gardner tells me knows nothing about racing and is designing a monstrosity. The Colonel tells me we need an architect more like the one who built your own house, but that your architect only designs on a small scale."

"The Colonel told you he'd visited me?"

"Most sensible thing he's done this year."

"You amaze me."

"I want you as an ally," she said. "Help me make the racecourse prosper."

I tried to sort out my own jumbled responses, and it was out of the jumble and not from thought-through reasons that I gave her my answer.

"All right, I'll try."

She held out a small hand to formalize the agreement, and I shook on it, a binding commitment.

MARJORIE WAS DRIVEN away without returning to the gutted garage, which was just as well as I found the mess unchanged and the boys, the Gardners and Dart all in the Gardners' kitchen with their attention on cake. Warm fragrant pale-colored fruitcake, that minute baked. Christopher asked for the recipe "so that Dad can make it in the bus."

"Dad can cook?" Dart asked ironically.

"Dad can do anything," Neil said, munching.

Dad, I thought to myself, had probably just impulsively set himself on a high road to failure.

"Colonel . . ." I started.

He interrupted. "Call me Roger."

"Roger," I said, "can I . . . I mean, may the architect of my house come here tomorrow and make a thorough survey of the grandstands as they are at present? I'm sure you have professional advisers about the state of the fabric and so on, but could we take a fresh detached survey with a view to seeing whether new stands are or are not essential for a profitable future?"

Dart's cake came to a standstill in mid-chew and Roger Gardner's face lost some of its habitual gloom.

"Delighted," he said, "but not tomorrow. I've got the course-builders coming, and the full complement of groundsmen will be here getting everything in shape for next Monday's meeting."

"Friday, then?"

He said doubtfully, "That'll be Good Friday. Easter, of course. Perhaps your man won't want to work on Good Friday."

"He'll do what I tell him," I said. "It's me."

Both Dart and Roger were surprised.

"I am," I said gently, "a qualified architect. I did five arduous years at the Architectural Association, one of the most thorough schools in the world. I do choose houses in preference to high rises, but that's because horizontal lines that fit in with nature please me better. I'm a Frank Lloyd Wright disciple, not a Le Corbusier, if that means anything to you."

"I've heard of them," Dart said. "Who hasn't?"

"Frank Lloyd Wright," I said, "developed the cantilever roof you see on all new grandstands everywhere."

"We don't have a cantilever," Roger said thoughtfully.

"No, but let's see what you *do* have, and what you can get away with not having."

Dart's view of me had changed a little. "You said you were a builder," he accused.

"Yes, I am."

Dart looked at the children. "What does your father do?" he asked.

"Builds houses."

"With his own hands, do you mean?"

"Well," Edward amplified, "with spades and trowels and a saw and everything."

"Ruins," Christopher explained. "We're on a ruin hunt for our Easter holidays."

Together they described the pattern of their lives to an ever more astonished audience. Their matter-of-fact acceptance of not every child's experience seemed especially to amaze.

"But we're going to keep the last one he did. Aren't we, Dad?"

"Yes."

*"Promise."*

I promised for roughly the twentieth time, which was an indication of the depth of their anxiety, as I'd always kept the promises I'd made them.

"You must all be so tired of moving on," Mrs. Gardner said sympathetically.

"It's not that," Christopher told her, "it's the house. It's brilliant." Brilliant in his teenage vocabulary meant only the opposite of awful (pronounced *ah-fal*, ironically).

Roger nodded and agreed, however. "Brilliant. Hell to heat, I should think, though, with all that space."

"It has a hypocaust," Neil said, licking his fingers.

The Gardners and Dart gazed at him.

"What," Dart asked, giving in, "is a hypocaust?"

"Central heating invented by the Romans," said my seven-year-old composedly. "You make hollow spaces and runways under a stone floor and drive hot air through, and the floor stays warm all the time. Dad thought it would work and it does. We ran about without shoes all winter."

Roger turned his head my way.

"Come on Friday, then," he said.

WHEN I DROVE the bus back to the same spot on a sunny morning two days later the ground outside the garage was cluttered not with the debris of decades but with horses.

My sons gazed out of their safe windows at a moving clutch of about six large quadrupeds and decided not to climb down among the hooves, even though every animal was controlled by a rider.

The horses, to my eyes, weren't fine-boned enough to be racehorses, nor were the riders as light as the average stable lad, and when I swung down from the cab Roger came hurrying across from his house, side-stepping round massive hindquarters, to tell me these were Conrad's working hunters out for their morning exercise. They were supposed to be out on the road, Roger said, but they'd been practically attacked by the six or seven woolen hats still stubbornly picketing the main gates.

"Where do they come from?" I asked, looking around.

"The horses? Conrad keeps them here on the racecourse in a yard down near the back entrance, where you came in."

I nodded. I'd seen the back of what could well have been the stables.

"They're trotting up and down the inner road instead," Roger said. "It's not ideal, but I won't let them out on the course, where they sometimes go, because everything is ready for Monday's meeting. Wouldn't your boys like to get out and see them?"

"I don't think so," I said. "Since the slaughter at the open ditch last Saturday they are a bit afraid of them. They were very shocked, you know, by that dead spectator's injuries."

"I'd forgotten they'd seen him, poor man. Will they just stay in the bus, then, while you and I go over the stands? I've spread out some of the original drawings in my office. We'll look at those first, if you like."

I suggested driving bus and boys as near to the office as possible, which resulted in our parking where the Stratton family's cars had been gathered two days earlier. The boys, relieved by the arrangement, asked if they could play a hide-and-seek game in the stands, if they promised not to do any damage.

Roger gave assent doubtfully. "You'll find many of the doors are locked," he told them. "And the whole place was cleaned yesterday, ready for Monday, so don't make any mess."

They promised not to. Roger and I left them beginning to draw up rules for their game and made our way to a low white-painted wooden building on the far side of the parade ring.

"Is it pirates again?" Roger asked, amused.

"I think it's storming the Bastille this time. That's to say, rescuing a prisoner without being captured yourself. Then the rescued prisoner has to hide and not be recaptured."

I looked back as Roger unlocked his office door. The boys waved. I waved back and went in, and began to sort my way through ancient building plans that had been rolled up so long that straightening them out was like six bouts with an octopus.

I took off my jacket and hung it on the back of a chair, so as to come to grips with things more easily, and Roger made a comment about the warmth of the spring day and hoped the sunshine would last until Monday.

Most of the plans were in fact working drawings, which gave detailed specifications for every nut and bolt. They were thorough, complete and impressive, and I commented on it.

"The only problem is," Roger said, with a twisting smile, "that the builder didn't stick to the specs. Concrete that should be six inches thick with reinforcing bars well covered has recently proved to be barely four and a half inches and we're having endless trouble with the private balcony boxes with water getting in through cracks and rusting the bars, which then of course expand because of the rust and crack the concrete more. *Crumble* the concrete, in some places."

"Spalling," I nodded. "Can be dangerous."

"And," Roger went on, "if you look at the overall design of the water inlets and outlets and sewer lines, the drawings make very good sense, but the water and drain pipes don't actually go where they should. We had one set of ladies' lavatories backing up for no reason we could think of and flooding the floor, but the drain seemed clear, and then we found we were checking the wrong drain, and the one from the lavatories went in an entirely different direction and was blocked solid."

It was familiar territory. Builders had minds of their own and often ignored the architect's best instructions, either because they truly thought they knew better or because they could make a fatter profit by shaving the quality.

We uncurled a dozen more sheets and tried to hold them flat with pots of pens for paperweights, a losing battle. I acquired, all the same, an understanding of what should have been built, with some picture of stress points and weaknesses to look for. I'd studied ancient plans a great deal less trustworthy than these, and these grandstands weren't ruins after all: they'd withstood gales and rot for well over half a century.

Basically, the front of the stands, the viewing steps themselves, were of reinforced concrete supported by steel girders, which also held up the roof. Backing the concrete and steel, solid brick pillars formed the weight-bearers for the bars, dining rooms and private rooms for the owners and stewards. Centrally there was a stairway stretching upward through five stories giving access outwards and inwards throughout. A simple effective design, even if now out of date.

The door of the office was suddenly flung open, and Neil catapulted himself inside.

"Dad," he said insistently, "Dad . . ."

"I'm busy, Neil."

"But it's urgent. Really, really urgent."

I let a set of drawings recurl by accident. "How urgent?" I asked, trying to open them again.

"I found some white wires, Dad, going in and out of some walls."

"What wires?"

"You know when they blew up the chimney?"

I left the plans to their own devices and paid full attention to my observant son. My heart jumped a beat. I did indeed remember the blowing up of the chimney.

"Where are the wires?" I asked, trying for calmness.

Neil said, "Near that bar with the smelly floor."

"What on earth is he talking about?" Roger demanded.

"Where are your brothers?" I said briefly.

"In the stands. Hiding. I don't know where," Neil's eyes were wide. "Don't let them be blown up, Dad."

"No." I turned to Roger. "Can you switch on a public address system that can be heard everywhere in the stands?"

"What on earth . . ."

*"Can you?"* I felt my own panic rising: fought it down.

"But . . ."

"For God's sake," I half yelled at him, quite unfairly. "Neil's saying he's seen det cord and demolition charges in the stands."

Roger's own face went taut. "Are you *serious?*"

"Same as the factory chimney?" I asked Neil, checking.

"Yes, Dad. *Exactly* the same. Do come on."

"Public address system," I said with dreadful urgency to Roger. "I have to get those children out of there at once."

He gave me a dazed look but at last went into action, hurrying out of his office and half running across the parade ring towards the weighing room, sorting through his bunch of keys as he went. We came to a halt beside the door into Oliver Wells's office, the lair of the Clerk of the Course.

"We tested the system yesterday," Roger said, fumbling slightly. "Are you *sure?* This child's so young. I'm sure he's mistaken."

"Don't risk it," I said, practically ready to shake him.

He got the door open finally and went across to unlatch a metal panel which revealed banks of switches.

"This one," he said, pressing down with a click. "You can speak direct from here. Let me plug in the microphone."

He brought an old-fashioned microphone from a drawer, fitted plug to socket, and handed me the instrument.

"Just speak," he said.

I took a breath and tried to sound urgent but not utterly frightening, though utterly frightened was what I myself felt.

"This is Dad," I said as slowly as I could, so they could hear clearly, "Christopher, Toby, Edward, Alan, the grandstands are not safe. Wherever you're hiding, leave the stands and go to the gate in the rails where we went through and down the course last Saturday. Go out in front of the stands, and gather by that gate. The gate is the rallying point. Go *at once*. The Bastille game is over for now. It's *urgent* that you go at once to the gate where we went out onto the course. It's quite near the winning post. Go there now. The grandstands aren't safe. They might blow up at any moment."

I switched off temporarily and said to Neil, "Do you remember how to get to that gate?"

He nodded and told me how, correctly.

"Then you go there too, will you, so that the others can see you? And tell them what you saw."

"Yes, Dad."

I said to Roger, "Have you the key to the gate?"

"Yes, but . . ."

"I'd be happier if they could go out through that gate and across to the winning post itself. Even that might not be far enough."

"Surely you're exaggerating," he protested.

"I hope to God I am."

Neil hadn't waited. I watched his little figure run.

"We went to see an old factory chimney being blown up," I said to Roger. "The boys were fascinated. They saw some charges being set. It was only three months ago." I spoke again into the microphone, "Boys, go down to the gate. It's very, very urgent. The stands are unsafe. They might blow up. Just run." I turned to Roger. "Could you unlock the gate for them?"

He said, "Why don't you?"

"I'd better check those wires, don't you think?"

"But . . ."

"Look, I've got to make sure Neil is right, haven't I? And we don't know *when* the charges are set for, do we? Maybe five minutes, maybe five hours, maybe after dark. Can't risk it for the boys, though. Have to get them out at once."

Roger swallowed and made no more objections. Together we ran from his office round to the front of the stands, he taking the key with him, I wanting to check that all five were safe.

The little knot by the gate grew to four as Neil reached them. Four, not five.

Four. *Not Toby.*

I sprinted back to Oliver's office and picked up the microphone.

"Toby, this is not a game. Toby, get off the stands. The stands are not safe. Toby, for Christ's sake do what I say. *This is not a game.*"

I could hear my voice reverberating round and through the building and out in the paddocks. I repeated the urgent words once more and then ran round the stands again to check that Toby had heard and obeyed.

*Four* boys. Four boys and Roger, walking across the track to the winning post. Not running. If Toby were watching, he'd see no reason for haste.

"Come on, you little *bugger*," I said under my breath. "For once in your life, *be told.*"

I went back to the microphone and said it loud and baldly. "There are demolition charges in the stands, Toby, are you listening? Remember the chimney? The stands can blow up too. Toby, get out of there quickly and join the others."

I went back yet again to the front of the stands, and yet again Toby failed to appear.

I was not a demolitions expert. If I wanted to take a building down to its roots I usually did it brick by brick, salvaging everything useful. I'd have felt happier at that moment if I'd known more. The first priority, though, was obviously to look at what Neil had seen, and to do that I needed to enter and climb the central stairway, off which led the bar with the smelly floor; the members' bar which should have been much busier than it was.

It was the same staircase, I'd noticed, that on one landing led off through double doors to the Strattons' carpeted and cosseted private rooms. According to the plans and also from what I myself remembered of it, that staircase was the central vertical artery feeding all floors of the grandstand; the central core of the whole major building.

At the top was a large windowed room like a control tower from where the Stewards with massive binoculars watched the races. A modern offshoot from there ran up yet again to an eyrie inhabited by race-callers, television equipment and the scribbling classes.

At other levels on its upward progress the staircase branched off inwards to a members' lunch room and outwards to ranks of standing-only steps open to the elements. A corridor on the first floor led to a row of private balcony boxes where prim little light white wooden chairs gave respite to rich and elderly feet.

I went into the staircase from the open front of the stands and sprinted up to the level of the smelly members' bar. The door of the bar was locked, but along the white-painted landing wall outside, at about eighteen inches from the ground, ran a harmless-looking thick white filament that looked like the sort of washing line used for drying laundry in back gardens.

At intervals along the wall the line ran into the wall itself and out again, and finally a hole had been drilled from the landing through into the bar, so that the white line ran into it, disappearing from view.

Neil had made no mistake. The white washing line look-alike was in fact itself an explosive known as "det cord," short for detonating cord, along which detonation could travel at something like eighteen thousand meters a second, blowing apart everything it touched. At every spot where the cord went into the wall and out again there would be a compressed cache of plastic explosive. All explosives did more damage when compressed.

Det cord was not like old fuses spluttering slowly towards a bomb marked "BOMB," as in comics and ancient westerns. Det cord *was* the explosive; and it seemed to be winding up and down through the walls of the stairwell for at least one floor above me and another below.

I yelled "Toby" with full lungs and whatever power I could muster. I yelled "Toby" up the staircase and I yelled "Toby" down the staircase, and got no response at all.

"Toby, if you're here, this place is full of explosives." I yelled it up the stairs, and down.

Nothing.

He had to be somewhere else, I thought. But where? *Where?* There could be det cord festooned throughout the length of all the buildings; throughout the Club, through the big secondary enclosure known as "Tattersalls" where on race days the bookies had their pitches, through the cheapest of three enclosures where there were almost more bars than viewing steps.

"Toby," I yelled: and got silence.

There was no possibility that I could miraculously dismantle what looked like a thoroughly planned attack. I didn't know enough, nor where to start. My first priority, anyway, was the safety of my son, so with silence continuing, I turned to go back out into the open air, to run further down the sprawling complex and try again.

I'd already pivoted to run when I heard the tiniest noise, and it seemed to me it came from above, from somewhere up the stairs, over my head.

I sprinted up two levels, to the landing outside the Stewards' vantage point, and yelled again. I tried the Stewards' room door, but like so much else, it was locked. He couldn't be in there, but I yelled anyway.

"Toby, if you're here, *please* come out. This place can blow up at any moment. Please, Toby. *Please.*"

Nothing. False alarm. I turned to go down again, to start searching somewhere else.

A wavery little voice said, "Dad?"

I whirled. He was climbing with difficulty out of his perfect tiny hiding place, a small sideboard with spindly legs beside an empty row of pegs meant for the Stewards' hats and coats.

"Thank God," I said briefly. "Now come on."

"I was the escaped prisoner," he said, slithering out and standing up. "If they'd found me they would have put me back in the Bastille."

I hardly listened. I felt only urgency along with relief.

"Will it really blow up, Dad?"

"Let's just get out of here."

I reached for his hand and tugged him with me towards the stairs, and there was a sort of *crrrump* from below us, and then a brilliant flash of light and a horrendous bang and a swaying all about us, and it was like what I imagined it must be like to be caught in an earthquake.

I n the fraction of time when thought was possible, both knowledge and instinct screamed that the stairs themselves, wreathed and tied with explosive like a parcel, were the embrace of death.

Enclosing Toby in my arms I spun on the heaving floor and hurled us with slipping feet and every labor-trained muscle back towards Toby's hiding-place cupboard beside the Stewards' box door.

The core of Stratton Park racecourse imploded, folding inwards. The staircase ripped and cracked and crashed as its walls collapsed into the well, splitting open into jagged caverns all the rooms alongside.

The Stewards' door blew open, its glass viewing walls splintering and flying in slicing spears. The terrifying noise deafened. The stands shrieked as they tore apart, wood against wood against brick against concrete against stone against steel.

With Toby beneath me, I fell forwards, scrabbling and seeking for footing so as not to slide back towards the gutted stairs; and the high precarious tower atop all else, the press and television vantage point, came smashing down through the ceiling beams and plaster above us, plunging in sharp-edged pieces at crazy angles across my back and legs. I seemed to stop breathing. Sharp stabs of passing agony stapled me to the floor. Movement became impossible.

Billowing black smoke poured up from the stairs, lung-filling, choking, setting off convulsive coughing when there was no room to cough.

The thunderous noise gradually stopped. Far below, small creaks and intermittent crashes. Everywhere black smoke, gray dust. In me, pain.

"Dad," Toby's voice said, "you're squashing me." He was coughing also. "I can't breathe, Dad."

I glanced vaguely down. The top of his head, brownhaired, came up as far as my chin. Inappropriately, but how can one help the things one thinks, I thought of his mother's once frequent complaint—"Lee, you're squashing me"—and I would raise my weight off her by leaning on my elbows and I'd look into her gleaming laughing eyes and kiss her, and she'd say that I was too big and that one day I would collapse her lungs and break her ribs and suffocate her from love.

Collapse her lungs, snap her ribs, suffocate . . . dear God.

With a good deal of effort I levered my elbows up into the familiar supporting position and spoke to Amanda's twelve-year-old son.

"Wriggle out," I said, coughing. "Wriggle up this way, head first."

"Dad . . . you're too heavy."

"Come on," I said, "you can't lie there all day." I meant, I didn't know for how long I could lift myself off him, so as not to kill him.

I felt like Atlas, only the world lay not on my shoulders, but beneath them.

Incongruously, sunlight fell all around us. Blue sky above, glimpsed through the hole in the roof. The black smoke funneled up through there, slowly dispersing.

Toby made convulsive little heaves until his face came up level with mine. His brown eyes looked terrified and, uncharacteristically, he was crying.

I kissed his cheek, which normally he didn't like. This time he seemed not to notice and didn't wipe it away.

"It's all right," I said. "It's over. We're both all right. All we have to do is get out. Keep on wriggling, you're doing fine."

He inched out with difficulty, pushing bits of masonry out of his way. There were some sobs but no complaints. He made it onto his knees by my right shoulder, panting quietly, coughing now and then.

"Well done," I said. I let my chest relax onto the floor. Not an enormous relief, except for my elbows.

"Dad . . . you're bleeding."

"Never mind."

A few more sobs.

"Don't cry," I said.

"That man," he said. "The horse kicked his eyes out."

I moved my shirt-sleeved right forearm in his direction. "Hold my hand," I said. His own fingers slid slowly across my palm. "Look," I said, gripping lightly, "dreadful things do happen. There's never going to be a time in your whole life when you won't remember that man's face. But you'll remember it less and less often, not all the time, like now. And you'll remember us being here, with all the stands blown inwards. A lot of people's memories are full of truly awful things. Any time you want to talk about that man, I'll listen."

He squeezed my hand fiercely, and let it go.

"We can't just sit here forever," he said.

Despite our fairly disadvantaged state, I was smiling.

"It's quite likely," I remarked, "that your brothers and Colonel Gardner will have noticed the stands have been rearranged. People will come."

"I could go and wave out of those broken windows, to tell them where we are . . ."

"Stay right here," I said sharply. "Any floor might collapse."

"Not this one, Dad." He looked around wildly. "Not this one, that we're on, will it, Dad?"

"It'll be all right," I said, hoping I spoke the truth. The whole landing, however, now sloped towards where the stairs had been, and I wouldn't have cared to jump up and down on it with abandon.

The pressures of the chunks of ceiling roof and press tower were unremitting across my back and legs, pinning me comprehensively. I could, though, move my toes inside my shoes, and I could certainly feel. Unless the building subsided more from accumulated internal stress, it looked possible I might escape with a clear head, an intact spinal cord, both hands and feet and an undamaged son. Not bad, considering. I hoped, all the same, that rescuers would expedite.

"Dad."

"Mm?"

"Don't shut your eyes."

I opened them, and kept them open.

"When will people come?" he asked.

"Soon."

"It wasn't my fault the stands exploded."

"Of course not."

After a pause, he said, "I thought you were kidding."

"Yep."

"It's not my fault you're hurt, is it?"

"No." He wasn't, I saw, reassured. I said, "If you hadn't been hiding right up here I could have been lower down the stairs when the explosion happened, and would now very likely be dead."

"Are you sure?"

"Yes."

It seemed very quiet. Almost as if nothing had happened. If I tried to move, different story . . .

"How did you know the stands would explode?" Toby said.

I told him about Neil seeing the det cord. "It's thanks to him," I said, "that all five of you weren't killed."

"I didn't notice any cord."

"No, but you know what Neil's like."

"He *sees* things."

"Yes."

In the distance, at what seemed long last, we could hear sirens. One, at first, then several, then a whole wailing orchestra.

Toby wanted to move but again I told him to stay still, and before very long there were voices on the racecourse side, outside and below, calling my name.

"Tell them we're here," I told Toby, and he shouted with his high voice, "We're here. We're up here."

After a brief silence a man's voice yelled, "Where?"

"Tell them beside the Stewards' box," I said.

Toby shouted the information and got another question in return.

"Is your father with you?"

"Yes."

"Is he talking?"

"Yes." Toby looked at me and spontaneously gave them more news. "He can't move. Some roof fell in."

"Stay there."

"OK?" I said to Toby. "I told you they would come."

We listened to clanging and banging and businesslike shouting, all far away and outside. Toby was shivering, not with cold, as the midday sun still warmed us, but with accumulated shock.

"They won't be long," I said.

"What are they *doing?*"

"Putting up some sort of scaffolding, I should think."

They came up from the racecourse side, where the reinforced concrete viewing steps on the steel girders had, it transpired, survived the onslaught pretty well unscathed. A fireman in a big hard hat and a bright yellow jacket suddenly appeared outside the broken windows of the Stewards' box and peered inwards.

"Anyone home?" he cheerfully called.

"Yes." Toby stood up joyfully and I told him abruptly to stay still.

"But Dad . . ."

*"Stay still."*

"You stay there, young 'un. We'll have you out in no time," the fireman told him, and vanished as quickly as he'd come. Returning, he brought with him a colleague and a secure metal walkway for Toby to cross onto the window, and almost in no time, as he'd promised, he'd picked the boy out of the window and out of danger. As Toby disappeared from my view, I felt weak. I trembled from relief. A lot of strength seemed to drain away.

The colleague, a moment later, stepped through the window and crossed the walkway in reverse, stopping at the end of it, some several feet from where I lay.

"Lee Morris?" he asked. Dr. Livingstone, I presume.

"Yes," I said.

"It won't be long."

They came in personal harnesses with jacks and cantilevers and slings and cutting equipment and a mini-crane, and they knew what they were doing, but the whole area where I was lying proved wickedly unstable, and at one point another big section of the press box came crashing through the roof and, missing my feet by millimeters, bounced and plummeted down the five-story hole where the stairs were meant to be. One could hear it colliding with wrecked walls all the way down until it reached the bottom with a reverberating disintegrating thud.

The firemen sweated and put jacks from floor to ceiling wherever they could.

There were three men working, moving circumspectly, taking no sudden unpremeditated steps. One of them, I slowly realized, seemed to be operating a video camera, of all things. The whirring came and went. I twisted my head round to check and found the busy lens pointing straight at my face, which I found deeply embarrassing but could do nothing about. A fourth man arrived, again in yellow, again with a rope to his waist, and he too brought a camera. Too much, I thought. He asked the first three for a progress report and I read his identification—"Police"—in black on his yellow chest.

The building *creaked.*

The men all stopped moving, waiting. The sounds ceased and the firemen with extreme caution moved again, cursing, dedicated, brave, prosaically taking risks.

I lay gratefully inert on my stomach and thought I hadn't had a bad life, if this should prove to be the end of it. The firemen had no intention of letting me come to the end of it. They brought up and slid a harness under my chest and fastened it round my arms and across my shoulders so that if I slid I wouldn't go down the gaping hole and, bit by bit, they levered the extensive chunks of brick and plaster slightly off me and freed me from splintered beams until, by pulling on the harness, they could move me a couple of feet up the sloping floor towards the threshold of the Stewards' box. The footing was more solid there, they said.

I wasn't of much help to them. I'd lain squashed for so long that my muscles wouldn't move properly on demand. Many of them developed pins and needles and then throbbed as if released from tourniquets, which I didn't much mind. The cuts caused by spears of wood felt worse.

A man in a fluorescent green jacket came through the window, crossed the safe walkway and, pointing to the information lettered in black across his chest, told me he was a doctor.

Dr. Livingstone? No, Dr. Jones. Oh, well.

He bent down by my head, which I'd tired of holding up.

"Can you squeeze my hand?" he asked.

I squeezed his hand obligingly and told him I wasn't much hurt.

"Good."

He went away.

It wasn't until much later, when I watched one of the videotapes, that I learned he hadn't totally believed me because, except for the collar and sleeves, my white shirt showed scarlet and had been ripped here and there like bits of skin underneath. In any case, when he returned it wasn't to expect me to stand up and walk out: instead he brought what looked to me like a sled, not a flat stretcher that one could easily fall off, but with raised rails down the sides, better for carrying.

One way or another, with one of the fireman levering the last chunk of timber off my legs and the other two pulling me forwards by the harness, with me tugging myself forward handhold by handhold, I slithered along face down onto the offered transport. When my center of gravity was more or less onto the safe walkway, and I was supported from the thighs up, the ominous creaking started again in the building, this time worse, this time with tremors.

The fireman behind my feet said "Christ" and leapt onto the walkway, edging past me with infectious urgency. As if rehearsed he and the others abandoned slow care, caught hold of the side rails of my sled-stretcher and yanked it with me hanging on like a limpet across the narrow path to the windows.

The building shuddered and shook. The rest of the press room—by far the largest part—toppled up high, broke loose, smashed down lethally through what was left of the ceiling right onto the place where I'd been lying, and with its weight tore the whole landing away from its walls and, roaring and thundering, plunged horribly downwards. Grit, dust, bricks, chunks of splintered plaster and slivers of glass fog-filled the air. Mesmerized, I glanced back over my shoulder and saw Toby's hiding place, the small sideboard, topple over forwards and slide to oblivion. The floor of the Stewards' box subsided and left the cantilevered safe walkway protruding inward from the sill of the window, life-saving still but now with nothing beneath. My legs, from above the knees, stuck out over space.

Incredibly, the policeman, now just outside the window, went on filming.

I gripped the rails of the stretcher, my hands fierce with the elemental fear of falling. The firemen clutched the harness round my shoulders, lifted the stretcher, hurled themselves and me toward safety, and the whole lot of us popped out into sunshine, an untidy group, disorganized, coughing from dust, but alive.

Nothing even then proved simple. The concrete viewing steps of the stands reached only as far as a story below the Stewards' box, and to bring the rescue equipment up the last nine or ten feet had demanded many struts ingeniously bolted together. Below near the racecourse rails, where crowds on race days cheered the finishes, the asphalt and grass viewing areas were packed with vehicles—fire engines, police cars, ambulances—and, worst, a television station's van.

I said that it would be much easier and less embarrassing if I simply stood up and walked down, and no one paid any attention. The doctor reappeared talking about internal injuries and not giving me any chance to make things worse, so rather against my will I got covered with a dressing or two and a blanket and was secured to the stretcher with straps and slowly carried step by careful step to the ground and across to where the emergency vehicles waited. I thanked the firemen. They grinned.

At the end of the journey five boys stood in a row, frightened and terribly strained.

I said, "I'm fine, chaps," but they seemed unconvinced.

I said to the doctor, "They're my children. Tell them I'm OK."

He glanced at me and at their young distressed faces.

"Your father," he said with common sense, "is a big strong fellow and he's quite all right. He has some bruises and cuts which we'll stick a few bandages on. You don't need to worry."

They read the word "Doctor" on the front of his bright green jacket and they decided, provisionally, to believe him.

"We're taking him to the hospital," the man in green said, indicating a waiting ambulance, "but he'll be back with you soon."

Roger appeared beside the boys and said he and his wife would look after them. "Don't worry," he said.

Ambulance men began feeding me feet first into their vehicle.

I said to Christopher, "Do you want your mother to come and take you home?"

He shook his head. "We want to stay in the bus."

The others nodded silently.

"I'll phone her," I said.

Toby said urgently, "No, Dad. We want to stay in the bus." His anxiety level, I saw, was still far too high. Anything that would reduce it had to be right.

"Play marooned, then," I said.

They all nodded, Toby, looking relieved, included.

The doctor, writing notes to give the ambulance men to take with me asked, "What's play marooned?"

"Making do on their own for a bit."

He smiled over his notes. *"Lord of the Flies?"*

"I never let it get that far."

He gave the notes to one of the ambulance men and glanced back at the boys. "Good kids."

"I'll look after them," Roger said again. "Be glad to."

"I'll phone you," I said. "And thanks."

The busy ambulance men shut the door on me, and Mrs. Gardner, I found later, made fruitcake for the boys until they couldn't face another slice.

Judged solely as a medical casualty I was fairly low in priority in the hospital's emergency department but all too high on the local media's attention list. The airwaves were buzzing, it seemed, with "terrorist bombing of a racecourse." I begged the use of a telephone from some half-cross, half-riveted nurses and got through to my wife.

"What the *hell's* going on?" she demanded, her voice high. "Some ruddy newspaper just phoned me to ask if I knew my husband and sons had been blown up. Can you *believe* it?"

"Amanda . . ."

"You obviously *haven't* been blown up."

"Which paper?"

"What does it matter? I can't remember."

"I'll complain. Anyway, just listen. Someone with a grudge put some explosive in Stratton Park racecourse, and yes, the stands did slightly blow up."

She interrupted, "The *boys*. Are they all right?"

"Unharmed. Totally all right. Only Toby was anywhere near, and some fireman carried him out. I promise you, none of them has a scratch."

"Where are you now?"

"The boys are with the racecourse manager and his wife."

"Aren't they with *you?* Why aren't they with you?"

"I've just . . . um. I'll be back with them in no time. I've got a couple of grazes that the local hospital's putting stuff on, then I'm going back to them. Christopher will phone you."

Every evening, from the mobile phone in the bus, the boys talked to their mother; family routine on expeditions.

Amanda took a bit of placating as well as reassuring. It was obviously my fault, she said, that the children had been put in danger. I didn't deny it. I asked her if she wanted them home.

"What? No, I didn't say that. You know I've a lot of things planned this weekend. They'd better stay with you. Just take more care of them, that's all."

"Yes."

"So what do I say if any other newspapers ring up?"

"Say you talked to me and everything's fine. You might see something about it on television, there were news cameras on the racecourse."

"Do take more *care,* Lee."

"Yes."

"And don't phone this evening. I'm taking Jamie over to Shelly's for the night. It's her birthday dinner, remember?"

Shelly was her sister. "Right," I said.

We said goodbye; always polite. Acid, by effort, diluted.

The variety of gashes and grazes that I had minimized as much as possible eventually got uncovered and tut-tutted over. Dust and rubble got washed out, impressive splinters were removed with tweezers and rows of staples got inserted with local anesthetic.

"You'll be sore when this wears off," the stitcher cheerfully told me. "Some of these wounds are deceptively deep. Are you *sure* you won't stay here overnight? I'm certain we can find a bed for you."

"Thanks," I said, "but no thanks."

"Lie on your stomach for a few days then. Come back in a week and we'll take the staples out. You should be healed by then."

"Thanks a lot," I said.

"Keep on taking the antibiotics."

The hospital dredged up an ambulance to take me back to Roger Gardner's house (by the back road, at my insistence) and with a bit of help from a borrowed walker and dressed in a blue dressing gown/robe from the hospital shop, I made the end of the journey upright.

The bus, I gratefully noted, had been driven down and parked outside the tidied garage. Its five younger inhabitants were in the Gardners' sitting room watching television.

*"Dad!"* they exclaimed, springing up, then, at the sight of the walking aid to the elderly, falling uncertainly silent.

"Yes," I said, "we will have no giggles about this, OK? A lot of bricks and ceiling fell on my back and legs and made a few cuts, which have now been stitched up. Some cuts were on my back and quite a lot on my legs and one cut is straight across my bottom so that I can't very easily sit down, and we will *not laugh* about that."

They did, of course, chiefly from relief, which was fine.

Mrs. Gardner offered sympathy.

"What can I get you?" she asked. "Hot cup of tea?"

"Treble scotch?"

Her sweet face creased. She poured the hard stuff generously and told me Roger had been busy all day along at the stands and was worn out by the police and by the news people and by most of the Stratton family, who had flocked to the place in fury.

The boys and Mrs. Gardner were, it appeared, waiting for the television news to start, which presently happened, with the bombing of Stratton Park racecourse prominently featured. Various shots showed the rear of the stands, from where the central column of damage couldn't be missed. A five-second interview with Conrad revealed his innermost thoughts ("shocked and angry"). "Fortunately only one minor casualty," said a voice over a shot of myself (luckily unrecognizable) being carried down the steps.

"That's you, Dad," Neil told me excitedly.

A brief shot of Toby walking down hand in hand with a fireman had the boys cheering. Next, ten seconds of Roger—"Colonel Gardner, racecourse manager"—saying the Stratton family promised the Monday race meeting would be held as scheduled. "Important not to give in to terror tactics." Finally a shot of the woolly hats with their placards at the gates, leaving viewers with an unspoken but sinister implication. Unfair, I thought.

When the news slid away into a plethora of politicians, I told Mrs. Gardner and the boys that I would go and put some clothes on, and I limped slowly with the walker over to the bus and winced without it up the steps, and although I'd meant to get dressed I lay down instead on the long sofa that was also my bed, and felt shivery and ill, and finally admitted to myself that I was a good deal more injured than I wanted to be.

After a while the outer door opened and I expected a child, but it was in fact Roger who had come.

He sat on the other long sofa opposite and looked weary.

"Are you all right?" he asked.

"Yes," I said, not moving.

"My wife says you look gray."

"You don't look too rosy yourself."

He smiled briefly and massaged his nose with a finger and thumb; a lean, neat, disciplined soldier allowing himself a gesture of tiredness after a long day's maneuvers.

"The police and all the safety-first people came out like bloodhounds. Oliver dealt with them—I phoned him at once—and he's bloody marvelous with those sort of people always. He had them agreeing immediately that, taking precautions, we could hold the races on Monday. Silver-tongued magician, he is." He paused. "The police have driven off to the hospital to interview you," he said. "Surely there was a bed for you there, in your state?"

"I didn't want to stay."

"But I told you we would look after your boys."

"I know. One or two might have been all right, but not five."

"They're easy children," he protested.

"They're subdued, today. It was best I came back."

He made no more demur but, as if unready yet to talk of the things uppermost in his thoughts, asked which was which. "To get them straight in my mind," he said.

I answered him in much the same way, postponing for a breathing space the questions that would have to be asked and answered.

"Christopher, the tall fair one, he's fourteen. Like most oldest children, he looks after the others. Toby, the one with me today in the stands, he's twelve. Edward's ten. He's the quiet one. Any time you can't find him, he's sitting in a corner somewhere reading a book. Then there's Alan."

"Freckles and a grin," Roger said, nodding.

"Freckles and a grin," I agreed, "and a deficient sense of danger. He's nine. Leaps first. Oops after."

"And Neil," Roger said. "Little bright-eyed Neil."

"He's seven. And Jamie, the baby, ten months."

"We have two daughters," Roger said. "Both grown and gone and too busy to marry."

He fell silent, and I also. The respite from gritty life slowly evaporated. I shifted with sharp discomfort on the sofa and Roger noted it but made no comment.

I said, "The stands were cleaned yesterday."

Roger sighed. "They were cleaned. They were clean. No explosives. Certainly no det cord running round that staircase. I walked everywhere myself, checking. I make rounds continually."

"But not on Good Friday morning."

"Late yesterday afternoon. Five o'clock. Went round with my foreman."

"It wasn't a matter of killing people." I said.

"No," he agreed. "It was to kill one main grandstand, on one of the very few weekdays in the year when there are no race meetings anywhere in Britain. Precisely *not* to kill people, in fact."

"I expect you have a night watchman," I said.

"Yes, we do." He shook his head frustratedly. "He makes his rounds with a dog. He says he heard nothing. He didn't hear people drilling holes in the walls. He saw no lights moving in the stands. He clocked out at seven this morning and went home."

"The police asked him?"

"The police asked him. I asked him. Conrad asked him. The poor man was brought back here soggy with sleep and bombarded with accusing questions. He's not ultra-bright at the best of times. He just blinked and looked stupid. Conrad blames me for employing a thicko."

"Blame will be scattered like confetti," I said.

He nodded. "The air's dense with it already. Mostly, everything's my fault."

"Which Strattons came?" I asked.

"Which didn't?" He sighed. "All of them except Rebecca that were here for the shareholders' meeting, plus Conrad's wife, Victoria, plus Keith's wife Imogen who was squinting drunk, plus Hannah's layabout son Jack, plus Ivan's mousy wife, Dolly. Marjorie Binsham used her tongue like a whip. Conrad can't stand up to her. She had the police pulverized. She wanted to know why you, particularly, hadn't stopped the stands blowing up once your infant child had done the trouble-spotting for you."

"Dear Marjorie!"

"Someone told her you'd damn nearly been killed and she said it served you right." He shook his head. "Sometimes I think the whole family's un-hinged."

"There's some scotch and glasses in that cupboard above your head," I said.

He loosened into a smile and poured into two tumblers. "It won't make you feel better," he observed, placing one on the built-in table with drawers under it that marked the end of my bed. "And where did you get this splendid bus? I've never seen anything like it. When I drove it down here with the boys on board they showed me all round it. They seemed to think you built the interior with your own hands. I reckon you had a yacht designer."

"Both right."

He tossed off his drink neat in two gulps, army fashion, and put down the glass.

"We can't give your boys beds, not enough room, but we could do food."

"Thanks, Roger. I'm grateful. But there's enough food in this bus for a battalion, and the battalion's had a good deal of practice in do-it-yourself."

Despite his assurances I could see his relief. He was indeed, if anything, more exhausted than myself.

I said, "Do me a favor, though?"

"If I can."

"Be vague about my whereabouts tonight? If, say, the police or the Strattons should ask."

"Somewhere to the left of Mars do you?"

"One day," I said, "I'll repay you."

THE REAL WORLD, as Toby would have said, had a go in the morning.

Traveling uncomfortably, I went along with Roger in his jeep to his office beside the parade ring, having left the five boys washing the outside of the bus with buckets of detergent, long-handled brushes and mops and the borrowed use of the Gardners' outdoor tap and garden hose.

Such mammoth splashy activity terminated always in five contentedly soaked children (they loved water-clown acts in circuses) and an at least half-clean bus. I'd advised Mrs. Gardner to go indoors and close her eyes and windows, and after the first bucketful of suds had missed the windscreen and landed on Alan, she'd given me a wild look and taken my advice.

"Don't you mind their getting wet?" Roger asked as we left the scene of potential devastation.

"They've a lot of compressed steam to get rid of," I said.

"You're an extraordinary father."

"I don't feel it."

"How are the cuts?"

"Ghastly."

He chuckled, stopped beside the office door and handed me the walker once I was on my feet. I would have preferred not to have needed it, but the only strength left anywhere, it seemed, was in my arms.

Although it was barely eight-thirty the first carload of trouble drew up on the tarmac before Roger had finished unlocking his office door. He looked over his shoulder to see who had come, and said a heartfelt *"Bugger,"* as he recognized the transport. "Bloody Keith."

Bloody Keith had not come alone. Bloody Keith had brought with him his Hannah, and Hannah, it transpired, had brought with her her son Jack. The three of them climbed out of Keith's car and began striding purposefully round to Roger's office.

He finished unlocking, opened the door, and said to me abruptly, "Come inside."

At walker pace I willingly followed him around towards the far side of his desk, where, as it happened, my jacket still hung over the back of his chair, abandoned since the previous morning. A lifetime, almost a deathtime, ago.

Keith, Hannah and Jack crowded in through the door, all three faces angry. Keith had reacted to the sight of me as if to an allergy, and Hannah wouldn't have admired her own shrewish expression. Jack, a loose-lipped teenager, mirrored his grandfather too thoroughly; handsome and mean.

Keith said, "Gardner, get that damned man out of here! And you're sacked. You're incompetent. I'm taking over your job, and you can clear out. As for you . . ." He turned his glare fully my way. "Your bloody children had no right to be anywhere near the grandstands, and if you're thinking of suing us because you were stupid enough to get yourself blown up you've another think coming."

I hadn't thought of it at all, actually. "You've given me ideas," I said rashly.

Roger, too late, made a warning movement with his hand, telling me to cool it, not stir. I had myself seen the speed with which Keith's violence had risen in him at the shareholders' meeting, and I remembered the complacency with which I'd reflected that he'd have no physical chance against Madeline's thirty-five-year-old son.

Things had changed slightly since then. I now needed a walker if I were to stay upright. And besides, there were three of them.

# 7

Roger said *"Hell"* under his breath.

I muttered to him similarly, "Get out of here."

"No."

"Yes. Keep your job."

Roger stayed.

Keith kicked the office door shut and though he, for a second or two, seemed to hesitate, Hannah had no doubts or restraints. I was, to her, the hated symbol of every resentment she'd fed and festered on for forty years. Keith, who could and should have soothed from childhood her hurt feelings, had no doubt encouraged them. Hannah's loathing was beyond her control. A dagger between the shoulder blades . . . it was there in her eyes.

She came towards me fast in the same leonine stride I'd seen in Rebecca and used her full weight to thrust me back against the wall while at the same time aiming with sharp clawed fingernails to rip my face.

Roger tried civilized protest. "Miss Stratton . . ."

The stalking cat pounced, oblivious.

I'd have liked to have punched her hard at the base of the sternum and to have slapped her into concussion, but hindering taboos bristled in my subconscious, and maybe I couldn't floor that particular woman because of Keith's hitting my mother. My mother, Hannah's mother. A jumble. In any case, I tried merely to grasp my wretched half-sister's wrists, which involved taking both my hands off the walker, and this gave Keith an opportunity he had no qualms in seizing.

He tweaked up the frame, barged Hannah out of the way and delivered a damaging clout in my direction in the shape of sturdy chromium tubing with black rubber-tipped feet. Not good. On the stapled-shut cuts, rotten.

Roger held on to Keith's arm to prevent a second strike and I held Hannah's wrists and tried to avoid her spitting in my face. All in all it had developed into a poorish Saturday morning.

It got worse.

Keith lashed out at Roger with the frame. Roger ducked. Keith swung the tubes round my way and again connected and, what with Hannah tugging furiously to get free and Keith crowding in with the four black-tipped legs aimed roughly now at my stomach, my legs inefficiently decided against continued support and to all intents buckled, so that I wavered and wobbled and in the end folded up ignominiously onto the floor.

Hannah yanked her wrists out of my grasp and put her boot in. Her son, who didn't even know me, stepped into the fracas and kicked me twice with equal venom, but also without considering any consequences to himself. I grabbed the foot coming forward for a third time and jerked hard, and with a yell of surprise he overbalanced, falling down within my reach.

His bad luck. I grabbed him and hit him crunchingly in the face and banged his head on the floor, which set Hannah screeching over us like a banshee. Her shoes, I learned, had sharp toes and spikes for heels.

I was aware that Roger, somewhere above, was trying to stop the fray, but what the Colonel really needed was a gun.

Keith took his heavy feet to me, stamping and kicking. There were deep shudders in my body under his weight and his savagery. Roger to his credit did his best to pull him off, and roughly at that time, and not a moment too soon, the outer door opened again, bringing a welcome interruption.

"I say," a man's voice bleated, "what's going on here?"

Keith, shaking off Roger's clutch and undeterred, said, "Go away, Ivan. It's none of your business."

Ivan, I supposed, might have done as he was told, but on his heels came a much tougher proposition.

Marjorie's imperious voice rose above the general noise of battle.

"Keith! Hannah! What on earth do you think you're doing? Colonel, call the police. Call the police this minute."

The threat worked instantaneously. Hannah stopped kicking and screeching. Keith, panting, stepped back. Jack slithered away from me on all fours. Roger put the walker next to me and stretched out a hand to haul me to my feet. It took him more effort than he'd expected, but by martial perseverance he succeeded. I propped myself upright on the walker by force of arms and leaned wearily against the wall, and found that not only Ivan and Marjorie had arrived, but also Conrad and Dart.

For a moment of speechlessness Marjorie took stock of things, noting the still-scorching fury in Hannah's manner, the brutish force unspent in Keith and the sullen nose-bleeding vindictiveness of Jack. She glanced at Roger and lastly flicked her gaze over me, head to foot, coming to rest on my face.

"Disgraceful," she said accusingly. "Fighting like animals. You ought to know better."

"He shouldn't be here," Keith said thickly, and added, lying easily, "He punched me. He started it."

"He's broken my nose," Jack complained.

"Don't tell me he attacked all three of you," Dart mocked. "Serves you right."

"You shut up," Hannah told him with bile.

Conrad gave his opinion. "He must have done *something* to start all this. I mean, it's obvious." He became the examining magistrate, the heavyweight of the proceedings, the accuser; pompous.

"Well, Mr. Morris, why precisely did you punch my brother and attack his family? What have you to say?"

Time, I thought, for the prisoner at the bar to defend himself. I swallowed. I felt weak. Also angry enough not to give in to the weakness, or to let them all see it and enjoy it.

When I could trust my voice not to come out as a croak, I said neutrally, "I didn't punch your brother. I did nothing. They had a go at me for being who I am."

"That doesn't make sense," Conrad said. "People don't get attacked just for being who they are."

"Tell that to the Jews," Dart said.

It shocked them all, but not much.

Marjorie Binsham said, "Go outside, the lot of you. *I* will deal with Mr. Morris, in here." She turned her head to Roger. "You too, Colonel. Out."

Conrad said, "It's not safe."

"Rubbish!" Marjorie interrupted. "Off you go."

They obeyed her, shuffling out without looking at each other, losing face.

"Close the door," she commanded, and Roger, last out, closed it.

She sat down composedly, wearing that day a narrow tailored navy blue overcoat with a white band of collar again showing beneath. The waved white hair, the fragile-looking complexion and the piercing hawk eyes, all those were as before.

She inspected me critically. She said, "You got yourself blown up yesterday and trampled today. Not very clever, are you?"

"No."

"And get off the wall. You're bleeding on it."

"I'll paint it, later."

"From where, exactly, are you bleeding?"

I explained about the multitude of bruises, cuts and staples. "Some of those," I said, "feel as if they've popped open."

"I see."

She seemed for a few moments undecided, not her usual force. Then she said, "I will free you, if you like, from our agreement."

"Oh?" I was surprised. "No, the agreement stands."

"I did not expect you to be hurt."

I briefly considered things. Hurt, even if grievous, was in some ways immaterial. I ignored it as best I could. Concentrated on anything else.

"Do you know," I asked, "who set the explosive?"

"No, I don't."

"Which Strattons could have the knowledge?"

"None of them."

"What about Forsyth?"

Shutters came down in her, too.

"Whatever Forsyth is or isn't," she said, "he is not expert in blowing things up."

"Does he have a motive for getting someone else to do it?"

After a pause, she said, "I don't think so."

My forehead was sweating. I put a hand up automatically to wipe it and started swaying, and regripped the walker urgently, fighting to regain balance and not to fall down. Too many crushed muscles, too many cut fibers, too much damned battering overall. I stood quietly, breathing deeply, crisis over, my weight on my arms.

"Sit down," Marjorie commanded.

"That might be worse."

She stared. I smiled. "My children think it funny."

"But not."

"Not very."

She said slowly, "Are you going to charge Keith with assault? Hannah also?"

I shook my head.

"Why not? They were kicking you. I saw them."

"And would you say so in court?"

She hesitated. She had used the police as a threat to end the fight, but that was all it had been, a threat.

I thought of the pact my mother had made with Lord Stratton, to keep quiet about Keith's violent behavior. I had hugely benefited from that silence. My unthought-out instinct was to do the same as my mother.

I said, "I will even things one day, with Keith. But not by embroiling you against your family in public. It will be a private matter, between him and me."

With evident relief and formality, she said, "I wish you well."

There was a brief single wail of a police siren outside the window, more an announcement of arrival than of hurry.

The police had arrived anyway. Marjorie Binsham looked not enchanted and I felt very tired, and presently the office door opened to let in far more people than the space had been designed for.

Keith was making abortive attempts to persuade the law that I had caused actual bodily harm to his grandson, Jack.

"Jack," observed Roger calmly, "shouldn't try to kick people when they're down."

"And you," Keith said to him viciously, "you can clear out. I told you. You're sacked."

"Don't be ridiculous," Marjorie snapped. "Colonel, you are *not* sacked. We need you. Please stay here. Only by a majority vote of the Board can you be asked to leave, and there will be no such majority."

"One of these days, Marjorie," Keith said, his voice heavy and shaking with humiliation, "I will get rid of you."

"Look here, Keith . . ." Conrad began.

"And you shut up," Keith said with hatred. "It was you or your blackmailing architect that put paid to the stands."

Into the shocked silence, which left all Stratton mouths dropping open, the police with bathos consulted a notebook full of pre-arranged agenda and asked which of the family normally drove a dark green six-year-old Granada with rusted near fenders.

"What's that got to do with anything?" Dart demanded.

Without answering that question the police presence repeated their own.

"I do, then," Dart said. "So what?"

"And did you drive that car through the main gates of the racecourse at eight-twenty yesterday morning, and did you oblige Mr. Harold Quest to leap out of your path to avoid serious injury, and did you make an obscene gesture to him when he protested?"

Dart nearly laughed, and prudently thought better of it at the last moment. "No, I didn't," he said.

"Didn't do what, sir? Didn't drive through the gates? Didn't make Mr. Quest leap out of the way? Didn't make an obscene gesture?"

Dart said unworriedly, "I didn't drive through the main gates at twenty past eight yesterday morning."

"But you identified the car, sir . . ."

"I wasn't driving it at eight-twenty yesterday morning. Not through the main gates, here. Not anywhere."

The police asked the inevitable question, politely.

"I was in my bathroom, since you ask," Dart said, and left his actual activity there to the collective imagination.

I asked, "Is Mr. Quest a large man with a beard, a knitted hat and a placard reading 'HORSES RIGHTS COME FIRST'?"

The police admitted, "He does answer to that description, yes, sir."

"That man!" exclaimed Marjorie.

"Should be shot," Conrad said.

"He walks straight out in front of one's car," Marjorie told the policemen severely. "He will, no doubt, achieve his aim in the end."

"Which is, madam?"

"To be knocked down, of course. To fall down artistically at the slightest contact. To suffer for the cause. One has to be frightfully careful with that sort of man."

I asked, "Are you sure that Mr. Quest was actually outside the gates himself at twenty past eight yesterday morning?"

"He insisted that he was," said the policeman.

"On Good Friday? It's a day when no one goes to racecourses."

"He said he was there."

I left it. Lack of energy. Dart and the car had gone in and out of the gates often enough for every picketer to be able to describe it down to its tattered rear bumper-sticker, which read, "If you can read this, drop back." Dart had annoyed big-beard the day I'd been with him. Big-beard, Harold Quest, felt compelled to make trouble. Where lay the truth?

"And you, Mr. Morris . . ." The notebook's pages were flipped over and were consulted, "We were told you were to be detained in hospital but when we went to interview you they said you had discharged yourself. They hadn't officially released you."

"Such punitive words!" I said.

"What?"

"Detained and released. As in prison."

"We couldn't find you," he complained. "No one seemed to know where you'd gone."

"Well, I'm here now."

"And . . . er . . . Mr. Jack Stratton alleges that at approximately eight-fifty this morning you attacked him and broke his nose."

"Jack Stratton alleges nothing of the sort," Marjorie said with certainty. "Jack, speak up."

The sullen young man, dabbing his face with a handkerchief, took note of Marjorie's piercing displeasure and mumbled he might have walked into a door, like. Despite Keith's and Hannah's protestations, the policeman resignedly drew a line across the entry in his notebook and said his superiors wanted information from me on the whereabouts of the explosive charges "prior to detonation." Where, they asked, could I be found?

"When?" I asked.

"This morning, sir."

"Then . . . here, I suppose."

Conrad, looking at his watch, announced that he had summoned a demolitions expert and an inspector from the local council to come to advise how best to remove the old stands and clear the area ready for rebuilding.

Keith, in a rage, said, "You've no right to do that. It's my racecourse just as much as yours, and I want to sell it, and if we sell to a developer *he* will clear away the stands at no expense to us. We are *not* rebuilding."

Marjorie, fierce-eyed, said they needed an expert opinion on whether or not the stands could be restored as they had been, and whether the racecourse insurance would cover any other course of action.

"Add the insurance to the profit from selling, and we will all benefit," Keith obstinately said.

The policemen, uninterested, retired to their car outside and could be seen talking on their private phone line, consulting their superiors, one supposed.

I said doubtfully to Roger, *"Can* the stands be restored?"

He answered with caution "Too soon to say."

"Of course they can." Marjorie was positive. "Anything can be restored, if one insists on it."

Replaced as before, or copied, she meant. A mistake, I thought it would be, for Stratton Park's racing future.

The family went on quarreling. They had all turned up early, it appeared, precisely to prevent any unilateral decision making. They left the office in an arguing mass, bound together by fears of what any one could do on his own. Roger watched them go, his expression exasperated.

"What a way to run a business! And neither Oliver nor I have been paid since before Lord Stratton died. He used to sign our checks personally. The only person empowered to pay us since then is Mrs. Binsham. I explained it to her when we were walking round the course last Wednesday, and she said she understood, but when I asked her again yesterday after the stands blew up, when she came here with all the others, she told me not to bother her at such a time." He sighed heavily. "It's all very well, but it's over two months now since we had any salary."

"Who pays the racecourse staff?" I asked.

"I do. Lord Stratton arranged it. Keith disapproves. He says it's an invitation to fraud. Judges me by himself, of course. Anyway, the only paychecks I can't sign are Oliver's and my own."

"Have you made them out already?"

"My secretary did."

"Give them to me, then."

"To you?"

"I'll get the old bird to sign them."

He didn't ask how. He merely opened a desk drawer, took out an envelope and held it towards me.

"Put it in my jacket," I said.

He looked at the walker, shook his head at his thoughts, and tucked the checks into my jacket pocket.

"Are the stands," I asked, "a total loss?"

"You'd better see for yourself. Mind you, no one can get close. The police have cordoned everything off."

From the office window, little damage was visible. One could see the end wall, the roof and an oblique side view of the open steps.

"I'd rather see the holes unaccompanied by Strattons," I said.

Roger almost grinned. "They're all afraid to let the others out of their sight."

"I thought so too."

"I suppose you do know you're bleeding."

"Staining the wall, Marjorie said." I nodded. "It's stopped by now, I should think."

"But . . ." He fell silent.

"I'll go back for running repairs," I promised. "Though God knows when. They keep one waiting so long."

He said diffidently, "One of the racecourse doctors would be quicker. I could ask him for you, if you like. He's very obliging."

"Yes," I said tersely.

Roger reached for his telephone and reassured the doctor that racing was still going ahead as planned on Monday. Meanwhile, as a favor, could a casualty be stitched? When? At once, preferably. Thanks very much.

"Come on, then," he said to me, replacing the receiver. "Can you still walk?"

I could and did, pretty slowly. The police protested at my vanishing again. Back in an hour or so, Roger said soothingly. The Strattons were nowhere in sight, though their cars were still parked. Roger aimed his jeep towards the main gates, and Mr. Harold Quest refrained from planting his obsessions in our path.

The doctor was the one who had attended the fallers at the open ditch, businesslike and calm. When he saw what he was being asked to do, he didn't want to.

"GPs don't do this sort of thing any more," he told Roger. "They refer people to hospitals. He should be in a hospital. This level of pain is ridiculous."

"It comes and goes," I said. "And suppose we were out in the Sahara Desert?"

"Swindon is not the Sahara."

"All life's a desert."

He muttered under his breath and stuck me together again with what looked like adhesive tape.

"Haven't I seen you before?" he asked, puzzled, finishing.

I explained about the fence.

"The man with the children!" He shook his head regretfully. "They saw a horror, I'm afraid."

Roger thanked him for his services to me, and I also. The doctor told Roger that the racing authorities had received a complaint from Rebecca Stratton about his professional competency, or lack of it. They wanted a full report on his decision to recommend that she should be stood down for concussion.

"She's a bitch," Roger said, with feeling.

The doctor glanced my way uneasily.

"He's safe," Roger assured him. "Say what you like."

"How long have you known him?"

"Long enough. And it was Strattons that kicked his wounds open again."

It had to be hellish, I thought, being in even the smallest way reliant on the Strattons for employment. Roger truly lived on the edge of an abyss: and out of his job would mean out of his home.

He drove us carefully back to the racecourse, forbearing from lecturing me about the hand I clamped over my face, or my drooping head. As far as he was concerned, what I chose to do about my troubles was my own affair. I developed strong feelings of friendship and gratitude.

Big-beard stepped in front of the jeep. I wondered if his name were really Quest, or if he'd made it up. Not a tactful question to ask at that time. He barred our way through the main gates peremptorily, and Roger, to my surprise, smartly backed away from him, swung the jeep round and drove off down the road, continuing our journey.

"It just occurred to me," he said judiciously, "that if we go in by the back road we not only avoid words with that maniac, but you could call at your bus for clean clothes."

"I'm running out of them."

He glanced across doubtfully. "Mine aren't really big enough."

"No. It's OK."

I was down to a choice between well-worn working jeans and racegoing tidiness. I opted for the jeans and a lumberjack-type wool checked shirt and dumped the morning's bloodied garments in a washing locker already filled with sopping smaller clothes.

The boys had finished sluicing both the bus and themselves. The bus looked definitely cleaner. The boys must be dry, even though nowhere in sight. I descended slowly to the ground again and found Roger walking round the home-from-home, interested but reticent, as ever.

"It used to be a long-distance touring coach," I said. "I bought it when the bus company replaced its cozy old fleet with modern glass-walled crowd-pleasers."

"How . . . I mean, how do you manage the latrines?"

I smiled at the army parlance. "There were huge spaces for suitcases, underneath. I replaced some of them with water and sewage tanks. Every rural authority runs pump-out tankers for emptying far-flung cesspits. And there are boatyards. It's easy to get a pump-out, if you know who to ask."

"Amazing." He patted the clean coffee-colored paintwork, giving himself another interval, I saw again, before having to go back to the distasteful present.

He sighed. "I suppose . . ."

I nodded.

We climbed back into the jeep and returned to the grandstands, where, leaning again on the walker, I took my first objective look at the previous day's destructive mayhem. We stood prudently outside the police tapes, but movement had ceased in the pile.

First thought: *incredible* that Toby and I had come out of that mess alive.

The building had been centrally disemboweled, its guts spilling out in a monstrous cascade. The weighing room, changing rooms and Oliver Wells's office, which jutted forward from the main structure, had been crushed flat under the spreading weight of the collapsing floors above. The long unyielding steel and concrete mass of the course-facing viewing steps had meant that all the explosive force had been directed one way, into the softer resistance of the brick, wood and plaster of dining rooms, bars and staircase.

Above the solidly impacted rubble a hollow column of space rose through the upper floors like an exclamation mark, topped with a few stark remaining fingers of the Stewards' viewing box pointing skyward.

I said slowly, under my breath, "Jesus Christ."

After a while, Roger asked, "What do you think?"

"Chiefly," I said, "how the hell are you going to hold a race meeting here the day after tomorrow?"

He rolled his eyes in frustration. "It's Easter weekend. More weddings today than on any other day of the year. Monday, horse shows, dog shows, you name it, all over the place. I spent all yesterday afternoon trying to get hire firms to bring marquees. *Any* sort of tent. But every scrap of canvas is already out in service. We're shutting off the whole of this end of the stands, of course, and are having to move everyone and everything along into Tattersalls, but so far I've only managed a promise of a couple of Portakabins for the changing rooms and it looks as if we're going to have to have the scales out in the open air, as they used to do at point-to-points. And as for food and extra bars . . ." He shrugged helplessly. "We've told the caterers to make their own arrangements and they say they're stretched already. God help us if it rains, we'll be working under umbrellas."

"Where were you planning to put tents?" I asked.

"In the members' parking lot." He sounded disconsolate. "The Easter Monday holiday meeting is our biggest money-maker of the year. We can't afford to cancel it. And both Marjorie Binsham and Conrad are adamant that we go ahead. We've told all the trainers to send their runners for the races. The stables are all right. We'll still comply with all the regulations such as six security boxes, and so on. The saddling stalls are fine. The parade ring's OK. Oliver can use my office."

He turned away from his gloomy contemplation of the ruined grandstand and we began a slow traverse towards his telephone. He had to confirm some electrical plans, he said.

His office was full of Strattons. Conrad sat in Roger's chair behind the desk. Conrad was talking on Roger's telephone, taking charge.

Conrad was saying, "Yes, I know you told my manager that all your tents were out, but this is Lord Stratton himself speaking, and I'm telling you to dismantle and bring in a suitable marquee from anywhere at all, and put it up here tomorrow. I don't care where you get it from, just get it."

I touched Roger's arm before he could make any protest, and waved to him to retreat. Outside the office, ignored by all the Strattons, I suggested he drive us both back to the bus.

"I've a telephone in it," I explained. "No interruptions."

"Did you hear what Conrad was saying?"

"Yes, I did. Will he be successful?"

"If he is, my job's gone."

"Drive down to the bus."

Roger drove and, to save having to get in and out of the bus again, I told him where to find the mobile phone and asked him to bring it out, along with a book of private phone numbers he would find beneath it. When he climbed down the steps with the necessary, I looked up a number and made a call.

"Henry? Lee Morris. How goes it?"

"Emergency? Crisis? The roof's fallen in?"

"How did you guess?"

"Yes, but Lee, my usual big top is out as an indoor pony school. Little girls in hard hats. They've got it for the year."

"What about the huge one that takes so much moving?"

A resigned sigh came down the wire. Henry, long-time pal, general large-scale junk dealer, had acquired two big tops from a bankrupt traveling circus and would rent them out to me from time to time to enclose any thoroughly gutted ruin I wanted to shield from the weather.

I explained to him what was needed and why, and I explained to Roger who he was going to be talking to, and I leaned peacefully on the walker while they discussed floor space, budget and transport. When they seemed to be reaching agreement I said to Roger, "Tell him to bring all the flags."

Roger, mystified, relayed the message and got a reply that made him laugh. "Fine," he said, "I'll phone back to confirm."

We took the telephone and the numbers book with us in the jeep and returned to the office. Conrad was still shouting down the phone there but, judging from the impatience now manifest in the Stratton herd, was achieving nil results.

"You're on," I murmured to Roger. "Say *you* found the tent."

It didn't come naturally to him to take another man's credit, but he could see the point in it. The Strattons could perversely turn down any suggestion of mine, even if it were to their own advantage to adopt it.

Roger walked over to his desk as Conrad slammed down the receiver in fury.

"I . . . er . . . I've located a tent," he said firmly.

"About time!" Conrad said.

"Where?" Keith demanded, annoyed.

"A man in Hertfordshire has one. He can ship it here by tomorrow morning, and he'll send a crew to erect it."

Conrad was grudgingly pleased but wouldn't admit it.

"The only thing is," Roger continued, "that he doesn't supply this tent on short leases. We would need to keep it for a minimum of three months. However," he hurried on, sensing interruptions, "that condition could be to our advantage, as the grandstands will be out of operation for much longer than that. We could keep the tent for as long as we need. And this tent has a firm floor and versatile dividing partitions and sounds stronger than a normal marquee."

"Too expensive," Keith objected.

"Less expensive, actually," Roger said, "than erecting tents separately for each meeting."

Marjorie Binsham's gaze bypassed both Roger and her family and fastened on me.

"Any ideas?" she asked.

"Ignore him," Keith insisted.

I said neutrally, "All four directors are here. Hold a board meeting and decide."

A smile, quickly hidden, tugged at Marjorie's lips. Dart, though, grinned openly.

"Give us the details," Marjorie commanded Roger, and he, consulting his notes, told them the space and price involved, and said the insurance from non-availability of the stands would easily cover it.

"Who arranged that insurance?" Marjorie asked.

"Lord Stratton and I and the insurance brokers."

"Very well," Marjorie said crisply. "I put forward a motion that the Colonel arranges a contract for the tent on the terms proposed. And Ivan will second it."

Ivan, galvanized, said vaguely, "Oh? Yes, rather."

"Conrad?" Marjorie challenged him.

"Well . . . I suppose so."

"Carried," Marjorie said.

"I object," Keith seethed.

"Your objection is noted," Marjorie said. "Colonel, summon the tent."

Roger turned the leaves of my phone book and spoke to Henry.

"Very well done, Colonel!" Marjorie congratulated him warmly when all was arranged. "This place could not function without you."

Conrad looked defeated; Ivan, bewildered; and Keith, murderous.

Jack, Hannah and Dart, minor players, put no thoughts into words.

The brief ensuing pause in the proceedings came to an end with the arrival of two more cars, one containing, it transpired, two senior policemen with an explosives expert, and the other, Conrad's demolition man and a heavily mustached manifestation of local authority.

The Strattons, as a flock, migrated into the open air.

Roger wiped a hand over his face and said service in Northern Ireland had been less of a strain.

"Do you think we had an Irish bomb here?" I said.

He looked startled but shook his head. "The Irish boast of it. No one so far has done any crowing. And this one wasn't aimed at people, don't forget. The Irish bombers aim to maim."

"So who?"

"Crucial question. I don't know. And you don't need to say it . . . this may not be the end."

"What about guards?"

"I've press-ganged my groundsmen. There are relays of them in pairs patrolling the place." He patted the walkie-talkie clipped to his belt. "They're reporting all the time to my foreman. If anything looks wrong, he'll report it to me."

The newly arrived policemen came into the office and introduced themselves as a detective chief inspector and a detective sergeant. An accompanying intense-looking young man was vaguely and anonymously introduced as an explosives expert, a defuser of bombs. It was he who asked most of the questions.

I answered him simply, describing where the det cord had been and how it had looked.

"You and your young son both knew at once what it was?"

"We'd both seen it before."

"And how close to each other were the charges in the walls?"

"About three feet apart. In some places, less."

"And how extensive or widespread?"

"All round the stairwell and the landing walls on at least two floors. Perhaps more."

"We understand you're a builder. How long, do you think, would it have taken you personally to drill the holes for the charges?"

"Each hole? Some of the walls were brick, some were composition, like cinder block, all of them plastered and painted. Thick and load-bearing, but soft, really. You'd hardly need a hammer drill, even. The holes would probably have to be five inches deep, about an inch in diameter—given a wide drill bit and electricity, I could do perhaps two a minute if I was in a hurry." I paused. "Threading the holes with det cord and packing them with explosives obviously takes longer. I've been told you need to compress and tamp it all in very carefully with something wooden, no sparks, like a broom handle."

"Who told you?"

"Demolitions people."

The chief inspector asked, "How are you so sure the walls were made of brick and cinder block? How could you possibly tell, if they were plastered and painted?"

I thought back. "On the floor beneath each charge there was a small pile of dust caused by drilling the hole. Some piles were pink brick dust, others were gray."

"You had time to see that?"

"I remember it. At the time, it just made it certain that there was a good deal of explosive rammed into those walls."

The expert said, "Did you look to see where the circuit began or ended?"

I shook my head. "I was trying to find my son."

"And did you see anyone else at all in the vicinity of the stands near that time?"

"No. No one."

They asked me and Roger to walk with them as far as the safety cordon, so that we could explain to the expert where the staircase and walls had been before the explosion. The expert, it seemed, would then put on a protective suit and a hard hat and go in wherever he could to take a look from the inside.

"Rather you than me," I commented.

They watched the best I could do at walking with them. When we reached the point of maximum visual bad news, the bomb-defusing expert looked upwards to the fingers of the Stewards' box and down to my walker. He put on his large head-sheltering hat and gave me a twisting self-mocking smile.

"I'm old in my profession," he said.

"How old?"

"Twenty-eight."

I said, "All of a sudden, I can't feel a thing."

His smile broadened. "People sometimes get lucky."

"Good luck, then," I said.

# 8

Y ou know what?" Roger said to me.

"What?"

We were standing on the tarmac a little apart from the policemen but looking still at the rubble.

"I'd think our demolitionist got more bang for his bucks than he intended."

"How do you mean?"

He said, "High explosives are funny things. Unpredictable, often. They weren't my speciality in the army, but of course most soldiers learn about them. There's always a tendency to use too much explosive for the job in hand, just to make sure of effective results." He smiled briefly. "A colleague of mine had to blow up a bridge, once. Just to blow a hole in it, to put it out of action. He overestimated how much explosive it would take, and the whole thing totally disintegrated into invisible dust which was carried away in the river below. Not a thing left. Everyone thought he'd done a brilliant job, but he was laughing about it in private. *I* wouldn't have known how much to use to cause this much damage here in the grandstands. And I've been thinking that whoever did it probably meant only to put the stairway out of action. I mean . . . setting all those careful charges rounds its walls . . . if he'd meant to destroy the whole stand, why not use one single large bomb? Much easier. Less chance of being spotted setting it up. See what I mean?"

"Yes, I do."

He glanced directly at my face. "Look," he said awkwardly, "I know it's not my business, but wouldn't you be better lying down in your bus?"

"I'll go if I have to."

He nodded.

"Otherwise," I said, "it's better to have other things to think about."

He was happy with that. "Just say, then."

"Yes. Thanks."

The Strattons were suddenly all around us. Dart said in my ear, "Conrad's architect has come. Now for some fireworks!" I looked at his impish enjoyment. "Did Keith really *kick* you?" he asked. "Ivan says I missed a real pretty sight by a few seconds."

"Too bad. Where's the architect?"

"That man beside Conrad."

"And is he a blackmailer?"

"God knows. Ask Keith."

He knew as well as I did that I wouldn't ask Keith anything.

"I reckon Keith made that up," Dart said. "He's a terrible liar. He can't tell the truth."

"And Conrad? Does he lie?"

"My father?" Dart showed no anger at the possible slur. "My father tells the truth on principle. Or else from lack of imagination. Take your pick."

"The twins at the fork in the road," I said.

"What the heck are you talking about?"

"Tell you later."

Marjorie was saying formidably, "We do *not* need an architect."

"Face facts," Conrad pleaded. "Look at this radical destruction. It's a heaven-sent opportunity to build something meaningful."

Build something meaningful. The words vibrated in memory. "Build something meaningful" had been one of the precepts repeated ad nauseam by a lecturer at college.

I looked carefully at Conrad's architect, turning the inward eye back more than sixteen years. Conrad's architect, I slowly realized, had been a student like myself at the Architectural Association School of Architecture: senior to me, one of the elite, a disciple of the future. I remembered his face and his glittering prospects, and I'd forgotten his name.

Roger left my side and went across to put in a presence at the Marjorie-Conrad conflict, a hopeless position for a manager. Conrad's architect nodded to him coolly, seeing Roger as critic, not ally.

Dart, waving a hand towards the rubble, asked me, "What do you think they should do?"

"I, personally?"

"Yes."

"They don't care what I think."

"But I'm curious."

"I think they should spend their time finding out who did it, and why."

"But the police will do that."

"Are you saying that the family doesn't want to find out?"

Dart said, alarmed, "Can you see through brick?"

"Why don't they want to know? I wouldn't think it safe not to."

"Marjorie will do anything to keep family affairs private," Dart said. "She's worse than Grandfather, and he would pay the earth to keep the Stratton name clean."

Keith must have cost them a packet, I thought, from my own mother on-wards; and I wondered fleetingly again what Forsyth could have done to cause them such angst.

Dart looked at his watch. "Twenty to twelve," he said. "I'm fed up with all this. What do you say to the Mayflower?"

On reflection I said yes to the Mayflower, and without fanfare retreated with him to the green six-year-old Granada with rusted near fenders. Harold Quest, it seemed, never interfered with exits. We made an unhindered passage to imitation 1620 A.D., where Dart accepted a half pint and I ordered also fif-teen fat rounds of cheese, tomato, ham and lettuce homemade sandwiches and a quart tub of ice cream.

"You can't be *that* hungry!" Dart exclaimed.

"I've five beaks to fill."

"Good God. I'd forgotten."

We drank the beer while waiting for the sandwiches, and then he good-naturedly drove us down through the back entrance to park outside Roger's house, near the bus.

Beside the main door into the bus, in a small outside compartment, I'd long ago installed a chuck-wagon-type bell. Dart watched in amusement when I extended it on its arm outward, and set it clanging with vigor.

The cowboys came in from the prairie, hungry, dry and virtuous, and sat around on boxes and logs for their open-air lunch. I stood with the walker. Getting used to it, the boys took it for granted.

They had built a stockade from sticks, they said. Inside the fort were the United States cavalry (Christopher and Toby) and outside were the Indians (the rest). The Indians were (of course) the Good Guys, who hoped to over-run the stockade and take a few scalps. Sneaky tactics were needed, Chief Ed-ward said. Alan Redfeather was his trusty spy.

Dart, eating a sandwich, said he thought Neil's lurid warpaint (Mrs. Gardner's lipstick) a triumph for political correctness.

None of them knew what he meant. I saw Neil storing the words away, mouthing them silently, ready to ask later.

Locust-like, they mopped up the Mayflower's food and, as it seemed a good time for it, I said to them, "Ask Dart the riddle of the pilgrim. He'll find it interesting."

Christopher obligingly began, "A pilgrim came to a fork in the road. One road led to safety, and the other to death. In each fork stood a guardian."

"They were twins," Edward said.

Christopher, nodding, went on, "One twin always spoke the truth and the other always lied."

Dart turned his head and stared at me.

"It's a very *old* riddle," Edward said apologetically.

"The pilgrim was allowed only one question," Toby said. "Only one. And to save his life he had to find out which road led to safety. So what did he ask?"

"He asked which way was safe," Dart said reasonably.

Christopher said, "Which twin did he ask?"

"The one who spoke the truth."

"But how did he know which one spoke the truth? They both looked the same. They were twins."

"Conrad and Keith aren't identical," Dart said.

The children, not understanding, pressed on. Toby asked again, "What question did the pilgrim ask?"

"Haven't the foggiest."

*"Think,"* Edward commanded.

Dart turned my way. "Save me!" he said.

*"That's* not what the pilgrim said," Neil informed him with relish.

"Do you all know?"

Five heads nodded. "Dad told us."

"Then Dad had better tell *me.* "

It was Christopher, however, who explained. "The pilgrim could only ask one question, so he went to one of the twins and he asked, 'If I ask your brother which way leads to safety, which way will he tell me to go?' "

Christopher stopped. Dart looked flummoxed. "Is that all?" he asked.

"That's all. So what did the pilgrim do?"

"Well . . . he . . . I give in. What did he do?"

They wouldn't tell him the answer.

"You're *devils,"* Dart said.

"One of the twins was a devil," Edward said, "and the other was an angel."

"You just made that up," Toby accused him.

"So what? It makes it more interesting."

They all tired abruptly of the riddle and trooped off, as was their habit, back to their make-believe game.

"For Christ's sake!" Dart exclaimed. "That's not bloody fair."

I laughed in my throat.

"So what did the pilgrim do?"

"Work it out."

"You're as bad as your children."

Dart and I got back into his car. He put the walker onto the back seat and observed, "Keith really hurt you, didn't he?"

"No, it was the explosion. Bits of roof fell in."

"Fell in on you. Yes, I heard."

"From the shoulder blades down," I agreed. "Could have been worse."

"Oh, sure." He started the engine and drove up the private inner road. "What did the pilgrim do, then?"

I smiled. "Whichever road either twin told him was safe, he went down the other one. Both twins would have pointed to the road leading to death."

He thought very briefly. "How come?"

"If the pilgrim asked the truthful twin which way his brother would send him to safety, the truthful twin, knowing his brother would lie, would point to the road to death."

"You've lost me."

I explained over again. "And," I said, "if the pilgrim happened to ask the lying twin which way his brother would send someone to safety, the lying twin, though knowing his brother would speak the truth, lied about what he would say. So the lying twin also would point to the road to death."

Dart relapsed into silence. When he spoke he said, "Do your boys understand it?"

"Yes. They acted it out."

"Don't they ever quarrel?"

"Of course they do. But they've been moved around so much that they've made few outside friendships. They rely on each other." I sighed. "They'll grow out of it, shortly. Christopher's already too old for half their games."

"A pity."

"Life goes on."

Dart braked his rusty car gently to a halt in the impromptu parking lot outside Roger's office.

I said diffidently, "Did you, in fact, drive here yesterday morning in this car, as Harold Quest said?"

"No, I didn't." Dart took no offense. "And what's more I *was* in my bathroom from eight to eight-thirty, and don't bloody laugh, I'm not telling anyone else, but I've got a new scalp vibrator thing that's supposed to stop hair falling out."

"Snake oil," I said.

"Bugger you, I said don't laugh."

"I'm not laughing."

"Your face muscles are *twitching.*"

"I do believe, anyway," I said, "that because of your hair you didn't arrive at the racecourse at eight-twenty yesterday morning with your old jalopy bulging with detonating cord and plastic explosive."

"Thanks a bunch."

"The thing is, could anyone have borrowed your car without you knowing? And would you mind very much if the bomb expert or the police tested this car for the presence of nitrates?"

He looked aghast. "You can't mean it!"

"Someone," I pointed out, "brought explosives to the stairs in the grandstands yesterday. It's probably fair to say it was plugged into the walls after the night watchman went home at seven. It was fully light by then. There was no one else about because of its being Good Friday. There was only Harold Quest and his pals at the gate, and I don't know how much one can trust him."

"The lying twin," Dart said.

"Maybe."

I tried to imagine easygoing Dart, with his thickening frame and his thinning hair, his ironic cast of mind and his core of idleness, ever caring enough about anything to blow up a grandstand. Impossible. But to lend his car? To lend his car casually for an unspecified purpose, yes, certainly. To lend it knowing it would be used for a crime? I hoped not. Yet he would have let me open the locked cupboard in his father's study. Had taken me there and given me every illegal chance. Hadn't cared a jot when I'd backed off.

A sloppy sense of right and wrong, or a deep alienation that he habitually hid?

I liked Dart; he lifted one's spirits. Among the Strattons, he was the nearest to normal. The nearest, one should perhaps say, to a rose among nettles.

I said neutrally, "Where's your sister Rebecca today? I'd have thought she'd have been here, practically purring."

"She's racing at Towcester," he said briefly. "I looked in the newspaper. No doubt she's thrilled the stands have had it, but I haven't spoken to her since Wednesday. She's talked to Father, I think. She's riding one of his horses here on Monday. It's got a good chance of winning, so no way would she have put the meeting in jeopardy, with dynamite shenanigans, if that's what you're thinking."

"Where does she live?" I asked.

"Lambourn. Ten miles away, roughly."

"Horse country."

"She lives and breathes horses. Quite mad."

I lived and breathed building. I got fulfillment from putting brick on brick, stone on stone: from bringing a dead thing to life. I understood a single-minded encompassing drive. Not much in the world, for good or for evil, gets done without it.

The rest of the Strattons came round from the racecourse side of the grandstands, bringing Conrad's architect with them. The police and the bomb expert seemed to be sifting carefully through the edges of the rubble. The mustached local authority was scratching his head.

Roger came over to Dart's car and asked where we'd been.

"Feeding the children," I said.

"Oh! Well, the Honorable Marjorie wants to demolish you. Er . . ." He went on more prudently in the presence of Dart, "Mrs. Binsham wants to see you in my office."

I clambered stiffly onto the tarmac and plodded that way. Roger came along beside me.

"Don't let her eat you," he said.

"No. Don't worry. Do you happen to know that architect's name?"

"What?"

"Conrad's architect."

"It's Wilson Yarrow. Conrad calls him Yarrow."

"Thanks."

I stopped walking abruptly.

Roger said, "What's the matter? Is it worse?"

"No." I looked at him vaguely, to his visible alarm. I asked, "Did you tell any of the Strattons that I'm an architect?"

He was perplexed. "Only Dart. You told him yourself, remember? Why? Why does it matter?"

"Don't tell them," I said. I did a one-eighty back towards Dart, who got out of his car and came to meet us.

"What's the matter?" he said.

"Nothing much. Look . . . did you happen to mention to any of your family that I'm a qualified architect?"

He thought back, frowning. Roger, reaching us, looked thoroughly mystified. "What does it matter?" he asked.

"Yes," Dart echoed, "what does it matter?"

"I don't want Conrad to know."

Roger protested. "But Lee, why ever not?"

"That man he's brought here, Wilson Yarrow, he and I were trained at the same school. There's something about him . . ." I dried up, thinking hard.

"What's odd about him?" Roger demanded.

"That's the trouble, I can't quite remember. But I can easily find out. I'd just rather find out without his knowing about it."

"Do you mean," Dart asked, "that he blew up the stands to get the commission to build the new ones?"

"God," Roger said. "You do jump to conclusions."

"Keith thinks so. He said so."

"I think they just know you're a builder," Roger said to me thoughtfully, "and to be honest, at the moment that's just what you look like."

I glanced down at my loose checked shirt and my baggy faded working jeans and acknowledged the convenient truth of it.

"Won't he know *you*," Roger asked, "if you trained at the same place?"

"No. I was at least three years behind him and not very noticeable. He was one of the flashing stars. Different firmament to me. I don't think we ever spoke. People like that are too wrapped up in their own affairs to learn the faces and names of junior intakes. And it wasn't last week. It's seventeen years now since I enrolled there."

When two architects met, the most normal opening gambit between them was, "Where were you taught?" And one took preconceived ideas from the answer.

To have learned architecture at Cambridge, for instance, indicated a likelihood of cautious conservation; at Bath, of anatomy before beauty; and at the Mackintosh in Glasgow, of partisan Scottishness. People who'd been to any of them knew how their fellows had been influenced. One understood a stranger because of the experiences shared.

The Architectural Association, alma mater of both Yarrow and myself, tended to turn out innovative ultra-modernists who saw into the future and built people-coercive edifices cleverly of glass. The spirit of Le Corbusier reigned, even though the school itself stood physically in Bedford Square in London, in a Georgian, beautifully proportioned terraced mansion often at odds with the lectures within.

The library windows shone out, brightly lit always, into the night shadows of the square, celebrating distinction of knowledge, and if a certain arrogance crept into self-satisfied star students, perhaps the supreme excellence and thoroughness of the tuition excused it.

The Association was mostly outside the state education system, which meant few student grants, which in turn meant that chiefly paying students went there, the intake having consequently changed slowly over the years from a preponderance of indigenous bohemian English to the offspring of wealthy Greeks, Nigerians, Americans, Iranians and Hong Kong Chinese, and I reckoned I'd learned a good deal and made unexpected friends from the mixture.

I myself had emerged from the exhaustively practical, and sometimes metaphysical, teaching with Le Corbusier technology and humanist tendencies, and would never be revered in the halls that had nurtured me: restoring old ruins carved no fame for posterity.

Dart asked curiously, "Do you have letters after your name?"

I hesitated. "What? Yes, I do. They're AA Dipl, which stands for Architectural Association Diploma. It may not mean much to the outside world generally, but to other architects, and to Yarrow, it's pretty revealing."

"Sounds like Alcoholics Anonymous Dipsomaniac," Dart said.

Roger laughed.

"Keep that joke under wraps," I begged, and Dart said maybe he would.

Mark, Marjorie's chauffeur, joined us and told us disapprovingly that I was keeping Mrs. Binsham waiting. She was sitting in the office tapping her foot.

"Tell her I'll come instantly," I said, and Mark went off with the message.

"That brave man deserves the Victoria Cross," Dart grinned, "for conspicuous valor." I set off in Mark's wake. "So do you," Dart shouted.

Marjorie, stiff-backed, was indeed displeased but, it transpired, not with Mark or myself. The chauffeur had been told to go for a walk. As for myself, I was invited to sit.

"I'd rather stand, really."

"Oh, yes, I forgot." She gave me a short shirt-by-jeans inspection, as if uncertain how to categorize me because of my changing appearance.

"I believe you're a builder by trade," she began.

"Yes."

"Well, as a builder, now that you've had a good look at the extent of the damage to the grandstand, what do you think?"

"About restoring things as they were?"

"Certainly."

I said, "As much as I understand that that's what you'd like, I frankly think it would be a mistake."

She was obstinate. "But could it be done?"

I said, "The whole structure may prove to be unsafe. The building's old, though well built, I grant you. But there may be fractures that can't be seen yet, and undoubtedly there are new stresses. Once the rubble is removed, more of the building could fall in. It would all need shoring up. I'm really sorry, but my advice would be to take it down and rebuild it from scratch."

"I don't want to hear that."

"I know."

"But could it be done so it was the same as before?"

"Certainly. All the original plans and drawings are here, in this office." I paused. "But it would be a lost opportunity."

"Don't tell me you side with Conrad!"

"I don't side with anyone. I'm just telling you honestly that you could improve the old stands enormously for modern comfort if you redesigned them."

"I don't like the architect that Conrad's thrusting down our throats. I don't understand half of what he says, and the man's *condescending,* can you believe?"

I could certainly believe it. "He'll find out his mistake," I said, smiling. "And, incidentally, if in the end you decide to modify the stands, it would be sensible to announce a competition in magazines architects read, asking for suggestions and drawings to be submitted to a jury, which you could appoint. Then you'd have a choice. You wouldn't be in a take-it-or-leave-it situation with Wilson Yarrow who, the Colonel assures me, doesn't know a jot about racing. One wouldn't choose even a chair without sitting in it. The stands need to be comfortable as well as good-looking."

She nodded thoughtfully. "You were going to look into this Yarrow's background. Have you done it?"

"It's in hand."

"And about Keith's debts?"

"Working on it."

She made a "Hmph" noise of disbelief, justifiably. "I suppose," she added, trying to be fair, "you're finding it difficult to get about."

I shrugged. "It's a holiday weekend, that's another of the problems." I thought briefly. "Where does Keith live?"

"Above his expectations."

I laughed. Marjorie primly smiled at her own wit.

She said, "He lives in the Dower House on the estate. It was built for the widow of the first baron and, as she had a taste for ostentation, it is large. Keith pretends he owns it, but he doesn't, he rents it. Since my brother has died, ownership passes to Conrad, of course."

I asked tentatively, "And . . . Keith's source of income?"

Marjorie disapproved of the question but on reflection answered: it was she, after all, who'd set me in motion.

"His mother left him provided for. He was a beautiful-looking little boy and young man, and she doted on him. Forgave him anything. Conrad and Ivan were always clumsy and plain and never made her laugh. She died ten years ago, I suppose. Keith inherited his money then, and I'd say he's lost it."

I thought a bit, and asked, "Who is Jack's father?"

"That's none of your business."

"Not relevant?"

"Certainly not."

"Does Keith gamble on horses? Or anything? Cards? Backgammon?"

"Perhaps you'll find out," she said. "He will never, of course, tell me anything."

I could think of only one way of getting a window into Keith's affairs, and even that was problematical. I would have to borrow a car and drive it, for a start, when it was hard enough to walk. Give it two or three days, I thought. Say Tuesday.

"What does Keith do with his time?" I asked.

"He says he has a job in the City. He may have had once, but I'm sure he's lying about it now. He does lie, of course. He's sixty-five, anyway. Retiring age, I'm told." She more or less sniffed. "If one has obligations, my brother used to say, one *never* retires."

Retiring wasn't always one's own choice, but why argue? Not everyone was a hereditary baron with dependent Honorables and a paternal nature. Not everyone had wealth enough to oil wheels and calm storms. My non-grandfather, I thought, must have been a nice man, whatever his faults; and my mother had liked him, and Dart also.

"How about Ivan?" I asked.

"Ivan?" Her eyebrows rose. "What do you mean?"

"He has a garden center?"

She nodded. "My brother made over to him fifty acres of the estate. Years ago, that was, when Ivan was young. He's good at growing things." She paused, and went on, "One doesn't need to be intellectual to lead a contented and harmless life."

"One needs to be lucky."

She considered me, and nodded.

I asked her, as it seemed she had run out of inquisition, if she would sign Roger's and Oliver's paychecks.

"What? Yes, I said I would. Tell the Colonel to remind me sometime again."

"They're here," I said, picking the envelope out of my still-chair-draping jacket. "Do you have a pen with you?"

She resignedly rummaged in a large handbag for a pen, took the checks out of the envelope and wrote her name with precision, no flourish, on the lines provided.

I said diffidently, "To save you the trouble in future, you directors could enable Conrad or Ivan or Dart to sign checks. It only needs to have their signatures registered with the bank. There are bound to be many things, and not only salary checks, needing signatures in the future. The Colonel has to have authorizations, in order to run things."

"You seem to know a lot about it!"

"I know about business. I have a limited company."

She frowned. "Very well. All three of them. Will that do?"

"Make it any two of the four of you. Then you will have safeguards, and the Colonel's honesty will be beyond being queried by Keith or Rebecca."

She didn't know whether to be annoyed or amused. "It's taken you no time at all, has it, to lay bare our Stratton souls?"

Without warning, and before I could answer, the office door opened fast and Keith and Hannah came in. Ignoring my presence they complained loudly to Marjorie that Conrad was talking to his architect as if the new plans would definitely be agreed.

"He's saying *when,*" Keith griped, "not *if.* I'm wholly against this ridiculous project and you've got to stop it."

"Stop it yourself," his aunt told him tartly. "You make a lot of noise, Keith, but you don't get things done. You want to get rid of me one minute, and you ask me to fight battles for you the next. And as you and Hannah are both here, you can apologize to Mr. Morris for attacking him."

Keith and Hannah gave me matching looks of malevolence from between narrowed eyelids. From their point of view, I understood, their ultimate purpose had been frustrated by Marjorie and Ivan's fortuitous arrival. I was still present, still standing, still and forever the symbol of their having been detested and rejected unbearably. That their hatred was irrational made no difference. Irrational hatred, the world over, set the furrows flooding with an impure blood—though it was only France that actively encouraged massacre in its patriotic war cry, the "Marseillaise" still glorifying the sentiments of 1792.

The impure blood at that time had been Austrian. Two hundred or so years later, blood-hatred flourished around the globe. Blood-hatred could al-

most be smelled in the manager's office of Stratton Park. I had by my presence there already activated responses beyond Keith and Hannah's control, and
felt no confidence whatever that we'd come to the end of it.

Only Marjorie, at that moment, stood between me and a continuation of
what they'd intended to do earlier that morning. I thought wryly that every
big and usually powerful weakling should have a staunch octogenarian bodyguard.

Marjorie waited only briefly for the apology that would never come: and
I could happily dispense forever with apologies, I thought, if they would
clearly see that no amount of Stratton money could cancel charges of
manslaughter.

Or half-brother slaughter. Or ex-wife's son slaughter. Whatever.

Amoeba-like, Strattons followed Strattons as if components of one organic
mass, and Conrad with Jack and Ivan joined the company, also swelled by the
foreign substance of Wilson Yarrow and completed by Dart, looking mis-
chievously entertained, and Roger, trying to be inconspicuous. The crowd
again was too big for the space.

Wilson Yarrow didn't know me. I gave him a flicking glance only, but he'd
accorded me barely that. His attention was chiefly engaged by Conrad, whose
suspicions had been aroused by Keith's talking to Marjorie behind a closed
door.

Physically, Wilson Yarrow was remarkable not so much for his actual features as for his posture. His reddish brown hair, tall narrow-shouldered body,
and square heavy jaw made no indelible statement. The way he held his head
back, so that he could look down his nose, was unforgettable.

Condescending, Marjorie had said of him. Convinced of his own superi-
ority, I thought, and without modesty to cloak it.

Conrad said, "Wilson Yarrow is of the opinion we should clear the site and
start rebuilding immediately, and I've agreed to that proposal."

"My dear Conrad," Marjorie said in her stop-the-world voice, "you may
*not* make such a decision. Your father had the right to make such decisions because he owned the racecourse. It now belongs to us all, and before anything
is done, a majority of our Board must agree to it."

Conrad looked affronted and Wilson Yarrow impatient, obviously thinking the old lady a no-account interruption.

"It is clear," Marjorie went on in her crystal diction, "that we have to have
a new grandstand."

"No," Keith interrupted. "We sell!"

Marjorie paid him no attention. "I am sure Mr. Yarrow is a highly competent architect, but for something as important as new stands I propose we

put an advertisement in a magazine read by architects, inviting any who are interested to send us plans and proposals in a competition so that we could study various possibilities and then make a choice."

Conrad's consternation was matched by Yarrow's.

"But Marjorie . . ." Conrad began.

"It would be the normal course of activity, wouldn't it?" she asked with open-eyed simplicity. "I mean, one wouldn't buy even a chair without considering several for comfort and appearance and usefulness, would one?"

She gave me a short, expressionless, passing glance. Double bravo, I thought.

"As a director," Marjorie said, "I put forward a motion that we seek a variety of suggestions for a grandstand, and of course we will welcome Mr. Yarrow's among them."

Dead silence.

"Second the motion, Ivan?" Marjorie suggested.

"Oh! Yes. Sensible. Very sensible."

"Conrad?"

"Now look here, Marjorie . . ."

"Use common sense, Conrad," she urged.

Conrad squirmed. Yarrow looked furious.

Keith unexpectedly said, "I agree with you, Marjorie. You have my vote."

She looked surprised, but although she may have reckoned, as I did, that Keith's motive was solely to impede the rebuilding, she pragmatically accepted his help.

"Carried," she said without triumph. "Colonel, could you possibly find a suitable publication for an advertisement?"

Roger said he was certain he could, and would see to it.

"Splendid." Marjorie leveled a limpid gaze on the discomfited personage who'd made the error of condescension. "When you have your plans ready, Mr. Yarrow, we'd be delighted to see them."

He said with clenched teeth, "Lord Stratton has a set."

"Really?" Conrad squirmed further under a similar gaze. "Then, Conrad, we'd all like to see them, wouldn't we?"

Stratton heads nodded with various gradations of urgency.

"They're in my house," Conrad informed her grudgingly. "I suppose I could bring them to you sometime."

Marjorie nodded. "This afternoon, shall we say? Four o'clock." She looked at her watch. "My goodness! We're all terribly late for lunch. Such a busy morning." She rose to her small feet. "Colonel, as our private dining room in the stands is, as I suppose, out of action, perhaps you could arrange somewhere suitable for us on Monday? Most of us, I imagine, will be attending."

Roger said again, faintly, that he would see to it.

Marjorie, nodding benignly, made a grande dame exit and, surrendering herself to Mark's solicitous care, was driven away.

More or less speechlessly, the others followed, Conrad taking an angry Yarrow, leaving Roger and myself in quiet occupancy of the combat zone.

"The old battleaxe!" Roger said with admiration.

I handed him his paychecks. He looked at the signature.

"How did you do that?" he said.

Roger spent the afternoon with the racecourse's consultant electrician, whose men bypassed the main grandstand while restoring power to everywhere else. Circuits that hadn't fused by themselves had been disconnected prudently by Roger, it seemed. "Fire," he explained, "is the last thing we need."

A heavy-duty cable in an insulating tube was run underground by a trenching machine to the members' parking lot, for lights, power and refrigerators in the big top. "Never forget champagne on a racecourse," Roger said, not joking.

The investigators in the ruins had multiplied and had brought in scaffolding and cutters. At one point they erected and bolted together a long six-foot-high fence, replacing the cordoning tape. "We could lose priceless clues to souvenir hunters," one told me. "Monday's crowd, left alone, could put piranhas to shame."

I said to one of the bombfinders, "If you'd been drilling upwards of thirty holes into the walls of a stairway, would you have posted a lookout?"

"Christ, yes." He thought for a bit. "Course, you know, when you have someone drilling, you mostly can't tell where the noise is coming from. Drilling's deceptive, like. You can think it's next door and it's a hundred yards away; and the other way round. If anyone heard the drilling, is what I'm trying to say, one, they wouldn't know where it was happening, and two, they wouldn't think nothing of it, not in a place this big."

Only Roger, I thought, would have known drilling was wrong: and Roger had been in his house half a mile out of earshot.

I used my mobile phone, still in Roger's jeep, to try to locate friends and staff from my student days to ask about Yarrow, but almost no one answered. I raised one wife, who said she would give Carteret my number but, sorry, he was busy in St. Petersburg, and I spoke also to a very young daughter who told me Daddy didn't live with them any more. This sort of thing, I thought ruefully, didn't happen to the best private eyes.

In the office, Roger and I drew up plans for the positioning of the big top and of the two Portakabins he'd been promised. Jockeys were to change in one, with the scales and attendant officials given housing in the other. We placed both structures near the parade ring within a few steps of Roger's office, and agreed that if his men took down the fence between the paddock and the members' parking lot, the access to the big top would be unhampered for the public. It meant rerouting the horses round the big top to get them out onto the course, but all, Roger promised, could be accomplished.

"Rebecca!" he exclaimed at one point, clapping palm to aghast forehead. "Women jockeys! Where do we put them?"

"How many of them?"

"Two or three. Six, max."

I phoned Henry, got an answering machine, and left a message begging for side tents of any description. "Also send anything pretty," I added. "Send Sleeping Beauty's castle. We need to cheer people up."

"This is a racecourse, not a fairground," Roger said, a touch disapprovingly, as I finished the call.

"This is Easter Bank Holiday," I reminded him. "This is restore-confidence day. This is ignore-bombs day, feel-more-secure day, have-a-good-time day. On Monday people coming here are going to forget there's a frightening disaster lying behind that new fence." I paused. "And we're going to have lights over the whole area tonight and tomorrow night, and as many people patrolling the stables and Tattersalls and the cheap rings as you can possibly press-gang."

"But the expense!" he said.

"Make a success of Monday, and Marjorie will pay for the guards."

"You're infectious, you know that?" He gave me an almost lighthearted smile and was about to hurry back to his electricians when the telephone rang.

Roger said, "Hallo," and "Yes, Mrs. Binsham," and "At once, of course," and put down the receiver.

He relayed the news. "She says Conrad and Yarrow are with her, and they've shown her his plans, and she wants a copy made here on the office copier."

"And did Conrad agree?" I asked with surprise.

"It seems so, as long as we lock the copy in the office safe."

"She's amazing," I said.

"She's got Conrad in some sort of hammerlock. I've noticed before. When she applies pressure, he folds."

"They all blackmail each other!"

He nodded. "Too many secrets, paid for and hushed up."

"That's what Dart says, more or less."

Roger pointed to the door of his secretary's office. "Both the copier and the safe are in there. Conrad and Yarrow are coming straight over."

"In that case, I'll vanish," I said. "I'll wait in your jeep."

"And when they've gone—back to your bus?"

"If you don't mind."

"Long after time," he said briefly, and opened the door for my clip-clomping progress outwards.

I sprawled sideways in the jeep and watched Conrad and Wilson Yarrow arrive with a large-sized folder and later leave, both of them striding stiff-legged in annoyance.

When they'd gone, Roger brought the new copies over to the jeep and we looked at them together.

He said the plans had been on three large sheets, with blue lines on pale gray paper, but owing to the size of the office machine, the copies came on smaller sheets with black lines. One set of copies laid out a ground-floor plan. One set showed elevations of all four sides. The third looked a maze of thin threadlike lines forming a three-dimensional viewpoint, but hollow, without substance.

"What's *that?*" Roger asked, as I frowned over it. "I've never seen anything like that."

"It's an axonometric drawing."

"A what?"

"An axonometric projection is a method of representing a building in three dimensions that is easier than fiddling about with true perspectives. You rotate the plan of the building to whatever angle you like and project verti-cals upwards . . . Well," I apologized, "you did ask."

Roger was more at home with the elevations. "It's just one big slab of glass," he protested.

"It's not all that bad. Incomplete, but not bad."

"Lee!"

"Sorry," I said. "Anyway, I wouldn't build it in Stratton Park, and probably not anywhere in England. It's crying out for tropical weather, vast air-conditioning and millionaire members. And even those aren't going to be ultra-comfortable."

"That's better," he said, relieved.

I looked at the top left-hand corner of each set of copies. All three were inscribed simply "Club Grandstands, Wilson Yarrow, AA Dipl." A lone job. No partners, no firm.

"The best racing grandstands ever built," I said, "are at Arlington Park, near Chicago."

"I thought you didn't go racing much," Roger said.

"I haven't been there. I've seen pictures and prints of the plans."

He laughed. "Can we afford stands like that?"

"You could adapt their ideas."

"Dream on," he said, shuffling the copies into order. "Wait while I tuck these into the safe." He went off on the short errand and returned to drive the scant half-mile to his house, which was quiet and empty: no children, no wife.

We found them all in the bus. The boys had invited Mrs. Gardner to tea (tuna sandwiches with crusts on, potato chips and chocolate wafer biscuits) and they were all watching the soccer results unwaveringly on television.

When the guest of honor and her husband had gone, Christopher gave her the highest of accolades. "She understands even the off-side rule!"

Soccer coverage went on. I claimed my own bed, dislodging a viewer or two, and lay on my stomach to watch the proceedings. After the last possible report had been made (ad infinitum reruns of every goal that afternoon), Christopher made supper for everyone of tinned spaghetti on toast. The boys then chose a video from the half dozen or so I'd rented for the ruin-hunt journey and settled down to watch that. I lay feeling that it had been a pretty long day and, somewhere during the film, went to sleep.

I awoke at about three in the morning, still face down, fully dressed.

The bus was dark and quiet, the boys asleep in their bunks. I found that they had put a blanket over me instead of waking me up.

On the table by my head stood a full glass of water.

I looked at it with grateful amazement, with a lump in the throat.

The evening before, when I'd stood a glass there, Toby, to whom, since the explosion, anything out of routine was a cause of quivering anxiety, had asked what it was for.

"The hospital," I explained, "gave me some pills to take if I woke up in the night and the cuts started hurting."

"Oh. Where are the pills?"

"Under my pillow."

They'd nodded over the information. I hadn't slept much and I had taken the pills, which they'd commented on in the morning.

So now, tonight, the glass of water was back, standing ready, put there by my sons. I took the pills, drinking, and I lay in the dark feeling grindingly sore and remarkably happy.

IN THE MORNING, a fine one, the boys opened all the windows to air out the bus, and I gave them the Easter presents Amanda had packed into the locker under my bed. Each boy received a chocolate Easter egg, a paperback book and a small hand-held computer game, and all spoke to their mother to thank her.

"She wants to talk to you, Dad," Alan said, handing me the telephone, and I said, "Hi," and "Happy Easter," and "How's Jamie?"

"He's fine. Are you feeding the boys properly, Lee? Sandwiches and tinned spaghetti aren't enough. I asked Christopher . . . he says you didn't buy fruit yesterday."

"They've had bananas and cornflakes for breakfast today."

"Fruit and fresh vegetables," she said.

"OK."

"And can you stay out a bit longer? Say Wednesday or Thursday?"

"If you like."

"Yes. And take their clothes to a launderette, won't you?"

"Sure."

"Have you found a good ruin yet?"

"I'll keep looking."

"We're living on savings," she said.

"Yes, I know. The boys need new sneakers."

"You could get them."

"All right."

Conversation, as usual, confined itself mostly to child-care. I said, trying my best, "How did your sister's party go?"

"Why?" She sounded almost, for a moment, wary: then she said, "Great, fine. She sends you her love."

"Thanks."

"Take care of the boys, Lee."

"Yes," I said, and "Happy Easter," and "Goodbye, Amanda."

"She asked us to phone her tomorrow night," Christopher said.

"She cares about you. She wants us to go on hunting ruins for another day or two."

None of them objected, surprisingly. They were eyes-down, of course, to their bleep-bleeping flickering games.

There was a bang on the door, which was opened without pause by Roger, who stuck his head in while still standing outside.

"Your pal Henry," he told me, "has himself arrived with a crane on a low-loader and brought the big top on about six vast lorries and he won't unload a thing without talking to you first."

"Henry's big top!" Christopher exclaimed. "The one we had over the pub, before you built our house?"

"That's right."

The boys shut the windows instantly and presented themselves fast in the driveway, looking hopeful. Roger resignedly gestured towards the jeep and they all packed into the back, jostling and fighting for their favorite seats.

"Sit down or get out," Roger commanded in his best parade-ground bark and, subdued, they sat down.

"I'll swap you the boys for Marjorie," I suggested.

"Done." He careered in battle fashion up the private road, did a flourish of a four-wheel drift stop outside his office, and informed my progeny that any sign of disobedience would incur immediate banishment to the bus for the rest of the day. The troops, very impressed, took the warning respectfully, but ran off to greet Henry with out-of-school whoops.

Henry, huge, bearded, always made me feel short. He lifted Neil effortlessly to sit on his shoulders and beamed in my direction, walker and all.

"Nearly got yourself squelched, then?" he said.

"Yeah. Careless."

He gestured with a huge hand to his heavily laden monster trucks, currently cluttering the tarmac.

"I brought the whole razzmatazz," he said, pleased with it.

"Yes, but, look here . . ." Roger began.

Henry looked down on him kindly. "You trust Lee, here," he said. "He knows what people like. He's a bloody wizard, is Lee. You let him and me set you up here for tomorrow, and six weeks from now, when you've got another Bank Holiday meeting—I looked it up, so I know—you won't have enough room in the parking lot. Word of mouth, see? Now, do you want crowds here, or don't you?"

"Er . . . yes."

"Say no more."

Roger said to me despairingly, "Marjorie . . ."

"She'll love it. She wants the racecourse to prosper, above all."

"Are you sure?"

"Hundred per cent. Mind you, she'll take five seconds to get over the shock."

"Let's hope it takes longer for her to drop down dead from a heart attack."

"Did you get those electrical cables laid?" Henry asked him. "Heavy-duty?"

"As you specified," Roger said.

"Good. Then . . . site plans?"

"In the office."

For most of the day Roger directed his groundsmen to help where they could and himself stood in long spells of wonderment as Henry and his crew built before his eyes a revolutionary vision of grandstand comfort.

First they erected four pylon-like towers in crane-lifted sections, towers strong enough, Henry told Roger, for trapeze artists to swing from: then with thick wire cables and heavy electric winches they raised tons of strong white canvas and spread them wide. The final height and the acreage matched those of the old stands, and easily outdid them for splendor.

Henry and I discussed crowd movement, racegoers' behavior, provision for rain. We set out the essentials, rubbed out the bottlenecks, made pleasure a priority, gave owners their due, allocated prime space for Strattons, for Stewards, for trainers' bars. Throughout the big top we planned solid-seeming flooring, with a wide center aisle, firm partition walls, and tented ceilings in each "room" of pale peach-colored thin pleated silk-like material. "I buy it by the mile," Henry assured a disbelieving Roger. "Lee told me sunlight shining through canvas and peach was more flattering to old faces than yellow, and it's seniors who pay the bills, mostly. I used to use yellow. Never again. Lee says the right light is more important than the food."

"And what Lee says is gospel?"

"Have you ever seen anyone transform a derelict no-customer pub into a human beehive? He's done it twice before my eyes, and more times before that, so I'm told. He knows what *attracts* people, see? They don't know exactly *what* attracts them. They just feel attracted. But Lee knows, you bet your sweet life he knows."

"Just what attracts people?" Roger asked me curiously.

"A long story," I said.

"But *how* do you know?"

"For years I asked hundreds, literally hundreds of people, why they'd bought the old houses they lived in. What was the decider, however irrational, that made them choose that house and no other? Sometimes they said bits of trellis, sometimes hidden winding secondary staircases, sometimes Cotswold stone fireplaces, or mill wheels, or sometimes split levels and galleries. I asked them also what they disliked, and would change. I simply grew to know how to rebuild near-ruins so that people hunger to live in them."

Roger said slowly, "Like your own house."

"Well, yes."

"And pubs?"

"I'll show you one day. But with pubs it's not just rebuilding. It's good food, good prices, fast service and a warm welcome. It's essential to learn the customers' faces and greet them as friends."

"But you always move on?"

"Once they're up and running," I nodded. "I'm a builder, not a restaurateur."

To Henry's men, many of them circus people themselves and accustomed to raising magic from an empty field overnight, twenty-four hours to gate-opening time was a luxury. They heaved on ropes, they swung mallets, they sweated. Henry bought a barrel of beer from the Mayflower for his "good lads."

Henry had brought not only the big top but a large amount of the iron piping and planking that, bolted together, had formed the basis of the tiered seating round the circus ring.

"Thought you might need it," he said.

"Grandstands!" I breathed. "You broth of a boy."

Henry beamed.

Roger couldn't believe it. His own workmen, under Henry's circus men's direction, erected all the steps not round a ring but in the open air along beside the rails of the track, their backs to the big top and their slanting face towards the action, with a wide strip of grass for access between the bottom step and the racecourse rails.

"We could do better given more time," Henry said, "but at least some of the customers will be able to see the races from here, without all squeezing onto the Tattersalls' steps."

"We probably need planning permission," Roger said faintly. "Safety officers. Heaven knows what."

Henry waved a couple of licenses under his nose. "I'm a licensed contractor. This is a temporary structure. Get who you like. Get them on Tuesday. Everything I do is safe and legal. I'll show you."

Grinning, he waved a huge hand and hey-prestoed an army of fire extinguishers from one of the trucks.

"Happier?" he asked Roger.

"Speechless."

Henry at one point drew me aside. "Who are those arseholes blocking the
gates? We as near as buggery knocked one of them over when we came across
with the beer. He walked straight out. Raving lunatic."

I explained about Mr. Harold Quest, his followers and their quest to get
steeplechasing banned. "Weren't they here when you first arrived?" I asked.

"No, they weren't. Do you want them shifted?"

"You mean physically shifted?"

"What other way is there?"

"Persuasion?" I suggested.

"Come off it."

"If you stamp on one wasp, fifty come to the funeral."

He nodded. "See what you mean." He rubbed his beard. "What do we do,
then?"

"Put up with them."

"That's pathetic."

"You could tell them that banning steeplechasing would mean hundreds of
horses being killed, once there was no use for them. Not just one horse would
die occasionally, but all of them within a year. Tell Harold Quest he's advo-
cating equine massacre and turning horses into an endangered species."

"Right." He looked as if he would do it immediately.

"But," I said, "quite likely he's not really fussed about the horses. Quite
likely he's looking for a way to stop people enjoying themselves. *He's* enjoying himself, that's his main aim. He's been trying for days to get knocked down
gently. Tomorrow he may manage to get himself arrested. If he does, he'll be
ecstatic."

"All fanatics are nutters," he said.

"What about suffragettes and the twelve apostles?"

"Want a beer?" he said. "I'm not arguing with *you.*"

"What we really want is a counterdemonstration," I suggested. "People
marching alongside Harold Quest with placards saying, 'ADD TO UNEM-
PLOYMENT.' 'PUT STABLELADS OUT OF WORK.' 'SEND ALL
STEEPLECHASE HORSES TO THE GLUE FACTORY.' 'PUT BLACK-
SMITHS ON THE DOLE.' "

"Farriers," Henry said.

"What?"

"Farriers shoe horses. Blacksmiths make wrought-iron gates."

"Let's have that beer," I said.

Beer got postponed however by the arrival of two cars, both driven by boiling tempers as a result of near-contact with Harold Quest.

Stuck behind the leading bumper came the torn remains of a placard saying "BAN CRUELTY," but as so often in such confrontations, a bossy platitudinous admonition had evoked an opposite response.

In the driver, Oliver Wells, the veneer of gentlemanly affability had rawly peeled to disclose a darker, heavier authority; and I was seeing, I thought, the equivalent of the ramming force of the pistons usually hidden within a smooth-running engine. More power, more relentlessness than on display to the world. Cruelty, in this unveiling of the man, could be considered a possibility.

His long nose and sticking-out ears quivering with the strength of his anger, he gave me a brief dismissive glance and demanded, "Where's Roger?"

"In his office," I said.

Oliver strode towards the office door, seemingly oblivious to the hammering activity all around him. The second car, a scarlet Ferrari, arrived to park beside his with a burning of tires and from it, self-ejecting, came the scowling fury of Rebecca.

She was, it briefly occurred to me, the first Stratton of the day, infinitely less welcome to me than her hair-fixated brother.

Rebecca too, in well-cut fawn trousers and brilliant scarlet sweater, resonated hotly with maximum outrage.

"I'll kill that verminous cretin," she told the world. "He's begging to be run down, and I'll do it, I swear it, if he dares to call me 'ducky' again."

I had difficulty swallowing the inappropriate laugh. Henry, having no inhibitions and sizing up the bristling feminism instantly, simply guffawed.

She half lowered her expressive eyelids and delivered a look of wholehearted venom which left Henry unmoved.

"Where's Oliver?" Her voice, like her manner, conveyed uncontrolled arrogance. "The man who drove in ahead of me?"

"In that office," Henry said, pointing; and I swear the word "ducky" got as far as his teeth.

He watched her pantherish gait as she set off away from us and for comment raised comical eyebrows, a real dagger-between-the-shoulders invitation if she'd chanced to turn round.

"She's good-looking and brave," I said. "Pity about the rest."

"Who is she?"

"The Honorable Rebecca Stratton, steeplechase jockey."

Henry lowered his eyebrows and shrugged her out of his immediate attention.

"Beer," he announced.

Another car again frustrated him; a small black Porsche this time, coasting up like a shadow from the private inner road and coming to an inconspicuous halt half hidden by one of Henry's trucks. No driver emerged. The tinted side windows obstructed identification.

Henry frowned in the newcomer's direction. "Who's that skulking behind my trucks?"

"Don't know," I said. "Go and see."

He padded over, inspected briefly, padded back.

"He's thin, young, looks like Ducky. He's sitting in there with the doors locked. He wouldn't speak to me." Henry leered. "He made an Italian truck driver's gesture! Are you any the wiser?"

"He just might be Forsyth Stratton. Ducky's cousin. He looks very like her."

Henry shrugged, his interest waning. "What do you want done with the empties in the bars?"

"The caterers will deal with them."

"Beer, then."

"Beer."

We finally lifted the elbows, discussing things as yet undone. His crew would work to midnight or later, he promised. They would sleep in the cabs of the trucks, as they often did, and would finish setting up early in the morning. His trucks would be gone by nine-thirty, all except the smallest, his own personal traveling workshop, which contained everything for maintenance and urgent repairs.

"I'll stay for the races," he said. "Can't miss them, after all this."

Roger joined us, a lot of strain showing.

"Oliver's in one of his vilest tempers," he reported. "And as for Rebecca . . ."

Rebecca herself came fast on his heels but bypassed our group and tried to find a way through the bolted-together fence that hid the gutted grandstand. Failing, she powered back to Roger and said forcefully, "Let me through that fence. I want to see how much damage has been done."

"I'm not in charge of the fence," Roger said with restraint. "Perhaps you should ask the police."

"Where are the police?"

"On the other side of the fence."

She narrowed her eyelids. "Fetch me a ladder, then."

When Roger failed to move fast to obey her, she turned instead to a passing workman. "Fetch me a stepladder," she told him. She gave him no "please," nor "thank you" when he brought one. She merely told him where to place it and gave him the slightest nod of ungracious approval when he stepped back to let her climb.

She went up the steps with assured liquid movement and looked for a long time at what the fence hid.

Henry and Roger sloped off fast like wily old soldiers and left me alone to benefit from Rebecca's scalpel-sharp opinions. She descended the steps with the same athletic grace, cast a disparaging look at my still-useful walker and told me to leave the racecourse at once, as I had no right to be there. I had also had no right to be in the stands two days earlier, on Friday morning, and if I were thinking of suing the Strattons for damages because of my injuries, the Strattons would sue me for trespass.

"OK," I said.

She blinked. "OK what?"

"Have you been talking to Keith?"

"That's none of your business, and I'm telling you to leave."

"The prosperity of this racecourse is my business," I said, unmoving. "I own eight hundredths of it. You, after probate, will own three hundredths. So who has the better right to be here?"

She narrowed the brilliant eyes, impatiently ducking the majority-of-interest issue but targeting the truly significant. "What do you mean, after probate? Those shares are mine, in the will."

"Under English law," I said, having discovered it in settling my mother's affairs, "no one actually owns what has been bequeathed to them until the will has been proved genuine, until taxes have been paid and a certificate of probate issued."

"I don't believe you."

"Doesn't alter the facts."

"Do you mean," she demanded, "that my father and Keith and Ivan have no right to be directors? That all their stupid decisions are null and void?"

I dashed her awakening hopes. "No, it doesn't. Directors don't have to be shareholders. Marjorie could have appointed anyone she liked, whether or not she was aware of it."

"You know too damned much," Rebecca said with resentment.

"Are you pleased," I asked, "that the main stands are now rubble?"

She said defiantly, "Yes, I am."

"And what would you want done?"

"New stands, of course. Modern. Glass-walled. New everything. Get rid of bloody Oliver and fuddy-duddy Roger."

"And run things yourself?" I said it without seriousness, but she seized on it fervently.

"I don't see why not! Grandfather did. We need change, now. New ideas. But this place should be run by a Stratton." Her zeal shone out like a vision. "There's no one else in the family who knows a rabbet from a raceway. Father has to leave Stratton Hays to his heir, but the racecourse land is not entailed. He can leave his racecourse shares to *me.*"

"He's only sixty-five," I murmured, wondering what galvanizing effect this conversation would have had on Marjorie and Dart, not to mention Roger and Oliver, and Keith.

"I can wait. I want to ride for at least two more seasons. It's time a woman reached the top five on the jockeys' list, and I'm going to do that this year, bar falls and bloody stand-downs by stupid doctors. After that, I'll manage the place."

I listened to her confidence, not sure whether she were self-deluded or, in fact, capable.

"The directors would have to appoint you," I said prosaically.

She sharpened her gaze on me assessingly. "So they would," she said slowly. "And I've two whole years to make sure that they do." She paused. "Whoever they are, by then."

Deciding abruptly that she'd given me enough of her time she prowled back to her scarlet car, casting hungry looks left and right at the domain she aimed to rule. Marjorie, of course, would frustrate her: but couldn't forever, consequence of the difference in decades. Rebecca had had that in mind.

Henry and Roger cravenly returned as Rebecca's exhaust pipe roared towards the exit.

"What was she saying to you?" Roger asked curiously. "She looked almost human."

"I think she wants to take charge here, like her grandfather."

"Rubbish!" He began a laugh which turned uneasily into a frown. "The family won't let her."

"No, they won't." Not this year, I thought, nor next year: but thereafter?

Roger shrugged away the untenable thought. "Don't tell Oliver," he said. "He'd strangle her first."

A policeman and the twenty-eight-year-old bomb expert came through a section of the fence, swinging it partly open, revealing the slow sifting activity of others within.

Roger and I walked to meet them and looked curiously at what they were carrying.

"Remains of an alarm clock," the expert said cheerfully, holding up a cog wheel. "One nearly always comes across pieces of timing devices. Nothing actually vaporizes with this type of explosive."

"What type?" I asked.

"P.E.4. Not Semtex. Not fertilizer and diesel oil. Not do-it-yourself terrorism. I'd say we're handling regular army here, not Irish Republican."

Roger, the colonel, said stiffly, "The army keeps strict control of detonators. P.E.4 is pussy-cat stuff without detonators."

The expert nodded. "You can pat it and mold it like marzipan. I wouldn't hit it with a hammer, though. But detonators under lock and key? Don't make me laugh. My life would be easier if it were true. But the army's been known to mislay tanks. What's a little fulminate of mercury between friends?"

"Everyone is very careful about detonators," Roger insisted.

"Oh, sure." The expert grinned wolfishly. "Old soldiers could liberate a field-gun from under your nose. And—you know what they say—there's nothing as good as a fire."

From the look on Roger's face, the saying was all too familiar.

"When a certain large depot the size of five soccer fields went up in flames a few years ago," the expert enlarged to me with unholy relish, "enough stuff was reported lost to fill double the space. The army produced tons of constructive paperwork to prove that all sorts of things had been sent to the depot during the week before the fire. Things that had earlier gone missing, and might have had to be accounted for, were all reported as having been 'sent to the depot.' Things were reported to have been 'sent to the depot' that had, after the fire, marched out of their home bases by the suitcaseful to much nearer destinations. A good fire is a godsend, right, Colonel?"

Roger said formally, "You don't expect me to agree."

"Of course not, Colonel. But don't tell me it's impossible for a caseful of detonators to fail to be counted." He shook his head. "I'll grant you no one but a fool or an expert would handle them, but a word here, a word there, and there's a market for anything under the sun."

# 10

The work went on.

Electric cables snaked everywhere and were gradually assimilated invisibly into the canvas. Lighting grew, looking as if it belonged there inevitably. White silently whirling fans hung beneath roof vents, to get rid of smells and used air. Henry himself understood tent management and crowd comfort in a way that sweltering guests in sunbaked marquees had never imagined, and as I too put climate control near the top of all living priorities, the Stratton Park racegoers were going to breathe easily without knowing why.

The nineteenth-century chimney-born updraughts in houses had created a boom then in footstools, winged chairs and screens; twentieth-century wind tunnels meant gale-ridden city street corners.

Air pressure, air movement, air temperature, dust removal, mite reduction, dehumidification: all were not just a matter of soft self-indulgence indoors, but of positive no-allergy health and the deterrence of rot, rust, fungus and mildew. The Lazarus act on old buildings began, in my no doubt obsessional mind, with the provision of clean dry air, unobtrusively circulating.

We fed everyone from the Mayflower's kitchen. My sons fetched and carried, acted as waiters, willingly collected rubbish and generally behaved as they never did normally unless bullied.

Roger and I consulted the racecourse's water-main maps, and his men laid a branch pipe to the side-tents' catering areas, with a twiglet off to the female jockeys' changing room especially for Rebecca. Cold water, of course, but perhaps better than none. Persistent telephoning finally wrung out a promise of one Portalet van and, from Ivan, Roger bravely cajoled a truckload of garden center potted plants.

"He says it's one of the top-selling days in his year," Roger commented, putting down the receiver. "He says the racecourse must pay for what he sends."

"Charming."

We discussed a few more arrangements before Roger bustled away, leaving me in the office. I'd begun in the past hour to find walking easier but on the other hand I felt weary across the shoulders and glad of a chance to perch a rump on the desk, avoiding the worst winces but resting arms and legs. I thought of the admonition card back home in my workshop, given me in happier times by Amanda, which read "If everything is going well you have obviously overlooked something," and idly wondered what hadn't occurred to Roger and Henry and me that could become a hopeless disaster on the morrow.

The door opened abruptly to reveal Forsyth Stratton striding over the threshold. None of the Strattons seemed capable of entering a room slowly.

"What are you doing in here?" he demanded.

"Thinking," I said. Thinking in fact that I was not pleased to see him, particularly if he had similar ideas to Hannah and Keith. It appeared, however, and somewhat to my relief, that his attack would be verbal, not physical.

He said with rage, "You've no right to take charge here."

"The Colonel's in charge," I replied mildly.

"The Colonel consults you before he does anything." His dark eyes glittered in the same way as Rebecca's, and I wondered fleetingly whether either or both of them wore contact lenses. "And that huge man whose staff are putting up tents, he asks the Colonel for decisions, then they come and ask *you,* or he bypasses the Colonel and comes to you first. You're much younger than them, but whatever *you* say, that's what they do. I've been sitting for hours watching and getting angrier and angrier, so don't tell me I don't know what I'm talking about. None of us want you here . . . just who the hell do you think you are?"

I said dryly, "A builder."

"A sodding builder shouldn't be running our racecourse."

"A shareholder then. A part owner."

"Sod that! I'm a *Stratton.*"

"Bad luck," I said briefly.

He was furiously affronted. His voice rose a couple of octaves and, with a vindictive twist to his mouth, he practically shouted, "Your sodding mother had no right to those shares. Keith should have given her a good hiding instead. And Jack says that's just what you got from Keith yourself yesterday only not enough and you've a sodding nerve to stick your snout into our affairs and if you're thinking of screwing money out of us you can piss in the wind."

The incoherence of his speech only added to the bile pouring out of him. As far as I was concerned I'd taken one insult too many from the Strattons and it annoyed me into a brutality I seldom felt. I said, with intention to wound, *"You* don't have an ounce of authority in your own family. They ignore you. They won't even look at you. What have you done?"

His hands rose fast, closing into fists. He took a fierce step forward. I stood up straight, not looking (I hoped) the pushover I actually was and, regardless of the threat, and with hot blood, I taunted him, "I'd guess it's cost them a fortune to keep you free, walking about and out of prison."

He yelled, "Shut up, shut up. I'll complain to Aunt Marjorie." One of his fists made a pass near my chin.

"Complain," I said. I strove unsuccessfully to regain the tatters of my temper, but even to my own ears, my words came out hurtful and rough. "You're a fool, Forsyth, and no doubt also a knave, and Marjorie despises you enough already, without you sniveling to her to have your pitiful nose wiped. And if you could see the ugly mess hate's making of your face, you'd run a mile and hide."

That last childish jibe pierced him keenly. He clearly liked his own good looks. The spiteful facial contortions slackened, the lips lost their rigidity and covered the teeth and his sallow skin reddened.

"You *shit.*" He shook with humiliations past and present. The fists unclenched and fell away. He unraveled fast into a pathetic failure, all sound and posture, no substance.

I abruptly felt ashamed of myself. Oh great, I thought, unleashing the artillery on the least of the Strattons. Where were my brave words yesterday when I'd been faced with Keith?

"I make a better ally than enemy," I said, cooling down. "Why don't you try me?"

He looked confused besides defeated: softened enough maybe to answer a few questions.

I said, "Was it Keith who told you I'd come here to screw money out of your family?"

"Of course." He nodded weakly. "Why else would you come?"

I did not say, "Because your grandfather's money paid for my schooling."
I did not say, "Perhaps to avenge my mother." I said, "Did he say it before or
after the stands blew up?"

"What?"

I didn't repeat the question. He stared sullenly for a bit and finally answered,
"After, I suppose."

"When exactly?"

"Friday. The day before yesterday. In the afternoon. A lot of us came here
when we heard about the explosion. They'd taken you off to hospital. Keith
said you'd be exaggerating a few grazes far more than their worth. Bound to,
he said."

"Which you naturally believed?"

"Of course."

"All of you?"

He shrugged. "Conrad said we'd have to be prepared to buy you off and
Keith said they couldn't afford it, not after . . ." His voice stopped suddenly,
his confusion worsening.

"Not after what?" I asked.

He shook his head miserably.

"Not after," I guessed, "what it had cost them to get *you* out of trouble?"

"I'm not listening," he said, and like a child put his hands over his ears.
"Shut up."

He was twenty-something, I thought. Unintelligent, unemployed and apparently unloved. Also, primarily, a Stratton. Buying people off had become
standard Stratton behavior, but from the way the others had behaved to
Forsyth at the Wednesday board meeting, he had cost them too much. If they
had had any affection for him earlier, by that meeting it had turned to resentment.

Within the family there were levers and coercions: I could see they existed,
couldn't know what they were. Forsyth's actual sin was probably not as important to them as the expense of it on one hand, and the power gained over
him on the other. If the threat of disclosure could still be applied to him, he
would now do, I reckoned, whatever the family told him.

Roger had said that Marjorie held Conrad in some sort of hammerlock;
that he would always give in to her when she demanded it.

I myself had agreed, without realizing the possible significance of it, to try
to find out for her how much Keith owed and to whom, and also to discover
what pressure was being put on Conrad by the would-be architect of the new
stands, who had proved to be Wilson Yarrow, of whom I knew something but
had forgotten more.

Was I, I wondered, being used by Marjorie to seek out facts for her chiefly to give her more leverage for ruling her family? Had she shrewdly guessed I would help her if she engaged my interest in the prosperity of the race-course? Was she that clever, and was I that dumb? Probably, yes.

I still did believe, though, that she genuinely did want the racecourse to prosper, even if she'd intended to use me as a tool in the achievement of her no-change policy.

Marjorie herself would not, and could not, have blown the grandstand apart. If, through me or in any other way, she found out who had, or who had arranged it, and if it should turn out to be one of themselves, she would not necessarily, I now thought, seek any public or law-driven retribution. There would be no trial or conviction or official penal sentence for the culprit. The Stratton family, and Marjorie above all, would assimilate one more secret into the family pool, and use it for internal family blackmail.

I said to Forsyth, "When you were at school, did you join a cadet corps?"

He stared. "No, of course not."

"Why 'of course'?"

He said impatiently, "Only a fool wants to march around in uniform being shouted at."

"Field marshals begin that way."

He sneered, "Power-hungry cretins."

I tired of him. It was unlikely he'd ever handled det cord or explosives himself: boys in the cadet forces might have done. Forsyth didn't seem even to understand the drift of my question.

Christopher, Toby and Edward all came into the office, close together as if for strength, looking anxious.

"What's the matter?" I asked.

"Nothing, Dad." Christopher relaxed slightly, his gaze on Forsyth. "The Colonel asked us to bring you over to position the taps for the water."

"You see?" Forsyth said bitterly.

Still using the walker, I went past Forsyth and out of the door with my boys and, though I could hear Forsyth coming behind me, I neither expected nor received any more trouble from that quarter. Trouble enough manifested itself irritatingly in a bunch of the Strattons issuing from the big top's main entrance like a posse intent on intercepting me mid-way on the tarmac. My three sons stopped walking, too young, too inexperienced for this sort of thing.

I took one step past them and stopped also. The Strattons formed a semi-circle in front of me; Conrad on my left, then a woman I didn't know, then Dart, Ivan, Jack with a bruised swollen face, then Hannah and Keith. Keith, on my right, stood just out of my peripheral vision, to me an unsatisfying state of affairs. I took a half-pace backwards so that I could see if he made any un-welcome movement; a step that the Strattons seemed to interpret as a general retreat. They all, in fact, took an equal step forward, crowding a shade closer, with Keith again behind my vision unless I turned my head his way.

Christopher, Toby and Edward hesitated, wavered and separated from each other behind me. I could sense their fright and dismay. They sidled off and round into my view, backing away behind the Strattons, then frankly turning and running off, disappearing into the big top. I didn't blame them: felt like running myself.

"No Marjorie?" I asked flippantly of Dart. And where, I might have added, was my bodyguard when I might need her?

"We went to church," Dart said unexpectedly. "Marjorie, Father, Mother and I. Easter Sunday, and all that." He grinned insouciantly. "Marjorie gave us lunch afterwards. She didn't want to come here with us. She didn't say why."

No one bothered with introductions, but I gathered that the woman be-tween Conrad and Dart was Dart's mother, Lady Stratton, Victoria. She was thin, cool, well-groomed and looked as if she would rather be anywhere else. She regarded me with full-blown Stratton disdain, and I wondered fleetingly if Ivan's wife Dolly and Keith's fourth victim, Imogen, fitted as seamlessly into the family ethos.

Forsyth came to a halt on my left, beside Conrad, who paid him not the slightest attention.

Across the tarmac Roger appeared briefly in the big top entrance, took note of the Stratton formation, and went back inside.

I surveyed the half-circle of disapproving faces and hard eyes and decided on attack. Better one shot than none, I supposed.

"Which of you," I said flatly, "blew up the stands?"

Conrad said, "Don't be ridiculous."

Talking to Conrad meant turning too much of my back towards Keith, but though the skin on my neck might creep with alarm, it was Conrad, I reck-oned, who might deter Keith from action.

I said to him, "One of you did it, or otherwise arranged it. Blowing up the stands was Stratton work. Not outside terrorism. Homegrown."

"Rubbish."

"The real reason you want to be rid of me is fear that I'll find out who did it. You're afraid because I saw how the explosive charges looked before they were set off."

"No!" The strength of Conrad's denial was in itself an admission.

"And fear that if I find out who did it, I'll offer silence for money."

None of them uttered.

"Which you can't easily afford," I went on, "after Forsyth's adventure."

They looked furiously at Forsyth.

"I didn't tell him," he begged desperately. "I didn't say *anything*. He guessed." He summoned a flash of healthier rage. "He guessed because you've all been so *beastly* to me, so serve you all right."

"Shut up, Forsyth," Hannah said viciously.

I said to Conrad, "How do you like your tent grandstand?"

For half a second Conrad looked instinctively, genuinely pleased, but Keith said violently behind my right ear, "It won't stop us selling the land."

Conrad gave him a glance of disgusted dislike and told him that without the tents now, disgruntled racegoers would stay away in droves in the future, the course would go bust and be left with huge debts that would cut deep into anything the land could be sold for.

Keith fumed. Dart smiled secretly. Ivan said judiciously, "The tents are *essential*. We're lucky to have them."

All except Keith nodded agreement. Keith growled in his throat, much too close to my shoulder. I could feel his intent.

I said with fierceness to Conrad, "Keep your brother off me."

"What?"

"If he," I said, "or any of you lays another finger on me, the big top comes down."

Conrad stared.

I leaned on the walker. I said, "Your brother knows he can still knock me over. I'm telling you that if he or Hannah or Jack has any idea of continuing what they were stopped from doing yesterday, tomorrow morning you'll find an empty field over there." I nodded towards the canvas.

Hannah sneered, "Don't be stupid."

Conrad said to me, "You can't do that. It isn't in your power."

"Want to bet?"

Henry came out of the big top, all my boys with him. They stood near the entrance, watching, awaiting events. Conrad followed the direction of my gaze and looked back at me thoughtfully.

"Henry," I told him, "that giant of a man, he brought the big top here to help you out because I asked him to. He's a friend of mine."

Conrad protested, "The Colonel found the tent."

"I told him where to look. If I get one more threat, one more bruise from you lot, Henry takes everything home."

Conrad knew the truth when it battered his eardrums. He was, moreover, a realist when it came to being persuaded by a threat he knew could be carried out. He turned away, breaking the alarming half-circle, taking his wife and Dart with him. Dart, looking back, gave me a gleam from his teeth. The crown of his head showed pink under the thinning fuzz, which he would not like to know.

I turned towards Keith, who still stood with hunched shoulders, head sticking forward, jaw prominent, eyes angry; a picture overall of unstable aggression.

I had nothing to say. I simply stood there, not daring him, just trying to convey that I expected nothing at all: not any onslaught, not a backing down, no loss of face on his part or on mine.

Forsyth, from behind me, said meanly, "Go on, Keith, give it to him. What are you waiting for? Kick him again, while you can."

The spiteful urging had the opposite effect. Keith said as if automatically, "Keep your stupid mouth shut, Forsyth," and shook with frustration as much as rage, the dangerous moment defusing into a more general state of continuing hatred.

I found my son Alan appearing at my side, holding on to the walker and watching Keith apprehensively, and a moment later Neil joined us, on my other side, giving Keith a wide perplexed stare. Keith, for all his bullying years, looked slightly unnerved at being opposed by children.

"Come on, Dad," Alan said, tugging at the frame, "Henry wants you."

I said, "Right," with decisiveness and began moving forward, with Hannah and Jack straight ahead in my way. Uncertainly, they parted to let me go by: no lack of ill will in their faces, but not the unstoppable boiling fury of the previous morning.

The other three boys trickled across and crowded round also, so that I reached Henry finally as if guarded by a young human hedge.

"You saw them off, then," he said.

"Your size was the ultimate deterrent."

He laughed.

"Also I told them that you would pack up the big top and go home if there were any more messing about, and they can't afford that."

"Right little raver, aren't you?" he said.

"I'm not keen on their sort of football."

He nodded. "The Colonel told me about that. Why the heck do you bother to help them?"

"Cussedness."

Christopher said unhappily, "We left you, Dad."

"We went to get help," Edward assured me, believing it.

Toby, whispering as much to himself as to me, said, "We were frightened. We just . . . ran away."

"You came into the office to fetch me," I pointed out, "and that was brave."

"But afterwards . . ." Toby said.

"In the real world," I said mildly, "no one's a total hero day in and day out. No one expects it. You can't do it."

"But Dad . . ."

"I was glad you went to find the Colonel, so forget it."

Christopher and Edward sensibly believed me, but Toby looked doubtful. There were too many things, that Easter school holidays, that he would never forget.

Roger and Oliver Wells came out of the big top chatting amicably. The fireball of Oliver's temper had been extinguished that morning by a conducted tour of the emerging arrangements inside the tents. Who cared about Harold Quest, he finally said. Henry's work was miraculous: all would be well. He and Roger had planned in detail how best to distribute racecards to all, and entry badges to the Club customers. At Oliver's insistence a separate viewing stand for the Stewards was being bolted together directly behind the winning post on the inside of the course. It was imperative, he said, that since that high-up box was no more, the Stewards should have an unimpeded all-round view of every race. Roger had found a sign-painter who'd agreed to forfeit his afternoon's television viewing in favor of "Stewards Only," "Club Enclosure," "Private Dining Room," "Women Jockeys' Changing Room" and "Members' Bar."

Roger and Oliver crossed to Roger's jeep, started the engine and set off on an unspecified errand. They'd gone barely twenty yards in the direction of the private road, however, when they smartly reversed, did a U-turn and pulled up beside me and the boys.

Roger stuck his head out and also a hand, which grasped my mobile phone.

"This rang," he said. "I answered it. Someone called Carteret wants to speak to you. Are you at home?"

"Carteret! Fantastic!"

Roger handed me the instrument, and went on his way.

"Carteret?" I inquired of the phone. "Is it you? Are you in Russia?"

"No, dammit," a long-familiar voice spoke in my ear. "I'm here in London. My wife says you told her it was urgent. After years of nothing, not even Christmas cards, everything's urgent! So what gives?"

"Er . . . what gives is that I need a bit of help from your long-term memory."

"What the hell are you talking about?" He sounded pressed and not over-pleased.

"Remember Bedford Square?"

"Who could forget?"

"I've come across an odd situation, and I wondered . . . do you by any chance remember a student called Wilson Yarrow?"

"Who?"

"Wilson Yarrow."

After a pause Carteret's voice said indecisively, "Was he the one three years or so ahead of us?"

"That's right."

"Something not right about him."

"Yes. Do you remember what, exactly?"

"Hell, it was too long ago."

I sighed. I'd hoped Carteret, with his oft-proven retentive memory, would come out snapping with answers.

"Is that all?" Carteret asked. "Look, sorry, mate, but I'm up to my eyes in things here."

Without much hope, I said, "Do you still have all those diaries you wrote at college?"

"I suppose so, well, yes, somewhere."

"Could you just look at them and see if you wrote anything about Wilson Yarrow?"

"Lee, have you *any* idea what you're asking?"

"I've seen him again," I said. "Yesterday. I *know* there's something I ought to remember about him. Honestly, it might be important. I want to know if I should . . . perhaps . . . *warn* some people I know."

A few moments of silence ended with, "I got back from St. Petersburg this morning. I've tried the number you gave my wife several times without success. Nearly gave up. Tomorrow I'm taking my family to Euro Disney for six days. After that, I'll look in the diaries. Failing that, come to think of it, if you're in more of a hurry, you could come over here, tonight, and take a quick look yourself. Would that do? You *are* in London, I suppose?"

"No. Near Swindon, actually."

"Sorry, then."

I thought briefly and said, "What if I came up to Paddington by train? Will you be at home?"

"Sure. All evening. Unpacking and packing. Will you come? It'll be good to see you, after all this time." He sounded warmer, as if he suddenly meant it.

"Yes. Great. I'd like to see you, too."

"All right then." He gave me directions for coming by bus from Paddington Station and clicked himself off. Henry and the children gave me blank stares of disbelief.

"Did I hear right?" Henry said. "You hang on to a walker with one hand and plan to catch a train to London with the other?"

"Maybe," I said reasonably, "Roger could lend me a stick."

"What about us, Dad?" Toby said.

I glanced at Henry who nodded resignedly. "I'll see they come to no harm."

"I'll be back by their bedtime, with a bit of luck."

I phoned Swindon railway station and asked about timetables. If I ran, it seemed, I could catch a train in five minutes. Otherwise, yes, possibly I could get to London even on the reduced Sunday service and be back in Swindon by bedtime. Just. With luck.

Roger, returning from his errand, offered not one but two walking sticks, plus, at my cajoling, a copy of Yarrow's grandstand plans ("You'll get me *shot*"), plus a ride to the station, though as we set off he said he doubted my sanity.

"Do you want to know if Wilson Yarrow can be trusted?" I asked.

"I'd be happy to know he can't be."

"Well, then."

"Yes, but . . ."

"I'm healing," I said briefly.

"I'll say no more."

I paid for my ticket by credit card, tottered onto the train, took a taxi from Paddington and arrived without incident on Carteret's doorstep near Shepherd's Bush. (Bay-windowed terrace built for genteel but impoverished Edwardians.)

He opened the door himself and we took stock of each other, the years of no contact sliding away. He was still small, rounded, bespectacled and black-haired, an odd genetic mixture of Celt and Thai, though born and educated in England. We had paired as strangers to share digs together temporarily during our first year in architectural school and had gone through the whole course helping each other where necessary.

"You look just the same," I said.

"So do you." He eyed my height, curly hair and brown eyes; raised his eyebrows not at the working clothes but at the sticks I leaned on.

"Nothing serious," I said. "I'll tell you about it."

"How's Amanda?" he asked, leading me in. "Are you still married?"

"Yes, we are."

"I never thought it would last," he said frankly. "And how are the boys? Three, was it?"

"We have six, now."

"Six! You never did anything by halves."

I met his wife, busy, and his two children, excited about going to meet Mickey Mouse. I told him, in his untidy, much-lived-in sitting room, about the present and possible future of Stratton Park racecourse. I explained a good deal.

We drank beer. He said he hadn't remembered anything else about Wilson Yarrow except that he had been one of the precious elite tipped for immortality.

"And then . . . what happened?" he asked. "Rumors. A cover-up of some sort. It didn't affect us, personally, and we were always working so hard ourselves. I remember his name. If he'd been called Tom Johnson or something, I'd have forgotten that too."

I nodded. I felt the same. I asked if I could look at his diaries.

"I did find them for you," he said. "They were in a box in the attic. Do you seriously think I'd have written anything about Wilson Yarrow?"

"I hope you did. You wrote about most things."

He smiled. "Waste of time, really. I used to think my life would go by and I'd forget it, if I didn't write it down."

"You were probably right."

He shook his head. "One remembers the great things anyway, and all the dreadful things. The rest doesn't matter."

"My diaries are balance sheets," I said. "I look at the old ones and remember what I was doing, when."

"Did you go on with rebuilding old wrecks?"

"Yeah."

"I couldn't do that."

"I couldn't work in an office. I tried it."

We smiled ruefully at each other, old improbable friends, unalike in everything except knowledge.

"I brought an envelope," I said, having clutched its large brown shape awkwardly along with one of the walking sticks during the journey. "While I read the diaries, you look at the way Wilson Yarrow thinks a grandstand should be built. Tell me your thoughts."

"All right."

A sensible plan, but no good in the performance. I looked with dismay as he brought out his diaries and piled them on his coffee table. There were perhaps twenty large spiral-bound notebooks, eight inches by ten and a half, literally thousands of pages filled with his neat cramped handwriting; a task of days, not half an hour.

"I didn't realize," I said weakly. "I didn't remember . . ."

"I told you you didn't know what you were asking."

"Could you . . . I mean, *would* you, lend them to me?"

"To take away, do you mean?"

"You'd get them back."

"You swear?" he said doubtfully.

"On my diploma."

His face lightened. "All right." He opened the brown envelope and took a look at the contents, pausing with raised eyebrows at the axonometric drawing. "That's showing off!" he said.

"Yeah. Not necessary."

Carteret looked at the elevations and floor plans. He made no comment about the amount of glass: building in difficult ways with glass was typical Architectural Association doctrine. We'd been taught to regard glass as avant-garde, as the pushing back of design frontiers. When I'd murmured that surely building with glass had been old hat since Joseph Paxton stuck together the old Crystal Palace in Hyde Park in 1851, I'd been reviled as an iconoclast, if not ruthlessly expelled for heresy. In any case, glass was acceptable to Carteret in futuristic ways that I found clever for the sake of cleverness, not for grace or utility. Glass for its own sake was pointless to me: except as a source of daylight, it was normally what one could see through it that mattered.

"Where are the rest of the plans?" Carteret asked.

"This is all Yarrow showed the Strattons."

"How does he get crowds up five stories?"

I smiled. "Presumably they walk, like they did in the old grandstand that exploded . . ."

"No lifts. No escalators in the floor plan." He looked up. "No client would buy this, not in this day and age."

"I'd guess," I said, "that Conrad Stratton has committed himself and the racecourse to whatever Yarrow produced."

"Signed a contract, do you mean?"

"I don't know. If he did, it's not binding, as he hadn't the power to."

He frowned. "Bit of a mess, though."

"Not if Wilson Yarrow's disqualified himself in some way."

"Literally? Do you mean disbarred? Struck off?"

"More like dishonest."

"Well, good luck with the diaries. I don't remember anything like that."

"But . . . something?"

"Yes."

I looked at my watch. "Do you have a number I could ring for a taxi?"

"Sure. It's in the kitchen. I'll do it for you." He went away on the errand and presently returned, carrying a tote bag and followed by his wife, who hovered in the doorway.

"Take the diaries in this," he said, beginning to transfer them to the tote, "and my wife says I must drive you to Paddington myself. She says you're in pain."

Disconcerted, I glanced at his wife and rubbed a hand over my face while I sought for a response.

"She's a nurse," Carteret said. "She thought you had arthritis until I explained about the roof falling in. She says you're forcing yourself to move and you need to rest a bit."

"Haven't time."

He cheerfully nodded. "Like, I may have a roaring temperature today but I can't fit in flu until, let's say, next Tuesday?"

"Quite right."

"So I will drive you to Paddington."

"I'm truly grateful."

He nodded, satisfied that I meant it.

"Anyway," I said, "I thought the current medical theory was 'get up and go.' "

Carteret's wife gave me a sweetly indulgent smile and went away, and Carteret himself put the toteful of diaries in his car and on arrival at Paddington Station drove around the back taxi road to park close between platforms, among the trains.

On the way there I said, "Stratton Park racecourse will be advertising a competition for its new stands. Why don't you ask your firm to put in for it?"

"I don't know anything about grandstands."

"I do," I said. "I could tell you what's needed."

"Why don't you do it yourself?"

I shook my head. "Not my sort of thing."

"I'll see what my firm says," he remarked doubtfully.

"Tell them to write and express interest and ask for how large a crowd the stands are envisaged to cater. You can't even begin to design stands until you've an idea of the size needed. Someone must have told Yarrow, because he got that about right."

"My firm can but try, I suppose," Carteret said. "There are fifteen thousand architects in Britain currently out of work. People don't think they *need* architects. They don't want to pay the fees, then they complain if they knock down a wall and the bedrooms fall into the basement."

"Life's rotten," I said dryly.

"Still the same cynic, I see."

He carried the diaries to the train and stored them and me into a seat. "I'll phone you when I get back from Disney. Where will you be?"

I gave him my home number. "Amanda may answer. She'll take a message."

"Don't let's leave it another ten years," he said. "OK?"

SWAYING TOWARDS SWINDON I dipped into the diaries and finally drowned in nostalgia. How young we'd been! How unformed and trusting! How serious and certain.

I came to a deep thrust of the knife.

Carteret had written:

Lee and Amanda got married today in church, the whole bit, like she wanted. They're both nineteen. I think he's a fool but have to admit they looked very pleased with themselves. She's dreamy. Trust Lee. Her father, ultra pukkah, he paid for it all. Her young sister Shelly was bridesmaid, a bit spotty. Lee's mother came. Madeline. A knockout. Fancied her rotten. She says I'm too young. Went to Amanda's folks' house after, for champagne and cake etc. About forty people. Amanda's cousins, girl friends, old uncles, that sort of thing. I had to toast the bridesmaid. Who'd be a best man? Lee says they'll live on air. Must say they were walking on it. They went off to practice being Mr. and Mrs. in Paris for three days. Amanda's parents gave it to them for a wedding present.

God, I thought, I remembered that wedding day in every tiny detail. I'd been positive we'd be blissful for ever and ever. Sad, sad illusion.

On the next page, Carteret had written:

Lee and Amanda's party last night. Most of our year came. A rave up. Bit different from last week's wedding!! They still look ecstatic. Beer and pizza this time. Lee was paying. I went to bed at six and slept through old Hammond's lecture this morning. I miss Lee in our lodgings. Didn't realize what I'd got. Better start looking for a replacement, can't afford this place on my own, bleak though it is.

Watching lights flash by in the dark countryside outside the train's windows, I wondered what Amanda was doing at that moment. Was she quietly alone at home with Jamie? Or was she, as I couldn't help speculating, embarking on an adventure of her own; had she met a new man at her sister's party? Had she *been* to her sister's party? Why did she want me and the boys to stay away for two more days?

I wondered how I would deal with it if she had finally, after all these years, fallen seriously in love with someone else.

For all the fragile state of our marriage, I desperately wanted it to continue. Perhaps because I myself hadn't been engulfed by an irresistible new passion, I still saw only advantages in staying, even unsatisfactorily, together; and top of that list came stability for six young lives. My whole mind skittered away from the thought of breaking everything up, from division of property, loss of sons, uncertainty, unhappiness, loneliness, acrimony. That sort of pain would disintegrate me into uselessness as nothing physical could.

Let Amanda have a lover, I thought: let her light up with excitement, go off on trips, even bear a child not mine; but dear God, let her stay.

I would find out, I thought, when we went home on Thursday. I would see, then. I would know. I didn't want Thursday to come.

With an effort I turned back to dipping into Carteret's diaries for the rest of the journey, but Wilson Yarrow might never have existed for all I found of him.

It was after ten o'clock when I directed the Swindon taxi to drive into the racecourse by the back road and stop at the bus.

The boys were all there, drowsily watching a video, Neil fast asleep. Christopher, relieved, went off, as he'd promised, to tell the Gardners I'd come safely back. I lay down gratefully myself with an intense feeling that *this* was home, this bus, these children. Never regret that unwise wedding day, this had grown out of it. Now, keeping it together was all that mattered.

Sleep enfolded us all, peacefully; but there was a fire in the night.

# 11

The boys and I surveyed the smoking ruins of the fence at the open ditch. Black, scorched to stumps and ash, it stretched across the course, smelling healthily of garden bonfire, thirty feet long by three feet wide.

Roger was there, unworried, with three groundsmen who had apparently doused the flames earlier and were now waiting with spades and a truck for the embers to cool to dismantling point.

"Harold Quest?" I asked Roger.

He shrugged resignedly. "His sort of thing, I suppose, but he left no signature. I'd have expected a 'BAN CRUELTY' poster, at the least."

"Will you doll off the fence?" I asked.

"Lord, no. Once we get this mess cleared away, we'll rebuild it. No problem. It's just a nuisance, not a calamity."

"No one saw who set it alight?"

" 'Fraid not. The night watchman spotted the flames from the stands at about dawn. He phoned me, woke me up, and of course I drove up here, but there was no one about. It would have been handy to catch someone with a can of gasoline, but no dice. It was a pretty thorough job, as you see. Not a cigarette. The whole width of the fence burned at once. There isn't much wind. It had to be gasoline."

"Or firelighters," Christopher said.

Roger looked interested. "Yes. I didn't think of that."

"Dad won't let us light fires with gasoline," my son explained. "He says we could easily light ourselves."

"Firelighters," Roger said thoughtfully.

All the boys nodded.

"Lots of twigs," Neil said.

"Birch," Edward corrected.

Toby said, shuddering, "I don't like this place."

Roger and I both abruptly remembered that it was here that Toby had seen the racegoer with his eyes kicked out. Roger said briskly, "Jump in the jeep, boys," and as they tumbled to obey him, added to me, "You *walked* up here from the bus!"

"It's not far," I pointed out, "and it's getting easier all the time." I'd taken only one stick: felt stiff and creaky but definitely stronger.

Roger said, "Good. Well, get in the jeep yourself. Henry's a genius!"

He drove up to the by now familiar roadway and parked outside his office and positively beamed at the sight before us.

The fine weather, though cooling, had lasted. The sky was a washed pale blue with a few streaky clouds slowly thinning and vanishing. The morning sun shone unhampered on strings of bright flags, which fluttered gently from the ridge lines of the big top's spreading roof right down to the ground in a blizzard of strings, arcading the whole huge tent like an arch of honor. Merrie Englande come again to gorgeous lighthearted life, uplifting the spirits, making one laugh.

I breathed, "Oh, my boy," and Roger said, "There are your flags. Henry said he brought every last one. When his men unfurled them all less than an hour ago, and that big white spread of canvas blossomed like that . . . well, you'd have to have been a sneering misanthrope not to have been moved."

"Colonel, you're a sentimentalist!"

"Who's talking!"

"I'm a hard-headed businessman," I said, only half truthfully. "The flags make people ready to spend more. Don't ask for the psychology, it just happens."

He said contentedly, "That's the perfect squelch for possible cynics. Mind if I use it?"

"Be my guest."

Henry's vast trucks had gone. Henry's own personal van, Roger said, was now parked out of sight at the far end of the big top. Henry was somewhere about.

Two Portakabins now stood, neatly aligned end to end, where Henry's trucks had been. Into one of them jockeys' valets were carrying saddles and hampers from their nearby vans, setting up the changing room for the male riders. Through the open door of the other could be seen an official weighing machine, borrowed from an obliging Midlands course.

A row of caterers' vans were drawn up outside the small feeder tents on the side of the big top furthest from the track, with busy hands carrying tables and trestles and folding chairs through the specially made passages into what would soon be fully fledged dining rooms and bars.

"It's all working," Roger said in wonderment. "It's bloody amazing."

"It's great."

"And the stables, of course, are OK. Horses have been arriving as usual. The canteen for drivers and lads is open, serving hot food. The press are here. The stable security staff say that for once everyone seems to be in a holiday mood. Like the Blitz, there's nothing like a bloody disaster to make the English good-humored."

We climbed out of the jeep and went into the big top itself. Each "room" now had a high-rising Moorish-looking tented ceiling of pleated peach "silk" above white solid-seeming walls, some of which were in fact taut whitened canvas laced onto poles. The floor throughout was of brown matting glued onto wooden sections slotted levelly together, firm and easy to the feet. Lights shone everywhere, discreetly. The fans up by the high roof silently circled, changing the air. Each room had an identifying board at its entrance. It all looked spacious, organized and calm. A rebirth; marvelous.

"What have we forgotten?" I said.

"You're such a comfort."

"Can I ask you something?"

"Of course."

"You remember, a week or so ago, that you learned about the precise distribution of shares among the Strattons, that they wouldn't tell you before?"

He flicked a glance at me, mentally a fraction off balance.

"Yes," he said slowly. "You noticed."

"Was it Forsyth who told you?"

"What does it matter?"

"Was it?" I asked.

"As a matter of fact, yes. Why did you think it was him?"

"He resents the way the others treat him, which makes him untrustworthy from their point of view. He knows he thoroughly earned the way they treat him. They think they control him, but they could compress him too far."

"Like plastic explosive."

"Yeah. Too close to home."

Roger nodded. "He told me in a moment of spite against them, and then said he was only guessing. He's not very bright."

"Very unhappy, though."

"I don't like him, don't trust him and, no, I really don't know what he did. When the Strattons hide something, they do a good job."

We walked out of the big top and found a van and a car parked near the entrance. The van, green with white lettering, announced "Stratton Garden Center." The car, door opening, disgorged Ivan.

He stood with his hands on his hips, head back, staring up in utter amazement at the sunlit splendor of flags. I waited for his disapproval, forgetting the little boy in him.

He looked at Roger, his eyes shiny with smiling.

"Colonel," he said, "what *fun.*" He transferred his gaze first to my walking stick and then up to my face. "Would you mind," he said awkwardly, "if I reconsidered a bit?"

"In what way?"

"Actually," he said, "I think Keith's wrong about you, don't you know." He turned away, embarrassed, and instructed his driver to get out of the cab and open the rear doors of the van. "I talked it over with Dolly—that's my wife—last night," he went on, "and we thought it didn't make sense. If you were meaning to blackmail the family, why would you help us by getting this tent? And then, don't you know, you don't seem a bad fellow at all, and Hannah has had bees in her bonnet about her mother—*your* mother—all her life. So we decided I might just, don't you know, *apologize,* if the occasion arose."

"Thank you," I said.

His face lightened, his errand achieved. His man opened the van's rear doors and disclosed a packed blaze of color inside. A whole army of flourishing pots.

"Superb!" Roger said, genuinely delighted.

"You see," Ivan explained, pleased, "when I saw the big top yesterday I understood why you'd asked me for plants, and this morning I went along to the center myself and told my manager to load not just green stuff, but *flowers.* Lots of flowers. The least I could do, don't you know."

"They're wonderful," I assured him.

He beamed, a heavy-set man in his fifties, not clever, not charismatic, polished in a way, but at heart uncomplicated. He hadn't been much of an enemy and wouldn't be much of a friend, but any neutralized Stratton could, in my terms, be counted a blessing.

Under Ivan's happy direction, my children enthusiastically carried and positioned all the flowers. I guessed they would be missing when it became time to collect them up again, except that Ivan in good humor gave them a pound each for their labors, making anything possible.

"You don't *have* to," Christopher told him earnestly, pocketing his coin, "but thanks very much."

"Forsyth," Ivan told me wistfully, "was a nice little boy."

I watched Toby stagger by with a huge pot of hyacinths. I would give almost anything, I thought, to have my own problem son grow into a well-balanced man, but it had to come from within him. He would make his own choices, as Forsyth had, as everyone did.

The plants positioned, Ivan and his van drove away and Roger asked if I would like to see the burned fence rebuilt. I glanced down at Neil who happened to be holding my hand and Roger resignedly yelled "Boys!" in his parade-ground voice and waited while they came running and piled into the jeep.

Toby refused to get out when he found where we'd got to, but I and the others watched the ultimate in prefabrication.

"It used to take days to put a new fence together," Roger said. "That was when we positioned poles as framework and filled the frame with bundle after bundle of birch, finally cutting the rough top edges into shape. Now we build fences in sections away in a separate area, take them to wherever's needed, and stake them into the ground. We can replace a whole fence or part of one at very short notice. Today's fire was at dawn and we don't race over this fence until two-thirty this afternoon. Piece of cake!"

His men, already having cleared the embers, were busy manhandling the first of the new sections into place.

"All our fences are built like this, now," Roger said. "They're good to jump but not as hard and unforgiving as the old sort."

I asked, "Did your men find any . . . well, *clues* . . . in the ashes to say who started the fire?"

Roger shook his head. "We always have trouble with vandalism. It's hopeless bothering to find out who did it. It's nearly always teenagers, and the courts hardly give them a slap on the wrist. We simply write vandalism into the budget and find ways to minimize the nuisance."

"How many people would know you could replace a fence this fast?" I asked.

"Trainers might," he said judiciously. "Jockeys, perhaps. Not many others, unless they worked here."

Roger went to speak to his foreman who looked at his watch, nodded, and got on with the job.

"Right," Roger said, returning and shepherding us back to his jeep. "Now, boys, muster at the jeep up by my office at eleven-thirty, right? I'll drive you and your father down to the bus then, and go on to my house. We all change for racing. At noon precisely I drive you back to the paddock. Understand?"

The boys were near to saluting. Roger, the peak of his tweed cap well pulled down over his eyes like a guards officer, was, with his clipped, very civilized voice and his spare decisive manner, the sort of senior soldier it was natural to obey. I could see I was never going to achieve such effortless mastery of my children's behavior.

We returned to Roger's office to find a flourishing row in full progress out on the tarmac. All the protesters from outside the gate were now inside, all of them clustered around Henry who held Harold Quest's elbow in an unyielding grip. The fierce woman was using a placard saying "ANIMAL RIGHTS" to belabor Henry as with a paddle. Four or five others howled verbal abuse with stretched ugly mouths and Henry shook Harold Quest without respect or mercy.

When he saw us Henry yelled, his voice rising as effortlessly above the screeching din as his height above everyone else, "This fellow's an imposter! A bloody imposter. They all are. They're rubbish."

He stretched out the hand not busy with shaking Quest and tweaked the placard away from the harpy attacking him.

"Madam," he roared, "go back to your kitchen."

Henry stood eighteen inches above her. He towered over Quest. Henry's beard was bigger than Quest's, Henry's voice mightier, Henry's strength double, Henry's character—no contest.

Henry was laughing. Harold Quest, the scourge of entering vehicles, had more than met his match.

"This man," Henry yelled, shaking Quest's elbow, "do you know what he was doing? I went over to the Mayflower and when I came back I found him *eating a hamburger.*"

My sons stared at him in perplexity. Eating hamburgers came well within normal behavior.

"Animal rights!" Henry shouted joyously. "What about hamburgers' rights? This man was *eating an animal.*"

Harold Quest squirmed.

"*Three* of these dimwits," Henry yelled, glancing at the screeching chorus, "were *dripping* with hamburgers. Animal rights, my *arse.*"

My boys were fascinated. Roger was laughing. Oliver Wells came out of Roger's office primed to disapprove of the noise only to crease into a smile once he understood Quest's dilemma.

"This jacket he's wearing," Henry yelled, "feels like *leather.*"

"No." Quest shook his head violently, tipping his woolly hat over one ear.

"And," Henry yelled, "when I accused him of eating an animal he put the hamburger in his *pocket.*"

Alan jumped up and down, loving it, his freckled face grinning.

Henry flung the "ANIMAL RIGHTS" placard far and wide and plunged his hand into the pocket of Harold Quest's leather-like jacket. Out came a wrapper, a half-eaten bun, tomato ketchup and yellow oozing mustard and a half-moon of meat with the Quest bite marks all over it.

Out of the pocket, too, unexpectedly, fell a second ball of plastic wrapper which had never seen a short-order cook.

In the general melee, no one saw the significance of the second wrapper until Christopher, from some obscure urge to tidiness, picked it up. Even then it would have meant nothing to most people, but Christopher was different.

"Come on," Henry yelled at his hapless captive, "you're not a real protester. What are you doing here?"

Harold Quest didn't answer.

"Dad," Christopher said, pulling my sleeve, "look at this. Smell it."

I looked at the ball of wrapping material he'd picked up, and I smelled it. "Give it," I said, "to the Colonel."

Roger, hearing my tone of voice, glanced at my face and took the crumpled ball from Christopher.

There were two brown transparent wrappers scrunched together, with scarlet and yellow printing on them. Roger smoothed one of them out and looked up at Henry who, no slouch on the uptake, saw that more had been revealed than a hamburger.

"Bring him into the office," Roger told Henry.

Henry, receiving the message, roared at Quest's followers, "You lot, clear off before you get prosecuted for being a nuisance on the highway. You with the leather shoes, you with the hamburgers, next time get your act right. Shove off, the lot of you."

He turned his back on them, marching Quest effortlessly towards the office door, the rest of us interestedly watching while Quest's noisy flock collapsed and deserted him, straggling off silently towards the way out.

The office filled up again: Oliver, Roger, myself, five boys trying to look unobtrusive, Harold Quest and, above all, Henry who needed the space of three.

"Could you," Roger said to Henry, "search his other pockets?"

"Sure."

He must have loosened his grip a little in order to oblige because Quest suddenly wrenched himself free and made a dash for the door. Henry plucked him back casually by the collar and swung his arm before letting go. With any-one else's strength it wouldn't have much mattered, but under Henry's easy force Quest staggered across the room and crashed backwards against the wall. A certain amount of self-pity formed moisture round his eyes.

"Take the jacket *off*," Henry commanded, and Quest, fumbling, obeyed.

Roger took the jacket, searched the pockets and laid the booty out on the desk beside the blotter where Henry had parked the half-eaten hamburger. Apart from a meager wallet with a return bus ticket to London, there were a cigarette lighter, a box of matches and three further dark brown transparent wrappers with scarlet and yellow overprinting.

Roger smoothed out one of these flat on the desk and read the writing aloud.

" 'Sure Fire,' " he announced. " 'Clean. Non-toxic. Long-burning. Infalli-ble. A fire every time. Twenty sticks.' " He did brief sums. "Five empty wrap-pers; that means one hundred firelighters. Now what would anyone want with one hundred firelighters on a racecourse?"

Harold Quest glowered.

Henry stood over him, a threat simply by size.

"As you're *unreal*," he boomed, "what were you up to?"

"Nothing," Quest weakly said, mopping his face with his hand.

Henry's loud voice beleaguered him, "People who burn fences can blow up grandstands. We're turning you over to the force."

"I never blew up the grandstand," said Quest, freshly agitated.

"Oh really? You were here, Friday morning. You admitted it."

"I never . . . I wasn't here then."

"You definitely *were*," I said. "You told the police you saw Dart Stratton's car drive in through the gates between eight and eight-thirty in the morning."

Harold Quest looked baffled.

"And it was *pointless*," Roger added, "to be picketing the gates of a race-course at that hour on a day none of the public would come."

"A day the TV cameras came, though," I said, "after the explosion."

"We saw you," Christopher said vehemently. "They said on the telly you'd done it. You nearly got my brother killed and you hurt my dad badly."

"I *didn't!*"

"Who did, then?" Henry roared. "You did it! You've been a bloody nui-sance, you're not a real protester, you've destroyed racecourse property and you're heading for jail. Colonel, fetch the police, they're here already poking around behind that fence. Tell them we've caught their terrorist."

"No!" Quest squealed.

"Then *give*," Henry commanded. "We're listening."

"All right then. All right. I did burn the fence." Quest was not confessing, but pleading. "But I never touched the grandstand. I didn't, as God's my witness."

"As to God, that's one thing. You've got to convince *us.*"

"Why did you burn the fence?" Roger demanded.

"Why?" Quest looked around desperately as if the answer might be written on the walls.

*"Why?"* Henry bellowed. "Why? Why? Why? And don't give us any shit about animal rights. We know that's all crap as far as you're concerned." He waved a hand at the hamburger relics. "So *why* did you do it? You're in dead trouble unless you come up with the goods."

Quest saw hope. "If I tell you, then, will that be the end of it?"

"It depends," Henry said. "Tell us first."

Quest looked up at the big man and at all of us staring at him with sharp hostile eyes and at the wrappers and the hamburger on the desk and, from one second to the next, lost his nerve.

He sweated. "I got paid for it," he said.

We met this announcement with silence.

Quest cast an intimidated look round the accusing faces and sweated some more.

"I'm an actor," he pleaded.

More silence.

Quest's desperation level rose with the pitch of his voice. "You don't know what it's like, waiting and waiting for jobs and sitting by the telephone *forever* and living on *crumbs* . . . you take *anything,* anything . . ."

Silence.

He went on miserably. "I'm a good actor . . ."

I thought that none of us, probably, would refute that.

". . . but you have to be *lucky.* You have to *know* people . . ."

He pulled off his askew woolly hat and began to look more credibly like Harold Quest, out-of-work actor, and less like Harold Quest, psyched-up fanatic.

He said, "I got this phone call from someone who'd seen me play a hunt saboteur in a TV film . . . only a bit part, no dialogue, just screaming abuse, but my name was there in the credits, hunt saboteur leader, Harold Quest."

Extraordinarily, he was proud of it: his name in the credits.

"So this phone caller said would I demonstrate for real, for money? And I wouldn't have to pay any agents' fees as he'd looked me up in the phone directory and just tried my number on the off-chance . . ."

He stopped, searching our faces, begging for understanding but not getting much.

"Well," he said weakly, "I was being evicted from my flat for non-payment of rent and I'd nowhere to go and I lived rough on the streets once before and anything's better than that."

Something in this recital, some tinge in the self-pity, reminded me sharply that this was an actor, a good one, and that the sob-stuff couldn't be trusted. Still, I thought, let him run on. There might be truth in him somewhere.

He realized himself that the piteousness wasn't achieving an over-sympathetic response and reacted with a more businesslike explanation.

"I asked what was wanted, and they said to come here and make a bloody intolerable nuisance of myself . . ."

"*They?*" Roger asked.

"He, then. *He* said to try to get some real demonstrators together and per-suade them to come here and rant and rave a bit, so I went to a foxhunt and got that loud-mouthed bitch Paula to bring some of her friends . . . and I tell you, I've spent nearly a week with them and they get on my wick something chronic . . ."

"But you've been paid?" I suggested. "You've taken the money?"

"Well . . ." grudgingly, "some up front. Some every day. Yes."

"*Every day?*" I repeated, incredulously.

He nodded.

"And for burning the fence?"

He began to squirm again and to look mulishly sullen. "He didn't say any-thing about burning the fence, not to begin with."

"Who," Roger asked without threat, "is *he?*"

"He didn't tell me his name."

"Do you mean," Roger said in the same reasonable voice, "that you mounted a threatening demonstration here for someone unknown?"

"For *money*. Like I said."

"And you just trusted you'd get paid?"

"Well, I *was.*" His air of defiance was of no help to him; much the reverse. "If I *hadn't* been paid, all I'd have laid out was the bus fare from London, but he promised me, and he kept his promise. And every day that I caused trou-ble, I got more."

"Describe him," I said.

Quest shook his head, rear-guarding.

"Not good enough," Roger said crisply. "The racecourse will lay charges against you for willful destruction of property, namely burning down the fence at the open ditch."

"But you *said* . . ." began Quest, impotently protesting.

"We promised nothing. If you withhold the identity of your, er, *procurer,* we fetch the police across here immediately."

Quest, looking hunted, caved in.

"He told me," he said, seeking to persuade us, "to stop every car and be as much nuisance as I could, and one of the cars would be *his,* and he would wind down the window and tell me my telephone number, and I would know it was *him,* and I would put my hand into the car and he would put money into my hand, and I was not to ask questions or speak to him—as God's my judge."

"Your judge will be a damn sight nearer than God," Henry bellowed, "if you're not telling us straight."

"As God's my . . ." Quest began, and collapsed into speechlessness, unable to deal with so many accusers, with such complete disbelief.

"All right," Roger told him prosaically, "you may not have wanted to look at him in the face, to be able to identify him, but there's one thing you do now know, which you can tell us."

Quest simply looked nervous.

*"Which car?"* Roger said. "Describe it. Tell us its number."

"Well . . . I . . ."

"After the first payment," Roger said, "you'd have been looking out for that car."

I suppose that rabbits might look at snakes as Quest looked at Roger.

*"Which car?"* Henry yelled in Quest's ear.

"A Jaguar XJ6. Sort of silver." He mumbled the number.

Roger, slightly aghast but not disbelieving, said to me succinctly, *"Keith's."*

He and I digested the news. Henry raised his eyebrows our way. Roger flapped a hand, nodding. Henry, perceiving that the really essential piece of information had surfaced, looked more benignly upon his demoralized captive.

"Well, now," he said, at only medium fortissimo, "when did you get hold of the firelighters?"

After a moment, meekly, Quest said, "I bought them."

"When?" Roger asked.

"Saturday."

"On *his* instructions?"

Quest said feebly, "There was a piece of paper in with the money. He said to burn the open ditch fence, where a horse had been killed on the Saturday. He said douse it with gasoline, to make sure."

"But you didn't."

"I'm not *daft.*"

"Not far off it," Henry told him.

"Where do I get gasoline?" Quest asked rhetorically. "Buy a can from a garage, buy five gallons of gasoline, then burn a fence down? I ask you! He took me for daft."

"Eating a hamburger was daft," Henry said.

"Do you still have the paper with the instructions?" I asked.

"The paper said to burn the instructions."

"And you did?"

He nodded. "Of course."

"Silly," I said. "You're not much of a villain. Who's going to believe you, without those instructions?"

"But," he spluttered, "I mean, but . . ."

"How did you actually do it?" I asked. "I mean, how did you position the firelighters?"

He said matter-of-factly, "I pushed them into the fence in bunches. Then I lit a roll of newspaper and went along lighting the bunches all at once." He almost smiled. "It was easy."

He should have burned the wrappers as well, I thought, but then people were fools, especially actors who weren't practiced criminals.

"I think," I said to Roger and Henry and Oliver, "that we might do a spot of Strattoning here."

"How do you mean, exactly?"

"Could I borrow your typewriter?"

"Of course," Roger said, pointing to the inner office. "In there."

I went through to the machine, switched on the electricity and typed a short statement:

I, Harold Quest, actor, agreed that in return for money I would mount nuisance demonstrations at the main gates of Stratton Park racecourse, ostensibly but not actually in support of a movement to discredit the sport of steeplechasing. For this service I received payments on several occasions from a man driving a silver Jaguar XJ6, registration number as follows:          To comply with instructions received from this driver I also bought one hundred "Sure Fire" firelighters and, using them, burned to the ground the birch fence at the open ditch in the straight, at approximately six A.M. Monday, Easter Bank Holiday.

Roger, Oliver and Henry read it and presented it to Quest for signing. He was predictably reluctant. We told him to add the date and his address.

"You might as well," I said, when he shrank from it, "as you're in the phone book and we can find you any time, I should think, if your photo's in *Spotlight* with the name of your agent."

"But this is an admission of guilt," he protested, not disputing our ability to track him down, as one could with any actor, through their professional publication.

"Of course," I said, "but if you sign it, you can buzz off now, at once, and use your return bus ticket, and with luck we won't give your confession to the police."

Quest searched our faces, not finding much to reassure or comfort him; but he did sign the paper. He did, in his own handwriting, fill in the car registration (verified by Roger), and also his address and the date.

The others scrutinized the pages.

"Is that everything?" Roger asked me.

"I'd think so."

Roger said to Henry, "Let him go," and Henry opened the office door to freedom and jerked his thumb in that direction, giving Quest a last order, "Out!"

Quest, an amalgam of relief and anxiety, didn't wait for a change of heart on our part but took himself off at the double.

Henry looked at the abandoned bits of hamburger and said disgustedly, "We should have rubbed the little shit's nose in that mustard."

I said with mock seriousness, "Quest's not all bad. Remember, he did call Rebecca 'ducky.' "

Henry guffawed. "So he did."

Roger picked up the signed confession. "What do we do with this, then? Do we, in fact, give it to the police?"

"No," I said. "We give it to Marjorie Binsham."

# 12

Notwithstanding our threats to Quest, the police presence behind the partitioning wall had by that morning fallen to two constables, both there more to prevent the public from entering and hurting themselves in the unstable building than to investigate further for evidence.

As far as Roger and Oliver had been able to discover the previous afternoon, after I'd left, the higher ranks and the bomb expert had completed their work with the discovery and reassembling of a blown-apart clock face, and had said their further inquiries would be conducted "elsewhere," unspecified.

"They don't know who did it," Roger baldly interpreted.

In front of the boring and forbidding partition fence there now rose an inflated Sleeping Beauty's Bouncing Castle, complete with fairytale towers and a child-minder in the shape of Henry's one remaining maintenance man.

Ivan, in a flush of generosity, had returned with a second vanload of (free) plants, this time young bushy trees in pots, which he spread out on each side of the castle, making the fence in consequence a tamer, even decorative, part of the scenery.

By the time Roger drove us toward his house at eleven-thirty, neither he nor I nor Henry could think of any improvements that could be managed in time for that afternoon, though many that could be achieved afterwards, before the next meeting.

The boys changed into tidy clothes with only medium grumbles. I changed from navvy to gentleman and with my walking stick clumsily managed to knock to the floor the pile of Carteret's diaries that had been on the table by my bed. Edward obligingly picked them up for me, but held one awkwardly open, its pages tearing half-way along from the spiral wire binding.

"Hey, careful!" I said, taking it from him. "You'll get me shot."

I concentrated on closing the book to minimize the damage, and there, leaping out at me from the page, was the name I'd sought for unsuccessfully on the train.

Wilson Yarrow.

"Wilson Yarrow," Carteret had written, "that paragon we've had stuffed down our throats, they say he's a fraud!"

The next paragraph didn't explain anything but merely consisted of remarks about a lecture on miniaturization of space.

I groaned. "They say he's a fraud" got me no further. I flicked forward a few pages and came to:

> There's a rumor going round that Wilson Yarrow won the Epsilon Prize last year with a design he pinched from someone else! Red faces on the staff! They're refusing to discuss it, but perhaps we'll hear less about the *brilliant* Wilson Yarrow from now on.

The Epsilon Prize, I remotely remembered, had been given each year for the most innovative design of a building by a senior student. I hadn't won it. Nor had Carteret. I couldn't remember ever having submitted an entry.

Roger banged on the bus door, stuck his head in and said, "Ready?" and the Morris family, dressed to impress, trooped out for his inspection.

"Very good," he approved. He gave us all racecards, entry badges and lunch tickets out of an attaché case.

"I don't want to go to the races," Toby said, suddenly frowning. "I want to stay here and watch soccer."

Roger left the decision to me.

"OK," I said to my son peaceably. "Get yourself some lunch, and if you change your mind, walk up later to the office."

Toby's worried frown turned to a more carefree expression. "Thanks, Dad," he said.

"Will he be all right by himself?" Roger asked, driving away with the rest of us, and Edward assured him, "Toby *likes* being by himself. He hides from us often."

"He goes off on bike rides," Christopher said.

Roger's mind switched to the day ahead. "We've done all we could," he said dubiously.

"Don't worry so much," I told him. "Do you know a rabbet from a raceway?"

"What on earth are you talking about?"

"Testing a theory."

"Is it a riddle, Dad?" Neil asked.

"Sort of. But don't ask, it hasn't an answer."

Roger parked the jeep at the end of the office building, where it would be ready if he needed to drive around the course. The boys paired off, Neil with Christopher, Edward and Alan together, with a rallying point near the office door for after the first, third and fifth races.

People were coming: a busload of Tote operators, the St. John's Ambulance people, the squad of policemen for traffic control and the general prevention of fights in the betting rings, the bookies with their soapboxes and chalk-boards, the gate-men, the racecard sellers; and then the jockeys, the sponsors of the races, the Stewards, the trainers, the Strattons and, finally, the racego-ers with all bets still to lose.

I stood near the main entrance, watching the faces, seeing on almost all of them the holiday pleasure we'd aimed for. Even the TV crew, invited by Oliver, seemed visibly impressed, cameras whirring outside the big top and within.

Mark drove the Daimler right up to the gate into the paddock so that Mar-jorie wouldn't have to walk from the parking lot. She saw me standing not far away, and beckoned as one seldom refused.

Without comment she watched me limp, with the stick, to her side.

*"Flags,"* she said dubiously.

"Watch the faces."

She was sold, as I'd thought she would be, by the smiles, the chatter, the hum of excitement. A fairground it might be, but something to talk about, something to give Stratton Park races a more positive face than a bomb-blasted grandstand.

She said, "The Colonel promised us *lunch* . . ."

I showed her the way to the Strattons' own dining room, where she was greeted by the same butler and waitresses who always served her at the races, and obviously she felt instantly at home. She looked around carefully at every-thing, at the table the caterers had brought and laid with linen and silver, and up at the shimmering tent-ceiling with its soft oblique lighting and hidden air-vents.

"Conrad told me," she said slowly. "He said . . . a miracle. A miracle is saving us. He didn't say it was *beautiful.*" She stopped suddenly, swallowing, unable to go on.

"There's champagne for you, I think," I said, and her butler was already bringing her a glass on a salver and pulling out a chair for her to sit down—a collapsible plastic-seated chair at base, covered now, as were ten round the table, with flowery material tied with neat bows.

Since pleasing Marjorie herself would mean the success of the whole enterprise, nothing we could think of that would make her comfortable had been left undone.

She sat primly, sipping. After a while she said, "Sit down, Lee. That is, if you can."

I sat beside her, able by now to do it without openly wincing.

*Lee.* No longer Mr. Morris. Progress.

"Mrs. Binsham . . ."

"You can call me Marjorie . . . if you like."

My great old girl, I thought, feeling enormous relief. "I'm honored," I said.

She nodded, agreeing with my assessment.

"Two days ago," she said, "my family treated you shamefully. I can hardly speak of it. Then you do this for us." She gestured to the room. *"Why* did you do it?"

After a pause I said, "Probably you know why. You're probably the only person who does know."

She thought. "My brother," she said, "once showed me a letter you wrote to him, after Madeline died. You said his money had paid for your education. You thanked him. You did all this for *him,* didn't you? To repay him?"

"I suppose so."

"Yes. Well. He would be pleased."

She put down her glass, opened her handbag, took out a small white handkerchief and gently blew her nose. "I miss him," she said. She sniffed a little, put the handkerchief away and made an effort towards gaiety.

"Well now," she said. "Flags. Happy faces. A lovely sunny spring day. Even those horrid people at the gate seem to have gone home."

"Ah," I said, "I've something to show you."

I took Harold Quest's confession from my pocket and, handing it over, explained about Henry and the out-of-character hamburger.

She searched for spectacles and read the page, soon putting a hand over her heart as if to still it.

*"Keith,"* she said, looking up. "That's Keith's car."

"Yes."

"Did you give a copy of this to the police?"

"No," I said. "That's a copy too, incidentally. The original is in the safe in the Colonel's office." I paused and went on. "I don't think I can find out how much money Keith owes, or to whom, but I did think this might do for you as a lever instead."

She gave me a long inspection.

"You understand me." She sounded not pleased, nor displeased, but surprised, and accepting.

"It took me a while."

A small smile. "You met me last Wednesday."

A long five days, I thought.

A woman appeared in the entrance to the dining room, with a younger woman hidden behind her.

"Excuse me," she said, "I was told I could find Lee Morris in here."

I stood up in my unsprightly fashion.

"I'm Lee Morris," I said.

She was plump, large-bosomed, friendly-looking, about sixty, with large blue eyes and short grayish blonde curly hair. She wore layers of blue and beige clothes with brown low-heeled shoes, and had an untidy multicolored silk square scarf tied in a bunched knot round her neck. Under her arm she carried a large brown handbag with its gold shoulder-chain dangling down, and there was altogether about her an air of being at home with herself: no mental insecurity or awkwardness.

Her gaze casually slid past me and fell on Marjorie, and there was a moment of extraordinary stillness, of suspension, in both women. Their eyes held the same wideness, their mouths the same open-lipped wonder. I thought in a flash of enlightenment that each knew the identity of the other, even though they showed no overt recognition nor made any attempt at polite speech.

"I want to talk to you," the newcomer said to me, removing her gaze from Marjorie but continuing to be tinglingly aware of her presence. "Not here, if you don't mind."

I said to Marjorie, "Will you excuse me?"

She could have said no. If she'd wanted to, she would have done. She cast an enigmatic glance at the newcomer, thought things over, and gave me a positive "Yes. Go and talk."

The newcomer backed out into the central aisle of the big top, with me following.

"I'm Perdita Faulds," the newcomer said, once outside. "And this," she added, stepping to her right and fully revealing her companion, "is my daughter, Penelope."

It was like being hit twice very fast with a hammer; no time to take in the first bit of news before being stunned by the second.

Penelope Faulds was tall, slender, fair-haired, long-necked and almost the double of Amanda: the young Amanda I'd fallen in love with, the nineteen-year-old marvelous girl with gray smiling eyes going laughingly to her immature marriage.

I was no longer nineteen. I felt as breathless, however, as if I still were. I said, "How do you do," and it sounded ridiculous.

"Is there a bar in here?" Mrs. Faulds asked, looking around. "Someone outside told me there was."

"Er . . . yes," I said. "Over here."

I took her into one of the largest "rooms" in the big top, the members' bar, where a few early customers were sitting at small tables with sandwiches and drinks.

Perdita Faulds took easy charge. "Was it champagne that Mrs. Binsham was drinking? I think we should have some."

Faintly bemused, I turned towards the bar to do her bidding.

"My treat," she said, opening her handbag and providing the funds. "Three glasses."

Penelope followed me to the bar. "I'll carry the glasses," she said. "Can you manage the bottle?"

My pulse quickened. Stupid. I had six sons. I was too old.

The bar staff popped the cork and took the money. Mrs. Faulds watched in good-natured enjoyment while I poured her bubbles.

"Do you know who I am?" she demanded.

"You own seven shares in this racecourse."

She nodded. "And you own eight. Your mother's. I knew your mother quite well at one time."

I paused with the drinks. "Did you really?"

"Yes. Do get on. I'm thirsty."

I filled her glass, which she emptied fast. "And how well," I asked, refilling it, "do you know Marjorie Binsham?"

"I don't exactly know her. I met her once, years ago. I know who she is. She knows who I am. You noticed, didn't you?"

"Yes."

I watched Penelope. Her skin looked smooth and enticing in the softly diffused peach light. I wanted to touch her cheek, stroke it, to kiss it, as I had with Amanda. For God's sake, I told myself astringently, take a grip on things. Grow up, you fool.

"I've never been here before," Mrs. Faulds said. "We saw on the television about the grandstand being bombed, didn't we, Pen? I got all curious. Then it was in Saturday's papers of course, with your name and everything, and they said the races would go on as planned. They said you'd been in the stands when they blew up, and that you were a shareholder, and in hospital." She looked at the walking stick. "They got that wrong, obviously. Anyway, I phoned the office here to ask where you were and they said you'd be here today, and I thought I'd like to meet you, Madeline's son, after all these years. So I told Pen I had some old shares in this place and asked if she would like to come with me, and here we are."

I thought vaguely that there was much she'd left out, but Penelope held most of my attention.

"Pen, darling," her mother said kindly. "This must be pretty boring for you, Mr. Morris and I talking about old times, so why don't you buzz off for a look at the horses?"

I said, "It's too early for there to be any horses in the parade ring yet."

"Hop off, Pen," her mother said, "there's a love."

Penelope gave a resigned conspiratorial smile, sucked her glass dry and amicably departed.

"She's a darling," her mother said. "My one and only. I was forty-two when I had her."

"Er . . . lucky," I murmured.

Perdita Faulds laughed. "Do I embarrass you? Pen says I'm embarrassing. She says I tell total strangers things I should never tell anyone. I do like to shock people a bit, to be honest. There are so many tight-lipped fuddy-duddies about. But secrets, they're different."

"What secrets?"

"What secret do you want to know?" she bantered.

"How you came by seven shares," I said.

She put down her glass and regarded me with eyes that were suddenly shrewd, besides being benign.

"Now, there's a question!" She didn't answer it at once. She said, "A couple of weeks ago the papers were saying the Strattons were rowing over the future of this racecourse."

"Yes, I read that too."

"Is that why you're here?"

"Basically, I guess so, yes."

She said, "I was brought up here, you know. Not here on the racecourse, but on the estate."

I said, puzzled, "But the Strattons—except Marjorie—say they don't know you."

"No, silly, they don't. Years ago, my father was Lord Stratton's barber."

She smiled at the surprise I hadn't hidden.

"You don't think I look like a barber's daughter?"

"Well, no, but then I don't know any barbers' daughters."

"My father rented a cottage on the estate," she explained, "and he had shops in Swindon, and Oxford and Newbury, but he used to go to Stratton Hays himself to cut Lord Stratton's hair. We moved before I was fifteen and lived near the Oxford shop, but my father still went to Stratton Hays once a month."

"Do go on," I said. "Did Lord Stratton give your father the shares?"

She finished the pale liquid in her glass. I poured some more.

"No, it wasn't like that." She considered a little, but continued. "My father died and left me the barber business. You see, by that time I'd learned the whole beauty trade, got diplomas, everything. Lord Stratton just strolled into the Oxford shop one day when he was passing, to see how I was getting on without my father, and he stayed to have a manicure."

She smiled. She drank. I asked no more.

"Your mother used to come into the Swindon shop to have her hair done," she said. "I could have told her not to marry that vicious swine, Keith, but she'd done it by then. She used to come into the shop with bruises on her face and ask me personally to style her hair to hide them. I used to take her into a private cubicle, and she'd cling to me sometimes, and just cry. We were about the same age, you see, and we liked each other."

"I'm glad she had someone," I said.

"Funny, isn't it, what happens? I never thought I'd be sitting here talking to *you*."

"You know about me?"

"Lord Stratton told me. During manicures."

"How long did you . . . look after his hands?"

"Until he died," she said simply. "But things changed, of course. I met my husband and had Penelope, and William—I mean, Lord Stratton, of course—he got *older* and couldn't . . . well . . . but he still liked to have his nails done, and we would *talk*. Like old, old friends, you see?"

I saw.

"He gave me the shares at the same time he gave them to your mother. He gave them to his lawyers to look after for me. He said they might be worth something one day. It wasn't a great big deal. Just a present. A loving present. Better than money. I didn't ever want money from him. He knew that."

"He was a lucky man," I said.

"Oh, you *dear*. You're as nice as Madeline was."

I rubbed a hand over my face, finding no answer.

"Does Penelope know," I asked, "about you and Lord Stratton?"

"Pen's a *child!*" she replied. "She's eighteen. Of course she doesn't know. Nor does her father. I never told anyone. Nor did William . . . Lord Stratton. He wouldn't hurt his wife, and I didn't want him to."

"But Marjorie guesses."

She nodded. "She's known all these years. She came to see me in the Oxford shop. She made a special appointment. I think it was just to see what I was like. We just talked a bit, not about anything much. She never said anything afterwards. She loved William, as I did. She wouldn't have given him away. She didn't, anyway. She still hasn't, has she?"

"No, she hasn't."

After a pause, Perdita changed gears with her voice, shedding nostalgia, taking on business, saying crisply, "So what are we going to do now, about William's racecourse?"

"If the course is sold for development," I said, "you'll make a nice little capital gain."

"How much?"

"You can do sums as well as anyone. Seventy thousand pounds  for every million the land raises, give or take a little capital gain."

"And you?" she asked frankly. "Would you sell?"

"You can't say it's not tempting. Keith's pushing for it. He's actually trying to put people off coming here, so that there's no profit in the course staying open."

"That puts me off selling, for a start."

I smiled. "Me, too."

"So?"

"So if we get a brilliant new stand built—and by brilliant, I don't mean huge, but clever, so that the crowds like to come here—our shares should pay us more regular dividends than they have in the past."

"You think, then, that horseracing as such will go on?"

"It's lasted in England so far for more than three hundred years. It's survived scandals and frauds and all sorts of accidental disasters. Horses are beautiful and betting's an addiction. I'd build a new stand."

"You're romantic!" she teased.

"I'm not deeply in debt," I said, "and Keith may be."

"William told me Keith was the biggest disappointment of his life."

I looked at her in sudden speculation, fifty questions rising like sharp rays of light; but before I could do anything constructive a racecourse official came to my side and said Colonel Gardner would like me to go urgently to the office.

"Don't go away without telling me how to find you," I begged Perdita Faulds.

"I'll be here all afternoon," she reassured me. "If I miss you, this is the phone number of my Swindon shop. That'll reach me." She gave me a business card. "And how do I find *you?*"

I wrote my mobile phone number and the Sussex house number on the back of another of her cards, and left her contentedly continuing with her champagne while I went to find out what crisis had overcome us.

The trouble, essentially, was the state of Rebecca's nerves. She was pacing up and down outside the office and gave me an angry stare as I went past her and through the door, and I'd never seen her look more unstable.

Roger and Oliver were inside, steaming and grinding their teeth.

"You are not going to believe this," Roger said tautly, when he saw me. "We have all the normal sort of troubles—we've caught a would-be nobbler in the stables, the lights on the Tote board have fused and there's a man down in Tattersalls having a heart attack—and we also have Rebecca creating the father and mother of a stink because there are no hangers in the women jockeys' changing tent."

"*Hangers?*" I said blankly.

"Hangers. She says they can't be expected to hang their clothes and colors up on the floor. We gave her a table, a bench, a mirror, a basin, running water and a drain. And she's creating a stink about *hangers.*"

"Er . . ." I said helplessly. "How about a rope, for their clothes?"

Roger handed me a bunch of keys. "I wondered if you'd take the jeep down to my house—it's locked, my wife's somewhere here but I can't find her—and bring back some hangers. Take the clothes off them. It's madness, but do you mind? Can you do it? Will your legs be up to it?"

"Sure," I said, relieved. "I thought it was serious, when you sent for me."

"She's riding Conrad's horse in the first race. It would be serious enough for him—and for all of us—if she went completely off her rocker."

"OK."

Outside, I found Dart trying without success to pacify his sister. He gave it up when he saw me and walked with me to the jeep, asking where I was going. When I said to fetch some hangers he was at first incredulous and then offered to help, so I drove both of us on the errand.

"She gets into states," Dart said, excusing her.

"Yes."

"I suppose it's a strain, risking your life every day."

"Perhaps she should stop."

"She's just blowing off steam."

We disunited Roger's clothes from a whole lot of hangers and on the way back called at the bus, where I opened the door and stuck my head into a soccer roar, maximum decibels.

"Toby," I yelled, "are you all right?"

"Yes, Dad." He turned the volume down slightly. "Dad, they had Stratton Park on the telly! They showed all the flags and the bouncing castle and everything. They said people should come here, the racing was going ahead and it was a real Bank Holiday day out."

"*Great!*" I said. "Do you want to come up to the paddock?"

"No thanks."

"OK, see you later."

I told Dart about the television coverage. "That was Oliver's doing," he said. "I heard him screwing the arms off those camera guys to get them rolling. I must say, he and Roger and you, you've done a fantastic job here."

"And Henry."

"Father says the family got you wrong. He says they shouldn't have listened to Keith."

"Good."

"He's worried about Rebecca, though."

So would I be, I thought, if she were my daughter.

Dart gave the hangers to his sister who stalked off with them, tight-mouthed. He also, to save my legs, he said, took the jeep's keys back into the office and told Roger and Oliver the big top had been news. Finally he suggested a beer and a sandwich in the bar so that he could skip the Stratton lunch. "Keith, Hannah, Jack and Imogen," he said. "Yuk." Then, "Did you know the police took my old wheels away for testing?"

"No," I said, looking for signs of worry on Dart's face, and finding none. "I didn't know."

"It's a bloody nuisance," he said. "I've had to rent a car. I told the police I would send them the bill and they just sneered. I'm fed up with this bomb thing." He grinned at my walking stick. "You must be, too."

Perdita Faulds had left the bar and was nowhere in sight when we reached it. Dart and I drank and munched and I told him I'd read a recipe once for curing falling hair.

He looked at me suspiciously. "You're kidding me."

"Well," I said judiciously, "it might be on a par with tearing off tree barks to cure malaria, or using mold growing on jelly to cure blood poisoning."

"Quinine," he said, nodding, "and penicillin."

"Right. So this cure for baldness came from a Mexican medicine-man's handbook written in 1552."

"I'll try *anything,*" he said.

"You grind up some soap plant," I said, "and you boil it in dog's urine, and you throw in a tree frog or two and some caterpillars . . ."

"You're a *shit,*" he said bitterly.

"That's what the book says."

"You're a bloody liar."

"The Aztecs swore by it."

"I'll throw you to Keith," he said. "I'll stamp on you myself."

"The book's called *The Barberini Codex.* It was all serious medicine five hundred years ago."

"What is soap plant, then?"

"I don't know."

"I wonder," he said thoughtfully, "if it works."

WE LEANED ON the parade ring rails before the first race, Dart and I, watching his father and mother, Conrad and Victoria, talking to their daughter-jockey, Rebecca, in a concerned little group that also included the horse's trainer. Other concerned little groups similarly eyed their four-legged performers stalking patiently around them, and hid their wild hopes under judicious appraisals.

"He won last time out," Dart said, appraising judiciously from his own sidelines. "She can ride well, you know, Rebecca."

"She must do, to get so high on the list."

"She's two years younger than me, and I can't remember when she wasn't besotted by ponies. I got kicked by one once, and that was enough for me, thanks very much, but Rebecca . . ." his voice held the familiar mix of exasperation and respect, "she's broken her bones as if they were fingernails . . . I can't imagine *ever* wanting *anything* as much as she wants to win."

"I think," I said, "that all top achievers are like that, at least for a while."

He turned his head, assessing me. "Are you?"

"Afraid not."

"Nor am I."

"So we stand here," I said, "watching your sister."

Dart said, "You have such a *damned* clear way of looking at things."

The signal was given for the jockeys to mount. Rebecca, wearing the dis-

tinctive Stratton colors of green and blue checks on the body with mis-
matched orange and scarlet sleeves and cap, swung her thin lithe shape into
the saddle as softly as thistledown landing. The excessive strain brought on by
the trivial annoyance of a lack of hangers had vanished: she looked cool, concentrated, a star on her stage, in command of her performance.

Dart watched her with all his ambivalent feelings showing; the female sib-
ling whose prowess outshone him, whom he admired and resented, understood but couldn't love.

Conrad's runner, Tempestexi, a chestnut gelding, looked, by comparison
with some of the others in the ring, to have a long back and short legs. The
two-mile hurdle race, according to the card, was for horses that hadn't won a
hurdle race before January first. Tempestexi, who had won one since, carried
a seven-pound penalty for doing so, but had, all the same, been made favorite.

I asked Dart how many racehorses his father had in training and he said
five, he thought, though they came and went a bit, he said, according to their
legs.

"Tendons," he said succinctly. "Horses' tendons are as temperamental as vi-
olin strings. Tempestexi is Father's current white-hot hope. No leg problems,
so far."

"Does Conrad bet?"

"No. Mother does. And Keith. He'd have put the Dower House on this
one, if he'd owned it—the Dower House, that is. He'll have bet anything he
can lay his hands on. If Rebecca doesn't win, Keith will kill her."

"That wouldn't help."

Dart laughed. "You of all people must know that logic never interferes with
instinct, in Keith."

The horses streamed out of the parade ring on their way to the course, and
Dart and I went to watch the race from the makeshift stands Henry had
bolted together from the circus tiers.

The steps were packed to the point that I hoped Henry's boast of infalli-
ble safety would hold up. Crowds, in fact, had poured through the gates like
a river during the past hour and had spread over the tarmac and into the big
top and down to the betting rings in chattering thousands. The dining rooms
were full, with customers waiting. There were crushes in all the bars and long
lines at the Tote, and the booths by the entrance had sold out of regular racecards. The big office copier was churning out paper substitutes and running
red-hot. Oliver, glimpsed briefly, sweated ecstatically.

"The television did it," he said, gasping.

"Yes, your work, well done."

Waiting for the race to start I said to Dart, "Perdita Faulds is here at the races."

"Oh? Who is she?"

"The other non-Stratton shareholder."

He showed minimal interest. "Didn't someone mention her at the family Board meeting the other day? Why did she come?"

"Like me, to see what was happening about her investment."

Dart cast it out of his mind. "They're off!" he said. "Now, come on, Rebecca."

It looked an uneventful race from the stands, though no doubt not from the saddle. The runners stayed bunched throughout the first circuit, clattered safely over the flights of hurdles, swept in an overlapping ribbon past the winning post for the first time and set off again into the country.

Down the far side the less fit, the less speedy, fell back, leaving Rebecca in third place round the last bend. Dart's genuine wish for his sister to win couldn't be doubted. He made scrubbing, encouraging movements with his whole body, and when she reached second place coming towards the last flight he raised his voice like the rest and yelled to her to win.

She did. She won by less than a length, accelerating, a thin streak of neat rhythmic muscle against an opponent who flapped his elbows and his whip but couldn't hang on to his lead.

The crowd cheered her. Dart oozed reflected glory. Everyone streamed down towards the winner's unsaddling enclosure where Dart joined his parents and Marjorie in a kissing and back-slapping orgy. Rebecca, pulling off the saddle, ducked the sentiment and dived purposefully into the Portakabin weighing room to sit on the scales. Very professional, fairly withdrawn; rapt in her own private world of risk, effort, metaphysics and, this time, success.

I took myself over to the office door and found four boys faithfully reporting there.

"Did you have lunch OK?" I asked.

They nodded. "Good job we went early. There were no tables left, pretty soon."

"Did you see Rebecca Stratton win that race?"

Christopher said reproachfully, "Even though she called us brats, we wanted to back her with you, but we couldn't find you."

I reflected. "I'll pay you whatever the Tote pays on a minimum bet."

Four grins rewarded me. "Don't lose it," I said.

Perdita Faulds and Penelope, passing, stopped by my side, and I introduced the children.

"All yours?" Perdita asked. "You don't look old enough."

"Started young."

The boys were staring at Penelope, wide-eyed.

"What's the matter?" she asked. "Have I got mud on my nose?"

"No," Alan said frankly, "you look like Mummy."

"Like your mother?"

They all nodded, and they moved off with her, as if it were natural, to go and look at the horses walking round for the next race.

"Like your wife, is she, my Pen?" Perdita said.

I dragged my gaze back. Heart thudded. Idiotic.

"Like she was then," I said.

"And now?"

I swallowed. "Yes, like now, too."

Perdita gave me a look born of long, knowing experience. "You can never go back," she said.

I would do it again, I thought helplessly. I'd marry with my eyes and find an unsuspected stranger inside the package. Did one never grow up?

I wrenched my mind away from it and said to Perdita, "Did Lord Stratton happen to know—and tell you—what it was that Forsyth Stratton did that has tied the whole family into knots?"

Her generous red mouth formed an O of amused surprise.

"You don't mess about, do you? Why should I tell you?"

"Because if we're going to save his racecourse, we have to unravel the strings that work the family. They all know things about each other that they use as threats. They blackmail each other to make them do—or not do—what they want."

Perdita nodded.

"And as a part of that," I said, "they pay people off, to keep the Stratton name clean."

"Yes, they do."

"Starting with my own mother," I said.

"No, before that."

"So you *do* know!"

"William liked to talk," she said. "I told you."

"And . . . Forsyth?"

Penelope and the boys were on their way back. Perdita said, "If you come to see me in my Swindon shop tomorrow morning, I'll tell you about Forsyth . . . and about the others, if you think up the questions."

# 13

Keith's rage, when he discovered that the runners in the second race would be jumping the open ditch as scheduled, verged on the spectacular.

Henry and I happened to be walking along behind the caterers' tents when the eruption occurred (Henry having had to deal with a leak in the new water main) and we hurried down a caterers' passage towards the source of vocal bellowing and crockery-smashing noises; into the Stratton's private dining room.

The whole family had clearly returned, after their victory, to finish their lunch and toast the winner, and typically, but perhaps luckily, had invited no outsiders to join them.

Keith, legs astride, shoulders back, mane of hair flying, had flung the entire dining table over and swept an arm along the line of bottles and glasses on the serving sideboard. Tablecloths, knives, plates, cheese, champagne, coffee, whipped-cream puddings, lay in a mess on the floor. Wine poured out of opened bottles. The waitresses pressed their hands to their mouths and various Strattons grabbed napkins and tried to clean debris from laps, trousers and legs.

"Keith!" screeched Conrad, equally furious, quivering on his feet, thunderous as a bull before charging. "You *lout.*"

Victoria's cream silk suit ran with coffee and Bordeaux. "I'm presenting the Cup," she yelled, wailing, "and *look* at me."

Marjorie sat calm, unspattered, icily furious. Ivan, beside her, said, "I say, Keith, I *say* . . ."

Hannah, trifle dripping down her legs, used unfilial language to her father and also to her son, who turned ineffectively to help her. The thin woman who sat beyond Ivan, unconcernedly continuing a relationship with a large snifter of brandy, I provisionally guessed to be Imogen. Dart wasn't there. Forsyth, sullenly seeming to be relieved that someone other than he was the focus of family obloquy, made his way to the doorway into the main passage, where we'd arranged a flap of canvas that could be fastened across to give privacy.

People were pulling the flap aside, trying to see in, to find out the cause of the commotion. Forsyth shouldered his way out, telling people rudely to mind their own business which, of course, they didn't.

The whole scene was laughable but, not far below the farcical surface, as each family member uneasily knew, lay the real cause of destructive violence, the melt-down in Keith that had so far gained most expression in hitting his wives and taking a belt at Lee Morris, but would one day go too far for containment.

Marjorie was holding in plain sight the copy of Harold Quest's confession; the cause of the debacle.

Keith suddenly seized it out of her hand, snatched the brandy glass rudely from his wife, poured the alcohol over the letter, threw down the glass and with economic speed produced a lighter from his pocket and put a flame to the paper. Harold Quest's confession flared brightly and curled to ash and was dropped and stamped on, Keith triumphant.

"It was only a copy," Marjorie said primly, intentionally goading.

"I'll kill you," Keith said to her, his lower jaw rigid. His gaze rose over her and fastened on me. The animosity intensified, found a more possible, a more preferred target. "I *will* kill *you*," he said.

In the small following silence I turned and went out the back way with Henry, leaving the poor waitresses to clear up the garbage.

"That was only half funny," Henry said thoughtfully.

"Yes."

"You want to be careful. He might just kill you next time. And *why? You* didn't bring Harold Quest here. *You* didn't smell out the hamburger."

"No," I sighed. "My pal Dart Stratton says logic never interferes with instinct, in Keith. But then, half the world's like that."

"Including murderers," Henry said.

"How inflammable," I asked, "is the big top?"

Henry stopped walking. "You don't think he'd try . . . ? He's pretty handy with that lighter. And burning the fence . . ." Henry looked angry but after a moment shook his head.

"This big top won't go on fire," he said positively. "Everything I brought here is flame retardant, flame resistant or can't burn, like all the metal poles and the pylons. There were disasters in circuses in the past. The regs now are stringent. This big top won't burn by accident. Arson . . . well, I don't know. But we've got extinguishers all over the place, as you know, and I ran a bit of water main up to the roof in a sort of elementary sprinkler system." He took me along to see. "That bit of rising main," he pointed, "the pressure's very good in it. I fed a pipe up and connected it to a garden hose running along inside, below the ridge. The hose has small holes in it. The water squirts out OK."

"Henry! You're a genius."

"I had a bit of time yesterday, when you went off to London, and I reckoned the racecourse couldn't afford another calamity like the stands. A good precaution's never wasted, I thought, so I rigged up this very basic sprinkler. Don't know how long it would work. If ever flames got that high, they could melt the hose." He laughed. "Also, I, or someone who knows, has to be around to turn the tap on. I had to stick tape and those labels all over it saying, *'Do not touch this,'* in case someone turned it on while all the crowds were inside tucking into their smoked salmon sandwiches."

"My God!"

"Roger knows about it and Oliver, and now you."

"Not the Strattons?"

"Not the Strattons, I don't trust them."

Keith, definitely, would have soaked the paying customers to ruin their day.

Henry went on, trying to reassure me. "But Keith won't actually try to kill you, not after he said in public that he was going to."

"That wasn't public. That was the Stratton family."

"But *I* heard him, and the waitresses did."

"They would pay off the waitresses and swear you misheard."

"Do you mean it?"

"I'm certain they've done that sort of thing often. Maybe not for murder, but other crimes, certainly."

"But . . . what about newspapers?"

"The Strattons are rich," I said briefly. "Money will and does buy more than you'd think. Money's for using to get what you want."

"Well, obviously."

"The Strattons don't want scandal."

"But they can't bribe the press!"

"How about the sources that speak to the press? How about suddenly blind waitresses with healthy bank balances?"

"Not these days," he protested. "Not with our insatiable tabloids."

"I never thought I'd feel older than you, Henry. The Strattons can outbid the tabloids."

Henry's mind I knew to be agile, practical, inventive and straight, but of his home life and background I knew nothing. Henry the giant and I had worked together in harmony over a stretch of years, never intimate, always appreciative; on my part, at least. Henry's junk dealings had found me a whole untouched Adam room once, and dozens of antique fireplaces and door frames. Henry and I did business by telephone—"Can you find me . . ." or "I've come across this . . ." These Stratton Park days were the first I'd spent so much in his company and they would, I thought contentedly, lead to a positive friendship.

We rounded the far end of the big top and watched the runners for the second race walk by on their way out onto the track. I found I was liking more and more to watch them, having given them little thought for most of my life. Imagine the world without them, I thought: history itself would have been totally different. Land transport wouldn't have existed. Medieval battles wouldn't have been fought. No six hundred to ride into a valley of death. No Napoleon. The seafarers, Vikings and Greeks, might still rule the world.

Horses, fleet, strong, tamable, had been just the right size. I watched the way their muscles moved under the groomed coats; no architect anywhere could have designed anything as functional, economical, supremely proportioned.

Rebecca rode by, adjusting her stirrup leathers, her attentions inward on the contest ahead. I had never wanted to ride, but at that moment I envied her: envied her skill, her obsession, her absolute commitment to a physical—animal—partnership with a phenomenal creature.

People could bet; they could own, train, breed, paint, admire, write about thoroughbreds: the primeval urge to be first, in both runner and rider, was where the whole industry started. Rebecca on horseback became for me the quintessence of racing.

Henry and I stood on the ex–circus stands and watched the race together. The whole field jumped the restored open ditch without faltering. Rebecca finished well back, not taking part in the finish.

Henry said racing didn't grab him like rugger and went away to patrol his defenses.

The afternoon passed. "There were the usual disasters," Roger said, dashing about.

I came across the racecourse doctor taking a breather between casualties.

"Come to see me on Thursday," he suggested. "I'll take all those staples out. Save you waiting around in the hospital."

"Great."

Oliver, in the office, dealt with inquiries and wrathful trainers and arranged for a Stewards' inquiry into an objection to the winner to take place in the inner office among the computers, copier and coffee machine.

On the whole, the pros whose business was everyone else's pleasure made allowances for the stopgap provisions, though it was interesting, as the day wore on, that they took the truly remarkable conjured-up arrangements more and more for granted and began to complain about the cramped weighing room and the inadequate view from the improvised stands.

"You give them a man-made miracle," Roger complained, "and they want the divine."

"Human nature."

"Sod them."

I spent some of the time with Perdita and Penelope, feeling disjointedly crazy, and some with my sons, thrust back into adulthood and paternity; but no more, thankfully, being told I was for the fairly immediate chop.

I did speak to Marjorie, who stood in for Victoria in the cup-presenting ceremony, her neat upright little figure being protected through the throng by the solicitous bulks of Conrad and Ivan. Photographs flashed, a hand-held microphone produced fuzzy noises; the winning owners floated, the trainer looked relieved, the jockey prosaic (his tenth pair of cufflinks) and the horse excited. A regular prizewinning; irregular day.

"Lee," Marjorie said, beginning to make her way back to the big top but pausing when she saw me nearby. "A cup of tea?"

I went with her obediently, though the tea idea was quickly abandoned in favor of vintage Pol Roger from Stratton Hays's cellars. Dismissing Conrad and Ivan, she took me alone into the tidied-up dining room, where the trusting staff had righted the table and laid it freshly with crustless cucumber sandwiches and small coffee éclairs.

Marjorie sat on one of the chairs and came straight to the point.

"How much is this all costing?" she peremptorily inquired.

"What is it worth?"

"Sit down, sit down." She waited while I sat. "It is worth, as you well know, almost anything your huge friend asks. We have been *flooded* with compliments all afternoon. People love this tent. The future of the racecourse, no less, has been saved. We may not make a cash profit on the day, but we have banked priceless goodwill."

I smiled at her business metaphor.

"I have told Conrad," she said collectedly, "not to quibble about the bills. Oliver Wells is so busy, I'm giving you this message for him instead. I've called for a family meeting on Wednesday, the day after tomorrow. Can you and Oliver and the Colonel draw up a list of costs and expenses for me before then?"

"Probably."

"Do it," she said, but more with persuasion than bossiness. "I've told Conrad to instruct our accountants to present an up-to-date realistic audit of the racecourse as soon as possible and not to wait for the end of its financial year. We need a survey of our present position, and it's imperative we sort out what we intend to do next." The clear voice paused briefly. "You have shown us today that we should not rebuild the old stand as it was before. You have shown us that people respond to a fresh and unusual environment. We must build some *lighthearted* stands."

I listened in awe. Eighty-four, was she? Eighty-five? A delicate-looking tough-minded old lady with a touch of tycoon.

"Will you come to the meeting?" she asked, far from sure.

"I expect so."

"Will Mrs. Faulds?"

I looked at her dryly. "She said you recognized her."

"Yes. What did she say to you?"

"Not a great deal. She said chiefly that if the racecourse can be run prosperously, she won't press for the land to be sold."

"Good." Marjorie's interior relief surfaced in a subtle loosening of several facial muscles that I hadn't realized were tight.

"I don't think she'll want to come to the meeting," I added. "She had read about the family disputes in the newspapers. She just wanted to know how things stood."

"The newspapers!" Marjorie shook her head in disgust. "I don't know how they heard of our arguments. Those reports were disgraceful. We cannot *afford* any more discord. What's more, we cannot afford *Keith.*"

"Perhaps," I said tentatively, "you should just let him . . . sink."

"Oh, no," she said at once. "The family name . . ."

The dilemma remained, age-old; unresolvable, from their point of view.

AT THE END of the day the crowds straggled off, leaving litter in tons. The big top emptied. The caterers packed their tables and chairs and departed. The afternoon sun waned in deep yellow on the horizon, and Henry, Oliver, Roger and I sat on upturned plastic crates in the deserted expanse of the members' bar, drinking beer from cans and holding anticlimactic post-mortems.

The five boys roamed around scavenging, Toby having joined them belatedly. The Strattons had left. Outside, horseboxes were loading the last winner and losers. The urgency was over, and the striving, and the glories. The incredible weekend was folding its wings.

"And for our next act . . ." I declaimed like a ringmaster, waving an arm.

"We go home to bed," Roger said.

He drove me and the boys good-naturedly down to the bus, but in fact he himself returned to the buildings and the tents to oversee the clearing up, the locking, and the security arrangements for the night.

The boys ate supper and squabbled over a video. I read Carteret's diaries, yawning. We all phoned Amanda.

Carteret wrote:

Lee persuaded me to go to an evening lecture on the effects of bombing on buildings. (The I.R.A. work, more than air-strikes.) Boring, really. Lee said sorry for wasting my time. He's got a thing about tumbledown buildings. I tell him it won't get him bonus points here. He says there's life after college . . .

"Dad," Neil said, interrupting.

"Yes?"

"I asked Henry the riddle."

"What riddle?"

"Do you know a rabbit from a raceway?"

I gazed in awe at my super-retentive small son. "What did he say?"

"He said who wanted to know. I said you did, and he just laughed. He said if anyone knew the answer, you did."

I said, smiling, "It's like the Mad Hatter's riddle in *Alice in Wonderland*: 'What's the difference between a raven and a writing desk?' There's no answer at all."

"That's a silly riddle."

"I agree. I always thought so."

Neil, whose taste for Pinocchio had won the video fight (for perhaps the tenth time) returned his attention to the nose that grew longer with lying. Keith's nose, I reckoned, would in that line of fantasy make Cyrano de Bergerac a non-starter.

Carteret's diary:

The "great" Wilson Yarrow was there, asking questions to show off his own brilliance. Why the staff think he's so marvelous is a mystery. He

sucks up to them all the time. Lee will get himself chucked out for
heresy if the staff hear his comments on Gropius. Better stop writing this
and get on with my essay on political space.

Pages and pages followed in a mixture of social events and progress on our
courses: no more about Yarrow. I fast-forwarded in time to the partially ripped
notebook and read onwards from the exclamation marks about the Epsilon
Prize. There seemed, for all my searching, to be only one further comment,
though it was damning enough in its way.

Carteret wrote:

More rumors about Wilson Yarrow. He's being allowed to complete his
diploma! They're saying someone else's design was entered in his name
for the Epsilon Prize *by mistake!!* Then old Hammond says a brilliant talent like that shouldn't be extinguished for one little lapse! How's that for
giving the game away? Discussed it with Lee. He says choice comes from
inside. If someone chooses to cheat once, they'll do it again. What about
consequences, I asked? He said Wilson Yarrow hadn't considered consequences because he'd acted on a belief that he would get away with
it. No one seems to know—or they're not telling—how the "mistake"
was spotted. The Epsilon has been declared void for this year. Why
didn't they give it to whoever's design it was that won it?

★ Just heard a red hot rumor. The design was by Mies!!! Designed in
1925, but never built. *Some* mistake!!!

I read on until my eyes ached over his handwriting but nowhere had Carteret
confirmed or squashed the red-hot rumor.

One long-ago and disputed bit of cheating might be interesting, but even
Marjorie wouldn't consider Carteret's old diaries a sufficient lever, all these
years later, especially as no action had been taken at the time. To call Wilson
Yarrow a cheat now would sail too close to slander.

I couldn't see any way that a dead ancient scandal, even if it were true,
could have been used by Yarrow to persuade or coerce Conrad into giving
him, alone, the commission for new stands.

Sighing, I returned the diaries to their tote bag, watched the last five minutes of *Pinocchio* and settled my brood for the night.

ON TUESDAY MORNING, with pressing errands of their own to see to, the
Gardners took me and the boys with them to Swindon, dumping us outside

the launderette and arranging a rendezvous later at a hairdressing salon called Smiths.

While almost our entire stock of clothes circled around washing and drying, we made forays to buy five pairs of sneakers (difficult—and expensive— as, for the boys, the colors and shapes of the decorative flashing had to be *right,* though to my eyes the "Yuk, Dad" shoes looked much the same), and after that (making a brief stop to buy a large bag of apples), I marched them relentlessly towards haircuts.

Their total opposition to this plan vanished like fruitcake the second they stepped over the threshold of Smiths, as the person who greeted us first there was Penelope Faulds. Blonde, tall, young Penelope, slapping hands with my children and deconstructing my every vestige of maturity.

Smiths, which I had expected somehow to be quiet and old-fashioned because of its age, proved to have skipped a couple of generations and now presented a unisex front of street smarts, blow-dries and rap music. Hairstyles in photographs on the walls looked like topiary. Chrome and multiple mirrors abounded. Young men in pigtails talked like Eastenders. I felt old there, and my children loved it.

Penelope herself cut their hair, consulting with me first about Christopher's instructions to have his head almost shaved, leaving only a bunch of his natural curls falling over his forehead. "Compromise," I begged her, "or his mother will slay me. It's she who normally gets their hair cut."

She smiled deliciously. I desired her so radically that the pain made a nonsense of falling-in roofs. She cut Christopher's hair short enough to please him, too short to my eyes. It was *his hair,* he said. Tell that to your mother, I told him.

Toby, interestingly, asked for his cut to be "ordinary": no statement of rebellion. Vaguely pleased, I watched Penelope fasten a gown round his throat and asked if her mother were anywhere about.

"Upstairs," she said, pointing. "Go up. She said she was expecting you." She smiled. Hop, skip and jump, heart. "I won't make your kids look like freaks," she promised. "They've got lovely-shaped heads."

I went upstairs reluctantly to find Perdita, and it was there, out of sight, that the old order persisted: the ladies with their hair in rollers, sitting under driers reading *Good Housekeeping.*

Perdita, vibrant in black trousers, a bright pink shirt and a long rope of pearls, led me past the grandmotherly customers who watched a large man with a walking stick go by as if he'd come from a different species.

"Never mind my old loves," Perdita teased me, beckoning me into a sheltered be-chintzed sanctum on the far side of the beautification. "Tanqueray do you?"

I agreed a little faintly that it would, and she pressed into my hand a large glass holding lavish gin and little tonic with tinkling ice and a thick slice of lemon. Eleven-fifteen on a Tuesday morning. Ah, well.

She closed the door between us and the old loves. "They have ears like bats for gossip," she said blithely. "What do you want to know?"

I said tentatively, "Forsyth . . . ?"

"Sit down, dear," she commanded, sinking into a rose-printed armchair and waving me into its pair.

She said, "I've thought all night about whether I should tell you these things. Well, half the night. Several hours. William always trusted me not to repeat what he told me, and I never have. But now . . . I don't really know if he would say I should be silent forever, but things are different now. Someone blew up his beloved racecourse, and you saved the race meeting yesterday and I think . . . I really do think that, like you said, you can't finish the job for him unless you know what you're up against, so, well, I don't think he'd mind." She drank some gin. "I'll tell you about Forsyth first, and then we'll see."

"All right," I said.

She sighed deeply and began, gathering ease and momentum gradually as she went along.

"Forsyth," she said, "set out to defraud an insurance company, and the family had to come up with the whole pay-off or visit him behind bars for God knows how many years."

"I thought," I said slowly, "it might be something like that."

"William said . . ." She paused, still a little inhibited; uncertain, despite her decision. "It seems odd to be telling you these things."

I nodded.

"I wouldn't say a word if he were alive, but I don't care so much for his family. I often told him he ought to let them suffer properly for their criminal actions, but he wouldn't hear of it. Keeping the Stratton name clean . . . a sort of obsession."

"Yes."

"Well," she took a deep breath, "about a year ago, Forsyth borrowed a fortune from the bank, guaranteed by Ivan—his father—on the security of the garden center, and he started buying and selling radio-controlled lawn mowers. Ivan's no great businessman, but at least he listens to his manager and goes to Conrad or William . . . used to go, poor lamb . . . for advice, and has proper audits . . . but that know-it-all Forsyth, he went his own way and wouldn't listen to anybody and he bought a huge warehouse on a mortgage and thousands of lawn mowers that were supposed to cut the grass while you sat and watched, but they were already going out-of-date when he signed a contract for them, and also they kept breaking down. The people who sold them to him must have been laughing themselves sick, William said. William said Forsyth talked about 'cornering the market,' which no one can ever do, William said, in anything. It's a short cut to bankruptcy. So there is Forsyth with this vast stock he has contracted to buy but can't sell, paying a huge mortgage he can't afford, with the bank bouncing his checks and Ivan facing having to cover this enormous bank loan . . . and you can guess what happened." She paid attention to her drink.

"A little fire?" I suggested, swirling the ice around in my own glass.

"*Little!* Half an acre of it. Warehouse, mowers, radio controls, all cinders. William said everyone took it for granted it was arson. The insurance company sent investigators. The police were all over the place. Forsyth went to pieces and confessed to William in private."

She paused, sighing.

"So, what happened?" I asked.

"Nothing."

"*Nothing?*"

"No. It's not a crime to set fire to your own property. William paid it all off. He didn't claim the insurance. He paid off the warehouse mortgage with penalties and sold the land it had stood on. Paid off all the contracts for the rotten mowers, to avoid lawsuits. Repaid the money the bank had lent, plus all the interest, to save Ivan losing the garden center to the guarantee. It all cost an *enormous* amount. William told all the family that they would each inherit a good deal less from him because of Forsyth's business venture and criminal folly. None of them would speak to Forsyth after that. He whined to William about it and William told him it was Coventry or jail, and to be grateful. Forsyth said Keith had told him to burn the warehouse. Keith said Forsyth was lying. But William told me it was probably true. He said Keith always said you could get rid of things by burning them."

Like fences at open ditches, I thought. And grandstands, by blowing them up?

"There!" she said, as if surprised at herself for the ease of the telling, "I've told you! I can't feel William standing at my shoulder telling me to shut up. In fact . . . it's the other way round. I think he *approves,* dear, wherever he is."

I wasn't going to question that feeling. I said, "At least Forsyth's was a straightforward fraud. No rapes or drugs involved."

"Yes, dear, *much* harder to cover those up."

Some nuance in her voice, a quiet amusement, made me ask, "But not impossible?"

"You're encouraging me to be wicked!"

Once started, however, she'd been enjoying the saga.

"I won't tell them," I said. "I'll be like you, with William's secrets."

I don't know if she believed me. I don't know that I meant what I said. It encouraged her, all the same, to go on.

"Well . . . there was Hannah . . ."

"What about her?" I prompted, when she paused.

"She grew up so bitter."

"Yes, I know."

"No self-esteem, you see, dear."

"No."

"Keith never let her forget she'd been abandoned by her mother. By Madeline, poor dear. Madeline used to cry and tell me she'd give anything for a miscarriage, but we were both young then and we didn't know how to get her an abortion . . . you had to *know* someone in those days as you'd never get a family doctor to help you. No one would ever help a young married woman get rid of her first child. Keith got to hear she'd been *asking* about it and he flew into a terrible rage and knocked two of her teeth out." She drank deeply of gin at the memory. "William told me that Keith told Hannah her mother had wanted to abort her. Can you believe it? Keith had always been cruel, but saying that to your own daughter! He wanted Hannah to hate Madeline, and she did. William said he tried for Madeline's sake to love Hannah and bring her up properly, but Keith was there, poisoning her mind, and she was never a sweet little girl, William said, but always sullen and spiteful."

"Poor Hannah."

"Anyway, she grew up very pretty in a sharp sort of way, but William said young men were put off when they got to know her and she felt more and more rejected and hated everybody, and then she fell for this gypsy and let him have sex with her." Perdita shrugged, sighing. "William said he wasn't even a proper Romany, just a rough wanderer with a police record for thieving. William said he couldn't understand Hannah, but it was low self-esteem, dear. Low self-esteem."

"Yes."

"Well, she got pregnant of course. And this gypsy, he knew a good thing when it was shoved under his nose. He turned up on Keith's doorstep demanding money, else he'd go round the village telling everyone how he'd got Keith's posh daughter in the family way, and Keith knocked him down and kicked him and burst one of his kidneys."

Hell, I thought, I'd been lucky.

"Keith told William. Those three boys always loaded their troubles onto their father. William paid off the gypsy, and it cost ten times as much as the gypsy had been asking from Keith in the first place."

"Dire," I said.

"So Jack was born, and he didn't have much chance either of growing up decent. Hannah dotes on him. William, of course, paid and paid for his up-bringing."

"William told you all this?"

"Oh yes, dear. Not all at once, like I told you. In little bits. Sort of squeezed out of him, over the years. He would come to me very tired of them all, and unburden some of his thoughts, and we'd have a little gin and—if he felt like it, well, *you know*, dear—and he'd say he felt better, and go off home . . ."

She sighed deeply for times past.

"Conrad," she said surprisingly, "years ago, he got addicted to heroin."

"Can't believe it!"

Perdita nodded. "When he was young. Kids nowadays, they know they face terrible dangers all the time from drugs. When Conrad was twenty, he thought it a great adventure, William said. He was at university. He was with another young man, both of them injecting themselves, and his friend had too much, and died. William said there was a terrible stink, but he got Conrad out and hushed it all up and sent him to a very private and expensive clinic for treat-ment. He got Conrad to write him a letter describing his drug experiences, what he felt and saw when he was high. William didn't show me what Con-rad wrote, but he still had the letter. He said Conrad had been cured, and he was proud of him. Conrad didn't go back to university, though. William kept him at home on the estate."

Ah, I thought, *that* was Marjorie's hammerlock. Even after so many years, Conrad wouldn't want his youthful indiscretion made public.

Perdita finished her gin and poured some more. "Freshen your glass?" she asked me.

"No, I'm fine. Do go on, I'm riveted."

She laughed, talking easily now. "When Keith was about that age, when he was young and handsome and before all these really bad things, he spanked the daughter of one of the farm workers. Pulled down her knickers and spanked her. She hadn't done anything wrong. He said he wanted to know what it felt like. William paid her father a fortune—for those days—to keep him from going to the police. It wasn't a case of rape, though."

"Bad enough."

"Keith learned his lesson, William said. After that he only beat and raped his wives. You couldn't get done for it, then."

The fun went out of her face abruptly, and no doubt out of mine.

"Sorry, dear," she said. "I loved Madeline, but it was all forty years ago. And she did get out, and marry again and have you. William said Keith never forgave her for despising him."

Perhaps because I couldn't help having it on my mind, I said, "Keith said yesterday that he's going to kill me. Forty years on, he's trying to get even."

She stared. "Did he mean it?"

"He meant it when he said it."

"But dear, you have to take him seriously. He's a violent man. What are you going to do about it?"

I saw that she was basically more interested than anxious, but then it wasn't her life-or-death problem.

"It's the sight of me that enrages him," I said. "I could simply go away. Go home. Trust to luck he wouldn't follow me."

"I must say, dear, you take it very calmly."

I'd spent my own semi-wakeful night thinking about it, but I answered her casually. "It's probably because it seems so unreal. I mean, it's not exactly routine to be discussing the possibility of one's own murder."

"I do see that," she agreed. "So . . . are you going?"

I couldn't answer her, because I still didn't know. I had the five children to consider, and for their sakes I thought I should avoid any further confrontations as much as possible. The manic quality of Keith's hatred for me had been all too evident in the ferocity of his kicks and he had now also the justification for an attack—in his eyes—because of my involvement in the uncovering of Harold Quest and the delivery of Quest's confession to Marjorie. I had thrown him at her feet: he would kill me for it. I did deep down believe he would try, and, although I didn't want to, I feared him.

I could probably ensure the boys a live father by leaving the arena.

I could . . . run away.

It was unrealistic, as I'd told Toby, to expect to be steadfast every day of the week. It would be *prudent* to go.

The trouble was that though I might long to, the part of me that ultimately decided things *couldn't* go.

"I wish," I said fervently, "that I were able to do as the Strattons do, and *blackmail* Keith into leaving me alone."

"What a thought, dear!"

"No chance, though."

She put her head on one side, looking at my face and thinking on my behalf.

"I don't know if it's of much help, dear," she said slowly, "but Conrad might have something like that."

"What sort of thing? What do you mean?"

"I never knew exactly what it was," she said, "but William did have a way of keeping Keith in order during the past few years. Only, for once he didn't tell me everything. I'd have said he was too *ashamed* of Keith, that time. He sort of winced away from his name, even. Then one day he said there were things he didn't want people to know, not even after he died, and he thought he would have to give the knowledge to Conrad, his *heir*, you see, dear, so that Conrad could use it if he had to. I'd never seen him so troubled as he was that day. I asked him about it the next time he came to see me, but he still didn't want to talk about it much. He just said he would give a sealed packet to Conrad with very strict instructions about when or if ever it should be opened, and he said he had always done the best he could for his family. The very best."

She stopped, overcome. "He was such a *dear*, you know."

"Yes."

The secrets were out. Perdita wept a few tears of fondness and felt clearly at peace. I stood up, kissed her cheek, and went downstairs to collect my newly shorn children.

They looked great. Penelope's pleased professionalism liquified my senses. The boys laughed with her, loving her easily, and I, who ached for her body, paid for their haircuts (despite her protestations) and thanked her, and took my sons painfully away.

"Can we go back there, Dad?" they asked.

I promised, "Yes, one day," and wondered "Why not?" and "Perhaps she would love me" and thought that the children liked her anyway, and fell into a hopeless jumble of self-justification, and was ready to dump my unsatisfactory marriage, that so recently, on the train, I had prayed to preserve.

The Gardners picked us up and took the clean clothes, the apples, the new sneakers and the haircuts back to the racecourse and ordinary life.

In the evening we telephoned Amanda. At eight o'clock, she sounded languorously sleepy.

I spent a long night unhappily, thinking both of my own obligations and desires, but also of Keith and whatever he might be plotting. I searched for ways to defeat him. I thought of fear and the need for courage, and felt unready and inadequate.

# 14

By Wednesday morning Henry had gone home in his last truck, leaving everything so far accomplished ready for next time, and promising future improvements.

On Tuesday the flags over the big top had been furled into storage bags by ropes and pulleys and winches. The lights and the fans were switched off. The caterers' side-tents were laced tight, giving no casual access. The fire extinguishers remained in place, scarlet sentinels, unused. Henry's man and some of the groundsmen had scrubbed the tramp of a few thousand feet off the flooring with brooms and hoses.

On Wednesday morning Roger and I walked down the center aisle, desultorily checking the big empty rooms to each side. No chairs, no tables; a few plastic crates. The only light was daylight from outside, filtering through canvas and the peach roofing, and changing from dull to bright and to dull again as slow clouds crossed the sun.

"Quiet, isn't it?" Roger said.

A flap of canvas somewhere rattled in the wind but all else was silent.

"Hard to believe," I agreed, "how it all looked on Monday."

"We had the final gate figures yesterday afternoon," Roger said. "The attendance was eleven percent up on last year. Eleven percent! And in spite of the stands being wrecked."

"Because of them," I said. "Because of the television coverage."

"Yes, I suppose so." He was cheerful. "Did you see the papers yesterday? 'Plucky Stratton Park.' Goo like that. Couldn't be better!"

"The Strattons," I said, "said they were holding a meeting this morning. Do you know where?"

"Not here, as far as I've heard. There's only the office," he said doubtfully, "and it's really too small. Surely they'll tell you where, if they're meeting."

"I wouldn't bet on it."

We walked slowly back towards the office, unusually idle; and Dart in his beaten-up car drove onto the tarmac.

"Hello," he said easily, climbing out, "am I the first?"

Roger explained about his lack of instructions.

Dart's eyebrows rose. "When Marjorie said meeting, I took it for granted she meant here."

The three of us continued towards the office, amicably.

Dart said, "The police gave me my wheels back, as you see, but it's a wonder I'm not in the slammer. A matter of time, I dare say. They've decided I blew up the stands."

Roger paused briefly in mid-stride, astounded. *"You?"*

"Like, my car came up positive for HIV, hashish, mad cow disease, dirty finger-nails, you name it. Their dogs and their test-tubes went mad. Alarm bells all over the place."

"Nitrates," I interpreted.

"You've got it. The stuff that blew up the stands came to the racecourse in my car. Eight to eight-thirty, Good Friday morning. That's what they say."

"They can't mean it," Roger protested.

"Yesterday afternoon they gave me a bloody rough time." For all his bright manner, it was clear he'd been shaken. "They hammered away at where did I get the stuff, this P.E.4 or whatever. My accomplices, they kept saying. Who were they? I just goggled at them. Made a weak joke or two. They said it was no laughing matter." He made a comic-rueful face. "They accused me of having been in the army cadet corps at school. Half a lifetime ago! I ask you! I said so what, it was no secret. I marched up and down for a year or two to please my grandfather, but a soldier by inclination I am definitely *not*. Sorry, Colonel."

Roger waved away the apology. We all went into the office, standing around, discussing things.

Dart went on. "They said I would have handled explosives in the cadets. Not me, I said. Let others play at silly buggers. All I really remembered vividly of the cadets is crawling all over a tank once and having nightmares afterwards about falling in front of it. The *speed* it could go! Anyway, I said, talk to Jack, he's in the cadets for the same reason as I was, and he's still at school and hates it, and why didn't they ask *him* where you could get boom boom bang bangs, and they practically clicked on the handcuffs."

I said, when he paused, "Do you usually lock your car? I mean, who else could drive it at eight-thirty on a Good Friday morning?"

"Don't you believe me?" he demanded, affronted.

"Yes, I do believe you. I positively do. But if you weren't driving it, who was?"

"There *can't* have been explosives in my car."

"You'll have to face that there were."

He said obstinately, "I don't know anything about it."

"Well . . . er . . . *do* you lock your car?"

"Not often, no. Not when I'm outside my own door. I told the police that. I said it was just sitting there and yes, probably I'd left the key in it. I said *any-one* could have taken it."

Roger and I both looked away from Dart, not wanting to be accusatory. "Outside his own door" wasn't exactly in plain view of the general car-stealing public. Outside his own door was beside the back entrance of the family pile, Stratton Hays.

"What if it were Keith that took your car?" I asked. "Would your family loyalty stretch to *him?*"

Dart was startled. "I don't know what you're talking about. I don't know who took my car."

"And you don't want to find out."

He grinned a shade uneasily. "What sort of pal are you, anyway?"

Roger said neutrally, "Keith swore to Lee only the day before yesterday that he would kill him. There's no doubt he meant it. You can't blame Lee for wanting to know if Keith blew up the stands."

Dart gave me a long look. I smiled with my eyes.

"I don't think it was Keith," Dart said finally.

"I search under my bus," I said to him. "I won't let my children get into it before I'm as sure as I can be that it's safe."

"*Lee!*" It was a word full of shock. "No, he *wouldn't*. Not even Keith. I swear to you . . ." He stopped dead. He had, anyway, told me what I wanted to know. A fragment of truth, even if not whole knowledge.

"From family feeling," I said, aiming at lightness, "would you consider helping me find a way of preventing Keith from carrying out his unpleasant threat? To save him and all of you, one might say, from the consequences?"

"Well, of course."

"Great."

"But I don't see what I can do."

"I'll tell you a bit later. At the moment, where is your meeting?"

"Holy hell, yes."

He picked up the office telephone and got through, it was evident, to his parents' home, where he talked to a cleaner who didn't know where either Lord or Lady Stratton could be found.

"Damn," Dart said, trying another number. "Ivan? Where's this bloody meeting? In *your* house? Who's there? Well—tell them I'm late." He put the receiver down and gave Roger and me the old carefree grin. "My parents are there, so are Rebecca and Hannah, Imogen and Jack, and they're waiting for Aunt Marjorie. I could hear Keith shouting already. Tell you the truth, I'm not keen to go."

"Don't then," I said.

"It's a three-line whip, Ivan says. The whole family. That means I have to."

Carpe diem, they say. Seize the day. Seize the moment. I'd been handed an opportunity I had been wondering how to achieve.

"How about," I said, "if you drive me to your parents' house, tell the cleaner I'm a friend of the family, and leave me there while you go to the meeting?"

He said, puzzled, "What ever for?"

"For luck," I said.

"Lee . . ."

"OK. For that look at the grandstand plans that I backed away from last time."

Roger made the beginnings of a gesture to remind me I'd already seen the plans, and then, to my relief, subsided.

Dart said with furrowed brow, "I don't honestly understand . . ."

As I didn't *want* him to understand I said confusingly, "It's for the sake of your family. Like I said, if you're not keen for Keith to bump me off, just trust me."

He trusted me more than anyone else in his family did, and his easygoing nature won the day.

"If that's what you want," he agreed, still not understanding—as how could he? "Do you mean *now?*"

"Absolutely. Except, do you mind going down the back road, as I'd better tell my boys I'll be off the racecourse for a while."

"You're extraordinary," Dart said.

"They feel safer if they know."

Dart looked at Roger, who nodded resignedly. "Christopher, the eldest, told me that when they're away from home, in that bus, they don't mind their father leaving them, as long as they know he's gone, and roughly when he'll be back. They look after themselves then without worrying. It does seem to work."

Dart rolled his eyes comically at the vagaries of my domestic arrangements but accompanied me out to his car. Lying on the front seat, when I went round there, was a large glossy magazine entitled *American Hair Club,* with a young well-thatched model-type man smiling broadly on the cover.

Dart, removing it to the door pocket beside him, said defensively, "It's all about bonding hair on with polymers. It does seem to be a good idea."

"Follow it up," I suggested.

"Don't laugh at me."

"I'm not."

He gave me a suspicious look, but drove me down amiably enough to report to my sons, who proved not to be in the bus, where I called to pick up a small tool or two, but to be elbow-deep in flour in Mrs. Gardner's kitchen, making her perfect pale fruitcake and eating most of it raw. She gave me a flashing smile and a kiss and said, "I'm having such *fun* here. Don't hurry back."

"Where do you find a wife who'll give you five sons?" Dart asked moodily, driving away. "Who the hell wants a pudgy going-bald thirty-year-old with no talents?"

"Who wants a good-natured easygoing nice guy not ridden by demons?"

"Me, do you mean?" He was surprised.

"Yes."

"No girls really want me."

"Have you asked any?"

"I've *slept* with some, but they all seem to have their sights on huge old Stratton Hays, and they tell me how great it would be for parties there, and one even talked about our daughter's coming-out *ball . . .*"

"And it frightens you?"

"They want to marry a *house.*"

"When I go home," I said, "you can come and stay, and I'll see you meet people who've never heard of Stratton Hays, and don't know about your father's title or your own millions, and you can be Bill Darlington, or whatever name you like, and see how you go."

"Are you *serious?*"

"Yes, I am." I thought for a moment and said, "What will happen in your family when Marjorie dies?"

"I don't think about it."

"You should be married by then. You'll be the head of the family one day, and the others should take that for granted, and respect you and your wife, and look ahead to a good well-rooted future."

"God," he protested, "you don't ask much!"

"You're the best of the Strattons," I said.

He swallowed; reddened; fell silent. He drove between the gateposts of his parents' ugly striped house and parked, and we walked round to the rear as before.

The back door was unlocked. We went past the plumbing and through into the black-and-white-floored hall, and Dart shouted out loudly, "Mrs. Chinchee? Mrs. Chinchee!"

A small middle-aged woman in a pink overall appeared at the top of a long flight of stairs saying, "Mr. Dart, I'm up here."

"Mrs. Chinchee," Dart called up to her, "this friend and I will be in the house for a while, but just carry on with the cleaning."

"Yes, sir. Thank you, sir."

Dart turned away and Mrs. Chinchee retreated towards her upstairs tasks, any awkward curiosity well neutralized.

"Right," Dart said. "Now what? I'm not going off to that meeting. You might need me here."

"OK," I said, vaguely relieved. "Now you go out to your car, and if either of your parents should come back sooner than we expect from the meeting, you put your palm on the horn and you give five or six urgent blasts to warn me."

"You mean . . . I'm just a lookout?"

"If your parents come back, blow the horn, then tell them you've lent me the phone, or the bathroom, or something."

"I don't like it," he frowned. "Suppose they find you looking at the plans?"

"You didn't mind before. You encouraged me, in fact."

He sighed. "Yes, I did. I didn't know you so well, then, or care . . . Look, don't be too long."

"No."

Still hesitantly he turned away and went back towards the rear door, and I went on into Conrad's private room where horse pictures crowded the walls and endless shiny bric-a-brac suggested a magpie disposition. Miniature silver horses, antique gold coins on a tray, a tiny gold hunting scene; every surface held treasures.

Without wasting time, I skirted the large cluttered desk and attended to the illegal act of picking someone else's lock, the keyhole fortunately living up to the promise of easy access. The small flat tool I'd brought with me slid obligingly past the ward that guarded the simple works and moved the tongue back from the socket. For picking simple locks, any flat filed-down narrow version of an ordinary key will do the job; the simpler, the better.

The paneled door, so like the walls, pushed easily open, revealing a cupboard large enough to walk into. Leaving the walking stick lying on the desk, I limped into the cupboard and pressed a light switch I found there, activating an overhead bulb in a simple shade.

Inside, the walls were lined throughout by shelves, on which stood endless boxes, all of different sizes, colors and shapes, and all unhelpfully unlabeled.

The drawings for the proposed new stands were in clear view, the large folder that Conrad and Wilson Yarrow had taken to Roger's office standing on the floor, leaning against one of the shelf-walls. Untying the pink tape bow that held the folder shut, I took out the drawings, laying them flat, outside, on Conrad's desk.

They were, I had to confess, a sort of window-dressing in case Dart came to find me, as the drawings were those I had already seen, without any additions.

The chief object of my risky enterprise had been to try to find the packet that Perdita had said William, Lord Stratton, third baron, had intended to entrust to Conrad, fourth baron; the packet containing enough dirt on Keith to keep him controlled. If I could but find it, I thought, I could use it perhaps to preserve my own life, promising for instance that if I should die violently, the packet's contents would become public knowledge inexorably.

Faced with the actual array of random containers, I had to rethink. Finding any particular packet in those could take hours, not minutes, particularly as I'd been given no clear description of what sort of packet I was looking for.

I took the lid off a box straight ahead. The box was the size of a large shoe box, made of stiff decorative cardboard in a mottled maroon color; the sort of box my mother had stored photographs in.

This box held no photographs and no mysterious packets, but only mementos of social events to do with the hunt of which Conrad was joint master; stiff gilt-edged invitations, menus, order of speeches. A longer box next to it held dozens of loose clippings from newspapers and magazines, all showing either future hunting programs or accounts of past sport.

Box after box contained the same sort of thing: Conrad was not so much secretive, as Dart had described him, as a compulsive collector of the minutiae of his life, far outdoing Carteret's diaries or my balance-sheet memories as a proof of existence.

I tried to think my way into Conrad's mind, to imagine just where he would have stowed the most sensitive knowledge: and balked at wondering if I should simply be searching his desk or the bookshelves. If the packet's existence had been enough to worry William Stratton into passing it on, Conrad wouldn't leave it anywhere where an unsuspecting person could open it accidentally. Given the hidden cupboard, for all that its lock was child's play, Conrad would use it.

I hurried along the rows, tipping open the lids, turning over reams of irrelevant papers, finding nothing worth the risk. It was in an ordinary shoe box that I finally came across a gem that I'd been hoping for, though not the ultimate jackpot.

I found myself looking at a black-and-white glossy photograph of Rebecca: not by any means a portrait, but a picture of her in ordinary clothes, not jockey's colors, holding out her hand and receiving a wad of what looked like banknotes from a man whose back was to the camera, but who wore a trilby hat with hair curling from beneath the brim and a jacket cut from a distinctive check cloth. The background, a shade out of focus, was nevertheless identifiable as a racecourse.

I turned the photograph over: no notes, no provenance, nothing.

In the same box, where the photograph had been lying, lay a recording tape. Apart from those two objects, the box was empty.

The tape, ordinary-looking, bore no information as to what it carried.

Even without believing in extra-sensory perception, I felt an unusual frisson over the juxtaposition of photograph and tape, and their sole occupancy of a box. I took them out and put them on Conrad's desk, meaning to look around for a tape recorder; but meanwhile I returned to the cupboard, still obstinately seeking a packet that was quite likely not there to be found.

Old out-of-date lists of hounds. Years-old estate accounts. Boxes packed with Dart's school reports. On the maxim thieves work by, that everyone hides valuable things at the *bottom* of drawers, and that the quickest way of finding profit is to empty the drawer out onto the floor, I began, not emptying exactly, but tipping up all the contents to look at the bottom-most in each box, and it was by doing that that I finally came across an ordinary brown envelope with the single word "Conrad" written on it.

I drew it out from under a pile of similar envelopes holding ancient insurance policies, long out of date. The "Conrad" envelope had been slit open. I looked inside without excitement, having by then concluded I'd been clutching at straws, that anything of critical importance would be somewhere else after all. Sighing, I drew out a single sheet of paper with a short note handwritten on it. It said:

*Conrad,*
*This is the envelope I told you of.*
*Take care with it.*
*Knowledge is dangerous.*

S.

I looked into the brown envelope further. Inside it lay another brown envelope, this one smaller and unopened, but fatter, with more sheets than one or two inside.

Either it was what I was looking for, or it wasn't. In either case, I was taking it with me, and so as to conceal my pilfering even from Dart, I hid the outer envelope, with letter and unopened envelope inside it, in my clothes: in, to be exact, my close-fitting underpants, against the skin of my abdomen.

Looking round to make sure that all the boxes were closed and appeared undisturbed, I went out to Conrad's desk to put the grandstand plans back in their folder, to prop them where they had been, to relock the cupboard door and beat an undiscovered retreat.

The photograph of Rebecca and the tape lay on top of the plans. Frowning, I unzipped my trousers again and put the photograph face down against my stomach, where the glossy surface stuck to me, the brown envelope outside it, both of them held snugly, too large and flat to slide out down my legs.

It was at that point that I heard voices out in the hall, near, coming nearer.

"But, Father," Dart's voice reached me loudly, desperately, "I want you to come and look at the fence along the five-acre covert—"

"Not now, Dart," Conrad's voice said. "And why were you not at the meeting?"

*Bloody hell,* I thought. I snatched up the tape and stuck it into my trousers pocket, and leaned over the set of grandstand plans as if they were the only interest in my life.

Conrad pushed open the door of the room, his until-then friendly expression becoming rapidly surprised and then thunderous, as anyone's would on seeing their most private heartland invaded.

Worse; behind him came Keith.

Conrad looked at his open cupboard with the light shining within, and at me by his desk. His bullish features darkened, his heavy eyebrows lowered, his mouth hardened implacably.

"Explain yourself!" he demanded, his voice harsh and scathing.

"I'm very sorry," I said awkwardly. I put the plans into the folder and closed it. "I can't excuse myself. I can only apologize. I do, very sincerely, apologize."

"It's not good enough!" His anger was deep and all the worse for being alien to his everyday nature, which was not quick to violence, like Keith's. "That cupboard was locked. I *always* lock it. How did you open it?"

I didn't answer him. The shaved key I'd used was still in the keyhole. I felt appallingly embarrassed, which no doubt he could see.

In an access of real rage he snatched up my walking stick, which lay on his desk, and raised it as if he would strike me.

"Oh no, Conrad," I said. "Don't."

He hesitated, his arm high. "Why not? Why bloody not? You deserve it."

"It's not your sort of thing."

"It's mine," Keith said loudly. He tugged the walking stick unceremoniously from his unprotesting twin and took a quick slash at my head.

I put an arm up in a reflex parrying action, caught the stick in my hand and, with more force then he'd envisaged, pulled it vigorously towards me. He held on long enough to overbalance, his weight coming forward, and he let go only in order to put both hands on the desk to steady himself.

All three of them, Conrad, Keith and Dart, looked stunned, but in truth that morning I'd felt some of my old strength returning like an incoming, welcome and familiar tide. They'd grown used to my weakness: had been unprepared for anything else.

I leaned on the stick, nevertheless; and Keith straightened himself, and in his eyes promised me death.

I said to Conrad, "I wanted to look at the plans."

"But why?"

"He's an architect," Dart said, defending me, though I wished he hadn't.

"A builder," contradicted his father.

"Both," I said briefly. "I'm very sorry. Very. I should have asked you to give me a sight of them, and not broken in here. I'm humbled . . . mortified . . ." And so I was, but not repentant nor truly ashamed.

Conrad interrupted my groveling, saying, "How did you know where the plans were?" He turned to Dart. "How did he know? He couldn't have found that cupboard by himself. It's practically invisible."

Dart, looking as uncomfortable as I felt, came round the desk and stopped a pace behind my left shoulder, almost as if sheltering from the parental ire brewing in Conrad.

"You told him where to look," Conrad accused his son indignantly. "You *showed* him."

Dart said weakly, "I didn't think it would matter. What's the big deal?"

Conrad gaped at him. "How can I explain if you can't see? But *you*," he turned to me, "I'd just begun to think we might trust you." He shrugged defeatedly. "Get out, both of you. You disgust me."

"No," Keith protested, "how do you know he's not stolen anything?" He looked round the room. "You have all these silver and gold pieces in here. He's a *thief*."

Damn bloody Keith, I thought, smothering panic. I'd stolen better than gold, and intended to keep what I'd taken. Stronger I might be, but couldn't yet swear to the outcome of a straightforward brawl, one against two. *Guile,* I told myself: all I had in the locker.

I raised my chin, until then tucked down in abashment. I looked as unworried as I could manage. I propped the walking stick against the desk, unzipped the front of the easy jacket which had spent several days earlier draped over the chair in Roger's office, slid my arms out of it and threw it to Conrad.

"Search it," I said.

He caught the bunched cloth. Keith seized the jacket and went through the pockets. No silver or gold. Nothing stolen.

I was wearing my loose wool checked shirt. I unbuttoned the cuffs and undid the front buttons, tugged off the shirt and threw it too to Conrad.

I stood bare to the waist. I smiled. I unzipped my fly and began to unbuckle my belt.

"Trousers next?" I asked Conrad lightly. "Shoes? Socks? Anything else?"

"No. No." He was confused. He made an upzipping gesture. "Put your shirt on again." He threw the shirt back to me. "You may be untrustworthy—I'm disappointed, I admit—but not a petty thief." He turned to Keith. "Let him go, Keith. Pick your fight somewhere else. Not in this room."

I put my shirt on and did up the buttons, but left the tails hanging down, like a coat.

Dart said abjectly, "Father, I'm sorry."

Conrad made a dismissive gesture. Dart edged round the desk, looking warily at Keith, who still held my jacket.

I followed Dart, limping slowly, the walking stick both a prop and a defense.

Conrad said mordantly, "I don't want to see you again, Mr. Morris."

I ducked my head, acknowledging fault.

Keith clung onto my jacket.

I was not going to ask for it back. Don't push your luck, I thought: the slightest quiver could erupt the volcano. I was glad simply to reach the door unmolested and to creep through into the hall, and scuttle across it ignominiously, as low in Conrad's esteem as a cockroach.

I held my breath until we were out of the house, but no angry yells stopped us. Dart scurried into his car, now flanked by Keith's Jaguar, and waited impatiently during my slower progress.

He let out an agonized "Whew" of relief as his engine fired and we sped to the road. "My God, he was angry."

"You're a bloody lousy lookout," I said bitterly. "Where was my warning?"

"Yes, well, look, *sorry.*"

"Were you asleep?"

"No . . . no . . . I was reading."

Comprehension arrived. "You were reading that damned magazine about hair loss!"

"Well . . . I . . ." He grinned, shamefacedly, admitting it.

There was nothing to be done about it. The toots on the horn would have given me time to transfer from Conrad's sanctum to the innocence of the bathroom near the rear entrance. Being caught with my hand in the till, so to speak, had not only been a rotten experience but might set Conrad checking the contents of the boxes. The consequences could be utterly disastrous.

"You took such a long time," Dart complained. "What kept you so long?"

"Just looking around."

"And it was *Keith's* car they came back in," Dart said, excusing himself. "I was on the lookout for Father's."

"Not much of a lookout."

"You looked terribly guilty," Dart said accusingly, shifting the blame.

"Yes, I felt it."

"But as for Keith thinking you'd steal . . ." He paused. "When you took your shirt off . . . I mean, I knew parts of the stands fell on you, but all those stitches and bruises . . . they must *hurt.*"

"Not any more," I sighed. I'd forgotten, in the urgency of the moment, that he'd been standing behind me. "It's the cuts on my legs that have made walking difficult, but they're all getting better."

"You gave Keith a shock, catching that walking stick."

I had made him more careful, I thought ruefully, which might not be a good thing, from my point of view.

"Where are we going?" Dart asked. He'd turned out of the gates in the direction of the racecourse, automatically. "Back to the Gardners'?"

I tried to think, to pull together a few scattered wits.

I asked, "Is Rebecca racing today, do you know?"

He answered as if bewildered, "No, I don't think so. She was at the meeting, of course."

"I need to talk to Marjorie," I said. "And to go to Stratton Hays."

"I don't follow you."

"No, but will you *take* me?"

He laughed. "I'm your chauffeur, now?"

"You're a better chauffeur than lookout."

"Thanks very much."

"Or lend me your car," I suggested.

"No," he said. "I'll drive you. Life's never boring, with you around."

"The Gardners' first, then."

"Yes, *sir.*"

In the Gardners' kitchen Mrs. Gardner greeted my return with friendly dismay, saying I'd lent her the five cooks for less than an hour, not long enough. I offered their services for another few hours. Accepted, she said.

"Tell me if I'm leaving them with you too much," I begged her.

"Don't be silly. I love it. And besides, Roger says that but for you he'd be half-way out of his job and we'd be sick with worry."

"Does he think so?"

"He knows it."

Grateful and partially comforted, I left Dart in the kitchen and went over to the bus, and there in the privacy of the cab fed the tape I'd stolen into the tape-playing slot of the radio.

It proved to be a recording of a telephone call made on a cellular phone: the sort of spying that was diabolically easy if one listened on a scanner close to the transmitting and receiving cell.

I'd always had misgivings about the randomness of overheard conversations that had come to public light: what sort of person listened in to other people's privacy day in and day out *and taped it all,* hoping to overhear marketable secrets? Someone apparently had, in this case.

The conversation was between a voice provisionally identifiable as Rebecca's and a man speaking in a south-east accent, not cockney, but all glottal stops where d's, t's or c's occurred in the center of words. Stratton came out as "Stra-on." Rebecca as "Rebe-ah."

"Rebe-ah Stra-on?" said the man's voice.

"Yes."

"What have you got for me, darlin'?"

"How much is it worth?"

"Same as usual."

After a short pause, speaking quietly, she said, "I'm riding Soapstone in the fifth, it's got no chance, it's only half fit. Lay off all you can on Catch-as-Catch, it's jumping out of its skin and they're putting a bundle on it."

"That's the lot?"

"Yes."

"Thanks, darlin'."

"I'll see you at the races."

"Same place," the man agreed. "Before the first."

The tape clicked and fell silent. I ejected it grimly and returned it to my pocket, and, climbing back into the body of the bus, unzipped my trousers and retrieved the glossy photograph and also the packet of dangerous knowledge.

From that I took out the interior, fatter brown envelope and slit it open with a knife. Inside were yet another envelope, white this time, and another short letter from William Stratton, third baron, to his son Conrad, fourth.

It read:

Conrad,

This grieves me beyond measure. Remember always that Keith, to my despair, tells lies. I sought out knowledge, and now I don't know how to use it. You must decide. But take care.

S.

Apprehensively, I slit open the white envelope and read its lengthier contents and by the end found my hands trembling.

My non-grandfather had shown me a way, once and for all, of dealing with Keith.

I reassembled the packet in its original order and, finding some sticky-tape, sealed the outside brown envelope so that no one could open it by chance. Then I sat for a while with my head in my hands, realizing that if Keith knew what I'd got he would kill me immediately, and also that saving myself from him posed a dilemma I'd never imagined.

Dangerous knowledge. Not dangerous: deadly.

# 15

Dart drove me to Stratton Hays. On the way, using my own mobile phone (anyone listening?), I got through to Marjorie's house and found her at home, forthrightly displeased.

"You didn't come to the meeting!"

"No. Very sorry."

"It was a shambles," she said crossly. "Waste of time. Keith shouted continually and nothing got done. He couldn't ignore the gate receipts, which were *excellent,* but he's fanatical about selling. Are you *sure* you cannot uncover his debts?"

"Does Imogen know them?" I asked.

*"Imogen?"*

"If I got her paralytically drunk, would she know anything at all of her husband's affairs?"

"You're disgraceful!"

"I'm afraid so."

"I wish she did. But don't try it, because if Keith caught you at it . . ." She paused, then said without pressure, "Do you take his threats seriously?"

"I have to."

"Have you thought of . . . retreat?"

"Yes, I have. Are you busy? I need to tell you a few things."

She said if I gave her an hour I could come to her house, to which I agreed. Dart and I continued to Stratton Hays, where he parked in the same place as on my first visit and as usual left the key in the ignition.

The great graceful pile, full of forgotten lives and quiet ghosts, stood peacefully in the mottled sunlight, a house built for hundreds, lived in by one.

"What now?" the one said; Darlington Stratton, fifth baron to be.

"We've got almost an hour. Can we look at the north wing?"

"But it's a ruin. I told you."

"Ruins are my business."

"I forgot. Well, OK." He unlocked the rear door and took me again across the vast unfurnished, uncurtained front hall and along a wide windowed passage proportioned like a picture gallery, but with bare walls.

At the end of it we came to a heavy door, unpaneled, unpolished and modern, fastened by bolts. Dart wrestled with the bolts and creaked open the door, and we walked into the sort of desolation I went looking for: rotting wood, heaps of debris, saplings growing.

"They took the roof off sixty or more years ago," Dart said glumly, looking upwards to the sky. "All those years of rain and snow . . . the upper floor just rotted and fell in. Grandfather asked the National Trust and the Heritage people . . . I think they said the only thing to do was to demolish this wing and save the rest." He sighed. "Grandfather didn't like change. He just let time run on and nothing got done."

I clambered with difficulty over a hillock of weathered gray beams and looked along a wide storm-struck landscape flanked by high, still-standing but unbuttressed stone walls.

"Do be careful," Dart warned. "No one's supposed to come in here without hard hats."

The space gave me no creative excitement, no desire to restore it. All it did give me, in its majestic proportions, and its undignified death, was an interval of respite, of nerve-calming patience, a deep breathtaking perception of life passing, a drawing-in of the faith and industry that had designed and built here four hundred years earlier.

"OK." I said, stirring and rejoining Dart in the open doorway. "Thanks."

"What do you think?"

"Your grandfather was given good advice."

"I was afraid so."

He rebolted the heavy door and we returned across the great hall to the rear entrance.

"Can I borrow your bathroom?" I asked.

"Sure."

He continued on past the door, heading towards his own personal quarters, the ground floor of the south wing.

Here, present life went on very comfortably with carpets, curtains, antique furniture and a fresh polished smell. He led me to the door of his bathroom, a mixture of ancient and modern, a room converted from perhaps a sitting room, with a large free-standing Victorian bath and two new-looking wash-basins built into a marble-topped fitment. The surface of the fitment was covered with bottles of shampoo and conditioner, and every variety of snake oil.

Sympathetically I went over to the window, which was curtained in lace, and looked out. Away to the left, Dart's car stood in the driveway. Ahead, lawns and trees. To the right, open gardens.

"What is it?" he said, as I stood there. After a moment, when I didn't move, he came over to stand beside me, to see what I was looking at.

He came, and he saw. He switched his gaze to my face, searching, and without trouble read my thoughts.

"*Shit*," he said.

An appropriate word for a bathroom. I said nothing, however, but walked back the way we had come.

"How did you know?" Dart asked, following.

"Guessed."

"So what now?"

"Go to Marjorie's house."

"I mean . . . what about *me?*"

"Oh, nothing," I said. "It's not up to me."

"But . . ."

"You were in the bathroom seeing to your hair," I said. "And through the window you saw who took your car on Good Friday morning. No one's going to put you to the torture to find out who it was. Just pretend you saw nothing, as you've been doing so far."

"Do you know . . . who?"

I half smiled. "Let's go and see Marjorie."

"*Lee.*"

"Come and listen."

Dart drove us to Marjorie's house, which proved to be unadulterated early Georgian, as well-bred and trim as she was herself. Set four-square in weed-less grounds at one end of Stratton village, it had sash windows in disciplined rows, a central front door and a circular driveway that reached past gateposts with urns on them.

Dart parked near the front door and as usual left the key in the ignition.

"Don't you *ever* lock it?" I asked.

"Why bother? I wouldn't mind an excuse to get a new car."

"Why not just buy one?"

"One day," he said.

"Like your grandfather."

"What? Oh, yes. I suppose I'm like him, a bit. One day. Maybe."

Marjorie's front door was opened to us by a manservant ("She lives in the past," murmured Dart), who pleasantly guided us across a hall to her drawing room. As expected, faultless taste there in time-stands-still land, gentle colors overall in dim pinks, green and gold. The window embrasures still held the original shutters, but there were floor-length curtains as well, and swagged valances, and a view of sunlit spring gardens beyond.

Marjorie sat in a wide armchair that commanded the room, very much and always the person in charge. She wore, as often, dark blue with white at the neck, looking doll-like and exquisite and temporarily hiding the tough cookie.

"Sit down," she commanded, and Dart and I sat near her, I on a small sofa, Dart on a spindly chair—Hepplewhite, probably.

"Things to tell me," she began. "That's what you said, Lee."

"Mm," I said. "Well, you asked me to find out two things."

"And on the subject of Keith's finances, you've failed." She nodded decisively. "You've already told me."

"Yes. But . . . as regards your other assignment . . ."

"Go *on*," she said, as I stopped. "I remember exactly. I asked you to find out what pressure that wretched architect was putting on Conrad to get his new stands built."

Dart looked surprised. *"Assignment?"* he asked.

"Yes, yes." His great-aunt was impatient. "Lee and I had an agreement. We shook hands on it. Didn't we?" She turned her head to me. "An agreement you did not want to break."

"That's right," I said.

"Aunt Marjorie!" Dart looked flummoxed. "You've had Lee working for *you?*"

"And what's wrong with that? It was for the ultimate good of the family. How can we proceed, if we don't know the facts?"

The world's politicians could learn from her, I thought with admiration. The clearest of brains under the waved white hair.

"Along the way," I said, "I learned about Forsyth and the lawn mowers."

Dart gasped. Marjorie's eyes widened.

"Also," I went on, "I heard about Hannah's bit of rough trade, and its results."

"What are you talking about?" Dart asked me, lost.

Marjorie enlightened him. "Hannah went off into the bushes with a gypsy and got herself pregnant, the silly ninny. Keith assaulted the gypsy, who demanded money, of course. My brother paid him off."

"Do you mean . . ." Dart worked it out, "that Jack's father was a *gypsy?*"

"Near enough. Not even a Romany. A good-for-nothing tramp," Marjorie said.

"Oh, my God," Dart said, weakly.

"And don't speak of it again," Marjorie commanded severely. "Hannah tells Jack his father was a foreign aristocrat who would have been ruined by the scandal."

"Yes." Dart's voice sounded faint. "Jack told me that himself."

"And let him believe it. I hope, Lee," she said to me, "that that's all."

The telephone rang on the small table beside her chair. She picked up the receiver and listened.

"Yes . . . when? Dart is here. So is Lee. Yes." She put the receiver down and said to Dart, "That was your father. He says he is coming here. He sounds incredibly angry. What have you done?"

"Is Keith with him?" My words came out with a jerk, which she pounced on.

"You're afraid of Keith!"

"Not unreasonably."

"Conrad said Keith told him to come here but didn't say if Keith were with him. Do you wish to leave now, at once?"

Yes, I did, and no, I didn't. I thought of murder in her quiet drawing room and hoped she wouldn't allow it.

I said, "I brought a photograph to show you. It's in Dart's car. I'll just fetch it."

I stood up and walked to the door.

"Don't drive off and leave me here," Dart said, only half joking.

The temptation bit deep, but where would I go? I picked the photograph, in an envelope, out of the door pocket, where I'd placed it, and returned to the drawing room.

Marjorie took out the photograph and looked at it uncomprehendingly. "What does it mean?"

"I'll explain," I said, "but if Conrad's coming, I'll wait until he gets here."

The distance from Conrad's house to Marjorie's was short. He came very soon, and, to my relief, without Keith. He came armed, though, carrying a shotgun, the landowner's friend. He carried it not broken open, over his arm, as one should, but straightened, and ready.

He brushed past the manservant, who had opened the door for him and was saying, "Lord Stratton, madam," punctiliously, and strode across Marjorie's pale Chinese carpet, coming to a halt in front of me with the twin barrels pointing my way.

I rose to my feet. Barely three paces lay between us.

He held the gun not as if aiming at flying birds but down at his waist, easily familiar with shots from the hip. At that distance he couldn't miss a mosquito.

"You're a liar and a thief." He was growling with fury, his fingers frighteningly unsteady in the region of the trigger.

I didn't deny the charge. I looked past him and his gun to the photograph Marjorie held, and he followed my gaze. He recognized the picture, and the look he gave me was as murderous as any of Keith's. The barrels aimed straight at my chest.

"Conrad," Marjorie said sharply, "calm down."

"Calm down? *Calm down!* This *despicable* person broke into my private cupboard and stole from me."

"However, you may *not* shoot him in my house."

In a way it was funny, but farce was too close to tragedy always. Even Dart didn't laugh.

I said to Conrad, "I'll free you from blackmail."

*"What?"*

"What are you talking about?" Marjorie demanded.

"I'm talking about Wilson Yarrow blackmailing Conrad into giving him the go-ahead for the new grandstand."

Marjorie exclaimed, "So you did find out!"

"Is that gun loaded?" I asked Conrad.

"Yes, of course."

"Would you mind . . . uh . . . pointing it somewhere else?"

He stood four-square, bullish, unwavering: unmoving.

"Father," Dart protested.

"You shut up," his father said grittily. "You abetted him."

I said, risking things, "Wilson Yarrow told you that if he didn't get the commission for the stands, he would see that Rebecca was warned off as a jockey."

Dart goggled. Marjorie said, "That's ridiculous."

"No. Not ridiculous. That photograph is a picture of Rebecca receiving a wad of money on a racecourse from a man who might be a bookmaker."

I tried to work saliva into my mouth. I'd never before had a loaded gun pointed at me in anger. Even though I clung to the belief that Conrad's inner restraints existed where Keith's didn't, I could feel my scalp sweating.

"I listened to the tape," I said.

"You *stole* it."

"Yes," I agreed. "I stole it. It's damning."

"So now it's *you* who'll blackmail me." His trigger hand tightened.

"Oh for Christ's sake, Conrad," I said, almost exasperated. "Use some sense. I'll not blackmail you. I'll see that Yarrow doesn't."

*"How?"*

"If you'll put that bloody gun down, I'll tell you."

"What tape?" Dart asked.

"The tape you helped him steal from my cupboard."

Dart looked blank.

"Dart didn't know," I said. "He was outside in his car."

"But Keith searched your jacket," Dart protested.

I put my hand into my trousers pocket and brought out the tape. Conrad flicked a glance at it and went on scaring me silly.

"This tape," I told Marjorie, "is a recording of a telephone call of Rebecca selling information about the horses she would be riding. It's the worst of racing crimes. Sending it and that photograph to the racing authorities would end her career. She'd be warned off. The Stratton name would be mud."

"But she *wouldn't* do that," Dart wailed.

Conrad said, as if the words hurt his tongue, "She admitted it."

"No!" Dart moaned.

"I challenged her," Conrad said. "I played her the tape. She can be so hard. She listened like stone. She said I wouldn't let Yarrow use it." Conrad swallowed. "And . . . she was right."

"Put the gun down," I said.

He didn't.

I threw the tape to Dart, who fumbled it, dropped it and picked it up again.

"Give it to Marjorie," I said and, blinking, he obeyed.

"If you'll unload the gun and put it against the wall," I said to Conrad, "I'll tell you how to get rid of Yarrow, but I'm not doing it with your hand on the trigger."

"Conrad," Marjorie said crisply, "you're not going to shoot him. So put the gun down in case you do it by accident."

Blessed bodyguard. Conrad woke to realities as if in a cold shower, looking down indecisively at his hands. He undoubtedly would have laid down his firepower were it not that Rebecca, at that moment, swept in like a whirlwind, having outrun the manservant altogether.

"What's going on here?" she demanded. "I've a right to know!"

Marjorie stared at her with her customary disfavor. "Considering what you've done, you've no right to *anything.*"

Rebecca looked at the photograph of herself and the tape in Marjorie's hand, and at the shotgun in her father's, and at me, threatened.

"Keith told me that this . . . this . . ." she pointed at me, not finding words bad enough, "stole enough to get me warned off . . ."

I said fiercely to Conrad, "That tape is a *fake.*"

The effect on Rebecca was an increase in fury. While the rest of the family tried to understand what I'd said, she snatched the gun from her father, swung it round at shoulder height, took a quick aim at me and without pause pulled the trigger.

I saw the intention in her eyes and flung myself sideways full length onto the carpet, rolling onto my stomach, missing the ball of fizzing pellets by fractions, conscious of *two* barrels, two cartridges, and no way of escaping a shot in the back.

The room had filled with a thunderous cracking noise, with flame and smoke, with the acrid smell of cordite at close quarters. *Jesus,* I thought. God almighty. Not Keith, but Rebecca.

The second shot didn't come. I cringed on the floor—no other word for it. There was the smell, the ringing echo, and beyond that . . . silence.

I stirred, turned my head, saw her shoes, crawled my gaze upwards as far as her hands.

She was *not* pointing the second of the barrel holes at me.

Her hands were empty.

Eyes slowly right . . . Conrad himself held his gun.

Dart came down on his knees by my head, saying, "Lee," helplessly.

I said thickly, "She missed me."

"God, Lee."

I felt breathless, but I couldn't stay there forever. I rolled into a sitting position; felt too shaken to stand.

The shot had shocked them all, even Rebecca.

Marjorie, straight-backed, looked over-white, her mouth open, fixed, animation suspended. Conrad's eyes stared darkly at a bloody mess too narrowly averted. I couldn't . . . yet . . . look straight at Rebecca.

"She didn't mean to," Conrad said.

But she had indeed meant it; an act beyond caution.

I coughed once, convulsively. I said again, "The tape is a fake." And this time, no one tried to kill me for it.

Conrad said, "I don't understand."

I breathed deeply, slowly, trying to steady the racket of my pulse.

"She *couldn't* have done it," I said. "Wouldn't have. She wouldn't put in jeopardy the . . . the *citadel* of her most inner self."

Conrad said, in perplexity, "I don't really follow."

I looked at last at Rebecca. She stared back, her face hard and expressionless.

"I saw you race," I said. "You exult in it. And the other day, I listened to you say you would be in the top five this year on the jockeys' list. You were passionate about it. You're a Stratton, you're infinitely proud, and you're rich and don't need the money. There's no way you're ever going to sell sleazy information that could bring you unbearable disgrace."

Rebecca's eyes slitted narrowly under lowered eyelids, her face rigid.

"But she confirmed it was true!" Conrad said again.

I said regretfully, "She made the tape herself to put pressure on you to get new stands built, and she tried to shoot me to stop me telling you."

"Rebecca!" Conrad couldn't believe it. "This man's lying. Tell me he's lying."

Rebecca said nothing.

"You've been showing all the signs of intolerable strain," I said to her. "I would think it seemed a good idea to you to begin with, to let your father believe he was being blackmailed to save you from being warned off, but once you'd done it, and he had in fact allowed himself to be blackmailed, I'd guess you regretted it sorely. But you didn't confess *that* to him. You went straight on with your obsessive and drastic plan to modernize Stratton Park radically, and it's been tearing you apart for weeks and making you . . . lose balance."

"The hangers!" Dart said.

"But *why*, Rebecca?" Conrad begged, intensely disturbed. "I'd have done anything for you . . ."

"You might not have agreed," I said, "to build new stands at all, let alone have Wilson Yarrow design them. And it was he, wasn't it, who came to you and said, 'I have the dirt on your daughter, and all you have to do to save her honor is give me this commission'?"

Conrad didn't answer directly, but he broke open his shotgun and with unsteady fingers pulled out both cartridges, the spent one, blackened and empty, and the unfired one, orange and bright. He put them both in his pocket and stood the gun by the wall.

As he did so there was a quiet tap on the door. Conrad went to open it and found Marjorie's manservant there, worried. "Nothing wrong," Conrad assured him fruitily. "Gun went off by accident. Bit of a nuisance to clear up, I'm afraid. We'll see to it later."

"Yes, my lord."

The door closed. I noticed for the first time that the spreading shot had smashed a mirror on the wall and torn pieces of gold silk upholstery from chairs. Much too damned close.

I reached for the walking stick I'd laid beside the small sofa where I'd been sitting and, with its help, returned to my feet.

"You must have said something to Keith about blackmail," I told Conrad. "He used that word in connection with Yarrow. You all heard him."

Conrad made a helpless gesture. "Keith went on and on at me to abandon the idea of new stands and I said I *couldn't.*" He paused. "But *how* did you find all this out?"

"A lot of small things," I said. "For example, I went to the same school of architecture as Wilson Yarrow."

*"Architecture!"* Marjorie interrupted.

"Yes. When I saw him . . . heard his name . . . I knew there was something wrong about him. I only vaguely remembered, so I looked up a man I was at architectural school with, that I hadn't heard from for ten years, and asked him. He kept a diary all those years ago and he'd written down a rumor he'd heard, that Wilson Yarrow had won a prestigious prize with an architectural design he'd sent in, while knowing that it wasn't his own. The college took the prize away and hushed it all up a bit, but the stigma of cheating remained, and there must be several hundred architects, like me, who associate that name of Yarrow with something not right. The word goes around in professional circles, and memories are long—and better than mine—and the brilliant career once expected of Yarrow has not come to pass. There was his name alone on the plans he drew for you, which means he's probably not employed in a firm. He may very well be unemployed altogether, and there's a glut of architects now, with the schools every year training more than the market can absorb. I'd guess he saw the prestige of building new stands at Stratton Park as a way back into esteem. I think he was *desperate* to get that commission."

They listened, even Rebecca, as if spellbound.

I said, "Before I ever came to Stratton Park, Roger Gardner told me there was an architect designing new stands who knew nothing about racing and didn't understand crowd behavior, and that as he wouldn't listen to advice he would be the death of the racecourse, but that you, Conrad, wouldn't be deflected from him."

I paused. No one said anything.

"So," I went on, "I came to your shareholders' meeting last Wednesday, and met you all, and listened. I learned what you all wanted for the racecourse. Marjorie wanted things to remain as they were. You, Conrad, wanted new stands, actually to save Rebecca from ruin, though I didn't know that then. Keith wanted to sell, for the money. Rebecca, of course, wanted a clean sweep, as she said; new stands, new manager, new Clerk of the Course, a new image for old-fashioned Stratton Park. Marjorie managed that meeting in a way that would have had superpowers kneeling in admiration, and she manipulated you all so that she got *her* way, which was for Stratton Park to continue in its old manner for the foreseeable future."

Dart cast an admiring glance at his great-aunt, the grin very nearly appearing.

I said, "That was not good enough for Rebecca, nor for Keith. Keith had already enlisted the actor, Harold Quest, to make a nuisance of himself demonstrating against steeplechasing outside the main gates, so that people would be put off going to the races at Stratton Park and the course would lose its attraction and its income, and go bankrupt as a business so that you would have to sell its big asset, the land. He also got Harold Quest to burn a fence— the open ditch; symbolically the open ditch, as it was there that a horse had been killed at the last meeting—but that ploy was a dud, as you know. Keith isn't bright. But Rebecca . . ."

I hesitated. There were things that had to be said: I wished there were someone else . . . anyone else . . . to say them.

"In the Stratton family, as it is now," I resumed, approaching things sideways, "there are two good-natured harmless fellows, Ivan and Dart. There's one very clever person, Marjorie. There's Conrad, more powerful in appearance than fact. There's a strain of ruthlessness and violence in everyone else of Stratton blood, which has cost you all fortunes. When you ally those traits with stupidity and arrogance, you get Forsyth and his mowers. There is in many of the Strattons, as in him, a belief that you'll never be found out, and if you should be, you believe the family will use its money and muscle to save you, as it always has done in the past."

"And will again," Marjorie said firmly.

"And will again," I acknowledged, "if you can. You'll need all your skills soon, though, in damage control."

Surprisingly, they went on listening, not trying to make me stop.

I said carefully, "In Rebecca, that violence is chiefly controlled and comes out as a consuming competitiveness in a testing sport. In her, there's splendid courage and will-to-win. There's also a tremendous overpowering urge to get her own way. When Marjorie blocked her first plan for achieving new stands, she hit on a simple solution—get rid of the old ones."

This time, Conrad protested incredulously, and Marjorie also, but not Rebecca nor Dart.

"I'd guess," I said to Rebecca, "that you told Wilson Yarrow to do it, as, if he didn't, he could kiss the commission goodbye."

She glared at me unblinkingly, a tigress untamed.

I said, "Wilson Yarrow was in deep already with that blackmailing attempt. He saw, as you did, that destroying a part of the main grandstand would mean new ones had to be built. He knew those old grandstands and, as an architect, he saw how maximum damage could be achieved for minimum effort. The staircase in the center was the main artery of the building. Collapse that core, and the rooms round it would cave in."

"I had nothing to do with it," Rebecca yelled suddenly.

Conrad jumped. Conrad . . . aghast.

"I saw those charges before they exploded," I said to Rebecca. "I saw how they were laid. Very professional. I could have done it myself. And I know other dealers, not as responsible as my giant friend Henry, who'll sell you anything, few questions asked. But it's difficult, even for people whose whole job is demolition, to get right the amount of explosive needed. Every structure has its own strengths and weaknesses. There's pressure to use too much rather than too little. The amount Yarrow used tore half the building apart."

"No," Rebecca said.

"Yes," I contradicted her. "Between you, you decided it should be done early on Good Friday morning, when there would be no one about."

"No."

"Wilson Yarrow drilled the holes and set the charges, with you acting as lookout."

"No!"

"He couldn't do it without a lookout. If you go in for crime, it's much best to post a lookout you can trust."

Dart squirmed. Then he grinned. Irrepressible.

"You sat on watch in Dart's car," I said.

Rebecca's eyes opened wide, abruptly. The "no" she produced lacked the fire of the other denials.

"You thought," I said, "that if you went in your own bright scarlet Ferrari, and any stray groundsman, perhaps, saw it on the racecourse on that non-racing day, he would remember it and report it after the stands had exploded. So you drove to Stratton Hays, and parked your car there, and took Dart's, which always has the keys left in, and you drove that car into the racecourse, because Dart's car is so familiar there as to be practically invisible. But you didn't reckon with Harold Quest, actor and busybody, who wouldn't have been at the gates there anyway on that day if he'd been a genuine protester, and you must have been shattered when he said Dart's car had been there, and described it to the police. But not as shattered as you would have been if Harold Quest had reported your Ferrari."

"I don't believe all this," Conrad said faintly; but he did.

"I imagine," I said to Rebecca, "that somewhere you picked up Yarrow and took him and the explosive to the racecourse, because the police tested the car and found traces of nitrates."

Rebecca said nothing.

I said, "Dart has known all along that it was you—or you and Yarrow—who blew up the stands."

"Dart told you!" Rebecca shouted, furiously turning to Dart, who looked staggered and hurt. "You gave me away to this . . . this . . ."

"No, he didn't," I said fiercely. "Dart was unswervingly loyal to you. He went through a considerable grilling from the police yesterday and didn't say a word. They accused him of setting the explosives himself, and he's still their chief suspect, and they'll question him again. But he won't tell them about you. He's proud of you, he has mixed feelings, he thinks you're crack-brained, but he's a Stratton and he won't give you away."

"How do you *know?*" Dart wailed, agonized.

"I stood next to you when she won on Tempestexi."

"But . . . you couldn't tell from *that.*"

"I've lived and breathed Strattons for a week."

*"How* did you know?" Rebecca demanded of her brother.

"I saw your Ferrari from my bathroom, parked where my old car was supposed to be."

She said helplessly, "It was there for less than an hour."

Conrad's shoulders sagged.

"I was back in Lambourn long before the explosion," Rebecca said crossly. "And Yarrow was putting himself about in London by then."

"I want to know," Marjorie said to me, after a silence, "what made you first suspect Rebecca?"

"Such small things."

"Tell them."

"Well," I said, "she fanatically wanted things changed."

"And?" Marjorie prompted, when I stopped.

"She mentioned new stands made of glass. There are stands in Britain with glassed-in sections, aren't there, but not sheeted altogether in glass, as Yarrow's plans are, and I wondered if she had *seen* the plans, which Conrad had locked away so secretively. And then . . ."

"Then what?"

"Rebecca said she was the only one in the family who knew a rabbet from a raceway."

They all, except Rebecca, looked uncomprehending.

"I don't follow," Marjorie said.

"It's not a racing term," I explained. "It meant nothing to Roger Gardner."

"Nor to me," Conrad interposed, "and I've owned and ridden horses all my life."

"It's clear to an architect," I said, "and to a builder, to a carpenter, to an engineer. Not, I wouldn't have expected, to a jockey. So I wondered, but not very conclusively at that point, if she'd been talking a good deal to an architect, and if that architect might not be Yarrow. Just a vague passing speculation, but that sort of thing sticks in your brain."

"So what *are* a rabbit and a raceway?" Dart asked.

"A rabbet, with an 'e,' is a tongue and groove joint, mostly in wood, to enable you to slot boards, say, together, as in a fence, or floorboards, without using nails. Like the floor in the big top, in fact."

Marjorie looked bewildered, Conrad not.

"And a raceway?" she asked. "Not a racecourse?"

"I suppose it could be. But otherwise it's either a sort of gully for draining fast-flowing fluids, or it could be a sort of collar that houses ball bearings. In either case, it's not common racecourse parlance."

"A rabbet from a raceway," Dart said thoughtfully. "Wasn't your youngest son chanting that?"

"Quite likely."

"I should have killed you when I had the chance," Rebecca said to me bitterly.

"I thought you were going to," I agreed.

"She was aiming straight at you," Dart said. "Father snatched the gun away from her. If you ask him, he'll probably say that shooting you once in the chest might have been passed off as an accident, but putting a second shot into your back couldn't be anything but murder."

"Dart!" Marjorie remonstrated severely; but there was no doubt he'd got it right. Dart was one of them. He knew.

Conrad had a question for his daughter. "Where did you meet Yarrow in the first place? How did you get to know him?"

She shrugged. "At a party. He was doing stupid imitations in the accent you heard on the tape. Rebe-ah Stra-on, darlin'. Someone told me he was an exceptionally good architect, but flat broke. I wanted new stands. He wanted a job badly and he wasn't fussy how he got it. We did a deal."

"But you don't usually like men."

"I didn't like him," she said brutally. "I *used* him. I despise him, as a matter of fact. He's in a blue funk now, predictably."

"So . . . what next?" Conrad asked me wretchedly. "The police?"

I looked at Marjorie. "You," I said, "are the one who pulls the levers in the family. You've ruled them all for forty years. You ruled even your own brother, in the gentlest of ways."

"How?" Dart said, avid.

Marjorie beseeched me with wide-open eyes, but it was for Perdita Faulds's sake that I said to Dart, "Your grandfather's secret was his alone, and died with him. I can't tell you it."

"Won't," Dart said.

"Won't," I agreed. "Anyway, to go to the police or not must be Marjorie's decision, not mine. My brief was to give her a lever against Yarrow, and she has it. That's where I finish." I paused. "I'm sure," I said, "for what it's worth, that the police haven't got, and won't find, enough for a prosecution against you, Dart. Just go on knowing nothing, and you'll be all right."

"What about Yarrow, though?" Dart asked.

"Marjorie must decide," I said. "But if you prosecute Yarrow you give away Rebecca's schemes and your own involvement. I can't see her doing it."

"But Keith?" Marjorie said, not dodging the burden I'd placed on her. "What about *him?*"

Keith.

I turned to Conrad. "Did you tell Marjorie that *Keith* sent you here?"

"I did, yes."

"Sent you . . . with a gun?"

He looked faintly shamefaced. "You can't really blame me. I mean, after you and Dart had gone, Keith and I were standing in my room talking about you breaking into my cupboard, and we found that key sort of thing of yours in the lock and I was saying what a risk you'd taken just for a look at some plans . . . and it simply flashed into my mind that you'd been so *involved* in things, and although I couldn't believe you'd been searching for anything else, or that you knew *enough,* I went into the cupboard and looked into the box where I'd put the photograph and the tape, and I was so devastated that Keith asked what was the matter, and I told him. He said—we both thought—you would of course blackmail me."

"Oh, of course."

"Yes, but . . ."

"You all do it to each other; you think no one's capable of anything else."

Conrad shrugged his heavy shoulders as if he believed that to be self-evident. "Anyway," he said, "Keith asked me to give him the envelope our father had entrusted to me shortly before he died. I told Keith I couldn't do that. We had a bit of an argument, but Father had given me very explicit instructions about not letting anyone else see it. Keith asked me if I knew what was in it, but I don't, and I said so. He said he had to have it. He began opening the boxes and tipping everything out. I tried to stop him, but you know what he's like. Then he came to the box where I thought I'd put that letter but when he tipped everything out it didn't seem to be there . . . but how could you have taken it when you couldn't have known it existed? In the end, I helped him look for it. Everything's out on the floor, it's a terrible mess and I'll never put it straight . . ."

"But you did find the envelope?" Marjorie asked anxiously.

"No, we didn't." He turned to me, insisting, "I *know* it was in there, in one special box, under a pile of out-of-date *insurance policies*. Keith told me to bring the gun and kill you . . ."

"But he knew you wouldn't," I said positively.

Dart asked, "Why are you so sure?"

"One twin," I said, "would kill the pilgrim. The other wouldn't. They can't change their natures."

"The fork in the road! You . . . you *subtle* bastard."

Marjorie looked at me forthrightly, not understanding or caring what Dart had said. "Did you take that envelope?"

"Yes, I did," I said.

"Did you open it? Did you see what was inside?"

"Yes."

"Then give it to me."

"No." I shook my head. "This one . . ." I took a breath, "this one I have to do alone."

The telephone shrilled beside Marjorie. Mouth tightening with annoyance at the interruption, she lifted the receiver.

"Yes," she said, her face going blank. "Yes, he's here."

She held out the receiver to me. "It's Keith," she said, "He wants to talk to you."

He knows, I thought, that I must have taken that letter; and he knows what is in it.

With foreboding, I said, "Yes?"

He didn't speak at once, but he was there: I could hear him breathing. Long seconds passed.

He said five words only before the line went dead. The worst five words in the language.

*"Say goodbye to your children."*

# 16

My brain went numb.

A flush of fear zipped from my heels to my scalp in one of those dreadful physical disturbances that come with perceived irretrievable disaster.

I stood immobile, trying to remember the Gardners' telephone number. Couldn't do it. Squeezed my eyes shut and let it come without struggling, let it come subliminally, known as a rhythm, not by sight. Pressed buttons and sweated.

Roger's wife answered.

"Where are the boys?" I asked her abruptly.

"They should be with you at any minute," she said comfortingly. "They set off . . . oh . . . say, fifteen minutes ago. They'll be with you directly."

"With me . . . where?"

"Along at the big top, of course." She was puzzled. "Christopher got your message and they set off at once."

"Did Roger drive them?"

"No. He's around the course somewhere, I'm not sure where. The boys set off on foot, Lee . . . is something wrong?"

"What message?" I said.

"A phone call, for Christopher . . ."

I threw the receiver to Marjorie and sprinted out of her drawing room, across her calm hallway, and out of her front door and into Dart's car. Never mind that the sprint was a hobble, I'd never moved faster. Never mind that I knew I was heading for an ambush, for some thought-out fate. There was nothing to do but rush to it, hoping beyond hope that he'd be satisfied with me, that he would let the boys live . . .

I drove Dart's car like a madman through the village, but just when I could have done with a whole police posse, there was no police car to chase me for speeding.

In through the racecourse gates. Round onto the tarmac outside Roger's office. Keith's silver Jaguar was there. Nobody in sight . . . *Yes* . . . Christopher . . . and Edward . . . and Alan. All of them frightened to eye-staring terror. I scrambled out of the car, driven by demons.

"Dad!" Christopher's bottomless relief was not reassuring. "Dad, hurry."

"What's happening?"

"That man . . . in the big top."

I turned that way.

"He's lit fires in there . . . and Neil . . . and Toby . . . and Neil's screaming."

"Find Colonel Gardner," I shouted to him, running. "Tell him to turn on the sprinkler."

"But . . ." Despair in Christopher's voice, "we don't know where he is."

*"Find him."*

I could *hear* Neil screaming. Not words, nothing intelligible. High-pitched shrieks. *Screaming.*

How does one face such a thing?

I ran into the big top, into the center aisle, looking for the fire extinguisher that ought to have been there at the entrance, and not seeing it, running on and finding Alan running beside me.

"Go back," I yelled at him. "Alan, go *back.*"

There was smoke in the tent and small bright fires here and there on the floor; scarlet, orange and gold flames leaping in rivers and pools. And beyond, standing like a colossus with his legs apart, his weight braced and his mouth stretched wide in gleeful enjoyment . . . *Keith.*

He held Neil by the wrist, easily clamping the small bones in a vise-grip, and lifting him half-way into the air, holding my son at almost arm's length, the small body writhing and fighting to get free, but with only his toes touching the ground, giving no purchase.

"Let him go," I yelled, beyond pride, into begging, into any craven groveling needed.

"Come and get him, or I'll burn him."

Beside Keith, in a tall decorative wrought-iron container, stood a long-

handled torch flaring with a live naked flame, the sort designed for garden bar-
becues, for torchlight processions, for the evil firing of houses in raids; Neil
on one side, torch on the other. In the center Keith held a plastic jerry can
missing its cap.

"It's gasoline, Dad," Alan yelled beside me. "He was pouring it on the floor
and lighting it. We thought he might burn us . . . and we ran, but he caught
Neil . . . don't let him burn Neil, Dad."

"Go back," I screamed at him, frantic, and he wavered and stopped in his
tracks, tears on his cheeks.

I ran towards Keith, towards his terrible grin, towards my terrified son. I ran
towards certain fire, ran as fast as I could, ran from instinct.

If Keith wants to get rid of something, he burns it . . .

I would overrun him, I thought. I would crash down with him. He would
go with me . . . wherever I went.

He hadn't expected an onrush. He stepped back, looking less certain, and
Neil went on screaming. One will do, I realized later, almost insane things in
defense of one's children.

I was conscious then only of flames, of anger, of the raw smell of gasoline,
of a clear view of the outcome.

He would fling the gas can at me and swing the torch, and to do that he
would have to . . . *have* to let go of Neil. I would push him away beyond Neil,
who would live and be safe.

Six paces away, running towards him, I gave up all hope of not burning. But
Keith would burn too . . . and die . . . I would make sure of it.

A small dark figure launched itself in the shortening distance between us
like a goblin from nowhere, all arms and legs, ungainly but fast. He banged
into Keith and knocked him off balance, setting him reeling and windmilling
backwards.

Toby . . . *Toby.*

Keith let go of Neil. I shoved my small son away from him in a frenzy. The
gasoline spilled out of the can and over Keith's legs in a glittering stream. Stag-
gering, trying to evade the fuel, Keith knocked into the stand containing the
torch. It rocked; rocked back and forwards and then overbalanced; started the
flame falling in a deadly arc downwards.

I lunged forwards, snatched up Toby with my right arm, scooped Neil
into my left, lifted them both off their feet and turned in the same movement
to escape.

There was a great whoosh at our backs and a blast of heat and sizzling fire
as if the whole air were burning. I caught a split-second glimpse, looking over

my shoulder, of Keith with his mouth open as if he, this time, would scream. He seemed to take a deep breath to yell and fire rushed into his open mouth as if drawn by bellows into his lungs, and he made no sound at all, but clutched at his chest, his eyes wide, with white showing all round, and he fell face down in an accelerating fireball.

The back of my own shirt was scorching from neck to waist, and Toby's hair was on fire. I ran with the boys in my arms, ran far enough down the aisle and tripped and fell over, dropping Neil, rolling onto my back and rubbing Toby's hair with my hands.

Desperate moments. Neil smelled of gasoline, Toby also, and there were fires, a maze of fires, to traverse on the way out.

I lay momentarily panting for breath, collecting some strength, my left arm curving round Neil who was crying. I struggled to reassure Toby; and then from far above fell a blessed mist of drizzling drops of water, cooling, life-giving, spitting and sizzling on all the small fires around us, blackening the flames to extinction and turning to a smoking ruin the humped shape of Keith.

Toby leaned on my chest, staring into my face as if he couldn't bear to look anywhere else.

He said, "He was going to set fire to you, wasn't he, Dad?"

"Yes, he was."

"I thought so."

"Where did you come from?" I asked.

"Out of the dining room, where we had lunch. I was hiding . . ." His eyes were stretched. "I was *scared,* Dad." Water ran through his singed hair and into his eyes.

"Anyone would be." I rubbed my fist over his back, loving him. "You have the courage of ten thousand heroes." I fought for words. "It isn't every boy who knows he saved his father's life."

I could see it wasn't enough for him. There had to be more, something to give him a permanent feeling of self-worth, to steady him, keep him always in command of himself.

I thought of his little figure launching itself at an impossibly threatening target, arms and legs flying everywhere, but achieving the aim.

I said, "Would you like to learn karate, when we get home?"

His strained face split into a blazing smile. He wiped the trickling water away from his mouth. "Oh *yes,* Dad," he said.

I sat up, still hugging both of them, and Christopher came running, and the other two also, all of them staring beyond me to the blackened and unimaginable horror.

"Don't go down there," I said, pushing myself to my feet. "Where's Colonel Gardner?"

"We couldn't find him," Christopher said.

"But . . . the sprinkler?"

"I turned it on, Dad," Christopher said. "I saw Henry sticking all those labels on, the day you went on the train. I knew where the tap was."

*"Brilliant,"* I said; but there weren't any words good enough. "Well, let's get out of here, out of the rain."

Neil wanted to be carried. I picked him up and he wound his arms round my neck, clinging tightly, and all six of us, soaking wet, made our slowish way out to the tarmac.

Roger drove up in his jeep, got out, and stared at us.

We must, I supposed, have looked odd. One tall boy, one little boy, clinging, the three others close, all dripping.

I said to Christopher, "Run and turn off the tap," and to Roger, "We had a fire in the big top. Bits of gasoline-soaked matting and floorboards burned, but Henry was right, the canvas didn't."

"A *fire!*" He turned towards the entrance, to go and see for himself.

"Better warn you," I said. "Keith's in there. He's dead."

Roger paused for one stride and then went on. Christopher came back from the errand, and all of the boys and I began shivering, as much, I supposed, from shock and anxiety as from standing wet in the light April breeze, in air too cold for comfort.

"Get into the car," I said, pointing at Dart's beaten-up wheels. "You need to get dry."

"But Dad . . ."

"I'm coming with you."

They piled in as Roger came out of the tent looking worried.

"Whatever's happened?" he said urgently. "I'll have to get the police. Come into the office."

I shook my head. "First, I get the boys into dry clothes. I'll not have them catching pneumonia. I'll come back."

"But Lee . . ."

"Keith tried to burn the big top," I said. "But . . ."

"But," Roger finished, "people who try to start fires with gasoline can end up by burning themselves."

I smiled faintly. "Right."

I walked over to Dart's car and drove the boys down to the bus, where everyone, myself emphatically included, showered and changed into dry clothes down to the skin. My checked shirt, its back blackened as if pressed by a too-hot iron, went into the rubbish bin, not into a laundry bag. Underneath I felt as if sunburnt: a first-degree soreness, nothing worse. Dead lucky, I thought, that the shirt had been thick pure wool, not melting nylon.

When the boys were ready I marched them over to Mrs. Gardner and begged her to give them hot sweet drinks and cake, if she had any.

"My *dears,*" she said, embracing them, "come on in."

"Don't leave us, Dad," Edward said.

"I have to talk to the Colonel, but I won't be long."

"Can I come with you?" Christopher asked.

I looked at his height, listened to the already deepening voice, saw the emerging man in the boy and his wish to leave childhood behind.

"Hop in the car," I said and, deeply pleased, he sat beside me on the short return journey.

"When you went up to the big top," I asked him, "what did Keith Stratton say to you?"

"That man!" Christopher shuddered. "It seemed all right at first. He told us to go into the big top. He said you would be coming."

"So then?" I prompted, as he stopped.

"So we went in, and he came in behind us. He told us to go on ahead, and we did."

"Yes."

"Then . . ." he hesitated, "it got *weird,* Dad. I mean, he picked up a can that was lying there and took the cap off, and we could *smell* it was gasoline. Then he put the can down again and picked up that rod thing, and flicked his lighter, and the end of the rod lit up like those torches in Ku Klux Klan films."

"Yeah."

"Then he poured gasoline onto the floor and trailed the torch into it and of course it went on fire, but just in one place." He paused, remembering. "We began to be scared, Dad. You've always told us never to put fire near gasoline, and he had a big can of it in one hand and the torch in the other. He told us to go up further into the big top and he came along behind us and started another fire, and then another, and lots of them and we got really frightened, but all he said was that you would come soon. 'Your father will come.' He gave us the creeps, Dad. He didn't behave like a grown-up. He wasn't *sensible,* Dad."

"No."

"He told us to go on further in, past that sort of stand thing that was there, and he put the torch into it so that it just burned *there,* and wasn't swinging about, and that was better, but we still didn't *like* it. But he put the gasoline can down too, and then he just looked at us and *smiled,* and it was *awful,* I mean, I can't describe it."

"You're doing well."

"He frightened me rigid, Dad. We all wanted to be out of there. Then Alan darted past him suddenly and then Edward, and I did too, and he yelled at us and ran about to stop us and we dodged him and ran, I mean, *pelted,* Dad . . . and then Toby didn't come out after us, and Neil started screaming . . . and that's when you came."

I stopped the car beside Roger's jeep. Keith's Jaguar stood beyond, and beyond that, a police car.

"And he didn't say anything else?" I asked.

"No, only something about not being blackmailed by *you.* I mean, it was silly, you wouldn't blackmail anyone."

I smiled inwardly at his faith. Blackmail wasn't necessarily for money.

"No," I said. "All the same, don't repeat that bit, OK?"

"No, Dad, OK."

Feeling curiously lightheaded, I walked across to the office with Christopher and told the police, when they asked, that I had no idea why Keith Stratton had behaved as irrationally as he had.

IT WAS FRIDAY before I left Stratton Park.

All Wednesday afternoon I replied "I don't know" to relays of police questions, and agreed that I would return dutifully for an inquest.

I said nothing about rushing at Keith to overbalance him. It didn't sound sensible. I said nothing about Neil.

When asked, I said I hadn't used a fire extinguisher to try to save Keith's life, because I couldn't find one.

"Four of them were lying out of sight in the bar area," Roger told me.

"Who put them there?" the police asked.

"I don't know," I said.

Christopher told the law that Keith was a "nutter." They listened politely enough and decided he was too young to be called as an inquest witness, as he had anyway not himself been present at the moment of the accident.

The press came; took photographs; asked questions, got the same answers.

A policewoman, in my presence, asked the younger boys later, down at the Gardners', what they'd seen, but in the manner of children with questioning strangers they clammed up into big-eyed silence, volunteering nothing and answering mainly in nods. Yes—nod—there had been fires in the tent. Yes—

nod—Keith Stratton had lit them. Yes—nod—Toby's hair had got singed. Yes—nod—Christopher had turned on the sprinkler, and yes—nod—their father had looked after them.

The Strattons, I thought ironically at one point, had nothing on the Morris family when it came to keeping things quiet.

On Thursday the staples came out of my mostly healed cuts and, with Dart chauffeuring, I took Toby to Swindon to see what Penelope could do with his unevenly burned hair.

I watched her laugh with him and tease him. Watched her wash the still lingering singe smell out, and cut and brush and blow-dry the very short remaining brown curls. Watched her give him confidence in his new appearance and light up his smile.

I spent the whole time wondering where and how I could get her into bed.

Perdita came downstairs behaving like a mother hen defending her chick against predators, as if reading my mind.

"I told you too much, dear, on Tuesday," she said a shade anxiously.

"I won't give you away."

"And Keith Stratton is dead!"

"So sad," I agreed.

She laughed. "You're a rogue. Did you kill him?"

"In a way." With help from my twelve-year-old, I thought, whether he realized it or not. "Self-defense, you might say."

Her eyes smiled, but her voice was sober. She used only one word for an opinion. *"Good."*

Penelope finished the twelve-year-old's hair. I paid her. She thanked me. She had no idea what I felt for her, nor gave any flicker of response. I was six boys' father, almost double her age. Perdita, seeing all, patted my shoulder. I kissed the cheek of the mother and still lusted for the daughter, and walked away, with Toby, feeling empty and old.

Dart returned Toby to his brothers at the Gardners' and willingly took me on to see Marjorie.

The manservant, aplomb in place, let us in and announced us. Marjorie sat, as before, in her commanding armchair. The smashed looking-glass had been removed, the torn chairs were missing. Rebecca's shot at me had left no permanent traces.

"I came to say goodbye," I said.

"But you'll come back to Stratton Park."

"Probably not."

"But we need you!"

I shook my head. "You have a great racecourse manager in Colonel Gardner. You'll have record crowds at the next meeting, with Oliver Wells's flair for publicity. You'll commission superb new stands—and what I will do, if you like, is make sure any firms submitting proposals to you are substantial and trustworthy. And beyond that, as regards your family, you have more power than ever to hold things together. You don't have Keith, so you don't need any way of restraining him. You have control of Rebecca, who aimed—probably still aims—to run the racecourse herself. She has probably done herself in there, as, even after you're gone, Conrad and Dart can both hold blackmail and attempted murder over her head, enough to out-vote her at Board meetings."

Marjorie listened and came up with her own sort of solution.

"I want you," she said, "to be a director. Conrad and Ivan and I will vote for it. Unanimous decision of the Board."

"Hear, hear," Dart said, delighted.

"You don't need me," I protested.

"Yes, we do."

I wanted to disentangle myself from the Strattons. I did not want to step in any way into my non-grandfather's shoes. From beyond the grave his influence and way of doing things had sucked me into a web of duplicity, and three times in a week his family had nearly cost me my life. I'd paid my debt to him, I thought. I needed now to be free.

And yet . . .

"I'll think about it," I said.

Marjorie nodded, satisfied. "With you in charge," she said, "the racecourse will prosper."

"I have to talk to Conrad," I said.

HE WAS ALONE in his holy of holies, sitting behind his desk.

I'd left Dart again outside in his car, reading about hair loss, though not acting as lookout this time.

"With this American system," he said, deep in before-and-after photographs, "I would never worry again. You can go swimming—diving—your new hair is part of you. But I'd have to go to America every six weeks to two months to keep it right."

"You can afford it," I said.

"Yes, but . . ."

"Go for it," I said.

He needed encouragement. "Do you really think I should?"

"I think you should book your first ticket at once."

"Yes. *Yes.* Well, yes, I *will.*"

Conrad stood up when I went in. His cupboard door was closed, but boxes stood higgledy-piggledy on his carpet, their contents stirred up.

He didn't offer his hand. He seemed to feel awkward, as I did myself.

"Marjorie telephoned," he said. "She says she wants you on the Board. She says I'm to persuade you."

"It's your own wishes that matter."

"I don't know . . ."

"No. Well, I didn't come to talk about that. I came to return what I stole from you yesterday."

"Only yesterday! So much has happened."

I put on his desk the outer brown envelope marked "Conrad." He picked it up, looking at the sticky-tape closure.

"Like I told you," I said, "I did look inside. Keith knew I would look. I don't think he could bear the thought of my using what I learned. I confess that I'm glad I don't have to, as he's dead, but I would have done, and you'd better know that. But I'll not tell Marjorie what's in there—it's evident she doesn't know—and I'll never tell anyone else."

"I don't want to open it," Conrad said, putting the envelope down.

"I can't say that you should."

"But you think so."

"Keith would have burned it," I said.

"Burned." He shuddered. "What a death!"

"Anyway," I said, "the knowledge belongs here, whatever you do with it. Your father meant you to have it. So," I sighed, "read it or burn it, but don't leave it lying about." I paused. "I apologize again for breaking in here. I'll be leaving Stratton Park in the morning. I'm sorry," I made a vague gesture, "for everything."

I turned regretfully and made for the door.

"Wait," Conrad said.

I paused, half in, half out.

"I have to know what you know." He looked wretched. "He was my twin. I know he envied me . . . I know it wasn't fair that I had so much just for being twenty-five minutes older, I know he was violent and cruel and often dangerous, I know he beat your mother and all his wives. I know he nearly killed Hannah's gypsy. I saw him kick you abominably . . . I know all that and more, but he was my brother, my *twin.*"

"Yes."

The Strattons, whatever their faults, had their own tight indestructible loyalty; a family, whatever their internal fights, that closed ranks against the ordinary world.

Conrad picked up the envelope and ripped off the tape.

He reread the first letter, then drew out the second letter and the white
inner envelope.

"Remember," he murmured, reading, "that Keith always tells lies . . ."

He removed the five folded sheets of paper from the white envelope and
read the top one, yet another short note from his father.

It said:

This lie of Keith's cost me a great deal of money, which I gave to Keith
himself, too trustingly. It took me many years to suspect that he'd robbed
me. A small matter, compared with the truth.

Conrad put the note down and looked at the next sheet, another letter, but
in typescript.

"Arne Verity Laboratories?" Conrad said. "Who are they?"

He read the letter, which was addressed to his father, and dated two years
earlier.

In essence, it said that the laboratory had conducted the requested analy-
ses. The detailed results of each separate analysis were appended but, summa-
rizing, the results were as follows:

You sent us three hairs, labeled "A," "B," and "C."
The results of DNA analysis are:
"A" is almost certainly the parent of "B"
and
"A" and "B" are the parents of "C."

Conrad looked up. "What does it mean?"
"It means there was no gypsy. Keith invented him."
"But . . ."
"It means that Keith was the father of Jack."

CONRAD SAT DOWN and looked faint.
"I don't believe it," he breathed. "I can't. It's not true."
"Jack doesn't look like a gypsy," I said. "He looks like Keith."
"Oh dear God . . ."

"Hannah doesn't like the gypsy story. She tells Jack his father was a foreign aristocrat who would have been ruined by the scandal. Apart from the foreign bit, that's more or less true."

"Hannah!" He looked even more distressed. "What are you going to do about *her?*"

"Nothing," I said, surprised he should ask. "With Keith dead, I don't need to use what I know. Hannah is safe from it ever leaking out through me."

"But she attacked you!"

I sighed. "She never had a chance, did she? She was conceived in rape, abandoned by her mother and impregnated by her father. She was rejected by young men and not loved by her grandfather but, whatever he may be, she has Jack, her son. I'll not spoil that for her. In the same way that Keith was your twin, Hannah, whether I like it or not, is my half-sister. Let her alone."

Conrad sat without moving for a long minute, then he shoveled his father's letters and the laboratory reports into the outer brown envelope and held out the whole package in my direction.

"Take it," he said succinctly, "and burn it."

"Yes, OK."

I went back to the desk and, taking the envelope, set out again for the door.

"Come on the Board," Conrad said. "As usual, Marjorie has it right. We're going to need you."

THE BOYS AND Mrs. Gardner said farewells as lengthily as Romeo and Juliet, with many promises of meeting again. Roger and I, less effusively, were nonetheless pleased at the prospect of working together in the future. "Such a lot to see to," Roger said.

Dart produced a diary. He would come to stay, he said, *after* he had been to America. He had, he said, made bookings.

The boys piled into the bus and waved like maniacs through the windows, and I drove us all away, back home to the peaceful Surrey-Sussex border.

"Did you have a good time, my darlings?" Amanda asked, embracing the children. "What did you find to do while your father was busy getting himself into the newspapers?"

They gazed at her. Bit by bit they would no doubt tell her, but at that moment the question struck them dumb.

Neil finally said, earnestly, "We made brilliant fruitcakes."

Amanda told me reproachfully, "The phone here has been ringing non-stop." She looked me over without much concern. "I suppose you're all right?"

"Yes," I said. "Fine."

"Good."

She took the children indoors. I stood by the bus, its engine cooling, and after a while I went and climbed into the oak.

Other trees might be flushing into leaf, but the oak as always hung back, vying with the ash to be the last turning green. I sat in the cradle of the fuzzy boughs, feeling the residual aches and soreness in my body, stretching for quiet in my mind.

After a while Amanda came out of the house and crossed to the tree.

"What are you doing up there?" she asked.

"Considering things."

"Come down. I want to talk to you."

I climbed down, not wanting to hear.

I said, "I was afraid I would return to an empty house. Afraid you and Jamie might have gone."

Her eyes widened. "You always know too damned much."

"I was afraid you'd met someone else."

"Yes, I have."

She wasn't exactly defiant, but she had already thought out what she wanted to say. She still looked lovely. I wished things were different.

"I've decided," she said, "that a formal separation from you wouldn't be good for the children. Also . . ." she slightly hesitated and then screwed up the courage, ". . . he is married, and feels the same about his own family. So we will see each other often. Take it or leave it, Lee."

She waited.

Christopher, Toby, Edward, Alan, Neil and Jamie. Six reasons.

"I'll take it," I said.

She nodded, making a pact of it, and returned to the house.

At bedtime she went up to our room an hour earlier than I, as always, but when I went up she was for once wide awake.

"Did you find a ruin?" she asked, as I undressed.

"No. I'll go looking once the boys are back at school. I'll go off for a while."

"Good."

It wasn't good. It was terrible.

Instead of lying the customary five feet away from her I went round to her side of the huge bed and climbed in beside her: and I made love to Penelope in Amanda, in a turmoil of lust, deprivation, hunger, passion and penetration. A wild, rough sexual action unlike anything before in our marriage.

She responded, after the briefest of protestations and withdrawal, with some of her original ardor, and lay afterwards apart from me, separate again, not full of recriminations but with her mouth curving in a secretive, cat-with-cream smile.

Two months later she said, "I'm pregnant. Did you know?"

"I wondered," I said. I screwed myself to the question. "Is it mine . . . or *his?*"

"Oh, yours," she said positively. "He can't give me a child. He had a vasectomy too long ago."

"Oh."

"It might be a girl," Amanda said coolly. "You always wanted a daughter."

In the fullness of time she gave rapturous birth to her seventh child.

A boy.

Fine by me.

# WILD HORSES

*We are spirits clad in veils;*
*Man by man was never seen;*
*All our deep communing fails*
*To remove the shadowy screen.*

CHRISTOPHER PEARSE CRANCH

(1813–1893)

# 1

Dying slowly of bone cancer the old man, shriveled now, sat as ever in his great armchair, tears of lonely pain sliding down crepuscular cheeks.

That Tuesday, his last, his stringy grip on my wrist tightened convulsively in a long silence while I watched his mouth tremble and move in abortive struggles to speak.

"Father." The words finally wavered out; a whisper, desperate, driven by ultimate need. "Father, I must make my confession. I must ask . . . absolution."

In great surprise and with compassion I said, "But . . . I'm not a priest."

He paid no attention. The feeble voice, a truer measure of affairs than the fiercely clutching hand, simply repeated, "Father . . . forgive me."

"Valentine," I said reasonably, "I'm Thomas. Thomas Lyon. Don't you remember? I come to read to you."

He could no longer see newsprint or anything straight ahead, though peripheral vision partly remained. I called in more or less every week, both to keep him up to date with the racing columns in the newspapers and also to let his beleaguered and chronically tired old sister go out for shopping and gossip.

I hadn't actually read to him on that day. When I arrived he'd been suffering badly from one of his intermittent bouts of agony, with Dorothea, his sister, feeding him a teaspoon of liquid morphine and giving him whiskey and water to help the numbness work faster.

He hadn't felt well enough for the racing papers.

"Just sit with him," Dorothea begged. "How long can you stay?"

"Two hours."

She'd kissed me gratefully on the cheek, stretching on tiptoes, and had hurried away, plump in her late seventies, forthright in mind.

I sat as usual on a tapestry stool right beside the old man, as he liked the physical contact, as if to make up for sight.

The fluttery voice persisted, creeping effortfully into the quiet room, determined and intimate. "I confess to God Almighty and to Thee, my Father, that I have sinned exceedingly . . . and I must confess . . . before . . . before . . ."

"Valentine," I repeated more sharply, "I'm not a priest."

It was as if he hadn't heard. He seemed to be focusing all the energy left in him into one extraordinary spiritual gamble, a last throw of hell-defeating dice on the brink of the abyss.

"I ask pardon for my mortal sin . . . I ask peace with God . . ."

I protested no more. The old man knew he was dying; knew death was near. In earlier weeks he had discussed with equanimity, and even with humor, his lack of a future. He had reminisced about his long life. He'd told me he had left me all his books in his will. Never had he made any mention of even the most rudimentary religious belief, except to remark once that the idea of life after death was a load of superstitious twaddle.

I hadn't known he was a Roman Catholic.

"I confess," he said, ". . . that I killed him . . . God, forgive me. I humbly ask pardon . . . I pray to God Almighty to have mercy on me . . ."

"Valentine . . ."

"I left the knife with Derry and I killed the Cornish boy and I've never said a word about that week and I accuse myself . . . and I lied about everything . . . mea culpa . . . I've done such harm . . . I destroyed their lives . . . and they didn't know, they went on liking me . . . I despise myself . . . all this time. Father, give me a penance . . . and say the words . . . say them . . . *Ego te absolvo* . . . I forgive your sins in the name of the Father . . . I beg you . . . I beg you . . ."

I had never heard of the sins he was talking about. His words tumbled out as if on the edge of delirium, making no cohesive sense. I thought it most likely that his sins were dreams; that he was confused, imagining great guilt where none lay.

There was no mistaking, however, the frantic nature of his repeated plea.

"Father, absolve me. Father, say the words . . . say them, I beg you."

I couldn't see what harm it would do. He was desperate to die in peace. Any priest would have given him absolution: who was I cruelly to withhold it? I was not of his faith. I would square it later, I thought, with my own immortal soul.

So I said what he wanted. Said the words, dredging them from memory. Said them in Latin, as he would clearly understand them, because they seemed less of a lie that way than in bald English.

*"Ego te absolvo,"* I said.

I felt a shiver through my body. Superstition, I thought.

I remembered more words. They floated on my tongue. *"Ego te absolvo a peccatis tuis in nomine Patris et Filii et Spiritus Sancti.* Amen."

I absolve you from your sins in the name of the Father and of the Son and of the Holy Ghost. Amen.

The greatest blasphemy of my life to date. God forgive me my sin, I thought.

The dreadful tension subsided in the old man. The rheumy near-blind eyes closed. The grip on my wrist loosened: the old hand fell away. His face relaxed. He faintly smiled, and then grew still.

Alarmed, I felt for a pulse under his jaw and was relieved to feel the thread-like beat. He didn't move under my touch. I shook him a little, but he didn't wake. After five minutes I shook him again, more strongly, without results. Indecisively then I got up from my seat beside him and, crossing to the telephone, dialed the number prominently written on a notepad nearby, to get through to his doctor.

The medicine man was less than pleased.

"I've told the old fool he should be in hospital," he said. "I can't keep running out to hold his hand. Who are you, anyway? And where's Mrs. Pannier?"

"I'm a visitor," I said. "Mrs. Pannier is out shopping."

"Is he groaning?" demanded the doctor.

"He was, earlier. Mrs. Pannier gave him some painkiller before she went out. Then he was talking. Now he's in a sort of sleep from which I can't seem to wake him."

The doctor growled a smothered curse and crashed his receiver into its cradle, leaving me to guess his intentions.

I hoped that he wouldn't send a wailing ambulance with busy figures and stretchers and all the rough paraphernalia of making the terminally ill feel worse. Old Valentine had wanted to die quietly in his own bed. Waiting there, I regretted my call to the doctor, thinking that I'd probably set in motion, in my anxiety, precisely what Valentine had most wanted to avoid.

Feeling stupid and remorseful, I sat opposite the steadily sleeping man—no longer on a stool beside him but in a more comfortable armchair.

The room was warm. He wore blue cotton pajamas, with a rug over his knees. He sat near the window, bare-branched trees outside giving promise of a spring he wouldn't know.

The study-like room, intensely his own, charted an unusual journey through time that had begun in heavy manual labor and ended in journalism. Born the son of a farrier, he'd been apprenticed to the forge in childhood, working the bellows for his father, skinny arms straining, young eyes excited by the noise and the fire. There had never been any question that he would follow in the trade, nor had he in fact veered toward anything else until his working pattern had long been settled.

Framed, fading photographs on his walls showed a young Valentine with the biceps and pectorals of a giant, a prize-winning wielder of brute power with the wide happy grin of an innocent. But the idyll of the village smithy under the chestnut tree had already long gone. Valentine in his maturity had driven from job to job with his tools and portable brazier in a mobile working van.

He had for years shod a stableful of racehorses trained by my grandfather. He'd looked after the feet of the ponies I'd been given to ride. He had seemed to me to be already a wise man of incredible age, though I knew now he'd been barely sixty-five when I was ten.

His education had consisted of reading (the racing newspapers), writing (bills for his customers), and arithmetic (costing the work and materials so that he made a profit). Not until his forties had his mental capacity expanded to match his muscles. Not until, he'd told me during the past debilitated weeks, not decisively until in his job he was no longer expected to make individual shoes to fit the hooves of horses, but to trim the hooves to fit mass-produced uniform shoes. No longer was he expected to hammer white-hot iron bars into shape, but to tap softer metals cold.

He had begun to read history and biography, at first all to do with racing but later with wider horizons. He had begun in shy anonymity to submit observations and anecdotes to the newspapers he daily studied. He wrote about horses, people, events, opinions. One of the papers had given him a regular column with a regular salary and room to grow a reputation. While still plying his original trade, Valentine had become an honored institution in print, truly admired and enjoyed for his insights and his wit.

As physical strength waned, his journalistic prowess had grown. He'd written on into his eighties, written into semi-blindness, written indeed until four weeks earlier, when the cancer battle had entered the stage of defeat.

And this was the old man, amusing, wise, and revered, who had poured out in panic an apparently unbearable secret.

"I killed the Cornish boy . . ."

He must have meant, I thought, that he was blaming himself for an error in his shoeing, that by some mischance a lost nail in a race had caused a fatal accident to a jockey.

Not for nothing had Valentine adopted often enough the doctrine of doing things thoroughly, quoting now and then the fable of the horseshoe nail. For want of a nail the kingdom was lost . . . little oversights led to great disasters.

A dying mind, I thought again, was scrambling old small guilts into mountainous terrors. Poor old Valentine. I watched him sleep, the white hair scanty on his scalp, big blotchy freckles brown in his skin.

For a long time, no one came. Valentine's breathing grew heavier, but not to the point of snoring. I looked round the familiar room, at the horses' photographs I'd come to know well in the past few months, at the framed awards on the dark green wall, the flower-printed curtains, the worn brown carpet, the studded leather chairs, the basic portable typewriter on an unfussy desk, the struggling potted plant.

Nothing had changed from week to week: only the old man's tenure there was slipping away.

One wall, shelved from floor to ceiling, held the books that I supposed would soon be mine. There were years and years of form books listing thousands upon thousands of by-gone races, with a small red dot inked in beside the name of every horse Valentine had fitted with racing shoes for the test.

Winners, hundreds of them, had been accorded an exclamation mark.

Below the form books there were many volumes of an ancient encyclopedia and rows of glossily jacketed life stories of recently dead racing titans, their bustling, swearing vigor reduced to pale paper memories. I'd met many of those people. My grandfather was among them. Their world, their passions, their achievements were passing into oblivion and already the young jockeys I'd star-gazed at ten were grandfathers.

I wondered who would write Valentine's life story, a worthy subject if ever there was one. He had steadfastly refused to write it himself, despite heavy prompting from all around. Too boring, he'd said. Tomorrow's world, that was where interest lay.

Dorothea came back apologetically half an hour late and tried without success to rouse her brother. I told her I'd phoned the doctor fruitlessly, which didn't surprise her.

"He says Valentine should be in hospital," she said. "Valentine refuses to go. He and the doctor swear at each other." She shrugged resignedly. "I expect the doctor will come in time. He usually does."

"I'll have to leave you," I said regretfully. "I'm already overdue at a meeting." I hesitated. "Are you by any chance Roman Catholic?" I asked. "I mean . . . Valentine said something about wanting a priest."

"A priest?" She looked astounded. "He was rambling on all morning . . . his mind is going . . . but the old bugger would never ask for a *priest.*"

"I just thought . . . perhaps . . . last rites?"

Dorothea gave me a look of sweet sisterly exasperation.

"Our mother was Roman Catholic, but not Dad. Lot of nonsense, he used to say. Valentine and I grew up outside the church and were never the worse for it. Our mother died when he was sixteen and I was eleven. She had a mass said for her . . . Dad took us to that but it made him sweat, he said. Anyway, Valentine's not much of a sinner except for swearing and such, and I know that being so weak as he is he wouldn't want to be bothered by a *priest.*"

"I just thought I'd tell you," I said.

"You're a dear to come here, Thomas, but I know you're mistaken." She paused. "My poor dear boy is very ill now, isn't he?" She looked down at him in concern. "Much worse?"

"I'm afraid so."

"Going." She nodded, and tears came into her eyes. "We've known it would come, but when it happens . . . oh, dear."

"He's had a good life."

She disregarded the inadequate words and said forlornly, "I'll be so *alone.*"

"Couldn't you live with your son?"

"No!" She straightened herself scornfully. "Paul is forty-five and pompous and domineering, though I hate to say it, and I don't get on with his wife. They have three obnoxious teenagers who switch on deafening radios all the time until the walls vibrate." She broke off and smoothed her brother's unresponsive head fondly. "No. Me and Valentine, we set up home here together when his Cathy died and my Bill passed on . . . well, you know all that . . . and we always liked each other, Valentine and me, and I'll miss him. I'll miss him something awful, but I'll stay here." She swallowed. "I'll get used to being alone, same as I did after Bill went."

Dorothea, like many elderly women, it seemed to me, had a resolute independence that survived where youth quaked. With help once daily from the district nurse, she'd cared for her failing brother, taking on ever more personal tasks for him, exhausting herself to give him comfort and painkillers when he lay awake in the night. She might mourn him when he'd gone, but her dark-rimmed eyes showed she was much overdue on rest.

She sat down tiredly on the tapestry stool and held her brother's hand. He breathed slowly, shallowly, the sound rasping. Fading daylight from the window beside Valentine fell softly on the aged couple, light and shadow emphasizing the rounded commitment of the one and the skeletal dependence of the other, the hovering imminence of death as plain as if the scythe had hung above their heads.

I wished I had a camera. Wished indeed for a whole camera crew. My normal day-to-day life involved the catching of emotion on the wing, the recording of ephemeral images to illumine a bedrock of truth. I dealt with unreality to give illusion the insight of revelation.

I directed films.

Knowing that one day I would use and re-create the quiet drama before me, I looked at my watch and asked Dorothea if I might use her telephone.

"Of course, dear. On the desk."

I reached Ed, my earnest assistant, who as usual sounded flustered in my absence.

"It can't be helped," I said. "I'm running late. Is everyone there? Well, get some drinks sent over. Keep them happy, but don't let Jimmy have more than two G and Ts, and make sure we have enough copies of the script alterations. Right? Good. See you."

I regretted having to leave Dorothea at such a time, but in fact I'd squeezed my visit into a day's schedule that had made no provision for it, keeping the promise I'd given week after week.

Three months back, in the preliminary pre-production stage of the film I was currently engaged on, I'd called to see Valentine as a brief matter of courtesy, a gesture to tell him I remembered him in the old days in my grandfather's time, and had always admired, even if from a distance, his emergence as a sage.

"Sage my foot!" He'd disclaimed the flattery but enjoyed it all the same. "I can't see very well these days, boy. How about reading to me for a bit?"

He lived on the outer edge of the town of Newmarket, Suffolk, England, the town long held to be the home and heart of the horseracing industry worldwide. "Headquarters" the racing press called it. Fifteen hundred of the thoroughbred elite rocketed there over the windswept training gallops and over the wide, difficult tracks, throwing up occasional prodigies that passed their glorious genes to flying generations of the future. An ancient wealth-producing business, the breeding of fast horses.

I was on the point of leaving when the front doorbell rang, and to save Dorothea's tired feet I went to answer it.

A short thirtyish man stood there looking at his watch, impatient.

"Can I help you?" I asked.

He gave me a brief glance and called past me, "Dorothea?"

Regardless of fatigue, she appeared from Valentine's room and said miserably, "He's . . . in a coma, I think. Come in. This is Thomas Lyon, who's been reading to Valentine, like I told you." As if on an afterthought, she finished the introduction, flapping a hand and saying, "Robbie Gill, our doctor."

Robbie Gill had red hair, a Scots accent, no small talk, and a poor bedside manner. He carried a medical bag into Valentine's room and snapped it open. He rolled up the ill man's eyelids with his thumb and pensively held one of the fragile wrists. Then he silently busied himself with stethoscope, syringes, and swabs.

"We'd better get him to bed," he said finally. No mention, I was glad to notice, of transportation to hospital.

"Is he . . . ?" Dorothea asked anxiously, leaving the question hovering, not wanting an affirmative answer.

"Dying?" Robbie Gill said it kindly enough in his brusque way. "In a day or two, I'd say. Can't tell. His old heart's still fairly strong. I don't really think he'll wake again, but he might. It partly depends on what he wants."

"How do you mean, what he wants?" I asked, surprised.

He spent time answering me, chiefly, I thought, for Dorothea's sake, but also from a teacher's pleasure in imparting technical information.

"Old people," he said, "very often stay alive if there's something they particularly want to do, and then after they've done it they die quite quickly. This week I've lost a patient who wanted to see her grandson married. She went to the wedding and enjoyed it, and she was dead two days later. Common occurrence. If Valentine has no unfinished business, he may slip away very soon. If he were looking forward to receiving another award, something like that, it might be different. He's a strong-willed man, and amazing things can happen even with cancer as advanced as this."

Dorothea shook her head sadly. "No awards."

"Then let's get him settled. I've arranged for Nurse Davies to pop in late this evening. She'll give him another injection, which will keep him free from any pain he might feel in the night, and I'll come back first thing in the morning. The old codger's beaten me, dammit. He's got his way. I'll not move him now. He can die here at home."

Dorothea's tears thanked him.

"It's lucky he has you," the doctor told her, "and don't make yourself ill." He looked from her to my height assessingly, and said, "You look bigger than both of us. Can you carry him? Nurse Davies would help Dorothea move him, as she always does, but usually he's conscious and doing his best to walk. Can you manage him on your own?"

I nodded. He weighed pathetically little for a man once as strong as horses.

I lifted the tall sleeping figure in my arms and carried him from his armchair, through the small hallway, and into his bedroom, putting him down gently on the white sheet, revealed by Dorothea peeling back the bed covers. Her brother's breathing rasped. I straightened his pajamas and helped Dorothea cover him. He didn't wake. He had died inside, I thought, from the moment he'd believed in his absolution.

I didn't bring up the subject of a priest again with Dorothea, nor mention it to the doctor. I was convinced they would both disapprove of what I'd done, even though Valentine was now dying in peace because of it. Leave things as they are, I decided. Don't add to Dorothea's distress.

I kissed the old lady, shook hands with the doctor, and, offering vague but willing future help, drove back to my job.

LIFE, BOTH REAL and imaginary, was loud and vigorous along in New-market, where the company I was working for had rented an empty racing sta-ble for three months, paying the bankrupt owner-trainer enough to keep him in multiple child-support forever.

Although a good hour late for the script conference I'd called for five-thirty, I did not apologize, having found that the bunch I was working with took regrets for weakness, chiefly because of their own personal insecurities. It was essential, I understood, for them to regard me as rock, even if to my-self sometimes the rock was no more durable than compressed sand.

They were gathered in what had earlier been the dining room of the trainer's cavernous house (all the furniture having passed under the bankruptcy hammer, satiny green and gold-striped paper still adhering richly to the walls) and were variously draped around a basic trestle table sitting on collapsible white plastic garden chairs on the bare boards of the floor. The drinks pro-vided by the catering unit had barely lasted the hour: no one on the produc-tion was wasting money on excess comfort.

"Right," I said, ousting Ed from the seat I wanted, halfway along one side of the table, "have you all read the alterations and additions?"

They had. Three were character actors, one a cinematographer, one a pro-duction manager, one a note-taker, one an assistant director—Ed—and one a scriptwriter that I would like to have done without. He had made the cur-rent changes at my reasonable insistence, but felt aggrieved. He believed I was intent on giving a slant to the story that departed at ninety degrees from his original vision.

He was right.

It was disastrously easy to make bad horseracing pictures and only possible to do it at bankable level, in my view, if racing became the framing back-

ground to human drama. I'd been given the present job for three reasons that
I knew of, the third being that I'd previously stood two animal stories on their
heads with profitable results, the second being that I'd been trained in my
work in Hollywood, the source of finance for the present epic, and—firstly—
that I'd spent my childhood and teens in racing stables and might be considered to know the industrial terrain.

We were ten days into production: that is to say that we had shot about one
sixth of the picture, or, putting it another way, roughly twenty minutes a day
of usable footage, whole cloth from which the final film would be cut. We'd
been scheduled to finish in sixty working days; a span of under ten weeks, as
rest days were precious and rare. I, as director, decided which scenes would actually be shot on which days, though I'd made and distributed in advance a
shooting schedule to which we mostly adhered.

"As you've seen," I said generally, "these changes mean that tomorrow
we'll be shooting on the railed forecourt in front of the Jockey Club's headquarters in the High Street. Cars arrive and leave through the gates. The local
police will help with the town's regular traffic from eleven to twelve only, so
all of our arrivals and departures will be condensed into that time. The Jockey
Club has agreed to our using their front door for entering and leaving shots.
The internal sets have, of course, been built here in this house. You three," I
said to the actors, "can put some useful poison into your various encounters.
George, be sly. Iago stuff. You are now secretly engineering Cibber's down-
fall."

The scriptwriter moaned, "That's not the right interpretation. I don't like
what you've made me do. Those two are very good friends."

"Only up to the point of opportunist betrayal," I said.

Howard Tyler, the writer, had already complained about small earlier
changes to the producer, to the accountant, and to the film company's top
brass, all without getting me fired. I could put up with his animosity in the
same way as I stifled irritation at his round granny glasses, his relentlessly prim
little mouth, and his determination to insert long, pointless silences where
only movement and action would fill theater seats. He adored convoluted unspoken subtleties that were beyond most actors' powers. He should have stuck
to the voluminous moody novels from whence he came.

His book that he'd adapted for the present film was loosely based on a real-
life story, a twenty-six-year-old Newmarket racing scandal very successfully
hushed up. Howard's fictional version purported to be the truth, but almost
certainly wasn't, as none of the still living real participants had shown the
slightest sign of indignant rebuttal.

"You'll find you each have a plan of the Jockey Club forecourt," I said to the meeting. They nodded, flicking over pages. "Also," I went on, "you've a list of the order of shooting, with approximate times. The three cars involved will be driven to the forecourt first thing in the morning. Get all the crews alerted so that lights and cameras can be set up where shown on the plan. If everyone's willing and ready, we should finish well before the daylight yellows. Any questions?"

There were always questions. To ask a question meant attention had been paid and, as often happened, it was actors with the smallest parts who asked most. George, in this case, wanted to know how his character would develop from the extra scene. Only, I enlightened him, as just one more factor in Cibber's troubles. Cibber, eventually, would crack. Bang. Fireworks. Cibber said, "Hallelujah," gratefully. George compressed his mouth.

"But they were friends," Howard repeated stubbornly.

"As we discussed," I said mildly, "if Cibber cracks, your motivation makes better sense."

He opened his little mouth, saw everyone else nodding, folded his lips, and began to act as if Cibber's cracking was all his own idea.

"If it rains tomorrow," I said, "we'll shoot the internal Jockey Club scenes instead and trust it will be fine on Thursday. We are due to complete the first Newmarket segment on Saturday. On Sunday, as I think you know, we're shifting the horses forty miles west to Huntingdon racecourse; to the stable block there. Actors and technicians will travel early on Monday morning. Rehearsals, Monday, from noon onward. Shooting Tuesday to Friday, return here the following weekend. Ed will distribute times and running order to everyone concerned. OK? Oh, and by the way, the rushes from yesterday are fine. Thought you'd like to know. It was a lot of hard work, but worth it."

The resulting sighs round the table came from relief. We'd spent the whole day in the stable yard, the human action in the foreground taking place against a background of routine equine life. Never could rows of horses have been mucked out, fed, watered, and groomed more times in any twelve hours before: but we had enough shots in the can to give the fictional stable unending life.

The script meeting over, everyone dispersed except a tall, thin, disjointed-looking man in an untidy beard and unkempt clothes whose unimpressive appearance hid an artistic confidence as unassailable as granite. He raised his eyebrows. I nodded. He slouched in his seat and waited until all backs but our own had passed through the door.

"You wanted me to stay?" he asked. "Ed said."

"Yes."

Every film with any hope of acclaimed success needed an eye that saw all life as through a camera lens. Someone to whom focus and light intensities were extrasensory dimensions taken for granted. His title on the credits might variously be "cinematographer" or "director of photography." I'd had a mathematical friend once who said he thought in algebra; Moncrieff, director of photography, thought in moving light and shadows.

We were used to each other. This was our third film together. I'd been disconcerted the first time by his surrealist sense of humor, then seen that it was the aquifer of his geysers of visual genius, then felt that to work without him would leave me nakedly exposed in the realm of translating my own perceptions into revelations on the screen. When I told Moncrieff what I wanted an audience to understand, he could instinctively slant a lens to achieve it.

We had once staged a "last rites" scene for a man about to be murdered by terrorists; the ultimate cruelty of that wicked blasphemy had been underscored by Moncrieff's lighting of the faces: the petrified victim, the sweating priest, and the hard men's absence of mercy. *Ego te absolvo* . . . it had brought me death threats by post.

On that Tuesday in Newmarket I asked Moncrieff, "Have you seen the railings outside the Jockey Club? The ones enclosing the private parking forecourt?"

"Tall and black? Yes."

"I want a shot that emphasizes the barrier qualities. I want to establish the way the railings shut out everyone but the elite. Inside can be mandarins of racing. Outside, hoi polloi."

Moncrieff nodded.

I said, "I also want to give an impression that the people inside, Cibber and George, the Jockey Club members, are themselves prisoners in their own conventions. Behind bars, one might say."

Moncrieff nodded.

"And," I said, "take a five-second shot of the hinges of the gates as they open, also as they close."

"Right."

"The scene between Cibber and George is shot to begin with from outside the bars. I'd like the zoo aspect made clear. Then track the lens forward between the railings to establish where they're standing. The rest of that conversation is in close-ups."

Moncrieff nodded. He seldom made notes while we talked, but he would write a meticulous worksheet before bedtime.

"We're not being judgmental," I said. "Not heavy-handed. No great social stance. Just a fleeting impression."

"A feather touch," Moncrieff said. "Got you."

"Contributing to Cibber's crack-up," I said.

He nodded.

"I'll get Howard to write that crack-up tomorrow," I said. "It's mainly a matter of a shift in intensity from the calm scene already in the script. Howard just needs to put some juice into it."

"Howard's juice is watered cranberry." Moncrieff picked up a vodka bottle from among the drinks clutter and squinted at it against the light. "Empty," he commented morosely. "Have you tried vodka and cranberry juice? It's disgusting."

Howard drank it all the time.

"Howard," Moncrieff said, "is radioactive waste. You can't get rid of it safely."

He knew as well as I did that Howard Tyler's name on the billboards would bring to the film both the lending library audience and attention from up-market critics. Howard Tyler won prestigious prizes and had received honorary doctorates on both sides of the Atlantic. Moncrieff and I were considered lucky to be working with such a luminous figure.

Few authors could, or even wanted to, write screenplays of their own novels; Howard Tyler had been nominated for an Oscar at his first attempt and subsequently refused to sell his film rights unless the package included himself. Moncrieff and I were stuck with Howard, to put it briefly, as fast as it seemed he was stuck with me.

Our producer, bald, sixty, a heavily framed American, had put a canny deal together for the company. Big name author (Howard), proven camera wizard (Moncrieff), vastly successful producer (himself), and young-but-experienced director (T. Lyon), all allied to one mega-star (male) and one deliciously pretty new actress; money spent on the big names and saved on the actress and me. He, producer O'Hara, had told me once that in the matter of acting talent it was a waste of resources employing five big stars in any one picture. One great star would bring in the customers and maybe two could be afforded. Get more and the costs would run away with the gross.

O'Hara had taught me a lot about finance and Moncrieff a lot about illusion. I'd begun to feel recently that I finally understood my trade—but was realistic enough to know that at any minute I could judge everything wrong and come an artistic cropper. If public reaction could be reliably foretold, there would be no flops. No one could ever be sure about public taste: it was as fickle as horseracing luck.

O'Hara, that Tuesday, was already in the Bedford Lodge hotel dining room when I joined him for dinner. The studio bosses liked him to keep an eye on what I was doing and report back. He marched into operations accordingly week by week, sometimes from London, sometimes from California, spending a couple of days watching the shooting and an evening with me going over the state of the budget and the time schedule. Owing to his sensible planning in the first place, I hoped we would come in under budget and with a couple of days to spare, which would encourage any future employers to believe I had organizational talents.

"Yesterday's rushes were good, and this morning went well," O'Hara said objectively. "Where did you get to this afternoon? Ed couldn't find you."

I paused with a glass of studio-impressing Perrier halfway to my mouth, remembering vividly the rasping of Valentine's breath.

"I was here in Newmarket," I said, putting down the water. "I've a friend who's dying. I called to see him."

"Oh." O'Hara showed no censure, registering the explanation as a reason, not an excuse. He knew anyway—and took it for granted—that I'd started work at six that morning and would put in eighteen hours most days until we'd completed the shooting.

"Is he a film man?" O'Hara asked.

"No. Racing . . . a racing writer."

"Oh. Nothing to do with us, then."

"No," I said.

Ah well. One can get things wrong.

# 2

Fortunately, Wednesday morning dawned bright and clear, and Moncrieff, his camera crew, and I attended sunrise beside the Jockey Club's railings, filming atmospheric barred shadows without interruption.

Rehearsals with Cibber and George went fine later on the forecourt, with Moncrieff opening his floods easily to supplement the sun, and with me peering through the camera eyepiece to be sure the angles brought out the spite developing between the erstwhile "best friends." By eleven we were ready for the cars-inward, cars-outward sequences, the police cooperating efficiently in the spirit of things.

Our male mega-star, laconic as always, patiently made three arrivals behind the wheel of a car, and four times uncomplainingly repeated a marching-to-execution type entrance through the hallowed front door, switching his fictional persona on and off with the confidence and expertise of a consummate pro. As if absentmindedly, he finally gave me an encouraging pat on the shoulder and left in his personal Rolls-Royce for the rest of the day.

At midday we broke for a well-earned hour for lunch.

O'Hara came in the afternoon to watch George's Iago touch (which basically needed only an inoffensive "cool it just a bit" comment from myself) and sat smiling in a director's chair for most of the afternoon. O'Hara's hovering smile, though I was never sure he knew it, acted like oil on the actors and technical crews, getting things smoothly done; under his occasional slit-eyed disapproval, problems geometrically increased.

After wrapping things up on the forecourt, O'Hara and I went together to Bedford Lodge for an early beverage (light on alcohol, following the film company's overall puritanical ethos), discussing progress and plans before he left fantasy land en route for marketing and advertisement in offices in London. Making the film was never enough; one had to sell the product as well.

"I see you've booked our chief stuntman for Monday," he said casually, standing to leave. "What do you have in mind?"

"Untamed horses on a beach."

I answered him lightly, giving him the option of believing me or not.

"Do you mean it?" he asked. "It's not in the script."

I said, "I can fit in the beach reconnaissance with the stuntman very early on Monday morning. Dawn, in fact. I'll be back in good time for rehearsals. But . . ." I paused indecisively.

"But what?"

"In the past you've given me an extra day here or there," I said. "What if I could use one this time? What if I get an idea?"

Twice in the past, granted latitude, I'd slanted his productions into a dimension the public had liked. Without demanding to know details in advance of a process I found came only from spur-of-the-moment inspiration in myself, he gave me merely a five-second considering stare, then a brief nod, and then a virtual carte blanche.

"Three days," he said. "OK."

Time was very expensive. Three days equaled trust. I said, "*Great.*"

"If you hadn't asked," he said reflectively, "we'd be in trouble."

"Don't you think it's going well?" I had anxieties always.

"It's going professionally," he said. "But I hired you for something more."

I didn't feel flattered so much as increasingly pressured. The days when not much had been expected had been relatively restful; success had brought an upward spiral of awaited miracles, and one of these days, I thought, I would fly off the top of the unsteady tower and crash down in Pisa, and no sane finance department would consider my name again.

On the doorstep of the hotel, with his chauffeured car waiting, O'Hara said, "You very well know that in the matter of film making there's power and there's money. On big-budget productions the money men dictate what the directors may do. On medium-budget productions, like this one, the power lies in the director. So use your power. *Use* it."

I gazed at him dumbly. I saw him as the mover behind this film, saw *him* as the power. He, after all, had made the whole project possible. I saw that chiefly I had been trying to please *him,* more than myself; and he was telling me that that wasn't what he wanted.

"Stand or fall," he said. "It's your picture."

I thought that if I were shooting this scene, it would be clear, whatever he said, that the real power lay in the older, craggily self-assured, lived-in face atop a wide-shouldered gone-to-overweight but comfortable body, and not in the unremarkable thirty-year-old easily mistaken for an extra.

"The power is yours," he said again. "Believe it."

He gave me an uncompromising nod, allowing me no excuses, and went onward to his car, being driven away without a farewell glance.

I walked thoughtfully across the drive to my own car and set off along the road to Valentine's house aware of being at the same time powerful and obscure, an odd mixture. I couldn't deny to myself that I did quite often feel a spurting ability to produce the goods, a soaring satisfaction that could nosedive the next minute into doubt. I needed confidence if I were to give life to anything worthwhile, yet I dreaded arrogance, which could at once mislead into sterile *folie de grandeur.* Why, I often wondered, hadn't I settled for a useful occupation that didn't regularly lay itself open to public evaluation, like, say, delivering the mail?

VALENTINE AND DOROTHEA had bought a four-roomed single-story house, taking two rooms each as bedroom and sitting room, constructing an extra bathroom so that they had their privacy, and sharing one large kitchen furnished with a dining table. Living that way had, they had both told me, been an ideal solution to their widowed state, a separate togetherness that gave them both company and retreat.

Everything looked quiet there when I parked outside on the road and walked up the concrete path to the front door. Dorothea opened it before I could ring the bell, and she'd been crying.

I said awkwardly, "Valentine . . . ?"

She shook her head miserably. "He's still alive, the poor poor old love. Come in, dear. He won't know you, but come and see him."

I followed her into Valentine's bedroom, where she said she had been sitting in a wing chair near the window, so that she could see the road and visitors arriving.

Valentine, yellowly pale, lay unmoving on the bed, his heavy slow breath noisy, regular, and implacably terminal.

"He hasn't woken or said anything since you went yesterday," Dorothea said. "We don't need to whisper in here, you know, we're not disturbing him. Robbie Gill came at lunchtime, not that I had any lunch, can't eat, somehow.

Anyway, Robbie says Valentine is breathing with difficulty because fluid is collecting in his lungs, and he's slipping away now and will go either tonight or tomorrow, and to be ready . . . How can I be ready?"

"What does he mean by ready?"

"Oh, just in my feelings, I think. He said to let him know tomorrow morning how things are. He more or less asked me not to phone him in the middle of the night. He said if Valentine dies, just to phone him at home at seven. He isn't really heartless, you know. He still thinks it would be easier on me if Valentine were in hospital, but I know the old boy's happier here. He's peaceful, you can see it. I just know he is."

"Yes," I said.

She insisted on making me a cup of tea, and I didn't dissuade her because I thought she needed one herself. I followed her into the brightly painted blue and yellow kitchen and sat at the table while she set out pretty china cups and a sugar bowl. We could hear Valentine breathing, the slow rasping almost a groan, though Nurse Davies, Dorothea said, had been an absolute brick, injecting painkiller so that her brother couldn't possibly suffer, not even in some deep brain recess below the coma.

"Kind," I said.

"She's fond of Valentine."

I drank the hot weak liquid, not liking it much.

"It's an extraordinary thing," Dorothea said, sitting opposite me and sipping. "You know what you said about Valentine wanting a priest?"

I nodded.

"Well, I told you he couldn't have meant it, but then, I would never have believed it, this morning a neighbor of ours—Betty from across the road, you've met her, dear—she came to see how he was and she said, did he get his priest all right? Well! I just stared at her, and she said, didn't I know that Valentine had been rambling on about some priest our mother had had to give her absolution before she died, and she said he'd asked her to fetch that priest. She said, what priest? I mean, she told me she never knew either of us ever saw a priest and I told her of course we hadn't, hardly even with our mother, but she said Valentine was talking as if he were very young indeed and he was saying he liked to listen to bells in church. Delirious, she said he was. She couldn't make sense of it. What do you think?"

I said slowly, "People often go back to their childhood, don't they, when they're very old."

"I mean, do you think I should get Valentine a priest? I don't know any. What should I do?"

I looked at her tired, lined face, at the worry and the grief. I felt the exhaustion that had brought her to this indecision as if it had been my own.

I said, "The doctor will know of a priest, if you want one."

"But it wouldn't be any good! Valentine wouldn't know. He can't hear anything."

"I don't think it matters that Valentine can't hear. I think that if you don't get a priest, you'll wonder for the rest of your life whether you should have done. So yes, either the doctor or I will find one for you at once, if you like."

Tears ran weakly down her cheeks as she nodded agreement. She was clearly grateful not to have had to make the decision herself. I went into Valentine's sitting room and used the phone there, and went back to report to Dorothea that a man from a local church would arrive quite soon.

"Stay with me?" she begged. "I mean . . . he may not be pleased to be called out by a lapsed nonpracticing Catholic."

He hadn't been, as it happened. I'd exhorted him as persuasively as I knew how; so without hesitation I agreed to stay with Dorothea, if only to see properly done what I'd done improperly.

We waited barely half an hour, long enough only for evening to draw in, with Dorothea switching on the lights. Then the real priest, a tubby, slightly grubby-looking middle-aged man hopelessly lacking in charisma parked his car behind my own and walked up the concrete path unenthusiastically.

Dorothea let him in and brought him into Valentine's bedroom, where he wasted little time or emotion. From a bag reminiscent of the doctor's, he produced a purple stole which he hung round his neck, a rich color against the faded black of his coat and the white band around his throat. He produced a small container, opened it, dipped in his thumb, and then made a small cross on Valentine's forehead, saying, "By this holy anointing oil . . ."

"Oh!" Dorothea protested impulsively, as he began. "Can you say it in Latin? I mean, with our mother it was always in Latin. Valentine would want it in Latin."

He looked as if he might refuse, but instead shrugged his shoulders, found a small book in his bag, and read from that instead.

"*Misereatur tui omnipotens Deus, et dimissis peccatis tuis, perducat te ad vitam aeternam. Amen.*"

May Almighty God have mercy on you, forgive you your sins, and bring you to everlasting life.

"*Dominus noster Jesus Christus te absolvet . . .*"

Our Lord Jesus Christ absolve you . . .

He said the words without passion, a task undertaken for strangers, giving blanket absolution for he knew not what sins. He droned on and on, finally repeating, more or less, the words I'd used, the real thing now but without the commitment I'd felt.

"*Ego te absolvo ab omnibus censuris et peccatis in nomine Patris et Filii et Spiritus Sancti*. Amen."

He made the sign of the cross over Valentine, who went on breathing without tremor, then he paused briefly before removing the purple stole and replacing it, with the book and the oil, in his bag.

"Is that all?" asked Dorothea blankly.

The priest said, "My daughter, in the authority vested in me I have absolved him from all blame, from all his sins. He has received absolution. I can do no more."

I went with him to the front door and gave him a generous donation for his church funds. He thanked me tiredly, and he'd gone before I thought of asking him about a funeral service—a requiem mass—within a week.

Dorothea had found no comfort in his visit.

"He didn't *care* about Valentine," she said.

"He doesn't know him."

"I wish he hadn't come."

"Don't feel like that," I said. "Valentine has truly received what he wanted."

"But he doesn't *know.*"

"I'm absolutely certain," I told her with conviction, "that Valentine is at peace."

She nodded relievedly. She thought so herself, with or without benefit of religion. I gave her the phone number of the Bedford Lodge hotel, and my room number, and told her I would return at any time if she couldn't cope.

She smiled ruefully. "Valentine says you were a real little devil when you were a boy. He said you ran wild."

"Only sometimes."

She stretched up to kiss my cheek in farewell, and I gave her a sympathetic hug. She hadn't lived in Newmarket when I'd been young, and I hadn't known her before coming back for the film, but she seemed already like a cozy old aunt I'd had forever.

"I'm always awake by six," I said.

She sighed. "I'll let you know."

I nodded and drove away, waving to her as she stood in Valentine's window, watching forlornly in her sorrowful vigil.

I drove to the stable yard we were using in the film and stood in the dark there, deeply breathing cool March evening air and looking up at the night sky. The bright clear day had carried into darkness, the stars now in such brilliant 3-D that one could actually perceive the infinite depths and distances of space.

Making a film about muddy passions on earth seemed frivolous in eternity's context, yet, as we were bodies, not spirits, we could do no more than reveal our souls to ourselves.

*Spiritus sanctus.* "Spiritus" meant breath in Latin. Holy breath. *In nomine Spiritus Sancti.* In the name of the Holy Spirit, the Holy Breath, the Holy Ghost. As a schoolboy I'd liked the logic and discipline of Latin. As a man, I found in it mystery and majesty. As a film director I'd used it to instill terror. For Valentine, I'd usurped its power. God forgive me, I thought . . . if there is a God.

The mega-star's Rolls whispered gently into the yard and out he popped, door opened for him as always by his attentive chauffeur. Male mega-stars came equipped normally with a driver, a valet, a secretary/assistant and occasionally a bodyguard, a masseur, or a butler. For female mega-stars, add a hairdresser. Either could require a personal make-up artist. These retinues all had to be housed, fed, and provided with rented transport, which was one reason why wasted days painfully escalated the costs.

"Thomas?" he asked, catching sight of me in the shadows. "I suppose I'm late."

"No," I assured him. Mega-stars were *never* late, however overdue. Mega-stars were walking green lights, the term that in the film world denoted the capacity to bring finance and credence to a project, allied with the inability to do wrong. What green lights desired, they got.

This particular green light had so far belied his persnickety reputation and had delivered such goods that he'd been asked for in good humor and with sufficient panache to please his fans.

He was fifty, looked forty, and stood eye to eye with me at a shade over six feet. Though his features off-screen were good but unremarkable, he had the priceless ability of being able to switch on inside and act with his eyes. With tiny shifts of muscle he achieved huge messages in close-up, and the smile he constructed with his lower eyelids had earned him the tag of "the sexiest man in films," though to my mind that smile was simply where his talents began.

I'd never before been appointed to direct such an actor, which he knew and made allowances for; yet he'd told me, much as O'Hara had, to get on with things and use my authority.

The mega-star, Nash Rourke, had himself asked for this night's meeting.

"A bit of quiet, Thomas, that's what I want. And I need to get the feel of the Jockey Club room you've had built in the trainer's house."

Accordingly we walked together to the house's rear entrance, where the night watchman let us in and logged our arrival.

"All quiet, Mr. Lyon," he reported.

"Good."

Within the barn of a house the production manager, with my and O'Hara's approval and input, had reconstructed a fictional drawing room within the original drawing room space, and also re-created the former trainer's office as it had been, looking out to the stable yard.

Upstairs, removing a wall or two and using old photographs as well as a sight of the real thing, we had built a reproduction of the imposing room still to be found within the Jockey Club headquarters in the High Street, the room where, in the historic past, enquiries had been held, with reputations and livelihoods at stake.

Real official enquiries had for forty years or more been conducted in the racing industry's main offices in London, but in Howard Tyler's book, and in our film, a kangaroo court, an unofficial and totally dramatic and damning enquiry was taking place within the old forbidding ambience.

I switched on the few available lights, which gave only a deadened view of a richly polished wood floor, Stubbs and Herring on the walls, and luxurious studded leather armchairs ranged round the outer side of a large horseshoe-shaped table.

The constructed replica room, to allow space for cameras, was a good deal larger than the real thing. Also, complete with cornices and paintings, the solid-seeming walls could obligingly roll aside. Bulbs on ceiling tracks, dark now, waited with a tangle of floods, spots, and cables for the life to come in the morning.

Nash Rourke crossed to one side of the table, pulled out a green leather armchair and sat on it, and I joined him. He had brought with him several pages of newly rewritten script, which he slapped down on the polished wood saying, "This scene we're doing tomorrow is the big one, right?"

"One of them," I nodded.

"The man is accused, baffled, angry, and innocent."

"Yes."

"Yeah. Well, our friend, Howard Tyler, is driving me crazy."

Nash Rourke's accent, educated American, Boston overtones, didn't sit exactly with the British upper-class racehorse trainer he was purporting to be, a minor detail in almost everyone's eyes, including my own but excluding (un-surprisingly) Howard's.

"Howard wants to change the way I say things, and for me to play the whole scene in a throttled whisper."

"Is that what he said?" I asked.

Nash shrugged a partial negative. "He wants what he called 'a stiff upper lip.' "

"And you?"

"This guy would *yell,* for Christ's sake. He's a big powerful man accused of murdering his wife, right?"

"Right."

"Which he didn't do. And he's faced with a lot of stick-in-the-muds bent on ruining him one way or the other, right?"

"Right."

"And the chairman is married to his dead wife's sister, right?"

I nodded. "The chairman, Cibber, eventually goes to pieces. We established that today."

"Which Howard is spitting blue murder about."

"Tomorrow, here," I waved a hand around the make-believe courtroom, "you yell."

Nash smiled.

"Also you put a great deal of menace into the way you talk back to Chairman Cibber. You convince the Jockey Club members, *and* the audience, that you do have enough force of personality to kill. Sow a seed or two. Don't be long-suffering and passive."

Nash leaned back in his chair, relaxing. "Howard will bust a gut. He's mad as hell with what you're doing."

"I'll soothe him."

Nash wore, as I did, unpressed trousers, an open-necked shirt, and a thick loose sweater. He picked up the sheets of script, shuffled them a bit, and asked a question.

"How different is the whole script than the one I saw originally?"

"There's more action, more bitterness, and a lot more suspense."

"But my character—this guy—he still doesn't kill his wife, does he?"

"No. But there's doubt about it right to the end, now."

Nash looked philosophical. "O'Hara sweet-talked me into this," he said. "I had three months free between projects. Fill them, he said. Nice little movie about horseracing. O'Hara knows I'm a sucker for the horses. An old real-life scandal, he tells me, written by our world-famous Howard, who of course I've heard of. Prestige movie, not a sink-without-trace, O'Hara says. Director? I ask. He's young, O'Hara says. You won't have worked with him before. Too damn right, I haven't. Trust me, O'Hara says."

"Trust me," I said.

Nash gave me one of the smiles an alligator would be proud of, the sort that in his Westerns had the baddies flinging themselves sideways in shoot-outs.

"Tomorrow," I said, "is the opening day of the main Flat racing season in England."

"I know it."

"They run the Lincoln Handicap on Saturday."

Nash nodded. "At Doncaster. Where's Doncaster?"

"Seventy miles north of here. Less than an hour by helicopter. Do you want to go?"

Nash stared. "You're bribing me!"

"Sure."

"What about insurance?"

"I cleared it with O'Hara."

"Be damned!" he said.

He stood up abruptly in amused good humor and began measuring his distances in paces round the set.

"It says in the script," he said, "that I stand on the mat. Is this the mat, this thing across the open end of the table?"

"Yes. It's actually a bit of carpet. Historically the person accused at a Newmarket horse racing enquiry had to stand there, on the carpet, and that's the origin of the phrase, to be carpeted."

"Poor bastards."

He stood on the carpet and quietly said his lines, repeating and memorizing them, putting in pauses and gestures, shifting his weight as if in frustration, and finally marching the inside distance of the horseshoe to lean menacingly over the top chair, which would contain Cibber, the inquisitor.

"And I yell," he said.

"Yes," I agreed.

With the fury at that point silent, he murmured the shout of protest, and in time returned to his former seat beside me.

"What happened to those people in real life?" he asked. "Howard swears what he's written are the true events. O'Hara tells me you're sure they're not, because no one's screaming foul. So what really did happen?"

I sighed. "Howard's guessing. Also he's playing safe. For a start, none of the people who were really involved are called by their real names in his book. And I don't honestly know more than anyone else, because it all happened in this town twenty-six years ago, when I was only four. I can't remember even hearing about it then, and in any case the whole thing fizzled out. The trainer you're playing was a man called Jackson Wells. His wife was found hanged in one of the stalls in his stable yard, and a lot of people thought he'd done it. His wife had had a lover. His wife's sister was married to a member of the Jockey Club. That's about as far as the known facts go. No one could ever prove Jackson Wells had hanged his wife, and he swore he hadn't."

"Howard says he's still alive."

I nodded. "The scandal finished him in racing. He could never prove he *hadn't* hanged his wife and although the Jockey Club didn't actually take away his license, people stopped sending him horses. He sold his place and bought a farm in Oxfordshire, I think, and got married again. He must be nearly sixty now, I suppose. There apparently hasn't been any reaction at all from him, and Howard's book's been out over a year."

"So he won't come bursting onto the set here swinging a noose to lynch me."

"Believe in his innocence," I said.

"Oh, I do."

"Our film is fiction," I said. "The real Jackson Wells was a middle-ability man with a middle-sized training stable and no outstanding personality. He wasn't the upper-class powerful figure in Howard's book, still less was he the tough, wronged, resourceful conqueror we'll make of you before we're done."

"O'Hara promised an up-beat ending."

"He'll get it."

"But the script doesn't say who *did* hang the wife, only who didn't."

I said, "That's because Howard doesn't know and can't make up his mind what to invent. Haven't you read Howard's book?"

"I never read the books scripts are written from. I find it's too often confusing and contradictory."

"Just as well," I said, smiling. "In Howard's book your character is not having an affair with his wife's sister."

"Not?" He was astonished. He'd spent a whole busy day tumbling about in bedclothes half naked with the actress playing his wife's sister. "However did Howard agree to *that*?"

I said, "Howard also agreed that Cibber, the sister-in-law's husband, should find out about the affair so that Cibber could have an overpowering reason for his persecution of your character; in fact, for the scene you're playing here tomorrow."

Nash said disbelievingly, "And *none* of that was in Howard's book?"

I shook my head. O'Hara had leaned on Howard from the beginning to spice up the story, in essence warning him, "No changes, no movie." The shifts of mood and plot line that I'd recently introduced were as nothing compared with O'Hara's earlier manipulations. With me, Howard was fighting a rear-guard action, and with luck he would lose that too.

Nash said bemusedly, "Is the real Cibber still alive as well? And how about the wife's sister?"

"About her, I don't know. The real Cibber died three or so years ago. Apparently someone dug up this old story about him, which is what gave Howard the idea for his book. But the real Cibber didn't persecute Jackson Wells as relentlessly as he does in the film. The real Cibber had little power. It was all a pretty low-key story, in reality. Nothing like O'Hara's version."

"Or yours."

"Or mine."

Nash gave me a straight look verging on the suspicious and said, "What are you not telling me about more script changes?"

I liked him. I might even trust him. But I'd learned the hard way once that nothing was ever off the record. The urge to confide *had* to be resisted. Even with O'Hara, I'd been reticent.

"Devious," O'Hara had called me. "An illusionist."

"It's what's needed."

"I'll not deny it. But get the conjuring *right.*"

Conjurors never explained their tricks. The gasp of surprise was their best reward.

"I'll always tell you," I said to Nash, "what your character would be feeling in any given scene."

He perceived the evasion. He thought things over in silence for a long full minute while he decided whether or not to demand details I might not give. In the end, what he said was, "Trust is a lot to ask."

I didn't deny it. After a pause he sighed deeply as if in acceptance, and I supposed he'd embraced blind faith as a way out if the whole enterprise should fail. "One should *never* trust a director . . ."

In any case he bent his head to his script, reading it again swiftly, then he stood up, left the pages on the table, and repeated the whole scene, speaking the lines carefully, forgetting them only once, putting in the pauses, the gestures, the changes of physical balance, the pouncing advance down the horseshoe, and the over-towering anger at the end.

Then, without comment, he went through the whole thing again. Even without much sound, the emotion stunned; and he'd put into the last walk-through even the suggestion that he could be a killer, a murderer of wives, however passionately he denied it.

This quiet, concentrated mental vigor, I saw, was what had turned a good actor into a mega-star.

I hadn't been going to shoot the scene in one long take, but his perfor-mance changed my mind. He'd given it a rhythm and intensity one couldn't get from cutting. The close shot of Cibber's malevolence could come after.

"Thanks for this," Nash said, breaking off.

"Anything."

His smile was ironic. "I hear I'm the green light around here."

"I ride on your coattails."

"You," he said, "do not need to grovel."

We left the set and the house and signed ourselves out with the night watchman. Nash was driven away in the Rolls by his chauffeur, and I returned to Bedford Lodge for a final long session with Moncrieff, discussing the vi-sual impacts and camera angles of tomorrow's scene.

I was in bed by midnight. At five, the telephone rang beside my head.

"Thomas?"

Dorothea's wavery voice, apologetic.

"I'm on my way," I said.

# 3

Valentine was dead.

When I arrived in his house I found not the muted private grief I expected, but a showy car, not the doctor's or the priest's, parked at the curbside, and bright lights behind the curtains in every window.

I walked up the concrete path to the closed front door and rang the bell.

After a long pause the door was opened, but not by Dorothea. The man filling the entry was large, soft, and unwelcoming. He looked me up and down with a practiced superciliousness and said, almost insultingly, "Are you the doctor?"

"Er . . . no."

"Then what do you want so early?"

A minor civil servant, I diagnosed: one of those who enjoyed saying no. His accent was distantly Norfolk, prominently London-suburban and careful.

"Mrs. Pannier asked me to come," I said without provocation. "She telephoned."

"At this hour? She can't have done."

"I'd like to speak to her," I said.

"I'll tell her someone called."

Down in the hall behind him, Dorothea appeared from her bathroom and, seeing me, hurried toward the front door.

"Thomas! Come in, dear." She beckoned me to sidle past the blockage. "This is my son, Paul," she explained to me. "And Paul, this is Valentine's friend Thomas, that I told you about."

"How is he?" I asked. "Valentine?"

Her face told me.

"He's slipped away, dear. Come in, do, I need your help." She was flustered by this son whom she'd described as pompous and domineering; and nowhere had she exaggerated. Apart from his hard bossy stare he sported a thin dark moustache and a fleshy upturned nose with the nostrils showing from in front. The thrust-forward chin was intended to intimidate, and he wore a three-piece important dark blue suit with a striped tie even at that hour in the morning. Standing about five feet ten, he must have weighed well over two hundred pounds.

"Mother," he said repressively, "I'm all the help you need. I can cope perfectly well by myself." He gestured to me to leave, a motion I pleasantly ignored, edging past him, kissing Dorothea's sad cheek, and suggesting a cup of tea.

"Of course, dear. What am I thinking of? Come into the kitchen."

She herself was dressed in yesterday's green skirt and jumper, and I guessed she hadn't been to bed. The dark rings of tiredness had deepened round her eyes and her plump body looked shakily weak.

"I phoned Paul later, long after you'd gone, dear," she said, almost apologetically, running water into an electric kettle. "I felt so lonely, you see. I thought I would just warn him that his uncle's end was near . . ."

"So of course, although it was already late, I set off at once," Paul said expansively. "It was only right. My duty. You should never have been here alone with a dying man, Mother. He should have been in hospital."

I lifted the kettle from Dorothea's hands and begged her to sit down, telling her I would assemble the cups and saucers and everything else. Gratefully she let me take over while the universal coper continued to rock on his heels and expound his own virtues.

"Valentine had already died when I got here." He sounded aggrieved. "Of course I insisted on telephoning the doctor at once, though Mother ridiculously wanted to let him sleep! I ask you! What are doctors for?"

Dorothea raised her eyes in a sort of despair.

"The damned man was *rude* to me," Paul complained. "He should be struck off. He said Valentine should have been in hospital and he would be here at seven, not before."

"He couldn't *do* anything by coming," Dorothea said miserably. "Dying here was what Valentine wanted. It was *all right.*"

Paul mulishly repeated his contrary opinions. Deeply bored with him, I asked Dorothea if I could pay my respects to Valentine.

"Just go in, dear," she said, nodding. "He's very peaceful."

I left her listening dutifully to her offspring and went into Valentine's bedroom which was brightly and brutally lit by a center bulb hanging from the ceiling in an inadequate lampshade. A kinder lamp stood unlit on a bedside table, and I crossed to it and switched it on.

Valentine's old face was pale and smoothed by death, his forehead already cooler to the touch than in life. The labored breathing had given way to eternal silence. His eyes were fully closed. His mouth, half open, had been covered, by Dorothea, I supposed, with a flap of sheet. He did indeed look remarkably at peace.

I crossed to the doorway and switched off the cold overhead light. Dorothea was coming toward me from the kitchen, entering Valentine's room past me to look down fondly at her dead brother.

"He died in the dark," she said, distressed.

"He wouldn't mind that."

"No . . . but . . . I switched off his bedside light so that people wouldn't see in, and I was sitting in that chair looking out of the window waiting for Paul to come, listening to Valentine breathing, and I went to sleep. I just drifted off." Tears filled her eyes. "I didn't know . . . I mean, I couldn't help it."

"You've been very tired."

"Yes, but when I woke up it was so dark . . . and absolutely quiet, and I realized . . . it was *awful*, dear. I realized Valentine had stopped breathing . . . and he'd died while I was *asleep*, and I hadn't been there beside him to hold his hand or anything . . . " Her voice wavered into a sob and she wiped her eyes with her fist.

I put an arm round her shoulders as we stood beside Valentine's bed. I thought it lucky on the whole that she hadn't seen the jolt of her brother's heart stopping, nor heard the last rattle of his breath. I'd watched my own mother die, and would never forget it.

"What time did your son get here?"

"Oh . . . it must have been getting on for three. He lives in Surrey, you see, dear. It's quite a long drive, and he'd been ready for bed, he said. I told him not to come . . . I only wanted someone to talk to, really, when I rang him, but he insisted on coming . . . very good of him, dear, really."

"Yes," I said.

"He closed the curtains, of course, and switched on all the lights. He was quite cross with me for sitting in the dark, and for not getting Robbie Gill out. I mean, Robbie could only say officially that Valentine was dead . . . Paul didn't understand that I *wanted* just to be in the dark with Valentine. It was a sort of *comfort,* you see, dear. A sort of good-bye. Just the two of us, like when we were children."

"Yes," I said.

"Paul means well," she insisted, "but I do find him tiring. I'm sorry to wake you up so early. But Paul was so cross with me . . . so I phoned you when he went to the bathroom, because he might have stopped me, otherwise. I'm not myself somehow, I feel so weak."

"I'm happy to be here," I assured her. "What you need is to go to bed."

"Oh, I couldn't. I'll have to be awake for Robbie. I'm so afraid Paul will be rude to him."

A certainty, I thought.

The great Paul himself came into the room, switching on the overhead light again.

"What are you two doing in here?" he demanded. "Mother, do come away and stop distressing yourself. The old man's had a merciful release, as we all know. What we've got to talk about now is your future, and I've got plans made for that."

Dorothea's frame stiffened under my embracing arm. I let it fall away from her shoulders and went with her out of Valentine's room and back to the kitchen, flicking the harsh light off again as I went and looking back to the quiet old face in its semi-shadow. Permanent timeless shadow.

"Of *course* you must leave here," Paul was saying to his mother in the kitchen. "You're almost eighty. I can't look after you properly when you live so far away from me. I've already arranged with a retirement home that when Valentine died you would rent a room there. I'll tell them you'll be coming within a week. It's less than a mile from my house, so Janet will be able to drop in every day."

Dorothea looked almost frightened. "I'm not going, Paul," she contradicted. "I'm staying here."

Ignoring her, Paul said, "You may as well start packing your things at once. Why waste time? I'll put this house on the market tomorrow, and I'll move you immediately after the funeral."

"No," Dorothea said.

"I'll help you while I'm here," her son said grandly. "All Valentine's things will need sorting and disposing of, of course. In fact I may as well clear some of the books away at once. I brought two or three empty boxes."

"Not the books," I said positively. "He left his books to me."

"*What?*" Paul's mouth unattractively dropped open. "He can't have done," he said fiercely. "He left everything to Mother. We all know that."

"Everything to your mother except his books."

Dorothea nodded. "Valentine added a codicil to his will about two months ago, leaving his books to Thomas."

"The old man was gaga. I'll contest it!"

"You can't contest it," I pointed out reasonably. "Valentine left everything but the books to your mother, not to you."

"Then Mother will contest it!"

"No, I won't, dear," Dorothea said gently. "When Valentine asked me what I thought about him leaving his books and papers to Thomas, I told him it was a very nice idea. I would never read them or ever look at them much, and Valentine knew Thomas would treasure them, so he got a solicitor to draw up the codicil, and Betty—a friend of mine—and Robbie Gill—our doctor—witnessed his signature with the solicitor watching. He signed it here in his own sitting room, and there was no question of Valentine being gaga, which both the solicitor and the doctor will agree on, and I can't see what you're so bothered about, there's just a lot of old form books and scrapbooks and books about racing."

Paul was, it seemed to me, a great deal more disconcerted than seemed natural. He seemed also to become aware of my surprise, because he groped and produced a specious explanation, hating me while he delivered it.

"Valentine once told me there might be some value in his collection," he said. "I intend to get them valued and sold . . . for Mother's benefit, naturally."

"The books are for Thomas," Dorothea repeated doughtily, "and I never heard Valentine suggest they were valuable. He wanted Thomas to have them for old-time's sake, and for being so kind, coming to read to him."

*"Ah-hah!"* Paul almost shouted in triumph. "Valentine's codicil will be invalid, because he *couldn't see* what he was signing!"

Dorothea protested, "But he *knew* what he was signing."

*"How* did he know? Tell me that."

"Excuse me," I said, halting the brewing bad temper. "If Valentine's codicil is judged invalid, which I think unlikely if his solicitor drew it up and witnessed its signing, then the books belong to Dorothea, who alone can decide what to do with them."

"Oh, *thank you,* dear," she said, her expression relaxing, "then if they are mine, I will give them to you, Thomas, because I know that's what Valentine intended."

Paul looked aghast. "But you *can't.*"

"Why not, dear?"

"They . . . they may be *valuable.*"

"I'll get them valued," I said, "and if they really are worth an appreciable amount, I'll give that much to Dorothea."

"No, dear," she vehemently shook her head.

"Hush," I said to her. "Let it lie for now."

Paul paced up and down the kitchen in a fury and came to a halt on the far side of the table from where I sat with Dorothea beside me, demanding forcefully, "Just who are you, anyway, apart from ingratiating yourself with a helpless, dying old man? I mean, it's *criminal.*"

I saw no need to explain myself to him, but Dorothea wearily informed him, "Thomas's grandfather trained horses that Valentine shod. Valentine's known Thomas for more than twenty years, and he's always liked him, he told me so."

As if unable to stop himself, Paul marched his bulk away from this unwelcome news, abruptly leaving the kitchen and disappearing down the hall. One might have written him off as a pompous ass were it not for the fugitive impression of an underlying, heavy, half-glimpsed predator in the undergrowth. I wouldn't want to be at a disadvantage with him, I thought.

Dorothea said despairingly, "I don't *want* to live near Paul. I couldn't bear to have Janet coming to see me every day. I don't get on with her, dear. She bosses me about."

"You don't have to go," I said. "Paul can't put this house up for sale, because it isn't his. But, dearest Dorothea . . ." I paused, hesitating.

"But what, dear?"

"Well, don't *sign* anything."

"How do you mean?"

"I mean, don't sign *anything*. Ask your solicitor friend first."

She gazed at me earnestly. "I may *have* to sign things, now Valentine's gone."

"Yes, but . . . don't sign any paper just because Paul wants you to."

"All right," she said doubtfully.

I asked her, "Do you know what a power of attorney is?"

"Doesn't it give people permission to do things on your behalf?"

I nodded.

She thought briefly and said, "You're telling me not to sign a paper giving Paul permission to sell this house. Is that it?"

"It sure is."

She patted my hand. "Thank you, Thomas. I promise not to sign anything like that. I'll read everything carefully. I hate to say it, but Paul does try too hard sometimes to get his own way."

Paul, to my mind, had been quiet for a suspiciously long time. I stood up and left the kitchen, going in search of him, and I found him in Valentine's sitting room taking books off the shelves and setting them in stacks on the floor.

"What are you doing?" I asked. "Please leave those alone."

Paul said, "I'm looking for a book I loaned Valentine. I want it back."

"What's it called?"

Paul's spur-of-the-occasion lie hadn't got as far as a title. "I'll know it when I see it," he said.

"If any book has your name in it," I said politely, "I'll make sure that you get it back."

"That's not good enough."

Dorothea appeared in the doorway, saw the books piled on the floor, and looked aghast and annoyed at the same time.

"Paul! Stop that! Those books are Thomas's. If you take them you'll be *stealing.*"

Paul showed no sign of caring about such a minor accusation.

"He won't take them," I told her reassuringly.

Paul curled his lip at me, shouldered his way past, and opened the front door.

"What is he doing, dear?" Dorothea asked, perplexed, watching her son's back go purposefully down the path.

"It seems," I said, "that he's fetching one of his boxes to pack the books in." I closed the front door and shot its bolts, top and bottom. Then I hurried through into the kitchen and secured its outside door in the same way, and made a quick trip through all the rooms, and both bathrooms, to make sure the windows were shut and locked.

"But Paul's my son," Dorothea protested.

"And he's trying to steal Valentine's books."

"Oh *dear.*"

Paul began hammering on the front door. "Mother, let me in *at once.*"

"Perhaps I *should,*" Dorothea worried.

"He'll come to no harm out there. It's nowhere near freezing, and he can sit in his car. Or go home, of course."

"Sometimes Paul isn't *likeable,*" Dorothea said sadly.

I put the stacks of books back on Valentine's shelves. The ones that Paul had chosen to steal first were those with the glossiest covers, the recently published racing biographies, which were, in commercial resale terms, almost worthless. I guessed that chiefly it was Paul's vanity that was reacting against being thwarted by his mother and by me.

I had never underestimated the virulence of outraged vanity since directing a disturbing film about a real-life fanatical bodybuilder who'd killed his girlfriend because she'd left him for a wimp. I'd had to understand him, to crawl into his mind, and I'd hated it.

Paul's heavy hand banged repeatedly on the door, and he pressed unremittingly on the doorbell. This last resulted not in a shrill nerve-shredding single note, but in a less insupportable nonstop, quiet ding-dong; quiet because Dorothea had turned down the volume to avoid disturbing Valentine as he'd grown weaker.

I looked at my watch: five minutes to six. Perhaps an hour before we could expect the doctor but only thirty minutes before I should start my own workday.

"Oh, dear," Dorothea said for about the tenth time, "I do wish he'd stop."

"Tell him you'll let him in if he promises to leave the books alone."

"Do you think he'll agree?" she asked dubiously.

"A good chance," I said.

He wouldn't want to lose too much face with the awakening neighbors, I reckoned; only a fool would allow himself to be seen to be shut out like a naughty boy by his aged mother.

With evident relief she relayed the terms, to which her son with bad grace agreed. She unbolted the door and let him in, an entrance I carefully didn't watch, as the slightest smile on my face would be interpreted by him as a jeer, which would set him off again. Motorists had been shot for cutting in.

I stayed for a while in Valentine's sitting room with the door shut while mother and son sorted themselves out in the kitchen. I sat in the armchair opposite the one no longer occupied by the old man, and thought how easy it was to get embroiled in a senseless fracas. Without expecting it, I'd made an enemy of Paul Pannier; and I surmised that what he really wanted was not so much the books themselves, but to get me and my influence out of his mother's life, so that he could control and order her future as best suited his beneficent view of himself.

At least, I *hoped* that was the case. Anything worse was more than I felt like dealing with in the middle of making a film.

I stared vacantly at the wall of books, wondering if after all there were anything there of value. If so, I was sure Valentine had been unaware of it. When I'd mentioned the possibility of an autobiography and he'd vetoed the idea, he hadn't referred to any diaries or other raw material that could be used as sources by anyone else, but, sitting there, I wondered if by any chance Paul had made some sort of deal with a writer or publisher, to trade Valentine's papers for a share of the profits. No biography of Valentine's would make a fortune, but Paul, I guessed, would be content with modest pickings. Anything was better than nothing, one might hear him say.

Howard Tyler's book was not on the shelves.

Valentine had asked me, the first time I'd called on him, what had brought me back to Newmarket, and when I'd explained about Howard's book—*Unstable Times*—and the film we were to make of it, he'd said he'd heard of the book but he hadn't bought it, since at the time of its publication his eyesight had been fast deteriorating.

"I hear it's a load of rubbish," he said.

"Is it?"

"I knew Jacksy Wells. I often shod his horses. He never murdered that mousey wife of his, he hadn't got the guts."

"The book doesn't say he did," I assured him.

"And I hear it doesn't say he didn't, neither."

"Well, no."

"It wasn't worth writing a book about it. Waste of time making a film."

I'd smiled. Film makers notoriously and willfully distorted historical facts. Films knowingly based on lies could get nominated for Oscars.

"What was she like?" I asked.

"Who?"

"Jackson Wells's wife."

"Mousey, like I said. Funny, I can't remember her clearly. She wasn't one of those trainers' wives who run the whole stable. Mouths like cesspits, some of them had in the old days. Jackson Wells's wife, you wouldn't have known she existed. I hear she's halfway to a whore in the book, poor little bitch."

"Did she hang herself?"

"Search me," Valentine said. "I only shod the horses. The fuss died down pretty fast for lack of clues and evidence, but of course it did Jackson Wells in as a trainer. I mean, would *you* send your horses to a man who'd maybe killed his wife?"

"No."

"Nor did anyone else."

"The book says she had a lover," I said.

"Did she?" Valentine pondered. "First I've heard of it," he said. "But then, Dorothea could have a lover here under my nose and I wouldn't care. Good luck to her, if she did."

"You're a wicked old man, Valentine."

"Nobody's an angel," he said.

I looked at his empty chair and remembered his desperate half-whisper . . .

*I killed the Cornish boy . . .*

Maybe the Cornish boy was a horse.

Steps sounded on the path outside and the doorbell rang, ding-dong. I waited so as not to appear to be usurping Paul's desired status as head of the household, but it was in fact Dorothea who went to answer the summons.

"Come in, Robbie," she said, the loud relief in her voice reaching me clearly. "How dear of you to come."

"That son of yours!" The doctor's voice held dislike.

"Sorry, sorry," Dorothea said placatingly.

"Not your fault."

Dorothea let him in and closed the front door, and I opened the door of Valentine's sitting room to say hello.

Robbie Gill shook my hand perfunctorily. "Glad you've got company," he told Dorothea. "Now, about Valentine?"

All three of us went quietly into the old man's dimly lit room, followed importantly by Paul who immediately flooded the scene again with the overhead bulb. Perhaps it was only the director in me, I thought, that found this harsh insistence unpalatable. Certainly Robbie Gill made no protest but set about establishing clinically what was evident to any eye, that Valentine—the he who had lived in that chemical shell—had left it.

"What time did he die?" he asked Dorothea, his pen poised over a clipboard.

"I don't know to the minute," she said unhappily.

"Around one o'clock," I said.

"Mother was asleep," Paul accused unforgivingly. "She confessed it. She doesn't know when he died."

Robbie Gill gave him an expressionless stare and without comment wrote 01.00 on his clipboard, showing it to me and Dorothea.

"I'll see to the paperwork for you," he said to Dorothea. "But you'll need to get an undertaker."

"Leave it to me," Paul interrupted. "I'll take charge of all that."

No one demurred. Taking important charge of relatively minor matters suited Paul's character perfectly; and perhaps, I thought, he would be so fulfillingly involved that he would forget about the books. There was no harm, however, in seeking to give Dorothea a close line of defense.

"How about," I suggested to her, "letting me go across to your friend Betty's house, and asking her to come over to keep you company?"

"Good idea," Robbie Gill agreed emphatically.

"No need for that!" Paul objected.

"It's a bit *early*, dear," Dorothea protested, looking at the clock, but seeming hopeful nevertheless.

I crossed the road to the friend's house and woke the friend's husband, whose initial irritation turned to a resigned shrug.

"Poor old sod," he said, apparently referring to Valentine. "We'll look after Dorothea."

"Her son Paul is with her," I told him.

"Betty," he said intensely, "will be over *straight away.*"

I smiled at the owner of the bristly chin and the crumpled pajamas and dressing gown. Paul had a galvanic effect on everyone else's good nature, it seemed.

I waited until Betty had bustled across, plump and loving like Dorothea, and until Robbie Gill had left; during which period Paul half a dozen times told me I had no need to remain. While he was at one point busy patronizing the doctor, Dorothea confided to me guiltily that she had *locked* Valentine's sitting room door, dear, just in case, and had hidden the key in the pink vase in her bedroom.

I kissed her cheek, smiling, and drove off to work, half an hour late again but offering no apology.

Rehearsal and lighting took all morning. Each of the nonspeaking characters, Jockey Club members, had to be positioned in his armchair and taken through the responses to Nash Rourke's long vehement defense.

"Act scandalized here," I prompted, "then disbelieving, then throw up hands, throw down pencil, look angry, you think the man's guilty and lying. Right, everyone, we go through it again."

And again and again, with Nash's stand-in repeating the speech and pausing step by forward step for Moncrieff's lighting plans to be finalized. Cibber, at the head of the table, kept making fruity jokes as usual and running down the government in the normal bored manner of an old character actor who'd long abandoned hopes of Hamlet. Cibber—I called most of the cast by their script names as I found it less confusing all round—Cibber was going to give a crack-up later of such truth and misery that he would garner good critical mentions while detesting me for a long time after, but as yet he coasted along on "heard the one about the sperm and the lawyer, old boy?"

Cibber had been chosen by the casting director because of his upper-class appearance and voice; and I had no complaints about these, but only with his facile assumption that they were *enough,* when to me they were merely a start.

We broke briefly for lunch. Nash Rourke arrived in good time for make-up, and did one silent walk-through under the lights, for Moncrieff to check he had the same color temperatures as with the stand-in.

Owing to Nash's having rehearsed in private the evening before, the

"Jockey Club members" were not prepared for what they were going to see, and as I particularly wanted to record their spontaneous reactions in advance of their rehearsed version, I announced that the first "take" was in this case not to be considered to be a rehearsal, but would be the real thing: that action, failing only the set falling to pieces, would continue from start to finish, whatever was seeming to go wrong.

"Continuous," I said. *"No stops.* Right?"

Everyone nodded, even if doubt could be spotted here and there. Except for unrepeatable effects involving five hundred extras, first takes were rarely those seen on the screen.

With the world-weariness of unlimited experience, Nash understood what I wanted, but that didn't guarantee that he would deliver. That day, however, from some motive of his own, he decided generously to go along with the all-out take one, and performed with such vibrating power that the mouths round the table fell open with real incredulity. Moncrieff said the hairs on his own neck stood up, let alone those of the cast. Cibber instinctively slid down in his chair as Nash came to a thunderous halt leaning over him, and after a second or two of dead silence, when I said a shade breathlessly, "Cut, and print," the crews and actors as if of one mind *applauded*.

Nash shrugged it off. "Well, it's strongly written . . ."

He retraced his steps to leave the horseshoe and came over to where I stood.

"Well?" he said.

I was practically speechless.

"Go on," Nash said. "Say it. Say 'do it again.' "

His eyes smiled.

"Do it again," I said.

We repositioned and reloaded the cameras and repeated the scene twice more. All three takes went miraculously without glitches, and all three were printable, but it wasn't only I who thought the first electric beyond insulation.

"That man could murder," Moncrieff said of Nash thoughtfully.

"He was acting."

"No." He shivered slightly. "I mean, in fact."

Howard had heard that the enquiry scene had given a galvanizing, positively animating jolt to the whole production. He'd been told, by about ten different people, that Nash had said, "It's strongly written": and Howard knew that he hadn't written what Nash had yelled.

*"You,"* he said furiously, facing me after dinner across a small table in the Bedford Lodge Hotel bar, far too public a venue for his emotions, *"you* changed the script."

"Well," I said peaceably, "not very much. Most of it was your words exactly."

"But not the feeling," he complained. "You willfully misinterpreted my intention. You told Nash to lose control and threaten Cibber. *You* told him to look like a killer, you must have done, otherwise he wouldn't have thought of it, not from what I wrote."

"Look, Howard," I said with resignation, "we'd better come once and for all to an understanding. I don't want to quarrel with you. I want us to work together to produce a good film, but you did sign a contract . . ."

"What *you* think is a good film," he interrupted, "and what *I* think is a film truthful to my book, are totally opposite. All *you* care about is how much money it makes."

I took a large bracing mouthful of post-prandial cognac (to hell with the non-alcohol ethos) and decided to explain a few basic facts of movie life to the unrealistic idealist opposite me, his prim round glasses gleaming over earnest brown eyes and his small mouth contracting further in pique.

"I'm a *name,*" he insisted. "My readers expect subtlety, understatement, and psychological depth. What you're giving them is sex and violence."

"Have another vodka and cranberry juice?"

"No."

"Howard," I said. "Don't you understand what you agreed to? O'Hara put together a package that brought finance from one of the top seven studios. However much one may regret it, they don't fund moody films to play in art houses. They are strictly in the business for profit. The bottom line, Howard."

"Obscene," he said, disapprovingly.

I said, "O'Hara's chief bargaining promise with the big-seven movie company was that we would, between us, produce a film that at least wouldn't *lose* them money. Your own soft-focus view of an ancient scandal obviously worked fine as a novel, and there's much of that that I've insisted on retaining. I've fought for you, whatever you may think."

"What, precisely, have you retained?" he demanded, hurting.

"You wrote the whole first quarter as a semi–ghost story about the dream lovers of the wife who ended up hanged."

"Yes."

"Her dreams and illusions are in the screenplay," I reminded him. "Her lovers are jockeys, the way you wrote them. But who were the real jockeys? Did they ride the horses her husband trained?"

"They were in her mind."

"But why did she hang, Howard? Was she topped by one of the dream lovers? Did she do it herself? Did her husband kill her?"

After a pause he said, "No one knows."

"I know they don't," I said. "At least, no one ever told. But an ending of no explanation at all isn't going to get people paying to see the film."

He said sarcastically, "That bottom line again."

"I'll give you the dream lovers," I said. "And you'll allow me an earthly explanation."

"That's not fair."

I gazed at him. He was old enough to know that few things were fair. Most five-year-olds had already discovered it.

"What we are dealing with here," I said, changing tack, "is three versions of the same story."

"What do you mean?"

"We have the story you wrote in your book. We have the story we're shooting in the film. And somewhere out of sight, way back in history, is what actually happened. Three views of the same facts."

Howard didn't argue.

I said, "By Sunday, Howard, I'd like you to come up with a rational explanation of the wife's death."

"But it's already Thursday evening!" he exclaimed, horrified.

"You've had literally years to work it out."

"But no one knows!"

"Then guess."

"I can't," he protested belligerently. "I've tried."

"Then I'll do it," I said. "I'll work with you on the necessary scenes. We'll use most of your script as written, but your inconclusive ending is impossible."

"But it's what *happened*. There wasn't any ending to the story."

"For the film, there has to be."

"Don't you *care* about the facts?"

"Perhaps, if we look closely enough," I said, only half meaning it, "we might ourselves uncover those facts. What if we actually could find out what really happened?"

"You can't," Howard said flatly. "No one knows."

"No one's saying. That's different." I paused. "What did Jackson Wells tell you, when you went to see him?"

O'Hara had asked Howard the same thing, he'd told me, and Howard, to O'Hara's utter disbelief, had said he hadn't consulted Jackson Wells at all. Howard hadn't thought it necessary. Howard didn't want to risk unwelcome anti-climactic disclosures from Jackson Wells that might upset his lyrical tale of the dream lovers and the semi-mystical death.

Moncrieff, strolling into the bar, seeing us, and crossing without hesitation to join us, saved Howard from having to answer.

Howard and Moncrieff disliked each other without making much overt display of it. Moncrieff, no reader of novels, thought Howard a prissy, impractical, pseudo-intellectual nuisance on the set. Howard's expression made no attempt to disguise his disparagement of Moncrieff's unkempt appearance with the small straggly beard that was halfway between an artistic statement and a lazy approach to shaving.

Neither of them had the least understanding of the other's function. Moncrieff, endlessly creative within the effects of lighting, needed to be given the actors, the scene, and the intention of the storyline, but his enormous input was a moonshot outside the range of Howard's comprehension. Each of them,

being acclaimed as individualists, wholly believed that it was he who was in-
dispensable to any chance of esteem for the finished film.

As Nash Rourke tended to think the same, also O'Hara, also myself, and
also the film editor who would cut some of his own opinions into our work,
it was unlikely that anyone would end up wholly satisfied, even if the public
approved. Howard, though he didn't seem to appreciate it, at least had more
control of his own work than most authors.

"What about those dream lovers, then?" Moncrieff asked abrasively.

Howard became predictably defensive. "The wife imagines them. You don't
need to worry about it."

"Oh, yes, he does," I corrected mildly. *"She* may be imagining the jockeys,
but we, the onlookers, are going to see them standing in her bedroom."

Howard looked aghast, to Moncrieff's amusement.

"One at a time," I explained. "She sees one in her bedroom. Another time,
she sees another. And another. We have three tall ultra-handsome unknowns
coming to dress up as the dream lovers. They won't look like real jockeys.
They don't speak, and don't worry, Howard, they won't get into bed. The wife
watches her husband from her bedroom window as he rides out with his
string of horses to their morning exercise, then she turns into the room and
conjures up her dream jockey lover. Moncrieff will light the jockey to make
it clear that he's imaginary. Another day the wife will wave to her husband,
and then turn and imagine a *different* lover."

Moncrieff nodded. "Easy."

"She dances with the third lover. Slowly, orgasmically. She's transported," I
said.

Moncrieff happily nodded again.

"So there you are, Howard," I said. "The lovers are how you wrote them.
No sex."

"All highly unlikely," Moncrieff laughed. "Any jockey worth his salt would
have her nightie off before her husband was out of the stable yard."

"She hanged," I said. "No dream."

Both of them stared, silenced.

*Why* did she hang, I wondered. The further we went with the filming, the
more I wanted to know, yet until then it had been the results of that death,
the accusations against her husband, and his handling of them, that had been
the focus both of Howard's book and, more especially, of our film version.

I gave a mental shrug. I hadn't time for any inept detective work, trying to
unearth a secret twenty-six years buried. I had only to bully Howard into in-
venting a good reason and giving Nash a huge satisfactory last scene in which

he discovered the truth—Howard's version of the truth—and to end the film in perhaps cynical heroism.

"What made you write the book?" I asked Howard.

"You know what did. A newspaper article."

"Do you still have it?"

He looked surprised and, as usual, displeased. "Yes, I suppose so," he said grudgingly, "but not *here.*"

"What paper was it in?"

"I don't see that it matters."

Howard himself, in the ensuing pause, seemed to agree that he'd been unnecessarily ungracious.

"The *Daily Cable,*" he said. "It was an obituary of the member of the Jockey Club that I called Cibber in the book."

I nodded. That much I knew. "What was Cibber's real name?"

"Visborough." He spelled it.

"And who wrote the obituary?" I asked.

"I've no idea," Howard replied, still obstructively but this time with a surprise that gave his statement credence.

"Didn't you follow it up?" I asked.

"Of course not." Howard became condescending. "You've no idea how a creative author writes. The *inconclusiveness* of the obituary was its own inspiration. I received the *idea* from the obituary and the book grew in my mind."

"So," Moncrieff said, "you never even tried to find out what really happened?"

"Of course not. But I didn't *alter* the account given in the obituary, not like O'Hara and Thomas have made me alter things for the film." He was acridly bitter. "My readers will *hate* the film."

"No they won't," I said, "and hundreds of thousands of new readers will buy your paperbacks."

He liked that idea, however he might carp. He preened, smirking. Moncrieff's dislike of him visibly grew.

Howard had had enough of Moncrieff, and of me too, no doubt. He got to his feet and left us, making no pretense of social civility.

"He's an oaf," Moncrieff said, "and he's bellyaching all over the place, to anyone who will listen, about the bastardizing of his masterpiece. A few dream lovers won't shut him up."

"Who has he been bellyaching *to?*" I asked.

"Does it matter?"

"Yes, it does. His contract forbids him to make adverse criticism of the film in public until six months after it has had a general release. If he's talking to the actors and the crews, that's one thing. If he's complaining to strangers, say in the bar here, I'll have to shut him up."

"But can you?" Moncrieff asked with doubt.

"There are prickly punitive clauses in his contract. I had a sight of it, so I'd know what I could ask of him, and what I couldn't."

Moncrieff whistled softly through his teeth. "Did O'Hara write the contract?"

"Among others. It's pretty standard in most respects. Howard's agent agreed to it, and Howard signed it." I sighed. "I'll remind him tactfully tomorrow."

Moncrieff tired of the subject. "About tomorrow," he said. "Still the six-thirty dawn call out in the stable yard?"

"Definitely. The horses have to be exercised. I told all the stable lads this evening we'd be shooting them mounting and riding out through the gate to the exercise ground. They'll be wearing their normal clothes: jeans, anoraks, crash helmets. I reminded them not to look at the cameras. We'll take the overall scene of the lads mounting. Nash will come out of the house and be given a leg-up onto his mount. We'll rehearse it a couple of times, not more. I don't want to keep the horses circling too long. When Nash is mounted and comfortable, the assistant trainer can lead the string out through the gate. Nash waits for them to go, and follows, last. As he leaves, he'll look backward and up to the window from where his wife is supposedly watching. You've arranged for a camera crew up there to do the wife's point of view? Ed will be up there, supervising."

Moncrieff nodded.

I said, "We'll cut the main shot once Nash is through the gate. I hope we won't have to do many retakes, but when we're satisfied, the string can go on and get their regular exercise, and Nash can come back and dismount. We're going to be repeating the whole thing on Saturday. We'll need a new view from the wife's room and different jackets et cetera on Nash and the lads. We'll need close shots of hooves on the gravel, that sort of thing."

Moncrieff nodded. "And Sunday?"

"The Jockey Club people are letting us film out on the gallops, as there won't be many real horses-in-training working that day. You and I will go out by car on the roads on Saturday with a map for you to position the cameras. I know already where best to put them."

"So you should, if you were brought up here."

"Mm. Sunday afternoon, the horses go to Huntingdon racecourse. I hope to hell we have three fine mornings."

"What if it rains?"

"If it's just drizzle, we go ahead with filming. Horses do go out in all weathers, you know."

"You don't say."

"Tomorrow afternoon," I said, "we'll be indoors up in the enquiry room set again, like today. The schedule you've got is unchanged. There are more exchanges involving Cibber, Nash, and others. Apart from the wide establishing shots, it's mostly short close-ups of them speaking. The usual thing. We'll complete Nash's shots first. If the others don't fluff their lines too much, we might get through most of it tomorrow. Otherwise we'll have to carry on on Saturday afternoon as well."

"OK."

Moncrieff and I finished our drinks and went our separate ways, I upstairs to my room to make an arranged phone call to O'Hara in London.

"How did the Jockey Club scene go?" he asked immediately.

"Nash wowed them."

"Good, then."

"I think . . . well, we'll have to see the rushes tomorrow . . . but I think it was a sit-up-and-take-notice performance."

"Good boy."

"Yes, he was."

"No, I meant . . . well, never mind. How's everything else?"

"All right, but," I paused, "we need a better ending."

"I agree that the proposed ending's too weak. Hasn't Howard any ideas?"

"He *likes* the weak ending."

"Lean on him," O'Hara said.

"Yes. Um, you know he based his book on the obituary of the man he called Cibber? His real name was Visborough." I spelled it, as Howard had done. "Well, could you get me a copy of that obituary? It was published in the *Daily Cable,* Howard says. It must have been at least three years ago. Howard doesn't know who wrote it. He never followed anything up in any way. He says simply that the obituary, and especially its inconclusiveness, was what jolted his imagination into writing the book."

"You don't ask much!"

"The *Daily Cable* must have a cuttings library. You'll certainly be able to get that obituary. Could you fax it to me here at Bedford Lodge? If I knew exactly what started Howard's imagination working in the first place, perhaps I could help him find an explosive denouement."

"You'll have the obituary tomorrow," O'Hara promised.

"Thanks."

"How's your friend?" he asked.

"What friend?"

"The one who's dying."

"Oh." I paused. "He died during last night."

"Bad luck."

"He was old. Eighty something. A blacksmith turned top racing journal-ist, grand old character, great unusual life. Pity we can't make a film of *him.*"

"Films of good people don't have much appeal."

"Ain't that the truth."

"What was his name?"

"Valentine Clark," I said. "The *Daily Cable* might do an obituary of him too, you never know. He wrote for the *Racing Gazette.* Everyone in racing knew him. And . . . um . . . he knew the real trainer, Jackson Wells, the basis of the character that Nash is playing."

"Did he?" O'Hara's attention sharpened down the line. "So you surely asked him what he knew of the hanging?"

"Yes, I did. He knew no more than anyone else. The police dropped the case for lack of leads. Valentine said Jackson Wells's wife was an unmemorable mouse. He couldn't tell me anything helpful. It was all so very long ago."

O'Hara almost laughed. "It was very long ago for *you,* Thomas, because you're young. I'll bet twenty-six years is yesterday to Jackson Wells himself."

"I . . . er . . ." I said diffidently, "I did think of going to see him."

"Jackson Wells?"

"Yes. Well, Valentine, my dead friend, he was originally a blacksmith, as I told you. He used to shoe my grandfather's horses regularly, and he did say he'd also sometimes shod the horses Jackson Wells trained. So perhaps I could make some excuse . . . following Valentine's death . . . to make a nostalgic visit to Jackson Wells. What do you think?"

"Go at once," O'Hara said.

"He won't want to talk about the wife who hanged. He has a new life now and a second wife."

"Try, anyway," O'Hara said.

"Yes, I thought so. But he lives near Oxford . . . it'll take me half a day."

"Worth it," O'Hara said. "I'll OK the extra time."

"Good."

"Goodnight," he said. "I've a lady waiting."

"Good luck."

He cursed me—"You son of a bitch"—and disconnected.

I'D ALWAYS LOVED early mornings in racing stables. I'd been down in my grandfather's yard dawn by dawn for years, half my day lived before the first school bell. I tended, for the film, to make the horses more of a priority in my attention than perhaps I should have, moving about the yard, in close contact with the creatures I'd grown up among, and felt at home with.

I'd ridden as an amateur jockey in jump races from the age of sixteen, with most of my family expecting horses in some way to be my life forever, but fate and finance—or lack of it—had found me at twenty engaged in organizing horses in Arizona for the cavalry in a Western drama. By twenty-one I'd become the director of a bad minor film about rodeo riders, but that had led to the same post in a noble native-American saga that had modestly hit the jackpot. After that I'd spent a year working for film editors, learning their craft, followed by another year on sound tracks and music, and by twenty-six I'd been let loose as director on an unconsidered romance between a boy and a puma that had made astonishing profits. O'Hara had been the producer: I had never since been long out of work. "The boy's lucky," O'Hara would say, selling my name. "You can't buy luck. Trust me."

For this present film I'd suggested to O'Hara early in the pre-production stage that this time we should *buy*, not rent or borrow for fees, our stableful of horses.

"Too expensive," he'd objected automatically.

"Not necessarily," I'd contradicted. "We can buy cheap horses. There are hundreds that have never done well in races, but they *look* like good thoroughbreds, and that's what's important. Also we won't have any problems with insurance or recompense for injuries, we can travel them where and when we like, and we can work them without anxious owners fluttering round to fuss about their feed or exercise. We can sell them again, at the end."

One of O'Hara's chief virtues, in my eyes, was his ability to evaluate facts very fast and come up with quick decisions. So "Buy them," he said, and he'd liberated sufficient funds for a bloodstock agency to acquire the fourteen good-looking no-hopers currently eating oats and hay in our yard.

The actors' unions having agreed we should use real-life stable personnel for the horses, I'd recruited a young assistant trainer from a prestigious Newmarket yard and installed him in charge of our whole horse operation, giving him the title of horsemaster and also the riding but nonspeaking role of assistant trainer in the film.

He was already busy getting lads and horses ready for the morning action when I arrived in the yard at dawn. Moncrieff's crew had laid felt carpeting over the gravel to silence the progress of the rolling camera dolly. He himself had strategically planted his lighting. Ed, he reported, was already in position upstairs.

The weather was cold and windy with dark scudding clouds. Moncrieff liked the moodiness, humming happily as he arranged for ominous shadows to fall across Nash's stand-in, who looked hopelessly un-trainerlike in riding gear. When Nash himself—in character—strode out of the house and yelled bad-tempered instructions to the lads, it was as real as any such bona fide moment I'd ever seen.

There were annoyances with the camera truck—one of its wheels squeaked despite the felt path. Oil and oaths fixed it. Moncrieff and I fretted at the delay because of light values. Nash seemed less irritated than resigned.

Only two takes were necessary of the assistant trainer giving Nash a leg-up onto his hack; the horse amazingly stood still. Nash wheeled away and sat on his mount in and out of shot while the assistant trainer heaved himself into his own saddle and led the circling string of by now mounted lads out through wide open stable gates onto the Newmarket training grounds beyond. Nash followed last, remembering to look back and up to the bedroom window. When his horse had walked him well out of sight I yelled, "Cut," and the whole string ambled back into the yard, the hooves scrunching on the gravel, the lads joshing each other like kids out of school.

"How did it go?" I asked Moncrieff. "Cameras OK?"

"OK."

"Print, then." I walked among the horses to speak to their riders. "That was good," I said. "We'll do it again, now, though. Two snaps are better than one."

They nodded. By then they all considered themselves expert film makers. The second take didn't go as smoothly, but that didn't necessarily matter: we would use the version that looked more natural on film.

I followed them on foot out of the gate to where Nash and all the lads were circling, awaiting my verdict.

"Same again tomorrow morning," I said, patting horses' necks. "Different clothes. Off you all go, then. Remember not to get in the way of any real race-horses. Walk and trot only on the grounds we've been allotted."

The string filed off to exercise and Nash returned to the yard, dismounting and handing his reins to the lad left behind for the purpose.

"Is it still on for tomorrow?" he asked, turning in my direction.

"Doncaster, do you mean?"

He nodded.

"Of course it is," I said. "The Stewards have asked you to their lunch, so you can use their box all afternoon and have as much as or as little privacy as you want. They've sent tickets for two, for you to take a companion."

"Who?"

"Whoever you like."

"You, then."

"*What?* I meant a friend, or perhaps Silva?" Silva was the bewitching actress he'd tumbled around with in bed.

"Not her," he said vehemently. "You. Why not? And don't say you'll still be doing close shots in the enquiry room. Let's make damned sure they all get completed this afternoon. I want you because you know the drill on a British racecourse, and the racing people know *you.*"

Green lights got what they wanted. Moreover, I discovered it was what I wanted also.

"Fine, then," I said. "Helicopter at eleven-thirty."

Watching his familiar back walk off to his ever-waiting Rolls, I called Bedford Lodge from my mobile phone and by persuasive perseverance got the staff to find Howard Tyler, who was in the bar.

"Just a word, Howard," I said.

"Not *more* script changes?" He was acidly sarcastic.

"No. Um . . . simply a word of warning."

"I don't need your words of warning."

"Good, then. But . . . er . . . I just thought I might remind you, knowing how you feel, that you agreed not to bellyache about the film until after its release."

"I'll say what I damned well please."

"It's your privilege. I don't suppose you care about the penalties in your contract."

"What penalties?"

"Most film contracts include them," I said. "I'm sure yours does. Film companies routinely seek ways to stop a disgruntled writer from sabotaging the whole film just because he or she dislikes the changes made to the original work. They put in clauses allowing themselves to recover substantial damages."

After a lengthy pause Howard said, "I never signed such a contract."

"Fine, then, but you might check with your agent."

"You're trying to frighten me!" he complained.

"I'm just suggesting you might want to be careful."

Silence. Howard simply put down his receiver. So much for tactful advice!

True to his intention, Nash did make damned sure that we completed the enquiry room shots that day, even if not until past eight in the evening. In want of a shower and a reviving drink, I drove back to Bedford Lodge and found waiting for me a long fax from O'Hara, starting with the *Daily Cable's* obituary.

Rupert Visborough's life was dedicated to serving his country, his neighbourhood, and the Sport of Kings.

Commissioned into the Scots Guards, he retired with the rank
of major to enter local politics in his home county of Cambridge-
shire. Many committees benefitted from his expert chairmanship,
including . . .

The list was long, virtuous, and unexciting.

A landowner, he was elected a member of the Jockey Club following the
death of his father, Sir Ralph Visborough, knighted for his patronage of
many animal charities.

Highly respected by all who knew him, Rupert Visborough felt
obliged to remove his name from a shortlist of those being considered
for selection as parliamentary candidate, a consequence of his having in-
advertently been involved in an unexplained death closely touching his
family.

His wife's sister, married to Newmarket trainer Jackson Wells, was
found hanged in one of the stalls in her husband's stable yard. Exhaus-
tive police enquiries failed to find either a reason for suicide, or any motive or suspect for murder. Jackson Wells maintained his innocence
throughout. The Jockey Club, conducting its own private enquiry, concluded there was no justification for withdrawing Wells's licence to train.
Rupert Visborough, present at the enquiry, was justifiably bitter at the
negative impact of the death on his own expectations.

Reports that Jackson Wells's wife was entertaining lovers unknown to
her husband could not be substantiated. Her sister—Visborough's wife—
described the dead woman as "fey" and "a daydreamer." She said that as
she and her sister had not been close she could offer no useful suggestions.

Who knows what Rupert Visborough might not have achieved in life
had these events not happened? Conjectures that he himself knew more
of the facts behind the tragedy than he felt willing to disclose clung to
his name despite his strongest denials. The death of his sister-in-law is
unresolved to this day.

Visborough died last Wednesday of a cerebral haemorrhage, aged 76,
with his great potential sadly unfulfilled.

He is survived by his wife, and by their son and daughter.

O'Hara had handwritten across the bottom: "Pious load of shit! No one
on the paper knows who wrote it. Their obits often come in from outside."
The pages of fax continued, however.

O'Hara's handwriting stated: "This paragraph appeared in the *Cable*'s irreverent gossip column on the same day as the obituary."

Secrets going to grave in the Visborough family? It seems Rupert (76), Jockey Club member, dead Wednesday of a stroke, never discovered how his sister-in-law hanged twenty-three years ago in who-dunnit circs. Bereaved husband, Jackson Wells, now remarried and raising rape near Oxford, had 'no comment' re the Visborough demise. Answers to the twenty-three-year-old mystery *must* exist. Send us info.

O'Hara's handwriting: "The *Cable* got about 6 replies, all no good. End of story as far as they are concerned. But at great expense they searched their microfilmed records and found these accounts, filed and printed at the time of the hanging."

The first mention had earned a single minor paragraph: "Newmarket trainer's wife hanged."

For almost two weeks after that there had been daily revelations, many along the lines of "did she jump or was she pushed?" and equally many about the unfairness—and personal bitterness—of the nipping in the bud effect of Visborough's ambitions for a political career.

A hanging in the family, it seemed, had discouraged not only racehorse owners; the blight had spread beyond Jackson Wells to canvassers and prospective voters.

The story had extinguished itself from lack of fuel. The last mention of Jackson Wells's wife announced untruthfully, "The police expect to make an arrest within a few days." And after that, silence.

The basic question remained unanswered—*why* did she hang?

I had dinner and went to bed and dreamed about them, Visborough as Cibber, his cuckolding wife as the pretty actress Silva, Nash as Jackson Wells, and the fey hanged woman as a wisp of muslin, a blowing curtain by the window.

No insight. No inspiration. No solution.

# 5

---

Delays plagued the going-out-to-exercise scene the next morning. One of the horses, feeling fractious, dumped his lad and kicked one of the camera operating crew. Light bulbs failed in midshot. One of the stable lads loudly asked a silly question while the cameras were rolling, and a sound engineer, who should have known better, strolled, smoking, into the next take.

Nash, emerging from the house, forgot to bring with him the crash helmet he was supposed to put on before he mounted. He flicked his fingers in frustration and retraced his steps.

By the time we finally achieved a printable result it was no longer dawn or anywhere near it. Moncrieff, cursing, juggled relays of colored filters to damp down the exuberant sun. I looked at my watch and thought about the helicopter.

"Once more," I shouted generally. "And for Christ's sake get it right. Don't come back, go on out to exercise. Everyone ready?"

"Cameras rolling," Moncrieff said.

I yelled "Action," and yet again the lads led their long-suffering charges out of the loose stalls, hauled themselves into the saddle, formed a straggly line, and skittered out of the gate. Nash, following them, forgot to look up at the window.

I yelled, "Cut," and said to Moncrieff, "Print."

Nash came back swearing.

"Never mind," I said. "We'll cut it in. Would you ride out again and turn and look up *after* you're through the gate, as if the other horses had gone out of shot ahead of you? We'll also do a close shot of that look."

"Right now?"

"Yes," I said. "Now, because of having the same light. And how about a touch of exasperation with the wife?"

The close shot of the exasperation proved well worth the extra time taken in raising a camera high. Even Moncrieff smiled.

All Nash said was, "I hope the Doncaster Stewards wait lunch."

He whisked off in the Rolls but when I followed a minute or two later I found him still standing in the hotel lobby reading a newspaper, rigidly concentrated.

"Nash?" I enquired tentatively.

He lowered the paper, thrust it into my hands, and in explosive fury said, *"Shit."* Then he turned on his heel and stalked off, leaving me to discover what had upset him.

I saw. I read, and felt equally murderous.

## BUMMER OF A FILM ON THE TURF

First reports of *Unstable Times,* now in front of cameras in Newmarket, speak of rows, discord, and screeching nerves.

Author Howard Tyler's vibrant tale, ten weeks on best-seller lists, is mangled beyond recognition, my sources tell me. Nash Rourke, superstar, rues his involvement: says "Director Thomas Lyon (30), ineffectual, arrogant, insists on disastrous last-minute script changes."

Lyon vows to solve a twenty-six-year-old real-life mystery, basis of Tyler's masterpiece. The police failed at the time. Who is Lyon kidding?

Naturally those closely touched by the tragic unexplained hanging death of a leading Newmarket trainer's wife are distressed to have cold embers fanned to hurtful inaccurate reheat.

Lyon's version so far has the hanged wife's trainer-husband—Rourke—tumbling her sister, prompting apoplectic revenge from consequently cuckolded top Jockey Club steward, later gaga. None of this happened.

Why do the giants of Hollywood entrust a prestigious film-of-the-book to the incompetent mercies of an over-hyped bullyboy? Why is this ludicrous buffoon still strutting his stuff on the Heath? Who's allowing him to waste millions of dollars on this pathetic travesty of a great work?

Isn't Master Thomas Lyon ripe for the overdue boot?

There was a large photograph of Nash, looking grim.

Blindly angry I went up to my rooms and found the telephone ringing when I walked in.

Before I could speak into the receiver, Nash's voice said, "I didn't say that, Thomas."

"You wouldn't."

"I'll kill that son of a bitch Tyler."

"Leave him to O'Hara."

"Are we still going to Doncaster?"

"We certainly are," I said. Anywhere but Newmarket, I thought. "Ready in half an hour?"

"I'll be down in the lobby."

I phoned O'Hara's mobile phone and reached only his message service.

I said, "Read the *Daily Drumbeat,* page sixteen, feature column headed, 'Hot from the Stars.' Nash and I are going to the sports. I'll have my mobile. Take Prozac."

Howard Tyler's phone rang and rang in his room, unanswered.

I showered in record time, put on Steward-lunching clothes, and went down to ask questions of the helpful soul behind the reception desk.

"Mr. Tyler isn't here," she confirmed. "He left."

"*When* did he leave?"

"Actually," she said, "he picked up a newspaper from the desk here and went into the dining room to have breakfast, as he always does. It's so nice to have him here, and Mr. Rourke too, we can hardly believe it . . . So Mr. Tyler hurried out of the dining room five minutes later—he didn't eat his breakfast—he went upstairs and came down with his suitcase and said he didn't know when he'd come back." She looked worried. "I didn't ask him for payment. I hope I haven't done wrong, but I understood everything should be charged to the film company."

"Don't worry about that," I reassured her. "Did Mr. Tyler say where he was going?"

He hadn't of course. He'd been in a great hurry. The receptionist had asked him if he'd felt ill, but he hadn't answered. He'd taken the newspaper with him, but the staff had had another copy. They had all read the column. She'd thought it best to show it to Mr. Rourke. Her virtuousness nearly choked her.

"What will happen, do you think?" Nash asked, ready for the races, listening to a repeat from the receptionist.

"Short term, we've got Howard off our backs."

We went out to the Rolls and along to where the helicopter waited.

"I'll sue the bastard," Nash said furiously, strapping himself in. "Saying I rue my involvement!"

"Did you?"

"Did I what?"

"Say it."

"Shit, Thomas. I said I was sorry not to be staying home with my wife. And that was on day one. I don't in the least regret it now."

"She could have come with you."

He shrugged. We both knew why his wife had stayed at home: her insecurity in a four-months' pregnancy with complications. She'd been annoyed with him for agreeing to Newmarket. He'd made too public an apology.

"As for all that trash I was supposed to say about you personally . . ."

"Howard put his own words into your mouth," I said. "Forget it."

The helicopter lifted off from the Newmarket grass and swung round northwest.

However glibly I might say "forget it," I had uncomfortable suspicions that the parent movie company, our source of finance, would come thundering down like a posse to lynch me from the nearest crossbeam. Any bad odor clinging to their investment called for dismissals to exorcise it. O'Hara might have to dump me: might even want to.

Bye-bye career, I thought. It had been great while it lasted. I couldn't believe what was happening.

Smart move on Howard's part to decamp out of reach of my fists. I could have killed him. I sat quietly in the helicopter looking out at the county of Lincolnshire passing beneath and felt queasy from the turmoil in my gut.

I accepted that in general the most disliked person in the making of any film was the director. The director required people to do things they considered unnecessary/ridiculous/wrong. Directors (a) demanded too much from actors and (b) ignored their well-thought-out interpretations. Directors were never satisfied, wasted time on detail, worked everyone to death, ignored injured feelings, made no allowance for technical difficulties, expected the impossible, screamed at people.

I accepted also on the other hand that a director needed an overall vision of the work in progress, even if details got changed en route. A director had to fight to bring that vision to revelatory life. Excessive sympathy and tolerance on the set were unproductive, vacillating decisions wasted money, and inconsistency left an enterprise rudderless. A successful movie was a tight ship.

It was more in my nature to be a persuader than an ogre, but sometimes, as with Howard, when persuasion failed to work, the ogre surfaced. I knew, too, that it was what O'Hara expected and in fact required of me. Use your power, he'd said.

Now everyone working on the film would read the piece in the *Drumbeat*. Half of Newmarket also. Even if O'Hara left me in charge, my job would be difficult to impossible, all my authority gone. If I had to, I would fight to get that back.

The helicopter landed near the Doncaster winning post, where a senior official was waiting to give Nash a suitable greeting and to lead him to the mandarins. The minute I followed him onto the grass my mobile phone buzzed, and I told him to go ahead, I would join him after I'd talked to O'Hara; if it were in fact O'Hara.

He looked at me straightly and asked the official to pause for my call.

I answered the phone's summons. "Thomas," I said.

"Thomas!" O'Hara's voice was loud with annoyance. "Where are you?" Nash could hear him shouting: he winced.

"Doncaster racecourse."

"I've had Hollywood on the line. It's not yet five in the morning there but the company is already furious. Someone made a phone call and then sent a fax of the *Drumbeat*."

I said stupidly, "A *fax?*"

"A fax," he confirmed.

"Who sent it?"

"The mogul I talked to didn't say."

I swallowed. My heart raced. The hand holding the instrument visibly trembled beside my eye. Calm down, I thought.

"Who did Tyler talk to?" O'Hara demanded furiously.

"I don't know."

"You don't *know?*"

"No. He was grumbling to everyone who would listen. He may not have known he was spouting to a journalist—or to someone who *knew* a journalist."

"What does he say about it?"

"The hotel says he blasted off the minute he saw the paper. No one knows where he's gone."

"I tried his home number," O'Hara shouted. "They say he's in Newmarket."

"More likely the moon."

"The mogul I talked to is one of the very top guys, and he wants your head."

This was it, I thought numbly, and I couldn't think of anything to say. I needed an impassioned plea in mitigation. Drew a blank.

"Are you there, Thomas?"

"Yes."

"He says you're fired."

I was silent.

"Hell's teeth, Thomas, defend yourself."

"I warned Howard yesterday not to shoot his mouth off, but I think now that he'd already done it."

"Two weeks ago he tried to get the moguls to fire you, if you remember. I pacified them then. But *this!*" Words failed him.

I began finally to protest. "We're on target for time. We're within budget. The company themselves insisted on story changes. I'm making a commercial motion picture, and it isn't true that there are rows and discord, except with Howard himself."

"What's he saying?" Nash demanded impatiently.

"I'm sacked."

Nash snatched the phone out of my hand.

"O'Hara? This is Nash. You tell those brain-deads who are our masters that I did *not* say what the *Drumbeat* says I did. Your boy is doing an OK job on this movie and if you take him off it at this stage you *will* get a bummer of a film, and what's more, they can whistle for me to sign with them ever again."

Aghast, I snatched the phone back. "Nash, you can't do that. O'Hara, don't listen to him."

"Put him back on the line."

I handed the phone over, shaking my head. Nash listened to O'Hara for a while and finally said, "You told me to trust him. I do. This movie has a good feel. Now you trust *me,* trust my nose in these matters."

He listened a bit longer, said "Right," and pressed the power-off button.

"O'Hara says he'll call you back in five hours when they will have talked it through in Hollywood. They're going to hold a breakfast meeting there at nine o'clock, when the bigwigs are all up. O'Hara will sit in on a conference call."

"Thank you," I said.

He smiled briefly. "My reputation is at stake here, same as yours. I don't want my green light turning amber."

"It never will."

"Bad reviews give me indigestion."

We walked with the patient official across the track and up to the Stewards' privacy. Heads turned sharply all the way as racegoer after racegoer did a double take at the sight of Nash. We had asked for no advance publicity—the parent film company was security hyper-conscious—so that only the top echelon knew whom to expect. I was glad, I found, to have an anonymous face.

They hadn't waited lunch. Even for mega-stars, racing timetables couldn't be changed. About twenty Stewards and friends were at their roast beef and suitable Yorkshire pudding.

From behind the forks the welcome was as warm and impressed as the most inflated ego could desire, and Nash's ego, as I was progressively discovering, was far more normal and unassuming than seemed consistent with his eminence.

I'd been in awe of him before I'd met him. I'd metaphorically approached him on my knees; and I'd found, not the temperamental perfectionist I'd been ominously told to expect, but essentially the man I'd seen him play over and over again on the screen, a man, whatever the role or the make-up, of sane intelligence, mentally tough.

I forlornly hoped that the Doncaster Stewards and their wives and other guests weren't avid readers of *Drumbeat*'s "Hot from the Stars," and with relief I saw that the two papers most in evidence were the *Racing Gazette* and the *Daily Cable,* both of them lying open at the obituary page for Valentine.

Nash and I shook a fair number of hands and were seated in prestigious places, and while Nash asked a dumbstruck waitress for fizzy mineral water, nearly causing her to faint from her proximity to the sexiest eyes in screendom, I read both farewells to Valentine, and found they'd done the old man proud. Cremation, the *Gazette* also noted, was set for eleven a.m., Monday, and a memorial service would be arranged later. If I were truly out of work, I thought gloomily, I could go to both.

By the coffee stage the *Drumbeat*'s pages were fluttering across the table and inevitably someone commiserated with Nash over the mess his director was making of his film. My own identity, remarked on around the table behind sheltering hands, produced universally disapproving stares.

Nash said with authority, his expert voice production easily capable of silencing other conversations, "Never believe what you read in the papers. We're making an excellent film in Newmarket. We're being bad-mouthed by a spiteful little man. I did *not* say what I am reported to have said, and I have complete confidence in Thomas here. I shall complain to the paper and demand they print a retraction."

"Sue them," someone said.

"Perhaps I will."

"And as for you, Thomas," said one of the Stewards whom I knew personally, *"you* must definitely sue."

I said, "I'm not sure that I can."

"Of course you can!" He stabbed at the pages with a forefinger. "This is defamatory in the extreme."

I said, "It's difficult to sue anyone for asking questions."

*"What?"*

"Those defamations are written carefully in the form of questions. The question marks tend to take the certainty out of the slurs."

"I don't believe it!"

A head further along the large table was gravely nodding. "A scurrilous suggestion, if it is expressed as a question, may or may not be considered libel. There are gray areas."

My Steward friend said blankly, "That's not justice!"

"It's the law."

"You knew that," Nash said to me.

"Mm."

"Did Howard know it?"

"Whoever wrote that piece certainly did."

Nash said, *"Shit!"* and not a single face objected.

"What Nash really needs," I said, "is a reliable tip for the Lincoln."

They laughed and with relief turned to the serious business of the day. I half heard the knowledgeable form-talk and thought that five hours could be a long torture. Barely forty minutes of it had so far passed. My pulse still raced from anxiety. My whole professional life probably hung on whether the moguls who would be bidden to the breakfast table were putting in a good night's sleep. Saturday morning. Golf day. I would be doubly unpopular.

I went down with Nash and a couple of the Stewards' other lunch guests to see the horses walking round the parade ring before the first race. Nash looked at the horses: the race crowd progressively looked at Nash. He seemed to take the staring for granted, just as he would have done back home in Hollywood, and he signed a few autographs for wide-eyed teenagers with pleasant politeness.

"How do I put a bet on?" he asked me, signing away.

"I'll do it for you if you like. Which horse, how much?"

"Hell knows." He raised his eyes briefly and pointed to a horse being at that point mounted by a jockey in scarlet and yellow stripes. "That one. Twenty."

"Will you be all right if I leave you?"

"I'm a grown boy, you know."

Grinning, I turned away, walked to the Tote, and bet twenty pounds to win on the horse called Wasp. Nash, waiting for me to retrieve him, returned with me to the Stewards' room, from where we watched Wasp finish an unobtrusive fifth.

"I owe you," Nash said. "Pick me one yourself for the next race."

The races as always were being shown on closed-circuit television on sets throughout the bars and the grandstands. A set in the Stewards' room was busy with a replay of the just-finished race, Wasp still finishing fifth, the jockey busy to the end.

I stared breathlessly at the screen.

"Thomas? *Thomas,*" Nash said forcefully in my ear. "Come back from wherever you've gone."

"Television," I said.

Nash said ironically, "It's been around a while, you know."

"Yes, but . . ." I picked up a copy of the *Racing Gazette* that was lying on the table and turned from Valentine's obituary to the pages laying out the Doncaster program. Television coverage of the day's sport, I saw, was, as I'd hoped, by courtesy of a commercial station that provided full day-by-day racing for grateful millions. For the big-race opening of the Flat season, they would be there in force.

*"Thomas,"* Nash repeated.

"Er . . ." I said. "How badly do you want to save our film? Or, in fact . . . me?"

"Not badly enough to jump off a cliff."

"How about an interview on TV?"

He stared.

I said, "What if you could say on television that we're *not* making a bummer of a movie? Would you want to do it?"

"Sure," he said easily, "but it wouldn't reach every reader of the *Drumbeat.*"

"No. But what if O'Hara could get the interview transmitted to Hollywood? How about the moguls seeing it at breakfast? Your own face on the screen might tip things where O'Hara's assurances might not. Only . . . how do you feel about trying?"

"Hell, Thomas, get on with it."

I went out onto the viewing balcony and pressed the buttons to get O'Hara; and let me not get his message service, I prayed.

He answered immediately himself, as if waiting for calls.

"It's Thomas," I said.

"It's too early to hear from Hollywood."

"No. It's something else." I told him what I'd suggested to Nash, and he put his finger at once on the snags.

"First of all," he said doubtfully, "you'd have to get the TV company to interview Nash."

"I could do that. It's getting the interview onto the screen in the Hollywood conference room that I'm not sure of. Live pictures get transmitted regularly from England to the States, but I don't know the pathways. If we could get to an L.A. station we could have a tape rushed round for our moguls to play on a VCR . . ."

"Thomas, stop. I can fix the L.A. end. The transmission from England . . ." he paused, sucking his teeth. "What station are we talking about?"

I told him. "The people they'll have here are an outside broadcast unit. They'll have engineers and camera crews and a producer or two and three or four interviewers and commentators, but they won't have the authority or the equipment to transmit overseas. The OK would have to come from their headquarters, which are in London. They'll have Doncaster races on their screen there. They can transmit to anywhere. Their number will be in the phone book . . ."

"And you need me to use my clout." He sounded resigned, seeing difficulties.

"Um," I said, "if you want *Unstable Times* to reach the theaters, it might be worth trying. I mean, it's your picture too, you know. Your head on the block for engaging me."

"I see that." He paused. "All right, I'll start. It's a hell of a long shot."

"They've been known to win."

"Is Nash with you?"

"Five paces away."

"Get him, would you?"

Nash came outside and took the phone. "I'll do the interview. Thomas says he can fix it, no problem." He listened. "Yeah. Yeah. If he says he can, I guess he can. He doesn't promise what he can't deliver. O'Hara, you get off your ass and put Thomas and me into that meeting. It's damn stupid to let that son-of-a-bitch Tyler sink the ship." He listened again, then said, "Get it done, O'Hara. Hang the expense. I'll not be beaten by that *scribbler.*"

I listened in awe to the switched-on power of the ultimate green light and humbly thanked the fates that he saw me as an ally, not villain.

He disconnected, handed the phone back to me, and said, "Where do we find our interviewer?"

"Follow me." I tried to make it sound light-hearted, but I was no great actor. Nash silently came with me down to the unsaddling enclosure, from where the runners of the just-run race had already departed.

"Do you know who you are looking for?" he asked, as I turned my head one way and another. "Can't you ask?"

"I don't need to," I said, conscious, even if Nash ignored it, of everyone looking at *him*. "This television company travels with a race-caller, a paddock commentator who talks about the runners for the next race, and someone who interviews the winning jockeys and trainers afterward, and it's him I'm looking for . . . and I know him."

"That's something."

"And there he is," I said, spotting him. "Coming?"

I slid then between the groups of people chatting in the railed area outside the weighing room; slid where the groups parted like the Red Sea to clear a path for Nash. My acquaintance the interviewer began to say hello to me, saw who I was with, and ended with his mouth open.

"Nash," I introduced, "this is Greg Compass: Greg . . . Nash Rourke."

Greg came to his senses like any seasoned television performer should and with genuine welcome shook the hand that had fired a hundred harmless bullets.

"He's here to see the Lincoln," I explained. "How about some inside information?"

"Gallico," Greg suggested promptly. "He's bursting out of his skin, so they say." He looked thoughtfully at Nash and without pressing him asked, "Do you mind if I say you're here? I expect Thomas told you I do the ghastly chat stuff for all the couch potatoes?"

"I did tell him, yes."

"Thomas and I," Greg explained, "used to ride against each other, when I was a jockey and we were young."

"You're all so tall," Nash exclaimed.

"Jump jockeys are mostly taller. Ex–jump jockeys get to be racing commentators or journalists, things like that. Live it first. Talk about it after." He was comically self-deprecating, though in fact he'd been a top career jockey, not an amateur like me. He was forty, slender, striking, stylish. He took a breath. "Well . . ."

"You can certainly say I'm here," Nash assured him.

"Great . . . um . . ." He hesitated.

"Ask him," I said, half smiling.

Greg glanced at me and back to Nash. "I suppose . . . I couldn't get you in front of my camera?"

Nash gave me a dry sideways look and in his best slay-them gravelly bass said that he saw no reason why not.

"I did hear you were in Newmarket, making a film," Greg said. "I suppose I can say so?"

"Sure. Thomas is directing it."

"Yes. Word gets around."

I pulled a folded *Drumbeat* page from my pocket and handed it to Greg.

"If you'll let him," I said, "Nash would very briefly like to contradict what's written in that 'Hot from the Stars' column."

Greg read it through quickly, his expression darkening from simple curiosity to indignation.

"Difficult to sue," he exclaimed. "It's all questions. Is it true?"

"It's true the film story is different from the book," I said.

Nash assured him, "I didn't say those things and I don't think them. The film is going well. All I'd like to say, if you'll let me, is that one shouldn't believe newspapers."

"Thomas?" Greg raised his eyebrows at me. "You're using me, aren't you?"

"Yes. But that column's assassinating me. If Nash can say on screen that it's not true, we can beam him to the moneymen in Hollywood and hope to prevent them from taking the column seriously."

He thought it over. He sighed. "All right, then, but very casual, OK? I'll put you both together in shot."

"Innocence by association," I said gratefully.

"Always a bright boy." He looked at his watch. "How about after the Lincoln? An hour from now. After I've talked to the winning trainer and jockey and the owners, if they're here. We could slot it in at that point. I'll tell my producer. Thomas, you remember where the camera is? Come there after the Lincoln. And Thomas, you owe me."

"Two seats for the premier," I said. "Without you there may not be one."

"Four seats."

"A whole row," I said.

"Done." Greg looked at Nash. "What is this over-hyped buffoon of an ineffectual bullyboy really like as a director?"

"Worse," Nash said.

WE DID THE interview, Nash and I side by side. Greg introduced us to the viewers, asked if Nash had backed the winner of the Lincoln—Gallico—congratulated him, and said he hoped Nash was enjoying his visit to Britain.

Nash said, "I'm making a film here. Very enjoyable." He nodded affably. He added a few details casually, as Greg had wanted, but left no listeners in doubt that the racing film we were making in Newmarket was going well.

"Didn't I read an uncomplimentary report . . . ?" Greg prompted quizzi-cally.

"Yes," Nash agreed, nodding. "Words were put into my mouth that I never said. So what else is new? Never believe newspapers."

"You're playing a trainer, aren't you?" Greg asked the questions we had asked him to ask as if he'd just that minute thought of them. "How's it going with the riding?"

"I can sit on a horse," Nash smiled. "I can't ride like Thomas."

"Do you ride in the film?" Greg asked me helpfully.

"No, he doesn't," Nash said, "but he takes a horse out on the Heath to gal-lop it sometimes . . . Still, I can beat him at golf."

The affection in his voice said more than a thousand words. Greg wound up the interview good-naturedly, and expertly handed on the couch potatoes to the paddock commentator for profiles of the next race's runners.

"Thank you," I said. "Very much."

"A row of seats," he nodded. "Don't forget." He paused, and added cyni-cally, "Do you play golf, Thomas?"

"No."

"I can always beat him," Nash confirmed.

"You're a double act!" Greg said.

O'HARA HAD WATCHED the interview in the television company's head-quarters in London, and he buzzed my telephone before I'd found a quiet spot for reaching him.

"Brilliant!" he said, almost laughing. "Brotherly love all over the screen. Not a dry eye in the house."

"Will it work?"

"Of course it will work."

"Will it get to the meeting in time?"

"Cancel the anxiety, Thomas. The people here have been real helpful. Their fee would launch a Hubble telescope, but the moguls will see the show with their Wheaties."

"Thanks, O'Hara."

"Give me Nash."

I handed the phone over and watched Nash deliver a series of nods and yeses.

"Yes, of course he suggested my lines," Nash said, "and he got that pal of his to ask the right questions. How? Hell knows. The old jockey network, I guess."

The last few races crawled by and, having thanked our hosts, we flew back to Newmarket with still no further word from O'Hara. After breakfast time in Los Angeles. What were the moguls doing?

"Stop biting your nails," Nash said.

His chauffeured Rolls took us back to Bedford Lodge, where Nash suggested I join him in his rooms so that we might both hear what O'Hara might report.

The film company had engaged four comfortable suites in the hotel; the best for Nash, one for Silva, one for me, and one (often empty) for O'Hara or other visiting mogul. Rooms in the hotel were provided for Moncrieff and for Howard; the rest of the approximately sixty people working on the film— those in scene-setting, wardrobe, make-up, those in technical trades, those who were assistants or production staff or couriers, all those inescapably involved— were staying in various other hotels, motels, or private lodgings. Most of the stable lads were housed in a hostel. The horsemaster/assistant trainer went home to his wife. The overall logistics of keeping everyone fed and working within union guidelines were, thankfully, not my job.

Nash's rooms looked out over pleasant gardens and provided large armchairs fit for soothing limbs made weary by hours of pretending to be someone else; or rather by hours of waiting around in order to pretend to be someone else, for five minutes or so, now and then. Moncrieff and I might work frantically nonstop. Actors stood around getting bored, waiting for us to be ready. Actors, lengthily immobile, grew tired, while Moncrieff and I did not.

Nash sank into his favorite armchair and for about the four hundredth time looked at his watch.

Five hours had gone. Almost six. I'd spent a great deal of the time sweating.

My mobile phone buzzed. My mouth went dry. Buzz, buzz.

"Answer it!" Nash commanded crossly, seeing my reluctance.

I said, "Hello." More of a croak.

"Thomas?" O'Hara said. "You're not fired."

Silence.

"Thomas? Did you hear? Get on with the film."

"I . . . er . . ."

"For hell's sake! Is Nash there?"

I handed the phone to the green light, whose reaction to the news was a robust "I should damn well think so. Yes, of course he's been worried, he's only human."

He gave me the phone back. O'Hara said, "There are strings attached. I have to spend more time in Newmarket supervising you. One of the big boys is coming to visit, in order to be satisfied that their money is being spent reasonably. They waffled on for far too long about who they could put in to direct in your place. But in the end your television clip did the trick. Nash convinced them. They still think he can do no wrong. If Nash is happy, they'll keep you on."

"Thanks."

"I'm coming back to Newmarket tomorrow. It's a goddam nuisance as I was planning to fly to L.A., but there it is. Like you said, it's my head on the block alongside yours. What will you be doing tomorrow morning?"

"Horses galloping on the Heath."

"And Nash?"

"Sitting on a horse, watching. In the afternoon, we ferry the horses to Huntingdon racecourse. Monday we set up and rehearse the crowd scenes at the races . . . Some of the crews are moving to motels around Huntingdon, but Nash and I, and a few others, are staying in our rooms here in Newmarket."

"How far is it?"

"Only about thirty-eight miles. Where do you want to sleep?"

"Newmarket." No hesitation. "Get yourself a driver, Thomas. I don't want you falling asleep at the wheel with those long hours you work."

"I like to drive myself, and it's not very far."

"Get a driver."

It was an order. I said OK. I was grateful to be still employed. He said, "See you, fellow," and I said, "Thanks, O'Hara."

And he left one further report, "Howard will have his claws well clipped. Stupid son of a bitch."

"There you go," Nash said, smiling, when I switched the phone off. "Drink? Eat with me, why not?"

Nash had most of his meals alone upstairs, brought by room service. Unlike most actors he had a solitary streak to which, because of his wife's absence, he had given free rein. Surprised therefore, but pleased not to be dining alone myself, I stayed for soup, lamb, and claret, and a step into a positive friendship that I wouldn't, a couple of weeks earlier, have thought likely.

Relaxed after the day's troubles I decided to make a brief call on Dorothea, to see if she needed anything, before my scheduled meeting with Moncrieff to plan the morning's activities on the Heath.

I expected to find a quiet sorrowful house. Instead, when I arrived there, I found flashing lights, a police car, and an ambulance.

policeman barred my attempt to walk up the concrete path.

"What happened?" I asked.

"Clear the path, please sir." He was young, big, businesslike, and unsympathetic with unknown members of the public. He had kept—and was keeping—a small crowd of onlookers from stepping too close to the goings-on.

I tried again. "The people who live here are my friends."

"Stand back, if you please, sir." He scarcely looked at me, unintentionally impressive, a large physical barrier that I had no inclination to fight.

I retreated through the curious crowd and from behind them used my constant companion the portable telephone to ring Dorothea's number. After what seemed a very long time a distressed woman's voice said, "Hello."

"Dorothea?" I said. "It's Thomas."

"Oh. Oh no, I'm Betty. Where are you, Thomas? Can you come?"

I explained I was outside but obstructed, and in a few seconds she was hurrying down the path to collect me. The large policeman stepped aside, shrugging, not caring one way or the other, and I hastened with Betty toward the front door.

"What's happened?" I asked her.

"Someone broke in. It's *terrible* . . . they've nearly killed Dorothea . . . how *could* they? Dr. Gill has just come and the police too and there's so much blood and they're taking photographs and it's all *unbelievable* . . ."

We went into the house which looked inside as if it had been swept through by a tornado.

Valentine's bedroom by the front door had been wrecked: drawers were up-turned on the floor, their contents scattered. The wardrobe stood open, empty. Pictures had been torn from the walls, their frames smashed. Mattress and pillows were ripped, guts spilling.

"It's all like this," Betty wailed. "Even the bathrooms and the kitchen. I must go back to Dorothea . . . I'm afraid she'll die . . ."

She left me and vanished into Dorothea's bedroom, where I with hesitation followed, stepping round a wide drying sea of blood in the hall.

I needn't have felt I might be intruding: the room was full of people. Robbie Gill obstructed my view of most of Dorothea, who was lying unspeaking but in shoes and stockings on the sliced ruins of her bed. Two ambulancemen filled half the available space with a stretcher on wheels. A uniformed policewoman and a photographer were busy. Betty threaded a way into the throng, beckoning me to follow.

Robbie Gill glanced up, saw me, nodded recognition, and took a pace back with the result that I saw all of Dorothea, and became sickened and overwhelmingly angry.

She was bleeding, swollen, and unconscious, with great gashes in the flesh of her cheek and forehead and a red mess where her mouth was.

"Her right arm's broken," Robbie Gill dictated to the note-taking policewoman. "She has internal injuries . . ." He stopped. Even for a doctor, it was too much. Dorothea's clothes were ripped open, her old breasts and stomach bare, two slashed wounds on her body bleeding copiously, one so deep that a bulge of intestines protruded through the abdomen wall, a glistening pale swelling island in a wet scarlet ocean. The smell of blood was overpowering.

Robbie Gill took sterile dressings from his bag and told everyone except the policewoman to leave. She herself looked over pale, but stood her ground as the rest of us silently obeyed.

Betty was shaking, tears on her cheeks.

"I came over to make sure she'd given herself something to eat. She doesn't take care of herself, now Valentine's gone. I came in through the back door, into the kitchen, and it's *wrecked,* it's terrible, and I *found* her, she was bleeding on the floor in the hall, and I thought she was dead . . . so I phoned Dr. Gill because his number is right beside the phone in the kitchen, and he brought the police here and the ambulancemen, and they carried her into the bedroom . . . Do you think she'll be all right?" Her anxiety shook her. "She won't die, not like this. How *could* anyone do this?"

I had imagined and I had filmed scenes as bad or worse, but the blood we'd used had often been lipstick dissolved in oil—to give it viscosity—and intestines made of inflated sausage skin, and sweat sprayed through an atomizer onto gray grease-painted faces.

More people came, apparently plain-clothes policemen. Betty and I retreated to Dorothea's sitting room where again, comprehensive chaos paralyzed thought.

"How could anyone *do* this?" Betty repeated numbly. *"Why* would anyone do it?"

"Did she have anything valuable?" I asked.

"Of course she didn't. Just her little knickknacks. Trinkets and souvenirs. They've even torn the photo of her and Bill's wedding. How *could* they?" She picked up the ruins of a photo frame, crying for her friend's pain. "And her pretty pink vase . . . it's in splinters. She loved that vase."

I stared at the pink pieces, and then went down on one knee and fruitlessly searched the carpet around them.

*I've put the key in the pink vase in my sitting room.*

Dorothea's voice spoke clearly in my memory. The key of Valentine's study, in safekeeping to prevent her son Paul from taking the books.

Bitterly but silently swearing I went along the passage and pushed open the study's half-closed door. The key was in the lock. Inside, Valentine's sanctum had been ravaged like the rest of the house; everything breakable had been demolished, everything soft slashed, all his photographs destroyed.

Every book had gone.

I opened the cupboard where I knew he kept the scrapbooks containing every column he'd ever written for newspapers.

Every shelf was bare.

Betty, trembling, put her hand on my arm and said, "Dorothea told me Valentine wanted you to have his books. Where have they gone?"

With Paul, I automatically thought. But he *couldn't* have inflicted such wounds on his mother. A pompous, bombastic man, yes; but not to this extent vicious.

I asked Betty, "Where is Paul? Her son."

"Oh dear! Oh dear! He went home yesterday. He doesn't know . . . And I don't know his number . . ." She swayed. "I can't bear it."

"Don't worry," I said. "Sit down. I'll find his number. I'll get you some tea. Where's your husband?"

"It's his darts night . . . at the pub."

"Which pub?"

"Oh dear . . . The Dragon."

First things first, I thought, heading for the kitchen. Hot sweet tea prevented a lot of breakdowns from shock. No authority figure stopped me, though the little house seemed crowded with them. I took the cup and saucer to Betty, who held them clattering in both hands as she sat in Valentine's room.

In the old man's fortunately unshredded phone book I looked up The Dragon's number and spoiled Betty's husband's treble twenty by asking him to come home quickly. Then I searched around for Paul's number and ran it to earth on the notepad attached to the extension phone in the kitchen.

Paul answered, and I listened to his obnoxious voice with relief. If he were at home in Surrey he couldn't have attacked his mother a hundred miles away in Newmarket, not with her wounds so recent and bleeding. Even if she lived, she couldn't have mentally recovered from being attacked by her own son.

He sounded as appalled as he ought to be. He announced he would set off at once.

"I don't know which hospital they'll take her to," I said.

"Is she going to die?" he interrupted.

"Like I told you, I don't know. Hold on for a bit and I'll get Dr. Gill to talk to you."

"Useless man!"

"Stay on the line," I said. "Wait."

I left the kitchen, found the plain-clothes men starting to blow dust on things for fingerprints and hovered until Dorothea's door opened to let out the policewoman, who was beckoning to the men with the stretcher.

I said to her, "Mrs. Pannier's son is on the telephone. Please can Dr. Gill talk to him?"

She looked at me vaguely and retreated into Dorothea's room with the ambulance people, but it seemed that she did pass on the message because presently Robbie Gill opened the bedroom door again and asked me if Paul were actually on the line.

"Yes," I confirmed. "He's waiting to talk to you."

"Tell him I won't be long."

I relayed the message to Paul. He was impatiently displeased. I told him to wait and left him. Angry and anxious about Dorothea, and concerned about the missing books, I found reassuring Paul impossible. I couldn't even be decently sympathetic. I was sure he wouldn't give the books back unless I took him to court, and even then I had no list of what I'd lost.

Robbie Gill accompanied Dorothea on the rolling stretcher right out to the ambulance, solicitously making sure she was gently treated. Then, looking stern, he came back into the house, strode down the hall to where I waited by the kitchen door, walked over to the central table, and picked up the receiver.

"Mr. Pannier?" he asked, then grimaced crossly as Paul spoke on the other end.

"Mr. Pannier," Robbie said forcefully, "your mother has been beaten about the head. She's unconscious from those blows. Her right arm is broken. In addition, she has knife wounds to her body. I am sending her to Cambridge . . ." he named the hospital ". . . where she will receive the best attention. I cannot tell you whether or not she will survive." He listened with disgust to Paul's reply. "No, she was not sexually assaulted. I have done everything possible. I suggest you check with the hospital later. It is now out of my hands." He thrust the receiver back into its cradle, compressed his mouth as if physically restraining himself from swearing, and squeezed his eyes with finger and thumb.

"How is she really?" I asked.

He shrugged wearily, his expression relaxing. "I don't know. She put up a fight, I should think. Tried to defend herself with her arm. It's odd . . . it's almost as if she had *two* assailants . . . one that hit her arm and her head with something hard and jagged, and one that used a knife. Or perhaps there was only one assailant, but with two weapons."

"It's a useless question," I said, "but *why* attack her?"

"A dear good old lady! The world's grown vicious. Old ladies get attacked. I detest that son of hers. I shouldn't say that. Pay no attention. He wanted to know if she'd been raped."

"He's the ultimate four-letter case."

"The police want to know why the whole house is in this state." He waved an arm at the devastation around. "How do I know? They weren't poor, they weren't rich. Poor old bodies. They relied on you lately, you know. They loved you, in a way. Pity *you* weren't their son."

"Valentine was part of my childhood."

"Yes. He told me."

"Well . . . what happens next?"

"The police are talking about attempted murder, because of the knife wounds. But . . . I don't know . . ."

"What?" I prompted, as he hesitated.

"It may be fanciful . . . I don't know if I'll say it to the police . . . but it would have taken so little to finish her off. Just one stab in the right place." He paused. "You saw her, didn't you?"

"Yes, when you moved back from her bed."

He nodded. "I thought so. You saw those slashes. Two of them, one relatively superficial, one very deep. The first one cut her clothes open. Why wasn't there a third? You know what I think? I think it was an *aborted* murder. I think he changed his mind."

I stared.

"You can call me crazy," he said.

"No, I think you're clever."

"I've seen knife murders. They often look like frenzy. Dozens of stab wounds. Deranged mind at work. They can't stop. Do you see?"

"Yes," I said.

"I don't know why I'm telling you. Pay no attention. With luck Dorothea will live to tell us herself."

"How much luck does she need?"

"Frankly," he said dispiritedly, "quite a lot. Concussion's unpredictable. I don't think she has intracranial bleeding, but I can't be sure. But that abdominal wound . . . it's bad . . . it depends on infection . . . and she's eighty next month . . . but she's well in herself . . . healthy for her age, I mean. I've grown fond of them both, though I used to fight with Valentine on the surface, obstinate old cuss."

I thought Robbie Gill a good doctor, and I said so. He brushed off my words.

"Can I ask you something?" I said.

"Of course."

"Well . . . how long ago was Dorothea attacked?"

"How long ago?"

"Yes. I mean, was she attacked *before* the trashing of the house? All this damage must have taken quite a while to achieve. Or had she been out, and came back at the wrong moment? Or did someone try to beat some information out of her and go too far, and then pull the place apart looking for whatever he wanted?"

"Hey, slow down," he protested. "You think like a policeman."

Like a film maker, I thought. I said again, "How long since she was attacked?"

He pursed his lips. "The house was trashed first."

We digested it in silence.

"You're sure?" I asked finally.

Gill said, "Judging from the comparatively small amount of swelling and the rate of bleeding, Dorothea hadn't been in that state very long before her friend Betty found her. I came at once when Betty phoned me. I wasn't much longer than five minutes on the way. Betty might be lucky that she didn't arrive here ten minutes sooner." He sighed. "It isn't our problem, I'm glad to say. We can leave it to the police."

"Yes."

He looked at his watch and said it had been a long day, and I agreed with that too. When he told the police he was leaving, they decided to take his fingerprints. They took mine also, and Betty's; for elimination, they said. They wrote brief statements from Betty and me, and we told them Paul's fingerprints would be everywhere, like our own.

Betty's husband came to collect her with wide consoling arms, and at length I drove back to Bedford Lodge and downed a medicinal large one with Moncrieff.

SUMMONED BY ED on my say-so, all available crews, technicians, wardrobe people, and actors (except Nash) gathered in the stable yard at dawn on Sunday morning.

I mounted a wooden chair to address them, and in the fresh ever-moving East Anglian air wondered how Shakespeare could have expected Henry V's words before Agincourt to be heard by any but the nearest knights, given the clinking noises of armor on horseback and the absence of microphones.

I at least had a megaphone, equipment perhaps over-familiar to my audience.

"I expect," I said loudly, when movement in the company had diminished to restless impatience, "that most of you have by now read yesterday's 'Hot from the Stars' column in the *Daily Drumbeat.*"

I reaped stares, nods, and a good many sardonic smiles. No overt sneers. Something, at least.

"As you can guess," I went on, "the column badly disturbed our parent company in Hollywood. Fortunately our producer assured them that you are all doing a very good job here. Some of you may like it, some may not, but Hollywood has confirmed that I continue to direct. Nash Rourke has told them he is in favor of this. In consequence, nothing has changed. Whether or not you agree with the *Drumbeat*'s assessment of my character, if you want to continue to be employed on this enterprise, you will please make a private commitment to give this film your best shot. For all our sakes, the creation of a well-made, visually exciting commercial motion picture should take priority over any personal feelings. I want you to be able in the future to say with *satisfaction* that you worked on this film. So it's back to business as usual, which means will the lads now saddle the horses and everyone else continue with the schedule that Ed has distributed. OK? Good."

I lowered the megaphone, stepped off the chair, and turned my back to the company to join Moncrieff, who had been standing behind me in support.

"Socked it to them," he approved with irony. "We could make a film of making this film."

"Or a book," I said.

Our female star, Silva Shawn, loped across the stable yard to join us. As usual when not dressed in character she wore flapping dark voluminous layers of clothes reaching to her ankles, with black Doc Marten boots below and a charcoal hat above, a hat that looked like a soft collapsed topper sitting on her eyebrows. She walked with long strides and arrived at most meetings with her shapely chin thrust forward in the body language of belittle-me-if-you-dare.

O'Hara had strongly warned me not to pay her any compliment she could possibly construe as sexual harassment, which I found difficult to comply with, as the adjectives which sprang first and naturally to my mind were— apart from delicious—divine, bewitching, and ultra-desirable: but "Never call her darling," O'Hara had instructed.

"Why did you pick her if she's so touchy?" I'd asked him, and he had said succinctly, "She can act."

To date her acting in the film had chiefly consisted of the notably explicit bedroom scenes with Nash (punctuated by "No, no, no" moans, from Howard) that we had captured the previous week. We had in fact faithfully adhered to Howard's script in the matter of words: what infuriated him was that I had ignored his intention to have Nash and Silva deliver their lines fully clothed. He had set their restrained show of affection in the drawing room. I had transferred it to the bedroom, letting the verbal restraint remain, but contrasting it with growing physical desire. Silva, without self-consciousness ("bodies are *natural*") had allowed delicately lit shots of her nudity in the bathroom. The rushes had quickened many pulses, including my own. Whether she chose to admit it or not, there was a sensual quality in Silva's acting diametrically opposite to her chosen off-screen stance.

She had been away from Newmarket for the past week fulfilling an unbreakable commitment somewhere else, but was due to ride a horse on the Heath that morning, making use of an equestrian skill she was proud of. As happened in almost all films, we were not shooting the scenes chronologically: the coming encounter between the trainer and Cibber's wife was their first, their meeting all innocence at the start but with, in no time, a promise developing in their eyes.

Silva said disapprovingly, "I hope you got me a good horse."

"He's fast," I said, nodding.

"And good-looking?"

"Of course."

"And well-trained?"

"I've been riding him myself."

Without comment she transferred her near-universal disapproval to Moncrieff, whom she considered a male chauvinist despite his spectacular ability to make even ugly women look beautiful on screen.

After so many years spent studying female curves one might have expected Moncrieff to have grown an impervious skin, but every time we'd worked together he had fallen in love with the leading lady, and Silva looked like being no exception.

"Platonic," I'd advised him. "Strictly hands off. OK?"

"She needs me," he'd pleaded.

"Light her and leave her."

"Such cheekbones!"

Silva had fortunately so far given him the reverse of encouragement. I'd noticed from the first day I met her that she looked with more favor on men with suits, ties, short haircuts, and clean-shaven faces, an inclination that should ensure the comparative invisibility of straggle-bearded, shambling, sloppily dressed Moncrieff.

"I think," I said to Silva politely, "they're expecting you in make-up."

She demanded, "Are you telling me I'm late?"

I shook my head. "The meeting has set everyone back. But I hope to finish the Heath scenes by lunchtime."

She loped off, skirts flapping, making her own sort of statement.

"Gorgeous," Moncrieff breathed.

"Dangerous," I said.

Nash arrived, yawning in his Rolls, and went into the house to the wardrobe and make-up departments. He was followed into the stable yard almost immediately by a man of very similar build, riding a bicycle which braked hard with a spraying of gravel beside Moncrieff and me.

"Morning," the newcomer said briefly, dismounting. No deference in sight.

"Good morning, Ivan," I answered.

"Are we still in business?"

"You're late," I said.

He rightly took the comment as disapproval and wordlessly retreated, with his bicycle, into the house.

"I don't like him," Moncrieff said. "Saucy bugger."

"Never mind. Make him look like St. George, a shining champion."

Nash himself had great presence just sitting on a horse but any speed faster

than a walk revealed deficiencies, so for distance shots of him trotting or cantering we were using a stuntman, Ivan, instead. Ivan made a living riding in
front of cameras and had picked up a truculent manner that would prevent
his ever getting further in his profession. He had a habit, I'd been told, of holding forth in pubs about how *close* he was to Nash Rourke, for whom he had
doubled on an earlier picture. Nash this, Nash that, Nash and I . . . In actual
fact, they met seldom and conversed less. Ivan had mushroomed a relationship
from a few short businesslike exchanges.

Trainers in many other racing centers drove out in Land Rovers to watch
their horses work, but on Newmarket's mainly roadless Heath it was still the
norm to oversee everything from horseback, and there was no doubt Nash
looked more imposing in the saddle than operating a four-wheel drive. The
mega-star's sex appeal brought in the pennies. My job was to make it powerful while looking natural, which in Nash's case wasn't hard.

Moncrieff was driven off up one of the few roads in a camera truck, with
a second crew following, to positions we'd agreed the previous evening. The
string of horses would canter up a hill, be followed broadside by one camera
and head-on by a second as they came over the brow into the low-in-the-sky
sunlight; rather, I hoped, like an orchestral flourish of brass after a muted but
lyrical introduction. I often heard sound tracks in my head long before any
composer approached them.

Ed, knowing to the minute when to start the action, remained down by the
stable. Though I could easily have driven, I chose to ride up onto the Heath
to join Moncrieff; and I rode the horse we'd allotted to Silva, to get its back
down: that is to say, to warm him up so that he would go sweetly with her
and not buck. Silva might be proud of her riding, but O'Hara wouldn't thank
me for getting her dumped on her exquisite backside.

The terrible Ivan was to canter alone to the brow of the hill, riding Nash's
usual mount. He was to stop there, turn his horse, and stand silhouetted
against the brightening sky. I'd asked him particularly not to waste the precious
light-slot by getting it wrong.

He'd been insulted that I should expect him to get it wrong.

"Don't then," I said.

I joined Moncrieff by the truck positioned halfway up the hill, and
breathed sighs of relief when Ivan obliged us with a beautifully ridden canter up the hill, stopping and turning at the right place, horse and rider stark
and splendidly black against a halo of gold.

"Holy Moses," Moncrieff said, intently looking through the lens. "It's a
beaut." He ran a long fifteen seconds' worth before cutting.

"Again?" I suggested.

Moncrieff checked that the film had run properly through the camera gate and shook his head. "It was about perfect."

"Great. Print. Let's reload fresh stock for the next long shot of the rest of the horses."

I called down to Ed on our walkie-talkie system, told him to stick to schedule, had the shot numbered as always by the clapper board operator, and watched while the string was filmed streaming uphill at a fast canter. I called up the out-of-sight camera over the brow of the hill to start rolling, but perfection was an elusive quality and it was only after I'd ridden over the hill myself to organize things from up there, only after some huffing and puffing and two retakes, that I got my flourish of trumpets.

With the crowd shots at last in the can everyone on horseback milled around waiting for clearance and instructions. Ivan was still importantly riding Nash's horse, but a little apart, and I myself was now down on foot conferring with Moncrieff, eyes concentrating on his records of exposed footage.

I didn't see what happened. I heard an indignant shout from Ivan and a clamor from other voices. I sensed and felt a lot of startled movement among the riders, but at first I assumed it to be the sort of everyday commotion when one in a company of horses lets fly with his heels at another.

Ivan, swearing, was picking himself up off the ground. One horse with its rider detached itself from the group and raced off over the hill in the direction of Newmarket town. I thought with irritation that I'd need to rap a knuckle or two and grudged the waste of time.

Ivan came storming up to me with his complaint.

"That *madman*," he said furiously, "came at me with a knife!"

"He can't have done."

"Look, then." He raised his left arm so that I could see his jacket, the tweed coat identical to that usually worn in the training scenes by Nash. At about waist level the cloth was cut open for seven or eight inches from front to back.

"I'm telling you!" Ivan was rigid with fear on top of indignation. "He had a *knife*."

Convinced and enormously alarmed I glanced instinctively to find the horse I'd been riding, but he was being led around a good way off. Nearest in the matter of transport stood one of the camera trucks, though pointing in the wrong direction. I scrambled behind its steering wheel, made a stunt-worthy three-point turn, and raced across the turf in the direction of Newmarket, coming into view of the fleeing horseman in the distance as soon as I was over the hilltop.

He was too far ahead for me to have a realistic chance of catching up with him. Over grass, a horse was as fast as the truck; and he had only to reach the town and to slow to a walk to become instantly invisible, as Newmarket was threaded through and through with special paths known as horse-walks, which had been purpose-laid to allow strings of horses to transfer to the gallops on the Heath from their stables in the town without having to disrupt traffic on the roads. Any rider moving slowly on a horse-walk became an unremarkable part of the general scenery, even on a Sunday morning.

It crossed my mind that I should perhaps try to catch him on film, but the camera on the truck was bolted to face backward, as normally it was driven along in front of its subject, filming advancing cars, people, or horses. If I stopped to turn the truck and change places to operate the camera my quarry would be too far off even for blowups, if not entirely out of sight.

I was just about to give up when the distant horse was suddenly and violently reined to a halt, the rider reversing his direction and starting back toward me. The truck's engine raced. His head came up. He seemed to see me speeding down the hill toward him. He whirled his horse round again and galloped toward Newmarket at an even faster pace than before.

Even though the distance between us had closed, he'd traveled too far toward safety. It was already hard to distinguish his outline against the buildings ahead. I had to admit to myself that I wasn't going to catch him, and if so I would settle for second best and try to discover what had made him stop and reverse.

I braked the truck to a standstill as near as I could judge to the place where he'd turned, then jumped out onto the grass, trying to see what he might have seen, that could have been important enough to interrupt his flight.

He'd been facing the town. I looked that way and could see nothing to alarm him. There seemed no reason for him to have doubled back, but no one escaping at that pace would have stopped unless he had to.

If I were filming it . . . why might he stop?

Because he'd *dropped* something.

The uphill stretch of well-grassed exercise ground was as wide as an airport runway and almost as long. I couldn't be sure I was in the right place. If the rider had dropped something small, I could search all day. If he had dropped something insignificant, I wouldn't see any importance in anything I might come across. Yet he had *stopped*.

I took a few irresolute strides. There was simply too much space. Grass all round; miles of it. I looked up the hill, to the brow, and saw all the film horses and riders standing there, like Indians appearing on the skyline in an old pioneer movie. The sun was rising behind them.

I'd dropped my walkie-talkie up there in my hurry. I decided to drive the truck back up the hill, having left a mark where I was currently standing, and get all the lads to walk down in that strung-out sideways fashion, to see if they could find anything odd on the ground.

I marked the spot by taking off my light blue sweater and dropping it in a heap: anything smaller couldn't be seen. I walked back to climb into the truck.

The sun rose brilliantly over the hill, and in the grass twenty paces ahead of me, something *glinted*.

I went on foot to see what it was, as nothing should glint where racehorses worked; and I stood transfixed and breathless.

The escaping rider had dropped his *knife*.

No wonder he'd tried to retrieve it. I stared down at the thing which lay on the turf in front of my toes, and felt both awed and repelled. It was no ordinary knife. It had a wide double-edged blade about eight inches long, joined to a handle consisting of a bar with four finger holes like substantial rings attached to one side of it. The blade was steel and the grip yellowish, like dulled brass. Overall the knife, about a foot long, was thick, strong, frightening, and infinitely deadly.

I looked up the hill. The lads still stood there, awaiting instructions.

One behaves as one is, I suppose. I returned to the truck, climbed into it, and drove it round until it stood over the knife, so that no one could pick up that weapon or dislodge it; so that no horse could step on it and get cut.

Then I hopped into the back of the truck, set the camera rolling, and filmed the line of horsemen standing black against the risen sun.

Even though I was again staring unemployment in its implacable face, it seemed a shame to waste such a shot.

# 7

I rearranged the day.

Everyone returned to the stable yard except Moncrieff, whom I left stationed behind the steering wheel of the camera truck with strict instructions not to move the wheels even if it were demanded of him by irate men whose job it was to keep vehicles off the Heath. I had transgressed appallingly, I told him, by driving on the hallowed gallops. He was not to budge the truck an inch.

"Why not?"

I explained why not.

"Knife?" he said disbelievingly.

"Someone really did mean harm to Nash."

"Impossible!" Moncrieff exclaimed, though more in protest than disbelief.

"Tennis players, skaters, John Lennon," I said. "Who's safe?"

"Shit."

Without choice, though reluctantly, I phoned the police, *Drumbeat* headlines bannering themselves in my head—"Jinx strikes Newmarket film again." *Shit,* indeed. I met them in the stable yard where all the lads were waiting in groups and Ivan had come to grandiose terms with his possible nearness to injury.

The policemen who presently arrived were different from those who had come to attend Dorothea. I wondered how odd it would strike the force eventually to have been called to two knife incidents within twenty-four hours, however unconnected the events might appear. I wondered if they would realize I'd been on the scene of both.

Nash, beseeched by Ed, came out of the house in costume and make-up and stood side by side with Ivan. The policemen looked from one to the other and came, as we all had, to the only possible conclusion. In carefully matched riding breeches, tweed jacket, and large buckled crash helmet, they looked from ten paces identical. Only the slash along the side of Ivan's jacket distinguished them easily.

I said to Nash, *"This* may put paid to the film."

"No one is hurt."

"Someone was out to get you."

"They didn't manage it," he said.

"You're pretty calm."

"Thomas, I've lived through years of danger of this sort. We all do. The world's full of crazy fanatics. If you let it worry you, you'd never go out." He looked across to where the police were writing down what the lads were telling them. "Are we going on with today's work?"

I hesitated. "How will Silva react?"

"Tough."

I smothered a smile. "Do you want to come out on the Heath and see what someone intended to stick into you? And do you realize that from now on you have to have a bodyguard?"

"No. I never have a bodyguard."

"No bodyguard, no film. Very likely, no film anyway, once Hollywood gets to hear of this."

He looked at his watch. "It's the middle of the night over there."

"You'll go on, then?"

"Yes, I will."

"In that case, as soon as we can," I said gratefully.

Ed came across and said the police wanted to speak to the person really in charge. I went over; they were both older than I and seemed to be looking around for a father figure to relate to. I was not, it appeared, their idea of authority. O'Hara would have fitted their bill.

The lads had told them that an extra horseman had joined their group while they were haphazardly circling after their third canter over the hill. They'd thought nothing much of it, as with film making the normal routine of training-stable life was not adhered to. The newcomer, dressed in jeans, anorak, and crash helmet, had blended in with themselves. It was only when Ivan's horse had reared away, and Ivan himself had shouted and fallen off, that they'd thought anything was wrong. No one seemed to have seen the slash of the blade.

They couldn't do much toward describing the extra man. Crash helmets with heavy chin straps effectively hid half the face. The newcomer also, they remembered, had been wearing jockeys' goggles, as many of them frequently did themselves to shield their eyes from dust and kicked up debris. They thought he might have been wearing gloves: nothing unusual in that either.

Had I anything to add, the police wanted to know.

"He could ride well," I said.

They seemed to find that unimportant, being used to the many skills of Newmarket, though I thought it significant.

"He wasn't a jockey," I said. "He was too heavy. Too thickset."

Description of features? I shook my head. I hadn't seen his face, only his backview galloping away.

I waited until they had let the lads and the camera crew disperse out of earshot before I told them about the knife.

We drove up the road to get as near as possible to the camera truck which still stuck out like an illegal sore thumb. Thanks only to its being Sunday, I guessed, no groundsmen were hopping up and down in rage. Leading the police vehicle, I took Nash with me in my car, breaking all the film company's rigid insurance instructions. What with one thing and another, who cared?

Moncrieff backed the camera truck ten feet. The police peered in silence at the revealed peril. Moncrieff looked shocked. Nash grew still.

"He dropped it," I explained. "He turned to come back for it. Then he saw me chasing him and decided on flight."

Nash said, "He lunged at Ivan with *that?*"

I nodded. "You'll have a bodyguard from now on."

He looked at me and made no further protest. One of the policemen produced a large paper bag and with care not to smudge possible fingerprints lifted the knife from the grass.

"There weren't any touts," I remarked.

"What?" asked Nash.

"Every day except Sunday there are watchers down there on the edge of the town, with binoculars." I pointed. "Information is their trade. They know every horse on the Heath. They pass titbits of training progress to newspapermen and to bookmakers. If they'd only been here today, our knifeman wouldn't have been able to vanish so easily."

One of the policemen nodded. "So who knew, sir, that Mr. Rourke would be out here this Sunday morning?"

"About sixty people," I said. "Everyone working on the film knows the shooting schedule a couple of days in advance." I paused. "There *were* a few people out watching, as there always are with film making, but we have staff moving them away as far as possible if we don't want them in shot. Then, too, we started work today before sunrise." I looked round the Heath. Despite our activity, few people were about. Cars went past us on the road without slowing. The Heath looked wide and peaceful, the last place for death.

As Nash had pointed out, no one had been hurt. The police took their notes, the knife, and their possible theories back into Newmarket, and, with a feeling of imminent doom sitting like vultures on our shoulders, I summoned the camera crews back to work and made the magical initial meeting of Nash and Silva come to life.

It was nearly three in the afternoon by the time we'd finished on the Heath. Just as I returned to the stables, four large motor horsevans had arrived to transport to Huntingdon racecourse all the horses, their saddles, bridles, rugs, and other gear, and their feed and bedding, besides the lads and their own travel bags. Our horsemaster seemed to be managing fine. Despite the early morning upset, everyone involved seemed to hum in a holiday mood.

O'Hara banished the temporary euphoria, arriving in the yard by car and scrambling out angrily to demand of me loudly, "What in hell's teeth's going on?"

"Going to Huntingdon," I said.

*"Thomas.* I'm not talking about goddam Huntingdon. It's on the car radio that some maniac attacked Nash with a knife. What in buggery happened?"

I tried to tell him but he was too agitated to listen.

"Where's Nash?" he demanded.

"In the house getting his make-up off."

He strode impatiently away and through the house's rear door, leaving me to restart the transportation and set the wagon train rolling, even though the pioneers no longer sang.

Moncrieff was supposed to be having a rare afternoon off. I told him he deserved it and to disappear, which he rapidly did, hoping O'Hara wouldn't reappear too soon.

Alone for a change, I leaned against the bottom half of a stable door, listening to the unaccustomed silence and thinking of knives. Valentine's old voice murmured in my head . . . *I left the knife with Derry* . . .

The world was full of knives.

Who was Derry?

O'Hara and Nash came out of the house together looking more cheerful than I'd feared.

"I spent half the night talking to Hollywood," O'Hara announced. "I reminded them that yanking the director in mid film almost inevitably led to critical disaster, as reviewers always latch onto that fact firstly and spend most of their column speculating on how much better it would have been to have left things alone."

"However untrue," Nash commented dryly.

"In this case," O'Hara told him firmly, "you said, if I remember, that if they sacked Thomas they sacked you too."

"Yeah. Crazy."

O'Hara nodded. "Anyway, I'll be plugging the line that the attack on the stuntman is *positive* publicity, not bad. By the time this movie gets to distribution, the public will be fired up to see it."

He sounded, I thought, as though he had had to convince himself first, but I was certainly not going to argue.

I asked instead, "Do you need me around, then, for the next several hours?"

"I guess not." He sounded doubtful, stifling curiosity.

"Late Sunday afternoon," I explained, "is a fairly mellow time for surprise calls on farmers."

O'Hara worked it out. "Jackson Wells!"

"Right." I turned to Nash. "Do you want to meet the man you're playing?"

"No, I do *not*," he said positively. "I do *not* want to pick up the crusty mannerisms of some bitter old grouch."

As I didn't want him to either, I felt relieved rather than regretful. I said, "I'll be back by ten this evening. I've a meeting scheduled then with Moncrieff and Ziggy Keene."

"Ziggy who?" Nash asked.

"Stuntman," I said. "No one better on a horse."

"Better than Ivan?"

I smiled. "He costs ten times as much and he's worth twenty."

"This beach business?" O'Hara asked.

I nodded.

"What beach business?" Nash wanted to know.

"Don't ask," O'Hara told him humorously. "Our boy has visions. Sometimes they work."

"What vision?" Nash asked me.

"He can't tell you," O'Hara answered for me. "But when he sees it, so will we."

Nash sighed. O'Hara went on, "Talking of seeing, when will today's dailies be ready?"

"Tomorrow morning, as usual," I assured him. "When the van comes back."

"Good."

We were sending our exposed film to London every day by courier, to have it processed there overnight in a laboratory specializing in Technicolor. The film traveled each way in a London-based van, with the driver and an accompanying guard spending their nights in London and their days in Newmarket: and so far the arrangement had thankfully proved hitchless.

Each day, after seeing the previous day's rushes, I entered on a complicated chart the scenes and takes that I thought we should use on screen, roughly editing the film as I went along. It both clarified my own mind and saved a great deal of time in the overall editing period later on. Some directors liked to work with the film's appointed editor always at hand making decisions throughout on the dailies, but I preferred to do it myself, even if sometimes it took half the night, as it gave me more control over the eventual product. The rough cut, the bones and shape of the finished film, would be in that way my own work.

Stand or fall, my own work. Life on the leaning tower.

I SET OFF westward from Newmarket with only a vague idea of where I was headed and an even vaguer idea of what I would say when I got there.

Perhaps postponing the moment, but anyway because the city lay on my route, I drove first into Cambridge and stopped at the hospital housing Dorothea. Enquiries on the telephone had produced merely "she's comfortable" reports, which could mean anything from near death to doped to the eyeballs, and, predictably, my arrival at the nurses' desk gained me no access to their patient.

"Sorry, no visitors."

Nothing would budge them. Positively no visitors, except for her son. I could probably speak to *him,* if I liked.

"Is he here?" I asked, wondering why I should be surprised. Nothing, after all, would unstick Paul from a full-blown crisis.

One of the nurses obligingly went to tell him of my presence, coming back with him in tow.

"Mother is not well enough to see you," he announced proprietorially. "Also she is sleeping."

We eyed each other in mutual dislike.

"How is she?" I asked. "What do the doctors say?"

"She is in intensive care." His bulletin voice sounded over-pompous, even for him.

I waited. In the end he amplified, "Unless there are complications, she will recover."

*Great,* I thought. "Has she said who attacked her?"

"She is not yet lucid."

I waited again, but this time without results. After he began to show signs of simply walking off to end the exchange, I said, "Have you seen the state of her house?"

He answered with a frown, "I went there this morning. The police took my fingerprints!" He sounded outraged.

"They took mine also," I said mildly. "Please return my books."

"Do *what?*"

"Return Valentine's books and papers."

He stared with a mixture of indignation and hatred. *"I* didn't take Valentine's books. *You* did."

"I did *not.*"

He glared righteously. "Mother locked the door and refused—*refused*—to give me the key. Her own *son!*"

"The key was in the open door last night," I said. "And the books had gone."

"Because *you* had taken them. I certainly did *not.*"

I began to believe his protestations of innocence, unlikely as they were.

But if he hadn't taken the things, who on earth had? The damage inside the house and the attack on Dorothea spoke of violence and speed. Moving a wall of books and cupboardsful of papers out of the house spoke of thoroughness and time. And Robbie Gill had been sure the rampage had happened before the attack on Dorothea.

None of it made any sense.

"Why," I asked, "were you so extremely anxious to get your hands on those books?"

Somewhere in his brain warning bells sounded. I'd directed too many actors not to recognize the twitch of eye muscles that I'd so often prompted. Paul, I thought, had a motive beyond greed, but apart from seeing that it existed, I was not going to get any further.

"It's best to keep family possessions in the family," he pontificated, and fired a final shot before stalking off. "In view of my mother's condition, the cremation planned for tomorrow morning has been indefinitely postponed. And do not plague her or me by coming here again. She is old and frail, and *I* will look after her."

I watched his large backview bustle away, self-importance in every stride, the fronts of his suit jacket swinging out sideways in the motion.

I called loudly after him, "Paul!"

He stopped reluctantly and turned, standing four-square in the hospital passage and not returning. "What is it now?"

A forty-two-inch waist at least, I thought. A heavy leather belt held up his dark gray trousers. Cream shirt, diagonally striped tie. The podgy chin tilted upward aggressively.

"What do you want?"

"Nothing," I said. "Never mind."

He shrugged heavily with exasperation, and I went thoughtfully out to my car with my mind on telephones. I wore my mobile clipped to my belt, ready at all times. Paul, I'd noticed, carried a similar mobile, similarly clipped to his heavy belt.

Yesterday evening, I remembered, I'd been glad for Dorothea's sake that Paul had answered from his Surrey home when I'd told him of the attack on his mother. Surrey was rock-solid alibi land.

If I'd liked or even trusted Paul, it wouldn't have occurred to me to check. As it was, I strove to remember the number I'd called, but could get no further than the first four digits and the last two, which wasn't going to connect me anywhere.

I rang the operator and asked if the first four numbers were a regional exchange in Surrey.

"No, sir," a crisp female voice said, "those numbers are used for mobile telephones."

Frozen, I asked if she could find me Paul Pannier's mobile number: he lived near Godalming; the last two digits were seven seven. Obligingly, after a short pause for searching, she told me the numbers I'd forgotten, and I wrote them down and made my call.

Paul answered curtly, "Yes?"

I said nothing.

Paul said, "Who are you? What do you want?"

I didn't speak.

"I can't hear you," he said crossly and switched off his instrument.

So much for Surrey, I thought grimly. But even Paul—*even Paul*—couldn't have slashed open his mother.

Sons had been known to murder their mothers . . .

But not fat forty-five-year-old men with inflated self-esteem.

Disturbed, I drove westward to Oxfordshire and set about looking for Jackson Wells.

WITH HELP AGAIN from directory enquiries I discovered his general location, and, by asking at garages and from people out walking dogs, I arrived in the end at Batwillow Farm, south of Abingdon, south of Oxford, sleepy and peaceful in the late Sunday afternoon.

I bumped slowly down a rutted unmade lane which ended in an untidy space outside a creeper-grown house. Weeds flourished. A set of old tires leaned against a rotting wooden shed. An unsteady-looking stack of fencing timber seemed to be weathering into disintegration. A crusty old grouch of a man leaned on a farm gate and stared at me with disfavor.

Climbing out of the car and feeling depressed already, I asked, "Mr. Wells?"

"Eh?"

He was deaf.

"Mr. Wells," I shouted.

"Aye."

"Can I talk to you?" I shouted.

Hopeless, I thought.

The old man hadn't heard. I tried again. He merely stared at me impassively, and then pointed at the house.

Unsure of what he intended, I nevertheless walked across to the obvious point of access and pressed a conspicuous doorbell.

There was no gentle ding-dong as with Dorothea: the clamor of the bell inside Batwillow Farm set one's teeth rattling. The door was soon opened by a fair young blonde girl with ponytailed hair and to-die-for skin.

I said, "I'd like to talk to Mr. Jackson Wells."

"OK," she nodded. "Hang on." She retreated into a hallway and turned left out of my sight, prompting the appearance presently of a lean loose-limbed blond man looking less than fifty.

"You wanted me?" he enquired.

I looked back to where the old deaf grump still leaned on the gate.

"My father," the blond man said, following my gaze.

"Mr. Jackson Wells?"

"That's me," he said.

"Oh!"

He grinned at my relief with an easygoing light-heartedness a hundred miles from my expectations. He waited, untroubled, for me to introduce myself, and then said slowly, "Have I seen you somewhere before?"

"I don't think so."

"On the television," he said doubtfully.

"Oh. Well—were you watching the Lincoln at Doncaster yesterday?"

"Yes, I was, but . . ." He wrinkled his forehead, not clearly remembering.

"My name," I said, "is Thomas Lyon, and I was a friend of Valentine Clark."

A cloud crossed Jackson Wells's sunny landscape.

"Poor old bugger died this week," he said. My name finally registered. "Thomas Lyon. Not him that's making the film?"

"Him," I agreed.

"I did see you on the TV yesterday, then, with Nash Rourke."

He summed me up in a short silence, and rubbed the top of his nose indecisively on the back of his hand.

I said, "I don't want to do you any harm in the making of this film. I came to ask you if there is anything you particularly don't want said. Because sometimes," I explained, "one can invent things—or think one invents them—that turn out to be damagingly true."

He thought it over and finally said, "You'd better come in, I reckon."

"Thank you."

He led me into a small room near the door; a room unlived-in and furnished only with an upright piano, a piano stool, a hard wooden chair, and a closed cupboard. He himself sat on the piano stool and waved me to the chair.

"Do you play?" I asked civilly, indicating the piano.

"My daughter does. Lucy, you met her."

"Mm," I nodded. I took a breath; said, "Actually, I came to ask you about Yvonne."

"Who?"

"Yvonne. Your wife."

"Sonia," he said heavily. "Her name was Sonia."

"It was Yvonne in Howard Tyler's book."

"Aye," he agreed. "Yvonne. I read it. The book."

He seemed to feel no anger or grief, so I asked, "What did you think of it?"

Unexpectedly, he laughed. "Load of rubbish. Dream lovers! And that upper-class wimp in the book, that was supposed to be me! Cobblers."

"You're going to be far from a wimp in the film."

"Is it true, then? Nash Rourke is *me?*"

"He's the man whose wife is found hanged, yes."

"You know what?" The sunniness shone in his manner and the smile in his eyes surely couldn't be faked. "It's all so bloody long ago. I don't give a piss what you say in the film. I can hardly remember Sonia, and that's a fact. It was a different life. I left it behind. Did a bunk, if you like. I got fed up with the whole bloody shooting match. See, I was twenty-two when I married Sonia and not yet twenty-five when she died, and I was only a kid really. A kid playing at being a big Newmarket racehorse trainer. After that business people started taking their horses away, so I packed it in and came here instead, and this life's OK, mate, no regrets."

As he seemed to discuss it quite easily I asked, "Why . . . er . . . why did your wife die?"

"Call her Sonia. I don't think of her as my wife. My wife's here in this house. Lucy's mother. We've been wed twenty-three years now and we'll stay that way."

There was an obvious self-contentment in his whole personality. He had the weathered complexion and thread-veined cheeks of an outdoors man, his eyebrows dramatically blond against the tanned skin. Blue eyes held no guile. His teeth looked naturally good, even and white. No tension showed in his long limbs or sturdy neck. I thought him no great brain, but one of nature's lucky accidents, a person who could be happy with little.

"Do you mind me asking about her?" I said.

"Sonia? Not really. I can't tell you why she died, though, because I don't know."

That was, I thought, the first lie he'd told me.

"The police had me in," he smiled. "Helping with their enquiries, they told the press. So of course everyone thought I'd done it. Questions! Days of them. I just said I didn't know why she died. I said it over and over. They did go on a bit. They thought they'd get me to confess, see?" He laughed. "Seems they do sometimes get fools to confess to things they haven't done. I can't see how that happens, can you? If you haven't done something, you just keep on saying it. In England, leastwise. No actual thumbscrews, see? They ban actual thumbscrews here, see?" He laughed again at his joke. "I told them to piss off and find out who really killed her, but they never managed *that*. They couldn't see farther than getting me to confess. I mean, it was daft. Would *you* confess to murdering someone if you hadn't?"

"I don't think so."

"Course you wouldn't. Hour after hour of it! I stopped listening. I wouldn't let them work me up into a state. I just sat there like a lump and told them to piss off at regular intervals."

"They must have loved it," I said dryly.

"You're laughing at me."

"Indeed I'm not," I assured him. "I think you were great."

"I was young," he said cheerfully. "They kept waking me up in the night. Silly sods didn't realize I was often up half the night with sick horses. Colic. Stuff like that. I just nodded off when they frothed on about Sonia. It annoyed them no end."

"Mm," I agreed, and asked tentatively, "Did you *see* . . . Sonia . . . I mean . . . er."

"Did I see her hanging? No, I didn't. I saw her in the morgue, hours after they took her down. They'd made her look peaceful by then."

"So it wasn't you who found her?"

"No. Reckon I was lucky, there. One of my stable lads found her while I was driving north to York races. The police drove me back, and they'd already decided I'd killed her. She'd been in a stall we weren't using at that point. The lad that found her brought his food up for a week after, poor sod."

"Did you think she'd hanged herself?"

"It wasn't like her." He showed a very long-lived old doubt. "There was a stack of hay bales there she could have jumped off of." He shook his head. "No one ever did know the truth of it, and, tell you no lie, it's better that way. I read in that *Drumbeat* rag that you're trying to find out. Well, I'd just as soon you didn't, to be honest. I don't want my wife and Lucy stirred up. Not fair to them, it isn't. You just get on and make up what story you like for your film. As long as you don't make out I killed her, it'll be all right with me."

"In the film you do *not* kill her," I said.

"That's fine, then."

"But I have to say why she died."

He said without heat, "I told you, I don't know why she died."

"Yes, I know you did, but you must have *thought* about it."

He gave me an unadulteratedly carefree smile and no information, and I had a clear picture of what the interrogating police had faced all those years ago; a happy unbroachable brick wall.

"In Howard Tyler's book," I said, "Yvonne daydreams about jockey lovers. Where . . . I mean . . . have you any idea where he got that idea?"

Internally this time, Jackson Wells laughed. "Howard Tyler didn't ask me about that."

"No," I agreed. "He told me he hadn't tried to see you at all."

"No, he didn't. First I knew of it, people were saying that that book, *Unstable Times,* was about me and Sonia."

"And did she . . . well . . . daydream?"

Again the secret, intense amusement. "I don't know," he said. "She might have done. That whole marriage, it was a sort of make-believe. We were kids playing at grown-ups. That writer, he got us dead wrong. I'm not complaining, mind."

"But the dream lovers are so striking," I persisted. "Where did he get the idea?"

Jackson Wells thought it over without any apparent anxiety.

"I reckon," he told me at length, "you should ask that stuck-up sister of hers."

"Sister . . . do you mean Rupert Visborough's widow?"

He nodded. "Audrey. Sonia's sister. Audrey was married to a member of the Jockey Club and never let me forget it. Audrey told Sonia not to waste herself on me. I wasn't good enough for her, see?" He grinned, not caring. "When I read that book I heard Audrey's prissy voice all through it."

Stunned by the simple depth of that perception, I sat in silence wondering what to ask him next; wondering whether I should or could ask why the hanging death of an obscure young sister-in-law had so thoroughly and permanently blighted Rupert Visborough's chances of political life.

How unacceptable in Westminster, in fact, were mysteriously dead relations? Disreputable family misfortunes might prove an embarrassment, but if the sins of sons and daughters could be forgiven, surely the more distant unsolved death should have been but a hiccup.

Before I'd found the words, the door opened to reveal Lucy, sunny like her father.

"Mum wants to know if you want anything, like for instance drinks."

I took it as the dismissal Mum had intended, and stood up.

Jackson Wells introduced me to his daughter with "Lucy, this is Thomas Lyon, the personification-of-evil film maker, according to yesterday's *Drumbeat.*"

Her eyes widened and, with her father's quiet mischief, she said, "I saw you on the tele with no horns or tails in sight! How cool to be making a film with Nash Rourke."

I said, "Do you want to be in it?"

"What do you mean?"

I explained that we were recruiting the local inhabitants of Huntingdon to be "crowd" at our version of a race meeting held on the course.

"We need people to ooh and aah . . ."

"And scream 'shift your arse'?" she grinned.

"Exactly."

"Dad?"

Her father's instinct was to say no. As he shook his head I said, "No one needs to know who you are. Give your name as Batwillow . . . and incidentally, what is a batwillow?"

"A tree you make cricket bats from," Lucy said, as if my question revealed my stupidity.

"You're kidding me?"

"Certainly not," her father said. "Where do you think cricket bats come from? They grow on trees."

They watched my face. "We grow the willows in wet lands near the brook," he said. "This farm has grown batwillows for generations."

Growing cricket bats, it seemed to me, entirely fitted his nature: wide shoulders hitting carefree sixes over the boundary with fast balls solidly blocked to prevent the breaking of the wicket.

Lucy's mother appeared with curiosity in the doorway, a friendly woman in fawn trousers and an enormous brown sweater over a cream turtleneck. Unconscious style, I thought, just like her daughter.

Jackson Wells explained my presence. His wife enjoyed the tale.

"Of course we'll all come," she said decisively, "if you promise we'll see Nash Rourke!"

"How corny can you get?" Lucy demanded of her.

I said, "Tomorrow at two o'clock we hold crowd rehearsals. Nash might be there, can't promise. On Tuesday and Wednesday we shoot the crowd scenes. We offer breakfast, lunch, and expenses to everyone who turns up, and Nash Rourke will definitely be there."

"It's near a two-hour drive from here to Huntingdon racecourse," Jackson Wells protested.

"You're outvoted, Dad," Lucy told him. "What time Tuesday? Is it OK if we miss the rehearsal?"

I gave them one of my cards, writing on the back "Priority entry. Batwillow family." "Nine in the morning, on Tuesday," I said. "Follow the crowd, who'll know what to do. When we break for lunch, use this card, and find me."

"Wow," Lucy said.

She had freckles on her nose. Quizzical blue eyes. I wondered how mature she was on the piano.

I said to her father, "Do you know why anyone would do violence to get this film abandoned?"

He answered blandly, "Like I heard on the radio? Someone tried to take a knife to your star? Total madman. To my knowledge, no one's afraid of your film."

I thought that that was probably the second lie he'd told me, or at least the second I'd noticed.

Lucy said, "Can Dad's brother come as well?"

Her father made a dismissive gesture and said, "He wouldn't want to."

"Yes, he would." To me she said, "My Uncle Ridley lives in Newmarket.

He goes to the cinema all the time, and he'd *rave* to be in a film with Nash Rourke."

"Then bring him in with you," I agreed. "We need the largest crowd we can get."

Her parents, I saw, didn't share her enthusiasm for her Uncle Ridley.

"Is he free," I asked, fishing, "to spend a day at Huntingdon on Tuesday or Wednesday?"

Lucy guilelessly answered, "Uncle Ridley bums around, Dad says."

Her father shook his head at her shortage of worldliness and amplified, "My brother Ridley breaks in horses and acts as a general nagsman. He's not exactly high powered, but he makes a living."

I smiled, half interested. "I'll be glad to meet him." I paused and returned to what more closely concerned me. "Could you lend me a photo of . . . er . . . Sonia? Just so we don't make Yvonne too like her in the film."

"Haven't got one," Jackson Wells said promptly.

"Not even . . . Excuse me," I said to Mrs. Wells apologetically, ". . . not even a wedding photo?"

"No," Jackson Wells said. "They got lost when I moved here." His eyes were wide with innocence, and for the third time I didn't believe him.

Driving toward Newmarket and working out times, I thought I might squeeze in an empty half hour before my ten o'clock meeting, and accordingly telephoned Dr. Robbie Gill, whose number I did remember clearly from Dorothea's heavy black help-summoning handwriting.

"Do you feel," I asked, "like a quick jar somewhere?"

"When?"

I'd worked it out. "I'm in my car. I'll hit Newmarket around nine-thirty. Any good? I have to be at Bedford Lodge at ten."

"Is it important?"

"Interesting," I said. "About Dorothea's attacker."

"I'll square it with my wife." His voice smiled, as if that were no problem. "I'll come to Bedford Lodge at nine-thirty and wait in the lounge."

"Great."

"I heard someone attacked Nash Rourke with a knife."

"As good as. It was his stand-in, though. And no harm done."

"So I gathered. Nine-thirty, then."

He clicked off, his Scottish voice as brusque as ever; and red-headed and terrier-like, he was patiently waiting in the entrance lounge when I got back to Bedford Lodge.

"Come upstairs," I said, shaking his hand. "What do you drink?"

"Diet Coke."

I got room service to bring up his fizzy tipple and for myself poured cognac from a resident bottle. This film, I thought fleetingly, was driving me toward forty percent proof.

"Well," I said, waving him to an armchair in the neat sitting room, "I went to see Dorothea in Cambridge this afternoon and found my way barred by our friend Paul."

Robbie Gill grimaced. "She's basically my patient, and he's barring my way too, as far as possible."

"What can I do to preserve her from being shanghaied by him as soon as she's capable of being transported by ambulance? She told him, and me, that she didn't want to move into this retirement home he's arranging for her, but he pays no attention."

"He's a *pest.*"

"Can't you slap a 'don't move this patient' notice on Dorothea?"

He considered it doubtfully. "No one would move her at present. But a few days from now . . ."

"Any which way," I said.

"How much do you care?"

"A good deal."

"I mean . . . moneywise."

I looked at him over my brandy glass. "Are you saying that an application of funds might do the trick?"

He replied forthrightly, as was his Scottish nature, "I'm saying that as her doctor I could, with her permission, shift her into a private nursing home of my choice if I could guarantee the bills would be paid."

"Would it break me?"

He mentioned an alarming sum and waited without censure for me to find it too much.

"You have no obligation," he remarked.

"I'm not poor, either," I said. "Don't tell her who's paying."

He nodded. "I'll say it's free on the National Health. She'll accept that."

"Go ahead, then."

He downed his Diet Coke. "Is that the lot?"

"No," I said. "If I draw something for you, tell me what you think."

I took a large sheet of writing paper, laid it on the coffee table, and drew a picture of the knife I'd found on the Heath. A wickedly knobbed hand grip on eight sharp inches of steel.

He looked at the drawing in motionless silence.

"Well?" I asked.

"A knuckle-duster," he said, "that grew into a knife."

"And Dorothea's injuries?" I suggested.

He stared at me.

I said, "Not two assailants. Not two weapons. This one, that's both a blunt instrument *and* a blade."

"Dear God."

"Who would own such a thing?" I asked him.

He shook his head mutely.

"Do you know anyone called Derry?"

He looked completely perplexed.

I said, "Valentine once mentioned leaving a knife with someone called Derry."

Robbie Gill frowned, thinking. "I don't know any Derry."

I sighed. Too many people knew nothing.

He said abruptly, "How old are you?"

"Thirty. And you?"

"Thirty-six." He smiled wryly. "Too old to conquer the world."

"So am I."

"Ridiculous!"

"Steven Spielberg," I said, "was twenty-seven when he made *Jaws*. I'm not him. Nor Visconti, nor Fellini, nor Lucas. Just a jobbing storyteller."

"And Alexander the Great died at thirty-three."

"Of Diet Coke?" I asked.

He laughed. "Is it true that in America, if you die of old age, it's your fault?"

I nodded gravely. "You should have jogged more. Or not smoked, or checked your cholesterol, or abstained from the juice."

"And then what?"

"And then you exist miserably for years with tubes."

He laughed and rose to go. "I'm embarrassed," he said, "but my wife wants Nash Rourke's autograph."

"Done," I promised. "How soon can you realistically move Dorothea?"

He thought it over. "She was attacked yesterday evening. She's been sleepy from anesthetic all day today. It was a bad wound . . . they had to remove part of the intestine before repairing the abdomen wall. If all goes well she'll be fully awake tomorrow and briefly on her feet the day after, but I'd say it will be another week before she could travel."

"I'd like to see her," I said. "The wretched Paul must sleep *sometime.*"

"I'll fix it. Phone me tomorrow evening."

MONCRIEFF, ZIGGY KEENE, and I set off at four-thirty the next morning, heading north and east to the Norfolk coast.

Ed, instructed by O'Hara, had found me a driver, a silent young man who took my car along smoothly and followed the instructions I gave him as I map-read beside him in the front passenger seat.

Moncrieff and Ziggy slept in the back. Into the trunk we'd packed the heavy camera Moncrieff could carry on his shoulders like a toy, also a cold box full of raw film and a hot box full of coffee and breakfast. The outside air was cold; the warm car soporific. I was glad, after a while, for the driver.

We cleared Norwich and headed across the flat lands toward the North Sea, skirting the Broads and sliding eventually through the still-sleeping village of Happisburgh and slowing down a narrow lane that ended in sand dunes.

Moncrieff and Ziggy climbed stiffly out of the car and shivered. It was still completely dark outside the range of the car's lights, and the coastal breeze was as unrelenting as ever.

"You said to bring warm clothes," Moncrieff complained, zipping himself into a fur-lined parka. "You said nothing about playing Inuits." He pulled the fur-lined hood over his head and thrust his hands into Arctic-issue gauntlets.

Leaving the driver with his own separate breakfast in the car, the three of us walked onward through the sand dunes toward the open shore, Moncrieff carrying the camera and the film box, I leading with the hot box, and Ziggy between us toting polystyrene rectangles for sitting insulation on cold salt-laden ground.

"How did you find this God-forsaken place?" Moncrieff grumbled.

"I used to come here as a boy."

"Suppose it had sprouted casinos?"

"I checked."

Beyond the range of the car's lights we paused to establish night vision, then went on slowly until the sand dunes fell away, the breeze freshened, and the sound of the restless waves spoke of timeless desolation.

"OK," I said, "if there's any shelter, sit in it."

Moncrieff groaned, took a pallet from Ziggy, and folded himself with oaths into a shallow hollow on the sea side of the last dune. Ziggy, tougher and taciturn, found a similar place near him.

Ziggy, Ukrainian by birth, had from the nursery proved so spectacularly acrobatic on horses that he had been sent to the Moscow Circus school at the age of eight, and there, far from his rural roots, had received a first-class education along with endless practice in his special skill. Every pupil in the school, boys and girls alike, received daily ballet lessons to teach graceful movement in the circus ring. Ziggy could in consequence have joined any ballet company anywhere, but nothing interested him except horses.

Ziggy at twenty-two had left the circus behind: circuses everywhere had left town. Never political, though a favored son, he had somehow traveled with his trade to America, and it was there that I'd seen him first, turning somersaults on a cantering horse one afternoon in an ill-attended practice for the Ringling Brothers in Madison Square Garden.

I'd offered him a job in my rodeo film and, despite union protests, I'd secured him. I'd shortened his unpronounceable surname to Keene, and he'd quickly earned such a brilliant reputation in the horse stunt business that nowadays I had to beg him for his time.

Slender, light, and wiry, he took the Norfolk chill in his stride. Child's play, I supposed, after the Russian steppes. Alternately morose and laughing, he was intensely Ukrainian in temperament, and often told me he would return soon to his roots, a threat receding as years passed. His roots, as perhaps he acknowledged, were no longer there.

At a fairly brief meeting the evening before, I'd outlined what we were looking for.

"Film the sunrise!" Moncrieff exclaimed lugubriously. "We don't have to drive seventy miles for that! What's wrong with the Heath outside the door?"

"You'll see."

"And the weather forecast?"

"Cold, windy, and clear."

His objections, I knew, were not from the heart. Every lighting cameraman knew that directors could be both unreasonable and unmovable when it came to specific locations. If I'd demanded the slopes of K2, he would have sworn and strapped on his crampons.

I said, "As it's the time of the vernal equinox, the sun will rise due east. And that"—I consulted the small compass I'd brought—"is straight over there." I pointed. "At the moment, looking directly out to sea, we are facing a bit further north. The coast runs from northwest to southeast, so when the sun rises, horses galloping along the sand from our left will be backlit, but will also have the sun very slightly in their faces."

Moncrieff nodded.

"Can you catch gleams of sun in their eyes?"

"Close?"

"Heads, necks, and manes in shot."

"Thomas," Ziggy said, the bass notes in his voice always a surprise from the slightness of his body. "You ask for wild horses."

I'd asked him the previous evening to picture them and to suggest where we might find some. The trouble with sudden visions was that I'd had no idea of the scene while we were at the pre-production stage, and so had not arranged a wild herd in advance. Wild horses didn't grow on bat-willows.

Circus horses, Ziggy had said. Too fat and sleek, I'd objected. Moorland ponies no good, he'd said: too slow and stupid. Think, I'd urged him. Tell me in the morning.

"Thomas," Ziggy said, as always emphasizing the second syllable of my name, "I think it must be *Viking* horses, from Norway."

I gazed at him. "Did you know that Viking ships once regularly raided this coast?"

"Yes, Thomas."

Viking horses. Perfect. Where on earth could I get any? From Norway, of course. So easy.

I asked him, "Have you ever worked with Norwegian horses?"

"No, Thomas. But I think they are not true wild. They are not ridden, but they are, I think, handled."

"Could you ride one without a saddle?"

"Of course." There wasn't a horse alive, his expression said, that wouldn't do what he asked.

"You could ride one in a nightgown and a long blond wig?"

"Of course."

"Bare feet?"

He nodded.

"The woman is *dreaming* she is riding the wild horse. It must be romantic, not real."

"Thomas, she will *float* on the horse."

I believed him. He was simply the best. Even Moncrieff stopped grumbling about our mission.

We ate our hot vacuum-packed bacon breakfast rolls and drank steaming coffee while the black sky slowly grayed and lightened and grew softly crimson far out at sea.

With adjusted eyes we watched the world take shape. Around us and at our backs the irregularly heaped sand dunes were revealed as being patches of scrubby marram grass, fringes of long dried stalks leaning in the wind. Slightly below us the sand remained powdery, unwashed by the tide, but blowing back to add to the dunes; and below that, hard packed sand stretched away to distant white-fringed waves.

The tide, I reckoned, was as low as it ever went. Too low, really, for the best dramatic effect. One week ahead, the tide at dawn would be high, covering the sand. We needed, I thought, to arrange to film the horses on a mid-tide day: better, I supposed, during an ebb tide, as a flooding tide could race over these flat sands and maroon the cameras. Say ten days to the next mid-tide ebb at dawn. Too soon. Add two weeks to the next opportunity; twenty-four days. Perhaps.

I told Ziggy the time frame. "We need the horses here on the beach twenty-four days from now. Or else fourteen days later; thirty-eight days. OK?"

"I understand," he agreed.

"I'll send an agent to Norway to arrange the horses and the transport. Will you go with him, to make sure we get the sort of horses we need?"

He nodded. "Best to have ten," he said. "Or twelve."

"See what you can find."

Moncrieff stirred, abandoning breakfast in favor of art. Faint horizontal threads of clouds were growing a fiercer red against the still gray sky, and as he busied himself with camera speed and focus the streaks intensified to scarlet and to orange and to gold, until the whole sky was a breath-gripping symphony of sizzling color, the prelude to the earth's daily spin toward the empowerment of life.

I had always loved sunrise: was always renewed in spirit. For all my life I'd felt cheated if I'd slept through dawn. The primeval winter solstice on bitter Salisbury Plain had raised my childhood's goose pimples long before I understood why; and it had long seemed to me that dawn-worship was the most logical of primitive beliefs.

The glittering ball rimmed over the horizon and hurt one's eyes. The brilliant streaks of cloud flattened to gray. The whole sun, somehow losing its magic, nevertheless lit a shimmering pathway across the ruffled surface of the sea, and Moncrieff went on filming, breathing deeply with satisfaction. Slowly on the wind he and I became aware of a deep rhythmic humming that grew into a melody seeming age old and sad: and as if of one mind we understood and laughed.

Ziggy was *singing*.

This was a dangerous coast as, flat as it looked, a few miles out to sea, unrelenting sandbars paralleled the shore; underwater invisible hazards, shipwrecking the unwary. Graveyards in the coastal villages were heaped with memorials to sailors drowned before accurate depth charts were invented.

Too much background music, I decided, would ruin the atmospheric quality of this historic shore. All we would need would be the wind, the waves, the clip of the horses' hooves, and perhaps Ziggy's own distant song, or maybe a haunting plaintive chant from Norway. This was to be a dream: did one ever hear whole orchestras in dreams?

FULFILLED IN ALL sorts of ways, the three of us were driven back to Newmarket where everyday reality returned to the hotel lobby in the unwelcome shape of our author, Howard Tyler.

Howard was not repentant but incensed. The round glasses flashed as if with their own anger. The prissy little mouth puckered with injured feelings of injustice. Howard the great writer could produce temper tantrums like a toddler.

Moncrieff, at the sight of him, evaporated into the woodwork. Ziggy, communing only with himself, loped off on foot toward the Heath and horses. Howard stood in my path, flushed with grievance.

"O'Hara says the company will sue me for breach of contract!" he complained. "It's not *fair.*"

I said reasonably, "But you *did* breach your contract."

"No, I didn't!"

"Where did the *Drumbeat* get its opinions from?"

Howard opened his baby lips and closed them again.

"Your contract," I reminded him, "forbids you to talk about the film to outsiders. I did warn you."

"But O'Hara can't sue me!"

I sighed. "You signed with a major business corporation, not personally with O'Hara. The corporation has lawyers with flints for souls whose job it is to recover for the company any money they can squeeze from the most minor breaches of contract. They are not kind, compassionate fellows who will pat you forgivingly on the back. They can imagine damages you never thought of. You opened your undisciplined mouth to some avidly listening ear, and whether you've done any real box-office damage or not, they're going to act as if you've cost the company millions, and they'll try to recover every penny they are contracted to pay you, and if you're really unlucky, more."

It seemed finally to get through to him that his gripe would prove expensive.

"Then *do* something," he insisted. "Tell them no harm was done."

"You as near as dammit cost me not just this job but any work in the future."

"All I said was . . ." his voice died.

"All you said was that I was a tyrannical buffoon wasting the film company's money."

"Well . . . I didn't mean it."

"That's almost worse."

"Yes . . . but . . . you've *mangled* my book. And as an author I have *moral* rights." The air of triumph accompanying these last words made my next statement sound perhaps more brutal than I would have let it if he'd shown the slightest regret.

With vanishing patience I said, "Moral rights give an author the right to object to derogatory alterations being made to his work. Moral rights can be waived, and invariably this waiver is included in agreements between screenplay writers and film production companies. Often the screenplay writer is given the right to remove his name from the credits if he hates the film enough, but in your case, Howard, it's your name they're specifically paying for, and you waived that right also."

Stunned, he asked, "How do you know?"

"I was given a sight of your contract. I had to know where we each stood."

*"When?"* he demanded. "When did you see it?"

"Before I signed a contract myself."

"You mean . . . *weeks* ago?"

"Three months or more."

He began to look bewildered. "Then . . . what can I do?"

"Pray," I said dryly. "But for a start, you can say who you talked to. You can say how you got in touch with the writer of 'Hot from the Stars.' Who did you reach?"

"But I . . ." He seemed not far from tears. "I *didn't*. I mean, I didn't tell the *Drumbeat*. I didn't."

"Who, then?"

"Well, just a friend."

"A *friend*? And the friend told the *Drumbeat*?"

He said miserably, "I suppose so."

We had been standing all this time in the lobby with Monday morning coming and going around us. I waved him now toward the lounge area and found a pair of convenient armchairs.

"I want some coffee," he said, looking round for a waiter.

"Have some later, I haven't got time. Who did you talk to?"

"I don't think I should say."

I felt like shaking him. "Howard, I'll throw you to the corporation wolves. And besides that, I'll sue you personally for defamation."

"She said questions weren't libelous."

"She, whoever she is, got it at least half wrong. I don't want to waste time and energy suing you, Howard, but if you don't cough up some answers pronto you'll get a writ in tomorrow's mail." I took a breath, "So, who is *she?*"

After a long pause in which I hoped he faced a few realities, he said, "Alison Visborough."

"Who?"

"Alison Vis . . ."

"Yes, yes," I interrupted. "I thought her name was Audrey."

"That's her mother."

I shook my head to clear it, feeling I'd left my senses back on Happisburgh beach.

"Let's get this straight," I said. "You poured out your grudges to Alison Visborough, whose mother is Audrey Visborough, who is the widow of the deceased Rupert Visborough, known in your book as Cibber. Right so far?"

He unhappily nodded.

"And," I said, "when you read Rupert Visborough's obituary, and got the idea for your book, you did *not* go to see Jackson Wells, whose wife hanged, but you *did* go to see the dead woman's sister, Audrey Visborough."

"Well . . . I suppose so."

"Yes or no?"

"Yes."

"And it was she who told you about her sister having dream lovers?"

"Er . . ."

*"Howard!"*

"Look," he said, with a recurrence of petulance, "I don't have to answer all these questions."

"Why ever not?"

"They wouldn't like it."

"Audrey and Alison wouldn't, do you mean?"

He nodded. "And Roddy."

"Who's Roddy?"

"Alison's brother."

Give me strength, I thought. I said, "Is this right? Rupert Visborough married Audrey; they had a daughter Alison and a son Roddy?"

"I don't see why you make it sound so difficult."

"But you didn't put the children in your book."

"They're not *children,*" Howard objected. "They're as old as I am."

Howard was forty-five.

"When you bitched to Alison," I asked, "why did she get your complaints printed in the *Drumbeat?* And how?"

He stood up abruptly. "I didn't know she was going to do it. I didn't ask her to. If you want to know, I was shocked when I read the paper. I didn't mean what I said to her to be published like that."

"Have you talked to her since?"

He said defensively, "She thought she was helping me."

"Shit," I said.

He took offense and stalked off, heading for the way out to the world.

With a feeling of medium irritation I went upstairs and found my message light flashing. O'Hara, it seemed, would be pleased by my appearance in his suite.

I walked the carpeted passages. "Did you know," he asked, opening his door to my knock, "that Howard is back?"

We discussed Howard. O'Hara's use of words was profligate.

"Howard told me," I said, only half successfully damming O'Hara's flow, "that he poured out his woes to a lady friend who promptly relayed them to the *Drumbeat,* but without his knowledge."

"What?"

I told O'Hara about the Visboroughs.

He repeated in disbelief, *"Audrey, Alison, and Roddy?"*

"And God knows who else."

"Howard," he pronounced heavily, "is off his trolley."

"He's naive. Doesn't make him a bad writer."

O'Hara agreed gloomily. "Dream lovers are naive." He thought things over. "I'll have to discuss his breach of contract again with the moguls. I suppose you've never met this disastrous Alison?"

I shook my head.

"Someone will have to switch on her lights."

"Mm," I paused. "You?"

O'Hara ducked it. "What time do you have, yourself?"

"Oh no," I protested. "We know her opinion of *me.* "

"All the same," O'Hara smiled, "if you want to, you can charm the birds off the trees."

"I don't know where she lives."

"I'll find out," he promised, "and you can do the damage control."

He seemed all of a sudden happier. Suing Howard would have dragged on and on and could well have alienated the very lending-library customers his name was supposed to attract into the cinema. Never attack anyone, old Valentine had once written, unless you've counted the cost of winning.

O'Hara asked if I'd found Jackson Wells, but seemed disappointed in the sweetness and light of his household.

"Do you think he murdered his wife?" he asked curiously.

"No one could ever prove it."

"But do *you* think he did?"

I paused. "I don't know."

O'Hara shrugged the thought away and, as he wanted to see the previous day's rushes, we drove along to the stable yard. There, in the vast house, one small room had been rigged for projection, with a screen and six chairs but no luxury. The windows were blacked out to foil peepers, and the reels of previously printed film were secured in racks in there by every fancy lock and fireproofing invented. The moguls had in this case spent lavishly: no one could afford to start shooting all over again.

That morning I worked the projector myself. O'Hara sat impassively while the horses galloped up the training hill and breasted it into sunlight. I'd been right, I saw, about the third attempt, and my flourish of trumpets looked great. Moncrieff had stopped the cameras after that. The only shot left on the reel was the one I'd made myself; the line of horses on the skyline, black against sunshine. The worst of luck, I thought, that with all that raw film in our possession, we had no footage at all that included the rider whose frightful knife had slashed at Ivan.

O'Hara cursed over it, but hindsight, as always, was an unfruitful regret.

I left that reel for the regular projectionist to rewind, and set going the stuff we'd done later, the "first meeting" of Nash and Silva.

As always with dailies, the sound quality was imperfect; marrying the eventual sound track to the pictures came later, in the post-production stage. Dailies, in any case, with two or three or more takes printed of a single scene, could only be judged by experts, rather like wine buyers discerning an eventual vintage in the harsh juice straight from fermentation. O'Hara even made appropriate sucking noises with his teeth as he watched Silva joltingly rein-in her horse, nearly knocking down Nash as he, the trainer, stood near his own horses; watched her dismount, jerk off her helmet, and speak her lines with the character's initial aggravation awakening to quick sexual interest; watched the smile curve the blissful mouth in a way that would quadruple her sticker price next time out.

"Good girl," O'Hara murmured, pleased.

Nash, bareheaded in riding clothes, did his own lines in platinum, close to priceless.

Howard, goaded into writing this scene, which had of course not appeared in the book, had nevertheless written exchanges of a quality entirely to justify his high placing in the film's credits. Moncrieff had lit the faces with creative skill and had, as agreed, shot the horses slightly out of focus to give sharp prominence to each human figure in close-up. Somehow the uncaring, oblivious nature of the horses lent contrast and comment to the vivid emotion developing near them. A brief, fleeting impression, but an addition to the mood. Not bad, overall.

The reel ended, I switched the projector off and the regular lights on, and waited for O'Hara's verdict.

"Tell you something," he said casually. "If you're not careful, we'll have a success on our hands."

"A bit early to say." I was pleased, all the same, at his compliment.

"How do you get on personally with Silva?" O'Hara asked, standing and stretching, preparing to leave.

"She does ride very well," I said. "I told her that I thought so."

"And you did not, I hope, tell her she rides as well as any man."

I laughed. "I'm not suicidal."

"She looks good on screen."

I nodded. "You were right, she can act. She knows where the camera is. She's professional, she listens to me, she did the nude scene on the closed set last week with cool naturalness, she's ambitious in a sensible way, and I can tiptoe round the feminism."

"And do you like her?"

"It's not necessary."

"No, but do you?"

I smiled. "If I told her I liked her, she'd smack my face."

"That's no answer."

"Then yes, I do like her. Actually, very much. But she doesn't want to be liked, she wants to be thought a good actress. Which she is. A merry-go-round, don't you think?"

"She's sleeping with me," O'Hara said.

I looked, in a moment of stillness, at the craggy strength of his face and physique, understood the magnetic sexual quality of power, and said without resentment, "Are you telling me, hands off?"

He calmly nodded. "Hands off."

"OK."

He made no more of it. It altered little. We went upstairs to see how far the art director and his department had gone with dismantling the Jockey Club enquiry room set, ready to construct an approximation of the Athenaeum dining room in the space.

Several of the upstairs walls had earlier been removed, with steel joists now holding up the roof. Many of the ceilings also had been cut out to allow for overhead lights and cameras. The house's owner was warming himself with his nicely stuffed bank account while trusting his beams and plaster would re-assert themselves later.

The Athenaeum dining room remained embryonic but would be ready with tables, waiters, and roast beef on our return from Huntingdon.

O'Hara said, "I met Moncrieff in the passage at the hotel this morning after you returned from the ocean. Incredibly, he was *humming*. He said he'd seen a revelation and that you were sending Ziggy to import a herd of wild horses from Norway. Say it's not true."

I laughed. "It's true. Viking horses. If we have ten or twelve, we can make them look like fifty. I'll send Ziggy with an agent to find some. They'll come over in horsevans on the ferry from Bergen."

"But," O'Hara asked reasonably, "wouldn't it be cheaper to use *local* wild horses?"

"First of all," I said, "there aren't any. Second, genuine Viking horses will be worth their weight in publicity."

O'Hara picked his way across wobbling scraps of scenery and stood looking out of a high window at the gray-green expanse of the Heath. He turned eventually: I couldn't see his expression against the light.

"I'll arrange it," he said. "I'll send Ziggy. You just get on with the movie."

I said with satisfaction, "Right," and we made our way as colleagues down to the stable yard, signing out as usual with the guard on the outer door and crossing to the car.

"Did you know," I said conversationally, "that they used to hang witches?"

O'Hara stopped in mid-stride and after a pause said, "Howard didn't suggest such a thing in the book, did he?"

"No. I'm surprised, really, that he didn't. It would have jelled with the dream lovers, don't you think?"

O'Hara blinked.

"The last witch was hanged in Merrie England in 1685," I said. "By then they had strung up over a thousand people accused of witchcraft, mostly women. I looked it up. Witchcraft itself went on for a long time after that. Goya was painting witches flying, around the year eighteen hundred. People still follow the old practices to this day. I'd think it improbable that a witch-hanging took place in Newmarket only twenty-six years ago, but there's no harm in Howard inserting a scene or two to sow doubt."

Unexpectedly glad after all to have a driver, I traveled to Huntingdon making notes for the rehearsals ahead and thinking over my second conversation with Howard. He had been in his room when I returned with O'Hara and had agreed to come along to my sitting room, but with bad grace.

"Howard," I pointed out, "your name is immovable on this film. You can write brilliantly. Whether or not you disapprove of its plot, the *words* in this film are mostly yours, and you'll be judged by them."

"Some are *yours*," he objected.

"I prefer yours. I only write what you won't."

He could glare, but not dispute it.

"So," I said without fuss, "please will you write a scene suggesting that the dead wife was hanged for being a witch."

He was outraged. "But she *wasn't* a witch."

"How do you know?"

"She was Audrey Visborough's sister!" His tone said that that settled matters beyond doubt.

"Think it over, Howard. Put the thought into someone's mouth. Into someone's head. Just a shot of a magazine article might do the trick. Headline—'Is witchcraft dead?' Something like that. But don't place your scene in the Jockey Club enquiry room, they've already struck that set."

Howard looked as if he might comply: he even looked interested.

"Her real name was Sonia," I said.

"Yes, I know."

"Did the Visboroughs tell you?"

"Why shouldn't they?" His prickles rose protectively. "They were all very helpful."

I forbore to say that the *Drumbeat* was as unhelpful as one could get, and went on my way.

My assistant director, Ed, who normally had one assistant of his own, now had, as usual for crowd scenes, several extra deputized helpers. The townspeople of Huntingdon, having streamed to the racecourse in highly satisfactory numbers, were being divided, positioned, and generally jollied along by Ed, who had been given, and had passed on, my emphatic instruction that the people who had come should be *happy,* and should want to return the next day, and the next. Lollipops were to be dangled. Fun was to be had. Nash—ah, Nash *himself*—would sign autographs now and then.

The people in charge of Huntingdon racecourse had been welcoming and obliging. Contracts, payment, insurance, safety precautions, police: all had been arranged. Provided we finished and vacated the place by Friday, they would give us, if they could, everything we asked for. Repairs, if any were needed, could then be done before they opened the gates to bona fide racing the following Monday.

Our horses, our jockeys, our crowds, our drama, had realistically to play their parts by Thursday evening. Tight, but possible.

I prayed for it not to rain.

Ed chose people to stand in the parade ring in groups, looking like owners and trainers. Others were directed to crowd round and stare. Genuine professional steeplechase jockeys appeared in the parade ring in racing colors and scattered to each group. They weren't the absolute top jockeys, but tough, reliably expert, and being well paid. Our lads led round the horses, saddled, rugged, and carrying number cloths. It all began to look like a race meeting.

The real thing, of course, would be filmed separately on the following Monday, with Ed in charge of wide establishing shots of full stands, large crowd movement, and bookmakers shouting the odds. Cut in with our own scenes, the joins of real to acted would be invisible, given no rain.

Cibber stood in the parade ring with his wife (Silva), and I positioned Nash's stand-in within easy scowling distance. Moncrieff rolled his camera around on a dolly to get interesting architectural background. It all, as ever, took time, but as soon as possible I sent the townspeople home. Boredom was my enemy; bore them, and they wouldn't return. Every child received a helium balloon on leaving (*Unstable Times* in blue on silver) given with jokes and thanks.

The jockeys had been asked to stay in the parade ring for a briefing. I found them standing stiffly in a group there, their attitude distrustful and surly.

Not understanding this, I began, "Just pretend it's a normal race tomorrow. Do everything you normally do on the way down to the start."

One of them almost belligerently interrupted, "Is it true you raced once as an amateur?"

"Well, yes, for three seasons."

"Why did you stop?"

I frowned. It wasn't their business to ask such questions, and certainly not like an inquisition, but I needed their cooperation, so I said mildly, "I went to Hollywood to make films of horses instead."

Silence.

"What's the matter?" I asked.

After a long pause, one of them told me, "It says in the *Drumbeat* . . ."

"Ah." Light arrived. I looked at the cool faces, all highly cynical. I needed these jockeys to ride their hearts out the next day; and I could see with absolute clarity that they weren't going to.

How odd, I thought, that I'd feared losing my authority over the film crews, but in fact had had little difficulty in reestablishing it, only to find now that I'd lost it among men I thought I understood. I asked if they'd watched the Lincoln and seen me talking to Greg Compass. None had. They'd been too busy working, they said. They'd been riding in races.

I said, "If any of you has doubts about doing a good job for me tomorrow . . . I'll race him here and now."

I didn't know I was going to say it until I did. Once said, there was no going back.

They stared.

I said, "I'm not incompetent or a buffoon or a tyrant. Newspapers tell lies. Surely you know?"

They loosened up a little and a few began staring at their boots instead of my face, but one of them slowly and silently unbuttoned his shiny green and white striped shirt. He took it off and held it out. Underneath he wore the usual thin blue sweater, with a white stock round his neck.

I unclipped the walkie-talkie from my belt and whistled up Ed.

"Where are you?" I asked.

"In the stables."

"Good. Send three of the horses back, will you, with racing saddles and bridles, each led by a lad."

"Sure. Which three?"

"The three fastest," I said. "And find the doctor we brought with us. Ask him to come to the parade ring."

"You don't have to be an effing hero," one of the jockeys said. "We get your point."

The one who'd removed his colors, however, still held them out as a challenge.

I unzipped my navy windproof jacket, took it off, and dropped it on the grass. I pulled off my sweater, ditto, and unbuttoned my shirt, which followed. I wore no jersey underneath, but I didn't feel my bare skin chill in the wind: too much else to think about. I put on the offered green and white stripes and pointed to the stock. Silently, it was handed over, and I tied it neatly, thanking my stars that I remembered how.

As it had been only a rehearsal that afternoon, and all on foot, no one carried a whip and none of the jockeys was wearing the normal shock-absorbing body protector that shielded fallen riders from horses' hooves. No one mentioned this absence. I buttoned the shirt and pushed the tails down inside my trousers; and I was passed a crash helmet with a scarlet cap.

Ed, in the distance, was walking back with three horses.

Moncrieff suddenly arrived at my elbow and demanded, "What in hell are you doing?"

"Going for a ride." I put on the helmet and left the strap hanging.

"You can't!"

"Be a pal and don't film it in case I fall off."

Moncrieff threw his arms out and appealed to the jockeys. "You can't let him. Tell him to stop."

"They've read the *Drumbeat*," I said succinctly. "And do we want one hell of a race tomorrow, or do we not?"

Moncrieff understood all right, but made ineffectual noises about insurance, and moguls, and O'Hara, and what would happen to the movie if I broke my neck.

"Do shut up," I said.

"Thomas!"

I grinned at him. I said to the jockeys, "Two of you might care to race with me. Sorry I can't take you all on, but we have to race the whole string tomorrow and they'll need to be fresh. So just two. Whoever you like. We'll go one circuit over the fences, not the hurdles, just as long as there's no one roaming about on the course where they shouldn't be."

Silence.

Privately amused, I waited until Ed had drawn near with the horses and had got over his shock at my explicit clothes.

"Ed, get a car out onto that road along beside the far rails," I showed him where, "and drive round behind us. Take our doctor with you in case one of us falls." I pointed. "There he is. He's coming now."

Ed looked stricken. I unclipped both the walkie-talkie and my mobile phone from my belt, and gave them to him to look after.

"I don't believe this," Moncrieff said.

A jockey said, "We could lose our licenses, racing you."

"No, you can't," I contradicted. "You're employed by the film company, and you're out here for a rehearsal. We have permission from everyone for you to jump round the course. You're just doing it a day earlier than planned. There's a doctor in attendance, as we promised in your agreements. Who'll come with me?"

They had lost the worst of their antagonism but I'd thrown the challenge back in their faces, and they weren't having *that*. Two of them started for the horses and left me the third.

"O'Hara will *kill* you," Moncrieff told me.

It so happened that they'd left me the horse that Silva had ridden the previous morning: the undisputed fastest of our bunch. I'd ridden him often at a canter and, according to his history, he was supposed to know how to jump.

"You haven't any breeches or boots," Ed said, looking with bewilderment at my ordinary trousers and brown shoes.

"The horse won't mind," I said. A little light-headedness, I thought, wasn't a bad idea in the circumstances.

The horse's lad gave me a leg up, as he'd done many times. I tightened the girth and lengthened the stirrup leathers, and buckled the strap of my helmet.

The two jockeys holding me to my word were mounted and ready. I laughed down at the ring of other faces that had suddenly reverted to a better humor.

"You're a right lot of bastards," I said; and I got several grins back.

As none of the gates was locked we walked the horses without hindrance out to the track. The one-and-a-half-mile circuit ran right-handed, with nine assorted jumps on the way. I hadn't raced for eleven years. I was crazy. It felt great.

Nasty long words like "irresponsibility" swam like worms into the saner regions of my mind. I did carry this multi-million-dollar motion picture on my shoulders. I did know, arrogance aside, that the soufflé I was building would collapse if the cooker were switched off.

All the same, it seemed to me somehow that I'd grown old a long time ago after too brief a youth. For perhaps three minutes I would go back to my teens.

Ed, car, and doctor followed us onto the course.

One of my opponents asked me, "How much do you weigh?"

"Enough to give me an excuse for losing."

"Bugger that," he said, and he pointed his horse toward the task and dug him in the flanks with his heels.

I followed him immediately. I'd have no second chance; and I felt the old controlled recklessness swamp through brain and body as if I'd never been away.

I thought of the man in front as Blue, because of his colors, and the one behind me as Red. We'd had all the shiny shirts especially made for the film for eye-appeal and distinguishability, and the wardrobe people had given us the goods.

Both Blue and Red were younger than I and had not yet started their careers by the time I'd left. They were intent, I saw at once, on making no allowances, and indeed, if they had done so, the whole enterprise would have been without purpose. I simply dredged my memory for a skill that had once come naturally, and judged my horse's stride before the first of the fences with an easy practice I'd thought long forgotten.

There was speed and there was silence. No banter, no swearing from the others. Only the thud of hooves and the brush through the dark birch of the fences. Only the gritting determination and the old exaltation.

My God, I thought in midair, why ever did I give this up? But I knew the answer. At nineteen I'd been too tall and growing too heavy, and starving down to a professional riding weight had made me feel ill.

Half a mile and two jumps later I felt the first quiver of unfitness in my muscles and remembered that both Blue and Red had been at racing peak for several months. The speed they took in their stride used all my strength. We'd rounded the bottom turn and had straightened three abreast into the long far side before I seriously considered that I'd been a fool—or at least definitely foolhardy—to set off in this roller coaster, and I jumped the next four close-together fences concentrating mainly on desperately keeping my weight as far forward as possible.

Riding with one's center of gravity over the horse's shoulder was best for speed aerodynamically, but placed the jockey in a prime position for being catapulted off forward if his mount hit a fence. The alternative was to slow the pace before jumping, sit back, let the reins slide long through one's fingers, and maybe raise an arm up and back to maintain balance before landing. An habitually raised arm, termed "calling a cab," was the trademark of amateurism. To do it once couldn't be helped, but five or six raised arms would bring me pity, not in the least what I was out there trying to earn. I was going to go over Huntingdon's jumps with my weight forward if it killed me.

Which of course it might.

With this last mordant thought, and with straining muscles and laboring lungs, I reached the long last bend toward home: two more fences to jump, and the run-in and winning post after.

Experienced jockeys that they were, Blue and Red had waited for that last bend before piling on the ultimate pressure. I quickened with them, determined only not to be ignominiously tailed-off, and my mount responded, as most thoroughbreds do, with an inbred compulsion to put his head in front.

I don't know about the others, but I rode over the last two fences as if it mattered like the Grand National; but even so, it wasn't enough. We finished in order, Red, Green, Blue, flat out past the winning post, with half a length between first and second and between second and third.

We pulled up and trotted back to the gate. I felt weak enough for falling off. I breathed deeply through my nose, having told many actors in my time that the most reliable evidence of exhaustion was to gasp with the mouth open.

With Blue and Red leading the way we rejoined the other jockeys. No one said much. We dismounted and gave the reins to the lads. I could feel my fingers trembling as I unbuckled the helmet and hoped the jockeys couldn't see. I took off the helmet, returning it to the man who'd lent it, and brushed sweat off my forehead with my thumb. Still no sound above half-heard murmurs. I unbuttoned the striped colors, forcing my hands to the task, and fumbled too much over untying the stock. Still with breaths heaving in my belly, I handed shirt and stock back, and took my own clothes from someone who'd lifted them from the grass. I hadn't the strength to put them on, but simply held them over my arm.

It struck me that what everyone was feeling, including myself, was chiefly embarrassment, so I made my best stab at lightness.

"OK!" I said. "Tomorrow, then? You'll race?"

Blue said, "Yes," and the others nodded.

"Fine. See you."

I raised a smile that was genuine, even if only half wattage, and turned away to walk over to where Moncrieff, curse him, was trying to pretend he hadn't had a video camera on his shoulder the whole time.

A voice behind me called, "Mr. Lyon."

I paused and turned. Mr. Lyon, indeed! A surprise.

The one with the green and white stripes said, "You did make your point."

I managed a better smile and a flap of a hand and plodded across the grass to Moncrieff.

"Shit," he said.

"Anything but. We might now get a brilliant race tomorrow. They're not going to let themselves do worse than a panting amateur."

"Put your shirt on, you'll die of cold."

But not of a broken neck, I thought, and felt warm and spent and thunderously happy.

ED GAVE ME back the mobile phone, saying that O'Hara had called while he, Ed, was driving round the course, and had wanted to know where I was.

"What did you tell him?" I asked.

"I said you were riding. He wants you to call him back."

"Right."

I set off toward my car and its driver and called O'Hara as I went. He had spent time with Howard, it seemed, who was now enthusiastic over the witch-craft angle and wanted it emphasized. Scenes were positively dripping off his pen.

"Yeah," I said, "but restrain him. Witches do not hang *themselves,* and we still need our designated murderer."

"You have," O'Hara said dryly, "a habit of putting your finger on the button." He paused briefly. "Howard told me where Alison Visborough lives."

"Did you bargain with him? A deal?"

"It's possible," O'Hara said stiffly, "that we may not wring the last cent out of him."

I smiled.

"Anyhow, go see her, will you? Some place in Leicestershire."

"When? We're shooting all day tomorrow."

"Uh, now. Howard phoned her. She's expecting you."

"Now! Can't someone else do it?"

I'd been up since four that morning and it was by now five-forty in the afternoon and I needed a shower and I felt knackered, to put it politely. Leicestershire began a lot of miles in the wrong direction.

O'Hara said, "I thought you'd be interested to meet her, and she has her mother living with her."

"The Audrey?"

O'Hara confirmed it. "Silva's character in the movie."

"Well . . . yes, I'm interested. OK, I'll go. What's the address?"

He told it to me in detail, phone number included. "Howard's busting a gut trying to be helpful."

"I'll bet."

O'Hara said, changing the subject, "Ed said you were riding?"

Amused by his oblique question, I answered, "I rode round the course with a couple of the jockeys for them to see what we'll be needing tomorrow."

"You take care."

"Sure," I said. "Always."

We said good-bye and I walked onward to the car, making another phone call, this time to Robbie Gill.

"Thomas Lyon," I said, when I reached him. "How's my girl?"

"Still in intensive care. I've liaised with her surgeon. He's slapped a 'do not move' notice on her, which should hold while she needs drip feeds. Two or three days, anyway. I can't stand that son of hers. What a bully!"

"What's he been doing?"

"The nurses threaten a mutiny. He's so bloody *lordly.*"

"Is Dorothea awake yet?"

"Yes, she's talked briefly to the police. Apparently the last thing she remembers is setting off to walk home from supper with a widowed friend who lives only a quarter of a mile away. They watch TV together sometimes, and she felt like company with Valentine gone. Lucky she wasn't at home earlier."

"I guess so. Perhaps."

"Perhaps," he agreed.

"Anything else?" I asked.

"Nothing. I asked the police. They gave me the sort of guff which means they haven't a clue."

"I'd like to see her."

"I told her that you'd been asking. She was obviously pleased. Perhaps tomorrow evening, or the next day."

"I'll phone you," I said.

I reached the car, delivered the change of plans to the driver, and consulted the road map. A matter of turn right onto the A 14, go northwest, skirt Kettering, press onward. Forty miles perhaps to Market Harborough.

"Wake me when we reach that point," I said, and went to sleep on the back seat.

ALISON VISBOROUGH'S HIDEAWAY proclaimed her personality from the gateposts onward. A crumbling tarmac drive led to an old two-story house, brick built, possibly eighteenth century, but without distinction. Fields near the house were divided into many paddocks, all fenced with weathered wooden rails, some occupied by well-muscled but plain horses. A larger paddock to one side held a variety of flakily painted gates, poles, and fake walls, the paraphernalia of show jumping. At the far end a man in a tweed jacket and high-domed black riding hat cantered a horse slowly round in a circle, looking down and concentrating on the leading foreleg, practicing dressage. A child, watching him, held a workaday pony by the reins. Lesson, it appeared, being given and received.

Everything about the place looked tidy and efficient and spoke of a possible shortage of funds.

My driver drew up outside the undemonstrative front door. He had said he would check that we had arrived at the right place, but he had no need to. The door opened before he could reach it, to reveal a full-bosomed middle-aged woman dressed in jodhpurs, shirt, and dull green sweater, accompanied by two half-grown Labrador dogs.

"Mr. Lyon?" Her voice reached me, loud, imperious, displeased.

My driver gestured to the car, out of which I unenthusiastically climbed.

"I'm Thomas Lyon," I said, approaching her.

She shook my hand as an unwelcome social obligation and similarly invited me into her house, leaving my driver to look after himself.

"I am Alison Visborough. Howard warned me to expect you," she announced, leading me into a cold tidy room furnished with hard-stuffed, blue-green armchairs and sofas which looked inviting but repelled boarders, so to speak. I perched on the inhospitable edge of one of them, and she on another. The dogs had been unceremoniously left in the hall.

"You are younger than I expected," she pronounced, her vowels unselfconsciously plummy. "Are you sure you are who you say?"

"Quite often."

She stared.

I said, "I'm not the ogre you described to the *Drumbeat*."

"You were driving Howard to despair," she said crisply. "Something had to be done. I did not expect all this fuss. Still less did I intend to bring trouble to Howard. He has explained that your wretched film company is angry with me, but when I perceive an injustice, I must speak out."

"Always?" I asked with interest.

"Of course."

"And does it often get you into trouble?"

"I am not to be deterred by opposition."

"For Howard's sake," I said, "could you write a short apology to the film company?"

She shook her head indignantly, then thought it over, and finally looked indecisive, an unusual state for her, I guessed.

She had short dark hair with gray advancing, also unafraid brown eyes, weathered skin, no lipstick, and ringless work-roughened hands. A woman hard on herself and on everyone else, but admired by Howard.

I asked, "Who did you talk to, who works for the *Drumbeat?*"

She hesitated again and looked not overpleased. "I didn't say," she grudgingly answered, "exactly what she wrote in the paper."

"She?"

"She's an old acquaintance. We went to the same school. She works on the 'Hot from the Stars' team, and I thought it would *help* Howard in his fight against you. *She* didn't write what was printed. She just passed on the information to one of the columnists, as she always does. She gathers the material, you see, and then it gets *sensationalized,* she explained to me, by someone whose job it is to do that."

Sensationalized. What a process! Yet without it, I supposed, Howard's gripe wouldn't have been worth the space.

"How long," I enquired, "have you known Howard?"

"Why do you want to know?"

"I only wondered about the length of your commitment to him."

With a touch of the belligerence I was coming to expect, she said, "I can be committed to a good cause within five minutes."

"I'm sure."

"Actually, we've known Howard since he came to visit us after Daddy died."

The word Daddy came naturally: it was only I who found it odd and incongruous in someone of her age.

"He came to see your mother?"

"Principally, I suppose so."

"Because of the obituary?"

She nodded. "Howard found it interesting."

"Mm." I paused. "Have you any idea who wrote that obituary?"

"Why do you want to know?"

I shrugged. "Interest. It seemed to me it was written from personal feelings."

"I see." She let seconds pass, then said, "I wrote that myself. It was edited by the paper, but the gist of it was mine."

"Was it?" I was noncommittal. "You wrote about your father's potential career being blighted by Sonia's death?"

"Yes, I did."

"You wrote as if you cared."

"Of *course* I cared," she said vehemently. "Daddy wouldn't discuss it with me, but I knew he was bitter."

"Uh," I said, "but why did Sonia's death make him give up politics?"

Impatiently, as if it were self-evident, she said, "Scandal, of course. But he would never talk about it. He would never have let this film be made. Rodbury and I were also against it, but we were powerless. The book was Howard's, not ours. Our name, Daddy's name, doesn't appear in it. Howard says you *forced* him to make the ridiculously untrue changes to his work, so of *course* I felt someone had to stop you. For Howard's sake and yes, for Daddy's memory, I had to do it."

And nearly succeeded, I thought.

I said, without trying to defend either myself or film company policy, "Excuse me, but who is Rodbury?"

"My brother, Roddy."

Roddy, of course.

"Could I possibly," I asked, "meet your mother?"

"What for?"

"To pay my respects."

It hung in the balance, but it wasn't left to her to decide. The half-closed door was pushed open by a walking stick in the hands of a thin seventyish lady with a limp. She advanced slowly and forbiddingly and, while I rose to my feet, informed me that I was a monster.

"You are the person, aren't you," she accused with tight lips, "who says I was unfaithful to my husband with Jackson Wells? *Jackson Wells!*" There was a world of outraged class-distinction in her thin voice. "Dreadful man! I *warned* my sister not to marry him, but she was headstrong and wouldn't listen. He wasn't good enough for her. And as for you thinking that *I* . . . I . . ." Words almost failed her. "I could hardly even be *civil* to the man, and he was almost twenty years *younger* than I."

She shook with vibrant disapproval. Her daughter rose, took her mother's arm, and helped her toward one of the chairs whose overstuffed firmness suddenly made sense.

She had short white curling hair and high cheekbones, and must once have been pretty, but either pain or a general disapproval of life had given her mouth a pinched bad-tempered downturn. I thought of Silva and her glowing beauty, and reckoned the two women would probably not want to meet.

I said without emphasis, "The film company discussed with Howard Tyler the changes they wished made to certain elements of the published book. I did not myself arrange them. I was engaged after the main changes had been agreed. Still, I think they were necessary and that they'll make a strong and entertaining motion picture, even though I understand your reservations."

"*Reservations!*"

"Disapproval, then. But as your own name is nowhere used, and as the film is fiction, not many will connect you to it."

"Don't be ridiculous. We are the laughingstock of Newmarket."

"I don't think so," I said. "It was all so long ago. But I would like to ask you a question, and I do hope you will help with the answer, as it might soften for you your understandable outrage. Did your sister Sonia lead the strong fantasy life that Howard gave her in the book? Was she a dreamy young woman in real life?"

While the older woman hesitated, Alison said, "I've never met her husband, and I don't remember her much at all. I was only fourteen."

"Sixteen," her mother corrected sharply.

Alison darted a barb of irritation at her mother, who looked faintly complacent. An uneasy mother-daughter friction existed, I saw, that was only half stifled by good manners. Alison, odd though it seemed for one of her disposition, was woman enough to want me to believe her younger.

"Dreams?" I prompted.

"My sister," Audrey Visborough pronounced repressively, "tended to fall for any man in breeches. She would drool over men she could never have. Very silly. I daresay I mentioned it to Howard when he first came here. Jackson Wells looked good in breeches and of course he was flattered when Sonia made eyes at him. It was no basis for a marriage."

I said, "Er . . ." without opinion.

"I at least prevented my daughter from making the same mistake."

Alison, the unmarried daughter, flashed her a glance full of old and bitter resentment.

I cleared my throat diplomatically and asked, "Do you by any chance have a photograph of your sister?"

"I don't think so."

"Not even from when you were both young?"

Audrey said severely, "Sonia was a late and unexpected child, born when I was already grown. She was pleasant enough to begin with, I suppose. I didn't see much of her. Then I married Rupert, and really . . . ! Sonia's behavior became *insupportable.* She wouldn't *listen* to me."

"But . . . when she died in that way . . . ?" I left the question open, ready for any response.

Audrey shuddered a little. "Horrible," she said, but the word and the shudder were automatic, the emotion dead from age.

"Do you have any idea why she died?" I asked.

"We have said over and over again that we do not."

"And," Alison added in the same manner, "it is disgraceful that you and your film should be intruding on our lives."

Audrey nodded vigorously: mother and daughter were agreed on that at least.

I asked Alison, "For Howard's sake, then, will you write the short note of explanation to the film company?"

With asperity she countered, "You don't care about Howard. You just care about yourself."

With patience I spoke the truth. "Howard writes a good screenplay. His name is on the film. If he is worried about being sued by the film company, he will not do himself justice in scenes which still need expanding. He admires you, Miss Visborough. Give him a chance to do his best work."

She blinked, rose to her sturdy feet, and left the room, closing the door behind her.

Her mother gave a cough of implacable distrust and said, "May I ask why you want a photograph of my sister?"

"It would help because then I could be sure the actress who plays her in the film will not look like her. If your sister had red hair, for instance, we could get the actress a black wig."

Every response seemed to be squeezed out of her against her will. She said however, "My sister had naturally mousey brown hair. She disliked it and dyed it any color she could think of. My husband had a fierce disagreement with her once when she came here with a green crewcut."

I managed not to smile. "Upsetting," I said.

"I do not care what you say about Sonia," she went on, "but I mind very much that you are denigrating my husband's achievements. Gaga! He was *never* gaga. He was a man of sense and wisdom, with a spotless reputation."

And I had no need to wonder what he'd looked like, as there were photographs of Rupert Visborough at various ages in silver frames on almost every surface in the room. He'd been handsome, upright, and humorless: no twinkle in any of the eyes. I thought with a small twinge of guilt that I was going to make of Cibber something Visborough had never been: a charging bull traveling out of control to self-destruction.

The sitting room door opened to reveal, not Alison returning, but an unprepossessing man in hacking jacket and jodhpurs who entered as if thoroughly at home, crossing to a tray holding glasses and a single bottle of whiskey. He poured from bottle to glass and took a swig before looking me over and waiting for an introduction.

"Roddy," Audrey Visborough said from conditioned social reflex, "this man is Thomas Lyon, who is making that wretched film."

Roddy Visborough had his glass to his face so that I couldn't see his expression, but his body stiffened in annoyance. He was, I thought, the dressage rider from the show-jumping paddock: a man of medium height, neither fat nor thin, uncharismatic, with scanty gray-brown hair, going bald.

He lowered the glass to chest level and offensively said, "Bugger off." He said it phonetically, as bugger *orf.*

Audrey Visborough made not the slightest protest. She remarked, merely, "Mr. Lyon is leaving shortly."

Her son sank the rest of his undiluted drink and poured a second. "What are you doing here?" he said. "You're upsetting my mother."

I answered, "I came to help straighten things out for Howard Tyler."

"Oh, him." Roddy Visborough smiled superciliously. "Seems keen on Alison. I can't think what he sees in her."

His mother made no comment.

I thought that what Howard saw in Alison was a staunch woman who took a realistic but none too happy view of the world. There had been unlikelier alliances.

Alison herself returned with a white envelope which she held out for me to take. I thanked her; she nodded unenthusiastically and turned to her brother, asking, "How did the lesson go?"

"The child's stupid."

"We need her custom."

"I do not need your criticism."

Alison looked as if this level of brotherly love was customary. To me, rather to my surprise, she explained, "We prepare horses and riders for eventing and show-jumping. We keep horses and ponies here at livery."

"I see."

"*I* don't live here," Roddy said with a sort of throttled grudge. "I have a cottage down the road. I only work here."

"He's the show-jumper," Alison said, as if I should have heard of him. "I employ him to teach."

"Ah," I said vaguely.

"This house is mine," Alison said. "Daddy left our family home to me in his will. Mummy, of course, is now my guest."

I looked carefully at Alison's face. Under the no-nonsense exterior she let me see a buried but definite glimmer of mischief, of extreme satisfaction, of perhaps the sweetest revenge for a lifetime of snubs.

# 10

Next morning I awoke with a groan, every muscle stiffly lecturing me on the folly of proving points. I winced down toward my car but was stopped in the lobby by Nash, O'Hara, and Moncrieff, who seemed to have been holding a conference.

O'Hara didn't say good morning, he said, "You're goddam crazy, you know that."

I turned disillusioned eyes on Moncrieff, who said, "Yeah, well, nothing's off the record, you're always saying so yourself."

Nash said, "Midnight last night, when you'd gone to bed, Moncrieff played us the video."

I pinched sleepy eyes between finger and thumb and asked O'Hara if he'd faxed Alison's letter to Hollywood, as he'd intended.

He nodded. "If Howard stays in line, he's off the hook."

"Good." I paused. "OK. Today, then. It's not raining. We can shoot the race as planned. We can only do it once, so anyone loading fogged film or getting his f-stops wrong will be blindfolded for the firing squad. Moncrieff, I'll sincerely kill you if your crews bugger it up."

O'Hara said, "Did you phone that TV guy Greg Compass yesterday?"

I thought back and nodded. "From Huntingdon. I couldn't reach him."

"He sent a message. The reception desk says you didn't call down for it."

He handed me a piece of paper on which a phone number was written, and a time, 9 a.m.

By nine o'clock, each of us traveling in his own car with driver, we had long reached Huntingdon racecourse. Greg, as good as his message, answered immediately when I phoned.

I said, "I wanted to thank you for Saturday."

"No sweat. I gather you're still running things."

"Sort of." I explained about the Huntingdon scenes and invited him to come and drape his familiar figure in shot, if he cared to.

"When?"

"Today, tomorrow, or Thursday. Any or all."

"Too busy," he said.

"Never mind, then."

"Fee?"

"Of course."

"I'll be with you tomorrow." He laughed and clicked off, and I wondered if it would cost me another row of seats.

I drove round the track with Moncrieff to check the positions of the cameras and, in places, lights. Apart from our own two usual crews, we had rented three more cameras on dollies and planted two others, unmanned, in the fences for close action. Moncrieff himself would be on the camera truck, driving round ahead of the horses, filming them from head on. The last of the rented equipment was high on the stands from where it would follow the action from start to winning post. As always with scenes that could only be shot once, there would be glitches, but enough, I fervently hoped, would be usable.

Ed having briefed the jockeys to wait for me, I found them gathered in the jockeys' changing room, kitted as for an ordinary race. Fourteen of them. Every single one.

"Morning," I said, matter-of-factly.

"Morning."

No one referred to the day before. I said, "I know Ed's given you the gen but we'll just go over it once more. From your point of view, it will be a race like most others. Two miles over fences. You'll circle around at the starting gate, and the starter will call you into line. The starter is an actor. He's been well rehearsed, but if he makes a balls of it, don't stop and go back. Just keep on racing." I paused. "Same as usual, there's a groundsman and an ambulanceman at every fence. The groundsman and the ambulancemen are the real thing. The ambulance is real. So is the doctor. So is the vet. All the spectators out on the course and at the fences will be professional extras. All the crowds on the stands will be townspeople. OK so far?"

They nodded.

"Our fourteen horses are all fairly fit but, as you know, they were chosen for a safe jumping record and bought cheaply. They won't break any sound barriers, and the three of them that raced yesterday may not stay the course today. If you want to, you can draw lots in a minute to see who gets which horse; one to fourteen on the number cloths."

The faces were businesslike. They agreed to draw lots.

"This race won't work," I said, "unless you yourselves make it good. You want to be able to show the video of it all to your families, let alone see it in the cinema. You'll all get a CD or video tape later."

"Who's got to win?" one of them asked.

"Didn't Ed tell you?"

They shook their heads.

"It's got to be a bona fide race. Whoever wins, those are the colors we'll put on the actor who's playing the jockey in close-up. This actor looks OK sitting on a horse and he can trot at a pinch. Sorry, but it's he who'll be led into the unsaddling enclosure in the winner's colors. But . . . er . . . to make up for it, the one of you who wins this race will get a percentage same as usual. When you pull up, come off the course through the usual gate. All the also-rans can unsaddle in the usual place. There'll be some extras there acting as owners and trainers. The lads will take the horses. Just behave as normal. The first four will be led off toward the winners' enclosure. Any questions?"

"What if we fall?" It was Blue who asked.

"Why did you all turn up?"

Some laughed and some swore. No tension any more.

"Have fun," I said.

One asked, "And where will you be?"

I said with audible regret, "I'll be watching from the ground." I paused. "If you can possibly avoid it, don't give us any flagrant grounds for an enquiry. There's no enquiry in the script. Try not to cross. OK?"

I went outdoors through the deserted weighing room that on a real race day would have been crowded with officials and trainers, and I watched for a moment the helpful people of Huntingdon arrive in droves, all dressed in race-going clothes and carrying, in impressive numbers, binoculars. Ed, I saw, had done a fine job.

One of the film personnel came up to me and handed me an envelope, saying it was urgent. I thanked him perfunctorily, and he'd gone before I'd opened the message.

I unfolded the inside sheet of contents, and read the words.

Stop making this film or you will die by the knife today.

Oh, delightful.

It looked like a computer printout on anonymous white office paper.

O'Hara appeared, wanting to discuss a detail or two, and asked what was the matter. "Why are you frozen?"

I gave him the missive. "I've had death threats before," I pointed out.

"Those were after the movie had been distributed. But we have to take this seriously." He flicked the page with a fingernail. "What are we going to do about it?"

"What do you suggest?"

"If you leave the set," O'Hara said plainly, "the movie automatically goes into recess. It would give us all time to find this bozo and slap him behind bars."

"We can't stop the filming," I said. "After the *Drumbeat* article and the knife on the Heath . . . one more panic and the moguls will take complete fright and yank the whole movie forever."

O'Hara suspected it was true, but worriedly said, "This letter just doesn't say you'll die, it says you'll die *today.*"

"Mm."

"Thomas . . . you're no good to us dead."

"What strikes me," I said, half smiling at his pragmatism, "is that whoever sent this note doesn't actually want to kill me, he wants to stop the film without being driven to drastic action. If he—or I suppose, she—meant to stop the film by killing me, why not just do it? Why the preliminary melodrama? We'll ignore it and press on."

"I'll at least get you a bodyguard, like Nash."

Nash, that day, had not one but two bodyguards in attendance but, as I reminded O'Hara, both of these bodyguards were well known to us.

"If you bring in a stranger, you're risking what you're trying to avoid," I said. "In classic cases, it's the bodyguards themselves that kill the victim." I tried a lie that I hoped would be true, and said, "I don't think I'm in much danger, so just forget it."

"Difficult." He was mildly relieved, all the same, by my decision.

"Keep the paper," I told him, "and keep the envelope." I gave it to him. "And let's get on with the film."

"I still don't like it."

Nor did I, much; but delivering a death *threat* took little organization or courage, and delivering a death by knife took both.

The knife intended for Nash had been incompetently dropped. Cling to that. Forget—for Christ's sake forget—the intestines spilling out of Dorothea.

"Who gave you the letter?" O'Hara asked.

"One of the grips. I've seen him around but I don't know his name."

There was never time to know the names of the between sixty and a hundred people working on a film on location. I hadn't learned even the names of the horses, neither their registered names, nor the names the lads called them, nor their invented names for the film. I didn't know the jockeys' names, nor those of the bit-part actors. It was faces I remembered, horses' faces, jockeys' faces, actors' faces from way back: my memory had always been chiefly visual.

I did forget for a while about the death threat: too much else to do.

As always with scenes involving two or three hundred people, the race took forever to set up. I spent ages on the walkie-talkie checking the status of each far-flung section, but at last, toward noon, everything seemed to be ready. The lads brought the horses from the stables and the jockeys mounted their balloted numbers and cantered down to the start.

I decided to ride on the camera truck with Moncrieff, to be nearer the action: and to guard my back, I cravenly and privately acknowledged.

Ed, equipped with loudspeaker, alerted the Huntingdon multitude to put on race-day faces and cheer the finish. The commentary, we had explained, would be missing; we had to record it separately and afterward. Nevertheless, Ed urged, cheer whoever won.

Eventually it was he who shouted "Action," the command reverberating through the stands, and I, with raised pulse, who found myself begging unknown deities for perfection.

There were flaws, of course. One of the rented cameras jammed, and one of the two planted in fences got kicked to oblivion by a horse, but the race started tidily, and it was joyously clear from the first that my quasi-colleagues were playing fair.

They had seen me on the truck, when it was positioned for the start, seen me sitting on the edge of the roof of the cab, to get the best of views. They'd waved, in a way, I thought, to reassure me, and I'd waved back; and they did indeed ride their hearts out all the way round.

We had the truck driven for a lot of the way so that the camera was barely six feet from the leading horses' heads, then speeded it up to give a longer view, then slowed again, varying the angles.

Two horses fell on the backstretch second time round. I looked back with anxiety, but both jockeys got to their feet, the loose horses adding the unpremeditated facets that in the end proved the contest real.

The other riders again piled on the pressure rounding the last bend, and again they rode flat out over the last two fences and stretched every sinew to win. The finish was even faster and closer than the day before, but distinguishably Blue, Green with White stripes, and Yellow crossed the line in the first three places; and as the truck slowed I could hear the crowd shouting them home as if they'd gambled their shirts. Those jockeys had ridden with an outpouring of courage that left me dry mouthed and breathless, grateful beyond expression, bursting with admiration.

As agreed, when they trotted the tired horses back to unsaddle, another of Moncrieff's cameras continued to film them. I couldn't walk into shot to thank them, and thanks, in any form, would have been inadequate.

"Hell's teeth," Moncrieff exclaimed, moved by the proximity to the speed and sweating commitment. "And they do that for a *living?*"

"Day in, day out, several times an afternoon."

"Crazy."

"There's nothing like it," I said.

WE CHANGED THE actor-jockey into Blue's colors and had him led into the winners' enclosure, to applause from a throng of mixed extras and townspeople. We had to do the unsaddling at that point, while the horses still steamed and sweated and stamped from the excitement of racing. We filmed Nash patting the winner's neck. We filmed the actor-jockey unbuckling the saddle while showing, to my mind, unprofessional clumsiness. We filmed the four horses being rugged and led away by the lads; and we broke for lunch.

Nash, bodyguard close, signed a host of good-natured autographs, mostly on the race cards we'd lavishly distributed.

O'Hara, again at my elbow, breathed in my ear, "Satisfied?"

"Are you?"

"Nash and I watched the race from up in the Stewards' box. Nash says those first three jockeys rode beyond the call of duty."

"Yes, they did."

"He says it will give fantastic bite to the victory of *his* horse over Cibber's."

"It'll drive Cibber mad."

"The final straw?"

"Almost. Cibber can't stand to have his best horse beaten into second place like that by the man he hates."

"When I read the revised script, I thought Howard had overdone the hate. I couldn't see any race inducing that level of paranoia."

"Hate can corrode the soul to disintegration."

"Maybe. But to show that, you needed an *exceptional* race . . ." His voice tailed off momentarily. "And I guess you got it," he finished, "in your own way."

I half smiled. "Let's find some lunch."

"You're having it in the Stewards' box with Nash and me. Do you realize I could have come up behind you just now and put a knife through your ribs? Do you realize we have roughly three hundred strangers here wandering around?"

I did realize. I went with him and lunched high up in safety.

By the time we returned to ground level and to work, one of Ed's assistants had found the grip who'd passed on the letter. Some kid had given it to him. What kid? He looked around, bewildered. Kids were all over the place. The grip had no recollection of age, sex, or clothes. He'd been busy with the un-loading of equipment for the following day.

"Shit," O'Hara said.

Another of the film personnel approached as if apologetically and held out a card toward me. "Some people called Batwillow say you're expecting them." He looked across to where the little group stood. Jackson Wells, his wife, and Lucy, and a man I didn't know.

I took the card and waved them over and had time only to say to O'Hara, "This is our hanged lady's real husband," before shaking their hands. They had come dressed for the races and Jackson Wells himself, in tweeds and trilby, looked indefinably more a trainer than a farmer. He introduced the stranger as "Ridley Wells, my brother." I shook a leathery hand.

Ridley Wells was altogether less striking than Jackson, both in coloring and personality, and he was also, I thought, less intelligent. He blinked a lot. He was dressed in riding clothes as if he had come straight from his work, which Jackson described to O'Hara as "teaching difficult horses better manners."

Ridley nodded, and in an accent stronger than his brother's, said self-pityingly, "I'm out in all weathers on Newmarket Heath, but it's a thankless sort of job. I can ride better than most, but no one pays me enough. How about employing me in this film?"

Jackson resignedly shook his head at Ridley's underlying chip-on-the-shoulder attitude. O'Hara said sorry, no job. Ridley looked as if he'd been badly treated; a habitual expression, I guessed. I could see why Jackson hadn't welcomed Ridley's inclusion in the day's proceedings.

Jackson still had, it seemed, the old professional trainer's eye, because after a few "nice days" and so on, he said, "That was some race those jocks rode. More electrifying than most of the real thing."

"Could you see that?" O'Hara asked interestedly.

"Didn't you hear the cheering? That was no act, either. 'Cheer the winner,' we were told, but the cheers came easy as pie."

"Be darned," O'Hara said, no horseman himself. He looked at my guests thoughtfully and said impulsively to me, "Keep the Batwillow family around you, why not?"

He meant, use them as bodyguards. He hadn't heard Jackson Wells tell me he'd have preferred not to have the film made. I felt safe, though, with his wife and daughter, so I wrapped them as a living shield around me, Mrs. Wells on one arm, Lucy on the other, and walked them all off to meet Nash.

Although Nash hadn't wanted to meet the man he was playing, I introduced them straightforwardly, "Jackson Wells—Nash Rourke," and watched them shake hands with mutual reservations.

They were in several ways superficially alike: same build, same age bracket, same firm facial muscles. Jackson was blond where Nash was darker, and sunnily open, where Nash, from long mega-star status, had grown self-protectively wary. Easier with the women, Nash autographed race cards for wife and daughter and effortlessly melted their hearts. He signed for Ridley also, and didn't take to him.

We were due to film Nash walking up the steps to the stands to watch (supposedly) his horse run in the race. Slightly to O'Hara's dismay, he invited Mrs. Wells and Lucy to stand near him, in front of the bodyguards, for the scene. Ridley, unasked, followed them up the steps, which left Jackson Wells marooned on his feet by my side, looking as if he wished he hadn't come.

"It hasn't occurred to your wife," I said.

"What hasn't?" he said, but he knew what I meant.

"That's she standing next to you, twenty-six years ago."

"They're the wrong age," he said brusquely. "We were all kids at the time. And you're right, I don't like it."

He bore it, however, standing rigid but quiet, while Nash, taking over from his stand-in, walked up the steps and turned on exactly the right spot to bring his face into Moncrieff's careful lighting. We shot the scene three times and I marked the first and third takes to be printed: and O'Hara stood all the while at my left elbow, riding shotgun, so to speak.

I grinned at him. "I could get me some armor," I said.

"It's no laughing matter."

"No."

One can't somehow believe in one's own imminent death. I hadn't stopped the film and I went on shooting bits of it all afternoon; and for ages at a time, like ten minutes, I stopped thinking about steel.

At one point, waiting as ever for lights and camera to be ready, I found my-self a little apart from the center of activity, standing beside Lucy, gazing into her amazing blue eyes and wondering how old she was.

She said suddenly, "You asked Dad for a photo of Sonia so that you didn't copy her exactly in the film."

"That's right. He hadn't kept any."

"No," she agreed. "But . . . well . . . I've got one. I found it one day jammed at the back of a drawer. I meant to give it to Dad, but he won't talk about Sonia. He won't let us mention her, ever. So I just kept it." She opened the small handbag swinging from her shoulder and handed me a creased but clearly distinguishable snapshot of a pretty girl and a good-looking young man, not Jackson. "You won't make Yvonne look like her, will you?"

Shaking my head, I turned the photo over and read the penciled informa-tion on the back: "Sonia and Pig."

"Who is Pig?" I asked.

"No idea," Lucy said. "I've never heard Dad mention him. But that's Dad's handwriting, so he must have known him, long ago."

"Long ago before you were born."

"I'm eighteen," she said.

I felt old. I said, "Could I borrow the photo for a while?"

She looked doubtful. "I don't want to lose it."

"Until tomorrow?" I suggested. "If you came here again tomorrow . . ."

"I don't think there's a chance. Dad didn't really want to come at all. He only gave in to Mum so that she could meet Nash Rourke."

"Could you and your mother come tomorrow?"

"She won't do anything if Dad doesn't like it."

"And you?"

"I don't have a car of my own."

"Lend me the photo for an hour, then."

She brightened and agreed, and I gave the photo to Moncrieff with an on-my-knees expression, begging him to do me a clear negative from which we could get a positive print. It would take the usual day for traveling to London to the laboratory for development, but with reasonable luck I'd have it back in the morning.

In the morning. Die today. Shut up, I thought.

"Do you," I asked Lucy later, "have a computer and a printer at home?"

"Of course we do," she answered, puzzled. "No one can farm without one, nowadays. The paperwork drives Dad loco. Why do you ask?"

"Just wondered. We use one here all the time." I enlarged on it, defusing my enquiry. "Every inch of film, every lens used, every focal stop . . . we have a script supervisor entering the lot. We can lay our hands on any frame of film that way, and also make sure we have continuity if we shoot the next scene days later."

She nodded in partial understanding and said, "And who are all those odd people you see on the credits? Grips, gaffers . . . who are they?"

"Grips move equipment. The gaffer is in charge of the lighting equipment. The most important chap at the moment is the production manager. He's the person who arranges for vehicles and scenery and props and all sorts of things to be in the right place when we need them."

"And you," she said with unflattering doubt, "are in overall charge of the whole thing?"

"I and the producer." I pointed to O'Hara. "No us, no film."

She said baldly, "Dad said so, but Mum thought you were too young."

"Are you always so frank?"

"Sixteen was hell," she said. "Tongue-tied. Not long ago I broke out of the egg."

"Congratulations."

"Dad says I talk nonsense."

"No better time for it. Stay and have dinner. I'll take you home later."

"Sorry." The response was automatic, the blue eyes full of the warnings she'd been given about date rape and such. "Not on our own."

I smiled wryly. I'd thought only of not being knifed, not of bed. I'm losing it, I thought, wanting my life saved by an eighteen-year-old still half in the cradle. I fetched her snap from Moncrieff—thumbs up, he said—and returned it to her.

"I didn't mean," she said awkwardly, sixteen surfacing again after all. "I mean, I don't want to offend you . . ."

"But no casting couches. It's all right."

She blushed and retreated, sane and confused, to her parents, and I thought bed wouldn't have been such a bad idea after all.

The trouble with making films, I acknowledged, was the way the occupation gobbled time. For the three months of any pre-production, I worked flat out to put the film together, choosing locations, getting the feel—the vision—in place, altering the screenplay, living with the characters. During production, like now, I worked seven days a week with little sleep. Post-production—the recording of music and sound effects, the cutting together of scenes and parts of scenes to make an impact and tell a story, the debates and the meetings and the previews—all of those often had to be scrambled into just a further three months. And with one film done, another crowded on my heels. I'd made three films lately in under two years. This new one had by far the biggest budget. I loved the work, I was lucky to be wanted, I felt no flicker of regret: I just didn't seem to have time to look for a wife.

One day, I guessed, it might happen like a thunderbolt. The skies, however, had to date vouchsafed only scattered showers, and Lucy looked like a continuing drought.

Someone unexpectedly knocked my elbow. I whirled round with surging heartbeat and found myself face-to-face with Moncrieff.

"Jumpy!" he said, watching me reach for composure. "What were you expecting? A tiger?"

"With claws," I agreed. I got things under control and we discussed the next scene.

"Are you all right?" Moncrieff asked, puzzled. "Not ill?"

Not ill, I thought, but plain scared. I said, "Everything's fine. But . . . er . . . some nutter wants to get the film stopped, and if you see anyone in my area raising a blunt instrument, give me a holler."

His eyebrows rose. "Is that why O'Hara has been standing behind you whenever he can?"

"I guess so."

He thought it over. "Nasty knife, that, on the gallops." A pause. "It got effing close to Ivan."

"Do me a favor and don't remind me."

"Just keep my eyes open?"

"Got it."

We lit and shot some nonspeaking takes of Nash's emotions during the race. The block of crowd behind him, mostly bona fide extras but some townspeople, also Mrs. Wells, Lucy, Ridley, and Nash's bodyguards, responded faithfully to Ed's exhortations, looking for each shot to where he pointed, oohing and aahing, showing anxiety, showing excitement, and finally cheering wildly as they watched in memory the horses racing to the finish.

All of the faces except Nash's would be very slightly out of focus, thanks to Moncrieff's wizardry with lenses. One of his favorite lenses had to be focused principally on the light in the actor's eyes. Everything else on the actor's head would be a tiny shade fuzzy, his neck, hair, the lot.

"The daylight's going," Moncrieff told me eventually, though to any eye but his the change was too slight to notice. "We should wrap for today."

Ed through his megaphone thanked the citizens of Huntingdon for their work and invited them back for the morrow. They clapped. Happy faces all round. Nash signed autographs with the bodyguards at his shoulders.

Lucy, glowing with the day's pleasures, walked to where I was checking through the following day's schedule with O'Hara, and handed me a flat white box about a foot long by three inches wide, fastened shut with a rubber band.

"What is it?" I asked.

"I don't know," she said. "A boy asked me to give it to you."

"What boy?"

"Just a boy. A present, he said. Aren't you going to open it?"

O'Hara took it out of my hands, stripped off the rubber band, and cautiously opened the box himself. Inside, on a bed of crunched up white office paper, lay a knife.

I swallowed. The knife had a handle of dark polished wood, ridged round and round to give a good grip. There was a businesslike black hilt and a narrow black blade nearly six inches long: all in all, good-looking and efficient.

"Wow," Lucy said. "It's beautiful."

O'Hara closed the box without touching the knife and, restoring the rubber band, stuck it in his outside jacket pocket. I thought it was better to get a knife in a box than in the body.

"We should stop all boys from leaving," O'Hara said, but he could see, as I could, that it was already too late. Half of the crowd had already walked homeward through the gates.

"Is something the matter?" Lucy asked, frowning, sensing our alarm.

"No," I smiled at the blue eyes. "I hope you've had a good day."

"Spectacular!"

I kissed her cheek. In public, she allowed it. She said, "I'd better go, Dad's waiting," and made a carefree departure, waving.

O'Hara took the white box from his pocket and carefully opened it again, picking out of the raised lid a folded strip of the same white paper. He handed it to me and I looked at its message.

Again a computer print-out, it said: TOMORROW.

O'HARA AND I walked out together toward the cars, and I told him about Dorothea and her injuries. I described again for him, as I had two days earlier, the knife that had been dropped on the Heath.

He stopped dead in mid-stride. "Are you saying," he demanded, "that your friend was attacked with *that* knife? The one on the Heath?"

"I don't know."

"But," he protested, bemused, "what possible connection could there be between her and our film?"

"I don't know."

"It can't have been the same knife." He walked on, troubled but certain.

"The only connection," I said, going with him, "is the fact that long ago Dorothea's brother Valentine put shoes on Jackson Wells's racehorses."

"Much too distant to have any significance."

"And Valentine said he once gave a knife to someone called Derry."

"Hell's teeth, Thomas, you're rambling."

"Yes. Valentine was at the time."

"Valentine was what?"

"Rambling," I said. "Delirious."

*I killed the Cornish boy . . .*

Too many knives.

"You are *not*," O'Hara said strongly, "going to get knifed tomorrow."

"Good."

He laughed. "You're a jackass, Thomas."

He wanted me to travel in his car, but I called Robbie Gill's mobile and found I could briefly see Dorothea, if I arrived by seven.

At the hospital the egregious Paul had positioned himself in a chair outside the single room into which Dorothea had been moved. He rose heavily to his feet at the sight of me; but to my surprise made none of the objections I was expecting.

"My mother wants to see you," he said disapprovingly. "I've told her I don't want you here, but all she does is cry."

There had been, I thought, a subtle change in Paul. His pompous inner certainty seemed to have rocked: the external bombast sounded much the same, but half its fire had gone.

"You're not to tire her," he lectured. "Five minutes, that's all."

Paul himself opened Dorothea's door and came in with me purposefully.

Dorothea lay on a high bed, her head supported by a bank of pillows, her old face almost as colorless as the cotton except for dark disturbing bruises and threadlike minutely stitched cuts. There were tubes, a bag delivering drops of blood, another bag of clear liquid, and a system that allowed her to run painkillers into her veins when she needed it. Her hold on life looked negligible. Her eyes were closed and her white body was motionless, even the slow rise and fall of her chest seeming too slight to register on the covering sheet.

"Dorothea," I said quietly. "It's Thomas. I've come."

Very faintly, she smiled.

Paul's loud voice broke her peace. "I've told him, Mother, that he has five minutes. And of course I will remain here at hand."

Dorothea, murmuring, said she wanted to talk to me alone.

"Don't be silly, Mother."

Two tears appeared below her eyelids and trembled in the lashes.

"Oh, for heaven's sake," Paul said brusquely. "She does that all the time." He turned on his heel and gave her her wish, seeming hurt at her rejection. "Five minutes," he threatened as a parting shot.

"Paul's gone," I said, as the door closed behind him. "How are you feeling?"

"So tired, dear." Her voice, though still a murmur, was perfectly clear. "I don't remember how I got here."

"No, I've been told. Robbie Gill told me."

"Robbie Gill is very kind."

"Yes."

"Hold my hand, dear."

I pulled the visitor's chair to her side and did as she asked, vividly remembering Valentine's grasp of my wrist, exactly a week ago. Dorothea, however, had no sins to confess.

"Paul told me," she said, "that someone tore my house apart, looking for something."

"I'm afraid so. Yes, I saw it."

"What were they looking for?"

"Don't you know?"

"No, dear. The police asked me. It must have been something Valentine had. Sometimes I think I know. Sometimes I think I hear him shouting at me, to tell him. Then it all goes away again."

"Who was shouting?"

She said doubtfully, "Paul was shouting."

"Oh no."

"He does shout, you know. He means well. He's my son, my sweet baby." Tears of weakness and regret ran down her cheeks. "Why do precious little babies grow . . . ?" Her question ended in a quiet sob, unanswerable. "He wants to look after me."

I said, "Did Robbie Gill talk to you about a nursing home?"

"So kind. I'd like to go there. But Paul says . . ." She stopped, fluttering a white hand exhaustedly. "I haven't the strength to argue."

"Let Robbie Gill move you," I urged. "In a day or two, when you're stronger."

"Paul says . . ." She stopped, the effort of opposing him too much.

"Just rest," I said. "Don't worry. Just lie and drift and get stronger."

"So kind, dear." She lay quiet for a long minute, then said, "I'm sure I know what he was looking for, but I can't remember it."

"What Paul was looking for?"

"No, dear. Not Paul." She frowned. "It's all jumbled up." After another pause she said, "How many knives did I have?"

"How many . . . ?"

"The police asked me. How many knives in the kitchen. I can't remember."

"No one knows how many knives they have in the kitchen."

"No . . . they said there weren't any knives in the house with blood on them."

"Yes, I see."

"Perhaps when I go home I'll see which knife is missing."

"Yes, perhaps. Would you like me to tidy your house up a bit?"

"I can't ask you."

"I'd like to do it."

"Paul wants to. He keeps asking. He gets so angry with me, but I don't know who has the key. So silly, isn't it? I can't go home because I haven't got the key."

"I'll find the key," I said. "Is there anything you want from there?"

"No, dear. I just want to be at home with Valentine." The slow tears came. "Valentine's dead."

I stroked her soft hand.

"It was a photo album," she said suddenly, opening her eyes.

"What was?"

"What they were looking for." She looked at me worriedly, pale blue shadows round her eyes.

"What photo album?"

"I don't know. I haven't got one, just some old snaps I keep in a box. Some pictures of Paul when he was little. I never had a camera, but friends gave me snaps . . ."

"Where's the box?"

"In my bedroom, but it's not an *album* . . . I didn't think of it before. Everything's so confusing."

"Mm. Don't let it worry you. And Robbie Gill will be cross if I tire you, let alone Paul."

A smile shone briefly in the old eyes. "I might as well be tired. I've nothing else to do."

I laughed. "It's just a shame," I said, "that Paul took Valentine's books after all. He swears he didn't, but he must have done, because they aren't in the house."

Dorothea frowned. "No, dear, Paul didn't take them."

"Didn't he?" I was skeptical. "Did he send someone else?"

"No, dear." Her forehead wrinkled further. "Valentine wanted *you* to have his books and I know he would have been furious if Paul had taken them, because he wasn't very fond of Paul, only put up with him for my sake, such a pity."

"So . . . who took them?"

"Bill."

"Who?"

"Bill Robinson, dear. He has them safe."

"But Dorothea . . . who is Bill Robinson, and where and why does he have the books?"

She smiled guiltily. "I was afraid, you see, dear, that Paul would come back and persuade me to let him take them. He tires me out sometimes until I do what he wants, but he's my son, dear, after all . . . So I asked Bill Robinson to come and pick them all up and put them in his garage, and he's a chum of mine, dear, so he came and took them, and they'll be quite safe, dear, he's a nice young man, he mends motorbikes."

# 11

I went to bed after midnight, thinking that although I had not died today, it was now already tomorrow.

Nash and I had eaten dinner together in harmony over his scenes-to-come in the parade ring, where his jockey would be wearing blue, while Cibber's would be in the green and white stripes.

After the evening preparation for the Jockey Club enquiry scene, Nash had, without baldly saying so, let me realize that he much preferred to rehearse everything with me in private, so that on set little needed to be asked or answered, his performances being already clear in his mind. I didn't know if he worked in this way with every director, but between the two of us it was notably fruitful in regard to his readiness for every shot. That we were saving time and running ahead of schedule was in this way chiefly his doing.

As usual I'd spent the last two hours of the evening with Moncrieff, putting together with him the plan of positions and lights for the parade ring cameras, also for those catching the pre-race routines of horses being saddled and led from the saddling stalls, being led round the parade ring, being de-rugged and mounted. Multiple cameras, though not cheap in themselves, also saved time: I would later cut together, from several lengthy shots, the snippets and pieces that in shorthand would give an overall impression of the whole pre-race tension. The slap of leather straps into buckles, the brushing of oil to gloss the hoof, the close shots of muscle moving below shining coat . . . It needed only two seconds of graphic visual image to flash an impression of urgency and intent, but it took maybe ten long minutes of filming to capture each.

Pace had a lot to do with good film making. There would be no flash–flash–flash over the dream/fantasy sequences, only a slowly developing realization of their significances.

Well . . . so I hoped.

While my silent young driver took me toward Huntingdon in the morning I thought of Dorothea's preservation of Valentine's books, and of the new uncertainty beneath Paul's bluster. He hadn't tried to cut short my visit to the patient: the five allowed minutes had stretched to ten, until I myself thought that she'd talked enough.

Paul had walked with me from her room to the hospital exit, his breath agitated and deep as if he wanted to say something but couldn't bring himself entirely to the point. I gave him time and opportunity, but he was not, as his uncle had been, desperate enough for confession.

Paul was shouting, Dorothea had said. For her sake, I hoped to God she'd got things mixed up.

At Huntingdon racecourse, before eight o'clock, the gates were already wide open to admit the local inhabitants. Breakfast, provided free for all comers via the film's caterers, ran to endless hot dogs out of a raised-sided van. The weather, though cold, still smiled. Cheerful faces abounded. I needn't have worried that the townspeople would be too bored to return: word of mouth had acted positively and we ended with an even larger crowd than on the day before.

The publicity department of the film company had provided five hundred T-shirts, one to be given that day to thank every local helper on departure—(much to my amusement the front of each T-shirt carried the slogan UNSTABLE TIMES in large letters, but if one looked closely at some extra tiny letters it read "UNSTABLE at all TIMES")—and I began to think they hadn't ordered enough.

The Huntingdon racecourse officials having been generous and helpful throughout, we had had unlimited access to everything we'd wanted. I was so keen not to abuse their welcome that I'd screwed O'Hara's arm to provide an army of scavengers to clean up all trash left by us.

"They'll have their own cleaning staff," he'd protested. "We're paying them, after all."

"Goodwill is beyond price."

He'd instructed the production manager to have the place left spotless.

The weighing room and the jockeys' changing rooms were already unlocked when I arrived on the course, and the wardrobe people were there too, laying out the jockeys' bright colors alongside their breeches and boots.

We had had all their gear made especially for the film, not just the colors. Everything except the racing saddles, which had been hired, belonged to the company.

There were twenty sets across the board, as we'd allowed for tears and spares and hadn't, at time of ordering, known how many horses we would end with. When I was in the changing rooms I found none of the jockeys had already arrived—they'd been called for nine o'clock—and I had no difficulty at all in scooping up what I wanted and locking myself privately into the bathroom.

I had taken with me two of the body protectors designed to save fallen jockeys from the worst effects of kicks. Stripped down to shirt and underpants I put on the first and zipped it up the front.

In essence the body protector was a blue cotton lightweight vest padded throughout with flat polystyrene oblongs, about six inches by four, by half an inch thick. The polystyrene pieces, stitched into place, covered the trunk from the neck to below the waist, with a further extension at the back to cover the coccyx at the base of the spine. From there a soft wide belt led forward between the legs to fasten to the vest in front, a scheme which prevented the protector from being displaced. Extra pieces led like epaulettes over the shoulders and down the upper arms, to be fastened round the arm with Velcro.

Although I'd taken the largest available, the protector fitted tight and snugly. When I put the second on top, the front zip wouldn't meet to fasten across my chest; a problem I half solved by straining my trousers over both protectors and cinching my waist with my belt to hold everything together. I ended feeling like a hunch-shouldered quarterback, but with my ordinary sweater on top and my windproof blue jacket fastened over all, I didn't in the mirror look much bigger.

I had no idea how a jockey's kick protector would stand up to a knife, but psychologically an inch of polystyrene and four layers of sturdy cotton cloth was better than nothing, and I couldn't afford to spend the whole busy day worrying about something that would probably not happen.

I'd happily ridden flat out over jumps round the racecourse without a body protector, risking my neck. I would as happily have done it again. Odd how fear had different faces.

Outside, Moncrieff had already positioned his camera on its dolly for the first scene of the day, which was the exodus of the jockeys from the weighing room on their way out to the parade ring before the race. Halfway along their path a child extra was to dash forward to offer an autograph book to the actor-jockey. Ed, directing a second camera, would film the jockey's friendly reaction in close-up, registering his face, his blue colors, and his nice-guy status, while the other jockeys went on their way through the shot behind him.

In the event we shot the sequence twice, though thanks to rehearsal it went smoothly the first time. Insurance, though, to my mind, was never wasted.

Between the two takes, I talked to the jockeys, joining them where they waited in the weighing room. I thanked them for their brilliant race the day before and they made nothing of it, joking. All prickliness had vanished absolutely. They called me Thomas. They said several of them would be racing over the course for real at the Huntingdon meeting the following Monday, but it would be the old nitty-gritty, not the joys of make-believe land. Any time I made another racing film, they said with typically mocking humor, they would stampede in the opposite direction.

When they were recalled for the retake walk to the parade ring, I went out before them and watched from beside Moncrieff: then with the two printable shots in the can Moncrieff took the camera and crew into the parade ring itself, where the camera could swivel on a turntable to take an almost 360 degrees view of the horses being led round. I stood in the center of the ring beside him, overseeing things.

As always it was the setting up that took the time: the positioning of extras playing the small groups of owners and trainers, the extras playing racing officials and Stewards, the townspeople filling the viewing steps round the ring, the rehearsing of the jockeys so that each went to an allotted owner, the ensuring that the jockeys of the two deadly rivals would arrive in the ring together—the actor-jockey in blue, the other in green and white stripes—and part at a designated spot to join the two groups containing Nash and Cibber.

Nash's main two bodyguards, dressed as owners, carried binoculars as if they would rather have had guns. The apparently elderly lady completing that group was a twenty-eight-year-old martial arts champion with lioness instincts.

Cibber's group included Silva dressed as befitted a Jockey Club member's wife in well-cut wool coat, knee-high boots, and fur hat; warm and pretty in the chill wind. Cibber's "trainer," off-course, taught judo. O'Hara had taken these precautions. My own shadow, the one he'd insisted on the evening before, stood beside me in the ring, looking dim. He was supposed to be a black belt but I had more faith in polystyrene.

Later in the day we would do close-ups of Cibber's acrid fury at having to suffer Nash, his wife's lover, in unbearable proximity: close-ups of Silva looking lovingly at Nash, goading poor Cibber further; close-ups of Nash behaving with good manners, neutral toward Cibber, circumspect with Silva; short essential close shots that would take an age to light.

Meanwhile, with the horses being led round the ring and with everyone in their allotted places, we filmed the entry of the jockeys. Miraculously they all went to the right groups, touched their caps to the owners, made pretense conversations, watched the horses; behaved as jockeys do. The actor-jockey in blue joined Nash. Green and White Stripes went to Cibber. No one tripped over cables, no one wandered inappropriately into shot, no one swore.

"Hallelujah," Moncrieff breathed, sweating beside me when Ed yelled "Cut."

"And print," I added. "And do it again."

WE BROKE FOR lunch. Nash, in the center of the parade ring, signed autographs one by one for a well-behaved but apparently endless single line of people, shepherded closely by one of Ed's assistants. O'Hara, the bodyguard, and the lioness formed a human wall round the mega-star's back.

We ate again, Nash, O'Hara, and I, up high in the Stewards' box.

Threats to the film apart, it had been a satisfactory morning; we all knew that the scenes had gone well.

O'Hara said, "Howard's here, did you know?"

"Howard!" Nash exclaimed with disgust.

"A very quiet Howard," O'Hara amplified, grimly amused. "Howard is putty in our hands."

"I don't think his views have changed," I said. "He's been frightened. He'll keep his mouth shut. I'd describe it as a plug in a volcano. There's no doubt he passionately meant what he said to Alison Visborough. He stirred her up enough to relay his gripes to her friend on the *Drumbeat,* and what he said to her, that's how he still feels."

"But," O'Hara protested, "he wouldn't want the film actually stopped . . . would he?"

"His full screenplay fee became payable on the first day of principal photography—the first day of filming in Newmarket. It's normal, of course, and it's in his contract. Finished or abandoned, the film can't earn him more money unless it makes unlikely zillions. And I think he still wants me sacked. He's still convinced I'm butchering his best-seller."

"Which you are," Nash smiled.

"Yes. You don't get good meat without a good butcher."

O'Hara liked it. "I'll tell Howard that."

"Better not," I said resignedly, knowing that he would.

O'Hara's mobile phone buzzed, and he answered it. "What? What did you say? I can't hear you. Slow down." He listened a brief moment more and passed the instrument to me. "It's Ziggy," he said. "You talk to him. He goes too fast for me."

"Where is he?" I asked.

O'Hara shrugged. "He went to Norway yesterday morning. I outlined what you wanted to an agent, who whisked him off at once."

Ziggy's voice on the telephone was as staccato as automatic rifle fire, and just as fast.

"Hey," I said after a while, "have I got this straight? You've found ten wild Viking horses but they must come at once."

"They cannot come at twenty-four days, or at thirty-eight days. They are not free. They are free only next week, for the right tides. They are coming on the ferry on Monday from Bergen to Immingham."

"Newcastle," I corrected.

"No. The Bergen ferry goes usually to Newcastle, but for horses it must be Immingham. It is better for us, they say. It is on the River Humber. They will leave Bergen on Sunday. They have a trainer and five grooms. They are all coming in big horse vans. They will bring the horses' food. They can work on Wednesday and Thursday and on Friday they must return to Immingham. It is all arranged, Thomas. Is it good?"

"Brilliant," I said.

He laughed happily. "Good horses. They will run wild without bridles, but they are trained. I have ridden one without a saddle, as you want. They are perfect."

"Fantastic, Ziggy."

"The trainer must know where we are to go from Immingham."

"Er . . . are you meaning to travel with them?"

"Yes, Thomas. This week I work with the trainer. I learn his ways with the horses. They get to know me. I will practice with a blond wig and a night-gown. It is arranged. The horses will not then panic. Is it good?"

I was practically speechless. Good hardly described it. "You're a *genius*," I said.

He said modestly, "Yes, Thomas, I am."

"I'll arrange where the horses are to go. Telephone again on Saturday."

He said good-bye excitedly without giving me a number where I could call him back, but I supposed the agent might help in an emergency. I relayed Ziggy's news to O'Hara and Nash and said we would have to rearrange the following week's schedule, but that it shouldn't be much problem.

"We have the hanged-wife actress working next week," O'Hara reminded me. "We have to complete all her scenes in fourteen days."

I would take her to the beach, I thought. I'd have the nightgown diaphanously blowing against the sunrise. I'd have her standing on the shore, and have Ziggy galloping for her on the horse. Insubstantial. Unreal. All in her mind.

Pray for a sunrise.

"Sonia," I said.

"Yvonne," O'Hara corrected. "We have to call her Yvonne. That's her name in the book and in the script."

I nodded. "Howard wrote the usual hanging cliché of legs and shoes swaying unsupported, with onlookers displaying shock. But I've ideas for that."

O'Hara was silent. Nash shuddered.

"Don't get us an NC17 certificate," Nash finally said. "We'll have to cut that scene, if you do."

"I'm to make it tastefully horrifying?"

They laughed.

"She did hang," I said.

Downstairs again, one of the first people I saw was Lucy Wells, who was arguing with a man obstructing her way. I walked over and asked what was the matter.

"This man," Lucy said heatedly, "says he has instructions not to let anyone near you."

O'Hara's order, the man explained. I reassured him about Lucy and bore her off, holding her arm.

"I thought you weren't coming today," I said.

"Dad changed his mind. He and Mum are both here again. So is Uncle Ridley. Wild horses wouldn't keep him away, he said."

"I'm glad to see you."

"Sorry I was so uncouth."

I smiled at her blue eyes. "A wise child," I said.

"I am *not* a child."

"Stay beside me," I said. "I'll tell Moncrieff it's OK."

"Who's Moncrieff?"

"The director of photography. Very important man."

She looked at me dubiously when I introduced her to the untidy beard and the earthquake-victim clothes, but after allowing us one old-fashioned sideways look, he took a fancy to her and let her get in his way without cursing.

She looked colorfully bright in scarlet short coat over clean new blue jeans, and mentally bright with noticing eyes and a firm calm mouth. She watched the proceedings without senseless chatter.

"I told Dad about that knife," she told me after a while.

"What did he say?"

"Funny, that's exactly what he said. He said, 'What did he say?' "

"Did he?" I considered her guileless expression. "And what did you say I said?"

Her forehead wrinkled. "I told him the knife looked beautiful, but you hadn't said much at all. I told Dad it hadn't pleased the producer, O'Hara, and I didn't know why."

"O'Hara doesn't like knives," I said, dismissing it.

"Oh, I see. Dad said it might be because someone had tried to cut Nash Rourke, like he'd heard on the radio, but it was his stand-in, not Nash himself."

"That too," I agreed.

"Dad said directors don't have a stand-in," she was teasing, unaware, "and you don't know which they are until someone points them out."

"Or when they come to your home."

"Goodness, yes. Did the photo of Sonia come out all right?"

"I'm sure it did, but I won't see it until I go back to Newmarket this evening."

She said hesitantly, "I didn't tell Dad. He really wouldn't like it."

"I won't mention it. The actress playing Yvonne—that's Nash's wife, in the film—starts work on set next week. I promise she won't look like the photo. She won't upset your father."

She smiled her appreciation and thanks, exonerated from her deception. I hoped no deadly harm would come to her, but in so many lives, it did.

First on the afternoon's schedule was the last of the wide crowd shots round the parade ring; the mounting of the jockeys onto their horses and their walk out toward the course. Even though the action would in the end be peripheral to the human story, we had to get the race-day sequences right to earn credibility. We positioned the owner-trainer groups again as before, each of them attended by their allotted jockey. Moncrieff checked the swiveling camera and gently moved Lucy out of shot.

Nash arrived in the ring trailing clouds of security and detoured to tell me a friend of mine was looking for me.

"Who?" I asked.

"Your TV pal from Doncaster."

"Greg Compass?"

He nodded. "Outside the weighing room. He's been yacking with the jockeys. He'll meet you there, he said."

"Great."

We rehearsed the mounting scene twice and shot it three times from two camera angles until the horses grew restive, and then asked all the townspeople to go round to the course side of the stands, to watch the string cantering down to the start.

During the inevitable delay for camera-positioning I left Lucy with Moncrieff and walked over to the weighing room to meet Greg, whom I found in a milk-of-human-kindness mood, dressed in an expensive gray suit and wide open to suggestions from me that he might like to earn an unexpected fee by briefly taking on his usual persona and interviewing the winning trainer; in other words, Nash.

"It won't be more than a few seconds on screen," I said. "Just enough to establish your pretty face."

"Don't see why not." He was amused and civilized; friendly.

"In half an hour?"

"Done."

"Incidentally, do you yourself remember anything about the trainer whose wife was hanged, who we're making this saga about?"

"Jackson Wells?"

"Yes. He's here, himself, today. So is his present wife. So's his daughter. And his brother."

"Before my time, old lad."

"Not much," I assured him. "You must have been about sixteen when Jackson stopped training. You rode in your first race not long after that. So . . . did you hear anything from the older jockeys about . . . well . . . anything?"

He looked at me quizzically. "I can't say I haven't thought about this since last Saturday, because of course I have. As far as I know, the book, *Unstable Times,* is sentimental balls. The jockeys who knew the real Yvonne were not dream lovers, they were a randy lot of activists."

I smiled.

"You knew?" he asked.

"It sort of stands to reason. But they're still going to be dream lovers in the film." I paused. "Do you remember any names? Do you by any chance know *who?*"

"By the time I'd dried behind the ears in the changing room, no one was saying *anything.* All scared at being sucked into a murder. Clams weren't in it." He paused. "If Jackson Wells himself is truly here today, I'd like to meet him."

"His daughter says he's here."

I refrained from asking him why he wanted to meet Jackson Wells but he told me anyway. "Good television. Rivet the couch potatoes. Good publicity for your film."

"Jackson Wells isn't keen on the film."

Greg grinned. "All the better, old lad."

I returned to Moncrieff with Greg in tow and promptly lost Lucy's attention to the smooth commentator's allure. Lucy promised breathlessly to take him to find her father and, when they'd gone, Moncrieff and I went back to work.

We shot the scenes of the horses walking out onto the course and cantering off to the start. One of the horses bolted. One of the saddles slipped, dumping its rider. One of the rented cameras jammed. The crowd grew restive, the jockeys lost their cool, and Moncrieff cursed.

We got it done in the end.

I walked with drained energy back toward the weighing room and found O'Hara there, talking to Howard.

Howard, to my complete astonishment, had brought with him his three friends: Mrs. Audrey Visborough; her daughter, Alison; and her son, Roddy.

O'Hara gave me a wild look and said, "Mrs. Visborough wants us to stop making the film."

I said to Howard, "Are you mad?" which might not have been tactful but summed up my exasperation. I'd been afraid of a stiletto through the heart, and Howard had brought clowns.

All three of them, however, wore unremarkable race-going clothes, not white cone hats, bobbles, and red noses. Audrey Visborough leaned on her cane and continued with her complaint.

"Your director, Thomas Lyon," she flicked me a venomous glance, "has obviously no intention whatever of either returning to the facts or of stopping making this travesty of a film. I demand that you order him to cease at once."

Howard shuffled from foot to foot and ineffectually said, "Er . . . Audrey."

O'Hara, restraining himself amazingly, told her that he hadn't the power to stop the film himself (which I guessed he actually had) and that she should write her objections directly to the moguls of the film company: in other words, to the top.

She announced that she would do that and demanded names and addresses. O'Hara obligingly handed her two or three business cards with helpful and soothing advice that slid over her consciousness without sticking. Audrey Visborough felt personally and implacably insulted by the film's plot, and nothing would satisfy her short of preventing its completion.

Alison stood to one side of her, nodding. Roddy looked weakly supportive but from the glances he gave his mother I would have guessed he cared a good deal less than she did about the scurrilous suggestion that she would *ever* have contemplated going to bed with the unspeakable lower-class Jackson Wells.

I said to Howard, "Why on *earth* did you bring them here?"

"I couldn't stop them," he said huffily. "And I do agree with Audrey, of course, that you have made her almost *ill* with disgust."

"You agreed to the plot changes," I pointed out. "And you yourself wrote the love scenes between Nash and Silva."

"But they were supposed to be quiet, in the drawing room, not rutting about in bed." His voice whined with self-pity. "I wanted to *please* the Visborough family with this film."

With a second twinge of guilt I reflected that his troubles with Audrey Visborough hadn't yet reached a peak.

I said to her daughter, Alison, "Would you care to watch a scene being shot?"

"Me?" She was surprised and glanced at her mother before answering. "It won't change our minds. This film is a disgrace."

When I moved a pace away in irritation, however, she took a pace after me.

"Where are you going?" her mother demanded sharply. "I need you here."

Alison gave me a dark look and said, "I'll work on Mr. Lyon."

She walked resolutely beside me, sensible in tweed suit and flat shoes, earnestly committed to just causes.

"Daddy," she said, "was a *good* man."

"I'm sure."

"Not easygoing," she went on with approbation. "A man of principle. Some people found him boring, I know, but he was a good father to me. He believed that women are very badly treated by the English system of leaving family inheritances chiefly to sons, which is why he left his house to me." She paused. "Rodbury was furious. He's three years older than I am, and he'd taken it for granted he would inherit everything. He had been generously treated all his life. Daddy bought all his show jumpers for him, and only insisted that Rodbury should earn his own keep by giving lessons. Perfectly reasonable, I thought, as Daddy wasn't unduly rich. He divided his money among the three of us. None of us is rich." She paused again. "I expect you wonder why I'm telling you this. It's because I want you to be fair to Daddy's memory."

I couldn't be, not in the way she wanted.

I said, "Think of this film as being about fictional people, not about your father and mother. The people in the film are not in the least like your parents. They are not *them*. They are inventions."

"Mummy will never be persuaded."

I took her with me into the parade ring, where Moncrieff as ever was busy with lights.

"I'm going to show you two people," I said to Alison. "Tell me what you think."

She looked puzzled, but her gaze followed where I pointed to a nearby couple, and she looked without emotion at Cibber, a sober fifty, and at lovely young Silva in her well-cut coat and polished narrow boots and bewitching fur hat.

"Well?" Alison demanded. "They look nice enough. Who are they?"

"Mr. and Mrs. Cibber," I said.

*"What?"* She whirled toward me, halfway to fury. Then, thinking better of a direct physical attack, turned back thoughtfully and simply stared.

"Beyond them," I said, "is Nash Rourke. He plays the character loosely based on Jackson Wells."

Alison speechlessly stared at the broad-shouldered heartthrob whose benign intelligence was unmistakable from twenty feet.

"Come with me," I said.

Dazedly she followed, and I took her to where Greg Compass and Lucy seemed finally to have found Lucy's father.

"These people," I told Alison, "are Greg Compass, who interviews racing people on TV."

Alison briefly nodded in recognition.

"This family," I said neutrally, "are Mr. and Mrs. Jackson Wells and their daughter, Lucy."

Alison's mouth opened but no words came out. Jackson Wells, good-looking and smiling, stood between his two wholesome, well-groomed women, waiting for me to complete the introduction.

"Alison Visborough," I said.

Jackson Wells's sunny face darkened. He said, almost spitting, *"Her* daughter!"

"You see," I said to Alison, "Jackson Wells dislikes your mother as intensely as she dislikes *him.* No way in real life would they ever have had a love affair. The people in this film are *not them."*

Alison remained dumb. I took her arm, wheeling her away.

"Your mother," I said, "is making herself ill. Persuade her to turn her back on what we are doing. Make her interested in something else, and don't let her see the completed film. Believe that I mean no disrespect to her or to your father's memory. I am making a movie about fictional people. I have some sympathy with your mother's feelings, but she will not get the film abandoned."

Alison found her voice. "You are ruthless," she said.

"Quite likely. However, I admire you, Miss Visborough, as Howard does. I admire your good sense and your loyalty to your father. I regret your anger but I can't remove its cause. Cibber in the film is not a nice man at all, I have to warn you. All I can say again is, don't identify him with your father."

"Howard did!"

"Howard wrote Cibber as a good man without powerful emotions. There's no conflict or drama in that. Conflict is the essence of drama . . . first lesson of film making. Anyway, I apologize to you and your mother and brother, but until last week I hardly knew you existed."

"Oh, Roddy!" she said without affection. "Don't worry about *him*. He doesn't care very much. He and Daddy were pretty cold to each other. Too different, I suppose. Rodbury . . . and I call him by his full name because Roddy sounds like a nice little boy, but he would never let me join in his games when we were children, and other girls were so wrong when they said I was *lucky* having an older brother . . ." She broke off abruptly. "I don't know why I said that. I don't talk to people easily. Particularly not to people I disapprove of. Anyway, Rodbury wouldn't care what you said about Daddy as long as *he* didn't lose money over it. He only pretends to Mummy that he cares, because he's always conning her into buying things for him."

"He's not married?"

She shook her head. "He boasts about girls. More talk than action, I sometimes think."

I smiled at her forthright opinion and thought of her unfulfilled life: the disappointing brother, the adored but distant father, the mother who'd prevented a perhaps unsuitable match. An admirable woman overall.

"I like you, Miss Visborough," I said.

She gave me a straight look. "Stop the film, then."

I thought of her feelings, and I thought of knives.

"I can't," I said.

WE COMPLETED THE day's shooting schedule in time to hold the semi-planned good-public-relations final autographing session outside the weighing room. Nash, Silva, and Cibber scribbled there with maximum charm.

Many Huntingdon residents were already wearing their UNSTABLE (at all) TIMES T-shirts. Good humor abounded all around. The envisaged orderly line of autograph hunters dissolved into a friendly scrum. O'Hara signed books and race cards presented to him by people who knew a producer when they saw one, and I, too, signed my share. Howard modestly wrote in proffered copies of his book.

The happy crowd roamed around. Nash's bodyguards were smiling. The lioness tried to stop him being kissed. My black belt stood at my left hand so that I could sign with my right.

I felt a thud as if someone had cannoned into me, a knock hard enough to send me stumbling forward onto one knee and from there overbalancing to the ground. I fell onto my right side and felt the first pain, sharp and alarming, and I understood with searing clarity that I had a knife blade in my body and that I had fallen onto its hilt, and driven it in further.

# 12

O'Hara, laughing, stretched his hand down to help me up.

I took his hand in my right, and reflexly accepted his assistance, and he saw the strong wince round my eyes and stopped laughing.

"Did you hurt yourself?"

"No." His pull had lifted me back to my knees. I said, "Lend me your jacket." He wore an old flying type of jacket, army colored, zip fronts hanging open. "Jacket," I repeated.

"What?" He leaned down toward me from his craggy height.

"Lend me your jacket." I swallowed, making myself calm. "Lend me your jacket and get my driver to bring my car right up here to the weighing room."

"Thomas!" He was progressively concerned, bringing his head lower to hear me better. "What's the matter?"

Clear-headed beyond normal, I said distinctly, "There is a knife in my side. Drape your jacket over my right shoulder, to hide it. Don't make a fuss. Don't frighten the moguls. Not a word to the press. Don't tell the police. I am not dead, and the film will go on."

He listened and understood but could hardly believe it. "Where's the knife?" he asked as if bewildered. "You look all right."

"It's somewhere under my arm, above my elbow. Do lend me your jacket."

"I'll get our doctor."

"No, O'Hara. *No.* Just the jacket."

I put, I suppose, every scrap of the authority he'd given me into the words that were half plea, half order. In any case, without further objection, he took off his windproof jacket and draped it over my shoulder, revealing the heavy-knit army-colored sweater he wore underneath.

Other eyes looked curiously our way. I put my left hand on O'Hara's arm, as he was facing me, and managed the endless inches to my feet. I concentrated on his eyes, at the same height as my own.

"The bastard," I said carefully with obvious anger, "is not going to succeed."

"Right," O'Hara said.

I relaxed infinitesimally, but in fact bloody-mindedness was the best anesthetic invented, and too much sympathy would defeat me quicker than any pain from invaded ribs.

O'Hara sent one of Ed's assistants to bring my car and reassuringly told a few enquirers that I'd fallen and wrenched my shoulder but that it was nothing to worry about.

I saw a jumbled panorama of familiar faces and couldn't remember any of them having been near enough for attack. But crowd movement had been nonstop. Anyone I knew in England, or anyone they had employed—and professionals were for hire and invisible everywhere—could have stood among the autograph hunters and seized the moment. I concentrated mostly on remaining upright while rather wildly wondering what vital organs lay inwards from just above one's right elbow, and realizing that though my skin might feel clammy from the shock waves of an outraged organism, I was not visibly leaking blood in any large quantities.

"Your forehead's sweating," O'Hara observed.

"Never mind."

"Let me get the doctor."

"You'll get Greg Compass and television coverage, if you do."

He was silent.

"I know a different doctor," I promised. "Where's the car?"

Ed returned with it pretty soon, though it seemed an age to me. I asked him to thank everyone and see to general security, and said we would complete the close-ups the next day.

He nodded merely and took over, and I edged gingerly into the rear seat of the car.

O'Hara climbed in on the other side. "You don't need to," I said.

"Yes, I do."

I was glad enough of his company, and I gave him a number to call on his telephone, taking the mobile from him after he'd pressed buttons.

"Robbie?" I said, grateful not to get his message service. "Thomas Lyon. Where are you?"

"Newmarket."

"Um . . . could you come to the hotel in an hour? Fairly urgent."

"What sort of urgent?"

"Can't say, right now."

O'Hara looked surprised, but I nodded toward our driver, who might be economical with words, but was far from deaf.

O'Hara looked understanding, but also worried. "One of the moguls from L.A. has arrived at the hotel and will be waiting for us."

"Oh." I hesitated, then said, "Robbie . . . can you make it Dorothea's house instead? It's for a Dorothea sort of job, though not so radical."

"You've got someone with you, listening, that you don't want to know what you're talking about? And it's a knife wound?"

"Right," I said, grateful for his quickness.

"Who's the patient?"

"I am."

"Dear God . . . Have you got a key to Dorothea's house?"

"I'm sure her friend Betty must have one. She lives nearly opposite."

"I know her," he said briefly. "One hour. Dorothea's house. How bad is it?"

"I don't know the internal geography well enough, but not too bad, I don't think."

"Abdomen?" he asked worriedly.

"No. Higher, and to one side."

"See you," he said. "Don't cough."

I gave the phone back to O'Hara, who stifled all his questions with worry and difficulty. I sat sideways, propping myself as firmly as possible against the motion of the car, but all the same it was a long thirty-eight miles that time from Huntingdon to Newmarket.

I gave the driver directions to Dorothea's house. Robbie Gill's car was there already. Robbie himself opening the front door from inside when we pulled up, and coming down the path to meet us. O'Hara arranged with the driver to return for us in half an hour while I uncurled out of the car and steadied myself unobtrusively by holding Robbie's arm.

I said, "We're not keen for publicity over this."

"So I gathered. I haven't told anyone."

He watched O'Hara get out of the car and give the driver a signal to depart, and I said briefly, "O'Hara . . . Robbie Gill," which seemed enough for them both.

We walked up the path slowly and into the empty but still ravaged house. Dorothea, Robbie said, had told him of my offer to start tidying up. We went into the kitchen, where I sat on one of the chairs.

"Did you see the knife?" Robbie asked. "How long was the blade?"

"It's still in me."

He looked shocked. O'Hara said, "This is some crazy boy."

"O'Hara's producing the film," I said. "He would like me stitched up and back on set tomorrow morning."

Robbie took O'Hara's jacket off my shoulder and knelt on the floor to take a closer look at the problem.

"This is like no knife I ever saw," he pronounced.

"Like the one of the Heath?" I asked.

"Different."

"Pull it out," I said. "It hurts."

Instead he stood up and said something to O'Hara about anesthetics.

"For Christ's sake," I said impatiently, "just . . . pull . . . it . . . out."

Robbie said, "Let's take an inside look at the damage, then."

He unzipped my dark blue windcheater and cut open my sweater with Dorothea's kitchen scissors, and came to the body protectors underneath.

"What on earth . . . ?"

"We had death threats," I explained, "so I thought . . ." I closed my eyes briefly and opened them again. "I borrowed two of the jockeys' body protectors. In case of kicks."

*"Death threats?"*

O'Hara explained and asked me, "What made you think of these padded jackets?"

"Fear," I said truthfully.

They almost laughed.

"Look," I said reasonably, "this knife had to go through my windproof jacket, a thick sweater, two body protectors designed to minimize impact, and also one shirt in order to reach my skin. It has cut into me a bit but I'm not coughing blood and I don't feel any worse than I did an hour ago, so . . . Robbie . . . a bit of your well-known toughness . . . please . . ."

"Yes, all right," he said.

He spread open the front of the body protectors and found my white shirt wet and scarlet. He pulled the shirt apart until he could see the blade itself, and he raised his eyes to me in what could only be called horror.

"What is it?" I said.

"This blade . . . it's *inches* wide. It's pinning all the layers into your side."

"Go on then," I said, "get it out."

He opened the bag he'd brought with him and picked out a pre-prepared disposable syringe, which he described briefly, sticking the needle into me, as a painkiller. After that he sorted out a surgical dressing in a sterile wrapping. The same as for Dorothea, I thought. He checked his watch to give the injection time to work, then tore off the wrapping and positioned the dressing ready inside my shirt and with his left hand tugged on the protruding handle of the knife.

It didn't budge, and in spite of the injection it felt terrible.

"I can't get enough leverage from this angle," Robbie said. He looked at O'Hara. "You're strong," he said. "You pull it out."

O'Hara stared at him, and then at me.

"Think of moguls," I said.

He smiled twistedly and said to Robbie, "Tell me when."

"Now," Robbie said, and O'Hara grasped the knife's handle and pulled until the blade came free.

Robbie quickly put the dressing in place and O'Hara stood as if stunned, holding in disbelief the object that had caused me such trouble.

"Sorry," Robbie said to me.

I shook my head, dry mouthed.

O'Hara laid the knife on the kitchen table, on the discarded wrapping from the dressing, and we all spent a fairly long silence simply looking at it.

Overall it was about eight inches long, and half of that was handle. The flat blade was almost three inches wide at the handle end, tapering to a sharp point. One long side of the triangular blade was a plain sharp cutting edge: the other was wickedly serrated. At its wide end the blade extended smoothly into a handle which had a space through it big enough to accommodate a whole hand. The actual grip, with undulations for fingers to give a better purchase, was given substance by bolted-on, palm-width pieces of dark, richly polished wood; the rest was shiny metal.

"It's heavy," O'Hara said blankly. "It could rip you in half."

A stud embellishing the wider end of the blade bore the one word: FURY.

I picked up the awful weapon for a closer look and found it was indeed heavy (more than half a pound, we soon found, when Robbie weighed it on Dorothea's kitchen scales) and, according to letters stamped into it, had been made of stainless steel in Japan.

"What we need," I said, putting it down, "is a knife expert."

"And what you need first," Robbie said apologetically, "is a row of staples to stop the bleeding."

We took off all my protective layers for him to see what he was doing and he presently told me consolingly that the point of the blade had hit one of my ribs and had slid along it, not slicing down into soft tissue and through into the lung. "The rib has been fractured by the blow but you are right, and lucky, because this injury should heal quite quickly."

"Cheers," I said flippantly, relieved all the same. "Maybe tomorrow I'll get me a bullet-proof vest."

Robbie mopped a good deal of dried blood from my skin, damping one of Dorothea's tea towels for the purpose, then helped me into my one relatively unharmed garment, the windproof jacket.

"You look as good as new," he assured me, fitting together the bottom ends of the zip and closing it upward.

"The mogul won't notice a thing," O'Hara agreed, nodding. "Are you fit enough to talk to him?"

I nodded. It was necessary to talk to him. Necessary to convince him that the company's money was safe in my hands. Necessary to confound all suggestion of "jinx."

I said, "We do, all the same, have to find out just who is so fanatical about stopping the film that he—or she—will murder to achieve it. It's possible, I suppose, that the knife was meant only to frighten us, like yesterday's dagger, but if I hadn't been wearing the protectors . . ."

"No protection and an inch either way," Robbie nodded, "and you would likely have been history."

"So," I said, "if we take it that my death was in fact intended, I absolutely *must* find out who and why. Find it out among ourselves, I mean, if we're not bringing in the police. Otherwise . . ." I hesitated, then went on, ". . . if the reason for the attack on me still exists, which we have to assume is the case, they—he or she or they—may try again."

I had the feeling that the thought had already occurred to both of them, but that to save my peace of mind they hadn't liked to say it aloud.

"No film is worth dying for," O'Hara said.

"The film has stirred up mud that's been lying quiet for twenty-six years," I said. "That's what's happened. No point in regretting it. So now we have the choice of either pulling the plug on the film and retiring in disarray—and where is my future if I do that?—or . . . er . . . sifting through the mud for the facts."

"But," Robbie said doubtfully, "could you really find any? I mean, when it all happened, when it was fresh, the police got nowhere."

"The police are ordinary people," I said. "Not infallible supermen. If we try, and get nowhere also, then so be it."

"But how do you start?"

"Like I said, we look for someone who knows about knives."

It had been growing dark while we spoke. As Robbie crossed to flip the light switch, we heard the front door open and close, and footsteps coming heavily along the passage toward us.

It was Paul who appeared in the kitchen doorway: Paul annoyed, Paul suspicious, Paul's attention latching with furious astonishment onto my face. The indecisiveness of our last meeting had vanished. The bluster was back.

"And what do you think you're doing here?" he demanded. "I've told you to stay away, you're not wanted."

"I told Dorothea I would tidy up a bit."

"*I* will tidy the house. I don't want you here. And as for you, Doctor Gill, your services aren't needed. Clear out, all of you."

It was O'Hara's first encounter with Paul Pannier; always a learning experience.

"And where did you get a key from?" he demanded aggrievedly. "Or did you break in?" He looked at O'Hara directly for the first time and said, "Who the hell are you? I want you all out of here at once."

I said neutrally, "It's your mother's house, and I'm here with her permission."

Paul wasn't listening. Paul's gaze had fallen on the table, and he was staring at the knife.

There was barely a smear of blood on it as it had been more or less wiped clean by its outward passage through many layers of polystyrene and cloth, so it seemed to be the knife itself, not its use, that was rendering Paul temporarily speechless.

He raised his eyes to meet my gaze, and there was no disguising his shock. His eyes looked as dark as his pudgy features were pale. His mouth had opened. He found nothing at all to say but turned on one foot and stamped away out of the kitchen down the hall and out through the front door, leaving it open behind him.

"Who was *he?*" O'Hara asked. "And what was that all about?"

"His mother," Robbie explained, "was savagely cut with a knife in this house last Saturday. He may think that somehow we've found the weapon."

"And have you?" O'Hara turned to me. "What was it you were trying to tell me yesterday? But this isn't the knife you found on the Heath, is it?"

"No."

He frowned. "I don't understand any of it."

That made two of us; but somewhere there had to be an explanation. Nothing happened without cause.

I asked Robbie Gill, who was tidying and closing his medical case, "Do you know anyone called Bill Robinson who mends motorbikes?"

"Are you feeling all right?"

"Not a hundred percent. Do you?"

"Bill Robinson who mends motorbikes? No."

"You know the town. Who would know?"

"Are you serious?"

"He may have," I explained briefly, "what this house was torn apart for."

"And that's all you're telling me?"

I nodded.

Robbie pulled the telephone toward him, consulted a notebook from his pocket, and pressed some numbers. He was passed on, relay by relay, to four more numbers but eventually pushed the phone away in satisfaction and told me, "Bill Robinson works for Wrigley's garage, and lives somewhere in Exning Road. He tinkers with Harley-Davidsons for a hobby."

"Great," I said.

"But," O'Hara objected, "what has any of this to do with our film?"

"Knives," I said, "and Valentine Clark knew Jackson Wells."

"Good luck with the mud," Robbie said.

THE MOGUL PROVED to be a hard-nosed thin businessman in his forties with no desire even to look at the growing reels of printed film. He didn't like movies, he said. He despised film actors. He thought directors should be held in financial handcuffs. Venture capital was his field, he said, with every risk underwritten. Wrong field, I thought.

He had demanded in advance to have an accounting for every cent disbursed or committed since the first day of principal photography, with the result that O'Hara's production department had spent the whole day itemizing such things as food, transport, pay for stable lads, lipsticks, and light bulbs.

We sat round the dining table in O'Hara's suite, I having made a detour to my own rooms to exchange my windproof jacket for a shirt and sweater. Robbie had stuck only a light dressing over the mended damage. I felt still a shade trembly, but apparently nothing showed. I concentrated on justifying Ziggy's fare and expenses in Norway, while sipping mineral water and longing for brandy.

"Wild horses!" the mogul exclaimed in near-outrage to O'Hara. "You surely didn't sanction bringing horses all the way from Norway! They're not in the script."

"They're in the hanged woman's fantasy," O'Hara explained flatly. "Her dream life is what the company thought best about the plot, and what you expect on the screen. Viking horses hold glamor for publicity, and will earn more than they cost."

O'Hara's clout silenced the mogul, who scowled but seemed to realize that if he antagonized his high-grade producer beyond bearing, he would lose him and sink the whole investment. In any event, he moderated his aggressive approach and nodded through the bonus for the winning jockey with barely a grimace.

The accounts audited, he wanted to discuss Howard.

I didn't.

O'Hara didn't.

Howard proving to be usefully out of the hotel, the subject died. I excused myself on the grounds of the regular evening meeting with Moncrieff, and the mogul said in parting that he trusted we would have no further "incidents," and announced that he would be watching the action the next morning.

"Sure," O'Hara agreed easily, hardly blinking. "The schedule calls for dialogue and close-ups, and several establishing shots of people walking in and out of the weighing room at Huntingdon racecourse. No crowd scenes, though, they're in the can. No jockeys, they've finished also. The horses will be shipped back here tomorrow afternoon. Thanks to fine weather and Thomas's good management, we'll be through with the racetrack scenes a day early."

The mogul looked as if he'd bitten a wasp. I wondered, as I left, just what would make him happy.

The Moncrieff session swelled with the arrival of both Nash and Silva, each wanting to continue with the private rehearsals. Nash had brought his script. Silva wore no lipstick and a feminist expression. I wondered what she and O'Hara were like together in bed, a speculation that didn't advance my work any, but couldn't be helped.

We went through the scenes. Moncrieff and Nash discussed lighting. Silva thrust forward her divine jaw and to her pleasure Moncrieff assessed her facial bones in terms of planes and shadows.

I drank brandy and painkillers with dedication: possibly medicinally a bad combination, but a great distancer from tribulation. When everyone left I went to bed half sitting up, and stayed awake through a lot of o'clocks, throbbing and thinking and deciding that in the near future I would stand with my back to a wall at all times.

O'Hara woke me from a troubled sleep by phoning at seven-thirty. Late.

"How are you doing?" he asked.

"Lousy."

"It's raining."

"Is it?" I yawned. "That's good."

"Moncrieff phoned the weather people. It should be dry this afternoon. So we could watch all the Huntingdon rushes this morning, when the van comes from London."

"Yes . . . I thought the mogul couldn't be bothered."

"He's going to London himself. He's not keen on waiting for Huntingdon this afternoon. He told me everything seems to be going all right with the movie now, and he'll report back to that effect."

"Jeez."

O'Hara chuckled. "He thought you were businesslike. That's his highest word of praise. He says I can go back to L.A."

"Oh." I was surprised by the strength of my dismay. "And are you going?"

"It's your movie," he said.

I said, "Stay."

After a pause he said, "If I go, it shows you're totally in command." Another pause. "Think it over. We'll decide after the dailies. See you at eleven o'clock in the screening room . . . will you be fit enough?"

"Yes."

"I sure as hell wouldn't be," he said and disconnected.

By nine I'd decided against the great British breakfast and had located Wrigley's garage on a town road map: by nine-fifteen my driver had found it in reality. There was a canopy over the gas pumps: shelter from rain.

Bill Robinson had long hair, a couple of pimples, a strong East Anglian accent, a short black leather jacket covered in gold studs, and a belt of heavy tools strung round his small hips. He took in the fact that I had a chauffeur and offered opportunist respect.

"Wha' can I do for yer?" he enquired, chewing gum.

I grinned. "Mrs. Dorothea Pannier thinks you're a great guy."

"Yeah?" He moved his head in pleasure, nodding. "Not such a bad old duck herself."

"Did you know she's in hospital?"

His good humor vanished. "I heard some bastard carved her up."

"I'm Thomas Lyon," I said. "She gave me your name."

"Yeah?" He was wary. "You're not from that son of hers? Right turd, that son of hers."

I shook my head. "Her brother Valentine left me his books in his will. She told me she'd trusted them to you for safe keeping."

"Don't give them to no one, that's what she said." His manner was determined and straightforward. I judged it would be a bad mistake to offer him money, which conferred on him saintly status in the modern scheme of things.

"How about," I said, "if we could get her on the phone?"

He could see nothing wrong in that, so I used the mobile to reach the hospital and then, with many clicks and delays, Dorothea herself.

She talked to Bill Robinson in his heavy leather gear and studs, and Bill Robinson's face shone with goodness and pleasure. Hope for the old world yet.

"She says," he announced, giving me my phone back, "that the sun shines out of your arse and the books are yours."

"Great."

"But they aren't here," he said. "They're in the garage at home."

"When could I pick them up?"

"I could go home midday in my lunch hour." He gazed briefly aside at a gleaming monster of a motorbike, heavily wheel-chained to confound would-be thieves. "I don't usually, but I could."

I suggested buying an hour of his time at once from his boss and not waiting for lunch.

"Cor," he said, awestruck; but his boss, a realist, accepted the suggestion, and the money, with alacrity, and Bill Robinson rode to his house in my car with undoubted enjoyment.

"How do you know Dorothea?" I asked on the way.

"My girlfriend lives next door to her," he explained simply. "We do errands sometimes for the old luv. Carry her shopping, and such. She gives us sweets like we were kids."

"Er . . ." I said, "how old are you, then?"

"Eighteen. What did you think of my bike?"

"I envy you."

His smile was complacent, and none the worse for that. When we reached his home ("Ma will be out at work, the key's in this thing what looks like a stone") he unlocked a padlock on the solid doors of a brick-built garage and revealed his true vocation, the care and construction of bikes.

"I buy wrecks and rebuild them," he explained, as I stood inside the garage gazing at wheels, handlebars, twisted tubing, shining fragments. "I rebuild them as good as new and then I sell them."

"Brilliant," I said absently. "Do you want to be in a film?"

"Do I what?"

I explained that I was always looking for interesting backgrounds. Would he mind moving some of the parts of motorbikes out of the garage into his short driveway and getting on with some work while we filmed Nash Rourke walking down the street, thinking? "No dialogue," I said, "just Nash strolling by and pausing for a second or two to watch the work in progress. The character he's playing will be walking through Newmarket, trying to make up his mind about something." I was looking for real Newmarket backgrounds, I said.

"Nash *Rourke!* You're kidding me."

"No. You'll meet him."

"Mrs. Pannier did say you were the one making the film they're talking about. It was in the *Drumbeat.*"

"The tyrannical bullyboy? Yes, that's me."

He smiled broadly. "Your books are in all those boxes." He pointed to a large random row of cartons that announced their original contents as TV sets, electrical office equipment, microwave ovens, and bread-making machines. "A ton of paper, I shouldn't wonder. It took me the whole of Saturday morning to pack it all and shift it here, but Mrs. Pannier, dear old duck, she made it worth my while."

It was approbation rather than a hint, but I said I would do the same, particularly if he could tell me which box held what.

Not a snowball's chance, he said cheerfully. Why didn't I look?

The task was too much, both for the available time and my own depleted stamina. I said I'd wrenched my shoulder and couldn't lift the boxes, so asked him to stow as many as possible in the trunk of the car. He looked resignedly at the rain but splashed backward and forward efficiently, joined after hesitation by my driver who buttoned his jacket closely and turned up his collar.

The car, including the front passenger seat, absorbed half of the boxes. I asked what he'd used to transport them on Saturday.

"My dad's little old pickup," he said. "It needed three journeys. He takes it to work weekdays, so I can't borrow it till this evening."

He agreed to load and deliver the rest of the boxes in the pickup, and in cheerful spirits came along to the hotel and helped the porter there stack the cartons in the lobby.

"Do you mean it about me being in your film?" he asked on the way back to Wrigley's garage. "And . . . *when?*"

"Tomorrow, maybe," I said. "I'll send a message; I'll fix it with your boss, and the film company will pay you a fee for your help."

"Cor," he said.

NASH, SILVA, AND Moncrieff all joined O'Hara and me to watch the Huntingdon rushes.

Even without much sound the crowd scenes looked like an everyday race meeting and the race itself was still remarkable for the Victoria Cross riding of the jockeys. The race had been filmed successfully by five cameras and semi-successfully by another. There was easily enough to cut together a contest to stir the pulses of people who'd never seen jump-racing at close quarters: even Silva gasped at one sequence, and Nash looked thoughtful. Moncrieff fussed about shadows in the wrong places, which no one else had noticed.

The close shots with dialogue showed Silva at her most enticing. I praised her interpretation, not her looks, and got a brief nod of acknowledgment. The two days' work, all in all, had been worth the effort.

After the end of the rushes the film developers had joined on the thirty seconds' worth Moncrieff had shot of Lucy's photo. Large and in sharp focus, the two faces appeared on the screen.

"Who are they?" O'Hara asked, perplexed.

"The girl on the left," I said, "is Yvonne. Or rather, she was Sonia Wells, the girl who hanged. The real one."

"Christ," O'Hara said.

"And who's the man?" Nash asked.

"His name is Pig, I think." I explained about Lucy's photo. "I promised her that Yvonne wouldn't look like Sonia."

The girl on the screen had curly light-brown hair, not a green crewcut or other weirdness. We would give Yvonne a long straight blond wig and hope for the best.

The screen ran clear. We switched on the lights, talked about what we'd seen and, as always, went back to work.

At Huntingdon a photographer, who'd been engaged by the company to chart progress for the publicity department, brought a set of eight-by-ten-inch prints for O'Hara to see. He and I took them into the weighing room and sat at a table there, minutely searching the snapshots with a magnifying glass.

We saw nothing of any help. There were photos of Nash signing in the end-of-the-day autograph session. A shot of Howard looking smug, inscribing his own book. Silva being film-star charming. Greg signing race cards. A shot of O'Hara and myself standing together. The lens had been focused every time on the main subject's face: people around were present but not warts and all.

"We need blowups of the crowd," O'Hara said.

"We're not going to get nice clear views of the Fury."

Morosely, he agreed, but ordered blowups anyway.

No more knives appeared, in or out of bodies. We filmed the remaining scenes and shipped out the horses. We made sure the whole place was ship-shape, thanked Huntingdon racecourse management for their kindnesses, and were back in Newmarket soon after six o'clock.

The message light inexorably flashed in my sitting room: whenever did it not?

Robbie Gill wanted me to phone him, urgently.

I got his message service: he would be available at seven.

To fill in the time I opened the tops of a few of the cartons of Valentine's books, which now took up a good deal of the floorspace, as I'd particularly asked for them not to be put one on top of another. I'd forgotten, of course, that bending down used chest muscles also. On my knees, therefore, I began to inspect my inheritance.

There was too much of it. After the first three boxes had proved to hold part of the collection of biographies and racing histories, after I'd painstakingly taken out every volume, shaken it for insertions, and replaced it, I saw the need for secretarial help; for a record keeper with a laptop computer.

Lucy, I thought. If I had a fantasy, I would materialize her in my sitting room, like Yvonne's dream lovers. Lucy knew how to work a computer.

Impulsively I phoned her father's house and put a proposition to his daughter.

"You told me you'd left school and are waiting to do a business course. Would you care for a two-week temporary job in Newmarket?" I explained what I needed. "I am not trying to seduce you," I said. "You can bring a chaperone, you can stay anywhere you like, you can drive home every day to Oxfordshire if you prefer. I'll pay you fairly. If you don't want to do it, I'll get someone local."

She said a shade breathlessly, "Would I see Nash Rourke again?"

Wryly, I promised that she would, "Every day."

"He's . . . he's . . ."

"Yes," I agreed, "and he's married."

"It's not *that*," she said disgustedly, "he's just . . . nice."

"True. What about the job?"

"I could start tomorrow."

The boxes could wait that long, I thought.

At seven I phoned Robbie Gill's number again and reached him promptly.

"Which do you want first," he asked, "the good news or the appalling?"

"The good. I'm tired."

"You don't surprise me. The good news is a list of names of knife experts. Three in London, two in Glasgow, four in Sheffield, and one in Cambridge." He read them all out and took away what little breath I could manage with a broken rib.

I said weakly, "Say that Cambridge one again."

He repeated it distinctly, "Professor Meredith Derry, lecturer in medieval history, late of Trinity College, retired."

*Derry.*

Knives . . .

"Do you want the appalling?" Robbie asked.

"I suppose I have to hear it?"

"Afraid so. Paul Pannier has been murdered."

# 13

**M**urdered?"

" 'Fraid so."

"Where? And . . . er . . . how?"

As if it were inevitable, the Scot's voice informed me, "He was killed in Dorothea's house . . . with a knife."

I sighed; a groan. "Does Dorothea know?"

"The police sent a policewoman to the hospital."

"Poor, poor Dorothea."

He said bluntly, "She won't be bullied any more."

"But she loved him," I protested. "She loved the baby he'd been. She loved her little son. She will be devastated."

"Go and see her," Robbie said. "You seem to understand her. I never could see why she put up with him."

She needed a hug, I thought. She needed someone to hold her while she wept. I said, "What about Paul's wife, Janet?"

"The police have told her. She's on her way here now, I think."

I looked at my watch. Five past seven. I was sore and hungry and had tomorrow's shots to discuss with Nash and Moncrieff. Still . . .

"Robbie," I said, "does Professor Derry have an address?"

"There's a phone number." He read it out. "What about Dorothea?"

"I'll go to see her now. I could be at the hospital in about forty minutes. Can you fix it that they'll let me see her?"

He could and would. Who had discovered Paul's murder, I asked.

"I did, damn it. At about three o'clock this afternoon I went to pick up a notebook that I left in Dorothea's kitchen last night. I called to get the key again from her friend Betty, but she said she didn't have the key any more; she'd given it to Paul this morning early. I went across to Dorothea's house and rang the bell—that ruddy quiet ding-dong—and no one came, so I went round the back and tried the kitchen door, and it was open." He paused. "Paul was lying in the hall on almost the exact spot where Betty found Dorothea. There wasn't any blood, though. He'd died at once and he'd been dead for hours. He was killed with what looked like one of Dorothea's big kitchen knives. It was still in him, driven deep into his chest from behind at a point not far above his right elbow . . ."

"*Robbie*," I said, stunned.

"Yes. Almost the same place as you. The handle was sticking out. An ordinary chef's knife handle, nothing fancy. No Fury. So I phoned the police and they kept me hanging about in that house all afternoon, but I couldn't tell them why Paul had gone there. How could I know? I couldn't tell them anything except that it looked to me as if the knife had reached his heart and stopped it."

I cleared my throat. "You didn't tell them about . . . me?"

"No. You didn't want me to, did you?"

"I did not."

"But things are different now," he said dubiously.

"Not if the police find Paul's killer quickly."

"I've got the impression that they don't know where to look. They'll be setting up an incident room, though. There will be all sorts of questions. You'd better be ready for them, because you were there in that house after Dorothea was attacked, and they have your fingerprints."

"So they have." I thought a bit and asked, "Is it against the law not to report having a knife stuck into you?"

"I don't really know," Robbie said, "but I know it's mostly against the law to carry a knife like the Fury in a public place, which is what O'Hara did when the two of you took it away with you last night. He could be liable for a fine and six months in jail."

"You're kidding?"

"No. There are fierce laws now about carrying offensive weapons, and you can't get anything much more offensive than a Fury."

"Forget you ever saw it."

"So easy."

We had cleaned the kitchen the evening before by bundling the body protectors, my shirt, my sweater, and Robbie's medical debris into a trash bag, knotting the top; and we'd taken it with us, casually adding it to the heap of similar bags to one side of Bedford Lodge, from where mountains of rubbish and empty bottles were cleared daily.

Robbie in farewell said again he would tell the nurses it was OK to let me in to see Dorothea, and asked me to phone him back later.

Promising I would, I said good-bye to him and dialed the number of Professor Meredith Derry who, to my relief, could be brought to the phone and who would acquiesce to a half-hour's worth of knife expertise, especially if I were paying a consultancy fee.

"Of course," I said heartily. "Double, if it can be this evening."

"Come when you like," the professor said, and he gave me an address and directions.

DOROTHEA'S GRIEF WAS as deep and pulverizing as I'd feared. The tears flowed the minute she saw me, weak endless silent tears, not howls and sobs of pain, but an intense mourning as much for times past as for present loss.

I put my arm round her for a while and then simply held her hand and sat there in that fashion until she fumbled for a tissue lying on the bed and weakly blew her nose.

"Thomas."

"Yes, I know. I'm so sorry."

"He wanted what was best for me. He was a good son."

"Yes," I said.

"I didn't appreciate him enough . . ."

"Don't feel guilty," I said.

"But I do. I can't help it. I should have let him take me with him as soon as Valentine died."

"No," I said. "Stop it, dearest Dorothea. You are not to blame for anything. You mustn't blame yourself."

"But *why?* Why would anyone want to kill my Paul?"

"The police will find out."

"I can't *bear* it." The tears came again, preventing speech.

I went out of her room to ask the nurses to give Dorothea a sedative. She had already been given one. No more without a doctor's say-so, they said.

"Then get a doctor," I told them irritably. "Her son's been murdered. She's feeling guilty."

"Guilty? Why?"

It was too difficult to explain. "She will be seriously ill by morning if you don't do something."

I went back to Dorothea thinking I'd wasted my breath, but ten minutes later one of the nurses came in brightly and gave her an injection, which almost immediately sent her to sleep.

"That satisfy you?" the nurse asked me with a hint of sarcasm.

"Couldn't be better."

I left the hospital and helped my driver find the way to Professor Derry. The driver was on time-and-a-half for evening work and said he was in no hurry at all to take me home.

Professor Derry's retirement was no gold-plated affair. He lived on the ground floor of a tall house divided horizontally into apartments, himself occupying, it transpired, a study, a bedroom, a bathroom, and a screened-off kitchen alcove, all small and heavy-looking in brown wood, all the fading domain of an ancient academic living frugally.

He was white haired, physically stooped, and frail, but with eyes and mind in sharp array. He waved me into his study, sat me down on a wooden chair with arms, and asked how he could help.

"I came for information about knives."

"Yes, yes," he interrupted. "You said that on the phone."

I looked around but could see no phone in his room. There had, however, been one—a pay phone—out in the hallway, shared with the upstairs tenants.

I said, "If I show you a drawing of a knife, could you tell me about it?"

"I can try."

I took the drawing of the Heath knife out of my jacket pocket and handed it to him folded. He opened it, flattened it out, and laid it aside on his desk.

"I have to tell you," he said with many small, rapid lip movements, "that I have recently already been consulted about a knife like this."

"You are an acknowledged expert, sir."

"Yes." He studied my face. "Why do you not ask who consulted me? Have you no curiosity? I don't like students who have no curiosity."

"I imagine it was the police."

The old voice cackled in a wheezy sort of laugh. "I see I have to reassess."

"No, sir. It was I who found the knife on Newmarket Heath. The police took it into custody. I didn't know they had consulted you. It was curiosity, strong and undiluted, that brought me here."

"What did you read?"

"I never went to university."

"Pity."

"Thank you, sir."

"I was going to have some coffee. Do you want some coffee?"

"Yes. Thank you, I'd like some."

He nodded busily, pulled aside the screen, and in his kitchen alcove heated water, spooned instant powder into cups, and asked about milk and sugar. I stood and helped him, the small domesticity a signal of his willingness to impart.

"I didn't care for the two young policemen who came here," he said unexpectedly. "They called me Granddad. Patronizing."

"Stupid of them."

"Yes. The shell grows old, but not the inhabiting intellect. People see the shell and call me Granddad. And *dearie*. What do you think of *dearie?*"

"I'd kill 'em."

"Quite right." He cackled again. We carried the cups across to the chairs. "The knife the police brought here," he said, "is a modern replica of a trench knife issued to American soldiers in France in the First World War."

"Wow," I said.

"Don't use that ridiculous word."

"No, sir."

"The policemen asked why I thought it was a replica and not the real thing. I told them to open their eyes. They didn't like it."

"Well . . . er . . . how did you know?"

He cackled. "It had 'Made in Taiwan' stamped into the metal. Go on, say it."

I said, "Taiwan wasn't called Taiwan in World War One."

"Correct. It was Formosa. And at that point in its history, it was not an industrial island." He sat and tasted his coffee, which, like mine, was weak. "The police wanted to know who owned the knife. How could I possibly know? I said it wasn't legal in England to carry such a knife in a public place, and I asked where had they found it."

"What did they say?"

"They didn't. They said it didn't concern me. Granddad."

I told him in detail how the police had acquired their trophy and he said, mocking me, "Wow."

I was becoming accustomed to him and to his crowded room, aware now of the walls of bookshelves, so like Valentine's, and of his cluttered old antique walnut desk, of the single brass lamp with green metal shade throwing inadequate light, of rusty green velvet curtains hanging from great brown rings on a pole, of an incongruously modern television set beside a worn old typewriter, of dried faded hydrangeas in a cloisonné vase and a brass Roman-numeraled clock ticking away the remains of a life.

The room, neat and orderly, smelled of old books, of old leather, of old coffee, of old pipe smoke, of old man. There was no heating, despite the chilly evening. An old three-barred electric fire stood black and cold. The professor wore a sweater, a scarf, a shabby tweed jacket with elbow patches, and indoor slippers of brown checked wool. Bifocals gave him sight, and he had meticulously shaved: he might be old and short of cash, but standards had nowhere slipped.

On the desk, in a silver frame, there was an indistinct old photograph of a younger himself standing beside a woman, both of them smiling.

"My wife," he explained, seeing where I was looking. "She died."

"I'm sorry."

"It happens," he said. "It was long ago."

I drank my unexciting coffee, and he delicately brought up the subject of his fee.

"I haven't forgotten," I said, "but there's another knife I'd like to ask you about."

"What knife?"

"Two knives, actually." I paused. "One has a handle of polished striped wood that I think may be rosewood. It has a black hilt and a black double-edged blade an inch wide and almost six inches long."

"A *black* blade?"

I confirmed it. "It's a strong, purposeful, and good-looking weapon. Would you know it from that description?"

He put his empty cup carefully on his desk and took mine also.

He said, "The best known black-bladed knife is the British commando knife. Useful for killing sentries on dark nights."

I nearly said "wow" again, not so much at the content of what he said, but at his acceptance that the purpose of such knives was death.

"They usually come in olive-khaki webbing sheaths," he said, "with a slot for a belt and cords for tying the bottom of the sheath round the leg."

"The one I saw had no sheath," I said.

"Pity. Was it authentic, or a replica?"

"I don't know."

"Where did you see it?"

"It was given to me, in a box. I don't know who gave it, but I know where it is. I'll look for 'Made in Taiwan.'"

"There were thousands made in World War Two, but they are collector's items now. And of course, in Britain one can no longer buy, sell, advertise, or even give such knives since the criminal justice act of 1988. A collection can be confiscated. No one who owns a collection will have it on display these days."

"Really?"

He smiled dimly at my surprise. "Where have you been, young man?"

"I live in California."

"Ah. That explains it. Knives of all sorts are legal in the United States. Over there they have clubs for aficionados, and monthly magazines, and shops and shows, and also one can buy almost any knife by mail order. Here, it is illegal to make or import any knife with a point where the blade has two cutting edges and is over three inches long." He paused. "I would guess that both the trench knife the police showed me and your putative commando knife came here illegally from America."

I waited a few seconds, thinking things over, and then said, "I'd like to draw another knife for you, if you have a piece of paper."

He provided a notepad and I drew the Fury, giving it its name.

Derry looked at the drawing in ominous stillness, finally saying, "Where did you see this?"

"In England."

"Who owns it?"

"I don't know," I said. "I hoped you might."

"No, I don't. As I said, anyone who owns such a thing in Britain keeps them invisible and secret."

I sighed. I'd hoped much from Professor Derry.

"The knife you've drawn," he said, "is called the Armadillo. Fury is the manufacturer's mark. It's made of stainless steel in Japan. It is expensive, heavy, and infinitely sharp and dangerous."

"Mm."

After a silence, I said, "Professor, what sort of person likes to own such knives, even in secret? Or, perhaps, particularly in secret?"

"Almost anyone," he said. "It's easy to buy this knife in the United States. There are hundreds of thousands of knife buffs in the world. People collect guns, they collect knives, they like the feeling of power . . ." His voice faded on the edge of personal revelation, and he looked down at the drawing as if unwilling for me to see his eyes.

"Do you," I asked carefully, without inflection, "own a collection? A collection left over, perhaps, from when it was legal?"

"You can't ask that," he said.

A silence.

"The Armadillo," he said, "comes in a heavy black leather protective sheath with a button closure. The sheath is intended to be worn on a belt."

"The one I saw had no sheath."

"It isn't safe, let alone legal, to carry it without a sheath."

"I don't think safety was of prime importance."

"You talk in riddles, young man."

"So do you, Professor. The subject is one of innuendo and mistrust."

"I don't know that you wouldn't go to the police."

"And I," I said, "don't know that you wouldn't."

Another silence.

"I'll tell you something, young man," Derry said. "If you are in any danger from the person who owns these knives, be very careful." He considered his words. "Normally knives such as these would be locked away. I find it disturbing that one was *used* on Newmarket Heath."

"Could the police trace its owner?"

"Extremely unlikely," he said. "They didn't know where to begin, and I couldn't help them."

"And the Armadillo's owner?"

He shook his head. "Thousands will have been made. The Fury Armadillo does, I believe, have a serial number. It would identify when a particular knife was made and one might even trace it to its first owner. But from there it could be sold, stolen, or given several times. I cannot envisage these knives you've seen being allowed into the light of day if they were traceable."

Depressing, I thought.

I said, "Professor, please show me your collection."

"Certainly not."

A pause.

I said, "I'll tell you where I saw the Armadillo."

"Go on, then."

His old face was firm, his eyes unblinking. He promised nothing, but I needed more.

"A man I knew was murdered today," I said. "He was killed in a house in Newmarket with an ordinary kitchen knife. It is his mother's house. Last Saturday, in the same house, his mother was badly slashed by a knife, but no weapons were found. She lived, and she's recovering in hospital. On the Heath, as I told you, we believe the star of our picture was an intended victim. The police are investigating all three of these things."

He stared.

I went on. "At first sight there seems to be no connection between today's murder and the attack on the Heath. I'm not sure, but I think that there may be."

He frowned. "Why do you think so?"

"A feeling. Too many knives all at once. And . . . well . . . do you remember Valentine Clark? He died of cancer a week ago today."

Derry's stare grew ever more intense. When he didn't answer, I said, "It was Valentine's sister, Dorothea Pannier, who was slashed last Saturday, in the house she shared with Valentine. The house was ransacked. Today her son, Paul, Valentine's nephew, went to the house and was killed there. There is indeed someone very dangerous roaming around and if the police find him— or her—quickly . . . great."

Unguessable thoughts occupied the professor's mind for whole long minutes. Finally he said, "I became interested in knives when I was a boy. Someone gave me a Swiss army knife with many blades. I treasured it." He smiled briefly with small mouth movements. "I was a lonely child. The knife made me feel more able to deal with the world. But there you are, that's how I think many people are drawn toward collecting, especially collecting weapons that one could use if one were . . . bolder, perhaps, or criminal. They are a crutch, a secret power."

"I see," I said, as he paused.

"Knives fascinated me," Derry went on. "They were my companions. I carried them everywhere. I had them strapped to my leg, or to my arm under my sleeve. I wore them on my belt. I felt warm with them, and more confident. Of course it was adolescence . . . but as I grew older, I collected more, not less. I rationalized my feelings. I was a student, making a serious study, or so I thought. It went on for very many years, this sort of self-confidence. I became an acknowledged expert. I am, as you know, *consulted.*"

"Yes."

"Slowly, some years ago, my need for knives vanished. You may say that at about sixty-five I finally grew up. Even so, I've kept my knowledge of knives current, because consultancy fees, though infrequent, are welcome."

"Mm."

"I do still own a collection, as you realize, but I seldom look at it. I have left it to a museum in my will. If those young policemen had known of its existence, they had the power to take it away."

"I can't believe it."

With the long-suffering smile of a tutor for a dim student, he pulled open a drawer in his desk, fumbled around a little, and produced a photo-copied sheet of paper, finely printed, which he handed to me.

I read the heading. "Prevention of Crime Act 1953. Offensive Weapons."

"Take it and read it later," he said. "I give this to everyone who asks about knives. And now, young man, tell me where you saw the Armadillo."

I paid my dues. I said, "Someone stuck it into me. I saw it after it was pulled out."

His mouth opened. I had really surprised him. He recovered a little and said, "Was this a *game?*"

"I think I was supposed to die. The knife hit a rib, and here I am."

"Great God." He thought. "Then the police have the Armadillo also?"

"No," I said. "I've good reasons for not going to the police. So I'm trusting you, Professor."

"Tell me the reasons."

I explained about the moguls and their horror of jinxes. I said I wanted to complete the film, which I couldn't do with police intervention.

"You are as obsessed as anybody," Derry judged.

"Very likely."

He wanted to know where and how I had—er, *acquired*—my firsthand knowledge of the knife in question, and I told him. I told him about the body protectors, and all about Robbie Gill's ministrations; all except the doctor's name.

When I stopped, I waited another long minute for his reaction. The old eyes watched me steadily.

He stood up. "Come with me," he said and led the way through a brown door to an inner room, which proved to be his bedroom, a monastic-looking cell with a polished wood floor and a high old-fashioned iron bed with a white counterpane. There was a brown wooden wardrobe, a heavy chest of drawers, and a single upright chair against plain white walls. The right ambience, I thought, for a medievalist.

He creaked down onto his knees by the bed as if about to say his prayers, but instead reached under the bedspread at floor level, and tugged.

A large wooden box on casters slowly rolled out, its dusty lid padlocked to the base. Roughly four feet long by three wide, it was at least a foot deep, and it looked formidably heavy.

The professor fumbled for a key ring which bore four keys only, and removed the padlock, opening the lid until it leaned back against the bed. Inside there was an expanse of green baize, and below that, when he removed it, row upon row of thin brown cardboard boxes, each bearing a neat white label with typewritten words identifying the contents. He looked them over, muttering that he hadn't inspected them for months, and picked out one of them, very much not at random.

"This," he said, opening the narrow brown box, "is a genuine commando knife, not a replica."

The professor's commando knife was kept safe in bubble packing but, unwrapped, looked identical to the one sent me as a warning, except that this one did have its sheath.

"I no longer," he said unnecessarily, "keep my knives on display. I packed them all away when my wife died, before I came here. She shared my interest, you see. She *grew* to be interested. I miss her."

"I'm sure you do."

He closed the commando knife away and opened other treasures.

"These two knives from Persia, they have a curved blade, and handles and sheaths of engraved silver with lapis lazuli inserts. These are from Japan . . . these from America, with carved bone handles in the shape of animal heads. All handmade of course. All magnificent specimens."

All lethal, I thought.

"This beautiful knife is Russian, nineteenth century," he said at one point. "Closed, like this, it resembles, as you see, a Fabergé egg, but in fact five separate blades open from it." He pulled out the blades until they resembled a rosette of sharp leaves spreading out from the base of the egg-shaped grip, itself enameled in blue and banded in fine gold.

"Er . . ." I said, "your collection must be valuable. Why don't you sell it?"

"Young man, read the paper I gave you. It is *illegal* to sell these things. One may now only give them to museums, not even to other individuals; and then only to museums that don't make a profit from exhibiting them."

"It's amazing!"

"It stops law-abiding people in their tracks, but criminals take no notice. The world is as medieval as ever. Didn't you know?"

"I suspected it."

His laugh cackled. "Help me lift the top tray onto the bed. I'll show you some curiosities."

The top tray had a rope handle at each end. He grasped one end, I the other, and, at his say-so, we lifted together. The tray was heavy. Not good, from my point of view.

"What's the matter?" he demanded. "Did that hurt you?"

"Just the Armadillo," I apologized.

"Do you want to sit down?"

"No, I want to see your knives."

He knelt on the floor again and opened more boxes, removing the bubble wrapping and putting each trophy into my hand for me to "feel the balance."

His "curiosities" tended to be ever more fearsome. There were several knives along the lines of the American trench knife (the genuine thing, 1918) and a whole terrifying group of second cousins to the Armadillo, knives with whole-hand grips, semi-circular blades, and rows of spikes, all dedicated to tearing an opponent to shreds.

As I gave each piece back to him he rewrapped it and restored it to its box, tidying methodically as he went along.

He showed me a large crucifix fashioned in dark red cloisonné, handsome on a gold chain for use as a chest ornament, but hiding a dagger in its heart. He showed me an ordinary-looking belt that one could use to hold up one's trousers: ordinary except that the buckle, which slid easily out into my hand, proved to be the handle of a sharp triangular blade that could be pushed home to kill.

Professor Derry delivered a grave warning. "Thomas . . ." (we had progressed from "young man"), "Thomas, if a man—or woman—is truly obsessed with knives, you must expect that *anything* he or she carries on their person may be the sheath of a knife. One can get key rings, money clips, hair combs, all with hidden blades. Knives can be hidden even under the lapels of a coat, in special transparent sheaths designed to be stitched onto cloth. A dangerous fanatic will *feed* on this hidden power. Do you at all understand?"

"I'm beginning to."

He nodded several times and asked if I would be able to help him replace the top tray.

"Before we do that, Professor, would you show me one more knife?"

"Well, yes, of course." He looked vaguely at the sea of boxes. "What sort of thing do you want?"

"Can I see the knife that Valentine Clark once gave you?"

After another of his telltale pauses, he said, "I don't know what you're talking about."

"You did know Valentine, didn't you?" I asked.

He levered himself to his feet and headed back into his study, switching off the bedroom light as he went: to save electricity, I supposed.

I followed him, and we resumed our former positions in his wooden armchairs. He asked for my connection with Valentine, and I told him about my childhood, and about Valentine recently leaving me his books. "I read to him while he couldn't see. I was with him not long before he died."

Reassured by my account, Derry felt able to talk. "I knew Valentine quite well at one time. We met at one of those ridiculous fund-raising events, all for a good cause, where people stood around with tea or small glasses of bad wine, being civil and wishing they could go home. I hated those affairs. My dear wife had a soft heart and was always coaxing me to take her, and I couldn't deny her . . . So long ago. So long ago."

I waited through his wave of regret and loneliness, unable to comfort the nostalgia.

"Thirty years ago, it must be," he said, "since we met Valentine. They were raising funds to stop the shipment of live horses to the Continent to be killed for meat. Valentine was one of the speakers. He and I just liked each other . . . and we came from such different backgrounds. I began reading his column in the newspapers, though I wasn't much interested in racing. But Valentine was so *wise* . . . and still an active blacksmith . . . a gust of fresh air, you see, when I was more used to the claustrophobia of university life. My dear wife liked him, and we met him and his wife several times, but it was Valentine and I who *talked*. He came from one sort of world and I from another, and it was perhaps because of that that we could discuss things with each other that we couldn't have mentioned to our colleagues."

I asked without pressure, "What sort of things?"

"Oh . . . medical, sometimes. Growing old. I would never have told you this once, but since I passed eighty I've lost almost all my inhibitions, I don't *care* so much about things. I told Valentine I was having impotency problems, and I was not yet sixty. Are you laughing?"

"No, sir," I said truthfully.

"It was easy to ask Valentine for advice. One *trusted* him."

"Yes."

"We were the same age. I asked him if he had the same problem but he told me his problem was the opposite, he was aroused by young women and had difficulty in controlling his urges."

*"Valentine?"* I exclaimed, astonished.

"People hide things," Derry said simply. "My dear wife didn't really mind that I could no longer easily make love to her, but she used to joke to other people about how *sexy* I was. Such a dreadful word! She wanted people to admire me, she said." He shook his head in love and sorrow. "Valentine told me a doctor to go to. He himself knew of all sorts of ways to deal with impotence. He told me he'd learned a lot of them from stud farms! He said I must be more light-hearted and not think of impotence as an embarrassment or a tragedy. He told me it wasn't the end of the world." He paused. "Because of Valentine, I learned to be content."

"He was great to so many people," I said.

The professor nodded, still reminiscing. "He told me something I've never been able to verify. He swore it was true. I've always *wondered* . . . If I ask you something, Thomas, will you answer me truthfully?"

"Of course."

"You may be too young."

"Try me."

"In confidence."

"Yes."

Nothing, I'd told Moncrieff, was ever off the record. But confessions were, surely?

The professor said, "Valentine told me that restricting the flow of oxygen to the brain could result in an erection."

He waited for my comment, which took a while to materialize. I hesitantly said, "Er . . . I've heard of it."

"Tell me, then."

"I believe it's a perversion that comes under the general heading of auto-erotic mania, in this case self-inflicted partial asphyxia."

He said impatiently, "Valentine told me that thirty years ago. What I'm asking you is, does it work?"

"Firsthand, I don't know."

He said with a touch of bitterness, "Because you've never needed to find out?"

"Well, not yet, no."

"Then . . . has anyone told you?"

"Not firsthand."

He sighed. "I could never face doing it. It's one of those things I'm never going to know."

"There are others?"

"Don't be stupid, Thomas. I am a medievalist. I know the facts that were written down. I try to feel my way into that lost world. I cannot smell it, hear it, live it. I can't know its secret fears and its assumptions. I've spent a lifetime learning and teaching it secondhand. If I went to sleep now and awoke in the year fourteen hundred, I wouldn't understand the language or know how to cook a meal. You've heard the old saying that if Jesus returned to do a replay of the sermon on the mount, no one now living would understand him, as he would be speaking ancient Hebrew with a Nazareth carpenter's accent? Well, I've wasted a lifetime on an unintelligible past."

"No, Professor," I protested.

"Yes," he said resignedly. "I don't think I any longer care. And I no longer have anyone to talk to. I can't talk to boring social workers who think I need looking after, and who call me 'dearie.' But I find I'm talking to *you,* Thomas, and I'm an old fool who should know better."

"Please go on talking," I said. "Go on about Valentine."

"These last years, I haven't seen him much. His wife died. So did mine. You might think it would have drawn us together, but it didn't. I suppose it was our wives who had arranged our meetings. Valentine and I just drifted apart."

"But," I said, "years ago . . . he knew you were interested in knives?"

"Oh yes, of course. He was enthusiastic about my collection. He and his wife used to come over to our house and the women would chat together and I would show Valentine the knives."

"He told me he gave you one."

"He *told* you . . . ?"

"Yes."

The professor frowned. "I remember him saying I wasn't ever to say who had given me that knife. He said just to keep it in case he asked for it back . . . but he never asked. I haven't thought about it. I'd forgotten it." He paused. *"Why* do you want to see it?"

"Just curiosity . . . and fondness for my old friend."

The professor thought it over, and said, "I suppose if he told you, he wouldn't mind."

He got to his feet and returned to the bedroom, with me on his heels. The light went on dimly; an economical bulb.

"I'm afraid," my host said doubtfully, "that there are three levels of knives in this chest, and we have to lift out the second tray to reach the knife you want to see. Are you able to lift it out onto the floor? It doesn't have to go up onto the bed."

I assured him I could, and did it left-handed, a shade better. The third layer, revealed, proved not to be of brown cardboard boxes but of longer parcels, each wrapped only in bubble plastic, and labeled.

"These are mostly swords," Derry said. "And swordsticks, and a couple of umbrellas with swords in the handles. They were a defense against thieves a hundred or two hundred years ago. Now, of course, they are illegal. One has nowadays to allow oneself to be mugged." He cackled gently. "You mustn't hurt the poor robber, you know."

He surveyed the labels, running his fingers along the rows.

"Here we are. 'Present from V.C.' " He lifted out a bubble-wrapped package, snapped open a taped fastening, and unrolled the parcel to reveal the contents.

"There you are," Professor Derry said. "That's Valentine's knife."

I looked at it. It was like no knife I'd ever seen. It was at least fifteen inches long, possibly eighteen. Its blade, double-edged and clearly sharp, took up barely a third of the overall length and was of an elongated flat oval like a spear, with a sharp spear's point. The long handle was narrow and was twisted throughout its length in a close spiral. The end of the spiral had been flattened into a circular embellishment, perforated with several holes.

"It's not a knife," I said. "It's a spear."

Derry smiled. "It's not meant for throwing."

"What was it for?"

"I don't know. Valentine simply asked me if I'd like to put it in my collection. It's hammered steel. Unique."

"But where would he buy such a thing?"

"Buy it?" The full cackle rang out. "Have you forgotten Valentine's trade? He was a smith. He didn't buy it. He *made* it."

# 14

Early Friday morning I worked in peace from four o'clock to six-thirty in the projection room, cutting scenes into rough order, a process that apart from anything else always told me what necessary establishing shots hadn't been provided for in the screenplay. A five-second shot here and there could replace, also, patches of dialogue that hadn't gone well. I made notes, fiddled about, hummed with contentment, clarified the vision.

By six-thirty Moncrieff was setting up the cameras in the stable yard, by seven the horses (back from Huntingdon) were out at exercise on the Heath, by seven-thirty the wardrobe and make-up departments were at work in the house, and at eight-thirty O'Hara's car swept into the yard with the horn blowing.

The lads, back from the Heath to groom and feed their charges, came out of the open-doored stalls at the summons. Wardrobe and make-up appeared. The camera crews paused to listen. Actors and extras stood around.

Satisfied, O'Hara borrowed Ed's megaphone and announced that the Hollywood company was pleased with the way things were going, and that as he himself was now leaving for Los Angeles, Thomas Lyon would be in sole charge of the production.

He handed the megaphone back to Ed, waved everyone away to resume work, and gave me a challenging stare.

"Well?" he said.

"I'd rather you stayed."

"It's your film," he insisted. "But you will please not go anywhere without your driver and your bodyguard." He looked around. "Where are they, anyway?"

"I'm safe here," I said.

"You are not to think you're safe *anywhere,* Thomas." He handed me a key, explaining it was his hotel rooms' key. "Use my rooms if you need them. The two knives are in the safe in there. The combination is four five four five. Got it?"

"Yes . . . but how will I reach you?"

"Phone my secretary in L.A. She'll know."

"Don't go."

He smiled. "My airplane leaves at noon. See you, guy."

He climbed into his car with finality and was driven away, and I felt like a junior general left in charge of a major battlefield, apprehensive, half confident, emotionally naked.

The schedule that morning was for some of the earliest scenes of the film, the arrival of the police to investigate the hanging. Moncrieff set about lighting the actors—some in and some out of police uniform—explaining exactly where he wanted them to stop and turn toward the camera. He and they would be working from the plans and diagrams we'd drawn the evening before on my return from Cambridge.

Leaving Ed to supervise I drove back to Bedford Lodge for a quiet breakfast in my rooms and found my driver and black belt distractedly pacing the lobby and fearing the sack.

"Calm down," I said. "Your day starts in an hour."

"Mr. O'Hara said . . ."

"One hour," I reiterated and went upstairs thinking that as they hadn't saved me from the Armadillo I might do equally well on my own.

Room service brought my breakfast and a visitor, Robbie Gill.

"I should be listening to chests and prescribing cough mixture," he said. "My receptionist is dealing with a seething line of disgruntled patients. Take your clothes off."

"Do what?"

"Sweater and shirt off," he repeated. "Undo your trousers. I've come to save your unworthy life."

Busily he unpacked things from his case, moving my croissant and coffee aside and eating my ham with his fingers.

"Hope you're not hungry," he said, munching.

"Starving."

"Too bad. Get undressed."

"Er . . . what for?"

"Number one, fresh dressing. Number two, knife-proof vest. I tried to get a proper bullet-and-knife-proof vest but neither the police nor the army would let me have one without bureaucracy, so we'll have to trust to home-made."

I took off my sweater and shirt and he removed the dressing, raising his eyebrows at the revealed scenery but appearing not displeased.

"You're healing. Is it sore?"

"The broken rib is."

"Only to be expected," he added and stuck on a new dressing. "Now," he said, "what do you know about Delta-cast?"

"Nothing."

"It's used instead of the old plaster of paris for fractured arms and legs. It's rigid. It's a polymer, actually, and porous, so you won't itch. A knife won't go through it."

"A bullet?"

"That's another matter."

He worked for half an hour, during which time we discussed Dorothea and Paul, and came to no useful conclusions, though I explained how, via Bill Robinson, I was now surrounded by the army of boxes containing Valentine's books.

At the end of Robbie's work I was encased from chin to waist in a hard sleeveless jacket that I could take off and put on in two halves and fasten with strips of Velcro.

When I protested at its height round my neck he said merely, "Do you want your throat cut? Wear a turtle-necked sweater. I brought you this thin white one, in case you hadn't got one." He handed it over as if it were nothing.

"Thanks, Robbie," I said, and he could hear I meant it.

He nodded briefly. "I'd better get back to my mob of coughers, or they'll lynch me." He packed things away. "Do you think your hanged lady was lynched?"

"No, I don't think so."

"Did you trawl any useful mud with Professor Derry?"

"The knife that bust my rib is called an Armadillo. The one with the finger holes, from the Heath, is a replica from World War One. The police had already asked the professor about it."

"Wow."

"The professor's about eighty-five. He told me not to say 'wow.' "

"He sounds a riot."

"We got on fine, but he doesn't know who owns the Armadillo."

"Take care," he said, leaving. "I'm around if you need me."

I ate what was left of my breakfast, dressed slowly, shaved, and got gradually used to living like a turtle inside a carapace.

At about the time I was ready to leave again the people at the reception desk phoned up to tell me that a young woman was asking for me. She thought I was expecting her. A Miss Lucy Wells.

"Oh, yes." I'd temporarily forgotten her. "Please send her up."

Lucy had come in jeans, sweater, sneakers, and ponytail, chiefly with the cool eighteen-year-old young lady in charge but with occasional tongue-tied lapses. She looked blankly at the multitude of boxes and wanted to know where to begin.

I gave her a laptop computer, a notebook, a ballpoint, and a big black marker pen.

"Give each box a big number," I said, writing I. with the marker pen on a microwave oven carton. "Empty it out. Write a list of the contents on the pad, enter the list on the little computer, and then put everything back, topping each box with the list of contents. On another page, write me a general list, saying, for example, 'Box one, books, biographies of owners and trainers.' OK?"

"Yes."

"Shake out each book in case it has loose papers inside its pages, and don't throw anything away, not even pointless scraps."

"All right." She seemed puzzled, but I didn't amplify.

"Order lunch from room service," I said. "Don't leave any papers or books lying around when the waiter comes. OK?"

"Yes, but why?"

"Just do the job, Lucy. Here's the room key for here." I gave it to her. "If you leave this room, use the key to return. When I come back, I'll bring Nash Rourke in for a drink."

Her blue eyes widened. She wasn't a fool. She looked at the boxes and settled for the package I'd offered.

I went back to work, driver and bodyguard giving me a lot less confidence than Delta-cast. We spent all morning in the stable yard, with Nash patiently (both in and out of character) dealing with the actors playing at police.

The initial police doubts, called for in the script, took an age to get right. "I don't want these policemen to appear *thick*," I pleaded, but it was the actors, I concluded, who were slow. I'd had no hand in casting minor characters; the trick was to make the dumbest poodle jump through the hoops.

Moncrieff swore nonstop. Nash could turn and get the light across his forehead right every time, but Nash, I reminded my fuming director of photography, wasn't called a mega-star for nothing.

The level of muddle was not helped by the arrival of the real police asking why my fresh fingerprints were all over Dorothea's house. We could have played it for laughs, but no one was funny. I proved to have an alibi for whenever it was that Paul had died (they wouldn't or couldn't say exactly when) but the stoppage ate up my lunch hour.

Back at work we progressed at length to the first arrival (by car) of Cibber, and to his planting of suspicions against Nash in the (fictional) police mind. Cibber was a good pro, but inclined still to tell inappropriate fruity jokes and waste time. "Sorry, sorry," he would breezily say, fluffing his words without remorse.

I hung on grimly to forbearance and walked twice out onto the Heath breathing deeply with sore rib twinges while Moncrieff's men loaded the cameras for the eighth take of a fairly simple sequence. I phoned Wrigley's garage and asked if Bill Robinson could have the afternoon off, and I spoke to Bill himself, thanking him for the second safe delivery of the boxes and asking him to open his home garage and bring bits of motorbike out onto his drive.

"We've decided to film your stuff after dark," I said. "Can you spare us the evening? And will you have your big bike at home?"

Natch, fine, yes indeedy, and cor, he said.

Tired and a shade dispirited, I called it a day at five-thirty in the afternoon and invited Nash to my Bedford Lodge rooms for a reviver.

"Sure," he agreed easily and greeted Lucy with enough warmth to tongue-tie her into knock-knees.

"How did you get on?" I asked her, explaining the task briefly to Nash; and she apologized for being slow and having completed only five boxes. She had just discovered that one of the boxes held some clippings about Sonia's death. Wasn't that extraordinary? Box six, she said. She hadn't had time to go through them.

"That's fine," I said. "Come again tomorrow, will you? Are you going right home at nights? Or perhaps staying with your uncle Ridley?"

She made a face. "Not with him. Actually," she blushed perceptibly, "I'm staying here in this hotel. They had a room free and Dad agreed. I hope that's all right?"

"It's splendid," I said moderately, knowing enthusiasm would frighten her. "What about Sunday, day after tomorrow?"

"I can stay until the job's finished," she said. "Dad said it was better."

"Good for Dad," Nash smiled.

"He's awfully interested," Lucy said, and after a pause added, "It's really odd, Mr. Rourke, imagining you as my dad."

Nash smiled, the eyelids crinkling. Despite his pregnant wife, he didn't look at all like anyone's dad, certainly not Lucy's.

We drank briefly together and split up, Nash yawning as he went and saying the slave driver (T. Lyon) wanted him out working again in a couple of hours. Lucy, without making an issue of it, excused herself at the same time. Staying in the hotel, she was telling me, meant no more than convenience.

When she'd gone I looked at her master list of the boxes' contents. Since they had been well jumbled up on the journeys, and since she had started methodically at one end, the six boxes she'd worked on held mixed and random contents.

Box I.      Form books. Flat racing.
Box II.      Biographies, trainers, owners, and jockeys.
Box III.      Form books. National Hunt racing.
Box IV.      Weekly columns, *Racing Gazette*.
Box V.      Books, annuals, racing history.

With unstoppable curiosity I knelt on the floor and opened Box III, National Hunt form books, and found that by happy chance it contained the records of two of the years when I'd been racing.

A British racing form book, built up week by week throughout the season with loose-leaf inserts tied between soft leather covers, contained details of every single race run, identifying each runner by name, trainer, jockey, weight carried, age, and sex, and giving a start-to-finish commentary of performance.

There was no gainsaying the form book. If the form books said Mr. T. Lyon (the Mr. denoting amateur status) had finished fifth a long way back, it was no good Mr. T. Lyon in memory thinking he'd ridden a close contest to be beaten by half a length. Mr. T. Lyon, I read with nostalgia, had won a three-mile steeplechase by two lengths at Newbury racecourse, the horse carrying 146 pounds. The underfoot conditions that day had been classified as "soft," and the starting price had been a hundred to six, Mr. T. Lyon's mount having unaccountably beaten the hot favorite (weighted out of it, carrying twenty pounds more). Mr. T. Lyon, I remembered, had been ecstatic. The crowd, who'd mostly lost their bets, had been unenthusiastically silent.

I smiled. Here I was, twelve years later, clad in Delta-cast and trying not to be killed: and I didn't think I'd ever been happier than on that cold long-ago afternoon.

Valentine had put a red exclamation mark against my winner, which meant that he personally had fitted the horse with shoes especially for racing, probably on the morning of the race.

Horses wore thin aluminum shoes for racing, much lighter and thinner than the steel shoes they needed in the stable and out at exercise. Farriers would routinely change the shoes before and after a race.

Owing to chance the form books in Box III went back only as far as my seventeenth birthday. For the Mr. T. Lyon debut at sixteen to turn up, I would have to wait for Lucy.

I opened Box I, Flat racing form books, and found that in this instance the books were older. These, indeed, covered the few years when Jackson Wells had been training in Newmarket: one of them covered the year of Sonia's death.

Fascinated, I looked for Valentine's red dots (runners) and red exclamation marks (winners) and found my grandfather's name as trainer all over the place. Twenty-six years ago, when I'd been four. A whole generation ago. So many of them gone. So many horses, so many races, lost and forgotten.

Jackson Wells hadn't had large numbers of runners and precious few winners, as far as I could see. Jackson Wells hadn't had a regular jockey either: only successful wealthy stables could afford to retain a top-flighter. Several of the Wells horses had been ridden by a P. Falmouth, several others by D. Carsington, neither of whom I'd heard of, which wasn't surprising.

On the day of his wife's death Jackson Wells had set off to York races, where a horse from his stable had been entered. I looked up the actual day and found his horse hadn't started but was listed as a nonrunner. Trainer Wells had been on his way back to Newmarket when they'd run the race without him.

I flicked forward through the pages. Valentine's dots for Jackson Wells were scattered and diminishing in number. There was only one exclamation mark, a minor race on a minor track, ridden by the minor jockey, D. Carsington.

"A winner is a winner," my grandfather always said. "Never despise the lowliest."

I put the form books back in the box, dutifully collected my guardian shadows from the lobby, and went by car to Betty's house to ask if she by any chance had Dorothea's key. She shook her head. *Poor* Dorothea; that poor man, Paul.

Betty's husband wasn't grieving for Paul. If I wanted to start tidying Dorothea's house, he said, he could open her door in no time. Betty's husband was an all-round handyman. A little how's-your-father and a shove, he said, would circumvent most locks, and consequently he and I soon went from room to ravaged room righting the mess as best we could. The police, he said, had taken their photos and their fingerprints and left. The house, such as it was, and crammed with bad memories, was Dorothea's to come home to.

I spent most time in her bedroom, looking for the photographs she said she kept in a box. I couldn't find them. I told Betty's husband what I was looking for—Dorothea's only mementos of Paul when young—but neither of us succeeded.

"Poor love," Betty's husband said. "That son of hers was a brute, but she would never hear a strong word against him. Between you and me, he's no loss."

"No . . . but who killed him?"

"Yeah . . . I see what you mean. Gives you a nasty feeling, doesn't it, some geezer running around with a knife?"

"Yes," I said. "It does."


I STOOD IN the dark street outside Bill Robinson's garage, with the black belt at my back facing the crowd that had inevitably collected.

There were bright lights inside the garage where Bill Robinson himself stood, dressed in his accustomed black leather and studs and looking self-conscious. The monster Harley-Davidson stood to one side. Pieces of a second, that Bill was rebuilding, lay in clumps on the drive. Moncrieff was busy pointing arc lamps and spots to give dramatic shadows and gleams, and Nash's stand-in walked to the designated point and looked toward the garage. Moncrieff lit his profile first, and then a three-quarter face angle, one side bright, the other in darkness, only the liquid sheen of an eye showing.

Nash arrived, walked up beside me, and watched.

"You pause," I said. "You're wondering how the hell you're going to get out of the fix you're in. You're psyching yourself up. OK?"

He nodded. He waved a hand toward the scene. "It's striking," he said, "but why a bike?"

"It's what our movie is about."

"How do you mean? There aren't any bikes in it, are there?"

"Fantasy," I said. "Our movie is about the need for fantasy."

"The dream lovers?" he suggested doubtfully.

"Fantasy supplies what life doesn't," I said casually. "That boy there with his bike is eighteen, good-natured, has a regular job, carries his elderly neighbor's shopping home for her, and in his fantasy life he's a hell raiser with roaring power between his legs and the gear and the studs . . . he's playing at what he wouldn't really like to be, but the imagining of it fills and satisfies him."

Nash stood without moving. "You sound as though you approve," he said.

"Yes, I do. A good strong fantasy life, I'd guess, saves countless people from boredom and depression. It gives them a feeling of being individual. They invent themselves. You know it perfectly well. You *are* a fantasy to most people."

"What about serial killers? Aren't they fantasists?"

"There's a hell to every heaven."

Moncrieff called, "Ready, Thomas," and Nash, without comment, went to the place from where he would walk into shot, and pause, and turn his head, and watch Bill Robinson live in his courage-inducing dreamland.

Ed went round explaining the necessity of silence to the neighbors. He shouted, "Turn over." The cameras reached speed. Ed yelled, "Action." Nash walked, stopped, turned his head. Perfect. Bill Robinson dropped a piece of exhaust pipe out of nervousness and said, "Sorry."

"Cut," Ed said, disgusted.

"Don't say 'sorry,' " I told Bill Robinson, walking toward the garage to join him. "It doesn't matter if you drop something. It doesn't matter if you swear. It's normal. Just don't say 'sorry.' "

He grinned. We shot the scene again and he fitted two shining pieces of metal together as if he hadn't got fifty people watching.

"Cut," Ed yelled with approval, and the neighbors cheered. Nash shook Bill Robinson's hand and signed autographs. We sold a lot of future cinema tickets, and no one stuck a knife in my back. Not a bad evening, overall.

Returning to Bedford Lodge, Nash and I ate room service dinner together.

"Go on," he said, "about the need for fantasy."

"Oh . . . I . . ." I hesitated, and stopped, unwilling to sound a fool.

"Go on," he urged. "People say . . . in fact *I* say . . . that playacting isn't a suitable occupation for a serious man. So tell me why it is."

"You don't need me to tell you."

"Tell me why you make fantasies, then."

"Have some wine."

"Don't duck the issue, dammit."

"Well," I said, pouring lavishly, "I wanted to be a jockey but I grew too big. Anyway, one day I went to see a doctor about some damage I'd done to my shoulder in a racing fall, and she asked me what I wanted to do with my life. I said 'be a jockey' and she lectured me crossly on wasting my time on earth frivolously. I asked her what occupation she would recommend and she sternly told me that the only profession truly helpful and worthwhile was medicine."

"Rubbish!"

"She scorned me for wanting to be merely an entertainer."

Nash shook his head.

"So," I said, "I rationalized it, I suppose. I'm still an entertainer and always will be, I guess, and I've persuaded myself that I do at least as much good as tranquilizers. Everyone can go where their mind takes them. You can live in imaginary places without feeling the real terror or the real pain. I make the images. I open the door. I can inflame . . . and I can heal . . . and comfort . . . and get people to understand . . . and for God's sake don't remember a word of this. I've just made it up to entertain you."

He drank his wine thoughtfully.

"And in this movie that we're engaged in," I said, "the dream lovers make the spurned wife's existence happier . . . They're the best way she can face her husband's affair with her own sister. They're her refuge . . . and her revenge."

He smiled twistedly. "My character's a shit, isn't he?"

"Human," I said.

"And are you going to sell Howard on her suicide?"

I shook my head. "I'm sure she didn't kill herself. But don't worry, your character will avenge her death and come up smelling of roses."

"Has Howard written those extra scenes?"

"Not yet."

"You're a rogue, Thomas, you know that?"

We finished dinner peaceably, and together with Moncrieff mapped out the next day's scenes, which were due to take place in the Athenaeum's look-alike dining room, happily by now built and ready.

After that meeting I un-Velcroed my restricting knife repeller with relief and washed without soaking the dressing, and in sleeping shorts thought I'd just take a quick look at the newspaper cuttings about Sonia's death before inching into bed: and two hours later, warmed by a robe, I was still sitting in an armchair alternately amused and aghast and beginning to understand why Paul had desperately wanted to take away Valentine's books and why Valentine, perhaps, hadn't wanted him to have them. In leaving them to me, a comparative stranger, the old man had thought to safeguard the knowledge contained in them, since I couldn't have understood the significance of the clippings and might simply have thrown them away, a task he should have done himself but had left too late, until his progressing illness made action impossible.

Paul had wanted Valentine's books and papers, and Paul was dead. I looked at the Delta-cast jacket standing empty and mute on a table and felt a strong urge to fasten it on again, even at two in the morning.

In describing Sonia to me, Valentine had called her a mouse, but that couldn't have been how he'd thought of her when she was alive. The folder of clippings about her held two large photographs, both the likenesses of a vividly pretty young woman with a carefree spirit and, I would have said, considerable carnal knowledge.

One of the photographs was an expert, glossy, eight-by-ten black-and-white version of the colored photo Lucy had lent me of "Sonia and Pig." In Valentine's photo the young man's presence had been deleted. Sonia smiled alone.

The second photo was of Sonia in her bridal gown, again alone, and again with nothing virginal about her eyes. My mother, of all people, had once instructed me about the difference: once a woman had slept with a man, she said, the woman would develop little pouches in her lower eyelids which would show when she smiled. Sonia was smiling in both pictures, and the small pouches were there unmistakably.

Valentine had said the book made her out to be a poor little bitch, and, in saying that, he'd intended to mislead. The folder held clippings about her death from a myriad of newspapers, and, in the most derogatory of the various accounts, in those most overtly speculatory about Mrs. Wells's fidelity to Jackson, someone—and it had to have been Valentine himself—had stricken the accounts through and through with red ballpoint and had written "No! No!" as if in pain.

I took everything out of the Sonia folder and found that besides the photos and the whole sheaf of newspaper cuttings, there were two frail dried roses, a brief note about shoeing which started, "Darling Valentine," and a wisp of creamy lace-edged panties.

Valentine had confessed he'd been too easily aroused by young women, Professor Derry had said. According to Valentine's own collection of memories, one of those young women had been Sonia Wells.

Poor old sod, I thought. He had been sixty, nearly, when she died. I was young enough to have considered sixty the far side of acute sexual obsession: Valentine enlightened even from beyond the grave.

The emotional vigor of the thick Sonia file blinded me for a long while to the slim folder underneath which lay at the bottom of the box: but this folder proved, when I read the contents carefully, to be raw explosive material in search of a detonator.

In search of myself.

I SLEPT FOR five hours, put on the carapace, went back to work. Saturday morning. I struck it off in my mind's calendar as day nineteen of production, or almost a third of my time allowed.

It rained all day, which didn't matter as we were engaged indoors in the Athenaeum dining room, shooting the scene where Cibber's suspicions of his wife's canoodling jelled into inescapable certainty. Cibber and Silva endlessly said "yes, please" and "no, thank you" to actor-waiters, chewed endless mouthfuls of food, and in Silva's case spitting them out immediately when I said "cut"; drank endless sips of wine-colored water; waved (in Cibber's case) to unidentified acquaintances across the room; conducted a conversation of concentrated spite with rigidly smiling lips and a vivid awareness of social status. Jockey Club membership, to Cibber, meant not publicly slapping your wife's face in the most conservative dining room in London.

Howard, I thought, as I listened and watched, had surpassed himself in understanding and reproducing the constraints of class on the potentially dangerous ego of a rejected male.

Silva sneered at Cibber with her eyes, her mouth saccharine. Silva told him she couldn't bear his hands on her breasts. Cibber, destroyed within, looked around to make sure the waiters hadn't heard. Both players gave the film enormously good value for money.

Breaking for lunch, with the close-ups to do in the afternoon, I returned for a respite to Bedford Lodge and found Nash in my rooms sprawling in an armchair and having an easy time with Lucy. She, in consequence, had, as her morning's work, itemized the contents of barely one and a half cartons.

"Oh, hallo," she greeted me from her knees, "what would you like me to do with three boxfuls of huge old encyclopedias?"

"How old?"

She pulled out one large volume and investigated. "Forty years!" Her voice made forty years unimaginable. Nash reflexively winced.

"Just label them and leave them," I said.

"Right. Oh . . . and I haven't come across any photo albums, that you wanted me to look for, but I did find a lot of snaps in an old chocolate box. What do you want me to do with those?"

"In a chocolate box . . . ?"

"Well, yes. It's got flowers on the lid. Pretty old."

"Er . . . Where's the box?"

She opened a carton that had once held a fax machine, and from it produced several box files full of ancient race cards and newspaper clippings of winners that Valentine had regularly shod. "Here's the chocolate box," Lucy said, lifting out and handing me a faded and battered gold-colored cardboard box with flowers like dahlias on the lid. "I didn't make a list of the photos. Do you want me to?"

"No," I said absently, taking off the lid and finding small ancient pictures inside, many in long ago faded colors with curling edges. Pictures of Valentine and his wife, pictures of Dorothea and her husband, a photo or two of Meredith Derry and his wife, and several of Dorothea with her child: with her nice-looking little boy, Paul. Pictures when life was fine, before time loused it up.

"How about ordering us all some lunch?" I said.

Nash did the ordering. "What do you want to drink, Thomas?"

"Lethe," I said.

"Not until you've finished the movie."

"What's Lethe?" Lucy asked.

Nash said, "The river in the underworld that, if you drink it, makes you sleep and forget about living."

"Oh."

"Forever," Nash added. "But Thomas doesn't mean that."

Lucy covered noncomprehension in activity with the marker pen.

At the bottom of the chocolate box I came across a larger print, the colors still not razor sharp, but in a better state of preservation. It was of a group of young people, all looking about twenty. On the back of the photo were two simple words: THE GANG.

The Gang.

The Gang consisted of five young men and a girl.

I sat staring at it for long enough for the other two to notice.

"What is it?" Nash asked. "What have you found?"

I handed the photo to Lucy, who glanced at it, did a double take, and then exclaimed, "Why, that's Dad, isn't it? How *young* he looks." She turned the photo over. "The Gang," she read aloud. "That's his handwriting, isn't it?"

"You'd know better than I would."

"I'm sure of it."

"Who are the people with him? Who are the Gang?" I asked.

She studied the picture. "That's Sonia, isn't it? It must be."

Nash took the photo out of Lucy's hand and peered at it himself, nodding. "That's definitely your father, and the girl looks like the photo you lent us . . . and that boy next to her, that's the other one in that photo . . . that's surely 'Pig.' "

"I suppose so," Lucy said doubtfully. "And that one on the end, he looks like . . ." She stopped, both unsure and disturbed.

"Like who?" I asked.

"He's not like that any more. He's well . . . *bloated* . . . now. That's my Uncle Ridley. He looks lovely there. How *awful*, what time does to people."

"Yes." Nash and I said it in unison. An endless host of barely recognizable old actors and actresses lived on in Hollywood in inelastic skins, everything sagging but the memory of glamor, their youthful selves mocking them relentlessly from rented videos and movie channels.

"Who are the others?" I asked.

"I don't know them," Lucy said, handing the photo back to me.

I said, "They look people of your age."

"Yes, they do." She found it unremarkable. "Do you want me to repack this box?"

"Yes, please. But leave out the chocolate box."

"OK."

Lunch came and we ate. Ziggy phoned the hotel from Norway.

"I cannot reach O'Hara's number," he complained.

"He's gone back to L.A.," I said. "How are the horses?"

"Working well."

"Good. The production department has found a disused stable yard for them to stay in, only ten miles from our beach." I fished a piece of paper out of an inner pocket and spelled the address for him patiently, letter by letter. "Phone me after you've landed at Immingham on Monday if you have any problems."

"Yes, Thomas."

"Well done, Ziggy."

He laughed, pleased, and departed.

I left Nash and Lucy drinking coffee and, taking with me both the Gang photo and the lower file from the previous night's reading, went along to O'Hara's suite, let myself in with his key, and stowed Valentine's mementos in the safe, with the knives. All the rooms in the hotel were equipped with individual small safes, which each guest could set to open to his own choice of combination. I hardly liked to acknowledge the instinct for extra security that led me to use O'Hara's safe instead of my own, but anyway, I did it.

Still in O'Hara's rooms I looked up the number of Ridley Wells in the local phone directory, and tried it, but there was no answer.

On returning to my own rooms I found Nash, on the point of leaving, announcing that he was going to spend the afternoon watching racing on TV while betting by phone with a bookmaker I'd arranged for him.

"Is it still on, for tonight?" he asked, pausing in the doorway.

"Certainly is, if the rain stops, which it is supposed to."

"How do you expect me to ride a horse in the goddam dark?"

"There will be moonlight. Moncrieff's arranging it."

"What about goddam rabbit holes?"

"There aren't any on Newmarket's gallops," I assured him.

"But what if I fall *off?*"

"We'll pick you up and put you back in the saddle."

"I hate you sometimes, Thomas." He grinned and went on his way. I left Lucy up to her elbows in decades of form books, collected my minders in the lobby, and was driven the short mile back to the stables.

On my way back to the Athenaeum I detoured into the downstairs office, used chiefly by Ed, where we had the business paraphernalia of telephones, faxes, and large-capacity copier, and asked the young woman operating everything there to keep on trying Ridley Wells's number for me, and if he returned home and answered the summons, to put the call through to me upstairs immediately.

"But you said never to do that, in case the phone rang during a shot."

"We can reshoot," I said. "I want to catch this man. OK?"

She nodded, reassured, and I went upstairs to recoax Cibber and Silva into their most venomous faces.

Ridley Wells answered his telephone at three-thirty, and sounded drunk.

I said, "Do you remember you asked our producer, O'Hara, if we had any riding work for you in our film?"

"He said you hadn't."

"Right. But now we have. Are you still interested?" I mentioned a fee for a morning's work large enough to hook a bigger fish than Ridley, and he didn't even ask what the job entailed.

I said, "We'll send a car for you tomorrow morning at seven. It will bring you to the stables where we're keeping our horses. You don't need to bring anything with you. We'll supply you with clothes from our wardrobe department. We'll supply the horse for you to ride. We don't want you to do anything out of the ordinary or dangerous on the horse. We're just short of a rider for a scene we're shooting tomorrow."

"Got you," he said grandly.

"Don't forget," I insisted.

"Mum's the word, old boy."

"No," I said. "Mum's *not* the word. If you're not sober in the morning, then no job and no fee."

After a pause he said, "Got you," again, and I hoped he meant it.

When we'd finished the close-ups and the day's work was safely on its way to London for processing, I ran the previous day's rushes in the screening room, happy for Bill Robinson's sake that he and his monster bike positively quivered with shining power, filling Nash's character with the determination he needed if he were to take action.

From fantasy, courage, I thought. I wanted the film to assert that old idea, but without ramming it down anyone's throat. I wanted people to see that they had always known it. To open doors . . . A door-opener; that was my function.

It stopped raining more or less at the time forecast—miraculous—and Moncrieff busied himself in the stable yard supervising the loading of cameras, films, lights, and crews onto trucks for the "moonlit" shots of Nash on the Heath.

Nash arrived to the minute, no surprise, and came out of the house half an hour later in riding clothes and nighttime make-up, carrying his helmet and demanding a thoroughly tranquilized mount.

"If your fans could only hear you!" I remarked dryly.

"You, Thomas," he said, smiling, "can go try 6G in a brake turn at low level."

I shook my head. Nash could fly fast jet aircraft—when not under a restrictive contract in mid-film—and I couldn't. Nash's pre–mega-star hair-raising C.V. included air force service in fighters, all part of his mystique.

"The scene comes a night or two before the motorbikes," I said. "You have been accused. You are worried. OK?"

He nodded. The screenplay had included the night-on-the-horse scene from the beginning, and he was prepared.

We drove the camera truck slowly up the road by the hill, Nash in the saddle beside us (the horse in dim "moonlight") looking worried and thoughtful. We then filmed him sitting on the ground with his back to a wind-bent tree, the horse cropping grass nearby. We'd more or less finished when the thick clouds unexpectedly parted and blew in dramatic shapes across the real full moon, and Moncrieff turned his camera heavenward for more than sixty seconds, and beamed at me triumphantly through his straggly beard.

The long day ended. Back at Bedford Lodge, I found three more boxes itemized, plus a note from Lucy saying she hoped I didn't mind but her parents wanted her home for Sunday after all. Back Monday, she wrote.

Box VIII.    Form books, Flat racing.
Box IX.      Horseshoes.
Box X.       Encyclopedias, A–F.

The horseshoes were actual horseshoes, each saved in a plastic bag and labeled with the name of the horse that had worn it, complete with winning date, racecourse, and event. Valentine had been a true collector, squirreling his successes away.

I pulled out the first of the encyclopedias without anything particular in mind and, finding a slip of paper in it acting as a bookmark, opened it there. *Autocrat:* an absolute ruler. Multiple examples followed.

I closed the book, rested my head against the back of my armchair, decided it was time to take off the Delta-cast, and drifted toward sleep.

The thought that galvanized me to full wakefulness seemed to come from nowhere but was a word seen peripherally, unconsidered.

*Autocrat . . .*

Further down the page came *Auto-eroticism.*

I picked the volume out of the box and read the long entry. I learned much more than I wanted to about various forms of masturbation, though I could find nothing of much significance. Vaguely disappointed I started to replace the bookmarker, but glanced at it and kept it in my hand. Valentine's bookmarker bore the one word "Paraphilia."

I didn't know what paraphilia was, but I searched through several unopened boxes and finally found the P volume of the encyclopedia, following where Valentine had directed.

The P volume also had a bookmark, this time in the page for paraphilia.

*Paraphilia,* I read, consisted of many manifestations of perverted love. One of them was listed as "erotic strangulation—the starvation of blood to the brain to stimulate sexual arousal."

Valentine's knowledge of self-asphyxia, the process he had described to Professor Derry, had come from this book.

"In 1791 in London," I read, "in the time of Haydn, a well-known musician died as a result of his leaning toward paraphilia. One Friday afternoon he engaged a prostitute to tie a leash round his neck which he could then tighten to the point of his satisfaction. Unfortunately he went too far and throttled himself. The prostitute reported his death and was tried for murder, but acquitted, as the musician's perversion was well known. The judge ordered the records of the case not to be published, in the interests of decency."

One lived and learned, I thought tolerantly, putting the encyclopedia back in its box. Poor old Professor Derry. Just as well, perhaps, that he hadn't acted on Valentine's information.

Before throwing them both away I glanced at Valentine's second bookmark. On the strip of white paper he'd written, "Tell Derry this" and, lower down, "Showed this to Pig."

I went along to O'Hara's room, retrieved the folder and the gang photograph from the safe, and sat in his armchair looking at them and thinking long and hard.

Eventually, I slept in his bed, as it was safer.

# 15

The film company's car brought Ridley Wells to the stables on time and sober the next morning. We sent him into the house to the wardrobe department, and I took the opportunity to telephone Robbie Gill on my mobile.

I expected to get his message service at that early hour, but in fact he was awake and answered my summons himself.

"Still alive?" he asked chattily.

"Yes, thank you."

"So what do you need?"

As always with Robbie, straight to the point.

"First," I said, "who gave you the list of knife specialists?"

"My professional colleague in the police force," he said promptly. "The doctor they call out locally. He's a randy joker, ex-rugger, good for a laugh and a jar in the pub. I asked him for known knife specialists. He said the force had drawn up the list themselves recently and asked him if he could add to it. He couldn't. The people he knows who carry knives tend to be behind bars."

"Did he attend Dorothea?"

"No, he was away. Anything else?"

"How is she?"

"Dorothea? Still sedated. Now Paul's gone, do you still want to pay for the nursing home?"

"Yes, I do, and I want to see her soon, like this afternoon."

"No problem. Just go. She's still in a side ward because of Paul, but physically she's healing well. We could move her by Tuesday, I should think."

"Good," I said.

"Take care."

I said wryly, "I do."

In the stable yard the lads were readying for morning exercise, saddling and bridling the horses. As it was Sunday, I told them, we would again have the Heath gallops more or less to ourselves, but we wouldn't be filming exactly the same scenes as the week before.

"You were all asked to wear what you did last Sunday," I said. "Did you all check with our continuity girl if you couldn't remember?"

I got nods.

"Fine. Then all of you will canter up the hill and stop where you stopped and circled last week. OK?"

More nods.

"You remember the rider who came from nowhere and made a slash at Ivan?"

They laughed. They wouldn't forget it.

"Right," I said. "Today we don't have Ivan, but we're going to stage that attack ourselves, and put it into the film. Today it will be a fictional affair. OK? The knife used will not be a real knife but one that's been made out of wood by our production department. What I want you to do is exactly the sort of thing you were doing last Sunday—circling, talking, paying not much attention to the stranger. Right?"

They understood without trouble. Our young horsemaster said, "Who is going to stand in for Ivan?"

"I am," I said. "I'm not as broadshouldered as him or as Nash, but I'll be wearing a jacket like the one Nash usually wears as the trainer. I'll be riding the horse Ivan rode. When we're ready with the cameras, the man playing the knife attacker will mount and ride that slow old bay that finished last in our race at Huntingdon. The lad who usually rides him will be standing behind the cameras, out of shot. Any questions?"

One asked, "Are you going to chase him down the hill on the camera truck, like last week?"

"No," I said. "He will gallop off down the hill. The camera will film him."

I handed over command, so to speak, to the horsemaster, who organized the mounting and departure of the string. Ed and Moncrieff were already on the Heath. I went into the wardrobe section to put on Nash's jacket and, Ridley being ready, took him with me in my car up the road to the brow of the hill. Ridley and I, out of the car, walked over to the circling horses, stopping by the camera truck.

"What we need," I told Ridley, "is for you to ride into the group from somewhere over there . . ." I pointed. "Trot into the group, draw a make-believe knife from a sheath on your belt, slash at one of the group as if you intended to wound him badly, and then, in the ensuing melee, canter off over the brow of the hill and down the wide training ground toward the town. OK?"

Ridley stared, his eyes darkly intense.

"You will slash at *me,* OK? I'm standing in for Nash."

Ridley said nothing.

"Of course," I told him pleasantly, "when this scene appears in the finished film it will not look like one smooth sequence. There will be flashes of the knife, of horses rearing, of jumbled movement and confusion. There will be a wound. There will be blood. We will fake those later." Ed brought various props across to where I stood with Ridley, and handed them to him one by one.

"Make-believe knife in sheath on belt," Ed said, as if reading from a list. "Please put on the belt."

As if mesmerized, Ridley obeyed.

"Please practice drawing the knife," I said.

Ridley drew the knife and looked at it in horror. The production department had faithfully reproduced the American trench knife from my drawing, and although the object Ridley held was light-weight and of painted wood, from three paces it looked like a heavy knuckle-duster with a long blade attached to its index finger side.

"Fine," I said noncommittally. "Put it back in its sheath."

Ridley fumbled the knife back into place.

"Helmet," Ed said, holding it out.

Ridley buckled on the helmet.

"Goggles," Ed offered.

Ridley put them on slowly.

"Gloves."

Ridley hesitated.

"Anything the matter?" I asked.

Ridley said "no" hoarsely, and accepted a leg-up onto our slowest nag.

"Great," I said. "Off you go, then. When Ed yells 'action,' just trot straight toward me, draw the knife, take a slash, and canter away fast toward New-market. Do you want a rehearsal, or do you think you can get it right first time?"

The helmeted, begoggled, gloved figure didn't respond.

"We'll take a bet you can get it right," I said.

Ridley seemed incapable of action. I asked the lad whose horse he was riding to lead him over to the starting point, and then let go and clear the shot. While the lad intelligently followed the instruction, the lad on Nash's horse dismounted and gave me a leg-up. The cracked rib tugged sharply. I lengthened the stirrup leathers. Moncrieff opened his floodlights to bathe the scene and augment the daylight.

Ed yelled, "Action."

Ridley Wells kicked his horse into a canter, not a trot. He tugged the knife free with his right hand while holding the reins with his left. He steered his mount with his legs, expert that he was, and he aimed himself straight at me, as murderously intent as one could have hoped.

The "knife" hit my coat and the carapace beneath and because the imitation blade had no slicing power, the impact knocked the weapon flying out of Ridley's grasp.

"I dropped it," he shouted, and I pointed to the brow of the hill and yelled at him, "Never mind. Gallop."

He galloped. He sat down low in the saddle and galloped as if it were a genuine escape.

The lads on their horses crowded to the top of the hill to watch, just as before, and this time I went after the fugitive on a horse, not in a truck.

The truck was being driven down the road, camera whirring. The sequence I finally cut together for the film showed "Nash" closely chasing his assailant; Nash with a deep bleeding wound; Nash losing his quarry, blood dripping everywhere; Nash in pain.

"*Lovely stuff,*" O'Hara breathed when he saw it. "*God,* Thomas . . ."

On this Sunday morning, however, there was no blood. I had much the faster horse and I caught up with Ridley before he could vanish into Newmarket's streets.

He reined furiously to a halt. He tore off the gloves, the goggles, and the helmet and threw them on the ground. He struggled out of the anorak we'd dressed him in and flung it away from him.

"I'll *kill* you," he said.

I said, "I'll send your fee."

His bloated face wavered with irresolution as if he couldn't decide whether or not to attack me there and then, but sense or cowardice prevailed, and he dismounted in a practiced slide, facing me, right foot lifting over the horse's neck. He let go of the reins. He turned his back on me and walked off unsteadily in the direction of Newmarket, as if he couldn't feel his feet on the ground.

I leaned forward, picked up the dangling reins, and walked both horses back to the stables.

The lads came back from the hill chattering like starlings, wide-eyed.

"That man looked just the same!" "He was the same!" "He looked like that man last week!" "Didn't he look just like the same man?"

"Yes," I said.

FROM THE WARDROBE department, where I shed Nash's coat and helmet, I paid a brief visit upstairs to where the production people were stacking the Athenaeum scenery to one side and filling the space instead with a reproduction of any horse's stall in the stable yard.

As a real natural stall was far too small for camera, crew, lights, and technicians, let alone a couple of actors, we were fabricating our own version. It was as if a stall had been divided into thirds, then spread apart, leaving a large center area for camera maneuvering. One third had the split door to the outer world (back projection of the stable yard), one portion contained a manger and water bucket. One, the largest, encompassed the place where a horse would normally stand.

The walls of the stall were being constructed of actual whitewashed breeze blocks with an open ceiling of heavy rafters. Bales of hay, at present neatly stacked, would be placed on a platform on the rafters above the action. A floor of concrete sections, covered with straw, was being slotted into each setting. Artistic hoof marks and other signs of wear and habitation showed that this was a stall often in use.

"How's it going?" I asked, looking round with approval.

"Ready in the morning," they assured me. "It'll be as solid as a rock, like you asked."

"Great."

DOROTHEA'S CHEEKS WERE faintly pink; a great advance.

We had a few tears on my arrival, but not the racking distress of two days earlier. As her physical state had grown stronger, so had her strength of mind resurfaced. She thanked me for the flowers I'd brought her and said she was sick of a diet of tomato soup.

"They say it's good for me but I'm growing to hate it. It's true I can't eat meat and salad—have you ever endured a hospital salad?—but why not *mushroom* or *chicken* soup?—and none of it's homemade, of course."

She was longing, she said, to go to the nursing home dear Robbie Gill had suggested, and she hoped her daughter-in-law, Janet, would soon return home to Surrey.

"We don't like each other," Dorothea confessed, sighing. "Such a pity."

"Mm," I agreed. "When you're well, will you go back to your house?"

Tears quivered in her eyes. "Paul died there."

Valentine also, I thought.

"Thomas . . . I've been remembering things." She sounded almost anxious. "That night when I was attacked . . ."

"Yes?" I prompted, as she stopped. "What do you remember?"

"Paul was shouting."

"Yes, you told me."

"There was another man there."

I drew the visitor's chair to beside her bed and sat peacefully holding her hand, not wanting to alarm her and smothering my own urgent thoughts.

I said gently, "Do you remember what he looked like?"

"I didn't know him. He was there with Paul when I got home from Mona's house . . . I'd been watching television with her, you see, but we didn't like the program and I went home early . . . and I went in by the kitchen door as usual and I was so surprised and, well—*pleased,* of course—to see Paul, but he was so *strange,* dear, and almost *frightened,* but he couldn't have been frightened. Why should he have been frightened?"

"Perhaps because you'd come home while he and the other man were ransacking your house."

"Well, dear, Paul shouted . . . where was Valentine's photo album, and I'm sure I said he didn't have one, he just kept a few old snaps in a chocolate box, the same as I did, and Paul wouldn't believe me, he kept going on about an album."

"So," I said, "did Valentine ever have an album?"

"No, dear, I'm sure he didn't. We were never a great family for photos, not like some people who don't believe a thing's happened unless they take snaps of it. Valentine has dozens of pictures of horses, but it was horses, you see, dear, that were his life. Always horses. He never had any children, his Cathy *couldn't,* you see. He might have been keener on photos if he'd had children. I keep quite a lot of photos in a box in my bedroom. Photos of us all, long ago. Pictures of Paul . . ."

Tears came again, and I didn't tell her I hadn't been able to find those pathetically few mementos in her bedroom. I would give her Valentine's chocolate box instead.

"Did Paul say why he wanted the photo album?" I asked.

"I don't think so, dear. Everything was happening so fast and the other man was so *angry,* and shouting too, and Paul said to me—so *frightening,* dear, but he said, 'Tell him where the album is, he's got a knife.' "

I asked quietly, "Are you sure about that?"

"I believed it was a dream."

"And now?"

"Well, now . . . I think he must have said it. I can hear my Paul's voice . . . oh dear . . . oh my darling little boy."

I hugged her while she sobbed.

"That other man *hit* me," she said, gulping. "Hit my head . . . and Paul was shouting, 'Tell him, tell him,' and I saw . . . he really did have a knife, that man . . . or at least he was holding something shiny, but it wasn't a real knife, he had his fingers through it . . . dirty fingernails . . . it was horrid . . . and Paul was shouting, 'Stop it . . . *don't* . . .' and I woke up in the hospital and I didn't know what had happened, but last night . . . well, dear, when I was waking up this morning and thinking about Paul, well, I sort of *remembered."*

"Yes," I said. I paused, consolidating earlier impressions. "Dearest Dorothea," I said. "I think Paul saved your life."

"Oh! Oh!" She was still crying, but after a while it was from radiant joy, not grinding regret.

"I think," I said, "that Paul was so horrified by seeing you attacked with that knife, that he prevented a fatal blow. Robbie Gill thought that the attack on you looked like an *interrupted* murder. He said that people who inflicted such awful knife wounds were usually in a frenzy, and simply couldn't stop. I think Paul stopped him."

"Oh, *Thomas!"*

"But I'm afraid," I said regretfully, "that it means that Paul knew the man who attacked you, and he didn't identify him to the police. In fact, Paul pretended he was in Surrey when you were attacked."

"Oh dear."

"And," I said, "Paul tried hard to prevent you from talking to me or to Robbie, or anyone else, until he was sure you remembered nothing about the attack."

Dorothea's joy faded somewhat but, underneath, remained.

"He changed a bit," I said. "I think at one point he almost told me something, but I don't know what. I do believe, though, that he was feeling remorse over what had happened to you."

"Oh, Thomas, I do hope so."

"I'm sure of it," I said, more positively than I felt.

She thought things over quietly for a while and then said, "Paul would burst out sometimes with opinions as if he couldn't hold them in any more."

"Did he?"

"He said . . . I didn't like to tell you, Thomas, but the other day—when he was here with me—he burst out with, *Why* did you ever have to make your film? He was *bitter.* He said I would never have been attacked if you hadn't stirred everything up. Of course I asked *what* you had stirred up and he said it was all in the *Drumbeat,* but I was to forget what he'd said, only if anything happened to you it would be your own fault. He said . . . I'm really sorry . . . but he said he would be pleased if you were cut to ribbons like me . . . It wasn't like him, really it wasn't."

"I did bolt him out of your house," I reminded her. "He didn't like me much for embarrassing him."

"No, but . . . well, something was *worrying* him, I'm sure of it."

I stood up and wandered over to the window, looking out aimlessly at the institutionally regular pattern of the windows in the building opposite and the scrubby patch of garden between. Two people in white coats walked slowly along a path, conversing. Extras playing doctors, I thought automatically—and realized I often saw even real life in terms of film.

I turned and asked Dorothea, "While you've been here in the hospital, did Paul ask you about a photo album?"

"I don't think so, dear. Everything gets so muddled, though." She paused. "He said something about you having taken Valentine's books away, and I didn't tell him you hadn't. I didn't want to argue, you see, dear. I felt too tired."

I told her I'd found a photo among Valentine's possessions—which I had retrieved from her nice young friend, Bill Robinson—but I couldn't see that it was worth the damage to her house or to herself.

"If I show it to you," I said, "will you tell me who the people are?"

"Of course, dear, if I can."

I took the Gang photo out of my pocket and put it into her hand.

"I need my reading glasses," she said, peering at it. "That red case on the bedside table."

I gave her her glasses and she looked without much reaction at the picture.

"Did one of those people attack you?" I asked.

"Oh no, none of those. He was much older. All these people are so young. Why!" she exclaimed. "That's Paul! That one at the end, isn't that Paul? How young he was! So handsome, then." She let the hand holding the photo rest on the sheet. "I don't know any of the others. I wish Paul was here."

Sighing, I took back the photo, replaced it in my pocket, and produced the small memo pad I habitually carried.

I said, "I don't want to upset you, but if I draw a knife will you tell me if it's the one that might have been used on you?"

"I don't want to see it."

"Please, Dorothea."

"Paul was killed with a knife," she wailed and cried for her son.

"Dearest Dorothea," I said after a while. "If it will help to find Paul's killer, will you look at my drawing?"

She shook her head. I put the drawing close to her hand and, after a long minute, she picked it up.

"How *horrid,*" she said, looking at it, "I didn't see a knife like that." She sounded extremely relieved. "It wasn't anything like that."

I'd drawn for her the American trench knife from the Heath. I turned the paper over and drew the wicked Armadillo, serrated edge and all.

Dorothea looked at it, went white, and didn't speak.

"I'm so sorry," I said helplessly. "But you didn't die. Paul loved you . . . He saved your life."

I thought of the cataclysmic shock in Paul's face when he'd come to Dorothea's house and seen the Armadillo lying on the kitchen table. When he'd seen me sitting there, *alive.*

He'd blundered out of the house and gone away, and it was pointless now to speculate that if we'd stopped him, if we'd sat him down and made him talk, he might have lived. Paul had been near, once, to breaking open. Paul, I thought, had become a fragile danger, likely to crumble, likely to confess. Paul, overbearing, pompous, unlikable, had lost his nerve and died of repentance.

MY DRIVER, WITH the black belt beside him, aimed my car toward Oxfordshire while consulting from time to time my written directions, and I sat in the back seat looking again at the Gang photo and remembering what both Dorothea and Lucy had said about it.

"They're so *young.*"

Young.

Jackson Wells, Ridley Wells, Paul Pannier, were all at least twenty-six years younger in the photo than the living men I'd met. Sonia had died twenty-six years earlier, and Sonia was alive in the picture.

Say the photo had been taken twenty-*seven* years ago—that made Jackson Wells about twenty-three, with all the others younger than that. Eighteen, nineteen, twenty: that sort of age. Sonia had died at twenty-one.

I had been four when she died and I hadn't heard of her, and I'd come back at thirty and wanted to know *why* she had died, and I had said I might try and find out, and in saying that I'd set off a chain reaction that had put Dorothea into hospital and Paul into his grave and had earned me a knife in the ribs . . . and whatever else might come.

I hadn't known there was a genie in the bottle, but genies once let out couldn't be put back.

My driver found Batwillow Farm and delivered me to Jackson Wells's door.

Lucy again answered the summons of the overloud bell, her blue eyes widening with astonishment.

"I say," she said, "you didn't mind my coming home for the day, did you? You haven't come to drag me back by my ponytail?"

"No," I smiled. "I really wanted to talk to your father."

"Oh, sure. Come in."

I shook my head. "I wonder if he would come out?"

"Oh? Well, I'll ask him." Faintly puzzled, she disappeared into the house, to return soon with her blond, lean, farm-tanned enquiring parent looking exactly as he had looked there one week earlier.

"Come in," he said, gesturing a welcome, happy-go-lucky.

"Come for a walk."

He shrugged. "If you like." He stepped out of his house and Lucy, unsure of herself, remained in the doorway.

Jackson eyed the two agile men sitting in my car and asked, "Friends?"

"A driver and a bodyguard," I answered. "Film company issue."

"Oh."

We crossed from the house and came to rest by the five-barred gate on which deaf old Wells senior had been leaning the week before.

"Lucy's doing a good job," I said. "Did she tell you?"

"She likes talking to Nash Rourke."

"They get on fine," I agreed.

"I told her to be careful."

I smiled. "You've taught her well." Too well, I thought. I said, "Did she mention a photograph?"

He looked as if he didn't know whether to say yes or no, but in the end said, "What photograph?"

"This one." I brought it out of my pocket and gave it to him.

He looked at the front briefly and at the back, and met my eyes expressionlessly.

"Lucy says that's your handwriting," I commented, taking the picture back.

"What if it is?"

"I'm not the police," I said, "and I haven't brought thumbscrews."

He laughed, but the totally carefree manner of a week earlier had been un-
dermined by wariness.

I said, "Last week you told me no one knew why Sonia had died."

"That's right." The blue eyes shone, as ever, with innocence.

I shook my head. "Everyone in that photo," I said, "knew why Sonia died."

His utter stillness lasted until he'd manufactured a smile and a suitably
scornful expression.

"Sonia is in that photo; what you said is codswollop."

"Sonia knew," I said.

"Are you saying she killed herself?" He looked almost hopeful, as well he
might.

"Not really. She didn't intend to die. No one intended to kill her. She died
by accident."

"You know bloody nothing about it."

I knew too much about it. I didn't want to do any more harm, and I didn't
want to get myself killed, but Paul Pannier's death couldn't simply be ignored; and apart from considerations of justice, until his murderer had been
caught I would be wearing Delta-cast.

"You all look so young in that photo," I said. "Golden girl, golden boys, all
smiling, all with bright lives ahead. You were all kids then, like you told me.
All playing at living, everything a game." I named the light-hearted gang in
the photo. "There's you and Sonia, and your younger brother, Ridley. There's
Paul Pannier, your blacksmith's nephew. There's Roddy Visborough, the son
of Sonia's sister, which made Sonia actually his aunt. And there's your jockey,
P. Falmouth, known as Pig." I paused. "You were the eldest, twenty-two or
twenty-three. Ridley, Paul, Roddy, and Pig were all eighteen, nineteen, or
twenty when Sonia died, and she was only twenty-one."

Jackson Wells said blankly, "How do you know?"

"Newspaper reports. Doing sums. It hardly matters. What does matter is the
immaturity of you all . . . and the feeling some people have at that age that
youth is eternal, caution is for oldies, and responsibility a dirty word. You went
off to York and the others played a game . . . and I think this whole gang, except you, were there when she died."

"No," he said sharply. "It wasn't a gang thing. You're meaning gang rape.
That didn't happen."

"I know it didn't. The autopsy made it quite clear that there'd been no in-
tercourse. The newspapers all pointed it out."

"Well, then."

I said carefully, "I think one of those boys in some way throttled her, not meaning to do her harm, and they were all so frightened that they tried to make it look like suicide, by hanging her. And then they just—ran away."

"No," Jackson said numbly.

"I think," I said, "that to begin with you truly didn't know what had happened. When you talked to the police, when they tried to get you to confess, you could deal blithely with their questions because you knew you weren't guilty. You truly didn't know at that point whether or not she'd hanged herself, though you knew—and said—that it wasn't like her. I think that for quite a while it was a true mystery to you, but what is also evident is that you weren't psychologically pulverized by it. None of the newspaper reports—and I've now read a lot of them—not one says anything about a *distraught* young husband."

"Well . . . I . . ."

"By then," I suggested, "you knew she had lovers. Not dream lovers. Real ones. The Gang. All casual. A joke. A game. I'd guess she never thought the sex act more than a passing delight, like ice cream, and there are plenty of people like that, though it's not them but the intense and the jealous that sell the tabloids. When Sonia died, your playing-at-marriage was already over. You told me so. You might have felt shock and regret at her death, but you were young and healthy and blessed with a resilient nature, and your grief was short."

"You can't possibly know."

"Am I right so far?"

"Well . . ."

"Tell me what happened afterward," I said. "If you tell me, I promise not to put anything you say in the film. I'll keep the fictional story well away. But it would be better if I knew the truth because, like I told you before, I might reveal your innermost secrets simply by guessing. So tell me . . . and you won't find what you're afraid of on the screen."

Jackson Wells surveyed his creeper-covered house and his untidy drive and yard, and no doubt thought of his pleasant existence with his new wife and of his pride in Lucy.

"You're right." He sighed heavily. "They were all there, and I didn't find out for weeks."

I let time pass. He had taken the first great step; the rest would follow.

"Weeks afterward, they began to unravel," he said at length. "They'd sworn to each other they would never say a word. Never. But it got too much for them. Pig pissed off to Australia and left me with only Derek Carsington to ride my nags; not that it mattered much, the owners were leaving as if I had the pox, and then Ridley . . ." He paused. "Ridley got drunk, which wasn't a rarity even in those days, and spilled his guts from every possible orifice . . . Ridley *disgusts* me but Lucy still thinks he's a laugh, which won't last much longer as he'd have his hand up her skirt by now except that I've told her always to wear jeans, no fun being a girl these days, not like Sonia, she loved skirts down to her ankles and no bra most of the time and a green crewcut— and why the *hell* am I telling you this?"

I thought he might be mourning Sonia twenty-six years too late; but maybe nothing was ever too late in that way.

"She was *fun,*" he said. "Always good for a laugh."

"Yes."

"Ridley told me what they'd done." The pain of the revelation showed sharply in the sunny face. "I as good as killed him. I thrashed him. Hit him. Beat him with a riding whip. Anything I could lay my hands on. I kicked him unconscious."

"That was grief," I said.

"Anger."

"Same thing."

Jackson stared unseeingly at time past.

"I went to see Valentine to ask him what to do," he said. "Valentine was like a father to all of us. A better father than any of us had. Valentine loved Sonia like a daughter."

I said nothing. The way Valentine had loved Sonia had had nothing to do with fatherhood.

"What did Valentine say?" I asked.

"He already knew! He said Paul had told him. Paul was in pieces, like Ridley. Paul had told his uncle everything. Valentine said they could all either live with what they'd done or go to the police . . . and he wouldn't choose for them."

"Did Valentine know that Roddy Visborough had been there?"

"I told him," Jackson said frankly. "Sonia was Roddy's *aunt*. And whatever sort of sex orgy they'd all been planning—I mean, of course, it was nothing like that, forget I said it—Roddy couldn't be dragged in, they said it was impossible. She was his aunt!"

"You all knew Valentine well," I said.

"Yes, of course. His old smithy was only just down the road from my yard. He was always in and out with the horses and we'd drop in there at his house, all of us. Like I said, he was a sort of father. Better than a father. But everything broke up. Training died on me, and Paul left Newmarket and moved away with his mother and father, and Roddy went off to go on the show-jumping circuit . . . he'd been wanting to be an assistant racehorse trainer only he hadn't yet got a job, and Pig, like I said, he'd already gone off. And then Valentine was moving too. The old smithy needed impossible roof repairs, so he had it torn down and sold the land for building. I was there one day when he was watching the builders throw the junk of a lifetime down to fill up an old well that he had in the back there, that was a danger to children, and I said things were never going to be the same again. And of course they weren't."

"But they turned out all right for you."

"Well, yes, they did." He couldn't repress his grin for long. "And Valentine became the Grand Old Man of racing, and Roddy Visborough's won enough silver cups for an avalanche. Ridley's still bumming about and I help him out from time to time, and Paul got married . . ." He stopped uncertainly.

"And Paul got killed," I said baldly.

He was silent.

"Do you know who killed him?" I asked.

"No." He stared. "Do you?"

I didn't answer directly. I said, "Did any of them tell Valentine—or you—which of the four of them throttled Sonia?"

"It was an accident."

"Whose accident?"

"She was going to let them put their hands round her neck. She was laughing, they all agreed about that. They were sort of high, but not on drugs."

"On excitement," I said.

His blue eyes widened. "They were all going to . . . that's what broke them up . . . they were all going to have a turn with her, and she wanted it . . . she bet they couldn't all manage it, not like that when the lads had all ridden out for second morning exercise, not before they came back again in an hour, and not with all of the gang watching and cheering each other on, and not in a stall on hay as a bed . . . and they were all crazy, and so was she . . . and Pig put his hands round her neck and kissed her . . . and squeezed . . . and she choked . . . he went on too long . . . and she went dark . . . her skin went dark, and by the time they realized . . . they couldn't bring her back . . ." His voice died, and after a while he said, "You're not surprised, are you?"

"I won't put it in the film."

"I was so *angry,*" he said. "How *could* they? How could she let them? It wasn't drugs . . ."

"Do you realize," I asked, "that it's almost always men who die in that sort of asphyxia?"

"Oh God . . . They wanted to see if it worked the same for women."

The total foolishness of it blankly silenced us both.

I took a breath. I said, "The *Drumbeat* said I couldn't solve Sonia's death, and I have. So now I'll find out who killed Paul Pannier."

He pushed himself away from the gate explosively, shouting back at me, *"How?* Leave it alone. Leave all of us alone. Don't make this pissing film."

His raised voice brought my judo keeper out of the car like an uncoiling eel. Jackson looked both surprised and alarmed, even as I made soothing hand gestures to calm my minder's reflexes.

I said to Jackson, "My bodyguard's like a growling dog. Pay no attention. The film company insists on him because others besides you want this movie stopped."

"That bitch Audrey, Sonia's sneering sister, I bet *she* does, for one."

"She above all," I agreed.

Lucy reappeared at the front door and called to her father, "Dad, Uncle Ridley's on the phone."

"Tell him I'll come in a minute."

I said, as she dematerialized, "Your brother rode on the Heath this morning, for the film. He won't be pleased with me."

"Why not?"

"He'll tell you."

"I wish you'd never come," he said bitterly and strode off toward his house, his safe haven, his two normal nice women.

I spent the journey back to Newmarket knowing I'd been rash, but not really regretting it. I might think I knew who'd killed Paul, but proving it was different. The police would have to prove it, but I could at least direct their gaze.

I thought of one particular newspaper clipping that I'd found in the file now resting in O'Hara's safe.

Valentine had written it for his occasional gossip column. The paper was dated six weeks after Sonia's death, and didn't mention her.

It said:

Newmarket sources tell me that the jockey P.G. Falmouth (19), familiarly known as "Pig," has gone to Australia, and is seeking a work-permit to ride there, hoping to settle. Born and raised near the town of his name in Cornwall, Pig Falmouth moved to Newmarket two years ago, where his attractive personality and dedication to winning soon earned him many friends. Undoubtedly he would have prospered in England as his experience increased, but we wish him great success in his new venture overseas.

This item was accompanied by a smiling picture of a fresh-faced good-looking young man in jockey's helmet and colors; but it was the headline of the section that had been for me the drench of ice-cold understanding.

"Exit," it said, "of the Cornish boy."

# 16

We filmed the hanging scene the following morning, Monday, in the cut-and-separated stable stall upstairs in the house.

Moncrieff flung a rope over the rafters and swung on it himself to test the set's robustness, but owing to the solid breeze blocks and huge metal angle-iron braces anchoring the new walls to the old floor, there wasn't the slightest quiver in the scenery, to the audible relief of the production department. The straw-covered concrete in the set sections deadened all hollow give-away underfoot echoing noises, those reality-destroying clatterings across the floors of many a supposedly well-built Hollywood "mansion."

"Where did you get to after our very brief meeting last night?" Moncrieff enquired. "Howard was looking all over the hotel for you."

"Was he?"

"Your car brought you back, you ate a room-service sandwich while we discussed today's work, and then you vanished."

"Did I? . . . Well, I'm here now."

"I told Howard you would be sure to be here this morning."

"Thanks so much."

Moncrieff grinned. "Howard was *anxious.*"

"Mm. Did the Yvonne girl get here?"

"Down in make-up," Moncrieff nodded lasciviously. "And is she a *dish.*"

"Long blond hair?"

He nodded. "The wig you ordered. Where did you get to, in fact?"

"Around," I said vaguely. I'd slipped my minder and walked a roundabout way, via the Heath, to the stables, booking in with the guard on the house door and telling him I wanted to work undisturbed, and, if anyone asked, to say I wasn't there.

"Sure thing, Mr. Lyon," he promised, used to my vagaries, so I'd gone privately into the downstairs office and phoned Robbie Gill.

"Sorry to bother you on Sunday evening," I apologized.

"I was only watching the TV. How can I help?"

I said, "Is Dorothea well enough to be moved tomorrow instead of Tuesday?"

"Did you see her today? What did you think?"

"She's longing to go to the nursing home, she said, and a lot of her toughness of spirit is back. But medically . . . could she go?"

"Hm . . ."

"She's remembered a good deal more about being stabbed," I said. "She saw the attacker's face, but she doesn't know him. She also saw the knife that cut her."

"*God,*" Robbie exclaimed. "That knuckle-duster thing?"

"No. It was the one that ended in me."

"*Christ.*"

"So, move her tomorrow if you can. Give her a false name in the nursing home. She's at risk."

"Bloody hell."

"She remembers that Paul interrupted the attack on her and effectively saved her life. It's comforting her. She's amazing. She's had three terrible things happen, but she'll be all right, I think."

"Spunky old woman. Don't worry, I'll shift her."

"Great." I paused. "You remember the police took our fingerprints to match them with the prints in Dorothea's house?"

"Of course I do. They took Dorothea's and her friend Betty's and her husband's and worked out Valentine's from his razor."

"And," I said, "there were others they couldn't match."

"Sure. Several, I believe. I asked my police friend how their enquiries were progressing. Dead stop, I would guess."

"Mm." I said. "Some of the prints they couldn't match would have been O'Hara's, and some would have been Bill Robinson's." I explained Bill Robinson. "And there has to be another—Dorothea's attacker didn't wear gloves."

Robbie said breathlessly, "Are you sure?"

"Yes. She said she saw his hand through the knife, and he had dirty fingernails."

"Jeez."

"When he went to her house he didn't expect her to be there. He didn't plan in advance to attack her. He went to search with Paul for something Valentine might have had, and I guess they ripped the place to bits from fury and frustration that they couldn't find anything. Anyway, his prints must be all over the place."

Robbie, perplexed, asked, "Whose?"

"I'll tell you when I'm sure."

"Don't get yourself killed."

"Of course not," I said.

Yvonne came upstairs at the required time, and proved to be the regulation issue semi-anorexic California waif beloved of moguls, a culture concept a cosmos away from the real laughing reckless Sonia.

Sonia, at her death, had worn, according to the more conservative newspapers, "a rose-red satin slip," and, according to the titillators, in blackest type, "a shiny scarlet mini with shoestring shoulder straps, and black finely strapped sandals with high rhinestone heels."

No wonder, I'd thought, that suicide had been in doubt.

Yvonne of the dream lovers was wearing a loose white day dress described in American fashion circles as a "float": that is to say, it softly outlined only what it touched. She also wore, at my request, chandelier pearl and gold earrings and a long pearl necklace nearly to her waist.

She looked beautifully ethereal and spoke like Texas.

"This morning," I said, "we're shooting the scenes in the right sequence. That's to say, first you enter through that split door." I pointed. "There will be backlighting. When Moncrieff is ready, I'd like you to stand in the doorway and turn your head slowly until we say stop, then if you'll remember that position and stop your head right there for the take, we will get a dramatic effect. You will be entering but looking back. OK? I expect you know your lines."

She gave me a limpid unintelligent wide-eyed look: great for the film, not so good for technical speed while we made it.

"They say," she said, "you get mad if you have to shoot a scene more than three times. That so?"

"Absolutely so."

"Guess I'd better concentrate, then."

"Honey child," I said in her accent. "You do just that and I'll earn you talk-show spots."

"*The Today Show?*"

"Nothing's impossible."

Calculation clouded the peerless violet eyes, and she went quietly off to one side and studied her script.

Battle lines drawn, we proceeded. When Moncrieff was satisfied with his light placement, we stood Yvonne in the doorway and moved her inch by inch until the light outside the door shone through her flimsy float to reveal her body to the camera inside: too flat-chested for my interest, but of the dreamy other-world unreality I'd hoped for.

"Jeez," Moncrieff murmured, looking through his lens.

I said, "Can you put a glint on those earrings?"

"You don't ask much!"

He positioned an inkie—an inkie-dinkie, meaning a very small spotlight—to give a glitter below her ears.

"Great," I said. "Everyone ready? We'll do a rehearsal. Yvonne, don't forget you're being followed by an earthy man who is parsecs away from a dream lover. You are already laughing at him in your mind, though not openly, as he has power to make Nash's life—that's to say, your film husband's life—very difficult. Just imagine you're being followed by a man you sexually despise but can't be rude to . . ."

Yvonne giggled. "Who needs to act? I meet them every day."

"I'll bet you do," Moncrieff said under his breath.

"Right, then," I said, trying not to laugh. "We'll do a walk-through. Ready? And . . ." a pause, "Go."

Yvonne got it dead right at the second rehearsal and then we shot the scene for real twice, both times fit to print.

"You're a doll," I told her. She liked it, where Silva might have said "sexism" or "harassment." I liked women, all sorts; I'd simply discovered, as I had with male actors, that it saved time to accept, not fight, their views of themselves in the world.

In the scene, Yvonne, talking to a man out of shot, had been saying she'd promised to ready the stall for a soon-to-arrive horse, a job she'd forgotten earlier but was now doing before joining her husband at a drinks party, to be held somewhere on his way home from the races.

So silly about her white sandals, she said, on the rough flooring. Would he please help her move the stack of hay bales, since—eyelashes fluttering—he was so much *bigger* and *stronger* than little Yvonne?

"I'd lie down and die for her," Moncrieff observed.

"He more or less did."

"Such a cynic," Moncrieff told me, moving lights to a point high among the rafters.

I rehearsed Yvonne through the scene where she realized the man meant business against her wishes. We trekked through surprise, discomfort, revulsion, and, dangerously, mockery. I made sure she understood—and could personally relate to—every step.

"Most directors just yell at me," she said at one point, when she'd fluffed her lines in rehearsal for the fifth or sixth time.

"You look stunning," I said. "All you need to do is *act stunned*. Then *laugh* at him. Some men can't bear women laughing at them. He's full of lust for you, and you think he's *funny*. What you're doing is mocking him to madness. He's going to kill you."

Total comprehension lit her sweet features. "Get out the straitjacket," she said.

"Yvonne, I love you."

We took a long series of shots of her face, one emotion at a time, and many of negative messages of body language and of the growth of fright, of panic, of desperate disbelief; enough to cut together the ultimate terror of approaching unexpected death.

We gave Yvonne a rest for lunch, while Moncrieff and I filmed the crews slapping heavy ropes sharply over the rafters, and tying frightful knots, to show the violence, the speed, the lack of mercy that I wanted. Naturally each segment took many minutes to stage and get right, but later, in cinemas, with every successful impression strung together—slap, slap, slap—the horror of the hanging would strike the popcorn crunchers silent.

I sat beside Yvonne on a hay bale. I said, "This afternoon we are going to tie your wrists together with that thick rope now hanging free from that rafter."

She took it easily.

"The man has by now frightened you so much that you are almost relieved that it is your wrists he has tied."

She nodded.

"But suddenly he pulls some slack into the rope leading from the rafter, and he loops the slack round your neck, and does it a second time, and pulls the rope tight until your pearls break and slide down inside your dress, and he leans all his weight on the free end of rope swinging from the rafter, and . . . er . . . he lifts you off your feet . . . and hangs you."

Big-eyed, she said, "What do I say? Do I beg? It doesn't say this."

"You don't say anything," I said. "You scream."

"*Scream?*"

"Yes. Can you?"

She opened her mouth and screamed up a hair-raising scale, alarming everyone on set and bringing them galloping to her rescue.

She giggled.

"No one rescued Yvonne," I said regretfully, "but no one will forget that scream."

We filmed a brutal hanging, but short of the dreaded NC17 or 18 certificates. We showed no black asphyxiated face, no terrible bloating. I got Yvonne to wriggle frantically while we suspended her from the wrists, but I filmed her only from the roped neck to her feet that frantically stretched down to the out-of-reach floor. We arranged for one of her white shoes to fall off. We turned the camera onto the shoe while the shadow of her last paroxysms fell across the white-washed walls, and we filmed her broken pearls and one twisted earring in the straw with her bare jerking toes just above.

That done, I let her down and hugged her gratefully; and told her she was marvelous, ravishing, brilliant, moving, could play Ophelia in her sleep and would *undoubtedly* appear on *The Today Show* (which fortunately, later, she did).

I'd planned from the beginning to shoot the hanging separate from the murderer just in case we needed to make a radical plot re-think at a later stage. By filming murder and murderer apart, one could slot in anyone's face behind the rope. That afternoon, however, I'd invited Cibber to learn the murderer's few lines, and he arrived on set with them only vaguely in his mind, while he expansively smoked a large cigar and exercised his fruity larynx on inappropriate jokes.

He patted Yvonne's bottom. Silly old buffoon, I thought, and set about turning him into a lecherous bull.

I positioned him in the manger section, and gave him an ashtray to prevent him setting fire to the straw. We placed Yvonne so that her white dress, on the edge of the frame and out of focus from being too near the camera, nonetheless established her presence.

Moncrieff, concentrating on the lighting, added a sheet of blue gelatine across one of the spots. He looked through the lens and smiled, and I looked also, and there it was, the actor blinking, bored, waiting for us while we fiddled, but with the probability of his guilt revealed by a trick of light.

Cibber, as first written by Howard, had been a pillar of the Jockey Club, an upright, unfortunate victim of events. Reluctantly Howard, bowing to the film company, had agreed to write a (mild!) liaison between Cibber's wife (Silva) and Nash Rourke. Equally reluctantly he had agreed that Cibber should persecute Nash for supposedly having hanged his (Nash's) wife,

Yvonne. Howard still didn't know that it would be Cibber himself that did the hanging. I would have trouble with Howard. Nothing new.

To me, the character of Cibber lay at the center of the film's dynamic. The Cibber I saw was a man constrained by his position in society; a man forced by upbringing, by wealth, by the expectations of his peers to mold himself into a righteous puritan, difficult to love, incapable of loving. Cibber couldn't in consequence stand ridicule; couldn't bear to know his wife had rejected him for a lover, couldn't have waiters hearing his wife mock him. Cibber expected people to do his bidding. He was, above all, accustomed to deference.

Yet Cibber, underneath, was a raw and passionate man. Cibber hanged Yvonne in a burst of uncontrollable rage when she laughed at his attempt at rape. Appalled, unable to face his own guilt, Cibber persecuted Nash to the point of paranoia and beyond. Cibber, eventually, would be totally destroyed and mentally wrecked when Nash, after many tries, found that the one way to defeat his persecutor was to trap him into earning pitying sneers. Cibber would, at the end, disintegrate into catatonic schizophrenia.

I looked at Cibber the actor and wondered how I could ever dig out of him Cibber the man.

I started that afternoon by blowing away his complacency and telling him he didn't understand lust.

He was indignant. "Of course I do."

"The lust I want is uncontrollable. It's out of control, frenetic, frantic, raging, berserk. It's *murderous.*"

"And you expect *me* to show all that?"

"No, I don't. I don't think you can. I don't think you have the technique. I don't think you're a good enough actor."

Cibber froze. He stubbed out the cigar; and he produced for the camera that day a conception of lust that made one understand and pity his ungovernable compulsion even while he killed for having it mocked.

He would never be a grandee type-cast actor again.

"I hate you," he said.


LUCY WAS BUSY with the boxes when, on returning to the hotel, I opened the door of my sitting room and went in, leaving it ajar.

She was on her knees among the boxes and looked up as if guiltily, faintly blushing.

"Sorry for the mess," she said, flustered. "I didn't think you'd be back before six o'clock, as usual. I'll just tidy this lot away. And shall I close the door?"

"No, leave it open."

Books and papers were scattered over much of the floor, and many of

them, I was interested to see, had come out of boxes she had already investigated and itemized. The folder of clippings about Sonia's death lay open on
the table: the harmless clippings only, as Valentine's totally revealing souvenirs
were out of sight in O'Hara's safe.

"You had some messages," Lucy said jerkily, picking up and reading from
a notebook. "Howard Tyler wants to see you. Someone called Ziggy—I
think—wanted you to know the horses had come without trouble through
Immingham and had reached their stable. Does that sound right? Robbie—
he wouldn't give any other name—said to tell you the move had been accomplished. And the film crew you sent to Huntingdon races got some good
crowd and bookmaker shots, they said."

"Thanks."

I viewed the general clutter on the floor and mildly asked, "What are you
looking for?"

"Oh." The blush deepened. "Dad said . . . I mean, I hope you won't mind,
but my Uncle Ridley came in to see me."

"In here?"

"Yes. I didn't know he was coming. He just knocked on the door and
walked straight in when I opened it. I said you might not be pleased, and he
said he didn't care a f—, I mean, he didn't care what you thought."

"Did your father send him?"

"I don't know if he *sent* him. He told him where I was and what I was
doing."

I hid from her my inner satisfaction. I had rather hoped to stir Ridley to
action; hoped Jackson would perform the service.

"What did Ridley want?" I asked.

"He said I wasn't to tell you." She stood up, her blue eyes troubled. "I
don't like it . . . and I don't know what I should do."

"Perch on something and relax." I lowered myself stiffly into an armchair
and eased my constricted neck. "Bad back," I said, explaining it away. "Nothing to fuss over. What did Ridley want?"

She sat doubtfully sideways on the edge of the table, swinging a free leg.
The ubiquitous jeans were accompanied that day by a big blue sweater across
which white lambs gambolled: nothing could possibly have been less threatening.

She made up her mind. "He wanted that photo of the Gang that you
showed Dad yesterday. And he wanted anything Valentine had written about
Sonia. He emptied out all this stuff. And," her forehead wrinkled, "he wanted
the *knives.*"

"What knives?"

"He wouldn't tell me. I asked him if he wanted that one a boy asked me to give you at Huntingdon, and he said that one and others."

"What did you say?"

"I said I hadn't seen any others and anyhow, if you had anything like that you would keep it locked away safely . . . and . . . well . . . he told me to wheedle out of you the combination you're using for the safe here. He tried to open it, you see . . ." She stopped miserably. "I *know* I should never have let him in. What is it all *about?*"

"Cheer up," I said, "while I think."

"Shall I tidy the boxes?"

"Yes, do."

First catch your sprat . . .

"Lucy," I said, "why did you tell me what Ridley wanted?"

She looked uncomfortable. "Do you mean, why am I not loyal to my uncle?"

"Yes, I do mean that."

"I didn't like him saying *wheedle*. And . . . well . . . he's not as nice as he used to be."

I smiled. "Good. Well, if I tell you the combination number, will you please tell Ridley? And also tell him how clever you were, the way you wheedled it out of me! And tell him you do think I have knives in the safe."

She hesitated.

I said, "Give your allegiance one way or the other, but stick to one."

She said solemnly, "I give it to you."

"Then the combination is seven three five two."

"Now?" she asked, stretching toward the telephone.

"Now."

She spoke to her uncle. She blushed deeply while she lied, but she would have convinced me, let alone Ridley.

When she put down the telephone I said, "When I've finished all the work on this film, which will be in another four and a half months, I should think, would you like to spend a holiday in California? Not," I went on hastily, "with any conditions or expectations attached. Just a holiday. You could bring your mother, if you like. I thought you might find it interesting, that's all."

Her uncertainty over this suggestion was endearing. I was everything she'd been taught to fear, a young healthy male in a position of power, out for any conquest he could make.

"I won't try to seduce you," I promised lightly. But I might end by marrying her, I thought unexpectedly, when she was older. I'd been forever bombarded by actresses. An Oxfordshire farmer's freckled-nosed blue-eyed daughter who played the piano and lapsed occasionally into sixteen-year-old awkwardness seemed in contrast an unrealistic and unlikely future.

There was no thunderbolt: just an insidious hungry delight that never went away.

Her first response was abrupt and typical. "I can't afford it."

"Never mind, then."

"But . . . er . . . yes."

"Lucy!"

The blush persisted. "You'll turn out to be a frog."

"Kermit's not bad," I said, assessingly.

She giggled. "What do you want me to do with the boxes?"

Her work on the boxes had been originally my pathway to her father. I might not need her to work on them any longer, but I'd grown to like finding her here in my rooms.

"I hope you'll go on with the cataloging tomorrow," I said.

"All right."

"But this evening I have to work on the film . . . er, alone."

She seemed slightly disappointed but mostly relieved. A daring step forward . . . half a cautious step back. But we would get there one day, I thought, and was content and even reassured by the wait.

We left through the still slightly open doorway, and I walked down the passage a little way before waving her down the stairs; and, returning, I stopped to talk to my bodyguard whom O'Hara, for the company, had by now installed in the room opposite my own.

My bodyguard, half Asian, had straight black hair, black shiny eyes, and no visible feelings. He might be young, agile, well trained, and fast on his feet, but he was also unimaginative and hadn't saved me from the Armadillo.

When I pushed open his unlocked door to reveal him sitting wide awake in an upright chair facing me, he said at once, "Your door has all the time been open, Mr. Lyon."

I nodded. I'd arranged with him that if he saw my door closed he was to use my key and enter my rooms immediately. I couldn't think of a clearer or more simple demand for help.

"Have you eaten?" I asked.

"Yes, Mr. Lyon."

I tried a smile. No response.

"Don't go to sleep," I said tamely.

"No, Mr. Lyon."

O'Hara must have dug him up from central casting, I thought. Bad choice.

I retreated into my sitting room, left the door six inches open, drank a small amount of brandy, and answered a telephone call from Howard.

He was predictably raging.

"Cibber told me you've made him the murderer! It's impossible! You can't do it. I won't allow it! What will the Visboroughs say?"

I pointed out that we could slot in a different murderer, if we wanted to.

"Cibber says you tore him to *shreds.*"

"Cibber gave the performance of his life," I contradicted; and indeed, of the film's eventual four Oscar nominations, Cibber won the award for Best Supporting Actor—graciously forgiving me about a year later.

I promised Howard, "We'll hold a full script conference tomorrow morning; you, me, Nash, and Moncrieff."

"I want you to stop the film!"

"I don't have that authority."

"What if you're *dead?*" he demanded.

I said after a moment, "The company will finish the movie with another director. Killing me, believe me, Howard, would give this film massive publicity, but it would not stop it."

"It's not *fair,*" he said, as if he'd learned nothing.

And I said, "See you in the morning," and disconnected in despair.

The safe in my sitting room, as in O'Hara's, was out of casual sight in a fitment that housed a large TV set above and a mini-bar as well as the safe below. The mini-bar held small quantities of drinks for needy travelers—spirits, wine, champagne, and beer, also chocolate and nuts. The safe—my safe—held nothing. I programmed it to open at seven three five two, entrusted the Gang photo into its safekeeping, and closed it.

I sat then in the armchair in my bedroom and waited for a long time, and thought about the obligations of the confessional, and about how totally, or how little, I myself was bound by Valentine's dying and frantic admissions.

I felt the weight of the obligation of priesthood that so many priests themselves took lightly, knowing that their role absolved them from any dire responsibility, even while they dispensed regular indulgences. I had had no right to hear Valentine's confession nor to pardon his sins, and I had done both. I'd absolved him. *In nomine Patris . . . ego te absolvo.*

I could not evade feeling an absolute obligation to the spirit of those words. I should not—and could not—save myself with the knowledge Valentine had entrusted to me as a priest when he was dying. On the other hand, I could in good conscience use what he'd left me in his will.

I hadn't come across, in his books and papers, any one single revelation that could have been found by ransacking his house. The pieces had been there, but obscured and devious. I'd sorted those out a good deal by luck. I wished there were a more conclusive artifact than the Gang photo with which to bait the safe, but I'd come to the conclusion that there wasn't one. Valentine hadn't written down his ultimate sin; he'd confessed it in his last lucid breaths but he had never meant it to live after him. He hadn't left any exact concrete record of his twenty-six-year-old secret.

Two and a half hours after I'd talked to Howard, my visitor arrived. He came to my sitting room door calling my name, and when I didn't at first reply he walked in boldly and closed the door behind him. I heard it latch. I heard him open the fitment and press the buttons to open the safe.

I ambled to my bedroom door and greeted him.

"Hello, Roddy."

He was dressed in blazer, shirt, and tie. He looked a pillar of show-jumping rectitude; and he held the Gang photo.

"Looking for something?" I asked.

"Er . . ." Roddy Visborough said civilly, "Yes, actually. Bit of an imposition, I'm afraid, but one of the children I teach has begged me to get Nash Rourke's autograph. Howard swears you'll ask him for it."

He laid the photo on the table and came toward me holding out an autograph album and a pen.

It was so very unexpected that I forgot Professor Derry's warning—*anything he possesses may hide a knife*—and I let him get too close.

He dropped the autograph book at my feet, and when I automatically looked down at it, he pulled his gold-colored pen apart with a movement too fast for me to follow, and lunged at me with it.

The revealed stiletto point went straight through my jersey and shirt and hit solid polymer over my heart.

Himself flummoxed, disbelieving, Roddy dropped the pen and reached for his tie, and with a tug produced from under it a much larger knife, fearsomely lethal, which I later saw to be a triangular blade like a flat trowel fixed to a bar which led between his fingers to a grip within his hand.

At the time I saw only the triangular blade that seemed to grow like an integral part of his fist, the wide end across his knuckles, the point protruding five or more inches ahead.

He slashed at my throat instantly and found Robbie's handiwork foiling him there also, and with one quick movement flicked the blade higher so that it cut my chin and ran sharply up across my cheek to above my ear.

I hadn't meant to have to fight him. I wasn't good at it. And how could anyone fight an opponent so appallingly armed when one had no defense except fists?

He meant to kill me. I saw it in his face. He was going to get blood on his elegant clothes. One thinks such stupid non sequiturs at moments of maximum peril. He worked out that I wore a body protector from neck to waist and aimed at more vulnerable areas and punched his awful triangular blade into my left arm several times as I tried to shield my eyes from damage while unsuccessfully trying to get behind him to put my right arm round his throat.

I tried to evade him. We circled the bedroom. He sought to keep himself between me and the door while he killed me.

There were scarlet splatters all over the place; a scarlet river down my left hand. I yelled with what breath I could muster for my damned bodyguard to come to my rescue and nothing happened except that I began to believe that whatever happened to Roddy afterward I wouldn't be there to care.

I tugged the bedspread off the bed and threw it at him, and by good fortune it landed over his right hand. I sprang at him. I rolled against him, wrapping his right arm closely. I overbalanced him: I put one leg behind his and levered him backward off his feet, and scrambled with him on the floor, enveloping him ever more deeply in the bedspread until he was cocooned in it, until I lay over him bleeding while he tried to heave me off.

I don't know what would eventually have happened, but at that moment my bodyguard finally showed up.

He arrived in the bedroom doorway, saying enquiringly, "Mr. Lyon?"

I was past answering him sensibly. I said, "Fetch someone." Hardly a Nash Rourke hero sort of speech.

He took me literally, anyway. I vaguely heard him talking on the sitting room telephone and soon my rooms seemed full of people. Moncrieff, Nash himself, large men from the Bedford Lodge kitchen staff who sat on the wriggling bedspread, and eventually people saying they were policemen and paramedics and so on.

I apologized to the hotel manager for the blood. Oh well.

"Where the hell were you?" I asked my bodyguard. "Didn't you see that my door was shut?"

"Yes, Mr. Lyon."

"Well then?"

"But Mr. Lyon," he said in righteous self-justification, "sometimes I have to go to the bathroom."

# 17

Early on Thursday morning I sat on a windy sand dune waiting for the sun to rise over Happisburgh beach.

O'Hara, back in a panic from L.A., sat shivering beside me. About forty people, the various location crews, came and went from the vehicles parked close behind the dunes, and out on the wet expanse of firm sand left clean and unmarked by the ebbing tide, Moncrieff worked on the cameras, lights, and gantry that had been taken out there bolted onto a caterpillar-tracked orange beach-cleaning monster that could bulldoze wrecks if need be.

Far off to the left, Ziggy waited with the Viking horses. Between him and us, Ed commanded a second camera crew, one that would give us side-on shots.

We had held a rehearsal on the ebb tide the evening before and knew from the churned up state of the sand afterward that we needed to get the first shoot right. Ziggy was confident, Moncrieff was confident, O'Hara was confident: I fidgeted.

We needed a decent sunrise. We could fudge together an impression by using the blazing shots of the sky from the previous week; we could shine lights to get gleams in the horses' eyes, but we needed luck and the real thing to get the effect I truly wanted.

I thought over the events of the past few days. There had been a micro-surgeon in the Cambridge hospital who'd sewn up my face with a hundred tiny black stitches that at present looked as if a millipede was climbing from my chin to my hairline, but which he swore would leave hardly a scar. The gouges in my left arm had given him and me more trouble, but at least they were out of sight. He expected everything to be healed in a week.

Robbie Gill visited the hospital briefly early on Tuesday morning, taking away with him the Delta-cast jacket that had puzzled the night nursing staff the evening before. He didn't explain why I'd been wearing it beyond "an experiment in porosity—interesting." He also told me he'd mentioned to his police colleague that Dorothea could now identify her attacker, and that as two knife nuts suddenly active in Newmarket were unlikely, why didn't they try her with a photo?

I'd spent Tuesday afternoon talking to policemen, and by then (during Monday night) I'd decided what to say and what not.

I heard later that they had already searched Roddy Visborough's cottage in Leicestershire and had found it packed with hidden unusual knives. They asked why I thought Roddy had attacked me.

"He wanted the film stopped. He believes it harms his family's reputation."

They thought it not a good enough reason for attempted murder and, sighing at the vagaries of the world, I agreed with them. Did I know of any other reason? Sorry, no.

Roddy Visborough, I was certain, would give them no other reason. Roddy Visborough would not say, "I was afraid Thomas Lyon would find out that I connived at a fake hanging of my aunt to cover up a sex orgy."

Roddy, "the show-jumper," had had too much to lose. Roddy, Paul, and Ridley must all have been aghast when their buried crime started coming back to haunt them. They'd tried to frighten me off first with threats, and when those hadn't worked, with terminal action.

With knives.

The police asked if I knew that Mr. Visborough's fingerprints had been found all over Mrs. Pannier's house, along with my own. How *extraordinary!* I said; I'd never seen Mr. Visborough in her house.

They said that, acting on information, they had that morning interviewed Mrs. Pannier, who had identified a police photograph of Mr. Visborough as being the man who had attacked her.

*"Amazing,"* I said.

They asked if I knew why Mrs. Pannier had been attacked by Mr. Visborough. No, I didn't.

What connection was there between her and me?

"I used to read to her blind brother," I said. "He died of cancer . . ."

They knew.

They wondered if the knife I'd found on the Heath, that was now in their possession, had anything to do with what had happened to me.

"We all believed it was an attempt to get the film abandoned," I said. "That's all."

I believed, also, though I didn't say so, that it was Roddy who had given Ridley the trench knife and told him to frighten off Nash and, through him, the film.

I believed Roddy had coerced Paul to ransack Dorothea's house with him, both of them looking for any giveaway account Valentine might have left of Sonia's death.

Roddy had been the strongest of the three of them, and the most afraid.

Prompted by Lucy, Ridley had obligingly passed on to Roddy the combination of my safe, and had told him that I knew far too much.

Roddy, as I'd hoped, had revealed himself and his involvement, the mackerel coming to the sprat. I had lured him to come, had hoped he might bring with him another esoteric knife: I hadn't meant to get myself so cut.

The police went away as if dissatisfied, but they were sure at the very least of two convictions for grievous bodily harm, and if, with all the modern available detection techniques, they couldn't prove Roddy Visborough had killed Paul Pannier, too bad. As for motive, they might conclude Paul had threatened in remorse to give Roddy away to the police for attacking Dorothea: near enough for belief. Near enough, anyway, for Dorothea to believe it, and be comforted.

On Wednesday morning I discharged myself from the hospital and returned to Newmarket to be confronted by a furious Howard and an extremely upset Alison Visborough.

"I *told* you you shouldn't have made changes to my book," Howard raged. "Now see what you've done! Roddy is going to *prison.*"

Alison looked in disbelief at the long millipede track up my face. "Rodbury wouldn't have done that!"

"Rodbury did," I said dryly. "Did he always have knives?"

She hesitated. She was fair-minded under the outrage. "I suppose . . . perhaps . . . he was secretive . . ."

"And he wouldn't let you join in his games."

She said "Oh," blankly, and began reevaluating her brother's psyche.

Sitting on the Norfolk dunes I thought of her father, Rupert, and of his aborted political career. I thought it almost certain that the scandal that had caused his retreat was not that his sister-in-law had been mysteriously hanged, but that he'd learned—perhaps from Valentine or even from Jackson Wells— that his own son had been present at the mid-morning cover-up hanging, having intended to have sexual relations with his aunt. Rupert, upright man, had given his son show-jumpers with which to redeem himself, but had stopped short of loving forgiveness and had left his own house to his daughter. Poor Rupert Visborough . . . he hadn't deserved to become Cibber, but at least he would never know.

O'Hara, huddling into his padded ex-army jacket, said that while I'd been out on the beach rehearsing the previous evening, he'd got the projectionist to show him the rushes of the hanging.

"What sort of certificate did we earn?" I asked. "PG13? That's what we ideally want."

"Depends on the cutting. What gave you that view of her death?"

"Howard holds forth on the catharsis of the primal scream."

"Shit, Thomas. That death wasn't any sort of therapy. That hanging had gut-churning vigor."

"Good."

O'Hara blew on his fingers. "I hope these damn horses are worth this frigging cold."

The eastern sky turned from black to gray. I picked up the walkie-talkie and spoke again to Ed and also to Ziggy. Everything was ready. I wasn't to worry. All would be well.

I thought of Valentine's powerful muscles, years ago.

I had kept faith with his confession. No one through me would ever learn his truth.

*I left the knife with Derry . . .*

Valentine's strength had fashioned for his great friend Professor Derry a unique knife to add to his collection: a steel knife with a spear head and a candy-twisted handle, unlike any ordinary weapon.

*I killed the Cornish boy . . .*

One of the Gang, perhaps even Pig Falmouth himself, had told Valentine how Sonia had died, and in an overwhelming, towering tidal wave of anger and grief and guilt he had snatched up the spear and plunged it deep into the jockey's body.

It had to have happened in some way like that. Valentine had loved Sonia in secret. He'd learned about paraphilia to solve Derry's impotence problem, and he'd shown the encyclopedia article to Pig, no doubt light-heartedly— "I say, Pig, just look at this!"—and Pig had told his friends.

*I destroyed all their lives . . .* I guessed he might have meant he ruined their lives by giving them the idea of their fatal game. They had destroyed their own lives, but guilt could lack logic.

Valentine had killed Pig Falmouth in the wild uncontainable sort of anger and grief that had caused Jackson Wells to beat his brother Ridley near to death; and Valentine himself had then written the gossip column that reported Pig's departure to work in Australia, that everyone had believed.

Pig Falmouth, I guessed, had lain for twenty-six years at the bottom of the well that Valentine had had a firm of builders fill in to make it safe for children. Valentine had stood with Jackson Wells and watched them throw the junk of years down the hole to obliterate the carefree boy who had kissed and killed his golden girl.

Valentine had at the end unloaded his soul's burden of murder.

I laid them both to rest.

THE SKY'S AMORPHOUS gray was slowly suffused with a dull soft crimson in the east.

Moncrieff was holding a light meter to measure the changing intensity in minutes with the dedication that won him *Unstable Times*'s second Oscar, for cinematography. Howard, nominated for best adapted screenplay, lost the award by inches, as did our fourth nominee, the art director. O'Hara and the moguls were happy, however, and I got allotted a big-budget epic with megastar Nash.

Over Happisburgh beach the crimson in the sky blossomed to scarlet and colored the waves pink. There were fewer cloud streaks than the week before, fewer brilliant gold halos against the vermillion. We would merge the two sunrises, I thought.

Away to our right, far behind Moncrieff and his cameras, the trainer of the Viking horses had spread out on the sands great bowls of horse nuts: the wild horses would race, on our signal, to reach their breakfast, as they had been trained.

Moncrieff, raising light meters high, greeted the dawn like an ancient prophet. When he lowered his arms, I was to cue the action.

The blinding sun swam upward. Moncrieff's arms swept down.

I said, "Action, Ed," and "Now, Ziggy," into my walkie-talkie, and away down the beach the horses began their run.

We had dressed Ziggy in an all-over body suit of gray Lycra, to which, ballet trained, he'd adapted instantly. Over the body suit he wore a floating shapeless gown of translucent white silk voile, and on his head the light blond wig. His own dark features had been transformed to blondness by the make-up department, and he was riding, as he'd promised, without shoes, saddle, or reins.

The horses accelerated, bursting into the wide silence of the deserted seascape with the thud and suction of their galloping hooves.

Ziggy knelt on his horse's withers, his head forward above the horse's straining neck. Gown and hair streamed out, gathering to themselves all the light, the gray-clad man inside seeming almost invisible, a misty shadow.

Moncrieff ran two head-on cameras, one set for a speed of thirty-six frames a second, slow motion.

The rising sun shone in the horses' eyes. Light gleamed on the flying manes. The heads of the wild herd plunged forward in the urgency of racing, in the untamed compulsion to be *first,* to lead the pack. The herd parted and swept round Moncrieff, the plunging bodies close, the Viking heads wild and free.

Ziggy rode between Moncrieff and the maximum brilliance of light. On the finished film it looked as if the flying figure had evaporated there, had been absorbed and assimilated in luminescence; had become a part of the sun.

"Jesus *Christ,*" O'Hara said, when he saw it.

I cut some of the shots of the hanging scene into the wild horse sequences for the ending of the film.

Yvonne's scream dissolved into the high thin forlorn cry of a wheeling seagull.

The young woman of the fantasy lovers dreamed she was riding the wild horses as she swung to her death.

# COME TO GRIEF

# 1

I had this friend, you see, that everyone loved.

(My name is Sid Halley.)

I had this friend that everyone loved, and I put him on trial.

The trouble with working as an investigator, as I had been doing for approaching five years, was that occasionally one turned up facts that surprised and appalled and smashed peaceful lives forever.

It had taken days of inner distress for me to decide to act on what I'd learned. Miserably, by then, I'd suffered through disbelief, through denial, through anger and at length through acceptance; all the stages of grief. I grieved for the man I'd known. For the man I *thought* I'd known, who had all along been a façade. I grieved for the loss of a friendship, for a man who still looked the same but was different, alien . . . despicable. I could much more easily have grieved for him dead.

The turmoil I'd felt in private had on public disclosure become universal. The press, jumping instinctively and strongly to his defense, had given me, as his accuser, a severely rough time. On racecourses, where I chiefly worked, long-time acquaintances had turned their backs. Love, support and comfort poured out towards my friend. Disbelief and denial and anger prevailed: acceptance lay a long way ahead. Meanwhile I, not he, was seen as the target for hatred. It would pass, I knew. One had simply to endure it, and wait.

On the morning set for the opening of his trial, my friend's mother killed herself.

The news was brought to the Law Courts in Reading, in Berkshire, where the presiding judge, enrobed, had already heard the opening statements and where I, a witness for the prosecution, waited alone in a soulless side room to be called. One of the court officials came to give me the suicide information and to say that the judge had adjourned the proceedings for the day, and I could go home.

"Poor woman," I exclaimed, truly horrified.

Even though he was supposed to be impartial, the official's own sympathies were still with the accused. He eyed me without favor and said I should return the following morning, ten o'clock sharp.

I left the room and walked slowly along the corridor towards the exit, fielded on the way by a senior lawyer who took me by the elbow and drew me aside.

"His mother took a room in a hotel and jumped from the sixteenth floor," he said without preamble. "She left a note saying she couldn't bear the future. What are your thoughts?"

I looked at the dark, intelligent eyes of Davis Tatum, a clumsy, fat man with a lean, agile brain.

"You know better than I do," I said.

"*Sid.*" A touch of exasperation. "Tell me your thoughts."

"Perhaps he'll change his plea."

He relaxed and half smiled. "You're in the wrong job."

I wryly shook my head. "I catch the fish. You guys gut them."

He amiably let go of my arm and I continued to the outside world to catch a train for the thirty-minute ride to the terminus in London, flagging down a taxi for the last mile or so home.

Ginnie Quint, I thought, traveling through London. Poor, poor Ginnie Quint, choosing death in preference to the everlasting agony of her son's disgrace. A lonely slamming exit. An end to tears. An end to grief.

The taxi stopped outside the house in Pont Square (off Cadogan Square), where I currently lived on the second floor, with a balcony overlooking the central leafy railed garden. As usual, the small, secluded square was quiet, with little passing traffic and only a few people on foot. A thin early-October wind shook the dying leaves on the lime trees, floating a few of them sporadically to the ground like soft yellow snowflakes.

I climbed out of the cab and paid the driver through his open window, and as I turned to cross the pavement and go up the few steps to the front door, a man who was apparently quietly walking past suddenly sprang at me in fury, raising a long black metal rod with which he tried to brain me.

I sensed rather than saw the first wicked slash and moved enough to catch the weight of it on my shoulder, not my head. He was screaming at me, half-demented, and I fielded a second brutal blow on a raised defensive forearm. After that I seized his wrist in a pincer grip and rolled the bulk of his body backward over the leg I pushed out rigidly behind his knees, and felled him, sprawling, iron bar and all, onto the hard ground. He yelled bitter words; cursing, half-incoherent, threatening to kill.

The taxi still stood there, diesel engine running, the driver staring wide-mouthed and speechless, a state of affairs that continued while I yanked open the black rear door and stumbled in again onto the seat. My heart thudded. Well, it would.

*"Drive,"* I said urgently. "Drive on."

"But . . ."

"Just drive. Go *on*. Before he finds his feet and breaks your windows."

The driver closed his mouth fast and meshed his gears, and wavered at something above running pace along the road.

"Look," he said, protesting, half turning his head back to me, "I didn't see nothing. You're my last fare today, I've been on the go eight hours and I'm on my way home."

"Just drive," I said. Too little breath. Too many jumbled feelings.

"Well . . . but, drive where *to?"*

Good question. Think.

"He didn't look like no mugger," the taxi driver observed aggrievedly. "But you never can tell these days. D'you want me to drop you off at the police? He hit you something shocking. You could *hear* it. Like he broke your arm."

"Just drive, would you?"

The driver was large, fiftyish and a Londoner, but no John Bull, and I could see from his head movements and his repeated spiky glances at me in his rear-view mirror that he didn't want to get involved in my problems and couldn't wait for me to leave his cab.

Pulse eventually steadying, I could think of only one place to go. My only haven, in many past troubles.

"Paddington," I said. "Please."

"St. Mary's, d'you mean? The hospital?"

"No. The trains."

"But you've just come from there!" he protested.

"Yes, but please go back."

Cheering a little, he rocked round in a U-turn and set off for the return to Paddington Station, where he assured me again that he hadn't seen nothing, nor heard nothing neither, and he wasn't going to get involved, did I see?

I simply paid him and let him go, and if I memorized his cab-licensing number it was out of habit, not expectation.

As part of normal equipment I wore a mobile phone on my belt and, walking slowly into the high, airy terminus, I pressed the buttons to reach the man I trusted most in the world, my ex-wife's father, Rear Admiral Charles Roland, Royal Navy, retired, and to my distinct relief he answered at the second ring.

"Charles," I said. My voice cracked a bit, which I hadn't meant.

A pause, then, "Is that you, Sid?"

"May I . . . visit?"

"Of course. Where are you?"

"Paddington Station. I'll come by train and taxi."

He said calmly, "Use the side door. It's not locked," and put down his receiver.

I smiled, reassured as ever by his steadiness and his brevity with words. An unemotional, undemonstrative man, not paternal towards me and very far from indulgent, he gave me nevertheless a consciousness that he cared considerably about what happened to me and would proffer rocklike support if I needed it. Like I needed it at that moment, for several variously dire reasons.

Trains to Oxford being less frequent in the middle of the day, it was four in the afternoon by the time the country taxi, leaving Oxford well behind, arrived at Charles's vast old house at Aynsford and decanted me at the side door. I paid the driver clumsily owing to stiffening bruises, and walked with relief into the pile I really thought of as home, the one unchanging constant in a life that had tossed me about, rather, now and then.

Charles sat, as often, in the large leather armchair that I found too hard for comfort but that he, in his uncompromising way, felt appropriate to accommodate his narrow rump. I had sometime in the past moved one of the softer but still fairly formal old gold brocade armchairs from the drawing room into the smaller room, his "wardroom," as it was there we always sat when the two of us were alone. It was there that he kept his desk, his collection of flies for fishing, his nautical books, his racks of priceless old orchestral recordings and the gleaming marble-and-steel wonder of a custom-built, frictionless turntable on which he played them. It was there on the dark-green walls that he'd hung large photographs of the ships he'd commanded, and smaller photos of shipmates, and there, also, that he'd lately positioned a painting of me as a jockey riding over a fence at Cheltenham racecourse, a picture that summed up every ounce of vigor needed for race-riding, and which had hung for years less conspicuously in the dining room.

He had had a strip of lighting positioned along the top of the heavy gold frame, and when I got there that evening, it was lit.

He was reading. He put his book face down on his lap when I walked in, and gave me a bland, noncommittal inspection. There was nothing, as usual, to be read in his eyes: I could often see quite clearly into other people's minds, but seldom his.

"Hullo," I said.

I could hear him take a breath and trickle it out through his nose. He spent all of five seconds looking me over, then pointed to the tray of bottles and glasses which stood on the table below my picture.

"Drink," he said briefly. An order, not invitation.

"It's only four o'clock."

"Immaterial. What have you eaten today?"

I didn't say anything, which he took to be answer enough.

"Nothing," he said, nodding. "I thought so. You look thin. It's this *bloody* case. I thought you were supposed to be in court today."

"It was adjourned until tomorrow."

"Get a drink."

I walked obediently over to the table and looked assessingly at the bottles. In his old-fashioned way he kept brandy and sherry in decanters. Scotch—Famous Grouse, his favorite—remained in the screw-topped bottle. I would have to have scotch, I thought, and doubted if I could pour even that.

I glanced upward at my picture. In those days, six years ago, I'd had two hands. In those days I'd been British steeplechasing's champion jockey: whole, healthy and, I dared say, fanatical. A nightmare fall had resulted in a horse's sharp hoof half ripping off my left hand: the end of one career and the birth, if you could call it that, of another. Slow, lingering birth of a detective, while I spent two years pining for what I'd lost and drifted rudderless like a wreck that didn't quite sink but was unseaworthy all the same. I was ashamed of those two years. At the end of them a ruthless villain had smashed beyond mending the remains of the useless hand and had galvanized me into a resurrection of the spirit and the impetus to seek what I'd had since, a myoelectric false hand that worked on nerve impulses from my truncated forearm and looked and behaved so realistically that people often didn't notice its existence.

My present problem was that I couldn't move its thumb far enough from its fingers to grasp the large heavy cut-glass brandy decanter, and my right hand wasn't working too well, either. Rather than drop alcohol all over Charles's Persian rug, I gave up and sat in the gold armchair.

"What's the matter?" Charles asked abruptly. "Why did you come? Why don't you pour a drink?"

After a moment I said dully, knowing it would hurt him, "Ginnie Quint killed herself."

*"What?"*

"This morning," I said. "She jumped from sixteen floors up."

His fine-boned face went stiff and immediately looked much older. The bland eyes darkened, as if retreating into their sockets. Charles had known Ginnie Quint for thirty or more years, and had been fond of her and had been a guest in her house often.

Powerful memories lived in my mind also. Memories of a friendly, rounded, motherly woman happy in her role as a big-house wife, inoffensively rich, working genuinely and generously for several charities and laughingly glowing in reflected glory from her famous, good-looking successful only child, the one that everyone loved.

Her son, Ellis, that I had put on trial.

The last time I'd seen Ginnie she'd glared at me with incredulous contempt, demanding to know how I could *possibly* seek to destroy the golden Ellis, who counted me his friend, who liked me, who'd done me favors, who would have trusted me with his life.

I'd let her molten rage pour over me, offering no defense. I knew exactly how she felt. Disbelief and denial and anger . . . The idea of what he'd done was so sickening to her that she rejected the guilt possibility absolutely, as almost everyone else had done, though in her case with anguish.

Most people believed I had got it all wrong, and had ruined *myself,* not Ellis. Even Charles, at first, had said doubtfully, "Sid, are you *sure?*"

I'd said I was certain. I'd hoped desperately for a way out . . . for *any* way out . . . as I knew what I'd be pulling down on myself if I went ahead. And it had been at least as bad as I'd feared, and in many ways worse. After the first bombshell solution—a proposed solution—to a crime that had had half the country baying for blood (but not *Ellis's* blood, no, *no,* it was *unthinkable*), there had been the first court appearance, the remand into custody (a *scandal,* he should *of course* be let out immediately on bail), and after that there had fallen a sudden press silence, while the sub judice law came into effect.

Under British sub judice law, no evidence might be publicly discussed between the remand and the trial. Much investigation and strategic trial planning could go on behind the scenes, but neither potential jurors nor John Doe in the street was allowed to know details. Uninformed public opinion had consequently stuck at the "Ellis is innocent" stage, and I'd had nearly three months, now, of obloquy.

Ellis, you see, was a Young Lochinvar in spades. Ellis Quint, once champion amateur jump jockey, had flashed onto television screens like a comet, a brilliant, laughing, able, funny performer, the draw for millions on sports quiz programs, the ultimate chat-show host, the model held up to children, the glittering star that regularly raised the nation's happiness level, to whom everyone, from tiara to baseball cap worn backwards, responded.

Manufacturers fell over themselves to tempt him to endorse their products, and half the kids in England strode about with machismo in glamorized jockey-type riding boots over their jeans. And it was this man, this *paragon,* that I sought to eradicate.

No one seemed to blame the tabloid columnist who'd written, "The once-revered Sid Halley, green with envy, tries to tear down a talent he hasn't a prayer of matching. . . ." There had been inches about "a spiteful little man trying to compensate for his own inadequacies." I hadn't shown any of it to Charles, but others had.

The telephone at my waist buzzed suddenly, and I answered its summons.

"Sid . . . Sid . . ."

The woman on the other end was crying. I'd heard her crying often.

"Are you at home?" I asked.

"No . . . In the hospital."

"Tell me the number and I'll phone straight back."

I heard murmuring in the background; then another voice came on, efficient, controlled, reading out a number, repeating it slowly. I tapped the digits onto my mobile so that they appeared on the small display screen.

"Right," I said, reading the number back. "Put down your receiver." To Charles I said, "May I use your phone?"

He waved a hand permissively towards his desk, and I pressed the buttons on his phone to get back to where I'd been.

The efficient voice answered immediately.

"Is Mrs. Ferns still there?" I said. "It's Sid Halley."

"Hang on."

Linda Ferns was trying not to cry. "Sid . . . Rachel's worse. She's asking for you. Can you come? Please."

"How bad is she?"

"Her temperature keeps going up." A sob stopped her. "Talk to Sister Grant."

I talked to the efficient voice, Sister Grant. "How bad is Rachel?"

"She's asking for you all the time," she said. "How soon can you come?"

"Tomorrow."

"Can you come this evening?"

I said, "Is it that bad?"

I listened to a moment of silence, in which she couldn't say what she meant because Linda was beside her.

"Come this evening," she repeated.

This evening. Dear God. Nine-year-old Rachel Ferns lay in a hospital in Kent a hundred and fifty miles away. Ill to death, this time, it sounded like.

"Promise her," I said, "that I'll come tomorrow." I explained where I was. "I have to be in court tomorrow morning, in Reading, but I'll come to see Rachel as soon as I get out. Promise her. Tell her I'm going to be there. Tell her I'll bring six wigs and an angel fish."

The efficient voice said, "I'll tell her," and then added, "Is it true that Ellis Quint's mother has killed herself? Mrs. Ferns says someone heard it on the radio news and repeated it to her. She wants to know if it's true."

"It's true."

"Come as soon as you can," the nurse said, and disconnected.

I put down the receiver. Charles said, "The child?"

"It sounds as if she's dying."

"You knew it was inevitable."

"It doesn't make it any easier for the parents." I sat down again slowly in the gold armchair. "I would go tonight if it would save her life, but I . . ." I stopped, not knowing what to say, how to explain that I wouldn't go. Couldn't go. Not except to save her life, which no one could do however much they ached to.

Charles said briefly, "You've only just got here."

"Yeah."

"And what else is there, that you haven't told me?"

I looked at him.

"I know you too well, Sid," he said. "You didn't come all this way just because of Ginnie. You could have told me about her on the telephone." He paused. "From the look of you, you came for the oldest of reasons." He paused again, but I didn't say anything. "For sanctuary," he said.

I shifted in the chair. "Am I so transparent?"

"Sanctuary from what?" he asked. "What is so sudden . . . and urgent?"

I sighed. I said with as little heat as possible, "Gordon Quint tried to kill me."

Gordon Quint was Ginnie's husband. Ellis was their son.

It struck Charles silent, open-mouthed: and it took a great deal to do that.

After a while I said, "When they adjourned the trial I went home by train and taxi. Gordon Quint was waiting there in Pont Square for me. God knows how long he'd been there, how long he would have waited, but anyway, he was there, with an iron bar." I swallowed. "He aimed it at my head, but I sort of ducked, and it hit my shoulder. He tried again . . . Well, this mechanical hand has its uses. I closed it on his wrist and put into practice some of the judo I've spent so many hours learning, and I tumbled him onto his back . . . and he was screaming at me all the time that I'd killed Ginnie . . . I'd killed her."

  *"Sid."*

"He was half-mad . . . raving, really . . . He said I'd destroyed his whole family. I'd destroyed all their lives . . . he swore I would die for it . . . that he would get me . . . get me . . . I don't think he knew what he was saying, it just poured out of him."

Charles said dazedly, "So what did you do?"

"The taxi driver was still there, looking stunned, so . . . er . . . I got back into the taxi."

"You got back . . . ? But . . . what about Gordon?"

"I left him there. Lying on the pavement. Screaming revenge . . . starting to stand up . . . waving the iron bar. I . . . er . . . I don't think I'll go home tonight, if I can stay here."

Charles said faintly, "Of course you can stay. It's taken for granted. You told me once that this was your home."

"Yeah."

"Then believe it."

I did believe it, or I wouldn't have gone there. Charles and his certainties had in the past saved me from inner disintegration, and my reliance on him had oddly been strengthened, not evaporated, by the collapse of my marriage to his daughter Jenny, and our divorce.

Aynsford offered respite. I would go back soon enough to defuse Gordon Quint; I would swear an oath in court and tear a man to shreds; I would hug Linda Ferns and, if I were in time, make Rachel laugh; but for this one night I would sleep soundly in Charles's house in my own accustomed room—and let the dry well of mental stamina refill.

Charles said, "Did Gordon . . . er . . . hurt you, with his bar?"

"A bruise or two."

"I know your sort of bruises."

I sighed again. "I think . . . um . . . he's cracked a bone. In my arm."

His gaze flew instantly to the left arm, the plastic job.

"No," I said, "the other one."

Aghast, he said, "Your *right* arm?"

"Well, yeah. But only the ulna, which goes from the little-finger side of the wrist up to the elbow. Not the radius as well, luckily. The radius will act as a natural splint."

"But, *Sid* . . ."

"Better than my skull. I had the choice."

"How can you *laugh* about it?"

"A bloody bore, isn't it?" I smiled without stress. "Don't *worry* so, Charles. It'll heal. I broke the same bone worse once before, when I was racing."

"But you had two hands then."

"Yes, so I did. So would you mind picking up that damned heavy brandy decanter and sloshing half a pint of anesthetic into a glass?"

Wordlessly he got to his feet and complied. I thanked him. He nodded. End of transaction.

When he was again sitting down he said, "So the taxi driver was a witness."

"The taxi driver is a 'don't-get-involved' man."

"But if he *saw* . . . He must have heard . . ."

"Blind and deaf, he insisted he was." I drank fiery, neat liquid gratefully. "Anyway, that suits me fine."

"But, Sid . . ."

"Look," I said reasonably, "what would you have me do? Complain? Prosecute? Gordon Quint is normally a level-headed, worthy sixtyish citizen. He's not your average murderer. Besides, he's your own personal long-time friend, and I, too, have eaten in his house. But he already hates me for attacking Ellis, the light of his life, and he'd not long learned that Ginnie, his adored wife, had killed herself because she couldn't bear what lies ahead. So how do you think Gordon feels?" I paused. "I'm just glad he didn't succeed in smashing my brains in. And, if you can believe it, I'm almost as glad for *his* sake that he didn't, as for my own."

Charles shook his head resignedly.

"Grief can be dangerous," I said.

He couldn't dispute it. Deadly revenge was as old as time.

We sat companionably in silence. I drank brandy and felt marginally saner. Knots of tension relaxed in my stomach. I made various resolutions to give up chasing the deadlier crooks—but I'd made resolutions like that before, and hadn't kept them.

I'd stopped asking myself why I did it. There were hundreds of other ways of passing the time and earning one's keep. Other ex-jockeys became trainers or commentators or worked in racing in official capacities, and only I, it seemed, felt impelled to swim around the hidden fringes, attempting to sort out doubts and worries for people who for any reason didn't want to bother the police or the racing authorities.

There was a need for me and what I could do, or I would have sat around idle, twiddling my thumbs. Instead, even in the present general climate of ostracism, I had more offers of work than I could accept.

Most jobs took me less than a week, particularly those that involved looking into someone's credit and credibility rating: bookmakers asked me to do that frequently, before taking on new account customers, and trainers paid me fees to assure them that if they bought expensive two-year-olds for new owners at the Sales, they wouldn't be left with broken promises and a mountain of debt. I'd checked on all sorts of proposed business plans and saved a lot of people from confidence tricksters, and I'd uncovered absconding debtors, and thieves of all sorts, and had proved a confounded nuisance to imaginative felons.

People had sobbed on my shoulders from joy and deliverance; others had threatened and battered to make me quit: Linda Ferns would hug me and Gordon Quint hate me; and I also had two more investigations in hand that I'd spent too little time on. So why didn't I give it up and change to a life of quiet, safe financial management, which I wasn't bad at, either? I felt the effects of the iron bar from neck to fingers . . . and didn't know the answer.

The mobile phone on my belt buzzed and I answered it as before, finding on the line the senior lawyer I'd talked to in the corridor in the Law Courts.

"Sid, this is Davis Tatum. I've news for you," he said.

"Give me your number and I'll call you back."

"Oh? Oh, OK." He read off his number, which I copied as before, and also as before I borrowed Charles's phone on the desk to get back to square one.

"Sid," said Tatum, coming as usual straight to the point, "Ellis Quint is changing his plea from not guilty to guilty by reason of diminished responsibility. It seems his mother's powerful statement of no confidence in his innocence has had a laxative effect on the bowels of the counsel for the defense."

"Jeez," I said.

Tatum chuckled. I imagined his double chin wobbling. He said, "The trial will now be adjourned for a week to allow expert psychiatric witnesses to be briefed. In other words, you don't have to turn up tomorrow."

"Good."

"But I hope you will."

"How do you mean?"

"There's a job for you."

"What sort of job?"

"Investigating, of course. What else? I'd like to meet you somewhere privately."

"All right," I said, "but sometime tomorrow I have to go to Kent to see the child, Rachel Ferns. She's back in the hospital and it doesn't sound good."

"Hell."

"Yeah."

"Where are you?" he asked. "The press are looking for you."

"They can wait a day."

"I told the people from *The Pump* that after the mauling they've given you they haven't a prayer of you talking to them."

"I appreciate that," I said, smiling.

He chuckled. "About tomorrow . . ."

"I'll go to Kent in the morning," I said. "I don't know how long I'll stay, it depends on Rachel. How about five o'clock in London? Would that do you? The end of your business day."

"Right. Where? Not in my office. How about your place? No, perhaps not, if *The Pump*'s after you."

"How about, say, the upstairs bar of Le Meridien restaurant in Piccadilly?"

"I don't know it."

"All the better."

"If I need to change it," he said, "can I still get you on your mobile phone?"

"Always."

"Good. See you tomorrow."

I replaced Charles's receiver and sat on the gold armchair as before. Charles looked at the mobile instrument I'd laid this time on the table beside my glass and asked the obvious question.

"Why do you ring them back? Why don't you just talk?"

"Well," I said, "someone is listening to this gadget."

*"Listening?"*

I explained about the insecurity of open radio transmission, that allowed anyone clever and expert to hear what they shouldn't.

Charles said, "How do you know someone's listening to you?"

"A lot of small things people have recently learned that I haven't told them."

"Who is it?"

"I don't actually know. Someone has also accessed my computer over the phone lines. I don't know who did that, either. It's disgustingly easy nowadays—but again, only if you're expert—to suss out people's private passwords and read their secret files."

He said with slight impatience, "Computers are beyond me."

"I've had to learn," I said, grinning briefly. "A bit different from scudding over hurdles at Plumpton on a wet day."

"Everything you do astounds me."

"I wish I was still racing."

"Yes, I know. But if you were, you'd anyway be coming to the end of it soon, wouldn't you? How old are you now? Thirty-four?"

I nodded. Thirty-five loomed.

"Not many top jump jockeys go on much after that."

"You put things so delightfully bluntly, Charles."

"You're of more use to more people the way you are."

Charles tended to give me pep talks when he thought I needed them. I could never work out how he knew. He'd said something once about my looking like a brick wall: that when I shut out the world and retreated into myself, things were bad. Maybe he was right. Retreat inward meant for me not retreating outwardly, and I supposed I'd learned the technique almost from birth.

Jenny, my loved and lost wife, had said she couldn't live with it. She'd wanted me to give up race-riding and become a softer-shelled person, and when I wouldn't—or couldn't—we had shaken acridly apart. She had recently remarried, and this time she'd tied herself not to a thin, dark-haired, risk-taking bundle of complexes, but to a man to fit her needs, a safe, graying, sweet-natured uncomplicated fellow with a knighthood. Jenny, the warring unhappy Mrs. Halley, was now serenely Lady Wingham. A photograph of her with her handsome, beaming Sir Anthony stood in a silver frame next to the telephone on Charles's desk.

"How's Jenny?" I asked politely.

"Fine," Charles answered without expression.

"Good."

"He's a bore, after you," Charles observed.

"You can't say such things."

"I can say what I bloody well like in my own house."

In harmony and mutual regard we passed a peaceful evening, disturbed only by five more calls on my mobile phone, all demanding to know, with varying degrees of peremptoriness, where they could find Sid Halley.

I said each time, "This is an answering service. Leave your number and we'll pass on your message."

All of the callers, it seemed, worked for newspapers, a fact that particularly left me frowning.

"I don't know where they all got this number from," I told Charles. "It's not in any directory. I give it only to people I'm working for, so they can reach me day or night, and only to others whose calls I wouldn't want to miss. I tell them it's a private line for their use only. I don't hand this number out on printed cards, and I don't have it on my writing paper. Quite often I reroute calls to this phone from my phone in the flat, but I didn't today because of Gordon Quint bashing away outside and preventing me from going in. So how do half the newspapers in London know it?"

"How will you find out?" Charles asked.

"Um . . . engage Sid Halley to look into it, I daresay."

Charles laughed. I felt uneasy all the same. Someone had been listening on that number, and now someone had broadcast it. It wasn't that my phone conversations were excessively secret—and I'd started the semi-exclusive number anyway solely so that the machine didn't buzz unnecessarily at awkward moments—but now I had a sense that someone was deliberately crowding me. Tapping into my computer—which wouldn't get anyone far, as I knew a lot of defenses. Assaulting me electronically. *Stalking.*

Enough was enough. Five newspapers were too much. Sid Halley, as I'd said, would have to investigate his own case.

Charles's long-time live-in housekeeper, Mrs. Cross, all dimples and delight, cooked us a simple supper and fussed over me comfortably like a hen. I guiltily found her a bit smothering sometimes, but always sent her a card for her birthday.

I went to bed early and found that, as usual, Mrs. Cross had left warm welcoming lights on in my room and had put out fresh pajamas and fluffy towels.

A pity the day's troubles couldn't be as easily cosseted into oblivion.

I undressed and brushed my teeth and eased off the artificial hand. My left arm ended uselessly four inches below the elbow; a familiar punctuation, but still a sort of bereavement.

My right arm now twinged violently at every use.

Damn the lot, I thought.

# 2

The morning brought little improvement.

I sometimes used a private chauffeur-driven car-hire firm based in London to ferry around people and things I wanted to keep away from prying eyes and consequently, waking to a couple of faulty arms, I telephoned from Charles's secure number and talked to my friends at Teledrive.

"Bob?" I said. "I need to get from northwest of Oxford to Kent, Canterbury. There'll be a couple of short stops on the journey. And, sometime this afternoon, a return to London. Can anyone do it at such short notice?"

"Give me the address," he said briefly. "We're on our way."

I breakfasted with Charles. That is to say, we sat in the dining room where Mrs. Cross, in her old-fashioned way, had set out toast, coffee and cereals and a warming dish of scrambled eggs.

Charles thought mornings hadn't begun without scrambled eggs. He ate his on toast and eyed me drinking coffee left-handedly. From long acquaintance with my preference for no fuss, he made no comment on the consequences of iron bars.

He was reading a broad-sheet newspaper which, as he showed me, was making a good-taste meal of Ginnie Quint's death. Her pleasant, smiling face inappropriately spread across two columns. I shut out of my mind any image of what she might look like sixteen floors down.

Charles said, reading aloud, " 'Friends say she appeared depressed about her

son's forthcoming trial. Her husband, Gordon, was unavailable for comment.'
In other words, the press couldn't find him.'"

Ordeal by newsprint, I thought; the latter-day torture.

"Seriously, Sid," Charles said in his most calm, civilized voice, "was Gordon's rage at you transient or . . . er . . . obsessive?"

"Seriously," I echoed him, "I don't know." I sighed. "I should think it's too soon to tell. Gordon himself probably doesn't know."

"Do take care, Sid."

"Sure." I sorted through the flurry of impressions I'd gathered in the brief seconds of violence in Pont Square. "I don't know where Ginnie was when she jumped," I said, "but I don't think Gordon was with her. I mean, when he leaped at me he was wearing country clothes. Work-day clothes: mud on his boots, corduroy trousers, old tweed jacket, open-necked blue shirt. He hadn't been staying in any sixteen-story hotel. And the metal bar he hit me with . . . it wasn't a smooth rod, it was a five-foot piece of angle iron, the sort you thread wire through for fencing. I saw the holes in it."

Charles stared.

I said, "I'd say he was at home in Berkshire when he was told about Ginnie. I think if I'd loitered around to search, I would have found Gordon's Land-Rover parked near Pont Square."

Gordon Quint, though a landowner, was a hands-on custodian of his multiple acres. He drove tractors, scythed weeds to clear streams, worked alongside his men to repair his boundaries, re-fence his sheep fields and thin out his woodlands, enjoying both the physical labor and the satisfaction of a job most competently done.

I knew him also as self-admiring and as expecting—and receiving—deference from everyone, including Ginnie. It pleased him to be a generous host while leaving his guests in no doubt of his superior worth.

The man I'd seen in Pont Square, all "squire" manner stripped away, had been a raw, hurt, *outraged* and oddly more genuine person than the Gordon I'd known before: but until I learned for sure which way the explosively tossed-up bricks of his nature would come down, I would keep away from fencing posts and any other agricultural hardware he might be traveling with.

I told Charles I'd engaged Teledrive to come and pick me up. To his raised eyebrows I explained I would put the cost against expenses. Whose expenses? General running expenses, I said.

"Is Mrs. Ferns paying you?" Charles neutrally asked.

"Not anymore."

"Who is, exactly?" He liked me to make a profit. I did, but he seldom believed it.

"I don't starve," I said, drinking my coffee. "Have you ever tried three or four eggs whipped up in mushroom soup? Instant mushroom omelette, not at all bad."

"Disgusting," Charles said.

"You get a different perspective, living alone."

"You need a new wife," Charles said. "What about that girl who used to share a flat with Jenny in Oxford?"

"Louise McInnes?"

"Yes. I thought you and she were having an affair."

No one had affairs anymore. Charles's words were half a century out of date. But though the terms might now be different, the meaning was eternal.

"A summer picnic," I said. "The frosts of winter killed it off."

"Why?"

"What she felt for me was more curiosity than love."

He understood that completely. Jenny had talked about me so long and intimately to her friend Louise, mostly to my detriment, that I recognized—in retrospect—that the friend had chiefly been fascinated in checking out the information personally. It had been a lighthearted passage from mating to parting. Nice while it lasted, but no roots.

When the car came for me I thanked Charles for sanctuary.

"Anytime," he said, nodding.

We parted as usual without physically touching. Eye contact said it all.

Getting the driver to thread his way back and forth through the maze of shopping dead ends in the town of Kingston in Surrey, I acquired six dressing-up party wigs from a carnival store and an angel fish in a plastic tub from a pet shop; and, thus armed, arrived eventually at the children's cancer ward that held Rachel Ferns.

Linda greeted my arrival with glittering tears, but her daughter still lived. Indeed, in one of those unpredictable quirks that made leukemia such a roller coaster of hope and despair, Rachel was marginally better. She was awake, semi-sitting up in bed and pleased at my arrival.

"Did you bring the angel fish?" she demanded by way of greeting.

I held up the plastic bucket, which swung from my plastic wrist. Linda took it and removed the watertight lid, showing her daughter the shining black and silver fish that swam vigorously inside.

Rachel relaxed. "I'm going to call him Sid," she said.

She'd been a lively, blonde, pretty child once, according to her photographs: now she seemed all huge eyes in a bald head. Lassitude and anemia had made her frighteningly frail.

When her mother had first called me in to investigate an attack on Rachel's pony, the illness had been in remission, the dragon temporarily sleeping. Rachel had become someone special to me and I'd given her a fish tank complete with lights, aeration, water plants, Gothic castle arches, sand and brilliant tropical swimming inhabitants. Linda had wept. Rachel had spent hours getting to know her new friends' habits; the ones that skulked in corners, the one who bossed all the rest. Half of the fish were called Sid.

The fish tank stood in the Fernses' sitting room at home and it seemed uncertain now whether Rachel would see the new Sid among his mates.

It was there, in the comfortable middle-sized room furnished with unaggressively expensive modern sofas, with glass-topped end tables and stained-glass Tiffany lamps, that I had first met my clients, Linda and Rachel Ferns.

There were no books in the room, only a few magazines; dress fashions and horses. Shiny striped curtains in crimson and cream; geometrically patterned carpet in merging fawn and gray; flower prints on pale pink walls. Overall the impression was a degree of lack of coordination which probably indicated impulsive inhabitants without strongly formed characters. The Fernses weren't "old" money, I concluded, but there appeared to be plenty of it.

Linda Ferns, on the telephone, had begged me to come. Five or six ponies in the district had been attacked by vandals, and one of the ponies belonged to her daughter, Rachel. The police hadn't found out who the vandals were and now months had gone by, and her daughter was still very distressed and would I *please, please,* come and see if I could help.

"I've heard you're my only hope. I'll pay you, of course. I'll pay you *anything* if you help Rachel. She has these terrible nightmares. *Please.*"

I mentioned my fee.

"Anything," she said.

She hadn't told me, before I arrived in the far-flung village beyond Canterbury, that Rachel was ill unto death.

When I met the huge-eyed bald-headed slender child she shook hands with me gravely.

"Are you really Sid Halley?" she asked.

I nodded.

"Mum said you would come. Daddy said you didn't work for kids."

"I do sometimes."

"My hair is growing," she said; and I could see the thin fine blonde fuzz just showing over the pale scalp.

"I'm glad."

She nodded. "Quite often I wear a wig, but they itch. Do you mind if I don't?"

"Not in the least."

"I have leukemia," she said calmly.

"I see."

She studied my face, a child old beyond her age, as I'd found all sick young people to be.

"You will find out who killed Silverboy, won't you?"

"I'll try," I said. "How did he die?"

"No, no," Linda interrupted. "Don't ask her. I'll tell you. It upsets her. Just say you'll sort them out, those *pigs*. And, Rachel, you take Pegotty out into the garden and push him round so that he can see the flowers."

Pegotty, it transpired, was a contented-looking baby strapped into a buggy. Rachel without demur pushed him out into the garden and could presently be seen through the window giving him a close-up acquaintance with an azalea.

Linda Ferns watched and wept the first of many tears.

"She needs a bone-marrow transplant," she said, trying to suppress sobs. "You'd think it would be simple, but no one so far can find a match to her, not even in the international register set up by the Anthony Nolan Trust."

I said inadequately, "I'm sorry."

"Her father and I are divorced," Linda said. "We divorced five years ago, and he's married again." She spoke without bitterness. "These things happen."

"Yes," I said.

I was at the Ferns house early in a June of languorous days and sweet-smelling roses, a time for the lotus, not horrors.

"A bunch of vandals," Linda said with a fury that set her whole body trembling, "they maimed a lot of ponies in Kent . . . in this area particularly . . . so that poor loving kids went out into their paddocks and found their much-loved ponies *mutilated*. What sick, sick mind would *blind* a poor, inoffensive pony that had never done anyone any harm? Three ponies round here were blinded and others had had knives stuck up their back passages." She blinked on her tears. "Rachel was terribly upset. All the children for miles were crying inconsolably. And the police couldn't find who'd done any of it."

"Was Silverboy blinded?" I asked.

"No . . . No . . . It was worse . . . For Rachel, it was worse. She found him, you see . . . out in the paddock . . ." Linda openly sobbed. "Rachel wanted to sleep in a makeshift stable . . . a lean-to shed, really. She wanted to sleep there at nights with Silverboy tied up there beside her, and I wouldn't let her. She's been ill for nearly three years. It's such a *dreadful* disease, and I feel so helpless. . . ." She wiped her eyes, plucking a tissue from a half-empty box. "She keeps saying it wasn't my fault, but I know she thinks Silverboy would be alive if I'd let her sleep out there."

"What happened to him?" I asked neutrally.

Linda shook her head miserably, unable still to tell me. She was a pretty woman in a conventional thirty-something way: trim figure, well-washed short fair hair, all the health and beauty magazine tips come to admirable life. Only the dullness in the eyes and the intermittent vibrations in many of her muscles spoke plainly of the long strain of emotional buffeting still assailing her.

"She went out," she said eventually, "even though it was bitter cold, and beginning to rain . . . February . . . she always went to see that his water trough was filled and clean and not frozen over . . . and I'd made her put on warm clothes and gloves and a scarf and a real thick woolly hat . . . and she came back running, and screaming . . . *screaming* . . ."

I waited through Linda's unbearable memories.

She said starkly, "Rachel found his *foot.*"

There was a moment of utter stillness, an echo of the stunned disbelief of that dreadful morning.

"It was in all the papers," Linda said.

I moved and nodded. I'd read—months ago—about the blinded Kent ponies. I'd been busy, inattentive: hadn't absorbed names or details, hadn't realized that one of the ponies had lost a foot.

"I've found out since you telephoned," I said, "that round the country, not just here in Kent, there have been another half a dozen or so scattered vandalizing attacks on ponies and horses in fields."

She said unhappily, "I did see a paragraph about a horse in Lancashire, but I threw the paper away so that Rachel wouldn't read it. Every time anything reminds her of Silverboy she has a whole week of nightmares. She wakes up sobbing. She comes into my bed, shivering, crying. Please, please find out why . . . find out *who* . . . She's so ill . . . and although she's in remission just now and able to live fairly normally, it almost certainly won't last. The doctors say she needs the transplant."

I said, "Does Rachel know any of the other children whose ponies were attacked?"

Linda shook her head. "Most of them belonged to the Pony Club, I think, but Rachel didn't feel well enough to join the club. She loved Silverboy—her father gave him to her—but all she could do was sit in the saddle while we led her round. He was a nice, quiet pony, a very nice-looking gray with a darker, smoky-colored mane. Rachel called him Silverboy, but he had a long pedigree name, really. She needed something to *love,* you see, and she wanted a pony so *much.*"

I asked, "Did you keep any of the newspaper accounts of Silverboy and the other local ponies being attacked? If you did, can I see them?"

"Yes," she answered doubtfully, "but I don't see how they could help. They didn't help the police."

"They'd be a start," I said.

"All right, then." She left the room and after a while returned with a small blue suitcase, the size for stowing under the seats of aircraft. "Everything's in here," she said, passing me the case, "including a tape of a program a television company made. Rachel and I are in it. You won't lose it, will you? We never show it, but I wouldn't want to lose it." She blinked against tears. "It was actually the only good thing that happened. Ellis Quint came to see the children and he was utterly sweet with them. Rachel loved him. He was so *kind.*"

"I know him quite well," I said. "If anyone could comfort the children, he could."

"A really *nice* man," Linda said.

I took the blue suitcase with its burden of many small tragedies back with me to London and spent indignant hours reading muted accounts of a degree of vandalism that must have been mind-destroying when fresh and bloody and discovered by loving children.

The twenty-minute videotape showed Ellis Quint at his best: the gentle, sympathetic healer of unbearable sorrows; the sensible, caring commentator urging the police to treat these crimes with the seriousness given to murders. How good he was, I thought, at pitching his responses exactly right. He put his arms around Rachel and talked to her without sentimentality, not mentioning, until right at the end of the program, when the children were off the screen, that for Rachel Ferns the loss of her pony was just one more intolerable blow in a life already full of burdens.

For that program, Rachel had chosen to wear the pretty blonde wig that gave her back her pre-chemotherapy looks. Ellis, as a final dramatic impact, had shown for a few seconds a photo of Rachel bald and vulnerable: an ending poignant to devastation.

I hadn't seen the program when it had been broadcast: judging from the March date on the tape, I knew I'd been away in America trying to find an absconding owner who'd left a monstrous training account unpaid. There were, anyway, many of Ellis's programs I hadn't seen: he presented his twenty-minute twice-weekly journalistic segments as part of an hour-long sports news medley, and was too often on the screen for any one appearance to be especially fanfared.

Meeting Ellis, as I often did at the races, I told him about Linda Ferns calling me in, and asked him if he'd learned any more on the subject of who had mutilated the Kent ponies.

"My dear old Sid," he said, smiling, "all of that was months ago, wasn't it?"

"The ponies were vandalized in January and February and your program was aired in March."

"And it's now June, right?" He shook his head, neither distressed nor surprised. "You know what my life's like, I have *researchers* digging out stories for me. Television is insatiably hungry. Of course if there were any more discoveries about these ponies, I would have been told, and I would have done a follow-up, but I've heard nothing."

I said, "Rachel Ferns, who has leukemia, still has nightmares."

"Poor little kid."

"She said you were very kind."

"Well . . ." he made a ducking, self-deprecating movement of his head, ". . . it isn't so very difficult. Actually that program did marvels for my ratings." He paused. "Sid, do you know anything about this bookmaker kickback scandal I'm supposed to be doing an exposé on next week?"

"Nothing at all," I regretted. "But, Ellis, going back to the mutilations, did you chase up those other scattered cases of foals and two-year-old thoroughbreds that suffered from vandalism?"

He frowned lightly, shaking his head. "The researchers didn't think them worth more than a mention or two. It was copycat stuff. I mean, there wasn't anything as strong as that story about the children." He grinned. "There were no heartstrings attached to the others."

"You're a cynic," I said.

"Aren't we all?"

We had been close friends for years, Ellis and I. We had ridden against each other in races, he as a charismatic amateur, I as a dedicated pro, but both with the inner fire that made hurtling over large jumps on semi-wild half-ton horses at thirty miles an hour seem a wholly reasonable way of passing as many afternoons as possible.

Thinking, after three or four months of no results from the police or the Ellis Quint program, that I would probably fail also in the search for vandals, I nevertheless did my best to earn my fee by approaching the problem crabwise, from the side, by asking questions not of the owners of the ponies, but of the newspapermen who had written the columns in the papers.

I did it methodically on the telephone, starting with the local Kent papers, then chasing up the by-line reporters in the London dailies. Most of the replies were the same: the story had originated from a news agency that supplied all papers with condensed factual information. Follow-ups and interpretation were the business of the papers themselves.

Among the newspapers Linda Ferns had given me, *The Pump* had stirred up the most disgust, and after about six phone calls I ran to earth the man who'd practically burned holes in the page with the heat of his prose: Kevin Mills, *The Pump*'s chief bleeding-hearts reporter.

"A jar?" he said, to my invitation. "Don't see why not."

He met me in a pub (nice anonymous surroundings) and he told me he'd personally been down to Kent on that story. He'd interviewed all the children and their parents and also a fierce lady who ran one of the branches of the Pony Club, and he'd pestered the police until they'd thrown him out.

"Zilch," he said, downing a double gin and tonic. "No one saw a thing. All those ponies were out in fields and all of them were attacked sometime between sunset and dawn, which in January and February gave the vandals hours and hours to do the job and vamoose."

"All dark, though," I said.

He shook his head. "They were all done over on fine nights, near the full moon in each month."

"How many, do you remember?"

"Four altogether in January. Two of them were blinded. Two were mares with torn knife wounds up their . . . well, *birth passages,* as our squeamish editor had me put it."

"And February?"

"One blinded, two more chopped-up mares, one cut-off foot. A poor little girl found the foot near the water trough where her pony used to drink. Ellis Quint did a brilliant TV program about it. Didn't you see it?"

"I was in America, but I've heard about it since."

"There were trailers of that program all week. Almost the whole nation watched it. It made a hell of an impact. That pony was the last one in Kent, as far as I know. The police think it was a bunch of local thugs who got the wind up when there was so much fuss. And people stopped turning ponies out into unguarded fields, see?"

I ordered him another double. He was middle aged, half-bald, doing nicely as to paunch. He wiped an untidy mustache on the back of his hand and said that in his career he'd interviewed so many parents of raped and murdered girls that the ponies had been almost a relief.

I asked him about the later copycat attacks on thoroughbreds in other places, not Kent.

"Copycat?" he repeated. "So they say."

"But?" I prompted.

He drank, thought it over, confided.

"All the others," he said, "are not in bunches, like Kent. As far as I know—and there may be still others—there were about five very young horses, foals and yearlings, that had things done to them, bad enough mostly for them to have to be put down, but none of them was blinded. One had his muzzle hacked off. None of them were mares. But . . ." He hesitated; sure of his facts, I thought, but not of how I would react to them.

"Go on."

"See, three others were two-year-olds, and all of those had a foot off."

I felt the same revulsion that I saw in his face.

"One in March," he said. "One in April. One last month."

"Not," I said slowly, "at the full moon?"

"Not precisely. Just on moonlit nights."

"But why haven't you written about it?"

"I get sent to major disasters," he said patiently. "Air crashes, multiple deaths, dozens of accidents and murders. Some nutter driving around chopping off a horse's foot now and again—it's not my absolute priority, but maybe I'll get round to it. The news agency hasn't picked up on it, but I tend to read provincial papers. Old habit. There has been just a para or two here and there about animal vandals. It's always happening. Horses, sheep, dogs—weirdos get their mucky hands on them. Come to think of it, though, if there's another one this month I'll insist on giving it the both-barrel treatment. And now, don't you go feeding this to other papers. I want my scoop."

"Silence," I promised, "if . . ."

He asked suspiciously, "If what?"

"If you could give me a list of the people whose thoroughbreds have been damaged."

He said cautiously, "It'll cost you."

"Done," I said, and we agreed both on a fee and on my giving him first chance at any story I might come up with.

He fulfilled his commitment that same afternoon by sending a motorbike courier bearing a sealed brown envelope containing photocopies of several inconspicuous small paragraphs culled from provincial papers in Liverpool, Reading, Shrewsbury, Manchester, Birmingham and York. All the papers gave the names and vague addresses of the owners of vandalized thoroughbreds, so I set off by car and visited them.

Four days later, when I returned to Linda Ferns's house in Kent, I had heard enough about man's inhumanity to horses to last me for life. The injuries inflicted, from the hacked-off muzzle onwards, were truly beyond comprehension but, compared with three two-year-olds, were all random and without pattern. It was the severed feet that were connected.

"I came across his foot by the water trough in the field," one woman said, her eyes screwing up at the memory. "I couldn't *believe* it. Just a *foot*. Tell you the truth, I brought up my breakfast. He was a really nice two-year-old colt." She swallowed. "He wasn't standing anywhere near his foot. The off-fore, it was. He'd wandered away on three legs and he was eating grass. Just *eating,* as if nothing had happened. He didn't seem to feel any pain."

"What did you do?" I asked.

"I called the vet. He came . . . He gave *me* a tranquilizer. He said I needed it more than the colt did. He looked after everything for me."

"Was the colt insured?" I asked.

She took no offense at the question. I guessed it had been asked a dozen times already. She said there had been no insurance. They had bred the two-year-old themselves. They had been going to race him later in the year. They had been to Cheltenham races and had backed the winner of the Gold Cup, a great day, and the very next morning . . .

I asked her for the vet's name and address, and I went to see him at his home.

"How was the foot taken off?" I asked.

He wrinkled his forehead. "I don't rightly know. It was neat. The colt had bled very little. There was a small pool of blood on the grass about a yard away from the foot, and that was all. The colt himself let me walk right up to him. He looked calm and normal, except that his off-fore ended at the fetlock."

"Was it done with an axe?"

He hesitated. "I'd say more like a machete. Just the one cut, fast and clean. Whoever did it knew just where to aim for, unless he was simply lucky."

"Did you tell the police?"

"Sure. A detective sergeant came out. He vomited, too. Then I called the knackers and put the colt down. Bloody vandals! I'd like to cut off *their* foot, see if they liked life with a stump." He remembered suddenly about my own sliced-off hand, and reddened, looking confused and embarrassed. There had been a much publicized court case about my hand. Everyone knew what had happened. I had finally stopped wincing visibly when people referred to it.

"It's all right," I said mildly.

"I'm sorry. My big mouth . . ."

"Do you think the colt's amputation was done by a vet? By any sort of surgical expert? Was it done with a scalpel? Was the colt given a local anesthetic?"

He said, disturbed, "I don't know the answers. I'd just say that whoever did it was used to handling horses. That colt was loose in the field, though wearing a head collar."

I went to see the detective sergeant, who looked as if he might throw up again at the memory.

"I see a lot of injured people. Dead bodies, too," he said, "but that was different. Mindless. Fair turned my stomach."

The police had found no culprit. It had been an isolated event, not part of a pattern. The only report they'd had was of the presence of a blue Land-Rover driving away along the lane from the colt's field; and Land-Rovers were two a penny in the countryside. Case not closed, but also not being actively investigated. The colt and his hoof had long gone to the glue factory.

"Are there any photographs?" I asked.

The sergeant said that the photographs were a police matter, not open to the general public.

"I do know who you are," he said, not abrasively, "but to us you're the general public. Sorry."

The colt's owner, consulted, said she had been too upset to want photographs.

I drove onwards, northwards to Lancashire, into a gale of anger. Big, blustery and impressively furious, a hard competent large-scale farmer let loose his roaring sense of injustice, yelling in my face, spraying me with spittle, jabbing the air with a rigid forefinger, pushing his chin forward in a classic animal gesture of aggression.

"Best colt I ever owned," he bellowed. "He cost me a packet, but he was a good 'un. Breeding, conformation, the lot. And he was *fast,* I'll tell you. He was going to Newmarket the next week." He mentioned a prestigious trainer who I knew wouldn't have accepted rubbish. "A good 'un," the farmer repeated. "And then the sodding police asked if I'd killed him for the insurance. I ask you! He wasn't insured, I told them. They said I couldn't *prove* he wasn't insured. Did you know that? Did you know you can prove something *is* insured, but you can't prove it *isn't?* Did you know that?"

I said I'd heard it was so.

"I told them to bugger off. They weren't interested in finding who took my colt's foot off, only in proving I did it myself. They made me that *angry. . . ."* His words failed him. I'd met many people unjustly accused of setting fires, battering children, stealing and taking bribes, and by then I knew the vocal vibrations of truly outraged innocence. The angry farmer, I would have staked all on it, had not taken the foot off his own colt, and I told him so. Some of his anger abated into surprise. "So you *believe* me?"

"I sure do." I nodded. "The point is, who knew you'd bought a fine fast colt that you had at your farm in a field?"

"Who knew?" He suddenly looked guilty, as if he'd already had to face an unpalatable fact. "I'd blown my mouth off a bit. Half the county knew. And I'd been boasting about him at Aintree, the day before the Grand National. I was at one of those sponsors' lunch things—Topline Foods, it was—and the colt was fine that night. I saw him in the morning. And it was the next night, after the National, that he was got at."

He had taken his own color photographs (out of distrust of the police) and he showed them to me readily.

"The off-fore," he said, pointing to a close-up of the severed foot. "He was cut just below the fetlock. Almost through the joint. You can see the white ends of the bones."

The photographs jolted. It didn't help that I'd seen my own left wrist in much the same condition. I said, "What was your vet's opinion?"

"Same as mine."

I went to see the vet. One chop, he said. Only one. No missed shots. Straight through at the leg's most vulnerable point.

"What weapon?"

He didn't know.

I pressed onwards to Yorkshire, where, barely a month earlier, at the time of the York Spring Meeting, a dark-brown two-year-old colt had been deprived of his off-fore foot on a moonlit night. One chop. No insurance. Sick and angry owners. No clues.

These owners were a stiff-upper-lip couple with elderly manners and ancient immutable values who were as deeply bewildered as repelled by the level of evil that would for no clear reason destroy a thing of beauty; in this case the fluid excellence of a fleet, glossy equine princeling.

*"Why?"* they asked me insistently. *"Why* would anyone do such a pointlessly wicked thing?"

I had no answer. I prompted them only to talk, to let out their pain and deprivation. I got them to talk, and I listened.

The wife said, "We had such a lovely week. Every year we have people to stay for the York Spring Meeting . . . because, as you can see, this is quite a large house . . . so we have six or eight friends staying, and we get in extra staff and have a party—such fun, you see—and this year the weather was perfect and we all had a great time."

"Successful, don't you know," said her husband, nodding.

"Dear Ellis Quint was one of our guests," the hostess said with a smile, "and he lifted everyone's spirits in that easy way of his so that it seemed we spent the whole week laughing. He was filming for one of his television programs at York races, so we were all invited behind the scenes and enjoyed it all so much. And then . . . then . . . the very night after all our guests had left . . . well . . ."

"Jenkins came and told us—Jenkins is our groom—he told us while we were sitting at breakfast, that our colt . . . our colt . . ."

"We have three brood-mares," his wife said. "We love to see the foals and yearlings out in the fields, running free, you know . . . and usually we sell the yearlings, but that colt was so beautiful that we kept him, and he was going into training soon. . . . All our guests had admired him."

"Jenkins had made a splendid job of breaking him in."

"Jenkins was in *tears*," the wife said. "Jenkins! A tough, leathery old man. In *tears*."

The husband said with difficulty, "Jenkins found the foot by the gate, beside the water trough."

His wife went on. "Jenkins told us that Ellis had done a program a few months ago about a pony's foot being cut off and the children being so devastated. So we wrote to Ellis about our colt and Ellis telephoned at once to say how *awful* for us. He couldn't have been nicer. Dear Ellis. But there wasn't anything he could do, of course, except sympathize."

"No," I agreed, and I felt only the faintest twitch of surprise that Ellis hadn't mentioned the York colt when I'd been talking to him less than a week earlier about Rachel Ferns.

B ack in London I met Kevin Mills, the journalist from *The Pump*, at lunchtime in the same pub as before.

"It's time for both barrels," I said.

He swigged his double gin. "What have you discovered?"

I outlined the rest of the pattern, beyond what he'd told me about two-year-old colts on moonlit nights. One chop from something like a machete. Always the off-fore foot. Always near a water trough. No insurance. And always just after a major local race meeting: the Gold Cup Festival at Cheltenham; the Grand National at Liverpool; the Spring Meeting at York.

"And this Saturday, two days from now," I said levelly, "we have the Derby."

He put his glass down slowly, and after a full silent minute said, "What about the kid's pony?"

I shrugged resignedly. "It was the first that we know of."

"And it doesn't fit the pattern. Not a two-year-old colt, was he? And no major race meeting, was there?"

"The severed foot was by the water trough. The off-fore foot. Moon in the right quarter. One chop. No insurance."

He frowned, thinking. "Tell you what," he said eventually, "it's worth a *warning*. I'm not a sports writer, as you know, but I'll get the message into the paper somewhere. 'Don't leave your two-year-old colts unguarded in open fields during and after the Epsom meeting.' I don't think I can do more than that."

"It might be enough."

"Yeah. *If* all the owners of colts read *The Pump.*"

"It will be the talk of the racecourse. I'll arrange that."

"On Derby Day?" He looked skeptical. "Still, it will be better than nothing." He drank again. "What we really need to do is catch the bugger redhanded."

We gloomily contemplated that impossibility. Roughly fifteen thousand thoroughbred foals were born each year in the British Isles. Half would be colts. Many of those at two would already be in training for flat racing, tucked away safely in stables; but that still left a host unattended out of doors. By June, also, yearling colts, growing fast, could be mistaken at night for two-year-olds.

Nothing was safe from a determined vandal.

Kevin Mills went away to write his column and I traveled on to Kent to report to my clients.

"Have you found out *who?*" Linda demanded.

"Not yet."

We sat by the sitting-room window again, watching Rachel push Pegotty in his buggy around the lawn, and I told her about the three colts and their shattered owners.

"Three more," Linda repeated numbly. "In March, April and May? And Silverboy in February?"

"That's right."

"And what about *now?* This month . . . *June?*"

I explained about the warning to be printed in *The Pump.*

"I'm not going to tell Rachel about the other three," Linda said. "She wakes up screaming as it is."

"I inquired into other injured horses all over England," I said, "but they were all hurt differently from each other. I think . . . well . . . that there are several different people involved. And I don't think the thugs that blinded and cut the ponies round here had anything to do with Silverboy."

Linda protested. "But they must have done! There couldn't be *two* lots of vandals."

"I think there were."

She watched Rachel and Pegotty, the habitual tears not far away. Rachel was tickling the baby to make him laugh.

"I'd do anything to save my daughter," Linda said. "The doctor said that if only she'd had several sisters, one of them might have had the right tissue type. Joe—Rachel's father—is half Asian. It seems harder to find a match. So I had the baby. I had Pegotty five months ago." She wiped her eyes. "Joe has his new wife and he wouldn't sleep with me again, not even for Rachel. So he donated sperm and I had artificial insemination, and it worked at once. It seemed an omen . . . and I had the baby . . . but he doesn't match Rachel. . . . There was only ever one chance in four that he would have the same tissue type and anti-gens. . . . I hoped and prayed . . . but he *doesn't*." She gulped, her throat clos-ing. "So I have Pegotty . . . he's Peter, really, but we call him Pegotty . . . but Joe won't bond with him . . . and we still can't find a match anywhere for Rachel, and there isn't much time for me to try with another baby . . . and Joe *won't*, anyway. His wife objects . . . and he didn't want to do it the first time."

"I'm so sorry," I said.

"Joe's wife goes on and on about Joe having to pay child support for Pe-gotty . . . and now she's pregnant herself."

Life, I thought, brought unlimited and complicated cruelties.

"Joe isn't mean," Linda said. "He loves Rachel and he bought her the pony and he keeps us comfortable, but his wife says I could have *six* children with-out getting a match. . . ." Her voice wavered and stopped, and after a while she said, "I don't know why I burdened you with all that. You're so easy to talk to."

"And interested."

She nodded, sniffing and blowing her nose. "Go out and talk to Rachel. I told her you were coming back today. She liked you."

Obediently I went out into the garden and gravely shook hands with Rachel, and we sat side by side on a garden bench like two old buddies.

Though still warm, the golden days of early June were graying and grow-ing damp: good for roses, perhaps, but not for the Derby.

I apologized that I hadn't yet found out who had attacked Silverboy.

"But you will in the end, won't you?"

"I hope so," I said.

She nodded. "I told Daddy yesterday that I was sure you would."

"Did you?"

"Yes. He took me out in his car. He does that sometimes, when Didi goes to London to do shopping."

"Is Didi his wife?"

Rachel's nose wrinkled in a grimace, but she made no audible judg-ment. She said, "Daddy says someone chopped your hand off, just like Silverboy."

She regarded me gravely, awaiting confirmation.

"Er," I said, unnerved, "not exactly like Silverboy."

"Daddy says the man who did it was sent to prison, but he's out again now on parole."

"Do you know what 'on parole' means?" I asked curiously.

"Yes. Daddy told me."

"Your daddy knows a lot."

"Yes, but is it *true* that someone chopped your hand off?"

"Does it matter to you?"

"Yes, it does," she said. "I was thinking about it in bed last night. I have awful dreams. I tried to stay awake because I didn't want to go to sleep and dream about you having your hand chopped off."

She was trying to be grown up and calm, but I could feel screaming hysteria too near the surface; so, stifling my own permanent reluctance to talk about it, I gave her an abbreviated account of what had happened.

"I was a jockey," I began.

"Yes, I know. Daddy said you were the champion for years."

"Well, one day my horse fell in a race, and while I was on the ground another horse landed over a jump straight onto my wrist and . . . um . . . tore it apart. It got stitched up, but I couldn't use my hand much. I had to stop being a jockey, and I started doing what I do now, which is finding out things, like who hurt Silverboy."

She nodded.

"Well, I found out something that an extremely nasty man didn't want me to know, and he . . . er . . . he hit my bad wrist and broke it again, and that time the doctors couldn't stitch it up, so they decided that I'd be better off with a useful plastic hand instead of the useless old one."

"So he didn't really . . . not *really* chop it off. Not like with an axe or anything?"

"No. So don't waste dreams on it."

She smiled with quiet relief and, as she was sitting on my left, put her right hand down delicately but without hesitation on the replacement parts. She stroked the tough plastic, unfeeling skin and looked up with surprise at my eyes.

"It isn't *warm*," she said.

"Well, it isn't cold, either."

She laughed with uncomplicated fun. "How does it work?"

"I tell it what to do," I said simply. "I send a message from my brain down my arm saying open thumb from fingers, or close thumb to fingers, to grip things, and the messages reach very sensitive terminals called electrodes, which are inside the plastic and against my skin." I paused, but she didn't say she didn't understand. I said, "My real arm ends about there"—I pointed—"and

the plastic arm goes up round my elbow. The electrodes are up in my forearm, there, against my skin. They feel my muscles trying to move. That's how
they work."

"Is the plastic arm tied on or anything?"

"No. It just fits tightly and stays on by itself. It was specially made to fit me."

Like all children she took marvels for granted, although to me, even though
by then I'd had the false arm for nearly three years, the concept of nerve messages moving machinery was still extraordinary.

"There are three electrodes," I said. "One for opening the hand, one for
closing, and one for turning the wrist."

"Do electrodes work on electricity?" It puzzled her. "I mean, you're not
plugged into the wall, or anything?"

"You're a clever girl," I told her. "It works on a special sort of battery
which slots into the outside above where I wear my watch. I charge up the
batteries on a charger which *is* plugged into the wall."

She looked at me assessingly. "It must be pretty useful to have that hand."

"It's brilliant," I agreed.

"Daddy says Ellis Quint told him that you can't tell you have a plastic
hand unless you touch it."

I asked, surprised, "Does your daddy know Ellis Quint?"

She nodded composedly. "They go to the same place to play squash. He
helped Daddy buy Silverboy. He was really really sorry when he found out it
was Silverboy himself that he was making his program about."

"Yes, he would be."

"I wish . . . ," she began, looking down at my hand, "I do wish Silverboy
could have had a new foot . . . with electrodes and a battery."

I said prosaically, "He might have been able to have a false foot fitted, but
he wouldn't have been able to trot or canter, or jump. He wouldn't have been
happy just limping around."

She rubbed her own fingers over the plastic ones, not convinced.

I said, "Where did you keep Silverboy?"

"The other side of that fence at the end of the garden." She pointed. "You
can't see it from here because of those trees. We have to go through the house
and out and down the lane."

"Will you show me?"

There was a moment of drawing back, then she said, "I'll take you if I can
hold your hand on the way."

"Of course." I stood up and held out my real, warm, normal arm.

"No . . ." She shook her head, standing up also. "I mean, can I hold this
hand that you can't feel?"

It seemed to matter to her that I wasn't whole; that I would understand someone ill, without hair.

I said lightly, "You can hold which hand you like."

She nodded, then pushed Pegotty into the house, and matter-of-factly told Linda she was taking me down to the field to show me where Silverboy had lived. Linda gave me a wild look but let us go, so the bald-headed child and the one-handed man walked in odd companionship down a short lane and leaned against a five-barred gate across the end.

The field was a lush paddock of little more than an acre, the grass growing strongly, uneaten. A nearby standing pipe with an ordinary tap on it stood ready to fill an ordinary galvanized water trough. The ground around the trough was churned up, the grass growing more sparsely, as always happened around troughs in fields.

"I don't want to go in," Rachel said, turning her head away.

"We don't need to."

"His foot was by the trough," she said jerkily, "I mean . . . you could see *blood* . . . and white bones."

"Don't talk about it." I pulled her with me and walked back along the lane, afraid I should never have asked her to show me.

She gripped my unfeeling hand in both of hers, slowing me down.

"It's all right," she said. "It was a long time ago. It's all right now when I'm awake."

"Good."

"I don't like going to sleep."

The desperation of that statement was an open appeal, and had to be addressed.

I stopped walking before we reached the door of the house. I said, "I don't usually tell anyone this, but I'll tell you. I still sometimes have bad dreams about my hand. I dream I can clap with two hands. I dream I'm still a jockey. I dream about my smashed wrist. Rotten dreams can't be helped. They're awful when they happen. I don't know how to stop them. But one does wake up."

"And then you have leukemia . . . or a plastic arm."

"Life's a bugger," I said.

She put her hand over her mouth and, in a fast release of tension, she giggled. "Mum won't let me say that."

"Say it into your pillow."

"Do you?"

"Pretty often."

We went on into the house and Rachel again pushed Pegotty into the garden. I stayed in the sitting room with Linda and watched through the window.

"Was she all right?" Linda asked anxiously.

"She's a very brave child."

Linda wept.

I said, "Did you hear anything at all the night Silverboy was attacked?"

"Everyone asks that. I'd have said if I had."

"No car engines?"

"The police said they must have stopped the car in the road and walked down the lane. My bedroom window doesn't face the lane, nor does Rachel's. But that lane doesn't go anywhere except to the field. As you saw, it's only a track really, it ends at the gate."

"Could anyone see Silverboy from the road?"

"Yes, the police asked that. You could see him come to drink. You can see the water trough from the road, if you know where to look. The police say the thugs must have been out all over this part of Kent looking for unguarded ponies like Silverboy. Whatever you say about two-year-olds, Silverboy *must* have been done by thugs. Why don't you ask the police?"

"If you wholeheartedly believed the police, you wouldn't have asked me for help."

"Joe just telephoned," she confessed, wailing, "and he says that calling you in to help is a waste of money."

"Ah."

"I don't know what to think."

I said, "You're paying me by the day, plus expenses. I can stop right now, if you like."

"No. Yes. I don't *know.*" She wiped her eyes, undecided, and said, "Rachel dreams that Silverboy is standing in the field and he's glowing bright and beautiful in the moonlight. He's *shining,* she says. And there's a dark mass of monsters oozing down the lane . . . 'oozing' is what she says . . . and they are shapeless and devils and they're going to kill Silverboy. She says she is trying to run fast to warn him, and she can't get through the monsters, they clutch at her like cobwebs. She can't get through them and they reach Silverboy and smother his light, and all his hair falls out, and she wakes up and screams. It's always the same nightmare. I thought if you could find out who cut the poor thing's foot off, the monsters would have names and faces and would be in the papers, and Rachel would know who they were and stop thinking they're lumps that ooze without eyes and won't let her through."

After a pause, I said, "Give me another week."

She turned away from me sharply and, crossing to a desk, wrote me a check. "For two weeks, one gone, one ahead."

I looked at the amount. "That's more than we agreed on."

"Whatever Joe says, I want you to go on trying."

I gave her tentatively a small kiss on the cheek. She smiled, her eyes still dark and wet. "I'll pay anything for Rachel," she said.

I drove slowly back to London thinking of the cynical old ex-policeman who had taught me the basics of investigation. "There are two cardinal rules in this trade," he said. "One. Never believe everything a client tells you, and always believe they could have told you more if you'd asked the right questions. And two. Never, never get emotionally involved with your client."

Which was all very well, except when your client was a bright, truthful nine-year-old fighting a losing battle against a rising tide of lymphoblasts.

I BOUGHT A take-out curry on the way home and ate it before spending the evening on overdue paperwork.

I much preferred the active side of the job, but clients wanted, and deserved, and paid for, detailed accounts of what I'd done on their behalf, preferably with results they liked. With the typed recital of work done, I sent also my final bill, adding a list of itemized expenses supported by receipts. I almost always played fair, even with clients I didn't like: investigators had been known to charge for seven days' work when, with a little application, they could have finished the job in three. I didn't want that sort of reputation. Speed succeeded in my new occupation as essentially as in my old.

Besides bathroom and kitchen, my pleasant (and frankly, expensive) apartment consisted of three rooms: bedroom, big sunny sitting room and a third, smaller room that I used as an office. I had no secretary or helper; no one read the secrets I uncovered except the client and me, and whatever the client did with the information he'd paid for was normally his or her own business. Privacy was what drove many people to consult me, and privacy was what they got.

I listened to some unexciting messages on my answering machine, typed a report on my secure word processor, printed it and put it ready for mailing. For reports and anything personal I used a computer system that wasn't connected to any phone line. No one could in consequence tap into it and, as a precaution against thieves, I used unbreakable passwords. It was my second system that could theoretically be accessed; the one connected by modem to the big wide world of universal information. Any snooper was welcome to anything found there.

On the subject of the management of secrecy, my cynical mentor had said, "Never, ever tell your right hand what your left hand is doing. Er . . . ," he added, "whoops. Sorry, Sid."

"It'll cost you a pint."

"And," he went on later, drinking, "keep back-up copies of completed sensitive inquiries in a bank vault, and wipe the information from any computer systems in your office. If you use random passwords, and change them weekly, you should be safe enough while you're actually working on something, but once you've finished, get the back-up to the bank and wipe the office computer, like I said."

"All right."

"Never forget," he told me, "that the people you are investigating may go to violent lengths to stop you."

He had been right about that.

"Never forget that you don't have the same protection as the police do. You have to make your own protection. You have to be careful."

"Maybe I should look for another job."

"No, Sid," he said earnestly, "you have a gift for this. You listen to what I tell you and you'll do fine."

He had taught me for the two years I'd spent doing little but drift in the old Radnor detection agency after the end of my racing life and, for nearly three years since, I'd lived mostly by his precepts. But he was dead now, and Radnor himself also, and I had to look inward for wisdom, which could be a variable process, not always ultraproductive.

I could try to comfort Rachel by telling her I had bad dreams also, but I could never have told her how vivid and liquefying they could be. That night, after I'd eased off the arm and showered and gone peacefully to bed, I fell asleep thinking of her, and descended after midnight into a familiar dungeon.

It was always the same.

I dreamed I was in a big dark space, and some people were coming to cut off both my hands.

*Both.*

They were making me wait, but they would come. There would be agony and humiliation and helplessness . . . and no way out.

I semi-awoke in shaking, sweating, heart-thudding terror and then realized with flooding relief that it wasn't true, I was safe in my own bed—and then remembered that it had already half happened in fact, and also that I'd come within a fraction once of a villain's shooting the remaining hand off. As soon as I was awake enough to be clear about the present actual not-too-bad state of affairs I slid back reassured into sleep, and that night the whole appalling nightmare cycled again . . . and again.

I forced myself to wake up properly, to sit up and get out of bed and make full consciousness take over. I stood under the shower again and let cool water run through my hair and down my body. I put on a terry cloth bathrobe and poured a glass of milk, and sat in an armchair in the sitting room with all the lights on.

I looked at the space where a left hand had once been, and I looked at the strong whole right hand that held a glass, and I acknowledged that often, both waking as well as sleeping, I felt, and could not repress, stabs of savage, petrifying fear that one day it would indeed be both. The trick was not to let the fear show, nor to let it conquer, nor rule, my life.

It was pointless to reflect that I'd brought the terrors on myself. I had chosen to be a jockey. I had chosen to go after violent crooks. I was at that moment actively seeking out someone who knew how to cut off a horse's foot with one chop.

My own equivalent of the off-fore held a glass of milk.

I had to be mentally deranged.

But then there were people like Rachel Ferns.

In one way or another I had survived many torments, and much could have been avoided but for my own obstinate nature. I knew by then that whatever came along, I would deal with it. But that child had had her hair fall out and had found her beloved pony's foot, and none of that was her fault. No nine-year-old mind could sleep sweetly under such assaults.

Oh God, Rachel, I thought, I would dream your nightmares for you if I could.

IN THE MORNING I made a working analysis in five columns of the Ferns pony and the three two-year-olds. The analysis took the form of a simple graph, ruled in boxes. Across the top of the page I wrote: Factors, Ferns, Cheltenham, Aintree, York, and down the left-hand column, Factors, I entered "date," "name of owner," "racing program," "motive" and finally, "who knew of victim's availability?" I found that although I could *think* of answers to that last question, I hadn't the wish to write them in, and after a bit of indecision I phoned Kevin Mills at *The Pump* and, by persistence, reached him.

"Sid," he said heartily, "the warning will be in the paper tomorrow. You've done your best. Stop agitating."

"Great," I said, "but could you do something else? Something that could come innocently from *The Pump,* but would raise all sorts of reverberations if I asked directly myself."

"Such as what?"

"Such as ask Topline Foods for a list of the guests they entertained at a sponsors' lunch at Aintree the day before the National."

"What the *hell* for?"

"Will you do it?"

He said, "What are you up to?"

"The scoop is still yours. Exclusive."

"I don't know why I trust you."

"It pays off," I said, smiling.

"It had better." He put down his receiver with a crash, but I knew he would do what I asked.

It was Friday morning. At Epsom that day they would be running the Coronation Cup and also the Oaks, the fillies' equivalent of the Derby. It was also lightly raining: a weak warm front, it seemed, was slowly blighting southern England.

Racecourses still drew me as if I were tethered to them with bungee elastic, but before setting out I telephoned the woman whose colt's foot had been amputated during the night after the Cheltenham Gold Cup.

"I'm sorry to bother you again, but would you mind a few more questions?"

"Not if you can catch the bastards."

"Well . . . was the two-year-old alone in his field?"

"Yes, he was. It was only a paddock. Railed, of course. We kept him in the paddock nearest to the house, that's what is so infuriating. We had two old hacks turned out in the field beyond him, but the vandals left them untouched."

"And," I said neutrally, "how many people knew the colt was accessible? And how accessible was he?"

"Sid," she exclaimed, "don't think we haven't racked our brains. The trouble is, all our friends knew about him. We were excited about his prospects. And then, at the Cheltenham meeting, we had been talking to people about *trainers.* Old Gunners, who used to train for us in the past, has died, of course, and we don't like that uppity assistant of his that's taken over the stable, so we were asking around, you see."

"Yeah. And did you decide on a trainer?"

"We did, but, of course . . ."

"Such a bloody shame," I sympathized. "Who did you decide on?"

She mentioned a first-class man. "Several people said that with him we couldn't go wrong."

"No." I mentally sighed, and asked obliquely, "What did you especially enjoy about the festival meeting?"

"The Queen came," she said promptly. "I had thick, warm boots on, and I nearly fell over them, curtseying." She laughed. "And oh, also, I suppose you do know you're in the Hall of Fame there?"

"It's an honor," I said. "They gave me an engraved glass goblet that I can see across the room right now from where I'm sitting."

"Well, we were standing in front of that big exhibit they've put together of your life, and we were reading the captions, and dear Ellis Quint stopped beside us and put his arm round my shoulders and said that our Sid was a pretty great guy, all in all."

Oh *shit,* I thought.

Her warm smile was audible down the line. "We've known Ellis for years, of course. He used to ride our horses in amateur races. So he called in at our house for a drink on his way home after the Gold Cup. Such a *lovely* day." She sighed. "And then those *bastards* . . . You will catch them, won't you, Sid?"

"If I can," I said.

I left a whole lot of the boxes empty on my chart, and drove to Epsom Downs, spirits as gray as the skies. The bars were crowded. Umbrellas dripped. The brave colors of June dresses hid under drabber raincoats, and only the geraniums looked happy.

I walked damply to the parade ring before the two-year-old colts' six-fur-long race and thoughtfully watched all the off-fore feet plink down light-heartedly. The young, spindly bones of those forelegs thrust thousand-pound bodies forward at sprinting speeds near forty miles an hour. I had mostly raced on the older, mature horses of steeplechasing, half a ton in weight, slightly slower, capable of four miles and thirty jumps from start to finish, but still on legs scarcely thicker than a big man's wrist.

The anatomy of a horse's foreleg consisted, from the shoulder down, of forearm, knee, cannon bone, fetlock joint (also known as the ankle), pastern bone, and hoof. The angry Lancashire farmer's colored photograph had shown the amputation to have been effected straight through the narrowest part of the whole leg, just at the base of the fetlock joint, where the pastern emerged from it. In effect, the whole pastern and the hoof had been cut off.

Horses had very fast instincts for danger and were easily scared. Young horses seldom stood still. Yet one single chop had done the job each time. *Why* had all those poor animals stood quietly while the deed was done? None of them had squealed loud enough to alert his owner.

I went up on the stands and watched the two-year-olds set off from the spur away to the left at the top of the hill; watched them swoop down like a flock of starlings round Tattenham Corner, and sort themselves out into winner and losers along the straight with its deceptively difficult camber that could tilt a horse towards the rails if his jockey was inexperienced.

I watched, and I sighed. Five long years had passed since I'd ridden my last race. Would regret, I wondered, ever fade?

"Why so pensive, Sid lad?" asked an elderly trainer, grasping my elbow. "A scotch and water for your thoughts!" He steered me around towards the nearest bar and I went with him unprotestingly, as custom came my way quite often in that casual manner. He was great with horses and famously mean with his money.

"I hear you're damned expensive," he began inoffensively, handing me a glass. "What will you charge me for a day's work?"

I told him.

"Too damned much. Do it for nothing, for old times' sake."

I added, smiling, "How many horses do you train for nothing?"

"That's different."

"How many races would you have asked me to ride for nothing?"

"Oh, all *right,* then. I'll pay your damned fee. The fact is, I think I'm being *had,* and I want you to find out."

It seemed he had received a glowing testimonial from the present employer of a chauffeur/houseman/handyman who'd applied for a job he'd advertised. He wanted to know if it was worth bringing the man up for an interview.

"She," he said, "his employer is a woman. I phoned her when I got the letter, to check the reference, you see. She couldn't have been more complimentary about the man if she'd tried, but . . . I don't know . . . She was *too* complimentary, if you see what I mean."

"You mean you think she might be glad to see the back of him?"

"You don't hang about, Sid. That's exactly what I mean."

He gave me the testimonial letter of fluorescent praise.

"No problem," I said, reading it. "One day's fee, plus travel expenses. I'll phone you, then send you a written report."

"You still *look* like a jockey," he complained. "You're a damned sight more expensive on your feet."

I smiled, put the letter away in a pocket, drank his scotch and applauded the string of winners he'd had recently, cheering him up before separating him from his cash.

I drifted around pleasurably but unprofitably for the rest of the day, slept thankfully without nightmares and found on a dry and sunny Derby Day morning that my friendly *Pump* reporter had really done his stuff.

"Lock up your colts," he directed in the paper. "You've heard of foot fetishists? This is one beyond belief."

He outlined in succinct paragraphs the similarities in "the affair of the four severed fetlocks" and pointed out that on that very night after the Derby—the biggest race of all—there would be moonlight enough at three A.M. for flashlights to be unnecessary. All two-year-old colts should, like Cinderella, be safe indoors by midnight. "And if . . . ," he finished with a flourish, ". . . you should spy anyone creeping through the fields armed with a machete, phone ex-jockey turned gumshoe Sid Halley, who provided the information gathered here and can be reached via *The Pump*'s special hotline. Phone *The Pump!* Save the colts! Halley to the rescue!"

I COULDN'T IMAGINE how he had got that last bit—including a telephone number—past any editor, but I needn't have worried about spreading the message on the racecourse. No one spoke to me about anything else all afternoon.

I phoned *The Pump* myself and reached someone eventually who told me that Kevin Mills had gone to a train crash; sorry.

"Damn," I said. "So how are you rerouting calls about colts to me? I didn't arrange this. How will it work?"

"Hold on."

I held on. A different voice came back.

"As Kevin isn't available, we're rerouting all Halley hotline calls to this number," he said, and he read out my own Pont Square number.

"Where's your bloody Mills? I'll wring his neck."

"Gone to the train crash. Before he left he gave us this number for reaching you. He said you would want to know at once about any colts."

That was true enough—but hell's bloody bells, I thought, I could have set it up better if he'd warned me.

I watched the Derby with inattention. An outsider won.

Ellis teased me about the piece in *The Pump*.

"Hotline Halley," he said, laughing and clapping me on the shoulder, tall and deeply friendly and wiping out in a flash the incredulous doubts I'd been having about him. "It's an extraordinary coincidence, Sid, but I actually *saw* one of those colts. Alive, of course. I was staying with some chums for York, and after we'd gone home someone vandalized their colt. Such fun people. They didn't deserve anything like that."

"No one does."

"True."

"The really puzzling thing is motive," I said. "I went to see all the owners. None of the colts was insured. Nor was Rachel Ferns's pony, of course."

He said interestedly, "Did you think it was an insurance scam?"

"It jumps to mind, doesn't it? Theoretically it's possible to insure a horse and collect the lucre without the owner knowing anything about it. It's been done. But if that's what this is all about, perhaps someone in an insurance company somewhere will see the piece in *The Pump* and connect a couple of things. Come to think of it," I finished slowly, "I might send a copy to every likely insurance company's board of directors, asking, and warning them."

"Good idea," he said. "Does insurance and so on really take the place of racing? It sounds a pretty dull life for you, after what we used to do."

"Does television replace it for you?"

"Not a hope." He laughed. "Danger is addictive, wouldn't you say? The only dangerous job in television is reporting wars and—have you noticed?—the same few war reporters get out there all the time, talking with their earnest, committed faces about this or that month's little dust-up, while bullets fly and chip off bits of stone in the background to prove how brave they are."

"You're jealous." I smiled.

"I get sodding bored sometimes with being a chat-show celebrity, even if it's nice being liked. Don't you ache for speed?"

"Every day," I said.

"You're about the only person who understands me. No one else can see that fame's no substitute for danger."

"It depends what you risk."

Hands, I thought. One could risk hands.

"Good luck, Hotline," Ellis said.

It was the owners of two-year-old colts that had the good luck. My telephone jammed and rang nonstop all evening and all night when I got home after the Derby, but the calls were all from people enjoying their shivers and jumping at shadows. The moonlight shone on quiet fields, and no animal, whether colt or two-year-old thoroughbred or children's pony, lost a foot.

In the days that followed, interest and expectation dimmed and died. It was twelve days after the Derby, on the last night of the Royal Ascot meeting, that the screaming heebie-jeebies re-awoke.

On the Monday after the Derby I trailed off on the one-day dig into the overblown reference and, without talking to the lady-employer herself (which would clearly have been counterproductive) I uncovered enough to phone the tight-fisted trainer with sound advice.

"She wants to get rid of him without risk of being accused of unfair dismissal," I said. "He steals small things from her house which pass through a couple of hands and turn up in the local antique shop. She can't prove they were hers. The antique shop owner is whining about his innocence. The lady has apparently said she won't try to prosecute her houseman if he gets the heck out. Her testimonial is part of the bargain. The houseman is a regular in the local betting shop, and gambles heavily on horses. Do you want to employ him?"

"Like hell."

"The report I'll write and send to you," I told him, "will say only, 'Work done on recruitment of staff.' You can claim tax relief on it."

He laughed dryly. "Anytime you want a reference," he said, pleased, "I'll write you an affidavit."

"You never know," I said, "and thanks."

I had phoned the report from the car park of a motorway service station on my way home late in the dusky evening, but it was when I reached Pont Square that the day grew doubly dark. There was a two-page fax waiting on my machine and I read it standing in the sitting room with all thoughts of a friendly glass of scotch evaporating into disbelief and the onset of misery.

The pages were from Kevin Mills. "I don't know why you want this list of the great and good," he wrote, "but for what it's worth and because I promised, here is a list of the guests entertained by Topline Foods at lunch at Aintree on the day before the Grand National."

The list contained the name of the angry Lancashire farmer, as was expected, but it was the top of the list that did the psychological damage.

"Guest of Honor," it announced, "Ellis Quint."

All the doubts I'd banished came roaring back with double vigor. Back too came self-ridicule and every defense mechanism under the sun.

I couldn't, didn't, *couldn't* believe that Ellis could maim—and effectively kill—a child's pony and three young racehorses. Not Ellis! No! It was *impossible.*

There had to be *dozens* of other people who could have learned where to find all four of those vulnerable, unguarded animals. It was *stupid* to give any weight to an unreliable coincidence. All the same, I pulled my box chart out of a drawer, and in very small letters, as if in that way I could physically diminish the implication, I wrote in each "Who knew of victim's availability" space the unthinkable words, Ellis Quint.

The "motive" boxes had also remained empty. There was no apparent rational motive. Why did people poke out the eyes of ponies? Why did they stalk strangers and write poison-pen letters? Why did they torture and kill children and tape-record their screams?

I wrote "self-gratification," but it seemed too weak. Insanity? Psychosis? The irresistible primordial upsurge of a hunger for pointless, violent destruction?

It didn't fit the Ellis I knew. Not the man I'd raced against and laughed with and had deemed a close friend for years. One couldn't know someone that well, and yet not know them at all.

Could one?

No.

Relentless thoughts kept me awake all night, and in the morning I sent Linda Ferns's check back to her, uncashed.

"I've got no further," I wrote. "I'm exceedingly sorry."

Two days later the same check returned.

"Dear Sid," Linda replied, "Keep the money. I know you'll find the thugs one day. I don't know what you said to Rachel but she's much happier and she hasn't had any bad dreams since you came last week. For that alone I would pay you double. Affectionately, Linda Ferns."

I put the check in a pending file, caught up with paperwork and attended my usual judo training session.

The judo I practiced was the subtle art of self-defense, the shifting of balance that used an attacker's own momentum to overcome him. Judo was rhythm, leverage and speed; a matter sometimes of applying pressure to nerves and always, in the way I learned, a quiet discipline. The yells and the kicks of karate, the arms slapped down on the padded mat to emphasize aggression, they were neither in my nature nor what I needed. I didn't seek physical domination. I didn't by choice start fights. With the built-in drawbacks of half an arm, a light frame and a height of about five feet seven, my overall requirement was survival.

I went through the routines absentmindedly. They were at best a mental crutch. A great many dangers couldn't be wiped out by an ability to throw an assailant over one's shoulder.

Ellis wouldn't leave my thoughts.

I was wrong. Of *course* I was wrong.

His face was universally known. He wouldn't risk being seen sneaking around fields at night armed with anything like a machete.

But he was bored with celebrity. Fame was no substitute for danger, he'd said. Everything he had was not enough.

All the same . . . *he couldn't.*


IN THE SECOND week after the Derby I went to the four days of the Royal Ascot meeting, drifting around in a morning suit, admiring the gleaming coats of the horses and the women's extravagant hats. I should have enjoyed it, as I usually did. Instead, I felt as if the whole thing were a charade taking illusory place over an abyss.

Ellis, of course, was there every day: and, of course, he sought me out.

"How's it going, Hotline?"

"The hotline is silent."

"There you are, then," Ellis said with friendly irony, "you've frightened your foot merchant off."

"Forever, I hope."

"What if he can't help it?" Ellis said.

I turned my head: looked at his eyes. "I'll catch him," I said.

He smiled and looked away. "Everyone knows you're a whiz at that sort of thing, but I'll bet you—"

"Don't," I interrupted. "Don't bet on it. It's bad luck."

Someone came up to his other elbow, claiming his attention. He patted my shoulder, said with the usual affection, "See you, Sid," and was drawn away; and I couldn't believe, I *couldn't,* that he had told me *why,* even if not how.

"*What if he can't help it?*"

Could compulsion lead to cruel, senseless acts?

No . . .

Yes, it could, and yes, it often did.

But not in Ellis. No, *not* in Ellis.

Alibis, I thought, seeking for a rational way out. I would find out—somehow—exactly where Ellis had been on the nights the horses had been attacked. I would prove to my own satisfaction that it couldn't have been Ellis, and I would return with relief to the beginning and admit I had no pointers at all and would never find the thugs for Linda, and would quite happily chalk up a failure.

At five-thirty in the morning on the day after the Ascot Gold Cup, I sleepily awoke and answered my ringing telephone to hear a high agitated female voice saying, "I want to reach Sid Halley."

"You have," I said, pushing myself up to sitting and squinting at the clock.

"What?"

"You are talking to Sid Halley." I stifled a yawn. Five-bloody-thirty.

"But I phoned *The Pump* and asked for the hotline!"

I said patiently, "They reroute the hotline calls direct to me. This is Sid Halley you're talking to. How can I help you?"

"Christ," she said, sounding totally disorganized. "We have a colt with a foot off."

After a breath-catching second I said, "Where are you?"

"At home. Oh, I see, Berkshire."

"Where, exactly?"

"Combe Bassett, south of Hungerford."

"And . . . um . . ." I thought of asking, "What's the state of play?" and discarded it as less than tactful. "What is . . . happening?"

"We're all up. Everyone's yelling and crying."

"And the vet?"

"I just phoned him. He's coming."

"And the police?"

"They're sending someone. Then we decided we'd better call you."

"Yes," I replied. "I'll come now, if you like."

"That's why I phoned you."

"What's your name, then? Address?"

She gave them—"Betty Bracken, Manor House, Combe Bassett"—stumbling on the words as if she couldn't remember.

"Please," I said, "ask the vet not to send the colt or his foot off to the knackers until I get there."

"I'll try," she said jerkily. "For God's sakes, *why?* Why our colt?"

"I'll be there in an hour," I said.

*What if he can't help it . . .*

But it took such planning. Such stealth. So many crazy risks. Someone, sometime, would see him.

Let it not be Ellis, I thought. Let the compulsion be some other poor bastard's ravening subconscious. Ellis would be able to control such a vicious appetite, even if he felt it.

Let it not be Ellis.

Whoever it was, he had to be stopped: and I would stop him, if I could.

I shaved in the car (a Mercedes), clasping the battery-driven razor in the battery-driven hand, and I covered the eighty miles to southwest Berkshire in a time down the comparatively empty M4 that had the speedometer needle quivering where it had seldom been before. The radar speed traps slept. Just as well.

It was a lovely high June morning, fine and fresh. I curled through the gates of Combe Bassett Manor, cruised to a stop in the drive and at six-thirty walked into a house where open doors led to movement, loud voices and a general gnashing of teeth.

The woman who'd phoned rushed over when she saw me, her hands flapping in the air, her whole demeanor in an out-of-control state of fluster.

"Sid Halley? Thank God. Punch some sense into this lot."

This lot consisted of two uniformed policemen and a crowd of what later proved to be family members, neighbors, ramblers and half a dozen dogs.

"Where's the colt?" I asked. "And where's his foot?"

"Out in the field. The vet's there. I told him what you wanted but he's an opinionated Scot. God knows if he'll wait, he's a cantankerous old devil. He—"

"Show me where," I said abruptly, cutting into the flow.

She blinked. "What? Oh, yes. This way."

She set off fast, leading me through big-house, unevenly painted hinterland passages reminiscent of those of Aynsford, of those of any house built with servants in mind. We passed a gun room, flower room and mud room (ranks of green wellies) and emerged at last through a rear door into a yard inhabited by trash cans. From there, through a green wooden garden door, she led the way fast down a hedge-bordered grass path and through a metal-railing gate at the far end of it. I'd begun to think we were off to limbo when sud-

denly, there before us, was a lane full of vehicles and about ten people leaning on paddock fencing.

My guide was tall, thin, fluttery, at a guess about fifty, dressed in old cord
trousers and a drab olive sweater. Her graying hair flopped, unbrushed, over
a high forehead. She had been, and still was, beyond caring how she looked,
but I had a powerful impression that she was a woman to whom looks mattered little anyway.

She was deferred to. The men leaning on the paddock rails straightened and
all but touched their forelocks. "Morning, Mrs. Bracken."

She nodded automatically and ushered me through the wide metal gate
that one of the men swung open for her.

Inside the field, at a distance of perhaps thirty paces, stood two more men,
also a masculine-looking woman and a passive colt with three feet. All, except
the colt, showed the facial and body language of impatience.

One of the men, tall, white-haired, wearing black-rimmed glasses, took
two steps forward to meet us.

"Now, Mrs. Bracken, I've done what you asked, but it's past time to put
your poor boy out of his misery. And you'll be Sid Halley, I suppose," he said,
peering down as from a mountaintop. "There's little you can do." He shook
hands briefly as if it were a custom he disapproved of.

He had a strong Scottish accent and the manner of one accustomed to
command. The man behind him, unremarkably built, self-effacing in manner,
remained throughout a silent watcher on the fringe.

I walked over to the colt and found him wearing a head collar, with a rope
halter held familiarly by the woman. The young horse watched me with
calm, bright eyes, unafraid. I stroked my hand down his nose, talking to him
quietly. He moved his head upward against the pressure and down again as if
nodding, saying hello. I let him whiffle his black lips across my knuckles. I
stroked his neck and patted him. His skin was dry: no pain, no fear, no distress.

"Is he drugged?" I asked.

"I'd have to run a blood test," the Scotsman said.

"Which you are doing, of course?"

"Of course."

One could tell from the faces of the other man and the woman that no
blood test had so far been considered.

I moved around the colt's head and squatted down for a close look at his
off-fore, running my hand down the back of his leg, feeling only a soft area
of no resistance where normally there would be the tough bowstring tautness
of the leg's main tendon. Pathetically, the fetlock was tidy, not bleeding. I bent

up the colt's knee and looked at the severed end. It had been done neatly, sliced through, unsplintered ends of bone showing white, the skin cleanly cut as if a practiced chef had used a disjointing knife.

The colt jerked his knee, freeing himself from my grasp.

I stood up.

"Well?" the Scotsman challenged.

"Where's his foot?"

"Over yon, out of sight behind the water trough." He paused, then, as I turned away from him, suddenly added, "It wasn't found there. I put it there, out of sight. It was they ramblers that came to it first."

"Ramblers?"

"Aye."

Mrs. Bracken, who had joined us, explained. "One Saturday every year in June, all the local rambling clubs turn out in force to walk the footpaths in this part of the country, to keep them legally open for the public."

"If they'd stay on the footpaths," the Scot said forbiddingly, "they'd be within their rights."

Mrs. Bracken agreed. "They bring their children and their dogs and their picnics, and act as if they own the place."

"But . . . what on earth time did they find your colt's foot?"

"They set off soon after dawn," Mrs. Bracken observed morosely. "In the middle of June, that's four-thirty in the morning, more or less. They gather before five o'clock, while it is still cool, and set off across my land first, and they were hammering on my door by five-fifteen. Three of the children were in full-blown hysteria, and a man with a beard and a pony-tail was screaming that he blamed the elite. What elite? One of the ramblers phoned the press and then someone fanatical in animal rights, and a carload of activists arrived with 'ban horse racing' banners." She rolled her eyes. "I *despair*," she said. "It's bad enough losing my glorious colt. These people are turning it into a *circus.*"

Hold on to the real tragedy at the heart of the farce, I thought briefly, and walked over to the water trough to look at the foot that lay behind it. There were horse-feed nuts scattered everywhere around. Without expecting much emotion, I bent and picked the foot up.

I hadn't seen the other severed feet. I'd actually thought some of the reported reactions excessive. But the reality of that poor, unexpected, curiously lonely lump of bone, gristle and torn ends of blood vessels, that wasted miracle of anatomical elegance, moved me close to the fury and grief of all the owners.

There was a shoe on the hoof; the sort of small, light shoe fitted to youngsters to protect their forefeet out in the field. There were ten small nails tacking the shoe to the hoof. The presence of the shoe brought its own powerful message: civilization had offered care to the colt's foot, barbarity had hacked it off.

I'd loved horses always: it was hard to explain the intimacy that grew between horses and those who tended or rode them. Horses lived in a parallel world, spoke a parallel language, were a mass of instincts, lacked human perceptions of kindness or guilt, and allowed a merging on an untamed, untamable mysterious level of spirit. The Great God Pan lived in racehorses. One cut off his foot at one's peril.

On a more prosaic level I put the hoof back on the ground, unclipped the mobile phone I wore on my belt and, consulting a small diary/notebook for the number, connected myself to a veterinary friend who worked as a surgeon in an equine hospital in Lambourn.

"Bill?" I said. "This is Sid Halley."

"Go to sleep," he said.

"Wake up. It's six-fifty and I'm in Berkshire with the severed off-fore hoof of a two-year-old colt."

"Jesus." He woke up fast.

"I want you to look at it. What do you advise?"

"How long has it been off? Any chance of sewing it back on?"

"It's been off at least three hours, I'd say. Probably more. There's no sign of the Achilles tendon. It's contracted up inside the leg. The amputation is through the fetlock joint itself."

"One blow, like the others?"

I hesitated. "I didn't see the others."

"But something's worrying you?"

"I want you to look at it," I said.

Bill Ruskin and I had worked on other, earlier puzzles, and got along together in a trusting, undemanding friendship that remained unaltered by periods of non-contact.

"What shape is the colt in, generally?" he asked.

"Quiet. No visible pain."

"Is the owner rich?"

"It looks like it."

"See if he'll have the colt—and his foot, of course—shipped over here."

"She," I said. "I'll ask her."

Mrs. Bracken gaped at me mesmerized when I relayed the suggestion, and said "Yes" faintly.

Bill said, "Find a sterile surgical dressing for the leg. Wrap the foot in another dressing and a plastic bag and pack it in a bucket of ice cubes. Is it clean?"

"Some early-morning ramblers found it."

He groaned. "I'll send a horse ambulance," he said. "Where to?"

I explained where I was, and added, "There's a Scots vet here that's urging to put the colt down at once. Use honey-tongued diplomacy."

"Put him on."

I returned to where the colt still stood and, explaining who he would be talking to, handed my phone to the vet. The Scot scowled. Mrs. Bracken said "Anything, anything," over and over again. Bill talked.

"Very well," the Scot said frostily, finally, "but you do understand, don't you, Mrs. Bracken, that the colt won't be able to race, even if they do succeed in reattaching his foot, which is very, very doubtful."

She said simply, "I don't want to lose him. It's worth a try."

The Scot, to give him his due, set about enclosing the raw leg efficiently in a dressing from his surgical bag and in wrapping the foot in a businesslike bundle. The row of men leaning on the fence watched with interest. The masculine-looking woman holding the head collar wiped a few tears from her weather-beaten cheeks while crooning to her charge, and eventually Mrs. Bracken and I returned to the house, which still rang with noise. The ramblers, making the most of the drama, seemed to be rambling all over the ground floor and were to be seen assessing their chances of penetrating upstairs. Mrs. Bracken clutched her head in distraction and said, "Please, will everyone leave," but without enough volume to be heard.

I begged one of the policemen, "Shoo the lot out, can't you?" and finally most of the crowd left, the ebb revealing a large basically formal pale green and gold drawing room inhabited by five or six humans, three dogs and a clutter of plastic cups engraving wet rings on ancient polished surfaces. Mrs. Bracken, like a somnambulist, drifted around picking up cups from one place only to put them down in another. Ever tidy minded, I couldn't stop myself twitching up a wastepaper basket and following her, taking the cups from her fingers and collecting them all together.

She looked at me vaguely. She said, "I paid a quarter of a million for that colt."

"Is he insured?"

"No. I don't insure my jewelry, either."

"Or your health?"

"No, of course not."

She looked unseeingly around the room. Five people now sat on easy chairs, offering no help or succor.

"Would someone make a cup of tea?" she asked.

No one moved.

She said to me, as if it explained everything, "Esther doesn't start work until eight."

"Mm," I said. "Well . . . er . . . who is everybody?"

"Goodness, yes. Rude of me. That's my husband." Her gaze fell affectionately on an old bald man who looked as if he had no comprehension of anything. "He's deaf, the dear man."

"I see."

"And that's my aunt, who mostly lives here."

The aunt was also old and proved unhelpful and selfish.

"Our tenants." Mrs. Bracken indicated a stolid couple. "They live in part of the house. And my nephew."

Even her normal good manners couldn't keep the irritation from either her voice or her face at this last identification. The nephew was a teenager with a loose mouth and an attitude problem.

None of this hopeless bunch looked like an accomplice in a spite attack on a harmless animal, not even the unsatisfactory boy, who was staring at me intensely as if demanding to be noticed: almost, I thought fleetingly, as if he wanted to tell me something by telepathy. It was more than an interested inspection, but also held neither disapproval nor fear, as far as I could see.

I said to Mrs. Bracken, "If you tell me where the kitchen is, I'll make you some tea."

"But you've only one hand."

I said reassuringly, "I can't climb Everest but I can sure make tea."

A streak of humor began to banish the morning's shocks from her eyes. "I'll come with you," she said.

The kitchen, like the whole house, had been built on a grand scale for a cast of dozens. Without difficulties we made tea in a pot and sat at the well-scrubbed old wooden central table to drink it from mugs.

"You're not what I expected," she said. "You're *cozy.*"

I liked her, couldn't help it.

She went on, "You're not like my brother said. I'm afraid I didn't explain that it is my brother who is out in the field with the vet. It was he who said I should phone you. He didn't say you were cozy, he said you were flint. I should have introduced you to him, but you can see how things are. . . . Anyway, I rely on him dreadfully. He lives in the next village. He came at once when I woke him."

"Is he," I asked neutrally, "your nephew's father?"

"Goodness, no. My nephew . . . Jonathan . . ." She stopped, shaking her head. "You don't want to hear about Jonathan."

"Try me."

"He's our sister's son. Fifteen. He got into trouble, expelled from school . . . on probation . . . his step-father can't stand him. My sister was at her wits' end so I said he could come here for a bit. It's not working out, though. I can't get through to him." She looked suddenly aghast. "You don't think he had anything to do with the colt?"

"No, no. What trouble did he get into? Drugs?"

She sighed, shaking her head. "He was with two other boys. They stole a car and crashed it. Jonathan was in the back seat. The boy driving was also fifteen and broke his neck. Paralyzed. Joy-riding, they called it. Some joy! Stealing, that's what it was. And Jonathan isn't repentant. Really, he can be a *pig*. But not the colt . . . not that."

"No," I assured her, "positively not." I drank hot tea and asked, "Is it well known hereabouts that you have this great colt in that field?"

She nodded. "Eva, who looks after him, she talks of nothing else. All the village knows. That's why there are so many people here. Half the men from the village, as well as the ramblers. Even so early in the morning."

"And your friends?" I prompted.

She nodded gloomily. "Everyone. I bought him at the Premium Yearling Sales last October. His breeding is a dream. He was a late foal—end of April— he's . . . he *was* going into training next week. Oh *dear.*"

"I'm so sorry," I said. I screwed myself unhappily to ask the unavoidable question, "Who, among your friends, came here in person to admire the colt?"

She was far from stupid, and also vehement. "No one who came here could *possibly* have done this! People like Lord and Lady Dexter? Of course not! Gordon and Ginnie Quint, and darling Ellis? Don't be silly. Though I suppose," she went on doubtfully, "they could have mentioned him to other people. He wasn't a *secret*. Anyone since the Sales would know he was here, like I told you."

"Of course," I said.

*Ellis.*

We finished the tea and went back to the drawing room. Jonathan, the nephew, stared at me again unwaveringly, and after a moment, to test my own impression, I jerked my head in the direction of the door, walking that way; and, with hardly a hesitation, he stood up and followed.

I went out of the drawing room, across the hall and through the still-wide-open front door onto the drive.

"Sid Halley," he said behind me.

I turned. He stopped four paces away, still not wholly committed. His accent and general appearance spoke of expensive schools, money and privilege. His mouth and his manner said slob.

"What is it that you know?" I asked.

"Hey! Look here! What do you mean?"

I said without pressure, "You want to tell me something, don't you?"

"I don't know. Why do you think so?"

I'd seen that intense bursting-at-the-seams expression too often by then to mistake it. He knew something that he ought to tell: it was only his own contrary rebelliousness that had kept him silent so far.

I made no appeal to a better nature that I wasn't sure he had.

I said, guessing, "Were you awake before four o'clock?"

He glared but didn't answer.

I tried again, "You hate to be helpful, is that it? No one is going to catch you behaving well—that sort of thing? Tell me what you know. I'll give you as bad a press as you want. Your obstructive reputation will remain intact."

"Sod you," he said.

I waited.

"She'd kill me," he said. "Worse, she'd pack me off home."

"Mrs. Bracken?"

He nodded. "My Aunt Betty."

"What have you done?"

He used a few old Anglo-Saxon words: bluster to impress me with his virility, I supposed. Pathetic, really. Sad.

"She has these effing stupid rules," he said. "Be back in the house at night by eleven-thirty."

"And last night," I suggested, "you weren't?"

"I got probation," he said. "Did she tell you?"

"Yeah."

He took two more steps towards me, into normal talking distance.

"If she knew I went out again," he said, "I could get youth custody."

"If she shopped you, you mean?"

He nodded. "But . . . sod it . . . to cut a foot off a horse . . ."

Perhaps the better nature was somewhere there after all. Stealing cars was OK, maiming racehorses wasn't. He wouldn't have blinded those ponies: he wasn't that sort of lout.

"If I fix it with your aunt, will you tell me?" I asked.

"Make her promise not to tell Archie. He's worse."

"Er," I said, "who is Archie?"

"My uncle. Aunt Betty's brother. He's Establishment, man. He's the flogging classes."

I made no promises. I said, "Just spill the beans."

"In three weeks I'll be sixteen." He looked at me intently for reaction, but all he'd caused in me was puzzlement. I thought the cut-off age for crime to be considered "juvenile" was two years older. He wouldn't be sent to an adult jail.

Jonathan saw my lack of understanding. He said impatiently, "You can't be underage for sex if you're a man, only if you're a girl."

"Are you sure?"

*"She* says so."

"Your Aunt Betty?" I felt lost.

"No, stupid. The woman in the village."

"Oh . . . ah."

"Her old man's a long-distance truck driver. He's away for nights on end. He'd kill me. Youth custody would be apple pie."

"Difficult," I said.

"She *wants* it, see? I'd never done it before. I bought her a gin in the pub." Which, at fifteen, was definitely illegal to start with.

"So . . . um . . . ," I said, "last night you were coming back from the village . . . When, exactly?"

"It was dark. Just before dawn. There had been more moonlight earlier, but I'd left it late. I was *running*. She—Aunt Betty—she wakes with the cocks. She lets the dogs out before six." His agitation, I thought, was producing what sounded like truth.

I thought, and asked, "Did you see any ramblers?"

"No. It was earlier than them."

I held my breath. I had to ask the next question, and dreaded the answer.

"So, who was it that you saw?"

"It wasn't a 'who,' it was a 'what.' " He paused and reassessed his position. "I didn't go to the village," he said. "I'll deny it."

I nodded. "You were restless. Unable to sleep. You went for a walk."

He said, "Yeah, that's it," with relief.

"And you saw?"

"A Land-Rover."

Not a who. A what. I said, partly relieved, partly disappointed, "That's not so extraordinary, in the country."

"No, but it wasn't Aunt Betty's Land-Rover. It was much newer, and blue, not green. It was standing in the lane not far from the gate into the field. There was no one in it. I didn't think much of it. There's a path up to the house from the lane. I always go out and in that way. It's miles from Aunt Betty's bedroom."

"Through the yard with all the trash cans?" I asked.

He was comically astounded. I didn't explain that his aunt had taken me out that way. I said, "Couldn't it have been a rambler's Land-Rover?"

He said sullenly, "I don't know why I bothered to tell you."

I asked, "What else did you notice about the Land-Rover, except for its color?"

"Nothing. I told you, I was more interested in getting back into the house without anyone spotting me."

I thought a bit and said, "How close did you get to it?"

"I touched it. I didn't see it until I was almost on top of it. Like I told you, I was running along the lane. I was mostly looking at the ground, and it was still almost dark."

"Was it facing you, or did you run into the back of it?"

"Facing. There was still enough moonlight to reflect off the windshield. That's what I saw first, the reflection."

"What part of it did you touch?"

"The hood." Then he added, as if surprised by the extent of his memory, "It was quite hot."

"Did you see a number plate?"

"Not a chance. I wasn't hanging about for things like that."

"What else did you see?"

"Nothing."

"How did you know there was no one in the cab? There might have been a couple lying in there snogging."

"Well, there wasn't. I looked through the window."

"Open or shut window?"

"Open." He surprised himself again. "I looked in fast, on the way past. No people, just a load of machinery behind the front seats."

"What sort of machinery?"

"How the eff do I know? It had handles sticking up. Like a lawn mower. I didn't look. I was in a hurry. I didn't want to be seen."

"No," I agreed. "How about an ignition key?"

"Hey?" It was a protest of hurt feelings. "I didn't drive it away."

"Why not?"

"I don't take every car I see. Not alone, ever."

"There's no fun in it if you're alone?"

"Not so much."

"So there *was* a key in the ignition?"

"I suppose so. Yeah."

"Was there one key, or a bunch?"

"Don't know."

"Was there a key ring?"

"You don't ask much!"

"Think, then."

He said unwillingly, "See, I *notice* ignition keys."

"Yes."

"It was a bunch of keys, then. They had a silver horseshoe dangling from them on a little chain. A little horseshoe. Just an ordinary key ring."

We stared at each other briefly.

He said, "I didn't think anything of it."

"No," I agreed. "You wouldn't. Well, go back a bit. When you put your hand on the hood, were you looking at the windshield?"

"I must have been."

"What was on it?"

"Nothing. What do you mean?"

"Did it have a tax disk?"

"It must have done, mustn't it?" he said.

"Well . . . did it have anything else? Like, say, a sticker saying 'Save the Tigers'?"

"No, it didn't."

"Shut your eyes and think," I urged him. "You're running. You don't want to be seen. You nearly collide with a Land-Rover. Your face is quite near the windshield—"

"There was a red dragon," he interrupted. "A red circle with a dragon thing in it. Not very big. One of those sort of transparent transfers that stick to glass."

"Great," I said. "Anything else?"

For the first time he gave it concentrated thought, but came up with nothing more.

"I'm nothing to do with the police," I said, "and I won't spoil your probation and I won't give you away to your aunt, but I'd like to write down what you've told me, and if you agree that I've got it right, will you sign it?"

"Hey. I don't know. I don't know why I told you."

"It might matter a lot. It might not matter at all. But I'd like to find this bugger. . . ." God help me, I thought. I have to.

"So would I." He meant it. Perhaps there was hope for him yet.

He turned on his heel and went rapidly alone into the house, not wanting to be seen in even semi-reputable company, I assumed. I followed more slowly. Jonathan had not returned to the drawing room, where the tenants still sat stolidly, the difficult old aunt complained about being woken early, the deaf husband said, "Eh?" mechanically at frequent intervals and Betty Bracken sat looking into space. Only the three dogs, now lying down and resting their heads on their front paws, seemed fully sane.

I said to Mrs. Bracken, "Do you by any chance have a typewriter?"

She said incuriously, "There's one in the office."

"Er . . ."

"I'll show you." She rose and led me to a small, tidy back room containing the bones of communication but an impression of under-use.

"I don't know how anything works," Betty Bracken said frankly. "We have a part-time secretary, once a week. Help yourself."

She left, nodding, and I thanked her, and I found an electric typewriter under a fitted dust cover, plugged ready into the current.

I wrote:

*Finding it difficult to sleep, I went for a short walk in the grounds of Combe Bassett Manor at about three-thirty in the morning. [I inserted the date.] In the lane near to the gate of the home paddock I passed a Land-Rover that was parked there. The vehicle was blue. I did not look at the number plate. The engine was still hot when I touched the hood in passing. There was a key in the ignition. It was one of a bunch of keys on a key ring which had a silver horseshoe on a chain. There was no one in the vehicle. There was some sort of equipment behind the front seat, but I did not take a close look. On the inside of the windshield I observed a small transfer of a red dragon in a red circle. I went past the vehicle and returned to the house.*

Under another fitted cover I located a copier, so I left the little office with three sheets of paper and went in search of Jonathan, running him to earth eating a haphazard breakfast in the kitchen. He paused over his cereal, spoon in air, while he read what I'd written. Wordlessly, I produced a ball-point pen and held it out to him.

He hesitated, shrugged and signed the first of the papers with loops and a flourish.

"Why *three?*" he asked suspiciously, pushing the copies away.

"One for you," I said calmly. "One for my records. One for the on-going file of bits and pieces which may eventually catch our villain."

"Oh." He considered. "All right, then." He signed the other two sheets and I gave him one to keep. He seemed quite pleased with his civic-mindedness. He was rereading his edited deposition over his flakes as I left.

Back in the drawing room, looking for her, I asked where Mrs. Bracken had gone. The aunt, the tenants and the deaf husband made no reply.

Negotiating the hinterland passage and the dustbin yard again, I arrived back at the field to see Mrs. Bracken herself, the fence-leaners, the Scots vet and her brother watching the horse ambulance drive into the field and draw up conveniently close to the colt.

The horse ambulance consisted of a narrow, low-slung trailer pulled by a Land-Rover. There was a driver and a groom used to handling sick and injured horses and, with crooning noises from the solicitous Eva, the poor young colt made a painful-looking, head-bobbing stagger up a gentle ramp into the waiting stall.

"Oh *dear,* oh *dear,*" Mrs. Bracken whispered beside me. "My dear, dear young fellow . . . how *could* they?"

I shook my head. Rachel Ferns's pony and four prized colts . . . How could *anyone?*

The colt was shut into the trailer, the bucket containing the foot was loaded, and the pathetic twelve-mile journey to Lambourn began.

The Scots vet patted Betty Bracken sympathetically on the arm, gave her his best wishes for the colt, claimed his car from the line of vehicles in the lane and drove away.

I unclipped my mobile phone and got through to *The Pump,* who forwarded my call to an irate newspaperman at his home in Surrey.

Kevin Mills yelled, "Where the hell are you? They say all anyone gets on the hotline now is your answering machine, saying you'll call back. About fifty people have phoned. They're all rambling."

"Ramblers," I said.

"What?"

I explained.

"It's supposed to be my day off," he grumbled. "Can you meet me in the pub? What time? Five o'clock?"

"Make it seven," I suggested.

"It's no longer a *Pump* exclusive, I suppose you realize?" he demanded. "But save yourself for me alone, will you, buddy? Give me the inside edge?"

"It's yours."

I closed my phone and warned Betty Bracken to expect the media on her doorstep.

"Oh, no!"

"Your colt is one too many."

"Archie!" She turned to her brother for help with a beseeching gesture of the hand and, as if for the thousandth time in their lives, he responded with comfort and competent solutions.

"My dear Betty," he said, "if you can't bear to face the press, simply don't be here."

"But . . . ," she wavered.

"I shouldn't waste time," I said.

The brother gave me an appraising glance. He himself was of medium height, lean of body, gray in color, a man to get lost in a crowd. His eyes alone were notable: brown, bright and *aware*. I had an uncomfortable feeling that, far beyond having his sister phone me, he knew a good deal about me.

"We haven't actually met," he said to me civilly. "I'm Betty's brother. I'm Archie Kirk."

I said, "How do you do," and I shook his hand.

# 5

Betty Bracken, Archie Kirk and I returned to the house, again circumnavigating the trash cans. Archie Kirk's car was parked outside the manor's front door, not far from my own.

The lady of the manor refusing to leave without her husband, the uncomprehending old man, still saying "Eh?" was helped with great solicitude across the hall, through the front door and into an ancient Daimler, an Establishment-type conservative-minded political statement if ever I saw one.

My own Mercedes, milk-coffee colored, stood beyond: and what, I thought astringently, was it saying about *me?* Rich enough, sober enough, preferring reliability to flash? All spot on, particularly the last. And speed, of course.

Betty spooned her beloved into the back seat of the Daimler and folded herself in beside him, patting him gently. Touch, I supposed, had replaced speech as their means of communication. Archie Kirk took his place behind the wheel as natural commander-in-chief and drove away, leaving for me the single short parting remark, "Let me know."

I nodded automatically. Let him know *what?* Whatever I learned, I presumed.

I returned to the drawing room. The stolid tenants, on their feet, were deciding to return to their own wing of the house. The dogs snoozed. The cross aunt crossly demanded Esther's presence. Esther, on duty at eight and not a moment before, come ramblers, police or whatever, appeared forbiddingly in the doorway, a small, frizzy-haired worker, clear about her "rights."

I left the two quarrelsome women pitching into each other and went in search of Jonathan. What a household! The media were welcome to it. I looked but couldn't find Jonathan, so I just had to trust that his boorishness would keep him well away from inquisitive reporters with microphones. The Land-Rover he'd seen might have brought the machete to the colt, and I wanted, if I could, to find it before its driver learned there was a need for rapid concealment.

The first thing in my mind was the colt himself. I started the car and set off north to Lambourn, driving thoughtfully, wondering what was best to do concerning the police. I had had varying experiences with the force, some good, some rotten. They did not, in general, approve of freelance investigators like myself, and could be downright obstructive if I appeared to be working on something they felt belonged to them alone. Sometimes, though, I'd found them willing to take over if I'd come across criminal activity that couldn't go unprosecuted. I stepped gingerly around their sensitive areas, and also those of racing's own security services run by the Jockey Club and the British Horseracing Board. I was careful always not to claim credit for clearing up three-pipe problems. Not even one-pipe problems, hardly worthy of Sherlock Holmes.

Where the Jockey Club itself was concerned, I fluctuated in their view between flavor of the month and anathema, according as to who currently reigned as Senior Steward. With the police, collaboration depended very much on which individual policeman I reached and his private-life stress level at the moment of contact.

The rules governing evidence, moreover, were growing ever stickier. Juries no longer without question believed the police. For an object to be admitted for consideration in a trial it had to be ticketed, docketed and continuously accounted for. One couldn't, for instance, flourish a machete and say, "I found it in X's Land-Rover, therefore it was X who cut off a colt's foot." To get even within miles of conviction one needed a specific search warrant before one could even *look* in the Land-Rover for a machete, and search warrants weren't granted to Sid Halleys, and sometimes not to the police.

The police force as a whole was divided into autonomous districts, like the Thames Valley Police, who solved crimes in their own area but might not take much notice outside. A maimed colt in Lancashire might not have been heard of in Yorkshire. Serial rapists had gone for years uncaught because of the slow flow of information. A serial horse maimer might have no central file.

Dawdling along up the last hill before Lambourn, I became aware of a knocking in the car and pulled over to the side with gloomy thoughts of broken shock absorbers and misplaced trust in reliability, but after the car stopped the knocking continued. With awakening awareness, I climbed out, went around to the back and with difficulty opened the trunk. There was something wrong with the lock.

Jonathan lay curled in the space for luggage. He had one shoe off, with which he was assaulting my milk-coffee bodywork. When I lifted the lid he stopped banging and looked at me challengingly.

"What the hell are you doing there?" I demanded.

Silly question. He looked at his shoe. I rephrased it. "Get out."

He maneuvered himself out onto the road and calmly replaced his shoe with no attempt at apology. I slammed the trunk lid shut at the second try and returned to the driver's seat. He walked to the passenger side, found the door there locked and tapped on the window to draw my attention to it. I started the engine, lowered the electrically controlled window a little and shouted to him, "It's only three miles to Lambourn."

"No. Hey! You can't leave me here!"

Want to bet, I thought, and set off along the deserted downland road. I saw him, in the rear-view mirror, running after me determinedly. I drove slowly, but faster than he could run. He went on running, nevertheless.

After nearly a mile a curve in the road took me out of his sight. I braked and stopped. He came around the bend, saw my car and put on a spurt, racing this time up to the driver's side. I'd locked the door but lowered the window three or four inches.

"What's all that for?" he demanded.

"What's all what for?"

"Making me run."

"You've broken the lock on my trunk."

"What?" He looked baffled. "I only gave it a clout. I didn't have a key." No key; a clout. Obvious, his manner said.

"Who's going to pay to get it mended?" I asked.

He said impatiently, as if he couldn't understand such small-mindedness, "What's that got to do with it?"

"With what?"

"With the colt."

Resignedly I leaned across and pulled up the locking knob on the front passenger door. He went around there and climbed in beside me. I noted with interest that he was hardly out of breath.

Jonathan's haircut, I thought as he settled into his seat and neglected to buckle the seat belt, shouted an indication of his adolescent insecurity, of his desire to shock or at least to be *noticed*. He had, I thought, bleached inexpert haphazard streaks into his hair with a comb dipped in something like hydrogen peroxide. Straight and thick, the mop was parted in the center with a wing on each side curving down to his cheek, making a curtain beside his eye. From one ear backwards, and around to the other ear, the hair had been sliced off in a straight line. Below the line, his scalp was shaved. To my eyes it looked ugly, but then I wasn't fifteen.

Making a statement through hairstyle was universal, after all. Men with bald crowns above pigtails, men with plaited beards, women with severely scraped-back pinnings, all were saying "This is *me,* and I'm *different.*" In the days of Charles I, when long male hair was normal, rebellious sons had cut off their curls to have roundheads. Archie Kirk's gray hair had been short, neat and controlled. My own dark hair would have curled girlishly if allowed to grow. A haircut was still the most unmistakable give-away of the person inside.

Conversely, a wig could change all that.

I asked Jonathan, "Have you remembered something else?"

"No, not really."

"Then why did you stow away?"

"Come on, man, give me a break. What am I supposed to do all day in that graveyard of a house? The aunt's whining drives me insane and even Karl Marx would have throttled Esther."

He did, I supposed, have a point.

I thoughtfully coasted down the last hill towards Lambourn.

"Tell me about your uncle, Archie Kirk," I said.

"What about him?"

"You tell me. For starters, what does he do?"

"He works for the government."

"What as?"

"Some sort of civil servant. Dead boring."

Boring, I reflected, was the last adjective I would have applied to what I'd seen in Archie Kirk's eyes.

"Where does he live?" I asked.

"Back in Shelley Green, a couple of miles from Aunt Betty. She can't climb a ladder unless he's holding it."

Reaching Lambourn itself, I took the turn that led to the equine hospital. Slowly though I had made the journey, the horse ambulance had been slower. They were still unloading the colt.

From Jonathan's agog expression, I guessed it was in fact the first view he'd had of a shorn-off leg, even if all he could now see was a surgical dressing.

I said to him, "If you want to wait half an hour for me, fine. Otherwise, you're on your own. But if you try stealing a car, I'll personally see you lose your probation."

"Hey. Give us a break."

"You've had your share of good breaks. Half an hour. OK?"

He glowered at me without words. I went across to where Bill Ruskin, in a white coat, was watching his patient's arrival. He said, "Hello, Sid," absentmindedly, then collected the bucket containing the foot and, with me following, led the way into a small laboratory full of weighing and measuring equipment and microscopes.

Unwrapping the foot, he stood it on the bench and looked at it assessingly.

"A good, clean job," he said.

"There's nothing good about it."

"Probably the colt hardly felt it."

"How was it done?" I asked.

"Hm." He considered. "There's no other point on the leg that you could amputate a foot without using a saw to cut through the bone. I doubt if a single swipe with a heavy knife would achieve this precision. And achieve it several times, on different animals, right?"

I nodded.

"Yes, well, I think we might be looking at game shears."

"*Game shears?*" I exclaimed. "Do you mean those sort of heavy scissors that will cut up duck and pheasant?"

"Something along those lines, yes."

"But those shears aren't anywhere near big enough for this."

He pursed his mouth. "How about a gralloching knife, then? The sort used for disemboweling deer out on the mountains?"

"Jeez."

"There are signs of *compression,* though. On balance, I'd hazard heavy game shears. How did he get the colt to stand still?"

"There were horse nuts on the ground."

He nodded morosely. "Slimeball."

"There aren't any words for it."

He peered closely at the raw red and white end of the pastern. "Even if I can reattach the foot, the colt will never race."

"His owner knows that. She wants to save his life."

"Better to collect the insurance."

"No insurance. A quarter of a million down the drain. But it's not the money she's grieving over. What she's feeling is guilt."

He understood. He saw it often.

Eventually he said, "I'll give it a try. I don't hold out much hope."

"You'll photograph this as it is?"

He looked at the foot. "Oh, sure. Photos, X rays, blood tests on the colt, micro-stitching, every luxury. I'll get on with anesthetizing the colt as soon as possible. The foot's been off too long . . ." He shook his head. "I'll try."

"Phone my mobile." I gave him the number. "Anytime."

"See you, Sid. And catch the bugger."

He bustled away, taking the foot with him, and I returned to my car to find Jonathan not only still there but jogging around with excitement.

"What's up?" I asked.

"That Land-Rover that pulled the trailer that brought the colt . . ."

"What about it?"

"It's got a red dragon on the windshield!"

"What? But you said a *blue*—"

"Yeah, yeah, it wasn't the vet's Land-Rover I saw in the lane, but it's got a red dragon transfer on it. Not exactly the same, I don't think, but definitely a red dragon."

I looked around, but the horse ambulance was no longer in sight.

"They drove it off," Jonathan said, "but I saw the transfer close to, and it has *letters* in it." His voice held triumph, which I allowed was justified.

"Go on, then," I said. "What letters?"

"Aren't you going to say 'well done'?"

"Well done. What letters?"

"E.S.M. They were cut out of the red circle. Gaps, not printed letters." He wasn't sure I understood.

"I do see," I assured him.

I returned to the hospital to find Bill and asked him when he'd bought his Land-Rover.

"Our local garage got it for us from a firm in Oxford."

"What does E.S.M. stand for?"

"God knows."

"I can't ask God. What's the name of the Land-Rover firm in Oxford?"

He laughed and thought briefly. "English Sporting Motors. E.S.M. Good Lord."

"Can you give me the name of someone there? Who did you actually deal with?"

With impatience he said, "Look, Sid, I'm trying to scrub up to see what I can do about sticking the colt's foot back on."

"And I'm trying to catch the bugger that took it off. And it's possible he traveled in a Land-Rover sold by English Sporting Motors."

He said "Christ," wide-eyed, and headed for what proved to be the hospital's record office, populated by filing cabinets. Without much waste of time
he flourished a copy of a receipted account, but shook his head.

"Ted James in the village might help you. I paid *him*. He dealt direct with
Oxford. You'd have to ask Ted James."

I thanked him, collected Jonathan, drove into the small town of Lambourn
and located Ted James, who would do a lot for a good customer like Bill
Ruskin, it seemed.

"No problem," he assured me. "Ask for Roger Brook in Oxford. Do you
want me to phone him?"

"Yes, please."

"Right on." He spoke briefly on the phone and reported back. "He's busy.
Saturday's always a busy sales day. He'll help you if it doesn't take long."

The morning seemed to have been going on forever, but it was still before
eleven o'clock when I talked to Roger Brook, tubby, smooth and self-im-
portant in the carpeted sales office of English Sporting Motors.

Roger Brook pursed his lips and shook his head; not the firm's policy to
give out information about its customers.

I said ruefully, "I don't want to bother the police. . . ."

"Well . . ."

"And, of course, there would be a fee for your trouble."

A fee was respectable where a bribe wasn't. In the course of life I disbursed
a lot of fees.

It helpfully appeared that the red-dragon transparent transfers were slightly
differently designed each year: *improved* as time went on, did I see?

I fetched Jonathan in from outside for Roger Brook to show him the past
and present dragon logos, and Jonathan with certainty picked the one that had
been, Brook said, that of the year before last.

"Great," I said with satisfaction. "How many blue Land-Rovers did you sell
in that year? I mean, what are the names of the actual buyers, not the mid-
dlemen like Ted James?"

An open-mouthed silence proved amenable to a larger fee. "Our Miss
Denver" helped with a computer print-out. Our Miss Denver got a kiss from
me. Roger Brook with dignity took his reward in readies, and Jonathan and
I returned to the Mercedes with the names and addresses of two hundred and
eleven purchasers of blue Land-Rovers a little back in time.

Jonathan wanted to read the list when I'd finished. I handed it over, reck-
oning he'd deserved it. He looked disappointed when he reached the end, and
I didn't point out to him the name that had made my gut contract.

One of the Land-Rovers had been delivered to Twyford Lower Farms Ltd.

I had been to Twyford Lower Farms to lunch. It was owned by Gordon Quint.

Noon, Saturday. I sat in my parked car outside English Sporting Motors, while Jonathan fidgeted beside me, demanding, "What next?"

I said, "Go and eat a hamburger for your lunch and be back here in twenty minutes."

He had no money. I gave him some. "Twenty minutes."

He promised nothing, but returned with three minutes to spare. I spent his absence thinking highly unwelcome thoughts and deciding what to do, and when he slid in beside me smelling of raw onions and french fries I set off southwards again, on the roads back to Combe Bassett.

"Where are we going?"

"To see your Aunt Betty."

"But hey! She's not at home. She's at Archie's."

"Then we'll go to Archie's. You can show me the way."

He didn't like it, but he made no attempt to jump ship when we were stopped by traffic lights three times on the way out of Oxford. We arrived together in due course outside a house an eighth the size of Combe Bassett Manor; a house, moreover, that was frankly modern and not at all what I'd expected.

I said doubtfully, "Are you sure this is the place?"

"The lair of the wolf. No mistake. He won't want to see me."

I got out of the car and pressed the thoroughly modern doorbell beside a glassed-in front porch. The woman who came to answer the summons was small and wrinkled like a drying apple, and wore a sleeveless sundress in blue and mauve.

"Er . . . ," I said to her inquiring face, "Archie Kirk?"

Her gaze lengthened beyond me to include Jonathan in my car, a sight that pinched her mouth and jumped her to an instant wrong conclusion. She whirled away and returned with Archie, who said repressively, "What is *he* doing here?"

"Can you spare me half an hour?" I asked.

"What's Jonathan done?"

"He's been extraordinarily helpful. I'd like to ask your advice."

*"Helpful!"*

"Yes. Could you hold your disapproval in abeyance for half an hour while I explain?"

He gave me an intense inspection, the brown eyes sharp and knowing, as before. Decision arrived there plainly.

"Come in," he said, holding his front door wide.

"Jonathan's afraid of you," I told him. "He wouldn't admit it, but he is. Could I ask you not to give him the normal tongue-lashing? Will you invite him in and leave him alone?"

"You don't know what you're asking."

"I do," I said.

"No one speaks to me like this." He was, however, only mildly affronted.

I smiled at his eyes. "That's because they know you. But I met you only this morning."

"And," he said, "I've heard about your lightning judgments."

I felt, as on other occasions with people of his sort, a deep thrust of mental satisfaction. Also, more immediately, I knew I had come to the right place.

Archie Kirk stepped out from his door, took the three paces to my car, and said through the window, "Jonathan, please come into the house."

Jonathan looked past him to me. I jerked my head, as before, to suggest that he complied, and he left the safe shelter and walked to the house, even if reluctantly and frozen faced.

Archie Kirk led the way across a modest hallway into a middle-sized sitting room where Betty Bracken, her husband and the small woman who'd answered my ring were sitting in armchairs, drinking cups of coffee.

The room's overall impression was of old oak and books, a room for dark winter evenings and lamps and log fires, not fitted to the dazzle of June. None of the three faces turned towards us could have looked welcoming to the difficult boy.

The small woman, introducing herself as Archie's wife, stood up slowly and offered me coffee. "And . . . er . . . Jonathan . . . Coca-Cola?"

Jonathan, as if reprieved, followed her out to the next-door kitchen, and I told Betty Bracken that her colt was at that moment being operated on, and that there should be news of him soon. She was pathetically pleased: too pleased, I was afraid.

I said casually to Archie, "Can I talk to you in private?" and without question he said, "This way," and transferred us to a small adjacent room, again all dark oak and books, that he called his study.

"What is it?" he asked.

"I need a policeman," I said.

He gave me a long, level glance and waved me to one of the two hard oak chairs, himself sitting in the other, beside a paper-strewn desk.

I told him about Jonathan's night walk (harmless version) and about our tracing the Land-Rover to the suppliers at Oxford. I said that I knew where the Land-Rover might now be, but that I couldn't get a search warrant to examine it. For a successful prosecution, I mentioned, there had to be integrity of evidence; no chance of tampering or substitution. So I needed a policeman, but one that would listen and cooperate, not one that would either brush me off altogether or one that would do the police work sloppily.

"I thought you might know someone," I finished. "I don't know who else to ask, as at the moment this whole thing depends on crawling up to the machine-gun nest on one's belly, so to speak."

He sat back in his chair staring at me vacantly while the data got processed.

At length he said, "Betty called in the local police this morning early, but . . . ," he hesitated, "they hadn't the clout you need." He thought some more, then picked up an address book; he leafed through it for a number and made a phone call.

"Norman, this is Archie Kirk."

Whoever Norman was, it seemed he was unwilling.

"It's extremely important," Archie said.

Norman apparently capitulated, but with protest, giving directions.

"You had better be right," Archie said to me, disconnecting. "I've just called in about a dozen favors he owed me."

"Who is he?"

"Detective Inspector Norman Picton, Thames Valley Police."

"Brilliant," I said.

"He's off duty. He's on the gravel pit lake. He's a clever and ambitious young man. And I," he added with a glimmer, "am a magistrate, and I may sign a search warrant myself, if he can clear it with his superintendent."

He rendered me speechless, which quietly amused him.

"You didn't know?" he asked.

I shook my head and found my voice. "Jonathan said you were a civil servant."

"That, too," he agreed. "How did you get that boorish young man to talk?"

"Er . . . ," I said. "What is Inspector Picton doing on the gravel pit lake?"

"Water skiing," Archie said.

THERE WERE SPEEDBOATS, children, wet-suits, picnics. There was a clubhouse in a sea of scrubby grass and people sliding over the shining water pulled by strings.

Archie parked his Daimler at the end of a row of cars, and I, with Jonathan beside me, parked my Mercedes alongside. We had agreed to bring both cars so that I could go on eventually to London, with Archie ferrying Jonathan back to pick up the Brackens and take them all home to Combe Bassett. Jonathan hadn't warmed to the plan, but had ungraciously accompanied me as being a lesser horror than spending the afternoon mooching aimlessly around Archie's aunt-infested house.

Having got as far as the lake, he began looking at the harmless physical activity all around him, not with a sneer but with something approaching interest. On the shortish journey from Archie's house he had asked three moody questions, two of which I answered.

First: "This is the best day for a long time. How come you get so much done so quickly?"

No answer possible.

And second: "Did you ever steal anything?"

"Chocolate bars," I said.

And third: "Do you mind having only one hand?"

I said coldly, "Yes."

He glanced with surprise at my face and I saw that he'd expected me to say no. I supposed he wasn't old enough to know it was a question one shouldn't ask; but then, perhaps he would have asked it anyway.

When we climbed out of the car at the water-ski club I said, "Can you swim?"

"Do me a favor."

"Then go jump in the lake."

"Sod you," he said, and actually laughed.

Archie had meanwhile discovered that one of the scudding figures on the water was the man we'd come to see. We waited a fair while until a large presence in a blue wet-suit with scarlet stripes down arms and legs let go of the rope pulling him and skied free and gracefully to a sloping landing place on the edge of the water. He stepped off his skis grinning, knowing he'd shown off his considerable skill, and wetly shook Archie's hand.

"Sorry to keep you waiting," he said, "but I reckoned once you got here I'd have had it for the day."

His voice, with its touch of Berkshire accent, held self-confidence and easy authority.

Archie said formally, "Norman, this is Sid Halley."

I shook the offered hand, which was cold besides wet. I received the sort of slow, searching inspection I'd had from Archie himself: and I had no idea what the policeman thought.

"Well," he said finally, stirring, "I'll get dressed."

We watched him walk away, squelching, gingerly barefooted, carrying his skis. He was back within five minutes, clad now in jeans, sneakers, open-necked shirt and sweater, his dark hair still wet and spiky, uncombed.

"Right," he said to me. "Give."

"Er . . ." I hesitated. "Would it be possible for Mr. Kirk's nephew Jonathan to go for a ride in a speedboat?"

Both he and Archie looked over to where Jonathan, not far away, lolled un-prepossessingly against my car. Jonathan did himself no favors, I thought; self-destruction rampant in every bolshie tilt of the anti-authority haircut.

"He doesn't deserve any ride in a speedboat," Archie objected.

"I don't want him to overhear what I'm saying."

"That's different," Norman Picton decided. "I'll fix it."

Jonathan ungraciously allowed himself to be driven around the lake by Norman Picton's wife in Norman Picton's boat, accompanied by Norman Picton's son. We watched the boat race past with a roar, Jonathan's streaky mop blown back in the wind.

"He's on the fence," I said mildly to Archie. "There's a lot of good in him."

"You're the only one who thinks so."

"He's looking for a way back without losing face."

Both men gave me the slow assessment and shook their heads.

I said, bringing Jonathan's signed statement from my pocket, "Try this on for size."

They both read it, Picton first, Archie after.

Archie said in disbelief, "He never talks. He wouldn't have said all this."

"I asked him questions," I explained. "Those are his answers. He came with me to the Land-Rover central dealers in Oxford who put that red-dragon transfer on the windshield of every vehicle they sell. And we wouldn't know of the Land-Rover's presence in the lane, or its probable owner and whereabouts now, except for Jonathan. So I really do think he's earned his ride on the lake."

"What exactly do you want the search warrant *for?*" Picton asked. "One can't get search warrants unless one can come up with a good reason—or at least a convincing possibility or probability of finding something material to a case."

"Well," I said, "Jonathan put his hand on the hood of the vehicle standing right beside the gate to the field where Betty Bracken's colt lost his foot. If you search a certain Land-Rover and find Jonathan's hand-print on the hood, would that be proof enough that you'd found the right wheels?"

Picton said, "Yes."

"So," I went on without emphasis, "if we leave Jonathan here by the lake while your people fingerprint the Land-Rover, there could be no question of his having touched it this afternoon, and not last night."

"I've heard about you," Picton said.

"I think," I said, "that it would be a good idea to fingerprint that hood before it rains, don't you? Or before anyone puts it through a car-wash?"

"Where is it?" Picton asked tersely.

I produced the English Sporting Motors' print-out, and pointed. "There," I said. "That one."

Picton read it silently; Archie aloud.

"But I know the place. You're quite *wrong*. I've been a guest there. They're friends of Betty's."

"And of mine," I said.

He listened to the bleakness I could hear in my own voice.

"Who are we talking about?" Picton asked.

"Gordon Quint," Archie said. "It's rubbish."

"Who is Gordon Quint?" Picton asked again.

"The father of Ellis Quint," Archie said. "And you must have heard of *him.*"

Picton nodded. He had indeed.

"I suppose it's possible," I suggested tentatively, "that someone *borrowed* the Land-Rover for the night."

"But you don't believe it," Picton remarked.

"I wish I did."

"But where's the connection?" Picton asked. "There has to be *more*. The fact that Twyford Lower Farms Limited owned a blue Land-Rover of the relevant year isn't enough on its own. We cannot search that vehicle for hand-prints unless we have good reason to believe that it was that one and no other that we are looking for."

Archie said thoughtfully, "Search warrants have been issued on flimsier grounds before now."

He and Picton walked away from me, the professionals putting their distance between themselves and Sid Public. I thought that if they refused to follow the trail it would be a relief, on the whole. It would let me off the squirming hook. But there could be another month and another colt . . . and an obsession feeding and fattening on success.

They came back, asking why I should link the Quint name to the deed. I described my box chart. Not conclusive, Archie said judiciously, and I agreed, no.

Picton repeated what I'd just said: "Rachel's pony was bought by her father, Joe, on the advice of Ellis Quint?"

I said, "Ellis did a broadcast about Rachel's pony losing his foot."

"I saw it," Picton said.

They didn't want to believe it any more than I did. There was a fairly long, indeterminate silence.

Jonathan came back looking uncomplicatedly happy from his fast laps around the lake, and Norman Picton abruptly went into the clubhouse, returning with a can of Coke, which he put into Jonathan's hands. Jonathan held it in his left hand to open it and his right hand to drink. Norman took the empty can from him casually but carefully by the rim, and asked if he would like to try the skiing itself, not just a ride in the boat.

Jonathan, on the point of enthusiastically saying, *"Yes,"* remembered his cultivated disagreeableness and said, "I don't mind. If you insist, I suppose I'll have to."

"That's right," Picton said cheerfully. "My wife will drive. My son will watch the rope. We'll find you some swimming trunks and a wet-suit."

He led Jonathan away. Archie watched inscrutably.

"Give him a chance," I murmured. "Give him a challenge."

"Pack him off to the colonies to make a man of him?"

"Scoff," I said with a smile. "But long ago it often worked. He's bright and he's bored and he's not yet a totally confirmed delinquent."

"You'd make a soft and rotten magistrate."

"I expect you're right."

Picton returned, saying, "The boy will stay here until I get back, so we'd better get started. We'll take two cars, mine and Mr. Halley's. In that way he can go on to London when he wants. We'll leave your car here, Archie. Is that all right?"

Archie said he didn't trust Jonathan not to steal it.

"He doesn't think stealing's much fun without his pals," I said.

Archie stared. "That boy never says *anything.*"

"Find him a dangerous job."

Picton, listening, said, "Like what?"

"Like," I said, unprepared, "like . . . well . . . on an oil rig. Two years of that. Tell him to keep a diary. Tell him to write."

"Good God," Archie said, shaking his head, "he'd have the place in flames."

He locked his car and put the keys in his pocket, climbing into the front passenger seat beside me as we followed Norman Picton into Newbury, to his official place of work.

I sat in my car outside the police station while Archie and Picton, inside, arranged the back-ups: the photographer, the fingerprinter, the detective constable to be Inspector Picton's note-taking assistant.

I sat with the afternoon sun falling through the windshield and wished I were anywhere else, engaged on any other mission.

All the villains I'd caught before hadn't been people I knew. Or people—one had to face it—people I'd thought I'd known. I'd felt mostly satisfaction, sometimes relief, occasionally even regret, but never anything approaching this intensity of entrapped despair.

Ellis was loved. I was going to be hated.

Hatred was inevitable.

Could I bear it?

There was no choice, really.

Archie and Picton came out of the police station followed by their purposeful troop.

Archie, sliding in beside me, said the search warrant was signed, the Superintendent had given the expedition his blessing, and off we could go to the Twyford Lower Farms.

I sat without moving, without starting the car.

"What's the matter?" Archie demanded, looking at my face.

I said with pain, "Ellis is my friend."

Ginnie Quint was gardening in a large straw hat, businesslike gloves and gray overall dungarees, waging a losing war on weeds in flower beds in front of the comfortable main house of Twyford Lower Farms.

"Hello, dear Sid!" She greeted me warmly, standing up, holding the dirty gloves wide and putting her soft cheek forward for a kiss of greeting. "What a nice surprise. But Ellis isn't here, you know. He went to the races, then he was going up to the Regents Park apartment. That's where you'll find him, dear."

She looked in perplexity over my shoulder to where the Norman Picton contingent were erupting from their transport.

Ginnie said uncertainly, "Who are your friends, dear?" Her face cleared momentarily in relief, and she exclaimed, "Why, it's Archie Kirk! My dear man. How nice to see you."

Norman Picton, carrying none of Archie's or my social-history baggage, came rather brutally to the point.

"I'm Detective Inspector Picton, madam, of the Thames Valley Police. I've reason to believe you own a blue Land-Rover, and I have a warrant to inspect it."

Ginnie said in bewilderment, "It's no secret we have a Land-Rover. Of course we have. You'd better talk to my husband. Sid . . . Archie . . . what's all this about?"

"It's possible," I said unhappily, "that someone borrowed your Land-Rover last night and . . . er . . . committed a crime."

"Could I see the Land-Rover, please, madam?" Picton insisted.

"It will be in the farmyard," Ginnie said. "I'll get my husband to show you."

The scene inexorably unwound. Gordon, steaming out of the house to take charge, could do nothing but protest in the face of a properly executed search warrant. The various policemen went about their business, photographing, fingerprinting and collecting specimens of dusty earth from the tire treads. Every stage was carefully documented by the assisting constable.

The warrant apparently covered the machinery and anything else behind the front seat. The two sticking-up handles that had looked to Jonathan like those of a lawn mower were, in fact, the handles of a lawn mower—a light electric model. There were also a dozen or so angle iron posts for fencing, also a coil of fencing wire and the tools needed for fastening the wire through the posts. There was an opened bag of horse-feed nuts. There was a rolled leather apron, like those used by farriers. There were two spades, a heavy four-pronged fork and a large knife like a machete wrapped in sacking.

The knife was clean, sharp and oiled.

Gordon, questioned, growled impatiently that a good workman looked after his tools. He picked up a rag and a can of oil, to prove his point. What was the knife for? Clearing ditches, thinning woodland, a hundred small jobs around the fields.

There was a second, longer bundle of sacking lying beneath the fencing posts. I pointed to it noncommittally, and Norman Picton drew it out and unwrapped it.

Inside there were two once-varnished wooden handles a good meter in length, with, at the business end, a heavy arrangement of metal.

"Lopping shears," Gordon pronounced. "For lopping off small branches of trees in the woods. Have to keep young trees pruned, you know, or you get a useless tangle where nothing will grow."

He took the shears from Picton's hands to show him how they worked. The act of parting the handles widely away from each other opened heavy metal jaws at the far end; sharp, clean and oiled jaws with an opening wide enough to grip a branch three inches thick. Gordon, with a strong, quick motion, pulled the handles towards each other, and the metal jaws closed with a snap.

"Very useful," Gordon said, nodding, and rewrapped the shears in their sacking.

Archie, Picton and I said nothing.

I felt faintly sick.

Archie walked away speechlessly and Gordon, not understanding, laid the sacking parcel back in the Land-Rover and walked after him, saying, puzzled, "Archie! What is it?"

Picton said to me, "Well?"

"Well," I said, swallowing, "what if you took those shears apart? They look clean, but in the jaws . . . in that hinge . . . just one drop of blood . . . or one hair . . . that would do, wouldn't it?"

"So these shears fit the bill?"

I nodded faintly. "Mr. Kirk saw the colt's leg, like I did. And he saw the foot." I swallowed again. *"Lopping* shears. Oh, Christ."

"It was only a *horse,"* he protested.

"Some people love their horses like they do their children," I said. "Suppose someone lopped off your son's foot?"

He stared. I said wryly, "Betty Bracken is the fifth bereaved owner I've met in the last three weeks. Their grief gets to you."

"My son," he said slowly, "had a dog that got run over. He worried us sick . . . wouldn't eat properly . . ." He stopped, then said, "You and Archie Kirk are too close to this."

"And the Great British public," I reminded him, "poured their hearts out to those cavalry horses maimed by terrorists in Hyde Park."

He was old enough to remember the carnage that had given rise to the daily bulletins and to medals and hero status bestowed on Sefton, the wonderful survivor of heartless bombs set off specifically to kill harmless horses used by the army solely as a spectacle in plumed parades.

This time the Great British public would vilify the deed, but wouldn't, and couldn't, believe a national idol guilty. Terrorists, yes. Vandals, yes. Idol . . . *no.*

Picton and I walked in the wake of Archie and Gordon, returning to Ginnie in front of the house.

"I don't understand," Ginnie was saying plaintively. "When you say the Land-Rover may have been taken and used in a crime . . . what crime do you mean?"

Gordon jumped in without waiting for Picton to explain.

"It's always for robbery," he said confidently. "Where did the thieves take it?"

Instead of answering, Norman Picton asked if it was Gordon Quint's habit to leave the ignition key in the Land-Rover.

"Of course not," Gordon said, affronted. "Though a little thing like no ignition key never stops a practiced thief."

"If you did by any chance leave the key available—which I'm sure you didn't, sir, please don't get angry—but if anyone could have found and used your key, would it have been on a key ring with a silver chain and a silver horseshoe?"

"Oh, no," Ginnie interrupted, utterly guilelessly. "That's Ellis's key ring. And it's not a silver horseshoe, it's white gold. I had it made especially for him last Christmas."

I DROVE ARCHIE Kirk back to Newbury. The unmarked car ahead of us carried the four policemen and a variety of bagged, docketed, documented objects for which receipts had been given to Gordon Quint.

Lopping shears in sacking. Machete, the same. Oily rag and oil can. Sample of horse-feed nuts. Instant photos of red-dragon logo. Careful containers of many lifted fingerprints, including one sharply defined right full hand-print from the Land-Rover's hood that, on first inspection, matched exactly the right hand-print from the Coke can held by Jonathan at the lake.

"There's no doubt that it was the Quint Land-Rover in my sister's lane," Archie said. "There's no doubt Ellis's keys were in the ignition. But there's no proof that Ellis himself was anywhere near."

"No," I agreed. "No one saw him."

"Did Norman ask you to write a report?"

"Yes."

"He'll give your report and Jonathan's statement to the Crown Prosecution Service, along with his own findings. After that, it's up to them."

"Mm."

After a silence, as if searching for words of comfort, Archie said, "You've done wonders."

"I hate it."

"But it doesn't stop you."

*What if he can't help it . . . ?* What if I couldn't help it, either?

At the police station, saying good-bye, Archie said, "Sid . . . you don't mind if I call you Sid? And I'm Archie, of course, as you know . . . I do have some idea of what you're facing. I just wanted you to know."

"I . . . er . . . thanks," I said. "If you wait a minute, I'll phone the equine hospital and find out how the colt is doing."

His face lightened but the news was moderate.

"I've reattached the tendon," Bill reported. "I grafted a couple of blood vessels so there's now an adequate blood supply to the foot. Nerves are always difficult. I've done my absolute best and, bar infection, the foot could technically stay in place. The whole leg is now in a cast. The colt is semiconscious. We have him in slings. But you know how unpredictable this all is. Horses don't recover as easily as humans. There'll be no question of racing, of course, but breeding . . . I understand he's got the bloodlines of champions. Absolutely no promises, mind."

"You're brilliant," I said.

"It's nice," he chuckled, "to be appreciated."

I said, "A policeman will come and collect some of the colt's hair and blood."

"Good. Catch the bugger," he said.

I DROVE WILLY-NILLY without haste in heavy traffic to London. By the time I reached the pub I was half an hour late for my appointment with Kevin Mills of *The Pump* and he wasn't there. No balding head, no paunch, no drooping beer-frothed mustache, no cynical world-weariness.

Without regret I mooched tiredly to the bar, bought some whisky and poured into it enough London tap water to give the distiller fits.

All I wanted was to finish my mild tranquilizer, go home, find something to eat, and sleep. Sleep, I thought, yawning, had overall priority.

A woman's voice at my side upset those plans.

"Are you Sid Halley?" it said.

I turned reluctantly. She had shining black shoulder-length hair, bright light-blue eyes and dark-red lipstick, sharply edged. Naturally unblemished skin had been given a matte porcelain powdering. Black eyebrows and eyelashes gave her face strong definition, an impression her manner reinforced. She wore black clothes in June. I found it impossible to guess her age, within ten years, from her face, but her manicured red-nailed hands said no more than thirty.

"I'm from *The Pump*," she said. "My colleague, Kevin Mills, has been called away to a rape."

I said, "Oh," vaguely.

"I'm India Cathcart," she said.

I said "Oh" again, just as vaguely, but I knew her by her name, by her reputation and by her writing. She was a major columnist, a ruthless interviewer, a deconstructing nemesis, a pitiless exposer of pathetic human secrets. They said she kept a penknife handy for sharpening her ball-points. She was also funny, and I, like every *Pump* addict, avidly read her stuff and laughed even as I winced.

I did not, however, aim to be either her current or future quarry.

"I came to pick up our exclusive," she said.

"Ah. 'Fraid there isn't one."

"But you *said*."

"I hoped," I agreed.

"And you haven't answered your phone all day."

I unclipped my mobile phone and looked at it as if puzzled, which I wasn't. I said, making a discovery, "It's switched off."

She said, disillusioned, "I was warned you weren't dumb."

There seemed to be no answer to that, so I didn't attempt one.

"We tried to reach you. Where have you been?"

"Just with friends," I said.

"I went to Combe Bassett. What did I find? No colt, with or without feet. No Sid Halley. No sobbing colt owner. I find some batty old fusspot who says everyone went to Archie's house."

I gazed at her with a benign expression. I could do a benign expression rather well.

"So," continued India Cathcart with visible disgust, "I go to the house of a Mr. Archibald Kirk in the village of Shelley Green, and what do I find *there?*"

"What?"

"I find about five other newspapermen, sundry photographers, a Mrs. Archibald Kirk and a deaf old gent saying 'Eh?' "

"So then what?"

"Mrs. Kirk is lying, all wide-eyed and helpful. She's saying she doesn't know where anyone is. After three hours of that, I went back to Combe Bassett to look for ramblers."

"Did you find any?"

"They had rambled twenty miles and had climbed a stile into a field with a resident bull. A bunch of ramblers crashed out in panic through a hedge backwards and the rest are discussing suing the farmer for letting a dangerous animal loose near a public footpath. A man with a pony-tail says he's also suing Mrs. Bracken for not keeping her colt in a stable, thus preventing an amputation that gave his daughter hysterics."

"Life's one long farce," I said.

A mistake. She pounced on it. "Is that your comment on the maltreatment of animals?"

"No."

"Your opinion of ramblers?"

"Footpaths are important," I said.

She looked past me to the bartender. "Sparkling mineral water, ice and lemon, please."

She paid for her own drink as a matter of course. I wondered how much of her challenging air was unconscious and habitual, or whether she volume-adjusted it according to who she was talking to. I often learned useful things about people's characters by watching them talk to others than myself, and comparing the response.

"You're not playing fair," she said, judging me over the wedge of lemon bestriding the rim of her glass. "It was *The Pump*'s hotline that sent you to Combe Bassett. Kevin says you pay your debts. So pay."

"The hotline was his own idea. Not a bad one, except for about a hundred false alarms. But there's nothing I can tell you this evening."

"Not can't. Won't."

"It's often the same thing."

"Spare me the philosophy!"

"I enjoy reading your page every week," I said.

"But you don't want to figure in it?"

"That's up to you."

She raised her chin. "Strong men *beg* me not to print what I know."

I didn't want to antagonize her completely and I could forgo the passing pleasure of banter, so I gave her the benign expression and made no comment.

She said abruptly, "Are you married?"

"Divorced."

"Children?"

I shook my head. "How about you?"

She was more used to asking questions than answering. There was perceptible hesitation before she said, "The same."

I drank my scotch. I said, "Tell Kevin I'm very sorry I can't give him his inside edge. Tell him I'll talk to him on Monday."

"Not good enough."

"No, well . . . I can't do more."

"Is someone *paying* you?" she demanded. "Another paper?"

I shook my head. "Maybe Monday," I said. I put my empty glass on the bar. "Good-bye."

"Wait!" She gave me a straight stare, not overtly or aggressively feminist, but one that saw no need to make points in a battle that had been won by the generation before her. I thought that perhaps India Cathcart wouldn't have made it a condition of continued marriage that I should give up the best skill I possessed. I'd married a loving and gentle girl and turned her bitter: the worst, the most miserable failure of my life.

India Cathcart said, "Are you hungry? I've had nothing to eat all day. My expense account would run to two dinners."

There were many worse fates. I did a quick survey of the possibility of being deconstructed all over page fifteen, and decided as usual that playing safe had its limits. Take risks with caution: a great motto.

"Your restaurant or mine?" I said, smiling, and was warned by the merest flash of triumph in her eyes that she thought the tarpon hooked and as good as landed.

We ate in a noisy, brightly lit, large and crowded black-mirrored restaurant that was clearly the in-place for the in-crowd. India's choice. India's habitat. A few sycophantic hands shot out to make contact with her as we followed a lisping young greeter to a central, noteworthy table. India Cathcart acknowledged the plaudits and trailed me behind her like a comet's tail (Halley's?) while introducing me to no one.

The menu set out to amaze, but from long habit I ordered fairly simple things that could reasonably be dealt with one-handed: watercress mousse, then duck curry with sliced baked plantains. India chose baby eggplants with oil and pesto, followed by a large mound of crisped frogs' legs that she ate uninhibitedly with her fingers.

The best thing about the restaurant was that the decibel level made private conversation impossible: everything anyone said could be overheard by those at the next table.

"So," India raised her voice, teeth gleaming over a herb-dusted *cuisse,* "was Betty Bracken in tears?"

"I didn't see any tears."

"How much was the colt worth?"

I ate some plantain and decided they'd overdone the caramel. "No one knows," I said.

"Kevin told me it cost a quarter of a million. You're simply being evasive."

"What it cost and what it was worth are different. It might have won the Derby. It might have been worth millions. No one knows."

"Do you always play word games?"

"Quite often." I nodded. "Like you do."

"Where did you go to school?"

"Ask Kevin," I said, smiling.

"Kevin's told me things about you that you wouldn't want me to know."

"Like what?"

"Like it's easy to be taken in by your peaceful front. Like you having tungsten where other people have nerves. Like you being touchy about losing a hand. That's for starters."

I would throttle Kevin, I thought. I said, "How are the frogs' legs?"

"Muscular."

"Never mind," I said. "You have sharp teeth."

Her mind quite visibly changed gears from patronizing to uncertain, and I began to like her.

Risky to like her, of course.

After the curry and the frogs we drank plain black coffee and spent a pause or two in eye-contact appraisal. I expected she saw me in terms of adjectives and paragraphs. I saw her with appeased curiosity. I now knew what the serial reputation-slasher looked like at dinner.

In the way one does, I wondered what she looked like in bed; and in the way that one doesn't cuddle up to a potential cobra, I made no flicker of an attempt to find out.

She seemed to take this passivity for granted. She paid for our meal with a *Pump* business credit card, as promised, and crisply expected I would kick in my share on Monday as an exclusive for Kevin.

I promised what I knew I wouldn't be able to deliver, and offered her a lift home.

"But you don't know where I live!"

"Wherever," I said.

"Thanks. But there's a bus."

I didn't press it. We parted on the sidewalk outside the restaurant. No kiss. No handshake. A nod from her. Then she turned and walked away, not looking back: and I had no faith at all in her mercy.

ON SUNDAY MORNING I reopened the small blue suitcase Linda had lent me, and read again through all the clippings that had to do with the maimed Kent ponies.

I played again the videotape of the twenty-minute program Ellis had made of the child owners, and watched it from a different, and sickened, perspective.

There on the screen he looked just as friendly, just as charismatic, just as expert. His arms went around Rachel in sympathy. His good-looking face filled with compassion and outrage. Blinding ponies, cutting off a pony's foot, he said, those were crimes akin to murder.

Ellis, I thought in wretchedness, how *could* you?

*What if he can't help it?*

I played the tape a second time, taking in more details and attentively listening to what he had actually said.

His instinct for staging was infallible. In the shot where he'd commiserated with the children all together, he had had them sitting around on hay bales in a tack room, the children dressed in riding breeches, two or three wearing black riding hats. He himself had sat on the floor among them, casual in a dark open-necked jogging suit, a peaked cap pushed back on his head, sunglasses in pocket. Several of the children had been in tears. He'd given them his handkerchief and helped them cope with grief.

There were phrases he had used when talking straight to the camera that had brought the children's horrors sharply to disturbingly visual life: "pierced empty sockets, their eyesight running down their cheeks," and "a pure-bred silver pony, proud and shining in the moonlight."

His caring tone of voice alone had made the word pictures bearable.

"A silver pony shining in the moonlight." The basis of Rachel's nightmare.

"In the moonlight." He had *seen* the pony in the moonlight.

I played the tape a third time, listening with my eyes shut, undistracted by the familiar face, or by Rachel in his comforting hug.

He said, "A silver pony trotting trustfully across the field lured by a handful of horse nuts."

He shouldn't have known that.

He could have known it if any of the Fernses had suggested it.

But the Fernses themselves wouldn't have said it. They hadn't fed Silverboy on nuts. The agent of destruction that had come by night had brought the nuts.

Ellis would say, of course, that he had made it up, and the fact that it might be true was simply a coincidence. I rewound the tape and stared for a while into space. Ellis would have an answer to everything. Ellis would be believed.

In the afternoon I wrote a long, detailed report for Norman Picton: not a joyous occupation.

Early Monday morning, as he had particularly requested it, I drove to the police station in Newbury and personally delivered the package into the Detective Inspector's own hands.

"Did you talk about this to anybody?" he asked.

"No."

"Especially not to Quint?"

"Especially not. But . . . ," I hesitated, "they're a close family. It's more than likely that on Saturday evening or yesterday, Ginnie and Gordon told Ellis that you and I and Archie were sniffing round the Land-Rover and that you took away the shears. I think you must consider that Ellis knows the hunt is on."

He nodded disgustedly. "And as Ellis Quint officially lives in the Metropolitan area, we in the Thames Valley district cannot pursue our inquiries as freely as we could have."

"You mean, you can't haul him down to the local Regents Park nick and ask him awkward questions, like what was he doing at three A.M. on Saturday?"

"We can ask him ourselves if the Met agrees."

"I thought these divisions were being done away with."

"Cooperation is improving all the time."

I left him to sort out his problems and set off to drive to Kent. On the way, wanting to give Rachel Ferns a cheering-up present, I detoured into the maze of Kingston and, having parked, walked around the precincts looking for inspiration in the shops.

A windowful of tumbling puppies made me pause; perhaps Rachel needed an animal to love, to replace the pony. And perhaps Linda would *not* be pleased at having to house-train a growing nuisance that molted and chewed the furniture. I went into the pet shop, however, and that's how I came to arrive at Linda Ferns's house with my car full of fish tank, water weeds, miniature ruined castle walls, electric pump, lights, fish food, instructions, and three large lidded buckets of tropical fish.

Rachel was waiting by the gate for my arrival.

"You're half an hour late," she accused. "You said you'd be here by twelve."

"Have you heard of the M25?"

*"Everyone* makes that motorway an excuse."

"Well, sorry."

Her bald head was still a shock. Apart from that, she looked well, her cheeks full and rounded by steroids. She wore a loose sundress and clumpy sneakers on sticklike legs. It was crazy to love someone else's child so comprehensively, yet for the first time ever, I felt the idea of fatherhood take a grip.

Jenny had refused to have children on the grounds that any racing day could leave her a widow, and at the time I hadn't cared one way or another. If ever I married again, I thought, following Rachel into the house, I would long for a daughter.

Linda gave me a bright, bright smile, a pecking kiss and the offer of a gin and tonic while she threw together some pasta for our lunch. The table was laid. She set out steaming dishes.

"Rachel was out waiting for you two hours ago!" she said. "I don't know what you've done to the child."

"How are things?"

"Happy." She turned away abruptly, tears as ever near the surface. "Have some more gin. You said you'd got news for me."

"Later. After lunch. And I've brought Rachel a present."

The fish tank after lunch was the ultimate success. Rachel was enthralled, Linda interested and helpful. "Thank goodness you didn't give her a dog," she said. "I can't stand animals under my feet. I wouldn't let Joe give her a dog. That's why she wanted a pony."

The vivid fish swam healthily through the Gothic ruins, the water weeds rose and swelled, the lights and bubbles did their stuff. Rachel sprinkled fish food and watched her new friends eat. The pet shop owner had persuaded me to take a bigger tank than I'd thought best, and he had undoubtedly been right. Rachel's pale face glowed. Pegotty, in a baby-bouncer, sat wide-eyed and open-mouthed beside the glass. Linda came with me into the garden.

"Any news about a transplant?" I asked.

"It would have been the first thing I'd told you."

We sat on the bench. The roses bloomed. It was a beautiful day, heart-breaking.

Linda said wretchedly, "In acute lymphoblastic leukemia, which is what Rachel's got, chemotherapy causes remission almost always. More than ninety percent of the time. In seven out of ten children, the remission lasts forever, and after five years they can be thought of as cured for life. And girls have a better chance than boys, isn't that odd? But in thirty percent of children, the disease comes back."

She stopped.

"And it has come back in Rachel?"

"Oh, Sid!"

"Tell me."

She tried, the tears trickling while she spoke. "The disease came back in Rachel after less than two years, and that's not good. Her hair was beginning to grow, but it came out again with the drugs. They re-established her again in remission, and they're so good, it isn't so easy the second time. But I know from their faces—and they don't suggest transplants unless they have to, be-cause only about half of bone-marrow transplants are successful. I always talk as if a transplant will definitely save her, but it only *might*. If they found a tis-sue match they'd kill all her own bone marrow with radiation, which makes the children terribly nauseous and wretched, and then when the marrow's all dead they transfuse new liquid marrow into the veins and hope it will migrate into the bones and start making leukemia-free blood there, and quite often it *works* . . . and sometimes a child can be born with one blood group and be transfused with another. It's extraordinary. Rachel now has type A blood, but she might end up with type O, or something else. They can do so *much* nowa-days. One day they may cure *everybody*. But oh . . . oh . . ."

I put my arm around her shoulders while she sobbed. So many disasters were forever. So many Edens lost.

I waited until the weeping fit passed, and then I told her I'd discovered who had maimed and destroyed Silverboy.

"You're not going to like it," I said, "and it might be best if you can pre-vent Rachel from finding out. Does she ever read the newspapers?"

"Only Peanuts."

"And the television news?"

"She doesn't like news of starving children." Linda looked at me fearfully. "I've *wanted* her to know who killed Silverboy. That's what I'm paying you for."

I took out of my pocket and put into her hands an envelope containing her much-traveled check, torn now into four pieces.

"I don't like what I found, and I don't want your money. Linda . . . I'm so very sorry . . . but it was Ellis Quint himself who cut off Silverboy's foot."

She sprang in revulsion to her feet, immediate anger filling her, the shock hard and physical, the enormity of what I'd said making her literally shake.

I should have broken it more slowly, I thought, but the words had had to be said.

"How can you say such a thing?" she demanded. "How *can* you? You've got it all wrong. He couldn't possibly! You're *crazy* to say such a thing."

I stood up also. "Linda . . ."

"Don't say anything. I won't listen. I *won't.* He is so *nice.* You're *truly* crazy. And of course I'm not going to tell Rachel what you've accused him of, be-cause it would upset her, and you're *wrong.* And I know you've been kind to her . . . and to me . . . but I wouldn't have asked you here if I'd thought you could do so much awful harm. So please . . . *go.* Go, just *go."*

I shrugged a fraction. Her reaction was extreme, but her emotions were al-ways at full stretch. I understood her, but that didn't much help.

I said persuasively, "Linda, *listen."*

"No!"

I said, "Ellis has been my own friend for years. This is terrible for me, too."

She put her hands over her ears and turned her back, screaming, "Go away. Go away."

I said uncomfortably, "Phone me, then," and got no reply.

I touched her shoulder. She jerked away from me and ran a good way down the lawn, and after a minute I turned and went back into the house.

"Is Mummy crying?" Rachel asked, looking out of the window. "I heard her shout."

"She's upset." I smiled, though not feeling happy. "She'll be all right. How are the fish?"

"Cool." She went down on her knees, peering into the wet little world.

"I have to go now," I said.

"Good-bye." She seemed sure I would come back. It was a temporary farewell, between friends. She looked at the fishes, not turning her head.

" 'Bye," I said, and drove ruefully to London, knowing that Linda's rejection was only the first: the beginning of the disbelief.

In Pont Square the telephone was ringing when I opened my front door, and continued to ring while I poured water and ice from a jug in the refrigerator, and continued to ring while I drank thirstily after the hot afternoon, and continued to ring while I changed the battery in my left arm.

In the end, I picked up the receiver.

"Where the bloody hell have you *been?*"

The Berkshire voice filled my ear, delivering not contumely, but information. Norman Picton, Detective Inspector, Thames Valley Police.

"You've heard the news, of course."

"What news?" I asked.

"Do you live with your head in the sand? Don't you own a radio?"

"What's happened?"

"Ellis Quint is in custody," he said.

"He's *what?*"

"Yes, well, hold on, he's sort of in custody. He's in hospital, under guard."

"Norman," I said, disoriented. "Start at the beginning."

"Right." He sounded over-patient, as if talking to a child. "This morning two plainclothes officers of the Metropolitan Police went to Ellis Quint's flat overlooking Regents Park intending to interview him harmlessly about his whereabouts early Saturday morning. He came out of the building before they reached the main entrance, so, knowing him by sight, they approached him, identifying themselves and showing him their badges. At which point"—Picton cleared his throat but didn't seem able to clear his account of pedestrian police phraseology—"at which point Mr. Ellis Quint pushed one of the officers away so forcefully that the officer overbalanced into the roadway and was struck by a passing car. Mr. Quint himself then ran into the path of traffic as he attempted to cross the road to put distance between himself and the police officers. Mr. Quint caused a bus to swerve. The bus struck Mr. Quint a glancing blow, throwing him to the ground. Mr. Quint was dazed and bruised. He was taken to hospital, where he is now in a secure room while investigations proceed."

I said, "Are you reading that from a written account?"

"That's so."

"How about an interpretation in your own earthy words?"

"I'm at work. I'm not alone."

"OK," I said. "Did Ellis panic or did he think he was being mugged?"

Picton half laughed. "I'd say the first. His lawyers will say the second. But, d'you know what? When they emptied his pockets at the hospital, they found a thick packet of cash—and his passport."

"No!"

"It isn't illegal."

"What does he say?"

"He hasn't said anything yet."

"How's the officer he pushed?"

"Broken leg. He was lucky."

"And . . . when Ellis's daze wears off?"

"It'll be up to the Met. They can routinely hold him for one day while they frame a charge. I'd say that's a toss-up. With the clout he can muster, he'll be out in hours."

"What did you do with my report?"

"It went to the proper authorities."

Authorities was such a vague word. Who ever described their occupation as "an authority"?

"Thanks for phoning," I said.

"Keep in touch." An order, it sounded like.

I put down the receiver and found a handwritten scrawl from Kevin Mills on *Pump* letterhead paper in my fax.

He'd come straight to the point.

"Sid, you're a shit."

# 7

The week got worse, slightly alleviated only by a letter from Linda on Thursday morning.

Variably slanting handwriting. Jerky. A personality torn this way and that.

*Dear Sid,*

*I'm sorry I talked to you the way I did. I still cannot believe that Ellis Quint would cut off Silverboy's foot, but I remember thinking when he came here to do the TV program that he already knew a lot about what had happened. I mean things that hadn't been in the papers, like Silverboy liking horse nuts, which we never gave him, so how did he know, we didn't know ourselves, and I did wonder who had told him, but of course Joe asked Ellis who to buy a pony from, so of course I thought Ellis knew things about him from way back, like Silverboy being fed on horse nuts before he came to us.*

*Anyway, I can see how you got it wrong about Ellis, and it was very nice of you to bring the fish tank for Rachel, I can't tear her away from it. She keeps asking when you will come back and I don't like to tell her you won't, not as things are, so if you'll visit us again I will not say any more about your being wrong about Ellis. I ask you for Rachel.*

*We are both glad Ellis wasn't hurt today by that horrid bus.*

*Yours sincerely,*
*Linda Ferns.*

I wrote back thanking her for her letter, accepting her invitation and saying I would phone her soon.

ON TUESDAY ELLIS was charged with "actual bodily harm" for having in-
advertently and without intention pushed "an assailant" into the path of potential danger (under the wheels of a speeding motor) and was set free
"pending inquiries."

Norman Picton disillusionedly reported, "The only approximately good
thing is that they confiscated his passport. His lawyers are pointing their fingers up any police nose they can confront, screeching that it's a scandal."

"Where's Ellis now?"

"Look to your back. Your report is with the Crown Prosecution Service,
along with mine."

"Do you mean you don't know where he is?"

"He's probably in Britain or anywhere he can get to where he doesn't need
a passport. He told the magistrates in court that he'd decided to do a sports
program in Australia, and he had to have his passport with him because he
needed it to get a visa for Australia."

"Never underestimate his wits," I said.

"And he'd better look out for yours."

"He and I know each other too well."

ON WEDNESDAY AFTERNOON Ellis turned up at his regular television studio as if life were entirely normal and, on completion of an
audience-attended recording of a sports quiz, was quietly arrested by
three uniformed police officers. Ellis spent the night in custody, and on Thursday morning was charged with severing the foot of a colt: to be exact, the off-
fore foot of an expensive two-year-old thoroughbred owned by Mrs.
Elizabeth Bracken of Combe Bassett Manor, Berkshire. To the vociferous
fury of most of the nation, the magistrates remanded him in custody for another seven days, a preliminary precaution usually applied to those accused of
murder.

Norman Picton phoned me privately on my home number.

"I'm not telling you this," he said. "Understand?"

"I've got cloth ears."

"It would mean my job."

"I hear you," I said. "I won't talk."

"No," he said, "that, I believe."

"Norman?"

"Word gets around. I looked up the transcript of the trial of that man that smashed off your hand. You didn't tell *him* what he wanted to know, did you?"

"No . . . well . . . everyone's a fool sometimes."

"Some fool. Anyway, pin back the cloth ears. The reason why Ellis Quint is remanded for seven days is because after his arrest he tried to hang himself in his cell with his tie."

"He *didn't!*"

"No one took his belt or tie away, because of who he was. No one in the station *believed* in the charge. There's all hell going on now. The top brass are passing the parcel like a children's party. No one's telling anyone outside anything on pain of death, so, Sid . . ."

"I promise," I said.

"They'll remand him next week for another seven days, partly to stop him committing suicide and partly because . . ." He faltered on the brink of utter trust, his whole career at risk.

"I *promise,*" I said again. "And if I know what it is you want kept quiet, then I'll know what not to guess at publicly, won't I?"

"God," he said, half the anxiety evaporating, "then . . . there's horse blood in the hinges of the shears, and horse blood and hairs on the oily rag, and horse blood and hairs in the sacking. They've taken samples from the colt in the hospital at Lambourn, and everything's gone away for DNA testing. The results will be back next week."

"Does Ellis know?"

"I imagine that's why he tried the quick way out. It was a Hermès tie, incidentally, with a design of horseshoes. The simple knot he tied slid undone because the tie was pure smooth silk."

"For God's sake . . ."

"I keep forgetting he's your friend. Anyway, his lawyers have got to him. They're six deep. He's now playing the lighthearted celebrity, and he's sorrowful about *you,* Sid, for having got him all wrong. His lawyers are demanding proof that Ellis himself was ever at Combe Bassett by night, and we are asking for proof that he wasn't. His lawyers know we would have to drop the case if they can come up with a trustable alibi for any of the other amputations, but so far they haven't managed it. It's early days, though. They'll dig and dig, you can bet on it."

"Yeah."

"None of the Land-Rover evidence will get into the papers because the sub judice rule kicked in the minute they remanded him. Mostly that helps us, but you, as Sid Halley, won't be able to justify yourself in print until after the trial."

"Even if I can then."

"Juries are unpredictable."

"And the law is, frequently, an ass."

"People in the force are already saying you're off your rocker. They say Ellis is too well known. They say that wherever he went he would be recognized, therefore if no one recognized him, that in itself is proof he wasn't there."

"Mm," I said. "I've been thinking about that. Do you have time off at the weekend?"

"Not this weekend, no. Monday do you?"

"I'll see if I can fix something up with Archie . . . and Jonathan."

"And there's another thing," Norman said, "the Land-Rover's presence at Combe Bassett is solid in itself, but Jonathan, if he gets as far as the witness box, will be a *meal* for Ellis's lawyers. On probation for stealing cars! What sort of a witness is that?"

"I understood the jury isn't allowed to know anything about a witness. I was at a trial once in the Central Law Courts—the Old Bailey—when a beautifully dressed and blow-dried twenty-six-year-old glamour boy gave evidence—all lies—and the jury weren't allowed to know that he was already serving a sentence for confidence tricks and had come to court straight from jail, via the barber and the wardrobe room. The jury thought him a *lovely* young man. So much for juries."

"Don't you believe in the jury system?"

"I would believe in it if they were told more. How can a jury come to a prison-or-freedom decision if half the facts are withheld? There should be *no* inadmissible evidence."

"You're naive."

"I'm Sid Public, remember? The law bends over backwards to give the accused the benefit of the slightest doubt. The *victim* of murder is never there to give evidence. The colt in Lambourn can't talk. It's safer to kill animals. I'm sorry, but I can't stand what Ellis has become."

He said flatly, "Emotion works against you in the witness box."

"Don't worry. In court, I'm a block of ice."

"So I've heard."

"You've heard too damned much."

He laughed. "There's an old-boy internet," he said. "All you need is the password and a whole new world opens up."

"What's the password?"

"I can't tell you."

"Don't bugger me about. What's the password?"

"Archie," he said.

I was silent for all of ten seconds, remembering Archie's eyes the first time I met him, remembering the *awareness,* the message of knowledge. Archie knew more about me than I knew about him.

I asked, "What exactly does Archie do in the civil service?"

"I reckon," Norman said, amused, "that he's very like you, Sid. What he don't want you to know, he don't tell you."

"Where can I reach you on Monday?"

"Police station. Say you're John Paul Jones."

KEVIN MILLS DOMINATED the front page of *The Pump* on Friday—a respite from the sexual indiscretions of cabinet ministers but a demolition job on me. *"The Pump,"* he reminded readers, "had set up a hotline to Sid Halley to report attacks on colts. Owners had been advised to lock their stable doors, and to great effect had done so after the Derby. *The Pump* disclaimed all responsibility for Sid Halley's now ludicrously fingering Ellis Quint as the demon responsible for torturing defenseless horses. Ellis Quint, whose devotion to thoroughbreds stretches back to his own starry career as the country's top amateur race-rider, the popular hero who braved all perils in the ancient tradition of gentlemen sportsmen . . ."

More of the same.

"See also 'Analysis,' on page ten, and India Cathcart, page fifteen."

I supposed one had to know the worst. I read the leader column: "Should an ex-jockey be allowed free rein as pseudo sleuth? (Answer: no, of course not.)" and then, dredging deep for steel, I finally turned to India Cathcart's piece.

> *Sid Halley, smugly accustomed to acclaim as a champion, in short time lost his career, his wife and his left hand, and then weakly watched his friend soar to super-celebrity and national-star status, all the things that he considered should be his. Who does this pathetic little man think he's kidding? He's no Ellis Quint. He's a has-been with an ego problem, out to ruin what he envies.*

That was for starters. The next section pitilessly but not accurately dissected the impulse that led one to compete at speed (ignoring the fact that presumably Ellis himself had felt the same power-hungry inferiority complex).

My ruthless will to win, India Cathcart had written, had destroyed everything good in my own life. The same will to win now aimed to destroy my friend Ellis Quint. This was ambition gone mad.

*The Pump* would not let it happen. Sid Halley was a beetle ripe for squashing. *The Pump* would exterminate. The Halley myth was curtains.

———

DAMN AND BLAST her, I thought, and, for the first time in eighteen years, got drunk.

ON SATURDAY MORNING, groaning around the apartment with a headache, I found a message in my fax machine.

Handwritten scrawl, *Pump*-headed paper same as before . . . Kevin Mills.

*Sid, sorry, but you asked for it.*
   *You're still a shit.*

Most of Sunday I listened to voices on my answering machine delivering the same opinion.

Two calls relieved the gloom.

One from Charles Roland, my ex–father-in-law. "Sid, if you're in trouble, there's always Aynsford," and a second from Archie Kirk, "I'm at home. Norman Picton says you want me."

Two similar men, I thought gratefully. Two men with cool, dispassionate minds who would listen before condemning.

I phoned back to Charles, who seemed relieved I sounded sane.

"I'm all right," I said.

"Ellis is a knight in shining armor, though."

"Yeah."

"Are you *sure,* Sid?"

"Positive."

"But Ginnie . . . and Gordon . . . they're *friends."*

"Well," I said, "if *I* cut the foot off a horse, what would you do?"

"But you *wouldn't."*

"No."

I sighed. That was the trouble. No one could believe it of Ellis.

"Sid, come, anytime," Charles said.

"You're my rock," I said, trying to make it sound light. "I'll come if I need to."

"Good."

I phoned Archie and asked if Jonathan was still staying with Betty Bracken.

Archie said, "I've been talking to Norman. Jonathan is now addicted to water skiing and spends every day at the lake. Betty is paying hundreds and says it's worth it to get him out of the house. He'll be at the lake tomorrow. Shall we all meet there?"

We agreed on a time, and met.

When we arrived, Jonathan was out on the water.

"That's him," Norman said, pointing.

The flying figure in a scarlet wet-suit went up a ramp, flew, turned a somersault in the air and landed smoothly on two skis.

*"That,"* Archie said in disbelief, "is *Jonathan?"*

"He's a natural," Norman said. "I've been out here for a bit most days. Not only does he know his spatial balance and attitude by instinct, but he's fearless."

Archie and I silently watched Jonathan approach the shore, drop the rope and ski confidently up the sloping landing place with almost as much panache as Norman himself.

Jonathan grinned. Jonathan's streaky hair blew wetly back from his forehead. Jonathan, changed, looked blazingly *happy.*

A good deal of the joy dimmed with apprehension as he looked at Archie's stunned and expressionless face. I took a soft sports bag out of my car and held it out to him, asking him to take it with him to the dressing rooms.

"Hi," he said. "OK." He took the bag and walked off barefooted, carrying his skis.

"Incredible," Archie said, "but he can't ski through life."

"It's a start," Norman said.

After we'd stood around for a few minutes discussing Ellis we were approached by a figure in a dark-blue tracksuit, wearing also black running shoes, a navy baseball cap and sunglasses and carrying a sheet of paper. He came to within fifteen feet of us and stopped.

"Yes?" Norman asked, puzzled, as to a stranger. "Do you want something?"

I said, "Take off the cap and the glasses."

He took them off. Jonathan's streaky hair shook forward into its normal startling shape and his eyes stared at my face. I gave him a slight jerk of the head, and he came the last few paces and handed the paper to Norman.

Archie for once looked wholly disconcerted. Norman read aloud what I'd written on the paper.

" 'Jonathan, this is an experiment. Please put on the clothes you'll find in this bag. Put on the baseball cap, peak forward, hiding your face. Wear the sunglasses. Bring this paper. Walk towards me, stop a few feet away, and don't speak. OK? Thanks, Sid.' "

Norman lowered the paper, looked at Jonathan and said blankly, "Bloody hell."

"Is that the lot?" Jonathan asked me.

"Brilliant," I said.

"Shall I get dressed now?"

I nodded, and he walked nonchalantly away.

"He looked totally different," Archie commented, still amazed. "I didn't know him at all."

I said to Norman, "Did you look at the tape of Ellis's program, that one I put in with my report?"

"The tape covered with stickers saying it was the property of Mrs. Linda Ferns? Yes, I did."

"When Ellis was sitting on the floor with those children," I said, "he was wearing a dark tracksuit, open at the neck. He had a peaked cap pushed back on his head. He looked young. Boyish. The children responded to him . . . touched him . . . *loved* him. He had a pair of sunglasses tucked into a breast pocket."

After a silence Norman said, "But he *wouldn't*. He wouldn't wear those clothes on television if he'd worn them to mutilate the Ferns pony."

"Oh yes, he would. It would deeply amuse him. There's nothing gives him more buzz than taking risks."

"A baseball cap," Archie said thoughtfully, "entirely changes the shape of someone's head."

I nodded. "A baseball cap and a pair of running shorts can reduce any man of stature to anonymity."

"We'll never prove it," Norman said.

Jonathan slouched back in his own clothes and with his habitual half-sneering expression firmly in place. Archie's exasperation with him sharply returned.

"This is not the road to Damascus," I murmured.

"Damn you, Sid." Archie glared, and then laughed.

"What are you talking about?" Norman asked.

"Saint Paul's conversion on the road to Damascus happened like a thunderclap," Archie explained. "Sid's telling me not to look for instant miracles by the gravel pit lake."

Jonathan, not listening, handed me the bag. "Cool idea," he said. "No one knew me."

"They would, close to."

"It was still a risk," Norman objected.

"I told you," I said, "the risk is the point."

"It doesn't make sense."

"Cutting off a horse's foot doesn't make sense. Half of human actions don't make sense. Sense is in the eye of the beholder."

I DROVE BACK to London.

My answering machine had answered so many calls that it had run out of recording tape.

Among the general abuse, three separate calls were eloquent about the trouble I'd stirred up. All three of the owners of the other colt victims echoed Linda Ferns's immovable conviction.

The lady from Cheltenham: "I can't believe you can be so misguided. Ellis is absolutely innocent. I wouldn't have thought of you as being jealous of him, but all the papers say so. I'm sorry, Sid, but you're not welcome here anymore."

The angry Lancashire farmer: "You're a moron, do you know that? Ellis Quint! You're stupid. You were all right as a jockey. You should give up this pretense of being Sherlock Holmes. You're pitiful, lad."

The lady from York: "How *can* you? Dear Ellis! He's worth ten of you, I have to say."

I switched off the critical voices, but they went on reverberating in my brain.

The press had more or less uniformly followed *The Pump*'s lead. Pictures of Ellis at his most handsome smiled confidently from newsstands everywhere. Trial by media found Ellis Quint the wronged and innocent hero, Sid Halley the twisted, jealous cur snapping at his heels.

I'd known it would be bad: so why the urge to bang my head against the wall? Because I was human, and didn't have tungsten nerves, whatever anyone thought. I sat with my eyes shut, ostrich fashion.

Tuesday was much the same. I still didn't bang my head. Close-run thing.

On Wednesday Ellis appeared again before magistrates, who that time set him free on bail.

Norman phoned.

"Cloth ears?" he said. "Same as before?"

"Deaf," I assured him.

"It was fixed beforehand. Two minutes in court. Different time than posted. The press arrived after it was over. Ellis greeted them, free, smiling broadly."

"Shit."

Norman said, "His lawyers have done their stuff. It's rubbish to think the well-balanced personality intended to kill himself—his tie got caught somehow but he managed to free it. The policeman he pushed failed to identify himself adequately and is now walking about comfortably in a cast. The colt Ellis is accused of attacking is alive and recovering well. As bail is granted in cases of manslaughter, it is unnecessary to detain Ellis Quint any longer on far lesser charges. So . . . he's walked."

"Is he still to be tried?"

"So far. His lawyers have asked for an early trial date so that he can put this unpleasantness behind him. He will plead not guilty, of course. His lawyers are already patting each other on the back. And . . . I think there's a heavyweight maneuvering somewhere in this case."

"A heavyweight? Who?"

"Don't know. It's just a feeling."

"Could it be Ellis's father?"

"No, no. Quite different. It's just . . . since our reports, yours and mine, reached the Crown Prosecution Service, there's been a new factor. Political, perhaps. It's difficult to describe. It's not exactly a cover-up. There's already been too much publicity, it's more a sort of redirection. Even officially, and not just to the press, someone with muscle is trying to get you thoroughly and, I'm afraid I must say, *malignantly* discredited."

"Thanks a bunch."

"Sid, seriously, look out for yourself."

I FELT AS prepared as one could be for some sort of catastrophic pulverization to come my way, but in the event the process was subtler and long drawn out.

As if nothing had happened, Ellis resumed his television program and began making jokes about Sid Halley—"Sid Halley? That friend of mine! Have you heard that he comes from Halifax? Halley facts—he makes them up."

And "I like halibut—I eat it." And the old ones that I was used to, "halitosis" and "Hallelujah."

Hilarious.

When I went to the races, which I didn't do as often as earlier, people either turned their backs or *laughed,* and I wasn't sure which I disliked more.

I took to going only to jumping meetings, knowing Ellis's style took him to the most fashionable meetings on the flat. I acknowledged unhappily to myself that in my avoidance of him there was an element of cringe. I despised myself for it. All the same, I shrank from a confrontation with him and truly didn't know whether it was because of an ever-deepening aversion to what he had done, or because of the fear—the certainty—that he would publicly mock me.

He behaved as if there were never going to be a trial; as if awkward details like Land-Rovers, lopping shears and confirmed matching DNA tests tying the shears to the Bracken colt were never going to surface once the sub judice silence ended.

Norman, Archie and also Charles Roland worried that, for all the procedural care we had taken, Ellis's lawyers would somehow get the Land-Rover disallowed. Ellis's lawyers, Norman said, backed by the heavy unseen presence that was motivating them and possibly even paying the mounting fees, now included a defense counsel whose loss rate for the previous seven years was nil.

Surprisingly, despite the continuing barrage of ignominy, I went on being offered work. True, the approach was often tentative and apologetic—"Whether you're right or pigheaded about Ellis Quint . . ." and "Even if you've got Ellis Quint all wrong . . ."—but the nitty gritty seemed to be that they needed me and there was no one else.

Well, hooray for that. I cleaned up minor mysteries, checked credit ratings, ditto characters, found stolen horses, caught sundry thieves, all the usual stuff.

July came in with a deluge that flooded rivers and ruined the shoes of race-goers, and no colt was attacked at the time of the full moon, perhaps because the nights were wet and windy and black dark with clouds.

The press finally lost interest in the daily trashing of Sid Halley and Ellis Quint's show wrapped up for the summer break. I went down to Kent a couple of times, taking new fish for Rachel, sitting on the floor with her, playing checkers. Neither Linda nor I mentioned Ellis. She hugged me good-bye each time and asked when I would be coming back. Rachel, she said, had had no more nightmares. They were a thing of the past.

August came quietly and left in the same manner. No colts were attacked. The hotline went cold. India Cathcart busied herself with a cabinet member's mistress but still had a routinely vindictive jab at me each Friday. I went to America for two short weeks and rode horses up the Grand Tetons in Wyoming, letting the wide skies and the forests work their peace.

In September, one dew-laden early-fall English Saturday morning after a calm moonlit night, a colt was discovered with a foot off.

Nauseated, I heard the announcement on the radio in the kitchen while I made coffee.

Listeners would remember, the cool newsreader said, that in June Ellis Quint had been notoriously accused by ex-jockey Sid Halley of a similar attack. Quint was laughing off this latest incident, affirming his total ignorance on the matter.

There were no hotline calls from *The Pump,* but Norman Picton scorched the wires.

"Have you heard?" he demanded.

"Yes. But no details."

"It was a yearling colt this time. Apparently there aren't many two-year-olds in the fields just now, but there are hundreds of yearlings."

"Yes," I agreed. "The yearling sales are starting."

"The yearling in question belonged to some people near Northampton. They're frantic. Their vet put the colt out of his misery. But get this. Ellis Quint's lawyers have already claimed he has an alibi."

I stood in silence in my sitting room, looking out to the unthreatening garden.

"Sid?"

"Mm."

"You'll have to break that alibi. Otherwise, it will break *you.*"

"Mm."

"Say something else, dammit."

"The police can do it. Your lot."

"Face it. They're not going to try very hard. They're going to believe in his alibi, if it's anything like solid."

"Do you think, do you *really* think," I asked numbly, "that an ultra-respected barrister would connive with his client to mutilate . . . to kill . . . a colt—or pay someone else to do it—to cast doubt on the prosecution's case in the matter of a *different* colt?"

"Put like that, no."

"Nor do I."

"So Ellis Quint has set it up himself, and what he has set up, you can knock down."

"He's had weeks—more than two months—to plan it."

"Sid," he said, "it's not like you to sound defeated."

If he, I thought, had been on the receiving end of a long, pitiless barrage of systematic denigration, he might feel as I did, which, if not comprehensively defeated, was at least battle weary before I began.

"The police at Northampton," I said, "are not going to welcome me with open arms."

"That's never stopped you before."

I sighed. "Can you find out from the Northampton police what his alibi actually is?"

"Piece of cake. I'll phone you back."

I put down the receiver and went over to the window. The little square looked peaceful and safe, the railed garden green and grassy, a tree-dappled haven where generations of privileged children had run and played while their nursemaids gossiped. I'd spent my own childhood in Liverpool's back streets, my father dead and my mother fighting cancer. I in no way regretted the contrast in origins. I had learned self-sufficiency and survival there. Perhaps because of the back streets I now valued the little garden more. I wondered how the children who'd grown up in that garden would deal with Ellis Quint. Perhaps I could learn from them. Ellis had been that sort of child.

Norman phoned back later in the morning.

"Your friend," he said, "reportedly spent the night at a private dance in Shropshire, roughly a hundred miles to the northwest of the colt. Endless friends will testify to his presence, including his hostess, a duchess. It was a dance given to celebrate the twenty-first birthday of the heir."

"Damn."

"He could hardly have chosen a more conspicuous or more watertight alibi."

"And some poor bitch will swear she lay down for him at dawn."

"Why dawn?"

"It's when it happens."

"How do you know?"

"Never you mind," I said.

"You're a bad boy, Sid."

Long ago, I thought. Before Jenny. Summer dances, dew, wet grass, giggles and passion. Long ago and innocent.

Life's a bugger, I thought.

"Sid," Norman's voice said, "do you realize the trial is due to start two weeks on Monday?"

"I do realize."

"Then get a move on with this alibi."

"Yes, sir, Detective Inspector."

He laughed. "Put the bugger back behind bars."


ON TUESDAY I went to see the Shropshire duchess, for whom I had ridden winners in that former life. She even had a painting of me on her favorite horse, but I was no longer her favorite jockey.

"Yes, of *course* Ellis was here all night," she confirmed. Short, thin, and at first unwelcoming, she led me through the armor-dotted entrance hall of her drafty old house to the sitting room, where she had been watching the jump racing on television when I arrived.

Her front door had been opened to me by an arthritic old manservant who had hobbled away to see if Her Grace was in. Her Grace had come into the hall clearly anxious to get rid of me as soon as possible, and had then relented, her old kindness towards me resurfacing like a lost but familiar habit.

A three-mile steeplechase was just finishing, the jockeys kicking side by side to the finish line, the horses tired and straining, the race going in the end to the one carrying less weight.

The duchess turned down the volume, the better to talk.

"I cannot *believe,* Sid," she said, "that you've accused dear Ellis of something so *disgusting.* I know you and Ellis have been friends for years. Everyone knows that. I do think he's been a bit unkind about you on television, but you did *ask* for it, you know."

"But he *was* here . . . ?" I asked.

"Of course. All night. It was five or later when everyone started to leave. The band was playing still . . . we'd all had breakfast . . ."

"When did the dance start?" I asked.

"*Start?* The invitations were for ten. But you know how people are. It was eleven or midnight before most people came. We had the fireworks at three-thirty because rain was forecast for later, but it was fine all night, thank goodness."

"Did Ellis say good night when he left?"

"My dear Sid, there were over three hundred people here last Friday night. A succès fou, if I say it myself."

"So you don't actually remember when Ellis left?"

"The last I saw of him he was dancing an eightsome with that gawky Raven girl. Do drop it, Sid. I'm seeing you now for old times' sake, but you're not doing yourself any good, are you?"

"Probably not."

She patted my hand. "I'll always *know* you, at the races and so on."

"Thank you," I said.

"Yes. Be a dear and find your own way out. Poor old Stone has such bad arthritis these days."

She turned up the volume in preparation for the next race, and I left.

THE GAWKY RAVEN girl who had danced an eightsome reel with Ellis turned out to be the third daughter of an earl. She herself had gone off to Greece to join someone's yacht, but her sister (the second daughter) insisted that Ellis had danced with dozens of people after that, and wasn't I, Sid Halley, being a teeny-weeny *twit?*

I WENT TO see Miss Richardson and Mrs. Bethany, joint owners of the Windward Stud Farm, home of the latest colt victim: and to my dismay found Ginnie Quint there as well.

All three women were in the stud farm's office, a building separate from the rambling one-story dwelling house. A groom long-reining a yearling had directed me incuriously and I drew up outside the pinkish brick new-looking structure without relish for my mission, but not expecting a tornado.

I knocked and entered, as one does with such offices, and found myself in the normal clutter of desks, computers, copiers, wall charts and endless piles of paper.

I'd done a certain amount of homework before I went there, so it was easy to identify Miss Richardson as the tall, bulky, dominant figure in tweed jacket, worn cord trousers and wiry gray short-cropped curls. Fifty, I thought; despises men. Mrs. Bethany, a smaller, less powerful version of Miss Richardson, was reputedly the one who stayed up at night when the mares were foaling, the one on whose empathy with horses the whole enterprise floated.

The women didn't own the farm's two stallions (they belonged to syndicates) nor any of the mares: Windward Stud was a cross between a livery stable and a maternity ward. They couldn't afford the bad publicity of the victimized yearling.

Ginnie Quint, sitting behind one of the desks, leaped furiously to her feet the instant I appeared in the doorway and poured over me an accumulated concentration of verbal volcanic lava, scalding, shriveling, sticking my feet to the ground and my tongue in dryness to the roof of my mouth.

"He *trusted* you. He would have *died* for you."

I sensed Miss Richardson and Mrs. Bethany listening in astonishment, not knowing who I was nor what I'd done to deserve such an onslaught; but I had eyes only for Ginnie, whose long fondness for me had fermented to hate.

"You're going to go into court and try to send your best friend to prison . . . to destroy him . . . pull him down . . . ruin him. You're going to *betray* him. You're not fit to live."

Emotion twisted her gentle features into ugliness. Her words came out spitting.

It was her own son who had done this. Her golden, idolized son. He had made of me finally the traitor that would deliver the kiss.

I SAID ABSOLUTELY nothing.

I felt, more intensely than ever, the by now accustomed and bitter awareness of the futility of rebellion. Gagged by sub judice, I'd been unable all along to put up any defense, especially because the press had tended to pounce on my indignant protests and label them as "whining" and "diddums," and "please, Teacher, he hit me . . ." and "it's not fair, I hit him first."

A quick check with a lawyer had confirmed that though trying to sue one paper for libel might have been possible, suing the whole lot was not practical. Ellis's jokes were not actionable and, unfortunately, the fact that I was still profitably employed in my chosen occupation meant that I couldn't prove the criticism had damaged me financially.

"Grit your teeth and take it," he'd advised cheerfully, and I'd paid him for an opinion I gave myself free every day.

As there was no hope of Ginnie's listening to anything I might say, I unhappily but pragmatically turned to retreat, intending to return another day to talk to Miss Richardson and Mrs. Bethany, and found my way barred by two new burly arrivals, known already to the stud owners as policemen.

"Sergeant Smith reporting, madam," one said to Miss Richardson.

She nodded. "Yes, Sergeant?"

"We've found an object hidden in one of the hedges round the field where your horse was done in."

No one objected to my presence, so I remained in the office, quiet and riveted.

Sergeant Smith carried a long, narrow bundle which he laid on one of the desks. "Could you tell us, madam, if this belongs to *you?*"

His manner was almost hostile, accusatory. He seemed to expect the answer to be yes.

"What is it?" Miss Richardson asked, very far from guilty perturbation.

"This, madam," the sergeant said with a note of triumph, and lifted back folds of filthy cloth to reveal their contents, which were two long wooden handles topped by heavy metal clippers.

A pair of lopping shears.

Miss Richardson and Mrs. Bethany stared at them unmoved. It was Ginnie Quint who turned slowly white and fainted.

8

So here we were in October, with the leaves weeping yellowly from the trees.

Here I was, perching on the end of Rachel Ferns's bed, wearing a huge, fluffy orange clown wig and a red bulbous nose, making sick children laugh while feeling far from merry inside.

"Have you hurt your arm?" Rachel asked conversationally.

"Banged it," I said.

She nodded. Linda looked surprised. Rachel said, "When things hurt it shows in people's eyes."

She knew too much about pain for a nine-year-old. I said, "I'd better go before I tire you."

She smiled, not demurring. She, like the children wearing the other wigs I'd brought, all had very short bursts of stamina. Visiting was down to ten minutes maximum.

I took off the clown wig and kissed Rachel's forehead. " 'Bye," I said.

"You'll come back?"

"Of course."

She sighed contentedly, knowing I would. Linda walked with me from the ward to the hospital door.

"It's . . . *awful*," she said, forlorn, on the exit steps. Cold air. The chill to come.

I put my arms around her. Both arms. Hugged her.

"Rachel asks for you all the time," she said. "Joe cuddles her and cries. She cuddles *him,* trying to comfort him. She's her daddy's little girl. She loves him. But you . . . you're her *friend*. You make her laugh, not cry. It's you she asks for all the time—not Joe."

"I'll always come if I can."

She sobbed quietly on my shoulder and gulped, "Poor Mrs. Quint."

"Mm," I said.

"I haven't told Rachel about Ellis . . ."

"No. Don't," I said.

"I've been beastly to you."

"No, far from it."

"The papers have said such *dreadful* things about you." Linda shook in my arms. "I knew you weren't like that . . . I told Joe I have to believe you about Ellis Quint and he thinks I'm stupid."

"Look after Rachel, nothing else matters."

She went back into the hospital and I rode dispiritedly back to London in the Teledrive car.

Even though I'd returned with more than an hour to spare, I decided against Pont Square and took the sharp memory of Gordon Quint's attack straight to the restaurant in Piccadilly, where I'd agreed to meet the lawyer Davis Tatum.

With a smile worth millions, the French lady in charge of the restaurant arranged for me to have coffee and a sandwich in the tiny bar while I waited for my friend. The bar, in fact, looked as if it had been wholly designed as a meeting place for those about to lunch. There were no more than six tables, a bartender who brought drinks to one's elbow, and a calm atmosphere. The restaurant itself was full of daylight, with huge windows and green plants, and was sufficiently hidden from the busy artery of Mayfair downstairs as to give peace and privacy and no noisy passing trade.

I sat at a bar table in the corner with my back to the entrance, though in fact few were arriving: more were leaving after long hours of talk and lunch. I took some ibuprofen, and waited without impatience. I spent hours in my job, sometimes, waiting for predators to pop out of their holes.

Davis Tatum arrived late and out of breath from having apparently walked up the stairs instead of waiting for the elevator. He wheezed briefly behind my back, then came around into view and lowered his six-feet-three-inch bulk into the chair opposite.

He leaned forward and held out his hand for a shake. I gave him a limp approximation, which raised his eyebrows but no comment.

He was a case of an extremely agile mind in a totally unsuitable body. There were large cheeks, double chins, fat-lidded eyes and a small mouth. Dark, smooth hair had neither receded nor grayed. He had flat ears, a neck like a weight lifter, and a charcoal pin-striped suit straining over a copious belly. He might have difficulty, I thought, in catching sight of certain parts of his own body. Except in the brain-box, nature had dealt him a sad hand.

"First of all," he said, "I have some bad news, and I possibly shouldn't be here talking to you at all, according to how you read *Archbold.*"

"*Archbold* being the dos and don'ts manual for trial lawyers?"

"More or less."

"What's the bad news, then?" I asked. There hadn't been much that was good.

"Ellis Quint has retracted his 'guilty' plea, and has gone back to 'not guilty.' "

"*Retracted?*" I exclaimed. "How can one retract a confession?"

"Very easily." He sighed. "Quint says he was upset yesterday about his mother's death, and what he said about feeling guilty was misinterpreted. In other words, his lawyers have got over the shock and have had a rethink. They apparently know you have so far not been able to break Ellis Quint's alibi for the night that last colt was attacked in Northamptonshire, and they think they can therefore get the Bracken colt charge dismissed, despite the Land-Rover and circumstantial evidence, so they are aiming for a complete acquittal, not psychiatric treatment, and, I regret to tell you, they are likely to succeed."

He didn't have to tell me that my own reputation would never recover if Ellis emerged with his intact.

"And *Archbold?*"

"If I were the Crown Prosecuting counsel in this case I could be struck off for talking to you, a witness. As you know, I am the senior barrister in the chambers where the man prosecuting Ellis Quint works. I have seen his brief and discussed the case with him. I can absolutely properly talk to you, though perhaps some people might not think it prudent."

I smiled. " 'Bye-'bye, then."

"I may not discuss with you a case in which I may be examining you as a witness. But of course I will not be examining you. Also, we can talk about anything else. Like, for instance, golf."

"I don't play golf."

"Don't be obtuse, my dear fellow. Your perceptions are acute."

"Are we talking about angles?"

His eyes glimmered behind the folds of fat. "I saw the report package that you sent to the CPS."

"The Crown Prosecution Service?"

"The same. I happened to be talking to a friend. I said your report had surprised me, both by its thoroughness and by your deductions and conclusions. He said I shouldn't be surprised. He said you'd had the whole top echelon of the Jockey Club hanging on your every word. He said that, about a year ago, you'd cleared up two major racing messes at the same time. They've never forgotten it."

"A year last May," I said. "Is that what he meant?"

"I expect so. He said you had an assistant then that isn't seen around anymore. The job I'd like you to do might need an assistant for the leg-work. Don't you have your assistant nowadays?"

"Chico Barnes?"

He nodded. "A name like that."

"He got married," I said briefly. "His wife doesn't like what I do, so he's given it up. He teaches judo. I still see him—he gives me a judo lesson most weeks, but I can't ask him for any other sort of help."

"Pity."

"Yes. He was good. Great company and bright."

"And he got *deterred*. That's why he gave it up."

I went, internally, very still. I said, "What do you mean?"

"I heard," he said, his gaze steady on my face, "that he got beaten with some sort of thin chain to deter him from helping you. To deter him from all detection. And it worked."

"He got married," I said.

Davis Tatum leaned back in his chair, which creaked under his weight.

"I heard," he said, "that the same treatment was doled out to you, and in the course of things the Jockey Club mandarins made you take your shirt off. They said they had never seen anything like it. The whole of your upper body, arms included, was black with bruising, and there were vicious red weals all over you. And with your shirt hiding all that you'd calmly explained to them how and why you'd been attacked and how one of their number, who had arranged it, was a villain. You got one of the big shots chucked out."

"Who told you all that?"

"One hears things."

I thought in unprintable curses. The six men who'd seen me that day with my shirt off had stated their intention of never talking about it. They'd wanted to keep to themselves the villainy I'd found within their own walls; and nothing had been more welcome to me than that silence. It had been bad enough at the time. I didn't want continually to be reminded.

"Where does one hear such things?" I asked.

"Be your age, Sid. In the clubs . . . Bucks, the Turf, the RAC, the Garrick . . . these things get mentioned."

"How often . . . do they get mentioned? How often have you heard that story?"

He paused as if checking with an inner authority, and then said, "Once."

"Who told you?"

"I gave my word."

"One of the Jockey Club?"

"I gave my word. If you'd given your word, would *you* tell *me?*"

"No."

He nodded. "I asked around about you. And that's what I was told. Told in confidence. If it matters to you, I've heard it from no one else."

"It matters."

"It reflects your credit," he protested. "It obviously didn't stop you."

"It could give other villains ideas."

"And do villains regularly attack you?"

"Well, no," I said. "Physically no one's laid a finger on me since that time." Not until yesterday, I thought. "If you're talking about nonphysical assaults . . . Have you read the papers?"

"Scurrilous." Davis Tatum twisted in his seat until he could call the barman. "Tanqueray and tonic, please—and for you, Sid?"

"Scotch. A lot of water."

The barman brought the glasses, setting them out on little round white mats.

"Health," Davis Tatum toasted, raising his gin.

"Survival," I responded, and drank to both.

He put down his glass and came finally to the point.

"I need someone," he said, "who is clever, unafraid and able to think fast in a crisis."

"No one's like that."

"What about you?"

I smiled. "I'm stupid, scared silly a good deal of the time and I have night-mares. What you think you see is not what you get."

"I get the man who wrote the Quint report."

I looked benignly at my glass and not at his civilized face. "If you're going to do something to a small child that you know he won't like," I said, "such as sticking a needle into him, you *first* tell him what a brave little boy he is—in the hope that he'll then let you make a pincushion of him without complaint."

There was a palpable silence, then he chuckled, the low, rich timbre filling the air. There was embarrassment in there somewhere; a ploy exposed.

I said prosaically, "What's the job?"

He waited while four businessmen arrived, arranged their drinks and sank into monetary conversation at the table farthest from where we sat.

"Do you know who I mean by Owen Yorkshire?" Tatum asked, looking idly at the newcomers, not at me.

"Owen Yorkshire." I rolled the name around in memory and came up with only doubts. "Does he own a horse or two?"

"He does. He also owns Topline Foods."

"Topline . . . as in sponsored race at Aintree? As in Ellis Quint, guest of honor at the Topline Foods lunch the day before the Grand National?"

"That's the fellow."

"And the inquiry?"

"Find out if he's manipulating the Quint case to his own private advantage."

I said thoughtfully, "I did hear that there's a heavyweight abroad."

"Find out who it is, and why."

"What about poor old Archbold? He'd turn in his grave."

"So you'll do it!"

"I'll try. But why me? Why not the police? Why not the old-boy internet?"

He looked at me straightly. "Because you include silence in what you sell."

"And I'm expensive," I said.

"Retainer and refreshers," he promised.

"Who's paying?"

"The fees will come through me."

"And it's agreed," I said, "that the results, if any, are yours. Prosecution or otherwise will normally be your choice."

He nodded.

"In case you're wondering," I said, "when it comes to Ellis Quint, I gave the client's money back, in order to be able to stop him myself. The client didn't at first believe in what he'd done. I made my own choice. I have to tell you that you'd run that risk."

He leaned forward and extended his pudgy hand.

"We'll shake on it," he said, and grasped my palm with a firmness that sent a shock wave fizzing clear up to my jaw.

"What's the matter?" he said, sensing it.

"Nothing."

He wasn't getting much of a deal, I thought. I had a reputation already in tatters, a cracked ulna playing up, and the prospect of being chewed to further shreds by Ellis's defense counsel. He'd have done as well to engage my pal Jonathan of the streaky hair.

"Mr. Tatum," I began.

"Davis. My name's Davis."

"Will you give me your *assurance* that you won't speak of that Jockey Club business around the clubs?"

"Assurance?"

"Yes."

"But I told you . . . it's to your credit."

"It's a private thing. I don't like *fuss.*"

He looked at me thoughtfully. He said, "You have my assurance." And I wanted to believe in it, but I wasn't sure that I did. He was too intensely a club man, a filler of large armchairs in dark paneled rooms full of old exploded reputations and fruitily repeated secrets: "Won't say a word, old boy."

"Sid."

"Mm?"

"Whatever the papers say, where it really counts, you are respected."

"Where's that?"

"The clubs are good for gossip, but these days that's not where the power lies."

"Power wanders round like the magnetic North Pole."

"Who said that?"

"I just did," I said.

"No, I mean, did you make it up?"

"I've no idea."

"Power, these days, is fragmented," he said.

I added, "And where the power is at any one time is not necessarily where one would want to be."

He beamed proprietorially as if he'd invented me himself.

There was a quick rustle of clothes beside my ear and a drift of flowery scent, and a young woman tweaked a chair around to join our table and sat in it, looking triumphant.

"Well, well, well," she said. "Mr. Davis Tatum and Sid Halley! What a surprise!"

I said, to Davis Tatum's mystified face, "This is Miss India Cathcart, who writes for *The Pump*. If you say nothing you'll find yourself quoted repeating things you never thought, and if you say anything at all, you'll wish you hadn't."

"Sid," she said mock-sorrowfully, "can't you take a bit of kicking around?"

Tatum opened his mouth indignantly and, as I was afraid he might try to defend me, I shook my head. He stared at me, then with a complete change of manner said in smooth, lawyerly detachment, "Miss Cathcart, why are you here?"

"Why? To see you, of course."

"But why?"

She looked from him to me and back again, her appearance just as I remembered it: flawless porcelain skin, light-blue eyes, cleanly outlined mouth, black shining hair. She wore brown and red, with amber beads.

She said, "Isn't it improper for a colleague of the Crown Prosecutor to be seen talking to one of the witnesses?"

"No, it isn't," Tatum said, and asked me, "Did you tell her we were meeting here?"

"Of course not."

"Then how . . . why, Miss Cathcart, are you here?"

"I told you. It's a story."

"Does *The Pump* know you're here?" I asked.

A shade crossly she said, "I'm not a child. I'm allowed out on my own, you know. And anyway, the paper sent me."

"*The Pump* told you we'd be here?" Tatum asked.

"My editor said to come and see. And he was right!"

Tatum said, "Sid?"

"Mm," I said. "Interesting."

India said to me, "Kevin says you went to school in Liverpool."

Tatum, puzzled, asked, "What did you say?"

She explained, "Sid wouldn't tell me where he went to school, so I found out." She looked at me accusingly. "You don't sound like Liverpool."

"Don't I?"

"You sound more like Eton. How come?"

"I'm a mimic," I said.

If she really wanted to, she could find out also that between the ages of sixteen and twenty-one I'd been more or less adopted by a Newmarket trainer (who *had* been to Eton) who made me into a good jockey and by his example changed my speech and taught me how to live and how to behave and how to manage the money I earned. He'd been already old then, and he died. I often thought of him. He opened doors for me still.

"Kevin told me you were a slum child," India said.

589

"Slum is an attitude, not a place."

"Prickly, are we?"

Damn, I thought. I will *not* let her goad me. I smiled, which she didn't like. Tatum, listening with disapproval, said, "Who is Kevin?"

"He works for *The Pump*," I told him.

India said, "Kevin Mills is *The Pump*'s chief reporter. He did favors for Halley and got kicked in the teeth."

"Painful," Tatum commented dryly.

"This conversation's getting nowhere," I said. "India, Mr. Tatum is not the prosecutor in any case where I am a witness, and we may talk about anything we care to, including, as just now before you came, golf."

"You can't play golf with one hand."

It was Tatum who winced, not I. I said, "You can watch golf on television without arms, legs or ears. Where did your editor get the idea that you might find us here?"

"He didn't say. It doesn't matter."

"It is of the essence," Tatum said.

"It's interesting," I said, "because to begin with, it was *The Pump* that worked up the greatest head of steam about the ponies mutilated in Kent. That was why I got in touch with Kevin Mills. Between us we set up a hot-line, as a 'Save the *Tussilago farfara*' sort of thing."

India demanded, "What did you say?"

"*Tussilago farfara*," Tatum repeated, amused. "It's the botanical name of the wildflower coltsfoot."

"How did you know that?" she asked me fiercely.

"I looked it up."

"Oh."

"Anyway, the minute I linked Ellis Quint, even tentatively, to the colts, and to Rachel Ferns's pony, *The Pump* abruptly changed direction and started tearing me apart with crusading claws. I can surely ask, India, why do you write about me so ferociously? Is it just your way? Is it that you do so many hatchet jobs that you can't do anything else? I didn't expect kindness, but you are . . . every week . . . extreme."

She looked uncomfortable. She did what she had one week called me "diddums" for doing: she defended herself.

"My editor gives me guidelines." She almost tossed her head.

"You mean he tells you what to write?"

"Yes. No."

"Which?"

She looked from me to Tatum and back.

She said, "He subs my piece to align it with overall policy."

I said nothing. Tatum said nothing. India, a shade desperately, said, "Only saints get themselves burned at the stake."

Tatum said with gravitas, "If I read any lies or innuendos about my having improperly talked to Sid Halley about the forthcoming Quint trial, I will sue you personally for defamation, Miss Cathcart, and I will ask for punitive damages. So choose your stake. Flames seem inevitable."

I felt almost sorry for her. She stood up blankly, her eyes wide.

"Say we weren't here," I said.

I couldn't read her frozen expression. She walked away from us and headed for the stairs.

"A confused young woman," Tatum said. "But how did she—or her paper—know we would be here?"

I asked, "Do you feed your appointments into a computer?"

He frowned. "I don't do it personally. My secretary does it. We have a system which can tell where all the partners are, if there's a crisis. It tells where each of us can be found. I did tell my secretary I was coming here, but not who I was going to meet. That still doesn't explain . . ."

I sighed. "Yesterday evening you phoned my mobile number."

"Yes, and you phoned me back."

"Someone's been listening on my mobile phone's frequency. Someone heard you call me."

"Hell! But you called me back. They heard almost nothing."

"You gave your name . . . How secure is your office computer?"

"We change passwords every three months."

"And you use passwords that everyone can remember easily?"

"Well . . ."

"There are people who crack passwords just for the fun of it. And others hack into secrets. You wouldn't believe how *careless* some firms are with their most private information. Someone has recently accessed my own on-line computer—during the past month. I have a detector program that tells me. Much good it will do any hacker, as I never keep anything personal there. But a combination of my mobile phone and your office computer must have come up with the *possibility* that your appointment was with me. Someone in *The Pump* did it. So they sent India along to find out . . . and here we are. And because they succeeded, we now know they tried."

"It's incredible."

"Who runs *The Pump?* Who sets the policy?"

Tatum said thoughtfully, "The editor is George Godbar. The proprietor's Lord Tilepit."

"Any connection with Ellis Quint?"

He considered the question and shook his head. "Not that I know of."

"Does Lord Tilepit have an interest in the television company that puts on Ellis Quint's program? I think I'd better find out."

Davis Tatum smiled.

REFLECTING THAT, AS about thirty hours had passed since Gordon Quint had jumped me in Pont Square, he was unlikely still to be hanging about there with murderous feelings and his fencing post (not least because with Ginnie dead he would have her inquest to distract him), and also feeling that one could take self-preservation to shaming lengths, I left the Piccadilly restaurant in a taxi and got the driver to make two reconnoitering passes around the railed central garden.

All seemed quiet. I paid the driver, walked without incident up the steps to the front door, used my key, went up to the next floor and let myself into the haven of home.

No ambush. No creaks. Silence.

I retrieved a few envelopes from the wire basket clipped inside the letter box and found a page in my fax. It seemed a long time since I'd left, but it had been only the previous morning.

My cracked arm hurt. Well, it would. I'd ridden races—and winners—now and then with cracks: disguising them, of course, because the betting public deserved healthy riders to carry their money. The odd thing was that in the heat of a race one didn't feel an injury. It was in the cooler ebbing of excitement that the discomfort returned.

The best way, always, to minimize woes was to concentrate on something else. I looked up a number and phoned the handy acquaintance who had set up my computers for me.

"Doug," I said, when his wife had fetched him in from an oil change, "tell me about listening in to mobile phones."

"I'm covered in grease," he complained. "Won't this do another time?"

"Someone is listening to my mobile."

"Oh." He sniffed. "So you want to know how to stop it?"

"You're dead right."

He sniffed again. "I've got a cold," he said, "my wife's mother is coming to dinner and my sump is filthy."

I laughed; couldn't help it. "Please, Doug."

He relented. "I suppose you've got an analog mobile. They have radio signals that can be listened to. It's difficult, though. Your average bloke in the pub couldn't do it."

"Could you?"

"I'm not your average bloke in the pub. I'm a walking midlife crisis halfway through an oil change. I could do it if I had the right gear."

"How do I deal with it?"

"Blindingly simple." He sneezed and sniffed heavily. "I need a tissue." There was a sudden silence on the line, then the distant sound of a nose being vigorously blown, then the hoarse voice of wisdom in my ear.

"OK," he said. "You ditch the analog, and get a digital."

"I do?"

"Sid, being a jockey does not equip the modern man to live in tomorrow's world."

"I do see that."

"Everyone," he sniffed, "if they had any sense, would go digital."

"Teach me."

"The digital system," he said, "is based on two numbers, zero and one. Zero and one have been with us from the dawn of computers, and no one has ever invented anything better."

"They haven't?"

He detected my mild note of irony. "Has anyone," he asked, "reinvented the wheel?"

"Er, no."

"Quite. One cannot improve on an immaculate conception."

"That's blasphemous." I enjoyed him always.

"Certainly not," he said. "Some things are perfect to begin with. $E = mc^2$, and all that."

"I grant that. How about my mobile?"

"The signal sent to a digital telephone," he said, "is not one signal, as in analog, but is eight simultaneous signals, each transmitting one-eighth of what you hear."

"Is that so?" I asked dryly.

"You may bloody snigger," he said, "but I'm giving you the goods. A digital phone receives eight simultaneous signals, and it is *impossible* for anyone to decode them, except the receiving mobile. Now, because the signal arrives in eight pieces, the reception isn't always perfect. You don't get the crackle or the fading in and out that you get on analog phones, but you do sometimes get bits of words missing. Still, *no one* can listen in. Even the police can never tap a digital mobile number."

"So," I said, fascinated, "where do I get one?"

"Try Harrods," he said.

"*Harrods?*"

"Harrods is just round the corner from where you live, isn't it?"

"More or less."

"Try there, then. Or anywhere else that sells phones. You can use the same number that you have now. You just need to tell your service provider. And of course you'll need an SIM card. You have one, of course?"

I said meekly, "No."

"Sid!" he protested. He sneezed again. "Sorry. An SIM card is a Subscriber's Identity Module. You can't live without one."

"I can't?"

"Sid, I despair of you. Wake up to technology."

"I'm better at knowing what a horse thinks."

Patiently he enlightened me, "An SIM card is like a credit card. It actually *is* a credit card. Included on it are your name and mobile phone number and other details, and you can slot it into any mobile that will take it. For instance, if you are someone's guest in Athens and he has a mobile that accepts an SIM card, you can slot *your* card into *his* phone and the charge will appear on your account, not his."

"Are you serious?" I asked.

"With my problems, would I joke?"

"Where do I get an SIM card?"

"Ask Harrods." He sneezed. "Ask anyone who travels for a living. Your service provider will provide." He sniffed. "So long, Sid."

Amused and grateful, I opened my mail and read the fax. The fax being most accessible got looked at first.

Handwritten, it scrawled simply, "Phone me," and gave a long number.

The writing was Kevin Mills's, but the fax machine he'd sent it from was anonymously not *The Pump*'s.

I phoned the number given, which would have connected me to a mobile, and got only the infuriating instruction, "Please try later."

There were a dozen messages I didn't much want on my answering machine and a piece of information I *definitely* didn't want in a large brown envelope from Shropshire.

The envelope contained a copy of a glossy county magazine, one I'd sent for as I'd been told it included lengthy coverage of the heir-to-the-dukedom's coming-of-age dance. There were, indeed, four pages of pictures, mostly in color, accompanied by prose gush about the proceedings and a complete guest list.

A spectacular burst of fireworks filled half a page, and there in a group of heaven-gazing spectators, there in white tuxedo and all his photogenic glory, there unmistakably stood Ellis Quint.

My heart sank. The fireworks had started at three-thirty. At three-thirty, when the moon was high, Ellis had been a hundred miles northwest of the Windward Stud's yearling.

There were many pictures of the dancing, and a page of black and white shots of the guests, names attached. Ellis had been dancing. Ellis smiled twice from the guests' page, carefree, having a good time.

Damn it to hell, I thought. He had to have taken the colt's foot off early. Say by one o'clock. He could then have arrived for the fireworks by three-thirty. I'd found no one who'd seen him *arrive,* but several who swore to his presence after five-fifteen. At five-fifteen he had helped the heir to climb onto a table to make a drunken speech. The heir had poured a bottle of champagne over Ellis's head. Everyone remembered *that.* Ellis could not have driven back to Northampton before dawn.

For two whole days the previous week I'd traipsed around Shropshire, and next-door Cheshire, handed on from grand house to grander, asking much the same two questions (according to sex): Did you dance with Ellis Quint, or did you drink/eat with him? The answers at first had been freely given, but as time went on, news of my mission spread before me until I was progressively met by hostile faces and frankly closed doors. Shropshire was solid Ellis country. They'd have stood on their heads to prove him unjustly accused. They were not going to say that they didn't know when he'd arrived.

In the end I returned to the duchess's front gates, and from there drove as fast as prudence allowed to the Windward Stud Farm, timing the journey at two hours and five minutes. On empty roads at night, Northampton to the duchess might have taken ten minutes less. I'd proved nothing except that Ellis had had time.

Enough time was not enough.

As always before gathering at such dances, the guests had given and at-tended dinner parties both locally and farther away. No one that I'd asked had entertained Ellis to dinner.

No dinner was not enough.

I went through the guest list crossing off the people I'd seen. There were still far more than half unconsulted, most of whom I'd never heard of.

Where was Chico? I needed him often. I hadn't the time or, to be frank, the appetite to locate and question all the guests, even if they would answer. There must have been people—local people—helping with the parking of cars that night. Chico would have chatted people up in the local pubs and found out if any of the car-parkers remembered Ellis's arrival. Chico was good at pubs, and I wasn't in his class.

The police might have done it, but they wouldn't. The death of a colt still didn't count like murder.

The police.

I phoned Norman Picton's police station number and gave my name as John Paul Jones.

He came on the line in a good humor and listened to me without protest.

"Let me get this straight," he said. "You want me to ask favors of the Northamptonshire police? What do I offer in return?"

"Blood in the hinges of lopping shears."

"They'll have made their own tests."

"Yes, and that Northamptonshire colt is dead and gone to the glue factory. An error, wouldn't you say? Might they not do you a favor in exchange for commiseration?"

"You'll have my head off. What is it you actually *want?*"

"Er . . . ," I began, "I was there when the police found the lopping shears in the hedge."

"Yes, you told me."

"Well, I've been thinking. Those shears weren't wrapped in sacking, like the ones we took from the Quints."

"No, and the shears weren't the same, either. The ones at Northampton are a slightly newer model. They're on sale everywhere in garden centers. The problem is that Ellis Quint hasn't been reported as buying any, not in the Northamptonshire police district, nor ours."

"Is there any chance," I asked, "of my looking again at the material used for wrapping the shears?"

"If there are horse hairs in it, there's nothing left to match them to, same as the blood."

"All the same, the cloth might tell us where the shears came from. *Which* garden center, do you see?"

"I'll see if they've done that already."

"Thanks, Norman."

"Thank Archie. He drives me to help you."

"Does he?"

He heard my surprise. "Archie has *influence,*" he said, "and I do what the magistrate tells me."

When he'd gone off the line I tried Kevin Mills again and reached the same electronic voice: "Please try later."

After that I sat in an armchair while the daylight faded and the lights came on in the peaceful square. We were past the equinox, back in winter thoughts, the year dying ahead. Fall for me had for almost half my life meant the longed-for resurgence of major jump racing, the time of big winners and speed and urgency in the blood. Winter now brought only nostalgia and heating bills. At thirty-four I was growing old.

I sat thinking of Ellis and the wasteland he had made of my year. I thought of Rachel Ferns and Silverboy, and lymphoblasts. I thought of the press, and especially *The Pump* and India Cathcart and the orchestrated months of vilification. I thought of Ellis's relentless jokes.

I thought for a long time about Archie Kirk, who had drawn me to Combe Bassett and given me Norman Picton. I wondered if it had been from Archie that Norman had developed a belief in a heavy presence behind the scenes. I wondered if it could possibly be Archie who had prompted Davis Tatum to engage me to find that heavyweight. I wondered if it could possibly have been Archie who told Davis Tatum about my run-in with the bad hat at the Jockey Club, and if so, how did *he* know?

I trusted Archie. He could pull my strings, I thought, as long as I was willing to go where he pointed, and as long as I was sure no one was pulling *his*.

I thought about Gordon Quint's uncontrollable rage and the practical difficulties his fencing post had inflicted. I thought of Ginnie Quint and despair and sixteen floors down.

I thought of the colts and their chopped-off feet.

When I went to bed I dreamed the same old nightmare.

Agony. Humiliation. Both hands.

I awoke sweating.

Damn it all to hell.

# 9

In the morning, when I'd failed yet again to get an answer from Kevin Mills, I shunted by subway across central London and emerged not far from Companies House at 55 City Road, E.C.

Companies House, often my friend, contained the records of all public and private limited companies active in England, including the audited annual balance sheets, investment capital, fixed assets and the names of major shareholders and the directors of the boards.

Topline Foods, I soon learned, was an old company recently taken over by a few new big investors and a bustling new management. The chief shareholder and managing director was listed as Owen Cliff Yorkshire. There were fifteen non-executive directors, of whom one was Lord Tilepit.

The premises at which business was carried out were located at Frodsham, Cheshire. The registered office was at the same address.

The product of the company was foodstuffs for animals.

After Topline I looked up Village Pump Newspapers (they'd dropped the "Village" in about 1900, but retained the idea of a central meeting place for gossip) and found interesting items, and after Village Pump Newspapers I looked up the TV company that aired Ellis's sports program, but found no sign of Tilepit or Owen Yorkshire in its operations.

I traveled home (safely) and phoned Archie, who was, his wife reported, at work.

"Can I reach him at work?" I asked.

"Oh, no, Sid. He wouldn't like it. I'll give him a message when he gets back."

Please try later.

I tried Kevin Mills later and this time nearly got my eardrums perforated. "At last!"

"I've tried you a dozen times," I said.

"I've been in an old people's home."

"Well, bully for you."

"A nurse hastened three harpies into the hereafter."

"Poor old sods."

"If you're in Pont Square," he said, "can I call round and see you? I'm in my car not far away."

"I thought I was *The Pump*'s number one all-time shit."

"Yeah. Can I come?"

"I suppose so."

"Great." He clicked off before I could change my mind and he was at my door in less than ten minutes.

"This is *nice*," he said appreciatively, looking around my sitting room. "Not what I expected."

There was a Sheraton writing desk and buttoned brocade chairs and a couple of modern exotic wood inlaid tables by Mark Boddington. The overall colors were grayish-blue, soft and restful. The only brash intruder was an ancient slot machine that worked on tokens.

Kevin Mills made straight towards it, as most visitors did. I always left a few tokens haphazardly on the floor, with a bowl of them nearby on a table. Kevin picked a token from the carpet, fed it into the slot and pulled the handle. The wheels clattered and clunked. He got two cherries and a lemon. He picked up another token and tried again.

"What wins the jackpot?" he asked, achieving an orange, a demon and a banana.

"Three horses with jockeys jumping fences."

He looked at me sharply.

"It used to be the bells," I said. "That was boring, so I changed it."

"And do the three horses ever come up?"

I nodded. "You get a fountain of tokens all over the floor."

The machine was addictive. It was my equivalent of the psychiatrist's couch. Kevin played throughout our conversation but the nearest he came was two horses and a pear.

"The trial has started, Sid," he said, "so give us the scoop."

"The trial's only technically started. I can't tell you a thing. When the adjournment's over, you can go to court and listen."

"That's not exclusive," he complained.

"You know damned well I can't tell you."

"I gave you the story to begin with."

"I sought you out," I said. "Why did *The Pump* stop helping the colt owners and shaft me instead?"

He concentrated hard on the machine. Two bananas and a blackberry.

"Why?" I said.

"Policy."

"Whose policy?"

"The public wants demolition, they gobble up spite."

"Yes, but—"

"Look, Sid, we get the word from on high. And don't ask *who* on high, I don't know. I don't like it. None of us likes it. But we have the choice: go along with overall policy or go somewhere else where we feel more in tune. And do you know where that gets you? I work for *The Pump* because it's a good paper with, on the whole, fair comment. OK, so reputations topple. Like I said, that's what Mrs. Public wants. Now and then we get a *request,* such as 'lean hard on Sid Halley.' I did it without qualms, as you'd clammed up on me."

He looked all the time at the machine, playing fast.

"And India Cathcart?" I asked.

He pulled the lever and waited until two lemons and a jumping horse came to rest in a row.

"India . . . ," he said slowly. "For some reason she didn't want to trash you. She said she'd enjoyed her dinner with you and you were quiet and kind. Kind! I ask you! Her editor had to squeeze the poison out of her drop by drop for that first long piece. In the end he wrote most of her page himself. She was furious the next day when she read it, but it was out on the streets by then and she couldn't do anything about it."

I was more pleased than I would have expected, but I wasn't going to let Kevin see it. I said, "What about the continued stab wounds almost every week?"

"I guess she goes along with the policy. Like I said, she has to eat."

"Is it George Godbar's policy?"

"The big white chief himself? Yes, you could say the editor of the paper has the final say."

"And Lord Tilepit?"

He gave me an amused glance. Two pears and a lemon. "He's not a hands-on proprietor of the old school. Not a Beaverbrook or a Harmsworth. We hardly know he's alive."

"Does he give the overall policy to George Godbar?"

"Probably." A horse, a demon and some cherries. "Why do I get the idea that *you* are interviewing *me*, instead of the other way round?"

"I cannot imagine. What do you know about Owen Cliff Yorkshire?"

"Bugger all. Who is he?"

"Quite likely a friend of Lord Tilepit."

"Sid," he protested, "I do my job. Rapes, murders, little old ladies smothered in their sleep. I do not chew off the fingernails of my paycheck."

He banged the slot machine frustratedly. "The bloody thing hates me."

"It has no soul," I said. I fed in a stray token myself with my plastic fingers and pulled the handle. Three horses. Fountains of love. Life's little irony.

Kevin Mills took his paunch, his mustache and his disgusted disgruntlement off to his word processor, and I again phoned Norman as John Paul Jones.

"My colleagues now think John Paul Jones is a snitch," he said.

"Fine."

"What is it this time?"

"Do you still have any of those horse nuts I collected from Betty Bracken's field, and those others we took from the Land-Rover?"

"Yes, we do. And as you know, they're identical in composition."

"Then could you find out if they were manufactured by Topline Foods Limited, of Frodsham in Cheshire?"

After a short silence he said cautiously, "It could be done, but is it necessary?"

"If you could let me have some of the nuts I could do it myself."

"I can't let you have any. They are bagged and counted."

"Shit." And I could so easily have kept some in my own pocket. Careless. Couldn't be helped.

"Why does it matter where they came from?" Norman asked.

"Um . . . You know you told me you thought there might be a heavyweight somewhere behind the scenes? Well, I've been asked to find out."

"Jeez," he said. "Who asked you?"

"Can't tell you. Client confidentiality and all that."

"Is it Archie Kirk?"

"Not so far as I know."

"Huh!" He sounded unconvinced. "I'll go this far. If you get me some authenticated Topline nuts I'll see if I can run a check on them to find out if they match the ones we have. That's the best I can do, and that's stretching it, and you wouldn't have a prayer if you hadn't been the designer of our whole prosecution—and you can *not* quote me on that."

"I'm truly grateful. I'll get some Topline nuts, but they probably won't match the ones you have."

"Why not?"

"The grains—the balance of ingredients—will have changed since those were manufactured. Every batch must have its own profile, so to speak."

He well knew what I meant, as an analysis of ingredients could reveal their origins as reliably as grooves on a bullet.

"What interests you in Topline Foods?" Norman asked.

"My client."

"Bugger your client. Tell me." I didn't answer and he sighed heavily. "All right. You can't tell me now. I hate amateur detectives. I've got you a strip off that dirty Northampton material. At least, it's promised for later today. What are you going to do about it, and have you cracked Ellis Quint's alibi yet?"

"You're *brilliant,*" I said. "Where can I meet you? And no, I haven't cracked the alibi."

"Try harder."

"I'm only an amateur."

"Yeah, yeah. Come to the lake at five o'clock. I'm picking up the boat to take it home for winter storage. OK?"

"I'll be there."

"See you."

I phoned the hospital in Canterbury. Rachel, the ward sister told me, was "resting comfortably."

"What does that mean?"

"She's no worse than yesterday, Mr. Halley. When can you return?"

"Sometime soon."

"Good."

I spent the afternoon exchanging my old vulnerable analog mobile cellular telephone for a digital mobile receiving eight splintered transmissions that would baffle even the Thames Valley stalwarts, let alone *The Pump*.

From my apartment I then phoned Miss Richardson of Northamptonshire, who said vehemently that *no,* I certainly might *not* call on her again. Ginnie and Gordon Quint were her dear friends and it was *unthinkable* that Ellis could harm horses, and I was foul and *wicked* even to think it. Ginnie had told her about it. Ginnie had been very distressed. It was all my fault that she had killed herself.

I persevered with two questions, however, and did get answers of sorts.

"Did your vet say how long he thought the foot had been off when the colt was found at seven o'clock?"

"No, he didn't."

"Could you give me his name and phone number?"

"No."

As I had over the years accumulated a whole shelfful of area telephone directories, it was not so difficult via the Northamptonshire Yellow Pages to find and talk to Miss Richardson's vet. He would, he said, have been helpful if he could. All he could with confidence say was that neither the colt's leg nor the severed foot had shown signs of recent bleeding. Miss Richardson herself had insisted he put the colt out of his misery immediately, and, as it was also his own judgment, he had done so.

He had been unable to suggest to the police any particular time for the attack; earlier rather than later was as far as he could go. The wound had been clean: one chop. The vet said he was surprised a yearling would have stood still long enough for shears to be applied. Yes, he confirmed, the colt had been lightly shod, and yes, there had been horse nuts scattered around, but Miss Richardson often gave her horses nuts as a supplement to grass.

He'd been helpful, but no help.

After that I had to decide how to get to the lake, as the normal taken-for-granted act of driving now had complications. I had a knob fixed on the steering wheel of my Mercedes which gave me a good grip for one-(right)handed operation. With my left, unfeeling hand I shifted the automatic-gear lever.

I experimentally flexed and clenched my right hand. Sharp protests. Boring. With irritation I resorted to ibuprofen and drove to the lake wishing Chico were around to do it.

Norman had winched his boat halfway onto its trailer. Big, competent and observant, he watched my slow emergence to upright and frowned.

"What hurts?" he asked.

"Self-esteem."

He laughed. "Give me a hand with the boat, will you? Pull when I lift."

I looked at the job and said briefly that I couldn't.

"You only need one hand for pulling."

I told him unemotionally that Gordon Quint had aimed for my head and done lesser but inconvenient damage. "I'm telling you, in case he tries again and succeeds. He was slightly out of his mind over Ginnie."

Norman predictably said I should make an official complaint.

"No," I said. "This is unofficial, and ends right here."

He went off to fetch a friend to help him with the boat, and then busied himself with wrapping and stowing his powerful outboard engine.

I said, "What first gave you the feeling that there was some heavyweight meandering behind the scenes?"

"First?" He went on working while he thought. "It's months ago. I talked it over with Archie. I expect it was because one minute I was putting together an ordinary case—even if Ellis Quint's fame made it newsworthy—and the next I was being leaned on by the superintendent to find some reason to drop it, and when I showed him the strength of the evidence, he said the Chief Constable was unhappy, and the reason for the Chief Constable's unhappiness was always the same, which was political pressure from outside."

"What sort of political?"

Norman shrugged. "Not party politics especially. A pressure group. Lobbying. A bargain struck somewhere, along the lines of 'get the Quint prosecution aborted and such-and-such a good thing will come your way!' "

"But not a direct cash advantage?"

"Sid!"

"Well, sorry."

"I should frigging well hope so." He wrapped thick twine around the shrouded engine. "I'm not asking cash for a strip of rag from Northamptonshire."

"I grovel," I said.

He grinned. "That'll be the day." He climbed into his boat and secured various bits of equipment against movement en route.

"No one has entirely given in to the pressure," he pointed out. "The case against Ellis Quint has not been dropped. True, it's now in a ropy state. You yourself have been relentlessly discredited to the point where you're almost a liability to the prosecution, and even though that's brutally unfair, it's a fact."

"Mm."

In effect, I thought, I'd been commissioned by Davis Tatum to find out who had campaigned to defeat me. It wasn't the first time I'd faced campaigns to enforce my inactivity, but it was the first time I'd been offered a fee to save myself. To save myself, in this instance, meant to defeat Ellis Quint: so I was being paid for *that,* in the first place. And for what *else?*

Norman backed his car up to the boat trailer and hitched them together. Then he leaned through the open front passenger window of the car, unlocked the glove compartment there and drew out and handed to me a plastic bag.

"One strip of dirty rag," he said cheerfully. "Cost to you, six grovels before breakfast for a week."

I took the bag gratefully. Inside, the filthy strip, about three inches wide, had been loosely folded until it was several layers thick.

"It's about a meter long," Norman said. "It was all they would let me have. I had to sign for it."

"Good."

"What are you going to do with it?"

"Clean it, for a start."

Norman said doubtfully, "It's got some sort of pattern in it but there wasn't any printing on the whole wrapping. Nothing to say where it came from. No garden center name, or anything."

"I don't have high hopes," I said, "but frankly, just now every straw's worth clutching."

Norman stood with his legs apart and his hands on his hips. He looked a pillar of every possible police strength but what he was actually feeling turned out to be indecision.

"How far can I trust you?" he asked.

"For silence?"

He nodded.

"I thought we'd discussed this already."

"Yes, but that was months ago."

"Nothing's changed," I said.

He made a decision, stuck his head into his car again and this time brought out a business-sized brown envelope which he held out to me.

"It's a copy of the analysis done on the horse nuts," he said. "So read it and shred it."

"OK. And thanks."

I held the envelope and plastic bag together and knew I couldn't take such trust lightly. He must be very sure of me, I thought, and felt not complimented but apprehensive.

"I've been thinking," I said, "do you remember, way back in June, when we took those things out of Gordon Quint's Land-Rover?"

"Of course I remember."

"There was a farrier's apron in the Land-Rover. Rolled up. We didn't take that, did we?"

He frowned. "I don't remember it, but no, it's not among the things we took. What's significant about it?"

I said, "I've always thought it odd that the colts should stand still long enough for the shears to close round the ankle, even with head collars and those nuts. But horses have an acute sense of smell . . . and all those colts had shoes on—I checked with their vets—and they would have known the smell of a blacksmith's apron. I think Ellis might have worn that apron to reassure the colts. They may have thought he was the man who shod them. They would have *trusted* him. He could have lifted an ankle and gripped it with the shears."

He stared.

"What do you think?" I asked.

"It's you who knows horses."

"It's how I might get a two-year-old to let me near his legs."

"As far as I'm concerned," he said, "that's how it was done."

He held out his hand automatically to say good-bye, then remembered Gordon Quint's handiwork, shrugged, grinned and said instead, "If there's anything interesting about that strip of rag, you'll let me know?"

"Of course."

"See you."

He drove off with a wave, trailing his boat, and I returned to my car, stowed away the bag and the envelope and made a short journey to Shelley Green, the home of Archie Kirk.

He had returned from work. He took me into his sitting room while his smiling wife cooked in the kitchen.

"How's things?" Archie asked. "Whisky?"

I nodded. "A lot of water . . ."

He indicated chairs, and we sat. The dark room looked right in October: imitation flames burned imitation coals in the fireplace, giving the room a life that the sun of June hadn't achieved.

I hadn't seen Archie since then. I absorbed again the probably deliberate grayness of his general appearance, and I saw again the whole internet in the dark eyes.

He said casually, "You've been having a bit of a rough time."

"Does it show?"

"Yes."

"Never mind," I said. "Will you answer some questions?"

"It depends what they are."

I drank some of his undistinguished whisky and let my muscles relax into the ultimate of nonaggressive, noncombative postures.

"For a start, what do you do?" I said.

"I'm a civil servant."

"That's not . . . well . . . specific."

"Start at the other end," he said.

I smiled. I said, "It's a wise man who knows who's paying him."

He paused with his own glass halfway to his lips.

"Go on," he said.

"Then . . . do you know Davis Tatum?"

After a pause he answered, "Yes."

It seemed to me he was growing wary; that he, as I did, had to sort through a minefield of facts one could not or should not reveal that one knew. The old dilemma—does he know I know he knows—sometimes seemed like child's play.

I said, "How's Jonathan?"

He laughed. "I hear you play chess," he said. "I hear you're a whiz at misdirection. Your opponents think they're winning, and then . . . wham."

I played chess only with Charles at Aynsford, and not very often.

"Do you know my father-in-law?" I asked. "Ex–father-in-law, Charles Roland?"

With a glimmer he said, "I've talked to him on the telephone."

At least he hadn't lied to me, I thought; and, if he hadn't lied he'd given me a fairly firm path to follow. I asked about Jonathan, and about his sister, Betty Bracken.

"That wretched boy is still at Combe Bassett, and now that the water-skiing season is over he is driving everyone *mad*. You are the only person who sees any good in him."

"Norman does."

"Norman sees a talented water-skier with criminal tendencies."

"Has Jonathan any money?"

Archie shook his head. "Only the very little we give him for toothpaste and so on. He's still on probation. He's a mess." He paused. "Betty has been paying for the water skiing. She's the only one in our family with real money. She married straight out of school. Bobby's thirty years older—he was rich when they married and he's richer than ever now. As you saw, she's still devoted to him. Always has been. They had no children; she couldn't. Very sad. If Jonathan had any sense he would be *nice* to Betty."

"I don't think he's that devious. Or not yet, anyway."

"Do you like him?" Archie asked curiously.

"Not much, but I hate to see people go to waste."

"Stupid boy."

"I checked on the colt," I said. "The foot stayed on."

Archie nodded. "Betty's delighted. The colt is permanently lame, but they're going to see if, with his breeding, he's any good for stud. Betty's offering him free next year to good mares."

Archie's sweet wife came in and asked if I would stay to dinner; she could easily cook extra. I thanked her but stood up to go. Archie shook my hand. I winced through not concentrating, but he made no comment. He came out to my car with me as the last shreds of daylight waned to dark.

He said, "In the civil service I work in a small unacknowledged off-shoot department which was set up some time ago to foretell the probable outcome of any high political appointment. We also predict the future inevitable consequences of pieces of proposed legislation." He paused and went on wryly, "We call ourselves the Cassandra outfit. We see what will happen and no one believes us. We are always on the lookout for exceptional independent investigators with no allegiances. They're hard to find. We think you are one."

I stood beside my car in the dying light, looking into the extraordinary eyes. An extraordinary man of unimaginable insights. I said, "Archie, I'll work for you to the limit as long as I'm sure you're not sending me into a danger that you know exists but are not telling me about."

He took a deep breath but gave no undertaking.

"Good night," I said mildly.

"Sid."

"I'll phone you." It was as firm a promise, I thought, as "let's do lunch."

He was still standing on his gravel as I drove out through his gates. A true civil servant, I thought ruefully. No positive assurances could ever be given because the rules could at any time be changed under one's feet. I drove north across Oxfordshire to Aynsford and rang the bell of the side entrance of Charles's house. Mrs. Cross came in answer to the summons, her inquiring expression melting to welcome as she saw who had arrived.

"The Admiral's in the wardroom," she assured me when I asked if he was at home, and she bustled along before me to give Charles the news.

He made no reference to the fact that it was the second time in three days that I had sought his sanctuary. He merely pointed to the gold brocade chair and poured brandy into a tumbler without asking.

I sat and drank and looked gratefully at the austerity and restraint of this thin man who'd commanded ships and was now my only anchor.

"How's the arm?" he asked briefly, and I said lightly, "Sore."

He nodded and waited.

"Can I stay?" I said.

"Of course."

After a longish pause, I said, "Do you know a man called Archibald Kirk?"

"No, I don't think so."

"He says he talked to you on the telephone. It was months ago, I think. He's a civil servant and a magistrate. He lives near Hungerford, and I've come here from his house. Can you remember? Way back. I think he may have been asking you about *me*. Like sort of checking up, like a reference. You probably told him that I play chess."

He thought about it, searching for the memory.

"I would always give you a good reference," he said. "Is there any reason why you'd prefer I didn't?"

"No, definitely not."

"I've been asked several times about your character and ability. I always say if they're looking for an investigator they couldn't do better."

"You're . . . very kind."

"Kind, my foot. Why do you ask about this Archibald Church?"

"Kirk."

"Kirk, then."

I drank some brandy and said, "Do you remember that day you came with me to the Jockey Club? The day we got the head of the security section sacked?"

"I could hardly forget it, could I?"

"You didn't tell Archie Kirk about it, did you?"

"Of course not. I *never* talk about it. I gave you my word I wouldn't."

"Someone has," I said morosely.

"The Jockey Club didn't actually swear an oath of silence."

"I know." I thought a bit and asked, "Do you know a barrister called Davis Tatum? He's the head of chambers of the prosecuting counsel at Ellis's trial."

"I know *of* him. Never met him."

"You'd like him. You'd like Archie, too." I paused, and went on, "They both know about that day at the Jockey Club."

"But, Sid . . . does it really matter? I mean, you did the Jockey Club a tremendous favor, getting rid of their villain."

"Davis Tatum and, I'm sure, Archie, have engaged me to find out who is moving behind the scenes to get the Quint trial quashed. And I'm not telling you that."

He smiled. "Client confidentiality?"

"Right. Well, Davis Tatum made a point of telling me that he knew all about the mandarins insisting I take off my shirt, and why. I think he and Archie are trying to reassure themselves that if they ask me to do something dangerous, I'll do it."

He gave me a long, slow look, his features still and expressionless.

Finally he said, "And will you?"

I sighed. "Probably."

"What sort of danger?"

"I don't think they know. But realistically, if someone has an overwhelming reason for preventing Ellis's trial from ever starting, who is the person standing chiefly in the way?"

"*Sid!*"

"Yes. So they're asking me to find out if anyone might be motivated enough to ensure my permanent removal from the scene. They want me to find out *if* and *who* and *why.*"

"God, Sid."

From a man who never blasphemed, those were strong words.

"So . . . ," I sighed, "Davis Tatum gave me a name, Owen Yorkshire, and told me he owned a firm called Topline Foods. Now Topline Foods gave a sponsored lunch at Aintree on the day before the Grand National. Ellis Quint was guest of honor. Also among the guests was a man called Lord Tilepit, who is both on the board of Topline Foods and the proprietor of *The Pump,* which has been busy mocking me for months."

He sat as if frozen.

"So," I said, "I'll go and see what Owen Yorkshire and Lord Tilepit are up to, and if I don't come back you can kick up a stink."

When he'd organized his breath, he said, "Don't do it, Sid."

"No . . . but if I don't, Ellis will walk out laughing, and my standing in the world will be down the tubes forever, if you see what I mean."

He saw.

After a while he said, "I do vaguely remember talking to this Archie fellow. He asked about your *brains.* He said he knew about your physical resilience. Odd choice of words—I remember them. I told him you played a wily game of chess. And it's true, you do. But it was a long time ago. Before all this happened."

I nodded. "He already knew a lot about me when he got his sister to phone at five-thirty in the morning to tell me she had a colt with his foot off."

"So that's who he is? Mrs. Bracken's brother?"

"Yeah." I drank brandy and said, "If you're ever talking to Sir Thomas Ullaston, would you mind asking him—and don't make a drama of it—if he told Archie Kirk or Davis Tatum about that morning in the Jockey Club?"

Sir Thomas Ullaston had been Senior Steward at the time, and had conducted the proceedings which led to the removal of the head of the security section who had arranged for Chico and me to be thoroughly deterred from investigating anything ever again. As far as I was concerned it was all past history, and I most emphatically wanted it to remain so.

Charles said he would ask Sir Thomas.

"Ask him not to let *The Pump* get hold of it."

Charles contemplated that possibility with about as much horror as I did myself.

The bell of the side door rang distantly, and Charles frowned at his watch.

"Who can that be? It's almost eight o'clock."

We soon found out. An ultrafamiliar voice called "Daddy?" across the hall outside, and an ultrafamiliar figure appeared in the doorway. Jenny ... Charles's younger daughter . . . my sometime wife. My still embittered wife, whose tongue had barbs.

Smothering piercing dismay, I stood up, and Charles also.

"Jenny," Charles said, advancing to greet her. "What a lovely surprise."

She turned her cheek coolly, as always, and said, "We were passing. It seemed impossible not to call in." She looked at me without much emotion and said, "We didn't know *you* were here until I saw your car outside."

I took the few steps between us and gave her the sort of cheek-to-cheek salutation she'd bestowed on Charles. She accepted the politeness, as always, as the civilized acknowledgment of adversaries after battle.

"You look thin," she observed, not with concern but with criticism, from habit.

She, I thought, looked as beautiful as always, but there was nothing to be gained by saying so. I didn't want her to sneer at me. To begin with, it ruined the sweet curve of her mouth. She could hurt me with words whenever she tried, and she'd tried often. My only defense had been—and still was—silence.

Her handsome new husband had followed her into the room, shaking hands with Charles and apologizing for having appeared without warning.

"My dear fellow, anytime," Charles assured him.

Anthony Wingham turned my way and with self-conscious affability said, "Sid . . . ," and held out his hand.

It was extraordinary, I thought, enduring his hearty, embarrassed grasp, how often one regularly shook hands in the course of a day. I'd never really noticed it before.

Charles poured drinks and suggested dinner. Anthony Wingham waffled a grateful refusal. Jenny gave me a cool look and sat in the gold brocade chair.

Charles made small talk with Anthony until they'd exhausted the weather. I stood with them but looked at Jenny, and she at me. Into a sudden silence she said, "Well, Sid, I don't suppose you want me to say it, but you've got yourself into a proper mess this time."

"No."

"No what?"

"No, I don't want you to say it."

"Ellis Quint! Biting off more than you can chew. And back in the summer the papers pestered me, too. I suppose you know?"

I unwillingly nodded.

"That reporter from *The Pump*," Jenny complained. "India Cathcart, I couldn't get rid of her. She wanted to know all about you and about our divorce. Do you know what she wrote? She wrote that I'd told her that quite apart from being crippled, you weren't man enough for me."

"I read it," I said briefly.

"Did you? And did you like it? Did you like that, Sid?"

I didn't reply. It was Charles who fiercely protested. *"Jenny!* Don't."

Her face suddenly softened, all the spite dissolving and revealing the gentle girl I'd married. The transformation happened in a flash, like prison bars falling away. Her liberation, I thought, had dramatically come at last.

"I didn't say that," she told me, as if bewildered. "I really didn't. She made it up."

I swallowed. I found the reemergence of the old Jenny harder to handle than her scorn.

"What *did* you say?" I said.

"Well . . . I . . . I . . ."

*"Jenny,"* Charles said again.

"I told her," Jenny said to him, "that I couldn't live in Sid's hard world. I told her that whatever she wrote she wouldn't smash him or disintegrate him because no one had ever managed it. I told her that he never showed his feelings and that steel was putty compared to him, and that I couldn't live with it."

Charles and I had heard her say much the same thing before. It was Anthony who looked surprised. He inspected my harmless-looking self from his superior height and obviously thought she had got me wrong.

"India Cathcart didn't believe Jenny, either," I told him soothingly.

*"What?"*

"He reads minds, too," Jenny said, putting down her glass and rising to her feet. "Anthony, darling, we'll go now. OK?" To her father she said, "Sorry it's such a short visit," and to me, "India Cathcart is a bitch."

I kissed Jenny's cheek.

"I still love you," I said.

She looked briefly into my eyes. "I couldn't live with it. I told her the truth."

"I know."

"Don't let her break you."

"No."

"Well," she said brightly, loudly, smiling, "when birds fly out of cages they sing and rejoice. So . . . good-bye, Sid."

She looked happy. She laughed. I ached for the days when we'd met, when she looked like that always; but one could never go back.

"Good-bye, Jenny," I said.

Charles, uncomprehending, went with them to see them off and came back frowning.

"I simply don't understand my daughter," he said. "Do you?"

"Oh, yes."

"She tears you to pieces. *I* can't stand it, even if you can. Why don't you ever fight back?"

"Look what I did to her."

"She knew what she was marrying."

"I don't think she did. It isn't always easy, being married to a jockey."

"You forgive her too much! And then, do you know what she said just now, when she was leaving? I don't understand her. She gave me a hug—a hug—not a dutiful peck on the cheek, and she said, 'Take care of Sid.' "

I felt instantly liquefied inside: too close to tears.

"Sid . . ."

I shook my head, as much to retain composure as anything else.

"We've made our peace," I said.

"When?"

"Just now. The old Jenny came back. She's free of me. She felt free quite suddenly . . . so she'll have no more need to . . . to tear me to pieces, as you put it. I think that all that destructive anger has finally gone. Like she said, she's flown out of the cage."

He said, "I do hope so," but looked unconvinced. "I need a drink."

I smiled and joined him, but I discovered, as we later ate companionably together, that even though his daughter might no longer despise or torment me, what I perversely felt wasn't relief, but loss.

# 10

Leaving Aynsford early, I drove back to London on Thursday morning and left the car, as I normally did, in a large public underground car park near Pont Square. From there I walked to the laundry where I usually took my shirts and waited while they fed my strip of rag from Northampton twice through the dry-cleaning cycle.

What emerged was a stringy-looking object, basically light turquoise in color, with a non-geometric pattern on it of green, brown and salmon pink. There were also black irregular stains that had stayed obstinately in place.

I persuaded the cleaners to iron it, with the only result that I had a flat strip instead of a wrinkled one.

"What if I wash it with detergent and water?" I asked the burly, half-interested dry cleaner.

"You couldn't exactly *harm* it," he said sarcastically.

So I washed it and ironed it and ended as before: turquoise strip, wandering indeterminate pattern, stubborn black stain.

With the help of the Yellow Pages I visited the wholesale showrooms of a well-known fabric designer. An infinitely polite old man there explained that my fabric pattern was *woven*, while theirs—the wholesaler's—was *printed*. Different market, he said. The wholesaler aimed at the upper end of the middle-class market. I, he said, needed to consult an interior decorator, and with kindness he wrote for me a short list of firms.

The first two saw no profit in answering questions. At the third address I happened on an underworked twenty-year-old who ran pale long fingers through clean shoulder-length curls while he looked with interest at my offering. He pulled out a turquoise thread and held it up to the light.

"This is silk," he said.

"Real silk?"

"No possible doubt. This was expensive fabric. The pattern is woven in. See." He turned the piece over to show me the back. "This is remarkable. Where did you get it? It looks like a very old lampas. Beautiful. The colors are organic, not mineral."

I looked at his obvious youth and asked if he could perhaps seek a second opinion.

"Because I'm straight out of design school?" he guessed without umbrage. "But I studied *fabrics*. That's why they took me on here. I *know* them. The designers don't weave them, they use them."

"Then tell me what I've got."

He fingered the turquoise strip and held it to his lips and his cheek and seemed to commune with it as if it were a crystal ball.

"It's a modern copy," he said. "It's very skillfully done. It is lampas, woven on a Jacquard loom. There isn't enough of it to be sure, but I think it's a copy of a silk hanging made by Philippe de Lasalle in about 1760. But the original hadn't a blue-green background, it was cream with this design of ropes and leaves in greens and red and gold."

I was impressed. "Are you sure?"

"I've just spent three years learning this sort of thing."

"Well . . . who makes it now? Do I have to go to France?"

"You could try one or two English firms but you know what—"

He was brusquely interrupted by a severe-looking woman in a black dress and huge Aztec-type necklace who swept in and came to rest by the counter on which lay the unprepossessing rag.

"What are you doing?" she asked. "I asked you to catalog the new shipment of passementerie."

"Yes, Mrs. Lane."

"Then please get on with it. Run along now."

"Yes, Mrs. Lane."

"Do you want help?" she asked me briskly.

"Only the names of some weavers."

On his way to the passementerie my source of knowledge spoke briefly over his shoulder. "It looks like a solitary weaver, not a firm. Try Saul Marcus."

"Where?" I called.

"London."

"Thanks."

He went out of sight. Under Mrs. Lane's inhospitable gaze I picked up my rag, smiled placatingly and departed.

I found Saul Marcus first in the telephone directory and then in white-bearded person in an airy artist's studio near Chiswick, West London, where he created fabric patterns.

He looked with interest at my rag but shook his head.

I urged him to search the far universe.

"It might be Patricia Huxford's work," he said at length, dubiously. "You could try her. She does—or did—work like this sometimes. I don't know of anyone else."

"Where would I find her?"

"Surrey, Sussex. Somewhere like that."

"Thank you very much."

Returning to Pont Square, I looked for Patricia Huxford in every phone book I possessed for Surrey and Sussex and, for good measure, the bordering southern counties of Hampshire and Kent. Of the few Huxfords listed, none turned out to be Patricia, a weaver.

I really *needed* an assistant, I thought, saying good-bye to Mrs. Paul Huxford, wife of a double-glazing salesman. This sort of search could take hours. Damn Chico, and his dolly-bird protective missus.

With no easy success from the directories I started on directory inquiries, the central computerized number-finder. As always, to get a number one had to give an address, but the computer system contemptuously spat out Patricia Huxford, Surrey, as being altogether too vague.

I tried Patricia Huxford, Guildford (Guildford being Surrey's county town), but learned only of the two listed P. Huxfords that I'd already tried. Kingston, Surrey: same lack of results. I systematically tried all the other main areas; Sutton, Epsom, Leatherhead, Dorking . . . Surrey might be a small county in square-mile size, but large in population. I drew a uniform blank.

Huxfords were fortunately rare. A good job she wasn't called Smith.

Sussex, then. There was East Sussex (county town Brighton) and West Sussex (Chichester). I flipped a mental coin and chose Chichester, and could hardly believe my lucky ears.

An impersonal voice told me that the number of Patricia Huxford was ex-directory and could be accessed only by the police, in an emergency. It was not even in the C.O. grade-one class of ex-directory, where one could sweet-talk the operator into phoning the number on one's behalf (C.O. stood for calls offered). Patricia Huxford valued absolute grade-two privacy and couldn't be reached that way.

In the highest, third-grade, category, there were the numbers that weren't on any list at all, that the exchanges and operators might not know even existed; numbers for government affairs, the Royal Family and spies.

I yawned, stretched and ate cornflakes for lunch.

While I was still unenthusiastically thinking of driving to Chichester, roughly seventy more miles of arm-ache, Charles phoned from Aynsford.

"So glad to catch you in," he said. "I've been talking to Thomas Ullaston, I thought you'd like to know."

"Yes," I agreed with interest. "What did he say?"

"You know, of course, that he's no longer Senior Steward of the Jockey Club? His term of office ended."

"Yes, I know."

I also regretted it. The new Senior Steward was apt to think me a lightweight nuisance. I supposed he had a point, but it never helped to be discounted by the top man if I asked for anything at all from the department heads in current power. No one was any longer thanking me for ridding them of their villain: according to them, the whole embarrassing incident was best forgotten, and with that I agreed, but I wouldn't have minded residual warmth.

"Thomas was dumbfounded by your question," Charles said. "He protested that he'd meant you no harm."

"Ah!" I said.

"Yes. He didn't deny that he'd told someone about that morning, but he assured me that it had been only *one* person, and that person was someone of utterly good standing, a man of the utmost probity. I asked if it was Archibald Kirk, and he *gasped,* Sid. He said it was early in the summer when Archie Kirk sought him out to ask about you. Archie Kirk told him he'd heard you were a good investigator and he wanted to know *how* good. It seems Archie Kirk's branch of the civil service occasionally likes to employ independent investigators quietly, but that it's hard to find good ones they can trust. Thomas Ullaston told him to trust *you.* Archie Kirk apparently asked more and more questions, until Thomas found himself telling about that chain and those awful marks . . . I mean, sorry, Sid."

"Yeah," I said, "go on."

"Thomas told Archie Kirk that with your jockey constitution and physical resilience—he said physical resilience, Thomas did, so that's exactly where Kirk got that phrase from—with your natural inborn physical resilience you'd shaken off the whole thing as if it had never happened."

"Yes," I said, which wasn't entirely true. One couldn't ever forget. One could, however, ignore. And it was odd, I thought, that I never had nightmares about whippy chains.

Charles chuckled. "Thomas said he wouldn't want young master Halley on his tail if he'd been a crook."

Young master Halley found himself pleased.

Charles asked, "Is there anything else I can do for you, Sid?"

"You've been great."

"Be careful."

I smiled as I assured him I would. Be careful was hopeless advice to a jockey, and at heart I was as much out to win as ever.

On my way to the car I bought some robust adhesive bandage and, with my right forearm firmly strapped and a sufficient application of ibuprofen, drove to Chichester in West Sussex, about seven miles inland from the English Channel.

It was a fine spirits-lifting afternoon. My milk-coffee Mercedes swooped over the rolling South Downs and sped the last flat mile to the cathedral city of Chichester, wheels satisfyingly fast but still not as fulfilling as a horse.

I sought out the public library and asked to see the electoral roll.

There were masses of it: all the names and addresses of registered voters in the county, divided into electoral districts.

Where was Chico, blast him?

Resigned to a long search that could take two or three hours, I found Patricia Huxford within a short fifteen minutes. A record. I hated electoral rolls: the small print made me squint.

*Huxford, Patricia Helen, Bravo House, Lowell.*

Hallelujah.

I followed my road map and asked for directions in the village of Lowell, and found Bravo House, a small converted church with a herd of cars and vans outside. It didn't look like the reclusive lair of an ex-directory hermit.

As people seemed to be walking in and out of the high, heavy open west door, I walked in, too. I had arrived, it was soon clear, towards the end of a photographic session for a glossy magazine.

I said to a young woman hugging a clipboard, "Patricia Huxford?"

The young woman gave me a radiant smile. "Isn't she *wonderful?*" she said.

I followed the direction of her gaze. A small woman in an astonishing dress was descending from a sort of throne that had been built on a platform situated where the old transepts crossed the nave. There were bright theatrical spotlights that began to be switched off, and there were photographers unscrewing and dismantling and wrapping cables into hanks. There were effusive thanks in the air and satisfied excitement and the overall glow of a job done well.

I waited, looking about me, discovering the changes from church to modern house. The window glass, high up, was clear, not colored. The stone-flagged nave had rugs, no pews, comfortable modern sofas pushed back against the wall to accommodate the crowd, and a large-screen television set.

A white-painted partition behind the throne platform cut off the view of what had been the altar area, but nothing had been done to spoil the sweep of the vaulted ceiling, built with soaring stone arches to the glory of God.

One would have to have a very secure personality, I thought, to choose to live in that place.

The media flock drifted down the nave and left with undiminished good-will. Patricia Huxford waved to them and closed her heavy door and, turning, was surprised to find me still inside.

"So sorry," she said, and began to open the door again.

"I'm not with the photographers," I said. "I came to ask you about something else."

"I'm tired," she said. "I must ask you to go."

"You look beautiful," I told her, "and it will only take a minute." I brought my scrap of rag out and showed it to her. "If you are Patricia Huxford, did you weave this?"

"Trish," she said absently. "I'm called Trish."

She looked at the strip of silk and then at my face.

"What's your name?" she asked.

"John."

"John what?"

"John Sidney."

John Sidney were my real two first names, the ones my young mother had habitually used. "John Sidney, give us a kiss." "John Sidney, wash your face." "John Sidney, have you been fighting again?"

I often used John Sidney in my job: whenever, in fact, I didn't want to be known to be Sid Halley. After the past months of all-too-public drubbing I wasn't sure that Sid Halley would get me anything anywhere but a swift heave-ho.

Trish Huxford, somewhere, I would have guessed, in the middle to late forties, was pretty, blonde (natural?), small-framed and cheerful. Bright, observant eyes looked over my gray business suit, white shirt, unobtrusive tie, brown shoes, dark hair, dark eyes, unthreatening manner: my usual working confidence-inspiring exterior.

She was still on a high from the photo session. She needed someone to help her unwind, and I looked—and was—safe. Thankfully I saw her relax.

The amazing dress she had worn for the photographs was utterly simple in cut, hanging heavy and straight from her shoulders, floor length and sleeveless with a soft ruffled frill around her neck. It was the cloth of the dress that staggered: it was blue and red and silver and gold, and it *shimmered*.

"Did you weave your dress?" I asked.

"Of course."

"I've never seen anything like it."

"No, you wouldn't, not nowadays. Can I do anything for you? Where did you come from?"

"London. Saul Marcus suggested you might know who wove my strip of silk."

"Saul! How is he?"

"He has a white beard," I said. "He seemed fine."

"I haven't seen him for years. Will you make me some tea? I don't want marks on this dress."

I smiled. "I'm quite good at tea."

She led the way past the throne and around the white-painted screen. There were choir stalls beyond, old and untouched, and an altar table covered by a cloth that brought me to a halt. It was of a brilliant royal blue with shining gold Greek motifs woven into its deep hem. On the table, in the place of a religious altar, stood an antique spinning wheel, good enough for Sleeping Beauty. Above the table, arched clear glass windows rose to the roof.

"This way," Patricia Huxford commanded, and, leading me past the choir stalls, turned abruptly through a narrow doorway which opened onto what had once probably been a vestry and was now a small modern kitchen with a bathroom beside it.

"My bed is in the south transept," she told me, "and my looms are in the north. You might expect us to be going to drink China tea with lemon out of a silver teapot, but in fact I don't have enough time for that sort of thing, so the tea bags and mugs are on that shelf."

I half filled her electric kettle and plugged it in, and she spent the time walking around watching the miraculous colors move and mingle in her dress.

Intrigued, waiting for the water to boil, I asked, "What is it made of?"

"What do you think?"

"Er, it looks like . . . well . . . gold."

She laughed. "Quite right. Gold, silver thread and silk."

I rather clumsily filled the mugs.

"Milk?" she suggested.

"No, thank you."

"That's lucky. The crowd that's just left finished it off." She gave me a brilliant smile, picked up a mug by its handle and returned to the throne, where she sat neatly on the vast red velvet chair and rested a thin arm delicately along gilt carving. The dress fell into sculptured folds over her slender thighs.

"The photographs," she said, "are for a magazine about a festival of the arts that Chichester is staging all next summer."

I stood before her like some medieval page: stood chiefly because there was no chair nearby to sit on.

"I suppose," she said, "that you think me madly eccentric?"

"Not madly."

She grinned happily. "Normally I wear jeans and an old smock." She drank some tea. "Usually I work. Today is play-acting."

"And magnificent."

She nodded. "No one, these days, makes cloth of gold."

"The Field of the Cloth of Gold," I exclaimed.

"That's right. What do you know of it?"

"Only that phrase."

"The field was the meeting place at Guines, France, in June 1520, of Henry the Eighth of England and Francis the First of France. They were supposed to be making peace between England and France but they hated each other and tried to outdo each other in splendor. So all their courtiers wore cloth woven out of gold and they gave each other gifts you'd never see today. And I thought it would be historic to weave some cloth of gold for the festival . . . so I did. And this dress weighs a ton, I may tell you. Today is the only time I've worn it and I can't bear to take it off."

"It's breathtaking," I said.

She poured out her knowledge. "In 1476 the Duke of Burgundy left behind a hundred and sixty gold cloths when he fled from battle against the Swiss. You make gold cloth—like I made this—by supporting the soft gold on threads of silk, and you can recover the gold by burning the cloth. So when I was making this dress, that's what I did with the pieces I cut out to make the neck and armholes. I burnt them and collected the melted gold."

"Beautiful."

"You know something?" she said. "You're the only person who's seen this dress who hasn't asked how much it cost."

"I did wonder."

"And I'm not telling. Give me your strip of silk."

I took her empty mug and tucked it under my left arm, and in my right hand held out the rag, which she took; and I found her looking with concentration at my left hand. She raised her eyes to meet my gaze.

"Is it . . . ?" she said.

"Worth its weight in gold," I said flippantly. "Yes."

I carried the mugs back to the kitchen and returned to find her standing and smoothing her fingers over the piece of rag.

"An interior decorator," I said, "told me it was probably a modern copy of a hanging made in 1760 by . . . um . . . I think Philippe de Lasalle."

"How clever. Yes, it is. I made quite a lot of it at one time." She paused, then said abruptly, "Come along," and dived off again, leaving me to follow.

We went this time through a door in another white-painted partition and found ourselves in the north transept, her workroom.

There were three looms of varying construction, all bearing work in progress. There was also a business section with filing cabinets and a good deal of office paraphernalia, and another area devoted to measuring, cutting and packing.

"I make fabrics you can't buy anywhere else," she said. "Most of it goes to the Middle East." She walked towards the largest of the three looms, a monster that rose in steps to double our height.

"This is a Jacquard loom," she said. "I made your sample on this."

"I was told this piece was . . . a lampas? What's a lampas?"

She nodded. "A lampas is a compound weave with extra warps and wefts which put patterns and colors on the face of the fabric only, and are tucked into the back." She showed me how the design of ropes and branches of leaves gleamed on one side of the turquoise silk but hardly showed on the reverse. "It takes ages to set up," she said. "Nowadays almost no one outside the Middle East thinks the beauty is worth the expense, but once I used to sell quite a lot of it to castles and great houses in England, and all sorts of private people. I only make it to order."

I said neutrally, "Would you know who you made this piece for?"

"My dear man. No, I can't remember. But I probably still have the records. Why do you want to know? Is it important?"

"I don't know if it is important. I was given the strip and asked to find its origin."

She shrugged. "Let's find it then. You never know, I might get an order for some more."

She opened cupboard doors to reveal many ranks of box files, and ran her fingers along the labels on the spines until she came to one that her expression announced as possible. She lifted the box file from the shelf and opened it on a table.

Inside were stiff pages with samples of fabric stapled to them, with full details of fibers, dates, amount made, names of purchasers and receipts.

She turned the stiff pages slowly, holding my strip in one hand for comparison. She came to several versions of the same design, but all in the wrong color.

"That's it!" she exclaimed suddenly. "That's the one. I see I wove it almost thirty years ago. How time flies. I was so young then. It was a hanging for a four-poster bed. I see I supplied it with gold tassels made of gimp."

I asked without much expectation, "Who to?"

"It says here a Mrs. Gordon Quint."

I said, ". . . Er . . ." meaninglessly, my breath literally taken away.

Ginnie? *Ginnie* had owned the material?

"I don't remember her or anything about it," Trish Huxford said. "But all the colors match. It must have been this one commission. I don't think I made these colors for anyone else." She looked at the black stains disfiguring the strip I'd brought. "What a pity! I think of my fabrics as going on forever. They could easily last two hundred years. I love the idea of leaving something beautiful in the world. I expect you think I'm a sentimental old bag."

"I think you're splendid," I said truthfully, and asked, "Why are you ex-directory, with a business to run?"

She laughed. "I hate being interrupted when I'm setting up a design. It takes vast concentration. I have a mobile phone for friends—I can switch it off—and I have an agent in the Middle East, who gets orders for me. Why am I telling you all this?"

"I'm interested."

She closed the file and put it back on the shelf, asking, "Does Mrs. Quint want some more fabric to replace this damaged bit, do you think?"

Mrs. Quint was sixteen floors dead.

"I don't know," I said.

ON THE DRIVE back to London I pulled off the road to phone Davis Tatum at the number he'd given me, his home.

He was in and, it seemed, glad to hear from me, wanting to know what I'd done for him so far.

"Tomorrow," I said, "I'll give Topline Foods a visit. Who did you get Owen Yorkshire's name from?"

He said, stalling, "I beg your pardon?"

"Davis," I said mildly, "you want me to take a look at Owen Yorkshire and his company, so why? Why *him?*"

"I can't tell you."

"Do you mean you promised not to, or you don't know?"

"I mean . . . just go and take a look."

I said, "Sir Thomas Ullaston, Senior Steward last year of the Jockey Club, told Archie Kirk about that little matter of the chains, and Archie Kirk told *you*. So did the name Owen Yorkshire come to you from Archie Kirk?"

"Hell," he said.

"I like to know what I'm getting into."

After a pause he said, "Owen Yorkshire has been seen twice in the board-room of *The Pump*. We don't know why."

"Thank you," I said.

"Is that enough?"

"To be going on with. Oh, and my mobile phone is now safe. No more leaks. See you later."

I drove on to London, parked in the underground garage and walked along the alleyway between tall houses that led into the opposite side of the square from my flat.

I was going quietly and cautiously in any case, and came to a dead stop when I saw that the streetlight almost directly outside my window was not lit.

Boys sometimes threw stones at it to break the glass. Normally its darkness wouldn't have sent shudders up my spine and made my right arm remember Gordon Quint from fingers to neck. Normally I might have crossed the square figuratively whistling while intending to phone in the morning to get the light fixed.

Things were not normal.

There were two locked gates into the central garden, one opposite the path I was on, and one on the far side, opposite my house. Standing in shadow, I sorted out the resident-allocated garden key, went quietly across the circling roadway and unlocked the near gate.

Nothing moved. I eased the gate open, slid through and closed it behind me. No squeaks. I moved slowly from patch to patch of shaded cover, the half-lit tree branches moving in a light breeze, yellow leaves drifting down like ghosts.

Near the far side I stopped and waited.

There could be no one there. I was foolishly afraid over nothing.

The streetlight was out.

It had been out at other times. . . .

I stood with my back to a tree, waiting for alarm to subside to the point where I would unlock the second gate and cross the road to my front steps. The sounds of the city were distant. No cars drove into the cul-de-sac square.

I couldn't stand there all night, I thought . . . *and then I saw him.*

He was in a car parked by one of the few meters. His head—unmistakably Gordon Quint's head—moved behind the window. He was looking straight ahead, waiting for me to arrive by road or pavement.

I stood immobile as if stuck to the tree. It had to be obsession with him, I thought. The burning fury of Monday had settled down not into grief but revenge. I hadn't been in my flat for about thirty hours. How long had he been sitting there waiting? I'd had a villain wait almost a week for me once, before I'd walked unsuspectingly into his trap.

Obsession—fixation—was the most frightening of enemies and the hardest to escape.

I retreated, frankly scared, expecting him to see my movement, but he hadn't thought of an approach by garden. From tree to tree, around the patches of open grass, I regained the far gate, eased through it, crossed the road and drifted up the alleyway, cravenly expecting a bellow and a chase and, as he was a farmer, perhaps a shotgun.

Nothing happened. My shoes, soled and heeled for silence, made no sound. I walked back to my underground car and sat in it, not exactly trembling but nonetheless stirred up.

So much, I thought, for Davis Tatum's myth of a clever, unafraid investigator.

I kept always in the car an overnight bag containing the personality-change clothes I'd got Jonathan to wear: dark two-piece tracksuit (trousers and zip-up jacket), navy blue sneakers, and a baseball cap. The bag also contained a long-sleeved open-necked shirt, two or three charged-up batteries for my arm, and a battery charger, to make sure. Habitually around my waist I wore a belt with a zipped pocket big enough for a credit card and money.

I had no weapons or defenses like mace. In America I might have carried both.

I sat in the car considering the matter of distance and ulnas. It was well over two hundred miles from my London home to Liverpool, city of my birth. Frodsham, the base town of Topline Foods, wasn't quite as far as Liverpool, but still over two hundred miles. I had already, that day, steered a hundred and fifty—Chichester and back. I'd never missed Chico so much.

I considered trains. Too inflexible. Airline? Ditto. Teledrive? I lingered over the comfort of Teledrive but decided against, and resignedly set off northwards.

It was an easy drive normally; a journey on wide fast motorways taking at most three hours. I drove for only one hour, then stopped at a motel to eat and sleep, and at seven o'clock in the morning wheeled on again, trying to ignore both the obstinately slow-mending fracture and India Cathcart's column that I'd bought from the motel's newsstand.

Friday mornings had been a trial since June. Page fifteen in *The Pump*—trial by the long knives of journalism, the blades that ripped the gut.

She hadn't mentioned at all seeing Tatum and me in the Le Meridien bar. Perhaps she'd taken my advice and pretended we hadn't been there. What her column said about me was mostly factually true but spitefully wrong. I wondered how she could do it? Had she no sense of humanity?

Most of her page concerned yet another politician caught with his trousers at half-mast, but the far-right column said:

*Sid Halley, illegitimate by-blow of a nineteen-year-old window cleaner and a packer in a biscuit factory, ran amok as a brat in the slums of Liverpool. Home was a roach-infested council flat. Nothing wrong with that! But this same Sid Halley now puts on airs of middle-class gentility. A flat in Chelsea? Sheraton furniture? Posh accent? Go back to your roots, lad. No wonder Ellis Quint thinks you funny. Funny pathetic!*

*The slum background clearly explains the Halley envy. Halley's chip on the shoulder grows more obvious every day. Now we know why!*

*The Halley polish is all a sham, just like his plastic left hand.*

Christ, I thought, how much more? Why did it so bloody *hurt*?

My father had been killed in a fall eight months before my birth and a few days before he was due to marry my eighteen-year-old mother. She'd done her best as a single parent in hopeless surroundings. "Give us a kiss, John Sidney . . ."

I hadn't ever run amok. I'd been a quiet child, mostly. "Have you been fighting again, John Sidney . . . ?" She hadn't liked me fighting, though one had to sometimes, or be bullied.

And when she knew she was dying she'd taken me to Newmarket, because I'd been short for my age, and had left me with the king of trainers to be made into a jockey, as I'd always wanted.

I couldn't possibly go back to my Liverpool "roots." I had no sense of ever having grown any there.

I had never envied Ellis Quint. I'd always liked him. I'd been a better jockey than he, and we'd both known it. If anything, the envy had been the other way around. But it was useless to protest, as it had been all along. Protests were used regularly to prove *The Pump*'s theories of my pitiable inadequacy.

My mobile phone buzzed. I answered it.

"Kevin Mills," a familiar voice said. "Where are you? I tried your apartment. Have you seen today's *Pump* yet?"

"Yes."

"India didn't write it," he said. "I gave her the info, but she wouldn't use it. She filled that space with some pars on sexual stress and her editor subbed them out."

Half of my muscles unknotted, and I hadn't realized they'd been tense. I forced unconcern into my voice even as I thought of hundreds of thousands of readers sniggering about me over their breakfast toast.

"Then you wrote it yourself," I said. "So who's a shit now? You're the only person on *The Pump* who's seen my Sheraton desk."

"Blast you. Where are you?"

"Going back to Liverpool. Where else?"

"Sid, look, I'm sorry."

"Policy?"

He didn't answer.

I asked, "Why did you phone to tell me India didn't write today's bit of demolition?"

"I'm getting soft."

"No one's listening to this phone anymore. You can say what you like."

"Jeez." He laughed. "That didn't take you long." He paused. "You might not believe it, but most of us on *The Pump* don't any more like what we've been doing to you."

"Rise up and rebel," I suggested dryly.

"We have to eat. And you're a tough bugger. You can take it."

You just try it, I thought.

"Listen," he said, "the paper's received a lot of letters from readers complaining that we're not giving you a fair deal."

"How many is a lot?"

"Two hundred or so. Believe me, that's a *lot*. But we're not allowed to print any."

I said with interest, "Who says so?"

"That's just it. The ed, Godbar himself, says so, and he doesn't like it, either, but the policy is coming from the very top."

"Tilepit?"

"Are you *sure* this phone's not bugged?"

"You're safe."

"You've had a bloody raw mauling, and you don't deserve it. I know that. We all know it. I'm sorry for my part in it. I'm sorry I wrote today's venom, especially that bit about your hand. Yes, it's Tilepit. The proprietor himself."

"Well . . . thanks."

He said, "Did Ellis Quint *really* cut off those feet?"

I smiled ruefully. "The jury will decide."

"Sid, look here," he protested, "you *owe* me!"

"Life's a bugger," I said.

# 11

Nine o'clock Friday morning I drove into the town of Frodsham and asked for Topline Foods.

Not far from the river, I was told. Near the river; the Mersey.

The historic docks of Liverpool's Mersey waterfront had long been silent, the armies of tall cranes dismantled, the warehouses converted or pulled down. Part of the city's heart had stopped beating. There had been bypass surgery of sorts, but past muscle would never return. The city had a vast red-brick cathedral, but faith, as in much of Britain, had dimmed.

For years I'd been to Liverpool only to ride there on Aintree racecourse. The road I'd once lived in lay somewhere under a shopping mall. Liverpool was a place, but not home.

At Frodsham there was a "Mersey View" vantage point with, away to the distant north, some still-working docks at Runcorn on the Manchester Ship Canal. One of those docks, I'd seen earlier, was occupied by Topline Foods. A ship lying alongside bearing the flag and insignia of Canada had been unloading Topline grain.

I'd stopped the car from where I could see the sweep of river with the seagulls swooping and the stiff breeze tautening flags at the horizontal. I stood in the cold open air, leaning on the car, smelling the salt and the mud and hearing the drone of traffic on the roads below.

Were these roots? I'd always loved wide skies, but it was the wide sky of

Newmarket Heath that I thought of as home. When I'd been a boy there'd been no wide skies, only narrow streets, the walk to school, and rain. "John Sidney, wash your face. Give us a kiss."

The day after my mother died I'd ridden my first winner, and that evening I'd got drunk for the first and only time until the arrest of Ellis Quint.

Soberly, realistically, in the Mersey wind I looked at the man I had become: a jumble of self-doubt, ability, fear and difficult pride. I had grown as I was from the inside out. Liverpool and Newmarket weren't to blame.

Stirring and getting back into the car, I wondered where to find all those tungsten nerves I was supposed to have.

I didn't know what I was getting into. I could still at that point retreat and leave the field to Ellis. I could—and I couldn't. I would have myself to live with, if I did.

I'd better simply get on with it, I thought.

I drove down from the vantage point, located the Topline Foods factory and passed through its twelve-feet-high but hospitably open wire-mesh gates. There was a guard in a gatehouse who paid me no attention.

Inside there were many cars tidily parked in ranks. I added myself to the end of one row and decided on a clothing compromise of suit trousers, zipped-up tracksuit top, white shirt, no tie, ordinary shoes. I neatly combed my hair forward into a young-looking style and looked no threat to anybody.

The factory, built around three sides of the big central area, consisted of loading bays, a vast main building and a new-looking office block. Loading and unloading took place under cover, with articulated semi-trailers backing into the bays. In the one bay I could see into clearly, the cab section had been disconnected and removed; heavy sacks that looked as if they might contain grain were being unloaded from a long container by two large men who slung the sacks onto a moving conveyer belt of rollers.

The big building had a row of windows high up: there was no chance of looking in from outside.

I ambled across to the office building and shouldered open a heavy glass door that led into a large but mostly bare entrance hall, and found there the reason for the unguarded front gates. The security arrangements were all inside.

Behind a desk sat a purposeful-looking middle-aged woman in a green jumper. Flanking her were two men in navy blue security-guard suits with Topline Foods insignia on their breast pockets.

"Name, please," said the Green Jumper. "State your business. All parcels, carriers and handbags must be left here at the desk."

She had a distinct Liverpool accent. With the same inflection in my own voice, I told her that, as she could see, I had no bag, carrier or handbag with me.

She took the accent for granted and unsmilingly asked again for my name.

"John Sidney."

"Business?"

"Well," I said, as if perplexed by the reception I was getting, "I was asked to come here to see if you made some horse nuts." I paused. "Like," I lamely finished, dredging up the idiom.

"Of course, we make horse nuts. It's our business."

"Yes," I told her earnestly, "but this farmer, like, he asked me to come in, as I was passing this way, to see if it was you that made some horse nuts that someone had given him, that were very good for his young horse, like, but he was given them loose and not in a bag and all he has is a list of what's in the nuts and he wanted to know if you made them, see?" I half pulled a sheet of paper from an inside pocket and pushed it back.

She was bored by the rigmarole.

"If I could just *talk* to someone," I pleaded. "See, I owe this farmer a favor and it wouldn't take no more than a minute, if I could talk to someone. Because this farmer, he'll be a big customer if these are the nuts he's looking for."

She gave in, lifted a telephone and repeated a shortened version of my improbable tale.

She inspected me from head to foot. "Couldn't hurt a fly," she reported.

I kept the suitably feeble half anxious smile in place.

She put down the receiver. "Miss Rowse will be down to help you. Raise your hands."

"Eh?"

"Raise your hands . . . please."

Surprised, I did as I was told. One of the security guards patted me all over in the classic way of their job, body and legs. He missed the false hand and the cracked bone. "Keys and mobile phone," he reported. "Clean."

Green jumper wrote "John Sidney" onto a clip-on identity card and I clipped it dutifully on.

"Wait by the elevator," she said.

I waited.

The doors finally parted to reveal a teenage girl with wispy fair hair who said she was Miss Rowse. "Mr. Sidney? This way, please."

I stepped into the elevator with her and rode to the third floor.

She smiled with bright inexperienced encouragement and led me down a newly carpeted passage to an office conspicuously labeled Customer Relations on its open door.

"Come in," Miss Rowse said proudly. "Please sit down."

I sat in a Scandinavian-inspired chair of blonde wood with arms, simple lines, blue cushioning and considerable comfort.

"I'm afraid I didn't really understand your problem," Miss Rowse said trustingly. "If you'll explain again, I can get the right person to talk to you."

I looked around her pleasant office, which showed almost no sign of work in progress.

"Have you been here long?" I asked. (Guileless Liverpool accent, just like hers.) "Nice office. They must think a lot of you here."

She was pleased, but still honest. "I'm new this week. I started on Monday—and you're my second inquiry."

No wonder, I thought, that she'd let me in.

I said, "Are all the offices as plush as this?"

"Yes," she said enthusiastically. "Mr. Yorkshire, he likes things nice."

"Is he the boss?"

"The chief executive officer." She nodded. The words sounded stiff and unfamiliar, as if she'd only newly learned them.

"Nice to work for, is he?" I suggested.

She confessed, "I haven't met him yet. I know what he looks like, of course, but . . . I'm new here, like I said."

I smiled sympathetically and asked what Owen Yorkshire looked like.

She was happy to tell me, "He's ever so *big*. He's got a big head and a lovely lot of hair, wavy like."

"Mustache?" I suggested. "Beard?"

"No," she giggled. "And he's not *old*. Not a granddad. Everyone gets out of his way."

Do they indeed, I thought.

She went on, "I mean, Mrs. Dove, she's my boss really, she's the office manager, she says not to make him angry, whatever I do. She says just to do my job. She has a lovely office. It used to be Mr. Yorkshire's own, she says."

Miss Rowse, shaped like a woman, chattered like a child.

"Topline Foods must be doing all right to have rich new offices like these," I said admiringly.

"They've got the TV cameras coming tomorrow to set up for Monday. They brought dozens of potted plants round this morning. Ever so keen on publicity, Mrs. Dove says Mr. Yorkshire is."

"The plants do make it nice and homey," I said. "Which TV company, do you know?"

She shook her head. "All the Liverpool big noises are coming to a huge reception on Monday. The TV cameras are going all over the factory. Of course, although they're going to have all the machines running, they won't really make any nuts on Monday. It will all be pretend."

"Why's that?"

"Security. They have to be security mad, Mrs. Dove says. Mr. Yorkshire worries about people putting things in the feed, she says."

"What things?"

"I don't know. Nails and safety pins and such. Mrs. Dove says all the searching at the entrance is Mr. Yorkshire's idea."

"Very sensible," I said.

An older and more cautious woman came into the office, revealing herself to be the fount of wisdom, Mrs. Dove. Middle-aged and personally secure, I thought. Status, ability and experience all combining in priceless efficiency.

"Can I help you?" she said to me civilly, and to the girl, "Marsha dear, I thought we'd agreed you would always come to me for advice."

"Miss Rowse has been really helpful," I said. "She's going to find someone to answer my question. Perhaps you could yourself?"

Mrs. Dove (gray hair pinned high under a flat black bow, high heels, customer-relations neat satin shirt, cinched waist and black tights) listened with slowly glazing eyes to my expanding tale of the nutty farmer.

"You need our Willy Parrott," she said when she could insert a comment. "Come with me."

I waggled conspiratorial fingers at Marsha Rowse and followed Mrs. Dove's busy back view along the expensive passage with little partitioned but mostly empty offices on each side. She continued through a thick fire door at the end, to emerge on a gallery around an atrium in the main factory building, where the nuts came from.

Rising from the ground, level almost to the gallery, were huge mixing vats, all with paddles circulating, activated from machinery stretching down from above. The sounds were an amalgam of whir, rattle and slurp: the air bore fine particles of cereal dust and it looked like a brewery, I thought. It smelled rather the same also, but without the fermentation.

Mrs. Dove passed me thankfully on to a man in brown overalls who inspected my dark clothes and asked if I wanted to be covered in fall-out.

"Not particularly."

He raised patient eyebrows and gestured to me to follow him, which I did, to find myself on an iron staircase descending one floor, along another gallery and ending in a much-used battered little cubby-hole of an office, with a sliding glass door that he closed behind us.

I commented on the contrast from the office building.

"Fancy fiddle-faddle," he said. "That's for the cameras. This is where the work is done."

"I can see that," I told him admiringly.

"Now, lad," he said, looking me up and down, unimpressed, "what is it you want?"

He wasn't going to be taken in very far by the farmer twaddle. I explained in a shorter version and produced the folded paper bearing the analysis of the nuts from Combe Bassett and the Land-Rover, and asked if it was a Topline formula.

He read the list that by then I knew by heart.

*Wheat, oat feed, ryegrass, straw, barley, corn, molasses, salt, linseed.*
*Vitamins, selenium, copper, other substances and probably the antioxidant Ethoxyquin.*

"Where did you get this?" he asked.

"From a farmer, like I told you."

"This list isn't complete," he said.

"No . . . but is it enough?"

"It doesn't give percentages. I can't possibly match it to any of our products." He folded the paper and gave it back. "Your cubes might be our supplement feed for horses out at grass. Do you know anything about horses?"

"A little."

"Then, the more oats you give them, the more energy they expend. Racehorses need more oats. I can't tell you for sure if these cubes were for racehorses in training unless I know the proportion of oats."

"They weren't racehorses in training."

"Then your farmer friend couldn't do better than our Sweetfield mix. They do contain everything on your list."

"Are other people's cubes much different?"

"There aren't very many manufacturers. We're perhaps fourth on the league table but after this advertisement campaign we expect that to zoom up. The new management aims for the top."

"But . . . um . . . do you have enough space?"

"Capacity?"

I nodded.

He smiled. "Owen Yorkshire has plans. He talks to us man to man." His face and voice were full of approval. "He's brought the old place back to life."

I said inoffensively, "Mrs. Dove seems in awe of his anger."

Willy Parrott laughed and gave me a male chauvinist–type wink. "He has a flaming temper, has our Owen Yorkshire. And the more a man for that."

I looked vaguely at some charts taped to a wall. "Where does he come from?" I asked.

"Haven't a clue," Willy told me cheerfully. "He knows bugger all about nutrition. He's a salesman, and *that's* what we needed. We have a couple of nerds in white coats working on what we put in all the vats."

He was scornful of scientists as well as women. I turned back from the wall charts and thanked him for his time. Very interesting job, I told him. Obviously he ran the department that mattered most.

He took the compliment as his due and saved me the trouble of asking by offering to let me tag along with him while he went to his next task, which was to check a new shipment of wheat. I accepted with an enthusiasm that pleased him. A man good at his job often enjoyed an audience, and so did Willy Parrott.

He gave me a set of over-large brown overalls and told me to clip the identity card on the outside, like his own.

"Security is vital," he said to me. "Owen's stepped it all up. He lectures us on not letting strangers near the mixing vats. I can't let you any nearer than this. Our competitors wouldn't be above adding foreign substances that would put us out of business."

"D'you mean it?" I said, looking avid.

"You have to be specially careful with horse feed," he assured me, sliding open his door when I was ready. "You can't mix cattle feed in the same vats, for instance. You can put things in cattle feed that are prohibited for racehorses. You can get traces of prohibited substances in the horse cubes just by using the same equipment, even if you think you've cleaned everything thoroughly."

There had been a famous example in racing of a trainer getting into trouble by unknowingly giving his runners contaminated nuts.

"Fancy," I said.

I thought I might have overdone the impressed look I gave him, but he accepted it easily.

"We do nothing else except horse cubes here," Willy said. "Owen says when we expand we'll do cattle feed and chicken pellets and all sorts of other muck, but I'll be staying here, Owen says, in charge of the equine branch."

"A top job," I said with admiration.

He nodded. "The best."

We walked along the gallery and came to another fire door, which he lugged open.

"All these internal doors are locked at night now, and there's a watchman with a dog. Very thorough, is Owen." He looked back to make sure I was following, then stopped at a place from which we could see bags marked with red maple leaves traveling upward on an endless belt of bag-sized ledges, only to be tumbled off the top and be manhandled by two smoothly swinging muscular workers.

"I expect you saw those two security men in the entrance hall?" Willy Parrott said, the question of security not yet exhausted.

"They frisked me." I grinned. "Going a bit far, I thought."

"They're Owen's private bodyguards," Willy Parrott said with a mixture of awe and approval. "They're real hard men from Liverpool. Owen says he needs them in case the competitors try to get rid of him the old-fashioned way."

I frowned disbelievingly. "Competitors don't kill people."

"Owen says he's taking no risks because he definitely is trying to put other firms out of business, if you look at it that way."

"So you think he's right to need bodyguards?"

Willy Parrott turned to face me and said, "It's not the world I was brought up in, lad. But we have to live in this new one, Owen says."

"I suppose so."

"You won't get far with that attitude, lad." He pointed to the rising bags. "That's this year's wheat straight from the prairie. Only the best is good enough, Owen says, in trade wars."

He led the way down some nearby concrete stairs and through another heavy door, and I realized we were on ground level, just off the central atrium. With a smile of satisfaction he pushed through one more door and we found ourselves amid the vast mixing vats, pygmies surrounded by giants.

He enjoyed my expression.

"Awesome," I said.

"You don't need to go back upstairs to get out," he said. "There's a door out to the yard just down here."

I thanked him for his advice about the nuts for the farmer, and for showing me around. I'd been with him for half an hour and couldn't reasonably stretch it further, but while I was in midsentence he looked over my shoulder and his face changed completely from man-in-charge to subservient subject.

I turned to see what had caused this transformation and found it not to be a Royal Person but a large man in white overalls accompanied by several anxious blue-clad attendants who were practically walking backwards.

"Morning, Willy," said the man in white. "Everything going well?"

"Yes, Owen. Fine."

"Good. Has the Canadian wheat come up from the docks?"

"They're unloading it now, Owen."

"Good. We should have a talk about future plans. Come up to my new office at four this afternoon. You know where it is? Top floor, turn right from
the lift, like my old office."

"Yes, Owen."

"Good."

The eyes of the businessman glanced my way briefly and incuriously, and
passed on. I was wearing brown overalls and an identity card, after all, and
looked like an employee. Not an employee of much worth, either, with my
over-big overalls wrinkling around my ankles and drooping down my arms
to the fingers. Willy didn't attempt to explain my presence, for which I was
grateful. Willy was almost on his knees in reverence.

Owen Yorkshire was, without doubt, impressive. Easily over six feet tall, he
was simply large, but not fat. There was a lot of heavy muscle in the shoulders, and a trim, sturdy belly. Luxuriant closely waving hair spilled over his collar, with the beginnings of gray in the lacquered wings sweeping back from
above his ears. It was a hairstyle that in its way made as emphatic a statement
as Jonathan's. Owen Yorkshire intended not only to rule but to be remembered.

His accent was not quite Liverpool and not at all London, but powerful and
positive. His voice was unmistakably an instrument of dominance. One could
imagine that his rages might in fact shake the building. One could have sympathy with his yes-men.

Willy said "Yes, Owen," several more times.

The man-to-man relationship that Willy Parrott prized so much extended,
I thought, not much further than the use of first names. True, Owen Yorkshire's manner to Willy was of the "we're all in this together" type of management technique, and seemed to be drawing the best out of a good man;
but I could imagine the boss also finding ways of getting rid of his Willy Parrott, if it pleased him, with sad shrugs and "you know how it is these days, we
no longer *need* a production manager just for horse cubes; your job is computerized and phased out. Severance pay? Of course. See my secretary. No
hard feelings."

I hoped it wouldn't happen to Willy.

Owen Yorkshire and his satellites swept onwards. Willy Parrott looked after
him with pride tinged very faintly with anxiety.

"Do you work tomorrow?" I asked. "Is the factory open on Saturdays?"

He reluctantly removed his gaze from the Yorkshire back view and began
to think I'd been there too long.

"We're opening on Saturdays from next week," he said. "Tomorrow they're making more advertising films. There will be cameras all over the place, and on Monday, too. We won't get anything useful done until Tuesday." He was full of disapproval, but he would repress all that, it was clear, for man-to-man Owen. "Off you go then, lad. Go back to the entrance and leave the overalls and identity tag there."

I thanked him again and this time went out into the central yard, which since my own arrival had become clogged with vans and truckloads of television and advertising people. The television contingent were from Liverpool. The advertisement makers, according to the identification on their vans, were from Intramind Imaging (Manchester) Ltd.

One of the Intramind drivers, in the unthinking way of his kind, had braked and parked at an angle to all the other vehicles. I walked across to where he still sat in his cab and asked him to straighten up his van.

"Who says so?" he demanded belligerently.

"I just work here," I said, still in the brown overalls that, in spite of Willy Parrott's instructions, I was not going to return. "I was sent out to ask you. Big artics have to get in here." I pointed to the unloading bays.

The driver grunted, started his engine, straightened his vehicle, switched off and jumped down to the ground beside me.

"Will that do?" he asked sarcastically.

"You must have an exciting job," I said enviously. "Do you see all those film stars?"

He sneered. "We make *advertising* films, mate. Sure, sometimes we get big names, but mostly they're endorsing things."

"What sort of things?"

"Sports gear, often. Shoes, golf clubs."

"And horse cubes?"

He had time to waste while others unloaded equipment. He didn't mind a bit of showing off.

He said, "They've got a lot of top jockeys lined up to endorse the horse nuts."

"Have they?" I asked interestedly. "Why not trainers?"

"It's the jockeys the public know by their faces. That's what I'm told. I'm a football man myself."

He didn't, I was grateful to observe, even begin to recognize my own face, that in years gone by had fairly often taken up space on the nation's sports pages.

Someone in his team called him away and I walked off, sliding into my own car and making an uneventful exit through the tall unchecked outward gates. Odd, I thought, that the security-paranoid Owen Yorkshire didn't have a gate bristling with electronic barriers and ominous name gatherers; and the only reason I could think of for such laxity was that he didn't always *want* name takers to record everyone's visits.

Blind-eye country, I thought, like the private backstairs of the great before the India Cathcarts of the world floodlit the secretive comings and goings, and rewarded promiscuity with taint.

Perhaps Owen Yorkshire's backstairs was the elevator to the fifth floor. Perhaps Mrs. Green Jumper and the bouncers in blue knew who to admit without searching.

Perhaps this, perhaps that. I'd seen the general layout and been near the power running the business, but basically I'd done little there but reconnoiter.

I stopped in a public car park, took off the brown overalls and decided to go to Manchester.

THE JOURNEY WAS quite short, but it took me almost as long again to find Intramind Imaging (Manchester) Ltd., which, although in a back street, proved to be a much bigger outfit than I'd pictured; I shed the tracksuit top and the Liverpool accent and approached the reception desk in suit, tie and business aura.

"I've come from Topline Foods," I said. "I'd like to talk to whoever is in charge of their account."

Did I have an appointment?

No, it was a private matter.

If one pretended sufficient authority, I'd found, doors got opened, and so it was at Intramind Imaging. A Mr. Gross would see me. An electric door latch buzzed and I walked from the entrance lobby into an inner hallway, where cream paint had been used sparingly and there was no carpet underfoot. Ostentation was out.

Mr. Gross was "third door on the left." Mr. Gross's door had his name and a message on it: Nick Gross. What the F Do You Want?

Nick Gross looked me up and down. "Who the hell are *you?* You're not Topline Foods top brass, and you're over-dressed."

He himself wore a black satin shirt, long hair and a gold earring. Forty-five disintegrating to fifty, I thought, and stuck in a time warp of departing youth. Forceful, though. Strong lines in his old-young face. Authority.

"You're making advertising films for Topline," I said.

"So what? And if you're another of their whining accountants sent to beg for better terms, the answer is up yours, mate. It isn't our fault you haven't been able to use those films you spent millions on. They're all brilliant stuff, the best. So you creep back to your Mr. Owen effing Yorkshire and tell him there's no deal. Off you trot, then. If he wants his jockey series at the same price as before he has to send us a check every week. *Every week* or we yank the series, got it?"

I nodded.

Nick Gross said, "And tell him not to forget that in ads the magic is in the *cutting,* and the cutting comes *last.* No check, no cutting. No cutting, no magic. No magic, no message. No message, we might as well stop right now. Have you got it?"

I nodded again.

"Then you scurry right back to Topline and tell them no check, no cutting. And that means no campaign. Got it?"

"Yes."

"Right. Bugger off."

I meekly removed myself but, seeing no urgent reason to leave altogether, I turned the wrong way out of his office and walked as if I belonged there down a passage between increasingly technical departments.

I came to an open door through which one could see a screen showing startlingly familiar pieces of an ad campaign currently collecting critical acclaim as well as phenomenally boosting sales. There were bursts of pictures as short as three seconds followed by longer intervals of black. Three seconds of fast action. Ten of black.

I stopped, watching, and a man walked into my sight and saw me standing there.

"Yes?" he said. "Do you want something?"

"Is that," I said, nodding towards the screen, "one of the mountain bike ads?"

"It will be when I cut it together."

"Marvelous," I said. I took half a step unthreateningly over his threshold. "Can I watch you for a bit?"

"Who are you, exactly?"

"From Topline Foods. I came to see Nick Gross."

"Ah." There was a world of comprehension in the monosyllable: comprehension that I immediately aimed to transfer from his brain to mine.

He was younger than Nick Gross and not so mock-rock-star in dress. His certainty shouted from the zany speed of his three-second flashes and the wit crackling in their juxtaposition: he had no need for earrings.

I said, quoting the bike campaign's slogan, "Every kid under fifty wants a mountain bike for Christmas."

He fiddled with reels of film and said cheerfully, "There'll be hell to pay if they don't."

"Did you work on the Topline ads?" I asked neutrally.

"No, thank Christ. A colleague did. Eight months of award-worthy brilliant work sitting idle in cans on the shelves. No prizes for us, and your top man's shitting himself, isn't he? All that cabbage spent and bugger all back. And all because some twisted little pipsqueak gets the star attraction arrested for something he didn't do."

I held my breath, but he had no flicker of an idea what the pipsqueak looked like. I said I'd better be going and he nodded vaguely without looking up from his problems.

I persevered past his domain until I came to two big doors, one saying Sound Stage Keep Out and one, opening outward with a push-bar, marked Backlot. I pushed that door half-open and saw outside in the open air a huge yellow crane dangling a red sports car by a rear axle. Film cameras and crews were busy around it. Work in progress.

I retreated. No one paid me any attention on the way out. This was not, after all, a bank vault, but a dream factory. No one could steal dreams.

The reception lobby, as I hadn't noticed on my way in, bore posters around the walls of past and current purse-openers, all prestigious prize-winning campaigns. Ad campaigns, I'd heard, were now considered an OK step on the career ladder for both directors and actors. Sell cornflakes one day, play Hamlet the next. Intramind Imaging could speed you on your way.

I drove into the center of Manchester and anonymously booked into a spacious restful room in the Crown Plaza Hotel. Davis Tatum might have a fit over the expense but if necessary I would pay for it myself. I wanted a shower, room service and cosseting, and hang the price.

I phoned Tatum's home number and got an answering machine. I asked him to call back to my mobile number and repeated it, and then sat in an armchair watching racing on television—flat racing at Ascot.

There was no sight of Ellis on the course. The commentator mentioned that his "ludicrous" trial was due to resume in three days' time, on Monday. Sid Halley, he said, was sensibly keeping his head down as half Ellis's fan club was baying for his blood.

This little tid-bit came from a commentator who'd called me a wizard and a force for good not long ago. Times changed: did they ever. There were smiling close-ups of Ellis's face, and of mine, both helmetless but in racing colors, side by side. "They used to be the closest of friends," said the commentator sadly. "Now they slash and gore each other like bulls."

Sod him, I thought.

I also hoped that none of Mrs. Green Jumper, Marsha Rowse, Mrs. Dove, Willy Parrott, the Intramind van driver, Nick Gross and the film cutter had switched on to watch racing at Ascot. I didn't think Owen Yorkshire's sliding glance across my overalls would have left an imprint, but the others would remember me for a day or two. It was a familiar risk, sometimes lucky, sometimes not.

When the racing ended I phoned Intramind Imaging and asked a few general questions that I hadn't thought of in my brief career on the spot as a Topline Foods employee.

Were advertising campaigns originally recorded on film or on disks or on tape, I wanted to know, and could the public buy copies. I was answered helpfully: Intramind usually used film, especially for high-budget location-based ads, and no, the public could *not* buy copies. The finished film would eventually be transferred onto broadcast-quality videotape, known as Betacam. These tapes then belonged to the clients, who paid television companies for airtime. Intramind did not act as an agent.

"Thanks very much," I said politely, grateful always for knowledge.

Davis Tatum phoned soon after.

"Sid," he said, "where are you?"

"Manchester, city of rain."

It was sunny that day.

"Er . . . ," Davis said. "Any progress?"

"Some," I said.

"And, er . . ." He hesitated again. "Did you read India Cathcart this morning?"

"She didn't write that she'd seen us at Le Meridien," I said.

"No. She took your excellent advice. But as to the rest . . . !"

I said, "Kevin Mills phoned especially to tell me that she didn't write the rest. He did it himself. Policy. Pressure from above. Same old thing."

"But wicked."

"He apologized. Big advance."

"You take it so lightly," Davis said.

I didn't disillusion him. I said, "Tomorrow evening—would you be able to go to Archie Kirk's house?"

"I should think so, if it's important. What time?"

"Could you arrange that with him? About six o'clock, I should think. I'll arrive there sometime myself. Don't know when."

With a touch of complaint he said, "It sounds a bit vague."

I thought I'd better not tell him that with burglary, times tended to be approximate.

# 12

I phoned *The Pump,* asking for India Cathcart. Silly me.

Number one, she was never in the office on Fridays.

Number two, *The Pump* never gave private numbers to unknown callers.

"Tell her Sid Halley would like to talk to her," I said, and gave the switchboard operator my mobile number, asking him to repeat it so I could make sure he had written it down right.

No promises, he said.

I sat for a good while thinking about what I'd seen and learned, and planning what I would do the next day. Such plans got altered by events as often as not, but I'd found that no plan at all invited nil results. If all else failed, try Plan B. Plan B, in my battle strategy, was to escape with skin intact. Plan B had let me down a couple of times, but disasters were like falls in racing; you never thought they'd happen until you were nose down to the turf.

I had some food sent up and thought some more, and at ten-fifteen my mobile buzzed.

"Sid?" India said nervously.

"Hello."

"Don't say anything! I'll cry if you say anything." After a pause she said, "Sid! Are you there?"

"Yes. But I don't want you to cry so I'm not saying anything."

"Oh, God." It was half a choke, half a laugh. "How can you be so . . . so *civilized?*"

"With enormous difficulty," I said. "Are you busy on Sunday evening? Your restaurant or mine?"

She said disbelievingly, "Are you asking me out to dinner?"

"Well," I said, "it's not a proposal of marriage. And no knife through the ribs. Just food."

"How can you *laugh?*"

"Why are you called India?" I asked.

"I was conceived there. What has that got to do with anything?"

"I just wondered," I said.

"Are you *drunk?*"

"Unfortunately not. I'm sitting soberly in an armchair contemplating the state of the universe, which is C minus, or thereabouts."

"Where? I mean, where is the armchair?"

"On the floor," I said.

"You don't trust me!"

"No," I sighed, "I don't. But I do want to have dinner with you."

"Sid," she was almost pleading, "be sensible."

Rotten advice, I'd always thought. But then if I'd been sensible I would have two hands and fewer scars, and I reckoned one had to be *born* sensible, which didn't seem to have happened in my case.

I said, "Your proprietor—Lord Tilepit—have you met him?"

"Yes." She sounded a bit bewildered. "He comes to the office party at Christmas. He shakes everyone's hand."

"What's he like?"

"Do you mean to look at?"

"For a start."

"He's fairly tall. Light-brown hair."

"That's not much," I said when she stopped.

"He's not part of my day-to-day life."

"Except that he burns saints," I said.

A brief silence, then, "Your restaurant, this time."

I smiled. Her quick mind could reel in a tarpon where her red mouth couldn't. "Does Lord Tilepit," I asked, "wear an obvious cloak of power? Are you aware of his power when you're in a room with him?"

"Actually . . . no."

"Is anyone . . . *Could* anyone be physically in awe of him?"

"No." It was clear from her voice that she thought the idea laughable.

"So his leverage," I said, "is all economic?"

"I suppose so."

"Is there anyone that *he* is in awe of?"

"I don't know. Why do you ask?"

"That man," I said, "has spent four months directing his newspaper to . . . well . . . ruin me. You must allow, I have an interest."

"But you aren't ruined. You don't sound in the least ruined. And anyway, your ex-wife said it was impossible."

"She said *what* was impossible?"

"To . . . to . . ."

"Say it."

"To reduce you to rubble. To make you beg."

She silenced me.

She said, "Your ex-wife's still in love with you."

"No, not anymore."

"I'm an expert on ex-wives," India said. "Wronged wives, dumped mistresses, women curdled with spite, women angling for money. Women wanting revenge, women breaking their hearts. I know the scenery. Your Jenny said she couldn't live in your purgatory, but when I suggested you were a selfish brute she defended you like a tigress."

Oh God, I thought. After nearly six years apart the same old dagger could pierce us both.

"Sid?"

"Mm."

"Do you still love *her?*"

I found a calm voice. "We can't go back, and we don't want to," I said. "I regret a lot, but it's now finally over. She has a better husband, and she's happy."

"I met her new man," India said. "He's sweet."

"Yes." I paused. "What about your own ex?"

"I fell for his looks. It turned out he wanted an admiration machine in an apron. End of story."

"Is his name Cathcart?"

"No," she said. "Patterson."

Smiling to myself, I said, "Will you give me your phone number?"

She said, "Yes," and did so.

"Kensington Place restaurant. Eight o'clock."

"I'll be there."

WHEN I WAS alone, which was usual nowadays, since Louise McInnes and I had parted, I took off my false arm at bedtime and replaced it after a shower in the morning. I couldn't wear it in showers, as water wrecked the works. Taking it off after a long day was often a pest, as it fitted tightly and tended to cling to my skin. Putting it on was a matter of talcum powder, getting the angle right and pushing hard.

The arm might be worth its weight in gold, as I'd told Trish Huxford, but even after three years, whatever lighthearted front I might now achieve in public, in private the management of amputation still took me a positive effort of the "get on with it" ethos. I didn't know why I continued to feel vulnerable and sensitive. Too much pride, no doubt.

I'd charged up the two batteries in the charger overnight, so I started the new day, Saturday, with a fresh battery in the arm and a spare in my pocket.

It was by then five days since Gordon Quint had cracked my ulna, and the twinges had become less acute and less frequent. Partly it was because one naturally found the least painful way of performing any action, and partly because the ends of bone were beginning to knit. Soft tissue grew on the site of the break, and on the eighth day it would normally begin hardening, the whole healing process being complete within the next week. Only splintered, displaced ends caused serious trouble, which hadn't occurred in this case.

When I'd been a jockey the feel of a simple fracture had been an almost twice-yearly familiarity. One tended in jump racing to fall on one's shoulder, quite often at thirty miles an hour, and in my time I'd cracked my collarbones six times each side: only once had it been distinctly bad.

Some jockeys had stronger bones than others, but I didn't know anyone who'd completed a top career unscathed. Anyway, by Saturday morning, Monday's crack was no real problem.

Into my overnight bag I packed the battery charger, washing things, pajamas, spare shirt, business suit and shoes. I wore both pieces of the tracksuit, white shirt, no tie and the dark sneakers. In my belt I carried money and a credit card, and in my pocket a bunch of six keys on a single ring, which bore also a miniature flashlight. Three of the keys were variously for my car and the entry doors of my flat. The other three, looking misleadingly simple, would between them open any ordinary lock, regardless of the wishes of the owners.

My old teacher had had me practice until I was quick at it. He'd shown me also how to open the simple combination locks on suitcases; the method used by airport thieves.

I checked out of the hotel and found the way back to Frodsham, parking by the curb within sight of Topline Foods' wire-mesh gates.

As before, the gates were wide open and, as before, no one going in and out was challenged by the gatekeeper. No one, in fact, seemed to have urgent business in either direction and there were far fewer cars in the central area than on the day before. It wasn't until nearly eleven o'clock that the promised film crews arrived in force.

When getting on for twenty assorted vans and private cars had come to a ragged halt all over the place, disgorging film cameras (Intramind Imaging), a television camera (local station) and dozens of people looking purposeful with heavy equipment and chest-hugged clipboards, I got out of my car and put on the ill-fitting brown overalls, complete with identity badge. Into the trunk I locked my bag and also the mobile phone, first taking the SIM card out of it and stowing it in my belt. "Get into the habit of removing the SIM card," my supplier had advised. "Then if someone steals your phone, too bad, they won't be able to use it."

"Great," I'd said.

I started the car, drove unhesitatingly through the gates, steered a course around the assorted vans and stopped just beyond them, nearest to the un-loading bays. Saturday or not, a few other brown overall hands were busy on the rollers and the shelf escalator, and I simply walked straight in past them, saying "Morning" as if I belonged.

They didn't answer, didn't look up, took me for granted.

Inside, I walked up the stairs I'd come down with Willy Parrott and, when I reached the right level, ambled along the gallery until I came to his office.

The sliding glass door was closed and locked and there was no one inside.

The paddles were silent in the vats. None of the day before's hum and activity remained, and almost none of the smells. Instead, there were cameras being positioned below, with Owen Yorkshire himself directing the director, his authoritative voice telling the experts their job.

He was too busy to look up. I went on along the gallery, coming to the fire door up the flight of metal stairs. The fire doors were locked at night, Willy had said. By day, they were open. Thankful, I reached in the end the plush carpet of the offices.

There was a bunch of three media people in there, measuring angles and moving potted plants. Office work, I gathered, was due for immortality on Monday. Cursing internally at their presence, I walked on towards the elevator, passing the open door of Customer Relations. No Marsha Rowse.

To the right of the elevator there was a door announcing Office Manager, A. Dove, fastened with businesslike locks.

Looking back, I saw the measuring group taking their damned time. I needed them out of there and they infuriatingly dawdled.

I didn't like to hover. I returned to the elevator and, to fill in time, opened a nearby door which proved to enclose fire stairs, as I'd hoped.

Down a floor, and through the fire door there, I found an expanse of open space, unfurnished and undecorated, the same in area as the office suite above. Up two stories, above the offices, there was similar quiet, undivided, clean-swept space. Owen Yorkshire had already built for expansion, I gathered.

Cautiously, I went on upward to the fifth floor, lair of the boss.

Trusting that he was still down among the vats, I opened the fire door enough to put my head through.

More camera people moved around. Veritable banks of potted plants blazed red and gold. To the left, open, opulently gleaming double doors led into an entertaining and boardroom area impressive enough for a major industry of self-importance. On the right, more double doors led to Yorkshire's own new office; not, from what I could see, a place of paperwork. Polished wood gleamed. Plants galore. A tray of bottles and glasses.

I retreated down the unvarnished nitty-gritty fire stairs until I was back on the working-office floor, standing there indecisively, wondering if the mea-surers still barred my purpose.

I heard voices, growing louder and stopping on the other side of the door. I was prepared to go into a busy-employee routine, but it appeared they pre-ferred the elevator to the stairs. The lifting machinery whirred on the other side of the stairwell, the voices moved into the elevator and diminished to zero. I couldn't tell whether they'd gone up or down, and I was concerned only that they'd *all* gone up and not left one behind.

There was no point in waiting. I opened the fire door, stepped onto the carpet and right towards Mrs. Dove's domain.

I had the whole office floor to myself.

Great.

Mrs. Dove's door was locked twice: an old-looking mortise and a new knob with a keyhole in the center. These were locks I liked. There could be no nasty surprises like bolts or chains or wedges on the inside: also the em-phatic statement of *two* locks probably meant that there were things of worth to guard.

The mortise lock took a whole minute, with the ghost of my old master breathing disapprovingly down my neck. The modern lock took twenty sec-onds of delicate probing. One had to "feel" one's way through. False fingers for that, as for much else, were useless.

Once inside Mrs. Dove's office, I spent time relocking the door so that any-one outside trying it for security would find it as it should be. If anyone came in with keys, I would have warning enough to hide.

Mrs. Dove's cote was large and comfortable, with a wide desk, several of the Scandinavian-design armchairs and grainy blow-up black and white photographs of racing horses around the walls. Along one side there were the routine office machines—fax, copier, and large print-out calculator, and, on the desk, a computer, shrouded for the weekend in a fitted cover. There were multiple filing cabinets and a tall white-painted and—as I discovered—locked cupboard.

Mrs. Dove had a window with louvered blinds and a distant view of the Mersey. Mrs. Dove's office was managing director stuff.

I had only a vague idea of what I was looking for. The audited accounts I'd seen in Companies House seemed not to match the actual state of affairs at Frodsham. The audit did, of course, refer to a year gone by, to the first with Owen Yorkshire in charge, but the fragile bottom-line profit, as shown, would not suggest or justify expensive publicity campaigns or televised receptions for the notables of Liverpool.

The old French adage "look for the lady" was a century out of date, my old teacher had said. In modern times it should be "look for the money," and shortly before he died, he had amended that to "follow the paper." Shady or doubtful transactions, he said, always left a paper trail. Even in the age of computers, he'd insisted that paper showed the way; and over and over again I'd proved him right.

The paper in Mrs. Dove's office was all tidied away in the many filing cabinets, which were locked.

Most filing cabinets, like these, locked all drawers simultaneously with a notched vertical rod out of sight within the right-hand front corner, operated by a single key at the top. Turning the key raised the rod, allowing all the drawers to open. I wasn't bad at opening filing cabinets.

The trouble was that Topline Foods had little to hide, or at least not at first sight. Pounds of paper referred to orders and invoices for incoming supplies; pounds more to sales, pounds more to the expenses of running an industry, from insurance to wages, to electricity to general maintenance.

The filing cabinets took too long and were a waste of time. What they offered was the entirely respectable basis of next year's audit.

I locked them all again and, after investigating the desk drawers themselves, which held only stationery, took the cover off the computer and switched it on, pressing the buttons for List Files, and Enter. Scrolls of file names appeared and I tried one at random: "Aintree."

Onto the screen came details of the lunch given the day before the Grand National, the guest list, the menu, a summary of the speeches and a list of the coverage given to the occasion in the press.

Nothing I could find seemed any more secret. I switched it off, replaced the cover and turned my lock pickers to the tall white cupboard.

The feeling of time running out, however irrational, shortened my breath and made me hurry. I always envied the supersleuths in films who put their hands on the right papers in the first ten seconds and, this time, I didn't know if the right paper even existed.

It turned out to be primarily not a paper but a second computer.

Inside the white cupboard, inside a drop-down desk arrangement in there, I came across a second keyboard and a second screen. I switched the computer on and nothing happened, which wasn't astounding as I found an electric lead lying alongside, disconnected. I plugged it into the computer and tried again, and with a grumble or two the machine became ready for business.

I pressed List Files again, and this time found myself looking not at individual subjects, but at Directories, each of which contained file names such as "Formula A."

What I had come across were the more private records, the electronic files, some very secret, some not.

In quick succession I highlighted the "Directories" and brought them to the screen until one baldly listed "Quint": but no amount of button pressing got me any further.

*Think.*

The reason I couldn't get the Quint information onto the screen must be because it wasn't in the computer.

OK? OK. So where was it?

On the shelf above the computer stood a row of box files, numbered 1 to 9, but not one labeled Quint.

I lifted down number 1 and looked inside. There were several letters filed in there, also a blue computer floppy disk in a clear cover. According to the letters, box file number 1 referred to loans made to Topline Foods, loans not repaid on the due date. There was also a mention of "sweeteners" and "quid pro quos." I fed the floppy disk into the drive slot in the computer body and got no further than a single, unhelpful word on the screen: PASSWORD?

Password? Heaven knew. I looked into the box files one by one and came to Quint in number 6. There were three floppies in there, not one.

I fed in the first.

PASSWORD?

Second and third disks—PASSWORD?

Bugger, I thought.

Searching for anything helpful, I lifted down a heavy white cardboard box, like a double-height shoebox, that filled the rest of the box-file shelf. In there was a row of big black high-impact plastic protective coverings. I picked out one and unlatched its fastenings, and found inside it a videotape, but a tape of double the ordinary width. A label on the tape said Broadcast Quality Videotape. Underneath that was a single word, Betacam. Under that was the legend "Quint Series. 15 × 30 secs."

I closed the thick black case and tried another one. Same thing. Quint Series. 15 × 30 secs. All of the cases held the same.

These double-size tapes needed a special tape player not available in Mrs. Dove's office. To see what was on these expensive tapes meant taking one with me.

I could, of course, simply put one of them inside my tracksuit jacket and walk out with it. I could take all the "PASSWORD" disks. If I did I was (a) stealing, (b) in danger of being found carrying the goods, and (c) making it impossible for any information they held to be used in any later legal inquiry. I would steal the information itself, if I could, but not the software.

*Think.*

As I'd told Charles at Aynsford, I'd had to learn a good deal about computers just to keep a grip on the accelerating world, but the future became the present so fast that I could never get ahead.

*Someone tried to open the door.*

There was no time to restore the room to normal. I could only speed across the carpet and stand where I would be hidden by the door when it swung inward. Plan B meant simply running—and I was wearing running shoes.

The knob turned again and rattled, but nothing else happened. Whoever was outside had presumably been either keyless or reassured: in either case it played havoc with my breathing.

Oddly, the pumping adrenaline brought me my computer answer, which was, if I couldn't bring the contents of a floppy disk to the screen, I could transfer it whole to *another* computer, one that would give me all the time I needed to crack the password, or to get help from people who could.

Alongside the unconnected electric cable there had been a telephone cable, also unattached. I snapped it into the telephone socket on the computer, thereby connecting Mrs. Dove's modem to the world-wide Internet.

It needed a false start or two while I desperately tried to remember half-learned techniques, but finally I was rewarded by the screen prompting: "Enter telephone number."

I tapped in my own home number in the apartment in Pont Square, and pressed Enter, and the screen announced nonchalantly "Dialing in progress," then "Call accepted," then "Transfer," and finally "Transfer complete."

Whatever was on the first guarded "Quint" disk was now in my own computer in London. I transferred the other two "Quint" floppies in the same way, and then the disk from box-file number 1, and for good measure another from box 3, identified as "Tilepit."

There was no way that I knew of transferring the Betacam tapes. Regretfully I left them alone. I looked through the paper pages in the "Quint" box and made a photocopy of one page—a list of unusual racecourses—folding it and hiding it within the zipped pocket of my belt.

Finally I disconnected the electric and telephone cables again, closed the computer compartment, checked that the box files and Betacam tapes were as they should be, relocked the white cupboard, then unlocked and gently opened the door to the passage.

Silence.

Breathing out with relief, I relocked Mrs. Dove's door and walked along through the row of cubby-hole offices and came to the first setback: the fire door leading to brown-overalls territory was not merely locked but had a red light shining above it.

Shining red lights often meant alarm systems switched on with depressingly loud sirens ready to screech.

I'd been too long in Mrs. Dove's office. I retreated towards her door again and went down the fire stairs beside the elevator, emerging into the ground-floor entrance hall with its glass doors to the parking area beyond.

One step into the lobby proved to be one step too far. Something hit my head rather hard, and one of the beefy bodyguards in blue flung a sort of strap around my body and effectively pinned my upper arms to my sides.

I plunged about a bit and got another crack on the head, which left me unable to help myself and barely able to think. I was aware of being in the elevator, but wasn't quite sure how I'd got there. I was aware of having my ankles strapped together and of being dragged ignominiously over some carpet and dropped in a chair.

Regulation Scandinavian chair with wooden arms, like all the others.

"Tie him up," a voice said, and a third strap tightened across my chest, so that when the temporary mist cleared I woke to a state of near physical immobility and a mind full of curses.

The voice belonged to Owen Yorkshire. He said, "Right. Good. Well done. Leave the wrench on the desk. Go back downstairs and don't let anyone up here."

"Yes, sir."

"Wait," Yorkshire commanded, sounding uncertain. "Are you sure you've got the right man?"

"Yes, sir. He's wearing the identity badge we issued to him yesterday. He was supposed to return it when he left, but he didn't."

"All right. Thanks. Off you go."

The door closed behind the bodyguards and Owen Yorkshire plucked the identity badge from my overalls, read the name and flung it down on his desk.

We were in his fifth-floor office. The chair I sat in was surrounded by carpet. Marooned on a desert island, feeling dim and stupid.

The man-to-man, all-pals-together act was in abeyance. The Owen Yorkshire confronting me was very angry, disbelieving and, I would have said, *frightened*.

"What are you doing here?" he demanded, bellowing.

His voice echoed and reverberated in the quiet room. His big body loomed over me, his big head close to mine. All his features, I thought, were slightly oversized: big nose, big eyes, wide forehead, large flat cheeks, square jaw, big mouth. The collar-length black wavy hair with its gray-touched wings seemed to vibrate with vigor. I would have put his age at forty; maybe a year or two younger.

"Answer," he yelled. "What are you doing here?"

I didn't reply. He snatched up from his desk a heavy fifteen-inch-long silvery wrench and made as if to hit my head with it. If that was what his boys-in-blue had used on me, and I gathered it was, then connecting it again with my skull was unlikely to produce any answer at all. The same thought seemed to occur to him, because he threw the wrench down disgustedly onto the desk again, where it bounced slightly under its own weight.

The straps around my chest and ankles were the sort of fawn close-woven webbing often used around suitcases to prevent them from bursting open. There was no elasticity in them, no stretch. Several more lay on the desk.

I felt a ridiculous desire to chatter, a tendency I'd noticed in the past in mild concussions after racing falls, and sometimes on waking up from anesthetics. I'd learned how to suppress the garrulous impulse, but it was still an effort, and in this case, essential.

Owen Yorkshire was wearing man-to-man togs; that is to say, no jacket, a man-made-fiber shirt (almost white with vertical stripes made of interlocking beige-colored horseshoes), no tie, several buttons undone, unmissable view of manly hairy chest, gold chain and medallion.

I concentrated on the horseshoe stripes. If I could count the number of horseshoes from shoulder to waist I would not have any thoughts that might dribble out incautiously. The boss was talking. I blanked him out and counted horseshoes and managed to say nothing.

He went abruptly out of the room, leaving me sitting there looking foolish. When he returned he brought two people with him: they had been along in the reception area, it seemed, working out table placements for Monday's lunch.

They were a woman and a man; Mrs. Dove and a stranger. Both exclaimed in surprise at the sight of my trussed self. I shrank into the chair and looked mostly at their waists.

"Do you know who this is?" Yorkshire demanded of them furiously.

The man shook his head, mystified. Mrs. Dove, frowning, said to me, "Weren't you here yesterday? Something about a farmer?"

"This," Yorkshire said with scorn, "is Sid Halley."

The man's face stiffened, his mouth forming an O.

"*This,* Verney,*"* Yorkshire went on with biting sarcasm, "is the feeble creature you've spent months thundering on about. This! And Ellis said he was dangerous! Just look at him! All those big guns to frighten a mouse."

Verney *Tilepit.* I'd looked him up in *Burke's Peerage.* Verney Tilepit, Third Baron, aged forty-two, a director of Topline Foods, proprietor—by inheritance—of *The Pump.*

Verney Tilepit's grandfather, created a baron for devoted allegiance to the then prime minister, had been one of the old roistering, powerful opinion makers who'd had governments dancing to their tune. The first Verney Tilepit had put his shoulder to history and given it a shove. The third had surfaced after years of quiescence, primarily, it seemed, to discredit a minor investigator. Policy! His bewildered grandfather would have been speechless.

He was fairly tall, as India had said, and he had brown hair. The flicking glance I gave him took in also a large expanse of face with small features bunched in the middle: small nose, small mouth, small sandy mustache, small eyes behind large, light-framed glasses. Nothing about him seemed physically threatening. Perhaps I felt the same disappointment in my adversary as he plainly did about me.

"How do you know he's Sid Halley?" Mrs. Dove asked.

Owen Yorkshire said disgustedly, "One of the TV crew knew him. He swore there was no mistake. He'd filmed him often. He *knows* him."

Bugger, I thought.

Mrs. Dove pulled up the long left sleeve of my brown overalls, and looked at my left hand. "Yes. It must be Sid Halley. Not much of a champion now, is he?"

Owen Yorkshire picked up the telephone, pressed numbers, waited and forcefully spoke.

"Get over here quickly," he said. "We have a crisis. Come to my new office." He listened briefly. "No," he said, "just get over here." He slammed down the receiver and stared at me balefully. "What the sod are you doing here?"

The almost overwhelming urge to tell him got as far as my tongue and was over-ridden only by clamped-shut teeth. One could understand why people confessed. The itch to unburden outweighed the certainty of retribution.

"Answer," yelled Yorkshire. He picked up the wrench again. "Answer, you little cuss."

I did manage an answer of sorts.

I spoke to Verney Tilepit directly in a weak, mock-respectful tone. "I came to see you . . . sir."

"My lord," Yorkshire told me. "Call him 'my lord.' "

"My lord," I said.

Tilepit said, "What for?" and "What made you think I would be here?"

"Someone told me you were a director of Topline Foods, my lord, so I came here to ask you to stop and I don't know why I've been dragged up here and tied up like this." The last twenty words just dribbled out. Be *careful,* I thought. *Shut up.*

"To stop *what?*" Tilepit demanded.

"To stop your paper telling lies about me." Better.

Tilepit didn't know how to answer such naïveté. Yorkshire properly considered it barely credible. He spoke to Mrs. Dove, who was dressed for Saturday morning, not in office black and white, but in bright red with gold buttons.

"Go down and make sure he hasn't been in your office."

"I locked it when I left last night, Owen."

Mrs. Dove's manner towards her boss was interestingly like Willy Parrott's. All-equals-together; up to a point.

"Go and look," he said. "And check that cupboard."

"No one's opened that cupboard since you moved offices up here this week. And you have the only key."

"Go and check anyway," he said.

She had no difficulty with obeying him. I remembered Marsha Rowse's ingenuous statement—"Mrs. Dove says never to make Mr. Yorkshire angry."

Mrs. Dove, self-contained, confident, was taking her own advice. She was not, I saw, in love with the man, nor was she truly afraid of him. His temper, I would have thought, was to her more of a nuisance than life—or even job—threatening.

As things stood, or rather as I sat, I saw the wisdom of following Mrs. Dove's example for as long as I could.

She was gone a fair time, during which I worried more and more anxiously that I'd left something slightly out of place in that office, that she would know by some sixth sense that someone had been in there, that I'd left some odor in the air despite never using aftershave, that I'd closed the filing cabinets incorrectly, that I'd left visible fingerprints on a shiny surface, that I'd done *anything* that she knew she hadn't.

I breathed slowly, trying not to sweat.

When she finally came back she said, "The TV crews are leaving. Everything's ready for Monday. The florists are bringing the Lady Mayoress's bouquet at ten o'clock. The red-carpet people are downstairs now measuring the lobby. And, oh, the man from Intramind Imaging says they want a check."

"What about the office?"

"The office? Oh, the office is all right." She was unconcerned. "It was all locked. Just as I left it."

"And the cupboard?" Yorkshire insisted.

"Locked." She thought he was over-reacting. I was concerned only to show no relief.

"What are you going to do with *him?*" she asked, indicating me. "You can't keep him here, can you? The TV crew downstairs were talking about him being here. They want to interview him. What shall I say?"

Yorkshire with black humor said, "Tell them he's all tied up."

She wasn't amused. She said, "I'll say he went out the back way. And I'll be off, too. I'll be here by eight, Monday morning." She looked at me calmly and spoke to Yorkshire. "Let him go," she said unemotionally. "What harm can he do? He's pathetic."

Yorkshire, undecided, said, "Pathetic? Why pathetic?"

She paused composedly half-way through the door, and dropped a pearl beyond price.

"It says so in *The Pump.*"

NEITHER OF THESE two men, I thought, listening to them, was a full-blown criminal. Not yet. Yorkshire was too near the brink.

He still held the heavy adjustable wrench, slapping its head occasionally against his palm, as if it helped his thoughts.

"Please untie me," I said. At least I found the fatal loquaciousness had abated. I no longer wanted to gabble, but just to talk my way out.

Tilepit himself might have done it. He clearly was unused to—and disturbed by—even this level of violence. His power base was his grandfather's name. His muscle was his hire-and-fire clout. There were only so many top editorships in the British press, and George Godbar, editor of *The Pump*, wasn't going to lose his hide to save mine. Matters of principle were all too often an unaffordable luxury, and I didn't believe that in George Godbar's place, or even in Kevin Mills's or India's, I would have done differently.

Yorkshire said, "We wait."

He opened a drawer in his desk and drew out what looked bizarrely like a jar of pickles. Dumping the wrench temporarily, he unscrewed the lid, put the jar on the desk, pulled out a green finger and bit it, crunching it with large white teeth.

"Pickle?" he offered Tilepit.

The third baron averted his nose.

Yorkshire, shrugging, chewed uninhibitedly and went back to slapping his palm with the wrench.

"I'll be missed," I said mildly, "if you keep me much longer."

"Let him go," Tilepit said with a touch of impatience. "He's right, we can't keep him here indefinitely."

"We wait," Yorkshire said heavily, fishing out another pickle, and to the accompaniment of noisy munching, we waited.

I could smell the vinegar.

The door opened finally behind me and both Yorkshire and Tilepit looked welcoming and relieved.

I didn't. The newcomer, who came around in front of me blankly, was Ellis Quint.

Ellis, in open-necked white shirt; Ellis, handsome, macho, vibrating with showmanship; Ellis, the nation's darling, farcically accused. I hadn't seen him since the Ascot races, and none of his radiance had waned.

"What's *Halley* doing here?" he demanded, sounding alarmed. "What has he learned?"

"He was wandering about," Yorkshire said, pointing a pickle at me. "I had him brought up here. He can't have learned a thing."

Tilepit announced, "Halley says he came to ask me to stop *The Pump*'s campaign against him."

Ellis said positively, "He wouldn't have done that."

"Why not?" Yorkshire asked. "Look at him. He's a wimp."

"A *wimp!*"

Despite my precarious position I smiled involuntarily at the depth of incredulity in his voice. I even grinned at him sideways from below half-lowered eyelids, and saw the same private smile on his face: the acknowledgment of brotherhood, of secrecy, of shared esoteric experience, of cold winter af-

ternoons, perils embraced, disappointments and injuries taken lightly, of indescribable triumphs. We had hugged each other standing in our stirrups, ecstatic after winning posts. We had trusted, bonded and twinned.

Whatever we were now, we had once been more than brothers. The past—
our past—remained. The intense and mutual memories could not be erased.

The smiles died. Ellis said, "This *wimp* comes up on your inside and beats
you in the last stride. This wimp could ruin us all if we neglect our inside rail.
This wimp was champion jockey for five or six years and might have been still,
and we'd be fools to forget it." He put his face close to mine. "Still the same
old Sid, aren't you? Cunning. Nerveless. Win at all costs."

There was nothing to say.

Yorkshire bit into a pickle. "What do we do with him, then?"

"First we find out why he's here."

Tilepit said, "He came to get *The Pump* to stop—"

"Balls," Ellis interrupted. "He's lying."

"How can you tell?" Tilepit protested.

"I know him." He said it with authority, and it was true.

"What, then?" Yorkshire asked.

Ellis said to me, "You'll not get me into court, Sid. Not Monday. Not ever.
You haven't been able to break my Shropshire alibi, and my lawyers say that
without that the prosecution won't have a chance. They'll withdraw the
charge. Understand? I know you *do* understand. You'll have destroyed your
own reputation, not mine. What's more, my father's going to kill you."

Yorkshire and Tilepit showed, respectively, pleasure and shock.

"Before Monday?" I asked.

The flippancy fell like lead. Ellis strode around behind me and yanked
back the right front of my brown overalls, and the tracksuit beneath. He tore
a couple of buttons off my shirt, pulling that back after, then he pressed down
strongly with his fingers.

"Gordon says he broke your collarbone," he said.

"Well, he didn't."

Ellis would see the remains of bruising and he could feel the bumps of cal-
lus formed by earlier breaks, but it was obvious to him that his father had been
wrong.

"Gordon will kill you," he repeated. "Don't you care?"

Another unanswerable question.

It seemed to me as if the cruel hidden side of Ellis suddenly took over, ban-
ishing the friend and becoming the threatened star who had everything to
lose. He roughly threw my clothes together and continued around behind me
until he stood on my left side.

"You won't defeat me," he said. "You've cost me half a million. You've cost me lawyers. You've cost me *sleep.*"

He might insist that I couldn't defeat him, but we both knew I would in the end, if I tried, because he was guilty.

"You'll pay for it," he said.

He put his hands on the hard shell of my left forearm and raised it until my elbow formed a right angle. The tight strap around my upper arms and chest prevented me from doing anything to stop him. Whatever strength that remained in my upper left arm (and it was, in fact, quite a lot) was held in uselessness by that strap.

Ellis peeled back the brown sleeve, and the blue one underneath. He tore open my shirt cuff and pulled that sleeve back also. He looked at the plastic skin underneath.

"I know something about that arm," he said. "I got a brochure on purpose. That skin is a sort of glove, and it comes off."

He felt up my arm until, by the elbow, he came to the top of the glove. He rolled it down as far as the wrist and then, with concentration, pulled it off finger by finger, exposing the mechanics in all their detail.

The close-fitting textured glove gave the hand an appearance of life, with knuckles, veins and shapes like fingernails. The works inside were gears, springs and wiring. The bared forearm was bright pink, hard and shiny.

Ellis smiled.

He put his own strong right hand on my electrical left and pressed and twisted with knowledge and then, when the works clicked free, unscrewed the hand in several turns until it came right off.

Ellis looked into my eyes as at a feast. "Well?" he said.

"You *shit.*"

He smiled. He opened his fingers and let the unscrewed hand fall onto the carpet.

# 13

Tilepit looked shocked enough to vomit, but not Yorkshire: in fact, he laughed.

Ellis said to him sharply, "This man is not funny. Everything that has gone wrong is because of *him,* and don't you forget it. It's this Sid Halley that's going to ruin you, and if you think he doesn't care about what I've just done"—he put his toe against the fallen hand and moved it a few inches—"if you think it's something to laugh at, I'll tell you that for *him* it's almost unbearable . . . but *not* unbearable, is it, Sid?" He turned to ask me, and told Yorkshire at the same time, "No one yet has invented anything you've found actually unbearable, have they, Sid?"

I didn't answer.

Yorkshire protested, "But he's only—"

"Don't say *only,*" Ellis interrupted, his voice hard and loud. "Don't you understand it yet? What do you think he's doing here? How did he get here? What does he know? He's not going to tell you. His nickname's 'Tungsten Carbide'—that's the hardest of all metals and it saws through steel. I *know* him. I've almost loved him. You have no idea what you're dealing with, and we've got to decide what to do with him. How many people know he's here?"

"My bodyguards," Yorkshire said. "They brought him up."

It was Lord Tilepit who gave him the real bad news. "It was a TV crew who told Owen that Sid Halley was in the building."

"*A TV crew!*"

"They wanted to interview him. Mrs. Dove said she would tell them he'd gone."

"*Mrs. Dove!*"

If Ellis had met Mrs. Dove he would know, as I did, that she wouldn't lie for Yorkshire. Mrs. Dove had seen me, and she would say so.

Ellis asked furiously, "Did Mrs. Dove see him tied in that chair?"

"Yes," Tilepit said faintly.

"You *stupid* . . ." Words failed Ellis, but for only a few short seconds. "Then," he said flatly, "you can't kill him here."

"*Kill* him?" Tilepit couldn't believe what he'd heard. His whole large face blushed pink. "I'm not . . . are you talking about *murder?*"

"Oh yes, my lord," I said dryly, "they are. They're thinking of putting Your Lordship behind bars as an accessory. You'll love it in the slammer."

I'd meant only to get Tilepit to see the enormity of what Ellis was proposing, but in doing so I'd made the mistake of unleashing Yorkshire's rage.

He took two paces and kicked my unscrewed hand with such force that it flew across the room and crashed against the wall. Then he realized the wrench was still in his hand and swung it at my head.

I saw the blow coming but couldn't get my head back far enough to avoid it altogether. The wrench's heavy screw connected with my moving cheekbone and tore the skin, but didn't this time knock me silly.

In Owen Yorkshire, the half-slipping brakes came wholly off. Perhaps the very sight of me, left-handless and bleeding and unable to retaliate, was all it took. He raised his arm and the wrench again, and I saw the spite in his face and the implacably murderous intention and I thought of nothing much at all, which afterwards seemed odd.

It was Ellis who stopped him. Ellis caught the descending arm and yanked Owen Yorkshire around sideways, so that although the heavy weapon swept on downwards, it missed me altogether.

"You're *brainless*," Ellis shouted. "I said *not in here*. You're a raving lunatic. Too many people know he came here. Do you want to splatter his blood and brains all over your new carpet? You might as well go and shout from the rooftops. Get a grip on that frigging temper and find a tissue."

"A what?"

"Something to stop him bleeding. Are you terminally insane? When he doesn't turn up wherever he's expected, you're going to get the police in here looking for him. TV crew! Mrs. Dove! The whole frigging county! You get one drop of his blood on anything in here, you're looking at twenty-five years."

Yorkshire, bewildered by Ellis's attack and turning sullen, said there weren't any tissues. Verney Tilepit tentatively produced a handkerchief; white, clean and embroidered with a coronet. Ellis snatched it from him and slapped it on my cheek, and I wondered if ever, in any circumstances, I could, to save myself, deliberately kill *him,* and didn't think so.

Ellis took the handkerchief away briefly, looked at the scarlet staining the white, and put it back, pressing.

Yorkshire strode about, waving the wrench as if jerked by strings. Tilepit looked extremely unhappy. I considered my probable future with gloom and Ellis, taking the handkerchief away again and watching my cheek critically, declared that the worst of the bleeding had stopped.

He gave the handkerchief back to Tilepit, who put it squeamishly in his pocket, and he snatched the wrench away from Yorkshire and told him to cool down and *plan.*

Planning took them both out of the office, the door closing behind them. Verney Tilepit didn't in the least appreciate being left alone with me and went to look out of the window, to look anywhere except at me.

"Untie me," I said with force.

No chance. He didn't even show he'd heard.

I asked, "How did you get yourself into this mess?"

No answer.

I tried again. I said, "If I walk out of here free, I'll forget I ever saw you."

He turned around, but he had his back to the light and I couldn't see his eyes clearly behind the spectacles.

"You really are in deep trouble," I said.

"Nothing will happen."

I wished I believed him. I said, "It must have seemed pretty harmless to you, just to use your paper to ridicule someone week after week. What did Yorkshire tell you? To save Ellis at all costs. Well, it *is* going to cost you."

"You don't understand. Ellis is blameless."

"I understand that you're up to your noble neck in shit."

"I can't do anything." He was worried, unhappy and congenitally helpless.

"Untie me," I said again, with urgency.

"It wouldn't help. I couldn't get you out."

"Untie me," I said. "I'll do the rest."

He dithered. If he had been capable of reasoned decisions he wouldn't have let himself be used by Yorkshire, but he wasn't the first or last rich man to stumble blindly into a quagmire. He couldn't make up his mind to attempt saving himself by letting me free and, inevitably, the opportunity passed.

Ellis and Yorkshire came back, and neither of them would meet my eyes. Bad sign.

Ellis, looking at his watch, said, "We wait."

"What for?" Tilepit asked uncertainly.

Yorkshire answered, to Ellis's irritation, "The TV people are on the point of leaving. Everyone will be gone in fifteen minutes."

Tilepit looked at me, his anxieties showing plainly. "Let Halley go," he begged.

Ellis said comfortingly, "Sure, in a while."

Yorkshire smiled. His anger was preferable, on the whole.

Verney Tilepit wanted desperately to be reassured, but even he could see that if freeing me was the intention, why did we have to wait?

Ellis still held the wrench. He wouldn't get it wrong, I thought. He wouldn't spill my blood. I would probably not know much about it. I might not consciously learn the reciprocal answer to my self-searching question: Could *he* personally kill *me,* to save himself? How deep did friendship go? Did it ever have absolute taboos? Had I already, by accusing him of evil, melted his innermost restraints? He wanted to get even. He would wound me any way he could. But *kill* . . . I didn't know.

He walked around behind me.

Time, in a way, stood still. It was a moment in which to plead, but I couldn't. The decision, whatever I said, would be *his.*

He came eventually around to my right-hand side and murmured, "Tungsten," under his breath.

Water, I thought, I had water in my veins.

He reached down suddenly and clamped his hand around my right wrist, pulling fiercely upward.

I jerked my wrist out of his grasp and without warning he bashed the wrench across my knuckles. In the moment of utter numbness that resulted he slid the open jaws of the wrench onto my wrist and tightened the screw. Tightened it further, until the jaws grasped immovably, until they squeezed the upper and lower sides of my wrist together, compressing blood vessels, nerves and ligaments, bearing down on the bones inside.

The wrench was heavy. He balanced its handle on the arm of the chair I was sitting in and held it steady so that my wrist was up at the same level. He had two strong hands. He persevered with the screw.

I said, "Ellis," in protest, not from anger or even fear, but in disbelief that he could do what he was doing: in a lament for the old Ellis, in a sort of passionate sorrow.

For the few seconds that he looked into my face, his expression was flooded with awareness . . . and shame. Then the feelings passed, and he returned in deep concentration to an atrocious pleasure.

It was extraordinary. He seemed to go into a kind of trance, as if the office and Yorkshire and Tilepit didn't exist, as if there were only one reality, which was the clench of forged steel jaws on a wrist and the extent to which he could intensify it.

I thought: If the wrench had been lopping shears, if its jaws had been knives instead of flat steel, the whole devastating nightmare would have come true. I shut my mind to it: made it cold. Sweated, all the same.

I thought: What I see in his face is the full-blown addiction; not the cruel satisfaction he could get from unscrewing a false hand, but the sinful fulfillment of cutting off a live hoof.

I glanced very briefly at Yorkshire and Tilepit and saw their frozen, bottomless astonishment, and I realized that until that moment of revelation they hadn't wholly believed in Ellis's guilt.

My wrist hurt. Somewhere up my arm the ulna grumbled.

I said, *"Ellis"* sharply, to wake him up.

He got the screw to tighten another notch.

I yelled at him, *"Ellis,"* and again, *"Ellis."*

He straightened, looking vaguely down at fifteen inches of heavy stainless steel wrench incongruously sticking out sideways from its task. He tied it to the arm of the chair with another strap from the desk and went over to the window, not speaking, but not rational, either.

I tried to dislodge myself from the wrench but my hand was too numb and the grip too tight. I found it difficult to think. My hand was pale blue and gray. Thought was a crushed wrist and an abysmal shattering fear that if the damage went on too long, it would be permanent. Hands could be lost.

Both hands . . . Oh, God. Oh, *God*.

"Ellis," I said yet again, but in a lower voice this time: a plea for him to return to the old self, that was there all the time, somewhere.

I waited. Acute discomfort and the terrible anxiety continued. Ellis's thoughts seemed far out in space. Tilepit cleared his throat in embarrassment and Yorkshire, as if in unconscious humor, crunched a pickle.

Minutes passed.

I said, "Ellis . . ."

I closed my eyes. Opened them again. More or less prayed.

Time and nightmare fused. One became the other. The future was a void. Ellis left the window and crossed with bouncing steps to the chair where

I sat. He looked into my face and enjoyed what he could undoubtedly see there. Then he unscrewed and untied the wrench with violent jerks and dropped the abominable ratchet from a height onto the desk.

No one said anything. Ellis seemed euphoric, high, full of good spirits, striding around the room as if unable to contain his exhilaration.

I got stabbing pins and needles in my fingers, and thanked the fates for it. My hand felt dreadful but turned slowly yellowish pink.

Thought came back from outer space and lodged again earthily in my brain.

Ellis, coming down very slightly, looked at his watch. He plucked from the desk the cosmetic glove from my false arm, came to my right side, shoved the glove inside my shirt against my chest and, with a theatrical flourish, zipped up the front of my blue tracksuit to keep his gift from falling out.

He looked at his watch again. Then he went across the room, picked up the unscrewed hand, returned to my side and slapped the dead mechanism into my living palm. There was a powerful impression all around that he was busy making sure no trace of Sid Halley remained in the room.

He went around behind me and undid the strap fastening me into the chair. Then he undid the second strap that held my upper arms against my body.

"Screw the hand back on," he instructed.

Perhaps because they had bent from being kicked around, or perhaps because my real hand was eighty percent useless, the screw threads wouldn't mesh smoothly, and after three half turns they stuck. The hand looked reattached, but wouldn't work.

"Stand up," Ellis said.

I stood, swaying, my ankles still tied together.

"You're letting him go," Tilepit exclaimed, with grateful relief.

"Of course," Ellis said.

Yorkshire was smiling.

"Put your hands behind your back," Ellis told me.

I did so, and he strapped my wrists tight together.

Last, he undid my ankles.

"This way." He pulled me by the arm over to the door and through into the passage. I walked like an automaton.

Looking back, I saw Yorkshire put his hand on the telephone. Beyond him, Tilepit was happy with foolish faith.

Ellis pressed the call button for the elevator, and the door opened immediately.

"Get in," he said.

I looked briefly at his now unsmiling face. Expressionless. That made two of us, I thought, two of us thinking the same thing and not saying it.

I stepped into the elevator and he leaned in quickly and pressed the button for the ground floor, then jumped back. The door closed between us. The elevator began its short journey down.

To tie together the wrists of a man who could unscrew one of them was an exercise in futility. All the same, the crossed threads and my fumbling fingers gave me trouble and some severe moments of panic before the hand slipped free. The elevator had already reached its destination by the time I'd shed the tying strap, leaving no chance to emerge from the opening door with everything anywhere near normal.

I put the mechanical hand deep into my right-hand tracksuit trousers pocket. Surreal, I grimly thought. The long sleeve of brown overall covered the void where it belonged.

Ellis had given me a chance. Not much of one, probably, but at least I did have the answer to my question, which was no, he wouldn't personally kill me. Yorkshire definitely would.

The two blue-clad bodyguards were missing from the lobby.

The telephone on the desk was ringing, but the bodyguards were outside, busily positioning a Topline Foods van. One guard was descending from the driver's seat. The other was opening the rear doors.

A van, I understood, for abduction. For a journey to an unmarked grave. A bog job, the Irish called it. How much, I wondered, were they being paid?

Ellis's timing had given me thirty seconds. He'd sent me down too soon. In the lobby I had no future. Out in the open air . . . some.

Taking a couple of deep breaths, I shot out through the doors as fast as I could, and sprinted—and I ran not to the right, towards my own car, but veered left around the van towards the open gates.

There was a shout from one of the blue figures, a yell from the second, and I thought for a moment that I could avoid them, but to my dismay the gatekeeper himself came to unwelcome life, emerging from his kiosk and barring my exit. Big man in another blue uniform, over-confident.

I ran straight at him. He stood solidly, legs apart, his weight evenly balanced. He wasn't prepared for or expecting my left foot to knock aside the inside of his knee or for my back to bend and curl like a cannonball into his stomach: he fell over backwards and I was on my way before he struggled to his knees. The other two, though, had gained ground.

The sort of judo Chico had taught me was in part the stylized advances and throws of a regulated sport and in part an individual style for a one-handed victim. For a start, I never wore, in my private sessions with him, the loose white judogi uniform. I never fought in bare feet but always in ordinary shoes or sneakers. The judo I'd learned was how to save my life, not how to earn a black belt.

Ordinary judo needed two hands. Myoelectric hands had a slow response time, a measurable pause between instruction and action. Chico and I had scrapped all grappling techniques for that hand and substituted clubbing; and I used all his lessons at Frodsham as if they were as familiar as walking.

We hadn't exactly envisaged no useful hands at all, but it was amazing what one could do if one wanted to live. It was the same as it had been in races: win now, pay later.

My opponents were straight musclemen with none of the subtlety of the Japanese understanding of lift and leverage and speed. Chico could throw me every time, but Yorkshire's watchdogs couldn't.

The names of the movements clicked like a litany in my brain—*shintai, randori, tai-sabaki*. Fighting literally to live, I stretched every technique I knew and adapted others, using falling feints that involved my twice lying on the ground and sticking a foot into a belly to fly its owner over my head. It ended with one blue uniform lying dazed on his back, one complaining I'd broken his nose, and one haring off to the office building with the bad news.

I stumbled out onto the road, feeling that if I went back for my car the two men I'd left on the ground would think of getting up again and closing the gates.

In one direction lay houses, so I staggered that way. Better cover. I needed cover before anyone chased me in the Topline Foods van.

The houses, when I reached them, were too regular, the gardens too tidy and small. I chose one house with no life showing, walked unsteadily up the garden path, kept on going, found myself in the back garden with another row of houses over the back fence.

The fence was too high to jump or vault, but there was an empty crate lying there, a gift from the gods.

No one came out of any of the houses to ask me what I thought I was doing. I emerged into the next street and began to think about where I was going and what I looked like.

Brown overalls. Yorkshire would be looking for brown overalls.

I took them off and dumped them in one of the houses' brown-looking beech hedges.

Taking off the overalls revealed the nonexistence of a left hand.

Damn it, I thought astringently. Things are never easy, so *cope*.

I put the pink exposed end of arm, with its bare electrical contacts, into my left-hand jacket pocket, and walked, not ran, up the street. I wanted to run, but hadn't the strength. Weak . . . Stamina a memory, a laugh.

There was a boy in the distance roller-blading, coming towards me and wearing not the ubiquitous baseball cap but a striped woolen hat. That would do, I thought. I fumbled some money out of the zip pocket in my belt and stood in his way.

He tried to avoid me, swerved, overbalanced and called me filthy names until his gaze fell on the money in my hand.

"Sell me your hat," I suggested.

"Yer wha?"

"Your hat," I said, "for the money."

"You've got blood on your face," he said.

He snatched the money and aimed to roller-blade away. I stuck out a foot and knocked him off his skates. He gave me a bitter look and a choice of swear words, but also the hat, sweeping it off and throwing it at me.

It was warm from his head and I put it on, hoping he didn't have lice. I wiped my face gingerly on my sleeve and slouched along towards the road with traffic that crossed the end of the residential street . . . and saw the Topline Foods van roll past.

Whatever they were looking for, it didn't seem to be a navy tracksuit with a striped woolen hat.

Plan B—run away. OK.

Plan C—where to?

I reached the end of the houses and turned left into what might once have been a shopping street, but which now seemed to offer only realtors, building societies and banks. Marooned in this unhelpful landscape were only two possible refuges: a betting shop and a place selling ice cream.

I chose the ice cream. I was barely through the door when outside the window my own Mercedes went past.

Ellis was driving.

I still had its keys in my pocket. Jonathan, it seemed, wasn't alone in his car-stealing skill.

"What do you want?" a female voice said behind me.

She was asking about ice cream: a thin young woman, bored.

"Er . . . that one," I said, pointing at random.

"Cup or cone? Large or small?"

"Cone. Small." I felt disoriented, far from reality. I paid for the ice cream and licked it, and it tasted of almonds.

"You've cut your face," she said.

"I ran into a tree."

There were four or five tables with people sitting at them, mostly adolescent groups. I sat at a table away from the window and within ten minutes saw the Topline van pass twice more and my own car, once.

Tremors ran in my muscles. Fear, or over-exertion, or both.

There was a door marked Men's Room at the back of the shop. I went in there when I'd finished the ice cream and looked at my reflection in the small mirror over the sink.

The cut along my left cheekbone had congealed into a blackening line, thick and all too visible. Dampening a paper towel, I dabbed gently at the mess, trying to remove the clotted blood without starting new bleeding, but making only a partial improvement.

Locked in a cubicle, I had another try at screwing my wandering hand into place, and this time at length got it properly aligned and fastened, but it still wouldn't work. Wretchedly depressed, I fished out the long covering glove and with difficulty, because of no talcum powder and an enfeebled right hand, pulled that too into the semblance of reality.

Damn Ellis, I thought mordantly. He'd been right about some things being near to unbearable.

Never mind. Get on with it.

I emerged from the cubicle and tried my cheek again with another paper towel, making the cut paler, fading it into skin color.

Not too bad.

The face below the unfamiliar woolen hat looked strained. Hardly a surprise.

I went out through the ice cream shop and walked along the street. The Topline Foods van rolled past quite slowly, driven by one of the blue-clad guards, who was intently scanning the other side of the road. That bodyguard meant, I thought, that Yorkshire himself might be out looking for me in a car I couldn't recognize.

Perhaps all I had to do was go up to some sensible-looking motorist and say, "Excuse me, some people are trying to kill me. Please will you drive me to the police station?" And then, "Who are these people?" "The managing director of Topline Foods, and Ellis Quint." "Oh *yes?* And *you* are . . . ?"

I did go as far as asking someone the way to the police station—"Round there, straight on, turn left—about a mile"—and for want of anything better I started walking that way; but what I came to first was a bus shelter with several people standing in a line, waiting. I added myself to the patient half dozen and stood with my back to the road, and a woman with two children soon came up behind me, hiding me well.

Five long minutes later my Mercedes pulled up on the far side of the road with a white Rolls-Royce behind it. Ellis stepped out of my car and York-shire out of the Rolls. They conferred together, furiously stabbing the air, pointing up and down the street while I bent my head down to the children and prayed to remain unspotted.

The bus came while the cars were still there.

Four people got off. The waiting line, me included, surged on. I resisted the temptation to look out of the window until the bus was traveling again, and then saw with relief that the two men were still talking.

I had no idea where the bus was going.

Who cared? Distance was all I needed. I'd paid to go to the end of the line, wherever that was.

Peaceful Frodsham in Cheshire, sometime Saturday, people going shopping in the afternoon. I felt disconnected from that sort of life; and I didn't know what the time was, as the elastic metal bracelet watch I normally wore on my left wrist had come off in Yorkshire's office and was still there, I supposed.

The bus slowly filled at subsequent stops. Shopping baskets. Chatter. Where was I going?

The end of the line proved to be the railway depot in Runcorn, halfway to Liverpool, going north when I needed to go south.

I got off the bus and went to the depot. There was no Mercedes, no Rolls-Royce, no Topline Foods van in sight, which didn't mean they wouldn't think of buses and trains eventually. Runcorn railway depot didn't feel safe. There was a train to Liverpool due in four minutes, I learned, so I bought a ticket and caught it.

The feeling of unreality continued, also the familiar aversion to asking for help from the local police. They didn't approve of outside investigators. If I ever got into messes, besides, I considered it my own responsibility to get my-self out. Norman Pictons were rare. In Liverpool, moreover, I was probably counted a local boy who'd been disloyal to his "roots."

At the Liverpool railway depot I read the well-displayed timetable for trains going south.

An express to London, I thought; then backtrack to Reading and get a taxi to Shelley Green, Archie Kirk's house.

No express for hours. What else, then?

The incredible words took a time to penetrate: Liverpool to Bournemouth, departing at 3:10 P.M. A slow train, meandering southwards across England, right down to the Channel, with many stops on the way . . . and one of the stops was *Reading.*

I sprinted, using the last shreds of strength. It was already, according to the big depot clock, ticking away at 3:07. Whistles were blowing when I stumbled into the last car in the long train. A guard helped thrust me in and closed the door. The wheels rolled. I had no ticket and little breath, but a marvelous feeling of escape. That feeling lasted only until the first of the many stops, which I discovered with horror to be *Runcorn*.

Square one: where I'd started. All fear came flooding back. I sat stiff and immobile, as if movement itself would give me away.

Nothing happened. The train quietly rolled onwards. Out on the platform a blue-clad Topline Foods security guard was speaking into a hand-held telephone and shaking his head.

CREWE, STAFFORD, WOLVERHAMPTON, Birmingham, Coventry, Leamington Spa, Banbury, Oxford, Didcot, Reading.

It took four hours. Slowly, in that time, the screwed-tight wires of tension slackened to manageable if not to ease. At every stop, however illogical I might tell myself it was, dread resurfaced. Oversize wrenches could kill when one wasn't looking. . . . Don't be a fool, I thought. I'd bought a ticket from the train conductor between Runcorn and Crewe, but every subsequent appearance of his dark uniform as he checked his customers bumped my heart muscles.

It grew dark. The train clanked and swayed into realms of night. Life felt suspended.

There were prosaically plenty of taxis at Reading. I traveled safely to Shelley Green and rang Archie Kirk's bell.

He came himself to open the door.

"Hello," I said.

He stood there staring, then said awkwardly, "We'd almost given you up." He led the way into his sitting room. "He's here," he said.

There were four of them. Davis Tatum, Norman Picton, Archie himself, and Charles.

I paused inside the doorway. I had no idea what I looked like, but what I saw on their faces was shock.

"Sid," Charles said, recovering first and standing up. "Good. Great. Come and sit down."

The extent of his solicitude always measured the depth of his alarm. He insisted I take his place in a comfortable chair and himself perched on a hard one. He asked Archie if he had any brandy and secured for me a half-tumblerful of a raw-tasting own brand from a supermarket.

"Drink it," he commanded, holding out the glass.

"Charles . . ."

"Drink it. Talk after."

I gave in, drank a couple of mouthfuls and put the glass on a table beside me. He was a firm believer in the life-restoring properties of distilled wine, and I'd proved him right oftener than enough.

I remembered that I still wore the soft, stripey hat, and took it off; and its removal seemed to make my appearance more normal to them, and less disturbing.

"I went to Topline Foods," I said.

I thought: I don't feel well; what's wrong with me?

"You've cut your face," Norman Picton said.

I also ached more or less all over from the desperate exertions of the judo. My head felt heavy and my hand was swollen and sore from Ellis's idea of entertainment. On the bright side, I was alive and home, safe . . . and reaction was all very well but I was *not* at this point going to faint.

"Sid!" Charles said sharply, putting out a hand.

"Oh . . . yes. Well, I went to Topline Foods."

I drank some brandy. The weak feeling of sickness abated a bit. I shifted in my chair and took a grip on things.

Archie said, "Take your time," but sounded as if he didn't mean it.

I smiled. I said, "Owen Yorkshire was there. So was Lord Tilepit. So was Ellis Quint."

"Quint!" Davis Tatum exclaimed.

"Mm. Well . . . you asked me to find out if there was a heavyweight lumbering about behind the Quint business, and the answer is yes, but it is Ellis Quint himself."

"But he's a playboy," Davis Tatum protested. "What about the big man, Yorkshire?" Tatum's own bulk quivered. "He's getting known. One hears his name."

I nodded. "Owen Cliff Yorkshire is a heavyweight in the making."

"What do you mean?"

I ached. I hadn't really noticed the wear and tear until then. Win now, pay later.

"Megalomania," I said. "Yorkshire's on the edge. He has a violent, unpredictable temper and an uncontrolled desire to be a tycoon. I'd call it incipient megalomania because he's spending far beyond sanity on self-aggrandizement. He's built an office block fit for a major industry—and it's mostly empty—before building the industry first. He's publicity mad—he's holding a reception for half of Liverpool on Monday. He has plans—a *desire*— to take over the whole horse-feed nuts industry. He employs at least two bodyguards who will murder to order because he fears his competitors will assassinate him . . . which is paranoia."

I paused, then said, "It's difficult to describe the impression he gives. Half the time he sounds reasonable, and half the time you can see that he will simply get rid of anyone who stands in his way. And he is desperate . . . *desperate* . . . to save Ellis Quint's reputation."

Archie asked "Why?" slowly.

"Because," I said, "he has spent a colossal amount of money on an advertising campaign featuring Ellis, and if Ellis is found guilty of cutting off a horse's foot, that campaign can't be shown."

"But a few advertisements can't have cost that much," Archie objected.

"With megalomania," I said, "you don't make a few economically priced advertisements. You really go to town. You engage an expensive, highly prestigious firm—in this case, Intramind Imaging of Manchester—and you travel the world."

With clumsy fingers I took from my belt the folded copy of the paper in the "Quint" box file in Mrs. Dove's office.

"This is a list of racecourses," I said. "These racecourses are where they filmed the commercials. A thirty-second commercial gleaned from each place at phenomenal expense."

Archie scanned the list uncomprehendingly and passed it to Charles, who read it aloud.

"Flemington, Germiston, Sha Tin, Churchill Downs, Woodbine, Longchamps, K. L., Fuchu . . ."

There were fifteen altogether. Archie looked lost.

"Flemington," I said, "is where they run the Melbourne Cup in Australia. Germiston is outside Johannesburg. Sha Tin is in Hong Kong. Churchill Downs is where they hold the Kentucky Derby. K. L. is Kuala Lumpur in Malaysia, Woodbine is in Canada, Longchamps is in Paris, Fuchu is where the Japan Cup is run in Tokyo."

They all understood.

"Those commercials are reported to be brilliant," I said, "and Ellis himself wants them shown as much as Yorkshire does."

"Have you seen them?" Davis asked.

I explained about the box of Betacam tapes. "Making those special broadcast-quality tapes themselves must have been fearfully expensive—and they need special playing equipment, which I didn't find at Topline Foods, so no, I haven't seen them."

Norman Picton, with his policeman's mind, asked, "Where did you see the tapes? Where did you get that list of racecourses?"

I said without emotion, "In an office at Topline Foods."

He gave me a narrow inspection.

"My car," I told him, "is still somewhere in Frodsham. Could you get your pals up there to look out for it?" I gave him its registration number, which he wrote down.

"Why did you leave it?" he asked.

"Er . . . I was running away at the time." For all that I tried to say it lightly, the grim reality reached them.

"Well," I sighed, "I'd invaded Yorkshire's territory. He found me there. It gave him the opportunity to get rid of the person most likely to send Ellis to jail. I accepted that possibility when I went there but, like you, I wanted to know what was causing terrible trouble behind the scenes. And it is the millions spent on those ads." I paused, and went on, "Yorkshire and Ellis set out originally, months ago, not to kill me but to discredit me so that nothing I said would get Ellis convicted. They used a figurehead, Topline Foods director Lord Tilepit, because he owned *The Pump*. They persuaded Tilepit that Ellis was innocent and that I was all that *The Pump* has maintained. I don't think Tilepit believed Ellis guilty until today. I don't think *The Pump* will say a word against me from now on." I smiled briefly. "Lord Tilepit was duped by Ellis, and so, also, to some extent, was Owen Yorkshire himself."

"How, Sid?" Davis asked.

"I think Yorkshire, too, believed in Ellis. Ellis dazzles people. Knowing Ellis, to Yorkshire, was a step up the ladder. Today they planned together to . . . er . . . wipe me out of the way. Yorkshire would have done it himself in reckless anger. Ellis stopped him, but left it to chance that the bodyguards might do it . . . but I escaped them. Yorkshire now knows Ellis is guilty, but he doesn't care. He cares only to be able to show that brilliant ad campaign, and make himself king of the horse nuts. And of course it's not just horse nuts that it's all about. They're a stepping-stone. It's about being the Big Man with the power to bring mayors to his doorstep. If Yorkshire isn't stopped you'll find him manipulating more than *The Pump*. He's the sort of man you get in the kitchens of political clout."

After a moment, Archie asked, "So how do we stop him?"

I shifted wearily in the chair and drank some brandy, and said, "I can, possibly, give you the tools."

"What tools?"

"His secret files. His financial maneuverings. His debts. Details of bribes, I'd guess. Bargains struck. You scratch my back, I'll scratch yours. Evidence of leverage. Details of all his dealings with Ellis, and all his dealings with Tilepit. I'll give you the files. You can take it from there."

"But," Archie said blankly, "where are these files?"

"In my computer in London."

I explained the Internet transfer and the need for password cracking. I couldn't decide whether they were gladdened or horrified by what I'd done. A bit of both, I thought.

Charles looked the most shocked, Archie the least.

Archie said, "If I ask you, will you work for me another time?"

I looked into the knowing eyes, and smiled, and nodded.

"Good," he said.

# 14

I went home to Aynsford with Charles.

It had been a long evening in Archie's house. Archie, Davis, Norman and Charles had all wanted details, which I found as intolerable to describe as to live through. I skipped a lot.

I didn't tell them about Ellis's games with my hands. I didn't know how to explain to them that, for a jockey, his hands were at the heart of his existence . . . of his skill. One knew a horse by the feel of the bit on the reins, one listened to the messages, one interpreted the vibrations, one *talked* to a horse through one's hands. Ellis understood more than most people what the loss of a hand had meant to me, and that day he'd been busy punishing me in the severest way he could think of for trying to strip him of what he himself now valued most, his universal acclaim.

I didn't know how to make them understand that to Ellis the severing of a horse's foot had become a drug more addictive than any substance invented, that the risk and the power were intoxicating; that I'd been lucky he'd had only a wrench to use on me.

I didn't know how near he had come in his own mind to irrevocably destroying my right hand. I only knew that to me it had seemed possible that he would. I couldn't tell them that I'd intensely lived my own nightmare and still shook from fear inside.

I told them only that an adjustable wrench in Yorkshire's hands had cut my face.

I told them a little about the escape by judo, and all about the boy on Rollerblades and the ice cream cone and catching the bus within sight of Yorkshire and Ellis. I made it sound almost funny.

Archie understood that there was a lot I hadn't said, but he didn't press it. Charles, puzzled, asked, "But did they *hurt* you, Sid?" and I half laughed and told him part of the truth. "They scared me witless."

Davis asked about Ellis's Shropshire alibi. His colleague, the Crown Prosecutor, was increasingly concerned, he said, that Ellis's powerful lawyers would prevent the trial from resuming.

I explained that I hadn't had time to find out at what hour Ellis had arrived at the dance.

"Someone must know," I said. "It's a matter of asking the local people, the people who helped to park the cars." I looked at Norman. "Any chance of the police doing it?"

"Not much," he said.

"Round the pubs," I suggested.

Norman shook his head.

"There isn't much time," Davis pointed out. "Sid, couldn't you do it tomorrow?"

Tomorrow, Sunday. On Monday, the trial.

Archie said firmly, "No, Sid can't. There's a limit . . . I'll try and find someone else."

"Chico would have done it," Charles said.

Chico had undisputedly saved my pathetic skin that day. One could hardly ask more.

Archie's wife, before she'd driven over to spend the evening with her sister-in-law Betty Bracken, had, it appeared, made a mound of sandwiches. Archie offered them diffidently. I found the tastes of cheese and of chicken strange, as if I'd come upon them new from another world. It was weird the difference that danger and the perception of mortality made to familiar things. Unreality persisted even as I accepted a paper napkin to wipe my fingers.

Archie's doorbell rang. Archie went again to the summons and came back with a pinched, displeased expression, and he was followed by a boy that I saw with surprise to be Jonathan.

The rebel wings of hair were much shorter. The yellow streaks had all but grown out. There were no shaven areas of scalp.

"Hi," he said, looking around the room and fastening his attention on my face. "I came over to see you. The aunts said you were here. Hey, man, you look different."

"Three months older." I nodded. "So do you."

Jonathan helped himself to a sandwich, disregarding Archie's disapproval.

"Hi," he said nonchalantly to Norman. "How's the boat?"

"Laid up for winter storage."

Jonathan chewed and told me, "They won't take me on an oil rig until I'm eighteen. They won't take me in the navy. I've got good pecs. What do I do with them?"

"Pecs?" Charles asked, mystified.

"Pectoral muscles," Norman explained. "He's strong from weeks of water-skiing."

"Oh."

I said to Jonathan, "How did you get here from Combe Bassett?"

"Ran."

He'd walked into Archie's house not in the least out of breath.

"Can you ride a motorbike," I asked, "now that you're sixteen?"

"Do me a favor!"

"He hasn't got one," Archie said.

"He can hire one."

"But . . . what for?"

"To go to Shropshire," I said.

I was predictably drowned by protests. I explained to Jonathan what was needed. "Find someone—anyone—who saw Ellis Quint arrive at the dance. Find the people who parked the cars."

"He can't go round the pubs," Norman insisted. "He's under-age."

Jonathan gave me a dark look, which I steadfastly returned. At fifteen he'd bought gin for a truck driver's wife.

"Hey," he said. "Where do I go?"

I told him in detail. His uncle and everyone else disapproved. I took all the money I had left out of my belt and gave it to him. "I want receipts," I said. "Bring me paper. A signed statement from a witness. It's all got to be solid."

"Is this," he asked slowly, "some sort of test?"

"Yes."

"OK."

"Don't stay longer than a day," I said. "Don't forget, you may be asked to give evidence this week at the trial."

"As if I could forget."

He took a bunch of sandwiches, gave me a wide smile, and without more words departed.

"You *can't*," Archie said to me emphatically.

"What do *you* propose to do with him?"

"But . . . he's . . ."

"He's bright," I said. "He's observant. He's athletic. Let's see how he does in Shropshire."

"He's only *sixteen.*"

"I need a new Chico."

"But Jonathan steals cars."

"He hasn't stolen one all summer, has he?"

"That doesn't mean . . ."

"An ability to steal cars," I said with humor, "is in my eyes an asset. Let's see how he does tomorrow, with this alibi."

Archie, still looking affronted, gave in.

"Too much depends on it," Davis said heavily, shaking his head.

I said, "If Jonathan learns nothing, I'll go myself on Monday."

"That will be too late," Davis said.

"Not if you get your colleague to ask for one more day's adjournment. Invent flu or something."

Davis said doubtfully, "Are you totally committed to this trial? *The Pump*—or Ellis Quint—they haven't got to you in any way, have they? I mean . . . the hate campaign . . . do you want to back out?"

Charles was offended on my behalf. "Of course he doesn't," he said.

Such faith! I said plainly to Davis, "Don't let your colleague back down. That's the real danger. Tell him to insist on prosecuting, alibi or no alibi. Tell the prosecution service to dredge up some guts."

"Sid!" He was taken aback. "They're realists."

"They're shit-scared of Ellis's lawyers. Well, I'm not. Ellis took the foot off Betty Bracken's colt. I wish like hell that he hadn't, but he did. He has no alibi for that night. You get your colleague to tell Ellis's lawyers that the Northampton colt was a copycat crime. If we can't break Ellis's alibi, copycat is our story and we're sticking to it, and if you have any influence over your colleague the prosecutor, you make sure he gives me a chance in court to say so."

Davis said faintly, "I must not instruct him to do anything like that."

"Just manage to get it dripped into his mind."

"So there you are, Davis," Archie said dryly, "our boy shows no sign of the hate campaign having been successful. Rather the opposite, wouldn't you say?"

"Our boy" stood up, feeling a shade fragile. It seemed to have been a long day. Archie came out into the hall with Charles and me and offered his hand in farewell. Charles shook warmly. Archie lifted my wrist and looked at the swelling and the deep bruising that was already crimson and black.

He said, "You've had difficulty holding your glass all evening."

I shrugged a fraction, long resigned to occupational damage. My hand was still a hand, and that was all that mattered.

"No explanation?" Archie asked.

I shook my head.

"Stone walls tell more," Charles informed him calmly.

Archie, releasing my wrist, said to me, "The British Horseracing Board wants you to double-check some of their own members for loyalty. Ultra-secret digging."

"They wouldn't ask *me.*" I shook my head. "I'm not the new people's idea of reliable."

"They asked *me,*" he said, the eyes blazing with amusement. "I said it would be you or nobody."

"Nobody," I said.

He laughed. "You start as soon as the Quint thing is over."

The trouble, I thought, as I sat quietly beside Charles as he drove to Aynsford, was that for me the Quint thing would never be over. Ellis might or might not go to jail . . . but that wouldn't be the end for either of us. Gordon's obsession might deepen. Ellis might maim more than horses. In both of them lay a compulsive disregard of natural law.

No one could ever be comprehensively protected from obsession. One simply had to live as best one could and disregard the feral threat lying in wait—and I would somehow have to shake Gordon loose from staking out my Pont Square door.

Charles said, "Do you consider that transferring Yorkshire's secret files to your own computer was at all immoral? Was it . . . theft?"

He spoke without censure, but censure was implied. I remembered a discussion we'd had once along the lines of what was honorable and what was not. He'd said I had a vision of honor that made my life a purgatory and I'd said he was wrong, and that purgatory was abandoning your vision of honor and knowing you'd done it. "Only for you, Sid," he'd said. "The rest of the world has no difficulty at all."

It seemed he was applying to me my own rash judgment. Was stealing knowledge ever justified, or was it not?

I said without self-excuse, "It was theft, and dishonorable, and I would do it again."

"And purgatory can wait?"

I said with amusement, "Have you read *The Pump?*"

After about five miles he said, "That's specious."

"Mm."

*"The Pump*'s a different sort of purgatory."

I nodded and said idly, "The anteroom to hell."

He frowned, glancing across in distaste. "Has hell arrived, then?" He hated excess emotion. I cooled it.

I said, "No. Sorry. It's been a long day."

He drove another mile, then asked, "How *did* you hurt your hand?"

I sighed. "I don't want a fuss. Don't *fuss,* Charles, if I tell you."

"No. All right. No fuss."

"Then . . . Ellis had a go at it."

*"Ellis?"*

"Mm. Lord Tilepit and Owen Yorkshire watched Ellis enjoy it. That's how they now know he's guilty as charged with the colts. If Ellis had had shears instead of a wrench to use on my wrist, I would now have no hands—and for God's sake, Charles, keep your eyes on the road."

"But, *Sid* . . ."

"No fuss. You promised. There'll be no lasting harm." I paused. "If he'd wanted to kill me today, he could have done it, but instead he gave me a chance to escape. He wanted . . ." I swallowed. "He wanted to make me pay for defeating him . . . and he did make me pay . . . and on Monday in court I'll try to disgrace him forever . . . and I *loathe* it."

He drove to Aynsford in a silence I understood to be at least empty of condemnation. Braking outside the door, he said regretfully, "If you and Ellis hadn't been such good friends . . . no wonder poor Ginnie couldn't stand it."

Charles saw the muscles stiffen in my face.

"What is it, Sid?" he asked.

"I . . . I may have made a wrong assumption."

"What assumption?"

"Mm?" I said vaguely. "Have to think."

"Then think in bed," he said lightly. "It's late."

I thought for half the night. Ellis's revenge brutally throbbed in my fingers. Ellis had tied my wrists and given me thirty seconds . . . I would be dead, I thought, if we hadn't been friends.

AT AYNSFORD I kept duplicates of all the things I'd lost in my car—battery charger, razor, clothes and so on—all except the mobile phone. I did have the SIM card, but nothing to use it in.

The no-car situation was solved again by Teledrive, which came to pick me up on Sunday morning.

To Charles's restrained suggestion that I pass the day resting with him—"A game of chess, perhaps?"—I replied that I was going to see Rachel Ferns. Charles nodded.

"Come back," he said, "if you need to."

"Always."

"Take care of yourself, Sid."

RACHEL, LINDA TOLD me on the telephone, was home from the hospital for the day.

"Oh, do come," she begged. "Rachel *needs* you."

I went empty-handed with no new fish or wigs, but it didn't seem to matter.

Rachel herself looked bloodless, a white wisp of a child in the foothills of a far country. In the five days since I'd seen her, the bluish shadows under her eyes had deepened, and she had lost weight so that the round cheeks of the steroids under the bald head and the big shadowed eyes gave her the look of an exotic little bird, unlike life.

Linda hugged me and cried on my shoulder in the kitchen.

"It's good news, really," she said, sobbing. "They've found a donor."

"But that's *marvelous.*" Like a sunburst of hope, I thought, but Linda still wept.

"He's a Swiss," she said. "He's coming from Switzerland. He's coming on Wednesday. Joe is paying his airfare and the hotel bills. Joe says money's no object for his little girl."

"Then stop crying."

"Yes . . . but it may not work."

"And it *may,*" I said positively. "Where's the gin?"

She laughed shakily. She poured two glasses. I still didn't much care for gin but it was all she liked. We clinked to the future and she began talking about paella for lunch.

Rachel was half sitting, half lying, on a small sofa that had been repositioned in the sitting room so that she could look straight and closely into the fish tank. I sat beside her and asked how she felt.

"Did my mum tell you about the transplant?" she said.

"Terrific news."

"I might be able to run again."

Running, it was clear from her pervading lassitude, must have seemed at that point as distant as the moon.

Rachel said, "I begged to come home to see the fishes. I have to go back tonight, though. I hoped you would come. I begged God."

"You knew I would come."

"I meant *today*, while I'm home."

"I've been busy since I saw you on Tuesday."

"I know. Mummy said so. The nurses tell me when you phone every day."

Pegotty was crawling all around the floor, growing in size and agility and putting everything unsuitable in his mouth; making his sister laugh.

"He's so *funny*," she said. "They won't let him come to the hospital. I begged to see him and the fishes. They told me the transplant is going to make me feel sick, so I wanted to come home first."

"Yes," I said.

Linda produced steamy rice with bits of chicken and shrimps, which we all ate with spoons.

"What's wrong with your hand?" Linda asked. "In places it's almost black."

"It's only a bruise. It got a bit squashed."

"You've got sausage fingers," Rachel said.

"They'll be all right tomorrow."

Linda returned to the only important subject. "The Swiss donor," she said, "is older than I am! He has three children of his own. He's a schoolteacher . . . he sounds a nice man, and they say he's so pleased to be going to give Rachel some of his bone marrow."

Rachel said, "I wish it had been Sid's bone marrow."

I'd had myself tested, right at the beginning, but I'd been about as far from a match as one could get. Neither Linda nor Joe had been more than fifty percent compatible.

"They say he's a ninety percent match," Linda said. "You never get a hundred percent, even from siblings. Ninety percent is great."

She was trying hard to be positive. I didn't know enough to put a bet on ninety percent. It sounded fine to me; and no one was going to kill off Rachel's own defective bone marrow if they didn't believe they could replace it.

"They're going to put me into a bubble," Rachel said. "It's a sort of plastic tent over my bed. I won't be able to touch the Swiss man, except through the plastic. And he doesn't speak English, even. He speaks German. *Danke schoen*. I've learned that, to say to him. Thank you very much."

"He's a lucky man," I said.

Linda, clearing the plates and offering ice cream for dessert, asked if I would stay with Rachel while she took Pegotty out for a short walk in fresh air.

"Of course."

"I won't be long."

When she'd gone, Rachel and I sat on the sofa and watched the fish.

"You see that one?" Rachel pointed. "That's the one you brought on Tuesday. Look how fast he swims! He's faster than all the others."

The black and silver angel fish flashed through the tank, fins waving with vigor.

"He's you," Rachel said. "He's Sid."

I teased her, "I thought half of them were Sid."

"Sid is always the fastest one. That's Sid." She pointed. "The others aren't Sid anymore."

"Poor fellows."

She giggled. "I wish I could have the fishes in the hospital. Mummy asked, but they said no."

"Pity."

She sat loosely cuddled by my right arm but held my other hand, the plastic one, pulling it across towards her. That hand still wasn't working properly, though a fresh battery and a bit of tinkering had restored it to half-life.

After a long, silent pause, she said, "Are you afraid of dying?"

Another pause. "Sometimes," I said.

Her voice was quiet, almost murmuring. It was a conversation all in a low key, without haste.

She said, "Daddy says when you were a jockey you were never afraid of anything."

"Are you afraid?" I asked.

"Yes, but I can't tell Mummy. I don't like her crying."

"Are you afraid of the transplant?"

Rachel nodded.

"You will die without it," I said matter-of-factly. "I know you know that."

"What's dying like?"

"I don't know. No one knows. Like going to sleep, I should think." If you were lucky, of course.

"It's funny to think of not being here," Rachel said. "I mean, to think of being a *space.*"

"The transplant will work."

"Everyone says so."

"Then believe it. You'll be running by Christmas."

She smoothed her fingers over my hand. I could feel the faint vibrations distantly in my forearm. Nothing, I thought, was ever entirely lost.

She said, "Do you know what I'll be thinking, lying there in the bubble feeling awfully sick?"

"What?"

"Life's a bugger."

I hugged her, but gently. "You'll do fine."

"Yes, but tell me."

"Tell you what?"

"How to be brave."

What a question, I thought. I said, "When you're feeling awfully sick, think about something you like doing. You won't feel as bad if you don't think about how bad you feel."

She thought it over. "Is that all?"

"It's quite a lot. Think about fishes. Think about Pegotty pulling off his socks and putting them in his mouth. Think about things you've enjoyed."

"Is that what *you* do?"

"It's what I do if something hurts, yes. It does work."

"What if nothing hurts yet, but you're going into something scary?"

"Well . . . it's all right to be frightened. No one can help it. You just don't have to let being frightened stop you."

"Are you ever frightened?" she asked.

"Yes." Too often, I thought.

She said lazily, but with certainty, "I bet you've never been so frightened you didn't do something. I bet you're always brave."

I was startled. "No . . . I'm not."

"But Daddy said . . ."

"I wasn't afraid of riding in races," I agreed. "Try me in a pit full of snakes, though, and I wouldn't be so sure."

"What about a bubble?"

"I'd go in there promising myself I'd come out running."

She smoothed my hand. "Will you come and see me?"

"In the bubble?" I asked. "Yes, if you like."

"You'll make me brave."

I shook my head. "It will come from inside you. You'll see."

We went on watching the fish. My namesake flashed his fins and seemed to have endless stamina.

"I'm going into the bubble tomorrow," Rachel murmured. "I don't want to cry when they put me in there."

"Courage is lonely," I said.

She looked up into my face. "What does that mean?"

It was too strong a concept, I saw, for someone of nine. I tried to make things simpler.

"You'll be alone in the bubble," I said, "so make it your own palace. The bubble is to keep you safe from infection—safe from dragons. You won't cry."

She snuggled against me; happier, I hoped. I loved her incredibly. The transplant had a fifty-fifty chance of success. Rachel would run again. She *had* to.

Linda and Pegotty came back laughing from their walk and Linda built towers of bright plastic building blocks for Pegotty to knock down, a game of endless enjoyment for the baby. Rachel and I sat on the floor, playing checkers.

"You always let me be white," Rachel complained, "and then you sneak up with the black counters when I'm not looking."

"You can play black, then."

"It's disgusting," she said, five minutes later. "You're cheating."

Linda looked up and said, astounded, "Are you two *quarreling?*"

"He always wins," Rachel objected.

"Then don't play with him," Linda said reasonably.

Rachel set up the white pieces as her own. I neglected to take one of them halfway through the game, and with glee she huffed me, and won.

"Did you *let* me win?" she demanded.

"Winning's more fun."

"I hate you." She swept all the pieces petulantly from the board and Pegotty put two of them in his mouth.

Rachel, laughing, picked them out again and dried them and set up the board again, with herself again as white, and peacefully we achieved a couple of close finishes until, suddenly as usual, she tired.

Linda produced tiny chocolate cakes for tea and talked happily of the Swiss donor and how everything was going to be *all right*. Rachel was convinced, I was convinced, Pegotty smeared chocolate all over his face. Whatever the next week might bring to all of us, I thought, that afternoon of hope and or-dinariness was an anchor in reality, an affirmation that small lives mattered.

It wasn't until after she'd fastened both children into the back of her car to drive to the hospital that Linda mentioned Ellis Quint.

"That trial is on again tomorrow, isn't it?" she asked.

We stood in the chilly air a few paces from her car. I nodded. "Don't let Rachel know."

"She doesn't. It hasn't been hard to keep it all away from her. She never talks about Silverboy anymore. Being so ill . . . she hasn't much interest in anything else."

"She's terrific."

"Will Ellis Quint go to prison?"

How could I say "I hope so"? And *did* I hope so? Yet I had to stop him, to goad him, to make him fundamentally wake up.

I said, dodging it, "It will be for the judge to decide."

Linda hugged me. No tears. "Come and see Rachel in her bubble?"

"You couldn't keep me away."

"God . . . I hope . . ."

"She'll be all right," I said. "So will you."

PATIENT TELEDRIVE TOOK me back to London and, because of the fixed hour of Linda's departure to the hospital, I again had time to spare before meeting India for dinner.

I again ducked being dropped in Pont Square in the dark evening, and damned Gordon for his vigilance. He had to sleep *sometime* . . . but when?

The restaurant called Kensington Place was near the northern end of Church Street, the famous road of endless antique shops, stretching from Kensington High Street, in the south, up to Notting Hill Gate, north. Teledrive left me and my overnight bag on the northwest corner of Church Street, where I dawdled awhile looking in the brightly lit windows of Waterstone's bookshop, wondering if Rachel would be able to hear the store's advertised children's audio tapes in her bubble. She enjoyed the subversive Just William stories. Pegotty, she thought, would grow up to be like him.

A large number of young Japanese people were milling around on the corner, all armed with cameras, taking flash pictures of one another. I paid not much attention beyond noticing that they all had straight black hair, short padded jackets, and jeans. As far as one could tell, they were happy. They also surged between me and Waterstone's windows.

They bowed to me politely, I bowed unenthusiastically in return.

They seemed to be waiting, as I was, for some prearranged event to occur. I gradually realized from their quiet chatter, of which I understood not a word, that half of them were men, and half young women.

We all waited. They bowed some more. At length, one of the young women shyly produced a photograph that she held out to me. I took it politely and found I was looking at a wedding. At a mass wedding of about ten happy couples wearing formal suits and Western bridal gowns. Raising my head from the photo, I was met by twenty smiles.

I smiled back. The shy young woman retrieved her photo, nodded her head towards her companions and clearly told me that they were all on their honeymoon. More smiles all around. More bows. One of the men held out his camera to me and asked—I gathered—if I would photograph them all as a group.

I took the camera and put my bag at my feet, and they arranged themselves in pairs neatly, as if they were used to it.

Click. Flash. The film wound on, quietly whirring.

All the newlyweds beamed.

I was presented, one by one, with nine more cameras. Nine more bows. I took nine more photos. Flash. Flash. Group euphoria.

What was it about me, I wondered, that encouraged such trust? Even without language there seemed to be no doubt on their part of my willingness to give pleasure. I mentally shrugged. I had the time, so what the hell. I took their pictures and bowed, and waited for eight o'clock.

I left the happy couples on Waterstone's corner and, carrying my bag, walked fifty yards down Church Street towards the restaurant. There was a narrow side street beside it, and opposite, on the other side of Church Street, one of those quirks of London life, a small recessed area of sidewalk with a patch of scrubby grass and a park bench, installed by philanthropists for the comfort of footsore shoppers and other vagrants. I would sit there, I decided, and watch for India. The restaurant doors were straight opposite the bench. A green-painted bench made of horizontal slats.

I crossed Church Street to reach it. The traffic on Sunday evening was sporadic to nonexistent. I could see a brass plate on the back of the bench: the name of the benefactor who'd paid for it.

I was turning to sit when at the same time I heard a bang and felt a searing flash of pain across my back and into my right upper arm. The impact knocked me over and around so that I ended sprawling on the bench, half lying, half sitting, facing the road.

I thought incredulously, I've been *shot*.

I'd been shot once before. I couldn't mistake the *thud*. Also I couldn't mistake the shudder of outrage that my invaded body produced. Also . . . there was a great deal of blood.

I'd been shot by Gordon Quint.

He walked out of the shadows of the side street opposite and came towards me across Church Street. He carried a hand-gun with its black, round mouth pointing my way. He was coming inexorably to finish what he'd started, and he appeared not to care if anyone saw him.

I didn't seem to have the strength to get up and run away.

There was nowhere to run to.

Gordon looked like a farmer from Berkshire, not an obsessed murderer. He wore a checked shirt and a tie and a tweed jacket. He was a middle-aged pillar of the community, a judge and jury and a hangman . . . a raw, primitive walking act of revenge.

There was none of the screaming out-of-control obscenity with which he'd attacked me the previous Monday. This killer was cold and determined and *reckless.*

He stopped in front of me and aimed at my chest.

"This is for Ginnie," he said.

I don't know what he expected. He seemed to be waiting for something. For me to protest, perhaps. To plead.

His voice was hoarse.

"For Ginnie," he repeated.

I was silent. I wanted to stand. Couldn't manage it.

"Say something!" he shouted in sudden fury. The gun wavered in his hand, but he was too close to miss. "Don't you *understand?*"

I looked not at his gun but at his eyes. Not the best view, I thought inconsequentially, for my last on earth.

Gordon's purpose didn't waver. I might deny him any enjoyment of my fear, but that wasn't going to stop him. He stared at my face. He didn't blink. No hesitancy there. No withdrawal or doubt. None.

Now, I thought frozenly. It's going to be *now.*

A voice was shouting in the road, urgent, frantic, coming nearer, far too late. The voice shouted one despairing word.

*"Dad."*

Ellis . . . *Ellis* . . . Running across the road waving a five-foot piece of black angle-iron fencing and shouting in frenzy at his father, *"Dad . . . Dad . . . Don't . . . Don't do it."*

I could see him running. Nothing seemed very clear. Gordon could hear Ellis shouting but it wasn't going to stop him. The demented hatred simply hardened in his face. His arm straightened until his gun was a bare yard from my chest.

Perhaps I won't feel it, I thought.

Ellis swung the iron fencing post with two hands and all his strength and *hit his father on the side of the head.*

The gun went off. The bullet hissed past my ear and slammed into a shop window behind me. There were razor splinters of glass and flashes of light and shouting and confusion everywhere.

Gordon fell silently unconscious, face down on the scrubby patch of grass, his right hand with the gun underneath him. My blood ran into a scarlet and widening pool below the slats of the bench. Ellis stood for an eternity of seconds holding the fencing post and staring at my eyes as if he could see into my soul, as if he would show me his.

For an unmeasurable hiatus blink of time it seemed there was between us a fusing of psyche, an insight of total understanding. It could have been a hallucination, a result of too much stress, but it was unmistakably the same for him.

Then he dropped the fencing post beside his father, and turned, and went away at a slow run, across Church Street and down the side road, loping, not sprinting, until he was swallowed by shadow.

I was suddenly surrounded by Japanese faces all asking unintelligible questions. They had worried eyes. They watched me bleed.

The gunshots brought more people, but cautiously. Gordon's attack, that to me had seemed to happen in slow motion, had in reality passed to others with bewildering speed. No one had tried to stop Ellis. People thought he was going to bring help.

I lost further account of time. A police car arrived busily, lights flashing, the first manifestation of all that I most detested—questions, hospitals, forms, noise, bright lights in my eyes, clanging and banging and being shoved around. There wasn't a hope of being quietly stitched up and left alone.

I told a policemen that Gordon, though unconscious at present, was lying over a loaded gun.

He wanted to know if Gordon had fired the shots in self-defense.

I couldn't be bothered to answer.

The crowd grew bigger and an ambulance made an entrance.

A young woman pushed the uniforms aside, yelling that she was from the press. India . . . India . . . come to dinner.

"Sorry," I said.

"*Sid* . . ." Horror in her voice and a sort of despair.

"Tell Kevin Mills . . . ," I said. My mouth was dry from loss of blood. I tried again. She bent her head down to mine to hear above the hubbub.

With humor I said, "Those Japanese people took a load of photos . . . I saw the flashes . . . so tell Kevin to get moving . . . Get those photos . . . and he can have . . . his exclusive."

# 15

India wasn't a newspaperwoman for nothing. The front page of Monday's *Pump* bore the moderately accurate headline "Shot in the Back," with, underneath, a picture taken of Gordon Quint aiming his gun unequivocally at my heart.

Gordon's half–back view was slightly out of focus. My own face was sharp and clear, with an expression that looked rather like polite interest, not the fatalistic terror I'd actually felt.

Kevin and *The Pump* had gone to town. *The Pump* acknowledged that its long campaign of denigration of Sid Halley had been a mistake.

Policy, I saw cynically, had done a one-eighty U-turn. Lord Tilepit had come to such senses as he possessed and was putting what distance he could between himself and Ellis Quint.

There had been twenty eyewitnesses to the shooting of J. S. Halley. Kevin, arming himself with a Japanese interpreter, had listened intently, sorted out what he'd been told, and got it right. Throughout his piece there was an undercurrent of awe that no one was going to be able to dispute the facts. He hadn't once said, "It is *alleged*."

Gordon Quint, though still unconscious, would in due course be "helping the police with their inquiries." Kevin observed that Ellis Quint's whereabouts were unknown.

Inside the paper there were more pictures. One showed Ellis, arms and fence post raised, on the point of striking his father. The Japanese collectively, and that one photographer in particular, had not known who Ellis Quint was. Ellis didn't appear on the TV screens in Japan.

Why had there been so much photo coverage? Because Mr. Halley, Kevin said, had been kind to the honeymooners, and many of them had been watching him as he walked away down Church Street.

I read *The Pump* while sitting upright in a high bed in a small white side room in Hammersmith hospital, thankfully alone except for a constant stream of doctors, nurses, policemen and people with clipboards.

The surgeon who'd dealt with my punctures came to see me at nine in the morning, before he went off duty for the day. He looked a lot worse for wear by then than I did, I thought.

"How are you doing?" he asked, coming in wearily in a sweat-stained green gown.

"As you see . . . fine, thanks to you."

He looked at the newspaper lying on the bed. "Your bullet," he said, "plowed along a rib and in and out of your arm. It tore a hole in the brachial artery, which is why you bled so much. We repaired that and transfused you with three units of blood and saline, though you may need more later. We'll see how you go. There's some muscle damage but with physiotherapy you should be almost as good as new. You seem to have been sideways on when he shot you."

"I was turning. I was lucky."

"You could put it like that," he said dryly. "I suppose you do know you've also got a half-mended fracture of the forearm? And some fairly deep trauma to the wrist?"

I nodded.

"And we've put a few stitches in your face."

"Great."

"I watched you race," he said. "I know how fast jockeys heal. Ex-jockeys, too, no doubt. You can leave here when you feel ready."

I said "Thanks" sincerely, and he smiled exhaustedly and went away.

I could definitely move the fingers of my right hand, even though only marginally at present. There had been a private moment of sheer cowardice in the night when I'd woken gradually from anesthesia and been unable to feel anything in my arm from the shoulder down. I didn't care to confess or remember the abject dread in which I'd forced myself to *look*. I'd awoken once before to a stump. This time the recurrent nightmare of helplessness and humiliation and no hands had drifted horrifyingly in and out, but when I did finally look, there was no spirit-pulverizing void but a long white-wrapped bundle that discernibly ended in fingernails. Even so, they didn't seem to be connected to me. I had lain for a grim while, trying to consider paralysis, and when at length pain had roared back it had been an enormous relief: only whole healthy nerves felt like that. I had an arm . . . and a hand . . . and a life.

Given those, nothing else mattered.

In the afternoon Archie Kirk and Norman Picton argued themselves past the No Visitors sign on the door and sat in a couple of chairs bringing good news and bad.

"The Frodsham police found your car," Norman said, "but I'm afraid it's been stripped. It's up on bricks—no wheels."

"Contents?" I asked resignedly.

"No. Nothing."

"Engine?"

"Most of it's there. No battery, of course. Everything movable's missing."

Poor old car. It had been insured, though, for a fortune.

Archie said, "Charles sends his regards."

"Tell him thanks."

"He said you would be looking as though nothing much had happened. I didn't believe him. Why aren't you lying down?"

"It's more comfortable sitting up."

Archie frowned.

I amplified mildly. "There's a bullet burn across somewhere below my shoulder blade."

Archie said, "Oh."

They both looked at the tall contraption standing beside the bed with a tube leading from a high bag to my elbow. I explained that, too.

"It's one of those 'painkiller on demand' things," I said. "If I get a twinge I press a button, and bingo, it goes away."

Archie picked up the copy of *The Pump.* "All of a sudden," he commented, "you're Saint Sid who can do no wrong."

I said, "It's enough to make Ellis's lawyers weep."

"But you don't think, do you," Archie said doubtfully, "that Ellis's lawyers *connived* at the hate-Halley campaign?"

"Because they are ethical people?" I asked.

"Yes."

I shrugged and left it.

"Is there any news of Ellis?" I asked. "Or of Gordon?"

"Gordon Quint," Norman said in a policeman's voice, "was, as of an hour ago, still unconscious in a secure police facility and suffering from a depressed skull fracture. He is to have an operation to relieve the pressure on his brain.

No one is predicting when he'll wake up or what mental state he'll be in, but as soon as he can understand, he'll be formally charged with attempted murder. As you know, there's a whole flock of eyewitnesses."

"And Ellis?" I asked.

Archie said, "No one knows where he is."

"It's very difficult," I said, "for him to go anywhere without being recognized."

Norman nodded. "Someone may be sheltering him. But we'll find him, don't worry."

"What happened this morning," I asked, "about the trial?"

"Adjourned. Ellis Quint's bail is rescinded as he didn't turn up, and also he'll be charged with grievous bodily harm to his father. A warrant for his arrest has been issued."

"He wanted to prevent his father from murdering," I said. "He can't have meant to hurt him seriously."

Archie nodded. "It's a tangle."

"And Jonathan," I asked. "Did he go to Shropshire?"

Both of them looked depressed.

"Well," I said, "didn't he go?"

"Oh yes, he went," Norman said heavily. "And he found the car parkers."

"Good boy," I said.

"It's *not* so good." Archie, like a proper civil servant, had brought with him a briefcase, from which he now produced a paper that he brought over to the bed. I pinned it down with the weight of my still-sluggish left hand and took in its general meaning.

The car parkers had signed a statement saying that Ellis Quint had dined with media colleagues and had brought several of them with him to the dance at about eleven-thirty. The parkers remembered him—of course—not only because of who he was (there had been plenty of other well-known people at the party, starting with members of the Royal Family) but chiefly because he had given them a tip and offered them his autograph. They knew it was before midnight, because their employment as car parkers had ended then. People who arrived later had found only one car parker—a friend of those who'd gone off duty.

*Media colleagues!* Dammit, I thought. I hadn't checked those with the duchess.

"It's an unbreakably solid alibi," Norman observed gloomily. "He was in Shropshire when the yearling was attacked."

"Mm."

"You don't seem disappointed, Sid," Archie said, puzzled.

694

"No."

"But why not?"

"I think," I said, "that you should phone Davis Tatum. Will he be in his office right now?"

"He might be. What do you want him for?"

"I want him to make sure the prosecutors don't give up on the trial."

"You told him that on Saturday." He was humoring me, I thought.

"I'm not light-headed from bullets, Archie, if that's what you think. Since Saturday I've worked a few things out, and they are not as they may seem."

"What things?"

"Ellis's alibi, for one."

"But, Sid—"

"Listen," I said. "This isn't all that easy to say, so don't look at me, look at your hands or something." They showed no sign of doing so, so I looked at my own instead. I said, "I have to explain that *I* am not as I seem. When people in general look at me they see a harmless person, youngish, not big, not tall, no threat to anyone. Self-effacing. I'm not complaining about that. In fact, I choose to be like that because people then *talk* to me, which is necessary in my job. They tend to think I'm cozy, as your sister Betty told me, Archie. Owen Yorkshire considers me a wimp. He said so. Only . . . I'm not really like that."

"A *wimp!*" Archie exclaimed.

"I can look it, that's the point. But Ellis knows me better. Ellis calls me cunning and ruthless, and I probably am. It was he who years ago gave me the nickname of Tungsten Carbide because I wasn't easy to . . . er . . . intimidate. He thinks I can't be terrified, either, though he's wrong about that. But I don't mind him thinking it. Anyway, unlikely though it may seem, all this past summer, Ellis has been afraid of me. That's why he made jokes about me on television and got Tilepit to set his paper onto me. He wanted to defeat me by ridicule."

I paused. Neither of them said a word.

I went on. "Ellis is not what he seems, either. Davis Tatum thinks him a playboy. Ellis is tall, good-looking, outgoing, charming and *loved*. Everyone thinks him a delightful entertainer with a knack for television. But he's not only that. He's a strong, purposeful and powerful man with enormous skills of manipulation. People underestimate both of us for various and different reasons—I look weak and he looks frivolous—but we don't underestimate each other. On the surface, the easy surface, we've been friends for years. But in our time we rode dozens of races against each other, and racing, believe me, strips your soul bare. Ellis and I know each other's minds on a deep level that has nothing to do with afternoon banter or chit-chat. We've been friends on that level, too. You and Davis can't believe that it is Ellis himself who is the heavyweight, not Yorkshire, but Ellis and I both know it. Ellis has manipulated everyone—Yorkshire, Tilepit, *The Pump,* public opinion, and also those so-smart lawyers of his who think they're dictating the pace."

"And you, Sid?" Norman asked. "Has he pulled your strings, too?"

I smiled ruefully, not looking at him. "He's had a go."

"I'd think it was impossible," Archie said. "He would have to put you underground to stop you."

"You've learned a lot about me, Archie," I said lazily. "I do like to win."

He said, "So why aren't you disappointed that Ellis's Shropshire alibi can't be broken?"

"Because Ellis set it up that way."

"How do you mean?"

"Ever since the Northampton yearling was attacked, Ellis's lawyers have been putting it about that if Ellis had an unbreakable alibi for that night, which I bet he assured them he had, it would invalidate the whole Combe Bassett case. They put pressure on the Crown Prosecution Service to withdraw, which they've been tottering on the brink of doing. Never mind that the two attacks were separate, the strong supposition arose that if Ellis couldn't have done one, then he hadn't done the other."

"Of course," Norman said.

"No," I contradicted. "He made for himself a positively unbreakable alibi in Shropshire, and he got someone else to go to Northampton."

"But no one *would.*"

"One person would. And did."

"But *who,* Sid?" Archie asked.

"Gordon. His father."

Archie and Norman both stiffened as if turned to pillars of salt.

The nerves in my right arm woke up. I pressed the magic button and they went slowly back to sleep. Brilliant. A lot better than in days gone by.

"He *couldn't* have done," Archie said in revulsion.

"He did."

"You're just *guessing.* And you're *wrong.*"

"No."

"But, *Sid* . . ."

"I know," I sighed. "You, Charles and I have all been guests in his house. But he shot me last night. See it in *The Pump.*"

Archie said weakly, "But that doesn't mean . . ."

"I'll explain," I said. "Give me a moment."

My skin was sweating. It came and went a bit, now and then. An affronted body, letting me know.

"A moment?"

"I'm not made of iron."

Archie breathed on a smile. "I thought it was tungsten?"

"Mm."

They waited. I said, "Gordon and Ginnie Quint gloried in their wonderful son, their only child. I accused him of a crime that revolted them. Ginnie steadfastly believed in his innocence; an act of faith. Gordon, however reluctantly, faced with all the evidence we gathered from his Land-Rover, must have come to acknowledge to himself that the unthinkable was true."

Archie nodded.

I went on. "Ellis's wretched persecution of me didn't really work. Sure, I hated it, but I was still *there,* and meanwhile the time of the trial was drawing nearer and nearer. Whatever odium I drew onto myself by doing it, I was going to describe in court, with all the press and public listening, just how Ellis could have cut off the foot of Betty's colt. The outcome of the trial—whether or not the jury found Ellis guilty, and whether or not the judge sent him to jail—that wasn't the prime point. The trial itself, and all that evidence, would have convinced enough of the population of his guilt to destroy forever the shining-knight persona. Topline Foods couldn't have—and, in fact, won't be able to— use those diamond-plated round-the-world ads."

I took a deep couple of lungfuls of air. I was talking too much. Not enough oxygen, not enough blood.

I said, "The idea of the Shropshire alibi probably came about gradually, and heaven knows to which of them first. Ellis received an invitation to the dance. The plan must have started from that. They saw it as the one effective way to stop the trial from taking place."

Hell, I thought, I don't feel well. I'm getting old.

I said, "You have to remember that Gordon is a farmer. He's used to the idea of the death of animals being profitable. I dare say that the death of one insignificant yearling was as nothing to him when set beside the saving of his son. And he knew where to find such a victim. He would have to have long replaced the shears taken by the police. It must have seemed quite easy, and in fact he carried out the plan without difficulty."

Archie and Norman listened as if not breathing.

I started again. "Ellis is many things, but he's not a murderer. If he had been, perhaps he would have been a serial killer of humans, not horses. That urge to do evil—I don't understand it, but it *happens.* Wings off butterflies and so on." I swallowed. "Ellis has given me a hard time, but in spite of several opportunities he hasn't let me be killed. He stopped Yorkshire doing it. He stopped his father last night."

"People can hate until they make themselves ill," Archie nodded. "Very few actually murder."

"Gordon Quint tried it," Norman pointed out, "and all but succeeded."

"Yes," I agreed, "but that wasn't to help Ellis."

"What was it, then?"

"Have to go back a bit."

I'm too tired, I thought, but I'd better finish it.

I said to Norman, "You remember that piece of rag you gave me?"

"Yes. Did you do anything with it?"

I nodded.

"What rag?" Archie asked.

Norman outlined for him the discovery at Northampton of the lopping shears wrapped in dirty material.

"The local police found the shears hidden in a hedge," I said, "and they brought them into the stud farm's office while I was there. The stud farm's owners, Miss Richardson and Mrs. Bethany, were there, and so was Ginny Quint, who was a friend of theirs and who had gone there to comfort them and sympathize. Ginnie forcibly said how much she despised me for falsely accusing her paragon of a son. For accusing my *friend*. She more or less called me Judas."

"Sid!"

"Well, that's how it seemed. Then she watched the policeman unwrap the shears that had cut off the yearling's foot and, quite slowly, she went white . . . and fainted."

"The sight of the shears," Norman said, nodding.

"It was much more than that. It was the sight of the *material*."

"How do you mean?"

"I spent a whole day . . . last Thursday, it seems a lifetime away . . . I chased all over London with that little piece of cloth, and I finished up in a village near Chichester."

"Why Chichester?" Archie asked.

"Because that filthy old cloth had once been part of some bed hangings. They were woven as a special order by a Mrs. Patricia Huxford, who's a doll of the first rank. She has looms in Lowell, near Chichester. She looked up her records and found that that fabric had been made nearly thirty years ago especially—and exclusively—for a Mrs. Gordon Quint."

Archie and Norman both stared.

"Ginnie recognized the material," I said. "She'd just been giving me the most frightful tongue-lashing for believing Ellis capable of maiming horses, and she suddenly saw, because that material was wrapped round shears, that I'd been right. Not only that, she knew that Ellis had been in Shropshire the night Miss Richardson's colt was done. She knew the importance of his alibi . . . and she saw—she understood—that the only other person who could or would have wrapped lopping shears in that unique fabric was Gordon. Gordon wouldn't have thought twice about snatching up any old rag to wrap his shears in—and I'd guess he decided to dump them because we might have checked Quint's shears again for horse DNA if he'd taken them home. Ginnie saw that *Gordon* had maimed the yearling. It was too big a shock . . . and she fainted."

Archie and Norman, too, looked shocked.

I sighed. "I didn't understand that then, of course. I didn't understand it until the night before last, when everything sort of *clicked*. But now . . . I think it wasn't just because of Ellis's terrible guilt that Ginnie killed herself last Monday, but because it was Gordon's guilt and reputation as well . . . and then the trial was starting in spite of everything . . . and it was all too much . . . too much to bear."

I paused briefly and went on, "Ginnie's suicide sent Gordon berserk. He'd set out to help his son. He'd caused his wife's death. He blamed me for it, for having destroyed his family. He tried to smash my brains in the morning she'd died. He lay in wait for me outside my apartment . . . he was screaming that I'd killed her. Then, last night, in the actual moment that the picture in *The Pump* was taken, he was telling me the bullets were for Ginnie . . . it was my life for hers. He meant . . . he meant to do it."

I stopped talking.

The white room was silent.

LATER IN THE day I phoned the hospital in Canterbury and spoke to the ward sister.

"How is Rachel?" I asked.

"Mr. Halley! But I thought . . . I mean, we've all read *The Pump*."

"But you didn't tell Rachel, did you?" I asked anxiously.

"No . . . Linda—Mrs. Ferns—said not to."

"Good."

"But are you—"

"I'm absolutely OK," I assured her. "I'm in Hammersmith hospital. Du Cane Road."

"The best!" she exclaimed.

"I won't argue. How's Rachel?"

"You know that she's a very sick little girl, but we're all hopeful of the transplant."

"Did she go into the bubble?"

"Yes, very bravely. She says it's her palace and she's its queen."

"Give her my love."

"How soon . . . oh, dear, I shouldn't ask."

"I'll make it by Thursday."

"I'll tell her."

KEVIN MILLS AND India came to visit before ten o'clock the following morning, on their way to work.

I was again sitting up in the high bed but by then felt much healthier. In spite of my protests, my shot and mending arm was still held immobile in a swaddle of splint and bandages. Give it another day's rest, I'd been told, and just practice wiggling your fingers: which was all very well, except that the nurses had been too busy with an emergency that morning to reunite me with my left hand, which lay on the locker beside me. For all that it didn't work properly, I felt naked without it, and could do nothing for myself, not even scratch my nose.

Kevin and India both came in looking embarrassed by life in general and said far too brightly how glad they were to see me awake and recovering.

I smiled at their feelings. "My dear children," I said, "I'm not a complete fool."

"Look, mate . . ." Kevin's voice faded. He wouldn't meet my eyes.

I said, "Who told Gordon Quint where to find me?"

Neither of them answered.

"India," I pointed out, "you were the only person who knew I would turn up at Kensington Place at eight o'clock on Sunday evening."

"Sid!" She was anguished, as she had been in Church Street when she'd found me shot; and she wouldn't look at my face, either.

Kevin smoothed his mustache. "It wasn't her fault."

"Yours, then?"

"You're right about your not being a fool," Kevin said. "You've guessed what happened, otherwise you'd be flinging us out of here right now."

"Correct."

"The turmoil started Saturday evening," Kevin said, feeling secure enough to sit down. "Of course, as there's no daily *Pump* on Sundays there was hardly anyone in the office. George Godbar wasn't. No one was. Saturday is our night off. The shit really hit the fan on Sunday morning at the editorial meeting. You know editorial meetings . . . well, perhaps you don't. All the department

editors—news, sport, gossip, features, whatever, and the senior reporters—
meet to decide what stories will be run in the next day's paper, and there was
George Godbar in a positive *lather* about reversing policy on S. Halley. I mean,
Sid mate, you should've heard him swear. I never knew so many orifices and
sphincters existed."

"The boss had leaned on him?"

*"Leaned!* There was a panic. Our lord the proprietor wanted you *bought off."*

"How nice," I said.

"He'd suggested ten thousand smackers, George said. Try ten million, I said.
George called for copies for everyone of the complete file of everything *The
Pump* has published about you since June, nearly all of it in India's column on
Fridays. I suppose you've kept all those pieces?"

I hadn't. I didn't say so.

"Such *poison,"* Kevin said. "Seeing it all together like that. I mean, it silenced the whole meeting, and it takes a lot to do that."

"I wasn't there," India said. "I don't go to those meetings."

"Be fair to India," Kevin told me, "she didn't write most of it. I wrote some.
You know I did. Six different people wrote it."

India still wouldn't meet my eyes and still wouldn't sit in the one empty
chair. I knew about "policy" and being burned at the stake and all that, yet
week after week I'd dreaded her byline. Try as I would, I still felt sore from
that savaging.

"Sit down," I said mildly.

She perched uneasily.

"If we make another dinner date," I said, "don't tell anyone."

"Oh, Sid."

"She didn't mean to get you *shot,* for Chrissakes," Kevin protested. "The
Tilepit wanted you found. Wanted! He was shitting himself, George said. *The
Pump's* lawyer had passed each piece week by week as being just on the safe
side of actionable, but at the meeting, when he read the whole file at once,
he was *sweating,* Sid. He says *The Pump* should settle out of court for whatever you ask."

"And I suppose you're not supposed to be telling me that?"

"No," Kevin confessed, "but you did give me the exclusive of the decade."

"How did Gordon Quint find me?" I asked again.

"George said our noble lord was babbling on about you promising not to
send him to jail if you walked out free from somewhere or other, and you *had*
walked out free, and he wanted to keep you to your promise. George didn't
know what he was talking about, but Tilepit made it crystal that George's job
depended on finding you within the next five minutes, if not sooner. So

George begged us all to find you, to say *The Pump* would confer sainthood immediately and fatten your bank balance, and I phoned India on the off chance, and she said not to worry, she would tell you herself . . . and I asked her how . . . and where. There didn't seem to be any harm in it."

"And you told George Godbar?" I said.

Kevin nodded.

"And he," I said, "told Lord Tilepit? And *he* told Ellis, I suppose . . . because Ellis turned up, too."

"George Godbar phoned Ellis's father's house, looking for Ellis. He got an answering machine telling him to try a mobile number, and he reached Gordon Quint in a car somewhere . . . and he told Gordon where you would be, if Ellis wanted to find you."

Round and round in circles, and the bullets come out *here.*

I sighed again. I was lucky to be alive. I would settle for that. I also wondered how much I would screw out of *The Pump.* Only enough, I decided, to keep His Lordship grateful.

Kevin, the confession over, got restlessly to his feet and walked around the room, stopping when he reached the locker on my left side.

He looked a little blankly at the prosthesis lying there and, after a moment, picked it up. I wished he wouldn't.

He said, surprised, "It's bigger than I pictured. And heavier. And *hard.*"

"All the better to club you with," I said.

"Really?" he asked interestedly. "Straight up?"

"It's been known," I said, and after a moment he put the arm down.

"It's true what they say of you, isn't it? You may not look it, but you're one tough bugger, Sid mate, like I told you before."

I said, "Not many people look the way they are inside."

India said, "I'll write a piece about that."

"There you are then, Sid." Kevin was ready to go. "I've got a rape waiting. Thanks for those Japs. Makes us even, right?"

"Even." I nodded.

India stood up as if to follow him. "Stay a bit," I suggested.

She hesitated. Kevin said, "Stay and hold his bloody hand. Oh, shit. Well . . . sorry, mate. *Sorry.*"

"Get out of here," I said.

India watched him go.

"I'm really sorry," she said helplessly, "about getting you shot."

"I'm alive," I pointed out, "so forget it."

Her face looked softer. At that hour in the morning she hadn't yet put on the sharply outlined lipstick nor the matte porcelain makeup. Her eyebrows were as dark and positive, and her eyes as light-blue and clear, but this was the essential India I was seeing, not the worldly package. How different, I wondered, was the inner spirit from the cutting brain of her column?

She, too, as if compelled, came over to my left side and looked at the plastic arm.

"How does it work?" she asked.

I explained about the electrodes, as I had for Rachel.

She picked up the arm and put her fingers inside, touching the electrodes. Nothing happened. No movement in the thumb.

I swallowed. I said, "It probably needs a fresh battery."

"Battery?"

"It clips into the side. That boxlike thing"—I nodded towards the locker—"that's a battery charger. There's a recharged battery in there. Change them over."

She did so, but slowly, because of the unfamiliarity. When she touched the electrodes again, the hand obeyed the signals.

"Oh," she said.

She put the hand down and looked at me.

"Do you," she said, "have a steel rod up your backbone? I've never seen anyone more tense. And your forehead's sweating."

She picked up the box of tissues lying beside the battery charger and offered it to me.

I shook my head. She looked at the immobilized right arm and at the left one on the locker, and a wave of understanding seemed to leave her without breath.

I said nothing. She pulled a tissue out of the box and jerkily dabbed at a dribble of sweat that ran down my temple.

"Why don't you put this arm on?" she demanded. "You'd be better with it on, obviously."

"A nurse will do it." I explained about the emergency. "She'll come when she can."

"Let *me* do it," India said.

"No."

"Why not?"

"Because."

"Because you're too bloody *proud.*"

Because it's too private, I thought.

I was wearing one of those dreadful hospital gowns like a barber's smock that fastened at the back of the neck and shapelessly covered the body. A white flap covered my left shoulder, upper arm, elbow and what remained below.

Tentatively India lifted and turned back the flap so that we both could see my elbow and the short piece of forearm.

"You hate it, don't you?" India said.

"Yes."

"I would hate it, too."

I can't bear this, I thought. I can bear Ellis unscrewing my hand and mocking me. I can't bear love.

India picked up the electric arm.

"What do I do?" she asked.

I said with difficulty, nodding again at the locker, "Talcum powder."

"Oh." She picked up the white tinful of comfort for babies. "In the arm, or on you?"

"On me."

She sprinkled powder on my forearm. "Is this right? More?"

"Mm."

She smoothed the powder all over my skin. Her touch sent a shiver right down to my toes.

"And now?"

"Now hold it so that I can put my arm into it."

She concentrated. I put my forearm into the socket, but the angle was wrong.

"What do I do?" she asked anxiously.

"Turn the thumb towards you a bit. Not too far. That's right. Now push up while I push down. That top bit will slide over my elbow and grip—and keep the hand on."

"Like that?" She was trembling.

"Like that," I said. The arm gripped where it was designed to.

I sent the messages. We both watched the hand open and close.

India abruptly left my side and walked over to where she'd left her purse, picking it up and crossing to the door.

"Don't go," I said.

"If I don't go, I'll cry."

I thought that might make two of us. The touch of her fingers on the skin of my forearm had been a caress more intimate than any act of sex. I felt shaky. I felt more moved than ever in my life.

"Come back," I said.

"I'm supposed to be in the office."

"India," I said, "please . . ." Why was it always so impossible to plead? "Please . . ." I looked down at my left hand. "Please don't *write* about this."

"Don't *write* about it?"

"No."

"Well, I won't, but why not?"

"Because I don't like pity."

She came halfway back to my side with tears in her eyes.

"Your Jenny," she said, "told me that you were so afraid of being pitied that you would never ask for help."

"She told you too much."

"Pity," India said, coming a step nearer, "is actually about as far from what I feel for you as it's possible to get."

I stretched out my left arm and fastened the hand on her wrist.

She looked at it. I tugged, and she took the last step to my side.

"You're strong," she said, surprised.

"Usually."

I pulled her nearer. She saw quite clearly what I intended, and bent her head and put her mouth on mine as if it were not the first time, as if it were natural.

A pact, I thought.

A beginning.


TIME DRIFTED WHEN she'd gone.

Time drifted to the midday news.

A nurse burst into my quiet room. "Don't you have your television on? You're on it."

She switched on knobs, and there was my face on the screen, with a news-reader's unemotional voice saying, "Sid Halley is recovering in hospital." There was a widening picture of me looking young and in racing colors: a piece of old film taken years ago of me weighing in after winning the Grand National. I was holding my saddle in two hands and my eyes were full of the mystical wonder of having been presented with the equivalent of the Holy Grail.

The news slid to drought and intractable famine.

The nurse said, "Wait," and twiddled more knobs, and another channel opened with the news item and covered the story in its entirety.

A woman announcer whose lugubrious voice I had long disliked put on her portentous-solemn face and intoned: "Police today found the body of Ellis Quint in his car, deep in the New Forest in Hampshire. . . ."

Frozen, I heard her saying, as if from a distance, "Foul play is not suspected. It is understood that the popular broadcaster left a note for his father, still unconscious after an accidental blow to the head on Sunday night. Now over to our reporter in Hampshire, Buddy Bowes."

Buddy Bowes, microphone in hand, filled the foreground of the screen with, slightly out of focus in the distance behind him, woodland and activity and a rear view of a white car.

"This is a sad ending," Buddy Bowes said, appearing at least to show genuine regret, "to a fairy-tale life. Ellis Quint, thirty-eight, who gave pleasure to millions with his appearances on television, will also be remembered as the dashing champion amateur steeplechase jockey whose courage and gallantry inspired a whole generation to get out there and *achieve*. In recent months he has been troubled by accusations of cruelty to animals from his long-time colleague and supposed friend, Sid Halley, ex-professional top jockey. Quint was due to appear in court yesterday to refute those charges. . . ."

There was a montage of Ellis winning races, striding about in macho riding boots, wowing a chat-show audience, looking glowingly alive and handsome.

"Ellis will be mourned by millions," Buddy Bowes finished. "And now back to the studio . . ."

The nurse indignantly switched off the set. "They didn't say anything about your being shot."

"Never mind."

She went away crossly. The reputation Ellis had manufactured for me couldn't be reversed in a night, whatever *The Pump* might now say. Slowly perhaps. Perhaps never.

Ellis was dead.

I sat in the quiet white room.

Ellis was *dead*.


AN HOUR LATER a hospital porter brought me a letter that he said had been left by hand on the counter of the hospital's main reception desk and overlooked until now.

"Overlooked since when?"

Since yesterday, he thought.

When he'd gone I held the envelope in the pincer fingers and tore it open with my teeth.

The two-page letter was from Ellis, his handwriting strong with life.

It said:

*Sid, I know where you are. I followed the ambulance. If you are reading this, you are alive and I am dead. I didn't think you would catch me. I should have known you would.*

*If you're wondering why I cut off those feet, don't you ever want to break out? I was tired of goody-goody. I wanted the dark side. I wanted to smash. To ex-*

plode. To mutilate. I wanted to laugh at the fools who fawned on me. I hugged myself. I mocked the proles.

And that scrunch,

I did that old pony to make a good program. The kid had leukemia. Sob-stuff story, terrific. I needed a good one. My ratings were slipping.

Then I lusted to do it again. The danger. The risk, the difficulty. And that scrunch. I can't describe it. It gives me an ecstasy like nothing else. Cocaine is for kids. Sex is nothing. I've had every woman I ever wanted. The scrunch of bones is a million-volt orgasm.

And then there's you. The only one I've ever envied. I wanted to corrupt you, too. No one should be unbendable.

I know all you fear is helplessness. I know you. I wanted to make you help-less in Owen Yorkshire's office but all you did was sit there watching your hand turn blue. I could feel you willing me to be my real self but my real self wanted to hear your wrist bones crunch to dust. I wanted to prove that no one was good. I wanted you to crumble. To be like me.

And then, you'll think I'm crazy, I was suddenly glad you weren't sobbing and whining and I was proud of you that you really were how you are, and I felt happy and higher than a kite. And I didn't want you to die, not like that, not for nothing. Not because of me.

I see now what I've done. What infinite damage.

My father did that last colt. I talked him into it.

It's cost my mother's life. If my father lives they'll lock him up for trying to kill you. They should have let me hang, back in June, when I tried with my tie.

They say people want to be caught. They go on and on sinning until some-one stops them.

The letter ended there except for three words much lower down the page:

You win, Sid.

The two sheets of paper lay on the white bedclothes. No one else would see them, I thought.

I remembered Rachel saying how odd it would be to be dead. To be a *space*. The whole white room was a space.

Good and evil, he had been my friend. An enemy: but finally a friend.

The sour, cruel underside of him receded.

I had the win, but there was no one standing in the stirrups to share it with.

Regret, loss, acceptance and relief; I felt them all.

I grieved for Ellis Quint.